The Riser Saga

RISER

REAPER

RIPPER

BECCA C. SMITH

RISER
BOOK ONE

Okay, let me explain. My gift, or curse (I'll let you decide for yourself) to put it simply is: I can raise the dead. I know, sounds cheesy, but fortunately, or unfortunately it's true, and I don't mean just people. Basically, anything that had any kind of life: plants, animals, insects, plankton, *anything,* I can bring back. The only catch is, they're not really alive anymore they're just animated, like zombies I guess, but I control them. Plants are the easiest. My mom's garden is the prize of the trailer park, and she should take no credit whatsoever.

Animals and people are more complicated, maybe because there are so many working parts. I'm really not sure. My ability is still kind of a mystery to me. I have no clue why I have this power. It's not like I've ever heard of anyone else having this particular skill either, except in books and movies. I appear to be an anomaly in this world...

I was three-years-old when I knew I saw things differently than everyone else. My pet goldfish, Larry, died and a black spinning hole appeared in the center of his body. I thought it was just about the coolest thing I had ever seen. When I told my mother about it, she gave me a look that I'd never forget. It was a mixture of confusion and horror. She simply nodded and made me promise that I would never under any circumstances tell anyone else about what I saw. I was instantly ashamed and scared at her reaction, but something in the way that she had said it made me keep my promise.

After that, I saw the black holes everywhere, from the tiniest dead insects, to dead plants, to Ms. Thompkins when she died from a heart attack. The churning black masses had become second nature to me by then. At that point, I still didn't know *why* I could see them and I was scared to death to talk to anyone about it. I kept to myself mostly, afraid I would slip and say something to a neighbor or friend.

It was a very lonely childhood.

It wasn't until I killed my stepfather Bruce that I figured out that I could raise the dead. I never wanted to take Bruce's life: hurt maybe, kill no. And that was saying a lot seeing as he used to use my mom as a punching bag. He'd make me sit in the corner of our beat up trailer and watch him kick the living crap out of her. He'd laugh when I'd scream, he'd laugh when she'd scream, he'd laugh when *he'd* scream on the few occasions my mom fought back and actually inflicted pain on him.

Bruce was a jerk, but he didn't deserve to die, not like he did, not like how I killed him. I still can't believe it had been eleven years since it all happened. It felt like yesterday and forever ago all at once.

It was a day like any other day, Mom did some invisible transgression to piss Bruce off and he took it as a cue for another beating. Mom was having one of her comatose days, where I could tell she was just going to take it and hope that he got bored quickly from her unresponsiveness.

Bruce slammed her against the flimsy trailer wall of the kitchen with his beefy forearm. Tiny bits of ceiling floated down like snow on his greasy balding scalp. He sneered at her with glee, but she wouldn't give him the satisfaction of eye contact. She just kept her eyes down, arms dropped harmlessly at her side. Bruce went on a furious rampage. He punched her, pulled her hair, kicked her stomach, tried anything to get a response out of her, but she just lay there like a rag doll on the peeling linoleum floor.

Then he wheeled around to face *me*.

"NO!"

Finally, a reaction from my mother. Bruce was in ecstasy. He stormed towards me like an enraged bull. I could almost see steam coming out of his bulbous nose. Then WHACK!

I could literally feel every vertebra in my spine as all forty-five pounds of me slammed against the wall from the impact of Bruce's fist to my stomach. My world started to spin; everything was in blurred double vision. My mother's hysterical screams echoed in my head like a horrific nightmare. I couldn't focus.

PUNCH!

CRACK!

I could feel my nose crunch when he hit me a second time. It felt like it was running, but when I tried to wipe it clean my hands came away covered in blood. The combination of Bruce's frantic laughter and my mother's anguished screeches made it impossible to think clearly. I think I started to whimper at this point. My ribs were so bruised it hurt to breathe let alone move my chest to have a good cry like I wanted to.

These are the moments in life where you don't think rationally. In fact, you don't think at all, you just let your survival instinct take over. It becomes about you or your killer.

And I was no martyr.

I tried to blink fast enough to clear my vision.

THWACK!

My right eye started to swell from Bruce's backhand making it even more difficult to focus. At this point my mother, like a wailing Banshee, propelled herself onto Bruce's back and started pounding her fists onto any piece of flesh she could find. I could hear Bruce's low chuckle at my mom's feeble attempt to stop him. From the sound of his amusement I could tell that today was the most fun he'd had in years.

Taking short controlled breaths I took this moment of solace to regain my bearings. And that's when I saw it: a blurred swirling black hole in the corner of the trailer.

WHAM!

Bruce had thrown my mother clear across the room. Her body collapsed into unconsciousness as her head punched a hole through the trailer's wall.

I screamed a horrible, terrible scream: a scream that only a child could make whose world had just been crushed, whose mommy had just been smashed against a wall, leaving her daughter alone, defenseless, a scream that would make any human who possessed an ounce of parenting instincts come running, without thinking, without rational thought. And I couldn't stop. Even Bruce had to cover his ears from the onslaught of shrieking. But Bruce's instincts weren't to mother, they were to destroy and he started towards me.

And seeing him, fists raised, plowing forward, I suddenly felt inexplicably tied to that black swirling chasm across the room. I was a part of it. It was almost as if strings connected us together. And I did the only thing I could.

I made it attack Bruce.

At first I didn't know what I was doing, but I suddenly understood that I physically controlled the black holes. I was connected to them like they were an extension of my own body, like they were my own limbs.

Bruce bellowed in pain as we both realized at the same time what I had brought back to life.

A black widow spider, full of venom and ready to attack.

Over and over I made the spider tear its fangs into Bruce's body: his neck, his arms, his legs, his chest. Bruce swatted the spider, squished the spider, tore it in two, but nothing he did could stop it.

It was mine.

It was already dead.

He couldn't kill it again.

He fell to his knees. The poison was flowing through his body now. I could see a small black tornado forming in Bruce's chest.

Fear overtook every fiber of my soul as I realized what I had just done, what I was still doing. I dropped my connection to the spider instantly. It fell lifeless to the floor once more, the black void churning madly in its center.

I crawled over to Bruce's body, leaving a trail of blood from my broken nose. He was convulsing on the ground, his body seizing from the poison coursing through his veins. He was dying and there was nothing I could do about it.

"What did you do?" my mother's voice cut through the near silent grunting and gagging of Bruce's dying moments.

She had seen the whole thing.

"I…" I couldn't think of what to say. My mother looked relieved, guilty and horrified all in one condemning expression. I wasn't sure if she was upset about losing Bruce or that her seven-year-old child had just become a murderer. Bruce's eyes rolled back in his head. His last breath was rattling and eerily hushed. It seemed to last an eternity. As if the oxygen in his lungs didn't want to leave his body and clung to whatever life it could hold on to.

I stared into my mother's eyes. She couldn't speak. She couldn't move. A small line of blood trickled into her eye from a gash on her forehead, but she didn't flinch. She just looked into my eyes with a blankness more terrifying than any emotion could be.

"Chelsan…" she finally croaked. Her voice was gravelly from screaming.

That was all she could say. It was agony to see her so dead in the eyes, face, body… just staring. I would have given anything I had just to stop her from looking at me with those empty eyes. Her vacant stare felt like a howl of pain so excruciating I almost covered my ears from the silence. At least then I would have been able to hear my own muffled heartbeat. Any noise would have been better than the oppressive judging stillness.

And that was when I realized what I had to do. To break her out of this coma she was encasing herself into. I turned to Bruce. To his raging black abyss spiraling like a whirlpool deep inside his chest. And I switched him on. Just like the spider. He was a bit clumsy at first. I had to concentrate as hard as my seven-year-old brain would let me just to get him in a sitting position. But after a moment or two it became easier and easier and he began to feel like an extension of me. It was an eerie sensation as my thoughts mirrored Bruce's movements. I would think of his arm moving and it would move. I would think of him speaking and…

"Janet?" I made Bruce call to my mother.

His voice snapped her completely out of her stupor. She watched him in shock and overwhelming relief. "Bruce?"

And then I made him cry. Cry like he never could do when he was alive. I made him cry until his face and clothes were drenched with his tears. "I'm so sorry. I'm so sorry," I made him repeat over and over as he sobbed in the aftermath of the day's destruction.

Mom crawled over to the two of us, renewed hope in her eyes. Whether she knew what I was doing or not, she didn't say. All that mattered was that she wanted to believe it. She needed to believe it. I could see it in her face. I made Bruce embrace the two of us with a tenderness he was never capable of before. I was doing this for me as much as for my mother at this point. Feeling his strong arms around me, holding me close, affectionate, loving. It was the first time in my life I felt like I had a father: a real dad. I nestled in closer. When my mom saw this she did the same. We both had contented expressions on our bloody bruised faces. I let Bruce sputter and jabber about how much he loved the two of us, how he would never hurt us again, how he was a changed man…

And he was.

After that day he became the best father anyone could ever ask for.

I still find it funny in a strange and disturbing way, that Bruce is a better father dead than he ever was alive. He's the easiest for me to control now because he was my first, and I've had a lot of practice since then. It's almost as if he's really alive sometimes. But every time I watch his face go slack when he watches his holo-tv or he stinks so bad I have to puppeteer him in the shower, I remember.

He's dead. Truly dead.

And it was my fault.

"**B**reakfast, Chelsan. Hurry before it gets cold. You'll be late for school." Speak of the devil, that was Bruce calling me for breakfast. "Chelsan, I mean it. I made you eggs!" Bruce's voice called through my door from the kitchen.

"I'm coming," I said with a sigh. Dead people could be so pushy sometimes. But I had no one to blame but myself. I made him say those things just like I made him cook my breakfast. I had been controlling him for so long, I barely had to think about it anymore. It was like I had a second body to do all the crappy things in life, like cleaning and cooking and anything else annoying. How nice is that?

Bruce is awake when I am and asleep when I am, too. Or at least "alive" anyway, I just make him kind of lie there until I wake up. I can't control him when I'm asleep. I wish. Think of everything I could get done!

I quickly dressed in my usual tank top, jeans and Chuck Taylors (still popular after four-hundred years) and checked myself in the mirror. My hair was a mess so I ran a brush through it. I had been growing it out for the last three years now and it was just past my shoulders. I used to have a pixie cut that, unfortunately at the awkward age of fifteen made me look like a boy. So, three years later, I felt a little more feminine. It was chestnut brown and I soon realized brushing it was doing me no favors, so I tied it back in a high-ponytail. I had boring gray eyes (why couldn't they be blue?!), slightly fuller lower lip than upper lip, small straight nose, high cheekbones, and today, thank goodness, no zits. I remember having a pimple the size of a crater on my forehead just before school ended the year before that I didn't think I'd ever live down.

As I walked out of my room I blew a kiss to one of my many holo-pics of Jason Keroff (news reporter extraordinaire) plastered on my bedroom wall and entered the living room.

The new holographic-television was on as usual. Mom just had it installed and I was still getting used to the fact that the people were solid holographs as opposed to our old junky holo-tv where you could see right through them. Not to mention they'd flicker every five minutes making it impossible to really get into any kind of show. The only thing I could sit through was the news just because it didn't matter what the holographs looked like.

And there he was, the adorable reporter himself: Jason Keroff.

He worked for LA's own Channel 2 News and was a journalist for various magazines and newspapers. It was pretty embarrassing liking the guy that every other girl from the ages of nine to eighteen had a raging crush on.

But to be honest, thinking about Jason kept my mind off of my lost cause Ryan Vaughn. Ryan was ridiculously perfect in every way… Stop!

Ryan was waaaaaaaay out of my league!

Jason. Jason. Jason.

He was reporting live on my holo-tv on location at a Virtual Reality Bar, about some scandal and such. (I never really did pay attention.) He was looking perfect, as usual, with his short, cropped, messy, coal black hair, big green eyes, which would always feel like he was talking specifically to you through the hologram, slightly crooked nose that gave him that extra sexy "I just got into a bar fight" kind of edge, t-shirt and jeans with a nice dress jacket over the top, and a pair of Chuck Taylors. (Yes, I know, I'm a copycat.)

It was amazing how clear the holograms were on the new holo-tv. It was as if a ten-inch version of Jason stood in our living room, Virtual Bar behind him, hover cars flying over-head, all displayed on top of our entertainment stand.

Of course, no one knew how old Jason was. He kept that hidden from the press. He could be any age, really, since three-hundred years ago in 2030, a medical scientist named John Fortski found the cure for aging and put it in a tiny pill called, Age-pro.

Basically, this little white pill (if taken everyday) stops the aging process completely.

So if you take it at twenty, you're twenty *forever.*

You can still die, obviously: accidents, guns, murder, hurricanes, tidal waves, there's no pill for any of those things. But as long as you stay healthy and stay away from sharp objects, you could potentially live forever. I guess there used to be a bunch of diseases you could die from in the twentieth century, but after aging was cured supposedly the properties that were used for Age-pro were such a huge breakthrough in medical science that all of the killing diseases had a cure. But more importantly, they had preventative shots that everyone received as a baby so no one would die from some horrible illness.

People who had money were legally allowed to start taking Age-pro at eighteen, but people like us trailer-park-low-income types, usually started taking it when we were thirty. That w as w hen t he N ational Insurance kicked in and pretty much anyone could afford it. And let's face it, even people who had no money managed to find a way to get their hands on Age-pro. Who would want to miss out on immortality?

Jason was gone before I could really appreciate the crooked little smile he always gave at the end of each report and was replaced with boring Carleton Gordan, news anchor for the last hundred years not looking a day over nineteen.

Carleton droned on in his monotone, annoying voice, "Overpopulation has reached an all time high, and the death rate has dropped to a record low. The government c ommented t his morning about its terraforming project on Mars, but no other word or solution has been made…"

"Come on, eat your food before it gets cold." Bruce pulled my attention away from the news.

"Sure, thanks, Bruce." I sat down at the rusty Formica-topped kitchen table where my waiting eggs rested. The smell finally reached my nose and my stomach grumbled in response.

"You better hurry, sweetheart, that rich school of yours won't tolerate tardiness from a trailer kid." Mom came into the kitchen with her usual hostility toward the high school I went to. It was a private, richy-rich-school that we could never afford, but I worked at the ice-cream parlor off campus to pay the tuition that scholarships didn't cover. She wanted me to go to the public school about ten miles away.

But I physically couldn't. And I couldn't tell her why.

The first time I realized that my control of dead things had a proximity limit was when I was on my way to my friend's Aunt's house twenty miles away.

About five miles out, I got a call from my mother, screaming that Bruce had just dropped to the floor, dead. I cried hysterically until my friend's parents turned the car around. I concentrated as hard as I could until I could feel Bruce's black hole and brought him back to life. It was just shy of four miles away from the trailer park.

I knew then that I could never go beyond a four-mile radius of my home, or Bruce would become a corpse again. Not only that, but in the few minutes that I let him die for a second time, his body began to decay, as if it knew the exact date when he died.

Think if I left and let him die for good? He'd be a skeleton within minutes.

Luckily, he'd only rotted a bit on his upper arm and leg, so no one seemed to notice. Gross!

But this was my life, my existence, making sure all the dead things I'd brought back to life stay fresh so my loved ones weren't in excruciating emotional pain from their losses.

When I found out that the public high school was outside my "safety zone" I looked for another school I could go to.

Only one was exactly three miles away: *Geoffrey Turner High School,* a super elite, super expensive, private school named after the Vice President of Population Control, which was pretty much the most powerful position in the world, even more than the President, since population was the world's biggest concern today. He was the only man in the public eye who showed any sign of age. He was fifty when Fortski created Age-pro and Turner had been fifty ever since. I always tried to get a closer look at his wrinkles on the holo, but I think they did some kind of effect to hide most of them. He was a very distinguished man, always in a suit and tie, dark hair with flecks of white. His features were classic: straight nose, chiseled bone structure, strong chin.

Mom cringed every time I mentioned the fact that we had the same gray eyes. Even the shape was the same. In fact, she'd cringe every time I mentioned his name. She said it was because he was creepy to look at, being old and all, and not to *ever* compare myself to him again. And that was about all she'd say on the matter, but I suspected there was more to it than that. Vice President Turner must have done something political over the years to piss Mom off. Even though she looked thirty, she was about to have her sixtieth birthday soon, and Geoffrey Turner had been in office for over two hundred years. That was a lot of time to do something that my mom could hold a grudge for.

"Do you want to take the rest of your birthday cake for lunch?" Mom asked me as she was already packing it into my lunch box. I turned eighteen four days ago. I was the oldest in my senior class. It was always annoying starting the school year older than everyone else. By the end of the year everyone had caught up to me, but for some reason a year in high school was the equivalent of ten normal years. So for at least the first few months I'd be on the receiving end of jokes and condescending glares from all the seventeen-year-old seniors equating my "old" age to my intelligence or lack thereof according to them. I would say I couldn't wait to graduate and live on my own, but I knew if I left, Bruce would be bones and I still didn't think I could do that to my mother.

Mom handed me my lunch as she kissed the top of my head affectionately. She gave me her usual wink and a smile. Her way of saying she loved me. My mom was pretty gorgeous considering the time she began taking Age-pro. Her hair was brown like mine, but her eyes were light hazel. Her skin was ivory in color with a smattering of freckles across her nose.

She was thirty-one when she started Age-pro so she only had faint lines around her eyes, which I personally loved. Her face lit up when she laughed and the slight crinkles made her eyes sparkle. I used to think this was the reason my real father fell in love with her. I would sometimes imagine what he was like, what he looked like, what his voice sounded like. He died the day I was born and my mom didn't have any pictures of him. She said it was too painful a reminder. He was the love of her life and she always said it killed her the day he died. For some reason the way she'd say it always sounded like she meant it literally. Maybe that was why she ended up with Bruce, she picked the complete opposite of my father so she'd never be reminded of him again.

"Thanks, Mom. I better go. I have to work at the shop after school today. I took a shift for Jenny," I told her between mouthfuls as I shoveled down a few more bites of Bruce's eggs. "I'll see you around seven." I kissed her cheek and ran out the door.

The flimsy aluminum door slapped shut behind me as I left the trailer.

I made my way to the Hover-Shuttle waiting area just outside the park. The Hover-Shuttle came every five minutes or so and could take you pretty much anywhere in the larger city of Los Angeles. The trailer park was pretty dead at the moment. Most of the people who lived there had blue-collar jobs that required getting up at the crack of dawn. I resigned myself to working at the ice-cream shop for the rest of my life if I didn't figure out what to do about Bruce. And that could be a *very* long time, an eternity possibly. An eternity of working retail! I hoped at some point I could be honest with my mom and make her understand what I did and let Bruce rest in peace. Yeah right.

I reached the designated steel bench to wait for the Hover-Shuttle. The waiting area itself was circular, like a fifteen-foot bulls-eye made of gray asphalt.

A few seconds later, I could hear the whizzing sound of the Hover-Shuttle coming my way. Closer and closer the rectangular metal box buzzed toward me. It was clunky and old, but most things that came to the trailer park were. Society pretty much wanted to pretend we didn't exist, so when it came to public works and transportation we were last on the list of repairs. That was what happened when there were twenty-seven billion people on the planet and over half of them were rich and demanded their needs came first. The other half of us did all the menial work and shut our mouths. No one wanted to stir the pot in fear that the National Insurance for Age-pro would be cut. If the government decided to cut the funding, they could push the age minimum to forty or even fifty!

The orange-yellow glow and the whirling of ducted fans from the belly of the Hover-Shuttle lowered to the center of the waiting area. The propulsion fans ran on hydrogen fuel cell technology, so to kill two birds with one stone, there were containers under the vehicles collecting the steam and water from the cells to later dump into recycling plants. There the plants would send the water to all sorts of places from drinking water distribution facilities to watering tanks located in most suburban neighborhoods for their greens. Anywhere and everywhere they could use it.

The metal on the shuttle was chipped and dented giving the appearance of a beat up refrigerator. The passenger door lowered to the ground with a loud CLUNK and turned into a set of grated metal steps. Skipping two at a time, I climbed up the stairs and entered.

The interior wasn't much nicer than the exterior. The seats were arranged like any public transportation: two rows of two-seaters with a middle aisle in between. There was only one other passenger besides me: a businessman, suit and tie, reading from his electronic reader, keeping to himself. I sat down near the front. The driver waited a few moments as if someone from the trailer park would come running up the stairs at any second. Or maybe he just counted to ten in his head at every stop. Whatever it was, at some invisible marker of time, he closed the door of the craft and we were off.

The humming sound of the Hover-Shuttle was almost deafening as we sailed toward *Geoffrey Turner High School*, the next stop. I looked out the window as we traveled and admired the landscape. Where the trailer park was stark and devoid of much vegetation, once outside its perimeter, the ground became lush with bright green grass and a field of California Oaks. Once the International Law of 2142 was passed requiring the planting of a tree every twenty feet, most places decided to re-plant near extinct trees like the California Oak. The law was passed as soon as everyone realized the down sides to Age-pro.

Overpopulation.

This basically meant we'd run out of oxygen if we didn't start evening out the balance of the world. More people meant *more* things, which meant *more* natural resources being drained, trees being one of the highest for paper alone. The first law to be passed was in 2068 that outlawed anything printed on paper. Electronic reading devices were already a popular luxury item back then, but they soon became a requirement if you ever intended to read anything. Only e-books were legal. But there just wasn't enough plant life on the Earth to sustain the amount of people inhabiting it so they had to make planting more trees a worldwide law. It was hard for me to imagine living on this planet without the amount of trees we had now. I loved trees. I loved getting lost in the forest with a good e-book or to just sit under the shade and have a moment to myself.

The Hover-Shuttle flew past the oak forest and I could see my high school drawing near. It looked like something from a fairytale: early 1800s architecture (re-created of course: the school was only twenty-years-old) made entirely of brick and mortar, iron-wrought gates and ivy growing up the sides of the school like veins pumping life into the building.

I just wished the people inside it were as nice as the building was to look at. Being poor in a rich school didn't exactly lend itself to making friends. I had two people who were brave enough to socialize with the "leech" as I was so fondly referred to. And I truly considered them friends. Bill and Nancy. Bill was a sweetheart. He was loyal and simple in the kind of way that made it nice to be around him. He was also easy on the eyes with his perfectly messy brown hair, well-muscled body (I think the guy had a ten-pack if that was possible!) and a boyish face with long eyelashes. In the entire high school, his family was the richest by far! That was why they didn't give him much of a hard time hanging around with me. The one thing the rich kids had in common was the hierarchy of elitism. And since Bill could buy and sell almost everyone that attended Geoffrey Turner High, he'd get his usual kiss ass line of admirers every day whether I was with him or not. I always felt safest when I was with Bill since the worst kind of behavior I'd experience from the true nasties of the school was a total ignorance of my existence. When I wasn't with him it was an entirely different story. That's when the claws came out.

Bill and I met randomly sophomore year when I rounded a corner and slammed into his six-foot wall of a body. His stuff flew, my stuff flew, it was a mess. But the most tragic part about it was I broke my electronic reader, a lightning bolt shaped crack straight down the middle. Electronic readers weren't cheap mind you, I had to work double shifts at the ice-cream shop just to buy mine. I nearly cried between gulps of apologies. I thought I'd be crucified right then and there for daring to touch the precious Bill Merryweather, let alone knocking him on his butt. And without an electronic reader I'd have been kicked out of school for sure. I couldn't count the amount of times the school informed me, "Geoffrey Turner High is not a charity. If you can't purchase your own items, you will be excused."

Jill Forester (the ringleader of my torment for the last four years) was the first to kneel down and try to help Bill up, sending nasty glares at me about five times a second. Her hair was as black as her heart and she had bright green eyes that made her cruelly beautiful. Why are all the mean girls gorgeous?! She was thin and perfect and she knew it.

When she saw my broken reader she simply smirked and said, "Karma."

Karma, *this*! I wanted to say, but held my tongue and apologized to Bill again.

"You should be sorry." Jill couldn't help herself.

If ever I wanted to smack someone it was in that moment. But Bill did something I'll never forget. He shrugged Jill off and stood up. That alone caused a dramatic gasp from the crowd. He offered me his hand and smiled in a way that said, *don't listen to her. No harm, no foul, I'm fine.* I took his hand and he lifted me to my feet. He picked up my reader, handed it to me and genuinely looked like he was sorry. The group surrounding us already started to close in on Bill, shutting off any conversation, until I was standing alone in the middle of the hall with my broken reader. Later that day when I sat down in Geometry class there was a brand new, state of the art, grossly expensive, electronic reader lying on my desk with a card. The card simply said, "Sorry about your reader. Hope this will work for you. Bill." My heart had stopped. No one had ever done something like that for me before, especially someone as popular as Bill. He was really sticking his neck out on the social line for me. It was the nicest thing I had ever owned *and still own* to this day. I knew he had a ton of money and buying a reader was probably like spending a penny to him, but it was a kindness he was in no way obligated to do, and genuinely came from the goodness of his heart. Ever since then we've been close friends, despite Jill's agony over the union.

My friendship with Nancy was a different story. She was considered upper middle class which was still super rich compared to me, but not rich enough to give her the same immunity that Bill had. We met freshman year when we were forced to be lab partners in Biology. She wasn't happy about it. I was new and everyone knew I lived in the trailer park before I even arrived on campus. That put me in the below filth category on everyone's radar though no one would openly admit this for fear of looking like the prejudiced jerks they were. I knew they'd come up with a "real" reason for hating me later, but as for the moment of my arrival, it would just be an unsaid loathing toward me. Nancy did the usual: rolled her gorgeous blue eyes and flipped her long locks of blonde hair, in annoyance of my presence, audibly grunting exasperation, all for the pleasure of the rest of the class. Just another perfectly beautiful mean girl.

When the teacher handed out the dead frogs we were supposed to cut up, her face turned greener than their corpses. For me it was a room full of black swirling holes.

"Are you okay?" I asked.

Nancy tried to ignore the fact that I even spoke to her, but after a few moments she shook her head. "I don't think I can do it."

I didn't know what to say. I was afraid if I said anything she'd guffaw and tell me to shut up anyway, but as rude as she was to me, I could still see how much the frogs were upsetting her.

Then she spoke, her voice barely audible, her face growing paler by the second, "I had a pet frog that just died… Jimmy."

She said it with such emotion and heartache, all my feelings of annoyance toward her melted away.

"I don't think I can cut into him." Even though her voice was a whisper her eyes were screaming with panic and anguish.

That was when I decided to use my gift. There was no way I could let this poor girl cut into what she saw as her pet.

"We won't be cutting anything today," I said and I popped every single frog back into existence.

It was pure and utter chaos. There were jumping frogs everywhere: on the desks, on the students, on the stools, on the floor. Screams and laughter mixed together like a symphony of bedlam. The teacher tried to wrangle the frogs into the garbage receptor, but since I controlled the frogs, that didn't happen.

"Open the windows," I said very calmly to Nancy, whose expression had done a complete turn around. There were tears of joy streaming down her face: joy and relief. Whether she knew exactly what I was doing or not, she didn't say, but she did know I was somehow responsible. She nodded and walked over to the windows, opening them wide.

I made the frogs jump and whiz toward the windows like moths to a flame and within seconds they were gone. All that was left was a very excited and amped up biology class. Nancy sat down next to me, wonder in her eyes, but she didn't say anything.

"Calm down, okay, calm down, get in your seats." The biology teacher tried to bring some semblance of order back to the room. "We won't be dividing into lab partners today, obviously… I need to sit for a second." The teacher had finally grasped what had just happened and he couldn't seem to keep it together. After he sat he said, "You can sit in your regularly assigned seats if you like. Just read chapters four and five, I'll be right back." He left the classroom without another word.

The room broke out into chatter and laughter at what had happened. Jill Forester waltzed over to Nancy and said in the most condescending and superior voice she could, "You don't have to sit next to *that* anymore, Nancy. Come over and sit with Joan and me."

I waited for the inevitable rejection from Nancy. I expected it and I honestly wouldn't have been offended. Social ladders in high school are tricky things. If you were knocked down a few rungs, it was really difficult to climb back up, and being friends with me would probably knock her off the ladder completely.

But Nancy didn't even flinch, didn't even hesitate, she just turned to Jill and said in a cheerful voice, "No thanks." Then without another word of acknowledgement to Jill she turned to me with a smile, "What are you doing after school?"

Jill was in shock, standing there as if she had just been slapped in the face. After a moment she seemed to recover. "Nancy, this is your last chance. I'm serious."

Still smiling, acting completely oblivious, Nancy turned to her. "Serious about what?"

Jill didn't have a response to the directness of the question. As if spelling it out would somehow expose her as the raging bigot she was. In one fell swoop Nancy had beat Jill at her own social game by either making her admit to her prejudice against me, or back out and fight the fight in some other way. People were starting to stare at this strange confrontation, so she decided to back away, but not without an evil glare directed at the two of us. She was always full of those.

Ever since then, Nancy and I had been best friends.

The Hover-Shuttle landed at the station on the outskirts of Geoffrey Turner High. It was right next to the black iron wrought gate that served as metal open arms to the school. I did love this school, despite the people in it that made my life torture. There was something so comforting about its presence that I couldn't quite explain. Maybe it was because I earned my right to be there. I earned the scholarships, I worked a part-time job, I made the grades, I deserved to be there. I wasn't born into it; I made it happen and I was actually a little proud of that.

I exited the shuttle without a word to the driver and made my way through the gate to the front courtyard. It was pretty much deserted since above me was the carpool platform with a long line of hover-cars dropping off students. Most of the kids liked being driven, but a handful of students drove themselves and parked in the designated lot behind the school. You had to be seventeen to get your hover license and most of the rich kids waited until they were eighteen since they enjoyed having drivers taxi them around everywhere. Bill was the only person I knew that actually had his hover-license.

The courtyard was green and lush with classic maples and a hedge fence surrounding the entire circumference of the area. Two rows of cherry blossom trees lined the walkway ending at the large arched oak doors that led inside the school. My favorite time of year was spring when the trees become a forest of pink. There were benches scattered throughout to encourage students to study and socialize outdoors, but there were only a handful of us that took advantage of the space.

I walked through the oak doors and entered the bottom level of the school. The halls were quickly filling up as students made their way down from the hover platforms above. Mahogany lockers lined the hallways (no small feat considering the use of any kind of wood was limited by the law for environmental purposes) and white marble floors leading the way. I could only imagine the amount of money it took to maintain the beauty and quality of the wood and flooring with the wear and tear of high school students. Not that Vice President Turner had to worry about money. He was filthy rich and always had been, even before Age-pro. His family was old money, ancient money, like since the early fifteen hundreds kind of ancient.

When I reached my locker I opened the combination lock, pulled out my electronic reader and grabbed my fitted cardigan. Temperatures usually reached below freezing in Mr. Alaster's History class and I wanted something to protect me from the cold.

"Hey, did you read chapter eight?" Nancy suddenly appeared at my side. She had grown a few inches since freshman year, but her hair remained blonde, long and gorgeous. I still had pangs of guilt when I realized how popular Nancy would be if she wasn't friends with me. She was truly stunning to look at, giant blue eyes: a delicate straight nose and perfectly bowed lips that were always pinkish-red in color as if she wore lipstick, but she was just naturally flawless. Her tight jeans and fitted top showed off her picture-perfect body. I always felt like the ugly duckling little sister when I stood next to her.

"Yeah, I read it last night." I shut my locker and we began to walk down the hall toward class.

"Fill me in. I completely slacked." Nancy usually didn't do her homework and relied on me to keep her up to date. Her philosophy was that since she aced the tests what did it matter if she did the homework or not. She was one of those ridiculously smart people who never had to study for anything; everything came to her naturally. Somehow she'd manage to put all the pieces of the puzzle together just by looking at the question or the equation on the test. I, on the other hand, had to study for hours just to maintain my A status. If I didn't I'd lose my scholarships.

"We're just going over religious stuff since Age-pro," I told her.

Nancy rolled her eyes and made an exasperated groan. "Seriously? Haven't we covered that in *every class ever?*"

"I think we're going over the whole Voodoo thing today, so that'll be cool." I completely agreed with Nancy. The fascination of belief or lack of belief in religion since Age-pro was a topic that every teacher liked to discuss at some point in their classroom; from literature, to biology, to history, to social sciences, even the math teacher had something to say about it! At least Mr. Alaster delved into the interesting stuff, like the transformation of Vodun or Voodoo from a religion to black magic.

"Watch out for Jill today. She's on a rampage and you're her favorite target." Nancy didn't seem all that concerned, but confrontations with Jill tended to get ugly and I knew she genuinely wanted to avoid it at all costs.

"What's she on a rampage about?" I asked. Sometimes knowing what was bothering Jill helped me figure out how to avoid complete and total humiliation.

"Her mom found out she was taking Age-pro."

I shrugged. Most of the kids here illegally started to take Age-pro before the eighteen-year-old restriction. The fear of wrinkles and cellulite overrode health and good sense. The reason there was a restriction at all was because the International Health Board ruled it dangerous to stop aging before a person had fully grown. It could cause massive complications later in life. There were extreme cases, like in 2143 the "Alice Rose incident." Basically, this woman, Alice Rose, had a baby and decided she wanted a *baby* forever, so she started giving it Age-pro. When she was finally caught, the baby was nineteen-years-old and still an infant. Alice was arrested and sent to prison. That was when everyone started realizing the dangers of Age-pro. They immediately made the eighteen-year-old restriction punishable by life imprisonment, which meant no Age-pro, which meant dying of old age. Who knows when Jill started taking it? She was damn lucky her mom found out about it and not the police. By trying to stay forever young she came dangerously close to living a mere eighty to ninety years.

"I'll steer clear," I said to reassure Nancy. I really didn't want to be in Jill's warpath today.

The bell rang and everyone started shuffling into his or her designated classrooms. Nancy and I arrived at Mr. Alaster's door and entered.

Jill sat at the back of the class with her usual crowd of admirers hovering over her like bees to honey. As soon as I walked in I looked away trying to avoid eye contact.

"Just sit down," Nancy said under her breath, which indicated to me that Jill was staring me down. It was amazing when you could actually feel people staring at you. I refused to look in her direction. Meeting gazes with Jill would only give her an opening to use me as her verbal punching bag.

I did as Nancy said and we both sat in our seats near the front of the room just as Mr. Alaster walked in. Mr. Alaster started taking Age-pro around thirty and had a thin, wiry frame with curly brown hair on top, making him look like a human carrot. He wore his usual brown cardigan sweater with round suede elbow patches, typical khakis and dress shirt, and, of course, his wire frame glasses. Let's face it, he looked the way you'd imagine a history teacher to look. Sometimes I wondered if he did it on purpose or if he really, truly liked to dress that way.

"Punch up chapter eight." Mr. Alaster's enthusiastic, buoyant voice filled the room.

I pulled out my electronic reader and brought up chapter eight like everyone else in the room. The title of the chapter read: "The Fall of Religion and the Beginnings of Elemental Experimentation." Snore. Though Mr. Alaster didn't seem to think so, he was, in fact, more eager than I'd ever seen him before.

"What did you think of this chapter? Any thoughts? Questions? Come on, guys, don't be shy, this subject is fascinating, trust me." Mr. Alaster's smile was almost contagious. He might actually be right if we hadn't already heard it a bagillion times.

"No one? Really?" Mr. Alaster didn't seem upset, only surprised at our lack of enthusiasm.

That was when Ryan Vaughn raised his hand. I looked away and tried to ignore his perfect face. It was too torturous liking someone I had absolutely no shot at. He was the resident whiz kid of Geoffrey Turner High, and I had an enormously embarrassing crush on him. Like I said, most of my crush on the reporter Jason Keroff was to keep my mind off of my doomed liking of Ryan.

Ryan's family was on the same pay scale as Nancy's, which put him in the upper middle class range. He was a popular kid only because he agreed to do other people's homework for the right price. Ryan's I.Q.

was also fifty points above genius which put him as the smartest kid in school and rumor had it, in the world. Science scouts would come to our school all the time offering him jobs straight out of high school at the top research facilities in the world. Ryan didn't seem fazed by all the attention and no one knew if he took any of the offers.

He tutored me in math junior year and even though I was a social reject, he was still decent to me, which of course, made me like him all the more. I could barely speak when I was around him. He probably thought I was a complete idiot. Ryan was ridiculously cute and ridiculously brilliant. He kept his short, sandy-blonde hair in a kind of "planned messy" way and was taller than most boys our age (six-three). He was lean but muscular with big brown eyes and angular features. Okay, he was gorgeous, but way out of my reach. I seriously had a better chance with Jason Keroff than with him.

"Yes, Ryan." Mr. Alaster was thrilled that someone was participating, let alone the resident brainiac.

"Isn't all this *Elemental Experimentation* the same thing as religion? Just a bunch of mumbo jumbo made up to validate our existence." Ryan slumped in his chair and said this with a kind of arrogance that suggested he didn't have much conviction in his statement.

"That's a valid point, Ryan, but scientific Elemental Experimentation has tangible evidence that it truly produces results where as religion was always based on faith and imagination." You could almost see the saliva forming around Mr. Alaster's mouth from his passion on the topic. "The reason I'm so excited about this, guys, is because just this morning the Scientific Journal released the results of an extended study which began in 2247. It was run by a scientist named Lester Rankin who performed the Voodoo ritual of resurrection. He was actually able to bring a man back to life that had been dead for two days."

My interest immediately perked up. Nancy looked over at me with protective concern. We had never talked about the day I made the frogs come to life, but I could imagine she had wondered about it. And now as Mr. Alaster was telling me that there might be others who could do what I could do, I needed all the info I could get. I needed to download the Scientific Journal pronto.

"For how long?" I asked before I could stop myself. My curiosity overtook my sensibility of speaking up in a classroom where Jill Forester resided.

"For how long what?" Mr. Alaster wasn't upset by the disruption, he genuinely was curious as to where my mind was going with this.

"For how long has Chelsan been a complete moron?" Jill chimed in from the back.

The class laughed on cue, but I ignored them as usual. I turned my attention to Mr. Alaster. "How long was he able to bring him back to life?"

"Aaah!" Mr. Alaster was thrilled with the racing thoughts I instilled inside of his mind. "For only a few minutes. And the man wasn't really alive, more like an animated corpse. According to the study, the longest they were able to keep the corpses mobile was a maximum of five minutes."

Interesting. Somehow this had to have something to do with my gift. Maybe I had performed this spell or ceremony or whatever it was when I was a kid and didn't even realize it? Maybe my mom or my real dad… maybe something genetic because they had done this hoochimimbober Voodoo thing? I couldn't stop thinking about all the possibilities. I needed to know more.

Ryan raised his hand again, perplexed. "Correct me if I'm wrong, but I thought Vodun was a religion."

Mr. Alaster's eyes lit up with excitement. "You are very correct, Ryan. *But* Vodun or Voodoo is no longer considered a religion because of its tangible elements. Many people no longer believe in the Vodun creator, Mawu, or, God, in Christian religions anymore. Only the people who consider themselves truly faithful, like the Christian Coalition, who segregate themselves around the world in tiny towns and refuse to take Age-pro still worship their God and practice the ritual ceremonies."

There were a few gasps from Jill and her lackeys in the back of the room at the thought of not using Age-pro *on purpose*.

"Paganism and Wicca were also categorized as religions in the past, but are now seen as Elemental Experimentation. In the twentieth century people thought of them as hokum because death was such a driving factor in the way that people lived. They were on this planet for such a finite time that the afterlife was far more important to them than the mere seventy to ninety years they were alive. Once the factor of death was taken out of the equation, people found that there were far more interesting things to explore. Suddenly finding out if these rituals or spells, as they used to call them, actually worked became a priority. Most of the population found that when you had eternity, your goals and ambitions changed."

This was where I started to tune out. Mr. Alaster was now getting into familiar territory that all of us had heard too many times to count. I looked over at Ryan and even he had zoned, staring at his reader as if he were following along with Mr. Alaster.

At that moment though Ryan's eyes unexpectedly met mine and he smiled slightly. I could feel my face flush and I quickly turned away. My stomach did back flips and I could feel myself break into a slight sweat. What was my problem? A guy who wouldn't say "hi" to me in the hallway smiles at me and I was completely falling apart. And to boot, I just realized that when I turned away I didn't exactly smile back. I probably gave him some kind of look of disgust. Typical. It didn't matter anyway, it wasn't like Ryan would ever *like me like me*. He was almost certainly smiling at the fact that some moron stared at him like a complete dork. I was such an idiot. What was more annoying than that was the fact that I desperately wanted to look at him again. Was I a masochist or something? Don't do it!

"What's wrong with you?" Nancy whispered to me with a look of concern on her face.

"Nothing. Not feeling well, must've been breakfast." I tried to cover up, but I could tell Nancy wasn't buying it.

"Is it the study?" Nancy's expression indicated that she really *did* know more than she was letting on. I could tell we were going to have a discussion about my gift very soon. And a part of me looked forward to it. After four years I could trust her. Besides, she obviously already put most of it together if she was picking up on my interest in the study.

"Yeah. We'll talk," I promised.

Nancy's face changed from concern to excitement. Between her and Mr. Alaster's enthusiasm I could barely concentrate.

Okay, I could barely concentrate because I desperately wanted to turn around and stare at Ryan. My brain was a mess. I couldn't wrap my head around why I cared? I tried not to think of Ryan Vaughn all that often. In fact, after our tutoring time, I tried to block him out of my head completely for fear of becoming a stalker. But it was very hard to forget the rare moments when his hand brushed up against mine by accident and it would send tingles all the way to my toes.

IT WAS JUST A SMILE! STOP IT! I needed to clear my head.

I needed to focus on something else.

"Maybe Chelsan would know." Jill's voice cut through my inner hysteria.

Know what? Great. I hadn't been paying attention *at all*.

"Chelsan?" Mr. Alaster smiled at me with eagerness.

"Yes?" I asked.

I could tell Mr. Alaster immediately knew I had no idea what he was talking about. His face fell slightly as if he couldn't fathom how anyone could not have been engrossed in his lecture.

"I think she was too busy drooling over Ryan to pay attention." Jill laughed. And the class laughed with her.

Was I that obvious? Oh man, if Jill noticed my red face and sweats, Ryan *unquestionably* did. Thank goodness I had resisted my urge for a second sneak peek!

"I wasn't drooling." Did I *really* say that out loud?! I wanted to crawl under my desk and die.

"I see." Mr. Alaster realized that this was a feud between teenage girls and didn't want to have anything to do with it. "Let's continue forward, shall we? What religions took the biggest fall after Age-pro?" He droned on and the class quieted down from Jill's outburst.

Nancy tried to give me non-verbal support in the form of an encouraging smile, but nothing would make me feel better. Nothing except making Jill feel just as humiliated. I searched the room until I found the perfect thing.

A dead fly on the windowsill.

I brought it to life.

I started slow, just an irritating fly buzzing around Jill's face. She discreetly waved it away. Then I amped it up. I made it fly directly in her ear. SWAT! I kept the fly in her ear as if her swat had injured him. This freaked her out to the point of standing up in class trying to rid herself of the fly now stuck in her ear. Everyone stared in amusement.

"Jill? What's the problem?" Mr. Alaster asked.

Here goes. The fly raced out of her ear and flew around her face, up her nose, out of her nose, in her hair, in her clothes until Jill was flailing her arms and whole body in panic. She looked like a frenzied animal being attacked by an invisible force.

"GET IT OFF ME! GET IT OFF ME!" she wailed.

I made it land on her cheek.

WHACK! Jill's best friend, Joan, hit the fly with her reader thereby smacking Jill directly in the face.

I made the fly fall to the floor, dead once more.

Everyone stifled his or her laughter for fear of Jill's wrath, but I smiled as broadly as I could.

I win.

"Jill, you may want to go to the nurse, your cheek is looking a little red." Mr. Alaster looked as though he was trying to hide his own amusement. A lot of the teachers in the school liked Jill less than I did. Her father's influence in the government made it impossible to give Jill anything less than a B. Our math teacher freshman year tried to give her a D and needless to say he was fired the next day and replaced with a teacher that let her pass with flying colors. The teachers that didn't hate her simply sucked up to her any chance they got. Owen Forester (Jill's dad) was second in command to Geoffrey Turner himself, which meant he had influence in over-population "perks." Perks that included owning more than one hover-car, landscaping that fudged the "planting a tree every twenty feet" law, free passes to Virtual Reality Bars, just to name a few. And Jill's favorite teachers always cashed in any chance they could.

Jill gave Joan a look that could kill and made her way toward the exit just as the bell rang for the class to end.

"Is it that time already?" Mr. Alaster seemed disappointed to let us all go. It felt like leaving someone in mid-sentence.

Everyone began to move out of their seats and exit the classroom.

"Wait for Joan to leave," Nancy warned me and we pretended to gather our things a little bit more slowly than we normally would. "Okay, she's gone."

Everyone had left, including Ryan. I didn't even want to think about ever seeing him again for fear of dying of embarrassment. Why did I have to open my big mouth?

Nancy and I headed for the door. "Do you like Ryan?" she asked.

I tried my best to act shocked and appalled. "No!"

Nancy laughed out loud. "You totally do! That's cute."

"Cute?" I complained in exasperated disgust. "More like tragic. Guys like Ryan don't like girls like me."

Nancy rolled her eyes and practically guffawed. "Oh, please! Girls like you? Attractive, smart *and* have a personality? You're right, you should just give up on guys right now."

"Easy for you to say. You have money."

"Ha! I'll give you some. See how much it makes a difference in your love life," Nancy groaned.

"Being friends with me is what's messing up your love life. You may not care about money, but everyone else does." Which was true though Nancy didn't like hearing it.

She opened the door and we entered into the crowded halls.

And I ran straight into…

…Ryan.

I hit his chest full force. How could I not have seen him? How could Nancy not have warned me? Looking over at my best friend, I saw the triumphant smile on her face and knew she had done it on purpose. She had angled the door exactly so he'd be out of my view.

"Sorry," I sputtered.

Ryan smiled. I wished he wouldn't do that. It made my stomach churn in horrible ways.

"No problem. I actually wanted to talk to you for a minute. Can I walk you to class?"

My brain froze. What was that? Say something. Now would be the time to say something.

"She'd love to. Chelsan, I'll meet you later for lunch, okay?" Then Nancy eyed Ryan with a knowing smile, "Unless you have other plans," and she was off.

And I was alone. With Ryan. And I couldn't make myself say a single word.

Ryan's face seemed almost apologetic as if my silence was a

reprimand for something he'd done. "You must think I'm a jerk."

Really? Nothing? I couldn't even make something up, like, 'nice shoes.' Anything?! It was as if my mouth was paralyzed.

"Look. I'm really sorry I started ignoring you after tutoring last year. Jill's crew made it difficult for me," Ryan admitted sheepishly.

What was going on? Was this some sort of horrible prank where I'd start being nice to him and he'd laugh and tell me what a moron I was?

"Are you serious right now?" Wow. I really said that. And I said it so rudely. Ryan looked like I had punched him.

He shook his head and actually seemed embarrassed. "You're right. I'm sorry I bothered you."

And he started to leave. To leave!

And I still stood there, like someone had turned me into a statue. Come on! Do something!

"Ryan, wait!" Good. That was good.

Ryan turned around and he actually had hope in his eyes. Real, honest hope.

"I'm not used to people being nice to me," I confessed with as much sincerity as I could muster.

Ryan's face was immediately ridden with guilt. "I'm sorry," was all he could say.

He said it so sweetly my gut twisted with sympathy. "It's okay. It's just that in the past when people have been nice to me, it's been because Jill put them up to it to humiliate me in some way."

"I'm sick of Jill and her team of morons." Ryan practically spat out Jill's name to my pleasure. "Can I walk you to class?" He looked at me with those big brown eyes and I hoped my face wasn't turning bright red.

"Sure." Was this really happening? I still couldn't wrap my head around it. It had to be some kind of trick. I resolved myself to not get too excited until I was sure Ryan was on the level.

"Physics, right?"

He knew my schedule, which could be very bad or very good. Bad because Jill told him my schedule, so this would all be a part of the plan, or good because he *knew* my schedule… which meant he actually paid attention to what I was doing and where I was going.

"Yeah." Good. Cool and not too desperate. Like I wasn't about to vomit from nerves.

"Chelsan!"

I turned around to see Bill standing in front of Ryan and I like he was the Sheriff of Nottingham and Ryan was Robin Hood.

"Is he bothering you?!" Bill was actually angry. I had never seen him like this before. I was so surprised by his behavior I didn't know what to say. Unfortunately, he took that as a yes.

Bill slammed Ryan up against a set of mahogany lockers, pinning him with his arm. "Leave her alone." Bill was a couple inches shorter than Ryan, making him six-one, which was nothing to scoff at, but he was much more muscular and Ryan looked like a fly trapped by a spider.

My mouth had literally dropped. And as much torture as it was seeing Ryan wrongfully accused, it was almost a little exciting to see Bill so protective of me. I knew we were buds, but I didn't realize how far he would go to keep me safe. He was actually being violent. The angriest I had ever seen him was when Jill rigged it for him to be Homecoming King, and even then he had barely raised his voice.

"Bill. He's not bothering me, I swear! Let him go." I finally found my voice.

"Are you sure? It looked like you were about to throw-up."

Seriously? That actually showed?

"I'm sure. He was just walking me to class."

Bill let Ryan go with an apologetic shrug, but his eyes were still fuming.

Ryan, meanwhile, had let this whole event take place without so much as a peep or a struggle.

A crowd had formed and everyone waited with anticipation as to what would happen next.

Ryan straightened his shirt and combed his hand through his hair as if contemplating what his next move should be. Then he turned to me and did something that made every fiber of my being melt and tingle all at once.

He kissed me.

I felt like I was going to explode and collapse. There was no way my knees were going to function much longer if he kept this up.

Ryan pulled away, his hands cradling my face. He smiled. "See you later."

And then he was gone, down the hall, past the shocked observers and out of sight.

My whole body was shaky, including my brain. But as out of control as I felt, I didn't want the feeling to end. In fact, it just hit me that Ryan was gone. Hey!

"Chelsan?! What are you doing with Ryan Vaughn? Are you guys dating or something?" Bill looked at me with an emotion I couldn't quite place. One second it looked like anger, the next like I had killed his puppy.

The bell rang for class to start. The crowd dispersed, heading to their respective classes.

"No, Bill, Ryan and I aren't dating."

"Then why did he just kiss you?" Bill returned to his calmer demeanor as if me admitting that Ryan and I weren't dating comforted him in some way.

"I dunno, maybe because you slammed him against the lockers? He had to save face somehow." Damn it! That was probably it! It wasn't me that he wanted, he just didn't want to look like a wimp in front of the school. Uuugh! I felt like crap now.

Bill's face flushed with embarrassment. "Sorry about that. I really thought he was messing with you."

"It's okay. At least I know that you'll always have my back." And I meant it. Knowing *that* was the only thing keeping me from crawling into a hole and dying right now.

"Always."

The halls were empty.

"Better get to class." I smiled at Bill and he smiled back.

"I'll pick you up from work and drive you home. What time are you done?"

"Nine o'clock."

"See you then." Bill hurried toward his class until I was alone in the hallway.

With a deep and loud exasperated sigh, I made my way to Physics, knowing that the rest of the day would be spent re-playing Ryan's kiss.

Well meant or not, it was still achingly unforgettable.

***

The rest of school was highly uneventful. At lunch, Nancy made me give her a play by play of the Bill and Ryan showdown. She was most interested in the kiss, which apparently had spread throughout the high school pipelines like wild fire. I didn't go into too much detail, but I admitted that it was nice.

Nancy seemed a little disappointed by my lack of enthusiasm, but I didn't want word to get around that I was as flustered about it as I was. The only nice thing about the whole dramatic event was that Nancy appeared to have forgotten all about the conversation we were supposed to have about my gift. A small relief. I knew it was coming, but at least I wouldn't have to deal with it today. It would give me a chance to do the research about this new study myself and hopefully have more answers.

Besides, I was still paranoid about the whole Ryan thing. I needed more information before I moved forward. Ryan may want to have nothing to do with me after Bill smooshed him against the lockers. Most likely he was licking his wounds and would never see or speak to me again.

Probably for the best.

I took the Hover-Shuttle to work. *Mel's Ice Cream and Sodas.* It was still within my safety zone of the trailer park and it also happened to be the a popular hang-out for students from my school. They just loved to come in and have me serve them (like having money didn't already equip them with a hefty superiority complex over me).

Mel's was located on a beautiful cobblestone road lined with maple trees. Even though the need for roads and highways weren't necessary since all the vehicle traffic was sky level, they were still used as landing stations, decoration for shoppers, and more importantly, historical landmarks. I had to play sick my sophomore year when my history class took a field trip to a freeway called the 405. Supposedly, when people still drove land cars it was one of the busiest streets in the country and, according to my teacher, it was mainly a parking lot in its busiest times. As over-populated as our planet was, traffic wasn't really a problem since we had seven levels of hover airspace. Sometimes there were so many hovers above one area that it looked like cloud cover, blocking out the sun completely, 'But at least the cars are moving,' my mom would always say.

Mel's was one of the many little shops that were reminiscent of small cottages. The rooftops were thick clay tiles that gave the street the appearance of something out of a storybook. I had to admit there were worse places I could spend eternity.

I entered the shop, which was packed with people. I nearly cringed when I saw Jill sitting in the corner booth with her pack of hyenas. There was no way I going to avoid a confrontation with her. Not after the whole *Ryan* thing. She'd feel like I was encroaching on her territory.

I made my way past the red and white striped booths and black Formica-topped tables, lifted the flap of the bar, dropped it behind me, waved at Roger behind the cash register and walked into the back of the ice-cream shop.

Mel, the owner, sat at his desk in the corner doing paperwork with his usual large grin. He was heavy-set in a jolly way, balding (a rarity, but Mel started Age-pro at thirty-five and he was scared of hair implants), with small features that made him look like someone placed a tiny face on a large round canvas which happened to be his mug. Mel was just about the nicest person I'd ever met. He considered his employees his family since he had none of his own. I'd do anything for Mel, including taking Jill's abuse so as not to disturb the other customers. Oh boy. Better mentally prepare.

"You okay, Chelsan?

"I'm fine. I better get out there. Roger looks like he's going to explode."

Mel chuckled and nodded toward the giant-sized fridge next to me. "Better pull out more shake mix. I think we're running low out there."

I nodded, went into the freezing refrigerated chamber, grabbed a twenty-pound container full of shake mix and headed back to the melee of the shop.

Roger finished helping a customer and turned to me with a groan that could only come from someone who has worked in the service industry. Roger was a few years older than me and lived at a trailer park a couple miles away from mine. He was a good solid guy, always helped anyone in need, volunteered for just about anything: someone you could count on. His brown hair was short and curly, his face delicate, almost feminine-like in a pretty-boy kind of way. Very popular with the ladies. Even Jill would sometimes stoop to flirt with him.

"How long has it been busy?" I asked.

Normally, it wouldn't get crazy for another couple of hours.

"Since your school let out. I gotta warn you, I've been hearing your name come up *a lot*. Especially from your favorite." He nodded toward Jill.

"Yeah. Long story." I really didn't want to get into with Roger. He'd find the whole thing amusing, of course, but if Jill overheard me talking about Ryan, she'd find some way of turning it against me and embarrass me somehow. "I'll tell you later when it's not so crowded." I gave Roger a meaningful glance and he nodded in understanding.

"Gotcha. Don't you think it would have been easier if you went to regular school like the rest of us?"

"You have no idea, but Geoffrey Turner is one of the top schools in the country." I gave Roger the usual spiel. I had it memorized. I literally had a double life, the *fake* one where everyone thought I was an over-achiever that planned on going to the best schools and would have an amazing career, and the *real* one where I brought dead things to life and couldn't step out of a four mile radius from my home or my jerk step-dad would drop dead and rot on our trailer floor.

"I know. And just so you know, us *park people* are *really* proud of you. It's always an inspiration to see someone succeed and get out."

Roger smiled with pride, like he was living vicariously through me. My heart dropped slightly. There were a lot of people in the parks who saw me as an inspiration. I didn't want to think of how disappointed they'd be when I ended up staying at the ice-cream parlor and doing nothing with my life.

"Hey, no pressure. Relax, you look like you're going to cry."

I obviously hadn't perfected the art of hiding what I was thinking. I definitely needed to work on that. "I've just had a crazy day."

"You're killing me! What happened?" Roger salivated for the gossip.

"Later. Trust me."

"So, trying to sleep your way into money." Jill's voice came out of nowhere. How did she sneak up on me like that?

I turned to face her and there she was with Joan at her side sneering at me.

"Do you need a re-fill on that shake?" I asked in the most sickly sweet voice I could muster.

"Yes, but I don't want your dirty hands touching my glass. What's his name here will do just fine." Jill gave Roger the empty glass and he took it with a wink of encouragement to me.

"What do you want, Jill?" I wanted this to be over.

"I want you to stay away from Ryan Vaughn. Stick to your own kind, like *Shake Boy* here." Jill grew angrier by the second. I couldn't fathom why she hated me so much. She had everything: money, power, good looks. Why was she always so focused on making my life miserable?

Roger returned with Jill's shake and handed it to her. He had his back slightly turned so Jill couldn't see his lips and he mouthed to me, "Ryan Vaughn?" Then he made a face of genuine approval. "Nice."

I almost wanted to hug Roger. He was a friendly lifeline in the midst of attack.

"Okay. Will do. Is that all?" I raised my eyebrows in emphasis of the desire to end this.

Jill stood there, frozen in body, but eyes livid. I had seen that look before. It was the same expression Bruce used to make before he…

PUNCH!

Right in the face. Jill actually punched me! And it hurt!

"Oh crap!" Roger was stunned.

Even Joan and the rest of Jill's crew looked shocked.

And just when I thought that Jill had recovered from her freak-out, she leapt over the bar and tackled me to the floor.

This time I was a little more prepared, but not much. It was amazing at how awkward fighting actually was. In your mind you can imagine how you'd be, what you'd do, how you'd defend yourself, but when someone was actually on top of you, wrestling you to the ground, your basic instincts kicked in.

Fight or flight. Those are pretty much your two options, and as I knew from Bruce, mine was fight.

I grabbed Jill's wrists to stop her hands from wrapping themselves around my neck. Her face was distorted and snarling from anger. She had finally reached her limit. With the combination of being caught taking Age-pro, the fly that practically devoured her, Bill's protectiveness of me and Ryan's kiss had finally sent her over the edge.

Once I had a good hold on Jill's arms I used my whole body to flip her over so I was on top and…

BAM!

I punched her hard in the face.

That was when I felt the strong arms of Mel pulling me off of Jill's body.

Joan quickly ran around to the other side of the bar and helped Jill up, yelling, "YOU should fire her! She attacked Jill!"

"I did not! She punched me and then Amazon'd it over the bar!" I couldn't believe Joan was actually trying to go there.

"It's true, Mel, Chelsan didn't do anything but defend herself." Roger was obviously having none of Joan's shenanigans either.

"Like I would ever stoop to fighting!" Jill caught on to Joan's tactics. "And I have a room full of witnesses who will back me up." Jill smiled at me, regaining her evil calm and turned to Mel with as much malice as I've ever seen from her. "And if you don't fire her, my father will be coming down here and closing up this fine establishment, so I suggest you rid yourself of the scum that works here."

Mel looked like he wanted to kill Jill himself, but I knew Jill would make good on her promise of destruction. I turned to Mel before he had a chance to decide. "It's okay, Mel, I'll leave."

Mel's face burned with fury. He wheeled on Jill, but I stepped in front of him before he'd do anything he'd regret, and whispered so Jill couldn't listen. "Don't. You'll lose everything."

Mel did something then that I didn't expect. He hugged me and bent close so only I could hear, "I'll fix this." He pulled away and turned to the room full of staring customers. "Nothing more to see here. Go back to your business."

Everyone pretended to do just that, but there were still flickering glances of curiosity from the audience.

I gave one last look at Roger and could tell he was still enraged at the unfairness of it all.

"I might just have to press charges." Jill embraced this ruse full force now.

I turned to her with as much fury as I could evoke. "Then I might just have to report your Age-pro use to the proper authorities. It stays in your system for at least two weeks after you stop. All they'd have to do is a blood test." I totally lied. I had no idea if Age-pro stayed in your system or not, but from the horror on Jill's face, neither did she. "Even *daddy* can't get you out of that one," I added for measure.

It was the equivalent of another punch.

Jill fixed her hair and straightened out her clothing. "I suppose you being fired is enough punishment."

I shook my head and left. I had another semester's tuition due later this year and without a job there was no way I could pay it. Jill knew that. And then it hit me.

She had planned the whole thing.

That was why the shop was so full. Full of witnesses she controlled. I should have known something was up. She was waiting for me to hit her back and I fell for it. Though that look of rage on her face was real enough, and Joan acted pretty surprised when Jill punched me and leapt over the bar. Jill probably expected me to punch her first when she made the comments about Ryan and when I didn't bite she couldn't let the opportunity pass. I was still an idiot, but whether I hit her or not, she would have made everyone swear that I did, so it was pointless even thinking about it.

I made my way to the Hover-Shuttle stop which was located at the end of the street. I'd have to let Bill know that I didn't need that ride after all. I pulled out my cell phone and started to dial.

The phone rang a few feet behind me. I whirled around to see Bill holding his phone and smiling.

"You think a fist fight between you and Jill wouldn't be on every cell phone in our school in milliseconds," Bill laughed with amusement. "Come on. I'll take you home."

"Thanks," was all I could say. I had to admit it was nice seeing him there. Bill was quickly becoming a rock of support I didn't think I could live without.

"Tell me you got some good licks in." Bill tried to lighten my mood.

"I wish I could have done more." I smiled back at him.

"We're a pair today, me with Ryan, you with Jill."

"I seem to be the common denominator in all these equations."

"Something worth fighting for, I'd say." Bill leaned down and kissed the top of my head.

I was shocked. As innocent as it seemed, Bill had never touched me, let alone kiss me. And as surprised as I was, it was actually kind of nice. Unexpected, but comforting. I smiled up at him and gave him a playful nudge in the gut. "Let's just agree not to get into any more fights from now on."

"Agreed." Bill put his arm around me and gave me a supportive squeeze. It wasn't like the fire I felt with Ryan, but it was just as powerful. Like the fierceness you feel with a friend you know you'd do anything for. A surge of intense loyalty came over me and I squeezed Bill back.

"Thanks for picking me up. I really needed a friend."

"Any time."

We arrived at his hover-car without mishap and he opened my door for me like he always did. I sat inside while he smoothly walked around to the driver's side and slid into the car. He started the car and we were off.

"So, fired, huh?" Bill cringed.

"More like quit. Mel looked like he was going to throttle Jill himself for giving him an ultimatum like that. I didn't want her dad messing things up for him."

"If I could help you I would, you know that, right?" Bill was so sincere it made my heart hurt.

"Yeah, I know. Thanks, Bill."

"You need money? I think her plan was to get you to have to drop out due to lack of funds," Bill said this so quietly I had to strain my ears to hear.

"I figured. But I can't take your money. I'll figure it out somehow." The last thing I wanted to do was owe someone money. Especially since I was doomed to work crap jobs for the rest of my life. I'd be indebted to him *forever*.

"I wouldn't expect it back, if you're worried."

Did he just read my mind?

"But I, personally, would *have* to pay you back and that's why I can't. Thanks though, I really appreciate it."

"The offer will always be open if you need it." And he left it at that. Just like Bill: never pushy, never overbearing, just simple and to the point.

We arrived at my trailer and he lowered the hover-car to the ground. Bill quickly exited and ran around it to open my door.

"Thanks," I replied, a little embarrassed. He was being extra polite, probably because he felt bad about the whole Ryan debacle. I stepped out of the car.

"Try not to think about it." Bill tried to make me feel better.

And then he hugged me.

What was going on?

I hugged him back and pulled away, punching his arm to try and re-establish our normal buddy behavior. "See you Monday."

His face registered disappointment, but he hid it with a smile. "See you Monday."

Bill got in his hover-car and flew away.

"I thought you two were just friends," my mom's voice sounded from the doorway of the trailer.

I turned to face her and she looked angry.

"We are. What's your problem?" I didn't like the tone she was using to talk about Bill.

"Get in here."

I sighed and walked into the trailer. I kept Bruce sitting in front of the holo-tv and intended to keep him there during this soon-to-be painful conversation.

"Bill is a nice guy," I defended. I had this argument with my mom about five times a month. For some reason she didn't like Bill. Any time I'd mention him she'd ask me if there were any other boys at school that I liked. My reply would always be a groan and a giant no, but it was as if she knew I had a hopeless crush on Ryan and wanted me to do something about it.

"I know you think so, but I don't trust him. I see the way he looks at you. Aren't there any other boys at school that you like?"

SEE?!

"Mom, he doesn't look at me in any way but friendship." Which was true. Though he did just kiss the top of my head and that hug felt a little too tight.

"I saw that. I know you don't feel that way about him and you should tell him. Maybe he'll leave you alone after you deflate his ego a little."

"Charming, Mom."

"Well… wait a minute. What are you doing home so early?"

Uh oh. Here came another painful topic.

"I quit."

"Good. I don't like you working *and* going to school."

What? Not even a *why?* Or what happened? Just: *Good.*

"Good? I have no idea where my tuition is going to come from now." I was a little angry at her response.

"You'll just have to go to public school like the rest of us did," Mom responded with an air of pleasure.

I couldn't even stomach the rest of the conversation. "I'm going to bed."

I stalked past her and went into my room, slamming the flimsy aluminum door. I pulled out my reader, searched the directory for the Scientific Journal and downloaded the study Mr. Alaster referred to about resurrection.

After a few minutes my eyes grew heavy and I couldn't keep focused on what I was reading. I pulled my comforter on top of me and laid my head on my pillow, falling instantly asleep.

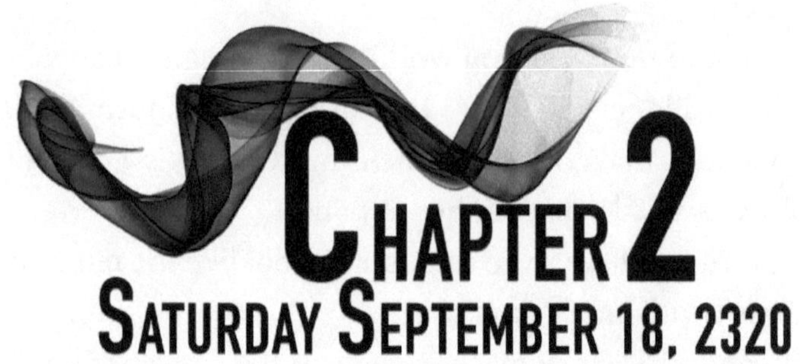

Chapter 2
Saturday September 18, 2320

I awoke to the sounds of clunking and clacking from the kitchen.

"Mom, seriously?!" I yelled through my wall. She was about to go fuss around in her garden and she was arranging her tools. The reason I knew this was because it had become an annoying Saturday tradition that would never fail to wake me up. She hated it when I slept in late. It was some kind of strange pet peeve of hers.

"Oh, did I wake you? Sorry, sweetie," her muffled voice came through the wall.

"Sure you are," I mumbled into my pillow.

My mother also knew that once I was up, I *was* up. I couldn't go back to sleep.

I suddenly thought of the Science Journal's report and I had a surge of excitement course through me. Maybe I could find some kind of clue as to how I had my powers. But the last place I wanted to read was in this dingy trailer. I suddenly thought of the perfect place, just outside of the trailer park, where no one ever went, where I could just be by myself and concentrate on the report.

I wore the same clothes as yesterday and I seriously debated on not changing. I wouldn't see anyone from school anyway. "Is it hot outside?" I called to my mother.

"It's already eighty-five degrees," she called back.

Shorts it was.

Grabbing a pair of cargo shorts from the floor, I quickly changed into them and replaced the tank top I wore for a sleeveless fitted top. I slipped on a pair of flip-flops, headed toward the kitchen, blanket and reader in hand.

Mom was arranging her bucket full of gardening supplies, about to head out front. "You going somewhere?" she asked thoughtfully.

"Just over to my tree to read."

Mom knew the spot.

She smiled, "Well, have fun. You should take some toast or an apple with you. Lunch won't be for another few hours and you'll be starving."

"Thanks, Mom." I grabbed an apple and left the trailer.

Walking through the trailer park, I felt a rush of contentment. This truly was my home and everyone in it felt like family.

A black swirling hole came running toward me as I recognized Buster, a golden retriever that belonged to a little girl named Katie. A couple of years ago he had been hit by a hover-car. The driver was drunk and swerved down too low to the ground, clipping Buster's head, killing him instantly. I knelt down and scratched behind Buster's ears. I made sure that he acted like he enjoyed it thoroughly.

Katie ran up to us slightly out of breath. "Buster! No more running away! You almost died last time!" Katie's long blond locks were tied in a neat ponytail. She had no idea he had actually died that day. When he was killed, everyone in the park came running out of their trailers from the screams of anguish flooding out of Katie. I just couldn't bear to see her giant brown eyes filled with such sadness and despair, so I kept Buster on my own leash and Katie had been happy ever since.

"Hi Katie, Buster looks good." I made Buster turn and lick Katie's face until she giggled and fell to the ground from his onslaught of affection.

After I was sure she'd had enough attention, I had Buster stop so she could regain her composure. She laughed when she said, "We're going to play Frisbee today."

"You guys have fun. I'm off to go read." I scratched Buster's head for emphasis.

Waving at Katie I walked to the outskirts of the park, a smile still on my face.

It took a while to arrive at my favorite spot. It was a field of rolling hills smattered with wild flowers and a large willow tree resting on top of the highest peak. The tree was a haven of shade on a particularly hot day. The only thing that could possibly break up the heat wave were the darkened clouds I could see on the horizon. Unfortunately, the clouds were making the air thick with humidity, but at least my willow tree would give me some comfort.

I walked up the incline of the color-filled hill leading to my tree. The flowers were gorgeous this time of year. Every color imaginable covered the landscape making me feel like I had stepped into a painting. Most people steered clear of this area because *with flowers came bees,* and lots of them. There was even a hive in my lovely willow tree. Thousands of these fields existed all over the world, another part of keeping the planet green and well oxygenated. I never minded the bees; they pretty much kept to themselves and if they buzzed around me, it was only out of curiosity, not the malice that most people assigned to the poor species. Even if you were stung, it was not like it was a life or death situation, unless you were allergic or something. But as many times as I'd frequented this spot not once had any bee killed itself by stinging me.

I pulled back the long hangings of leaf-covered branches that draped to the ground from the top of the willow. My private fortress. The buzzing of the beehive added a nice hum of life to the day. I laid my blanket on the ground, plopped down on my stomach and pulled out the reader.

I scrolled down to the Scientific Journal and brought it up on screen. I decided to start from the beginning since all the science mumbo jumbo went completely over my head last night. I had to admit, even awake and well rested I was having trouble understanding the terminology of the report. Words like neurotoxins and membrane proteins were cluttering the pages. I had to use the built-in dictionary just to read through two sentences. After the first pass, what I gathered was this: using certain forms of Voodoo rituals (i.e. ceremonial garb, prayers, herbs, blood, not specified whether human or animal, yuck) they were able to bring back the corpse for up to five minutes. No matter how hard I searched, I couldn't find anything that explained my power. It wasn't like my mom performed Voodoo. And my dad died before I was born. It was disheartening and I immediately felt defeated. Was I some random fluke of nature? Some misstep of evolution? I had no answers. Maybe I was missing something. I resolved myself to asking Mr. Alaster on Monday. Possibly he'd have some insight that I couldn't see. I could never tell him my secret, of course, but in a round about way I could at least find out what he knew. Not much, I'd guess, but it was worth a try.

Flipping through the pages of my reader, I found a news clipping of Jason Keroff. He droned on about Vice President Turner and his crusty old body and I didn't pay attention to the rest. I simply admired his adorable smiling eyes and that sarcastic smirk he was so good at.

And suddenly, Ryan popped into my head. The spontaneity of his kiss. The dirty blonde mess of his hair. Uuuuggh! He was ruining my perfect crush on Jason. It took me weeks to forget about Ryan after his tutoring ended, and that was a professional relationship. Now that he added a kiss in the mix (which could have been totally insincere) it was going to take me much longer to block him out of my head now.

I quickly thought about my strategy of how to avoid him at school. It worked before, it would work again. No talking, no close proximity and above all, no eye contact! It was those eyes that pulled me in every freakin' time and I was mad at myself for wanting to believe, even if just for a second, that he actually might like me. That was the biggest mistake I could ever make. I had to make him the enemy or I'd never get through this. Always remember, he ignored me and brushed me off last year. And even though he apologized, I had to believe that it wasn't heartfelt. Guilty feeling, maybe, but lying about it all the same.

THUMP!

I grabbed my head in pain. It felt as if someone had just hit my forehead with a steel hammer. What was that?

THUMP!

I began to panic. Was I dying? Was this some sort of brain hemorrhage? What was causing me this intense pain? It felt like an axe jammed into my brain and split it in two.

A green mist appeared in front of me, blinding me, seeping into my head through my nose and ears and mouth. I screamed in fear until the green fog started to clear and suddenly I was in the trailer park standing in front of my mother. She was in her garden, choking from the same green smoke. I reached out for her, but my hand went straight through her body as if she was a ghost.

Then I realized, I *was* the ghost.

I was at two places at the same time.

My body was still under the willow tree, but some other form of me was back in the trailer park watching my mother drop to the ground, coughing from the smoke filling her lungs.

I looked around and the green mist was everywhere and everyone in the park was choking and collapsing to the ground.

"Chelsan?"

I watched as a ghost of my mother stepped out of her writhing body.

"Mom! What's happening?" I couldn't hide the panic from my voice. Either I had fallen asleep and this was the worst nightmare I'd ever had, or something very unexplainable and weird was going on.

THUMP!

I cringed in pain and when I looked up, my mom and I were in an empty room. "Mom? What is going on?"

She wouldn't answer me. My brain squeezed with agony. I must have been having some kind of seizure and it was causing this insane delusion.

"I wanted to show you before it's too late," Mom spoke to me and her eyes met mine. There was a kind of desperation to her expression I couldn't quite put my finger on.

"Before what's too late?"

THUMP!

"Make it stop!" I cried out from the torment and suddenly Mom and I were in the most extravagant mansion I had ever seen. Almost every item from the stairway, to the tables, chairs, even the frames on the wall were all gold. It was like stepping into Fort Knox, melted down and molded into a house.

"Where is this place?"

Mom put her finger on her lips to quiet me and pointed.

I noticed a very pregnant version of my mom standing in front of Vice President Geoffrey Turner and his wife, Roberta. Uh oh.

Roberta was a Feline. A genuine cat lady. I had only heard about Felines in history class. Back in the early two-thousands (before Age-pro) women and men used to have surgeries to literally lift their skin off their skulls and pull it back to get rid of their wrinkles and sags. Gross. As a result the more they did it the less human they looked until eventually they started to resemble cats, hence the term Felines. On top of that they'd inject themselves with some kind of paralysis drug to freeze their faces in place. It was a horrendous sight; I had only seen pictures, but standing there in front of this woman with her long black hair pulled back tightly in a bun, midnight colored eyes and shiny-stretched-back alabaster skin, made me cringe.

Looking at Mom was a relief to the eyes, in her early thirties, fresh, vibrant, beautiful. The complete opposite of a Feline. Mom had obviously started her Age-pro by then and her face was timid and scared. She stood next to a man and my heart nearly jumped out of my body. I was positive with every fiber of my soul that it was my father. He had my eyes and my lips. I nearly choked from the emotion at seeing him.

The scene was surreal, as if watching it on a holo-tv and hitting pause. All four figures were frozen in time as if we had stepped into a three-dimensional photograph.

This was so confusing, why was my mom talking to the Vice President? What were they doing in his mansion? And then it hit me…

"This is your memory."

Mom reached out and touched my face, nodding once. "I know about your gift."

My eyes widened. "You what?"

"I need to show you everything I know."

"But why now?" I asked. Still trying to figure out what was happening.

"Just watch."

It was like she hit play. The four figures started moving.

WHACK! Geoffrey Turner slapped my father so hard, he actually fell backwards.

"HOW COULD YOU FRANKLIN?! After all these years?!" Turner roared in outrage.

I turned to the ghostly image of my mother to see her reaction, but she simply watched the scene in front of her, expressionless. As if these were events she had played over and over in her mind, eventually becoming numb to them.

"I LOVE HER!" My father screamed back. "AND I LOVE THE BABY SHE'S CARRYING!" He took a deep breath to calm himself and looked at Turner pleadingly, "She's your grandchild, father. Doesn't that mean anything to you?"

What? Did he just call Vice President Turner his father?

My mom from the past began to cry hysterically, holding her swollen belly, trying to regain her self-control. My father immediately supported her with his arms, keeping her steady.

"She's trash, Franklin, look what she did to you?! You know what must be done," Roberta replied quietly, but far more deadly than Turner's slap to the face.

My father's eyes seemed to pop from genuine terror. "You wouldn't dare," he hissed.

"You're back now and we forgive you, but we won't let you *mate* with this trash. These are the consequences you have to pay." Geoffrey Turner reached out and touched my mother's belly. "She'll be coming soon, I'd say my good-byes if I were you."

That seemed to crack whatever composure was left in my father. He punched the Vice President so hard in the face that he flew back five feet to land on his gold coffee table.

CRACK!

I cringed as I realized some kind of bone snapped in Turner.

Roberta wheeled on my parents.

And then the most frightening thing I had ever seen happened…

Roberta's eyes turned a deep solid purple. Out of her mouth a large boa constrictor slithered its way to the floor and moved with lightening speed toward my pregnant mother.

"Mom," I spoke in a quiet, frightened voice.

"Keep watching," was all she said.

My dad grabbed a gold statuette from the mantle and threw it as hard as he could at his mother. It hit with such terrifying impact that Roberta crumpled to the ground with only the sound of the THWAP to her head. The snake vanished only milliseconds from my mother's feet…

…THUMP!

I clenched my hands over my head from the tortured agony of the returning…

THUMP!

The surroundings started to swirl and change once more. I didn't know how much longer I could take the throbbing pain. My mind was racing and sluggish all at once. I wanted to vomit, but I could literally feel the disconnection between my body and this strange form I was currently in.

Red, orange and black churning colors swarmed around my eyes with dizzying force.

In an instant everything was in focus.

Mom and I stood next to a ten-foot bonfire. It was the only source of light in the pitch black dead of night. The flames licked up the side of a silhouetted cliff face and the sound of crashing waves filled the unnatural silence.

I saw Geoffrey Turner and Roberta standing in front of the fire. Their faces were painted like skeletons and they were dressed in long black robes embroidered with intricate tribal designs.

Their eyes were inhumanly pitch black and they began chanting unintelligible words. The fire responded in turn, flames rising higher and higher, crackling and snapping like a furious counterpart to the spine-chilling peace of the night.

Roberta's feline face was monster-like in the fire's glow. In her hands, she held a picture of my mom. She threw it into the flames and the fire roared in answer.

Turner reached down and picked up a cruelly serrated knife with symbols carved into the handle. He screamed in a kind of tortured pleasure as he tore into his arm with the saw-toothed blade. Blood poured from his wound into the fire.

The fire was alive with what could only be described as ecstasy. Flames leapt into the darkened sky. Turner's voice was hoarse and crackling as he said, "The mother and child will die."

Turner's wound closed like an imaginary zipper zipped his skin back together, forming a large white scar. Both Geoffrey and Roberta's eyes cleared.

WHOOSH!

The flames instantly extinguished and we were all plunged into darkness.

THUMP!

Ow. Seriously, ow.

Mom and I were in a delivery room. My delivery room.

There she was, dead on the gurney, and me, the baby me, dead in my father's arms.

The doctor was there. He placed one hand on my father's shoulder. "I'm so sorry."

When my father didn't respond the doctor shook his head in sympathy, "I'll give you a few moments."

The doctor left the room.

I was stunned by the memory. I turned to my mother. "But how?"

"This is how it happened," she answered and looked at me. Her eyes were filled with tears and then she turned back to the memory.

As soon as the door swung shut my father took a deep breath and placed my corpse on top of my mother. He leaned down and kissed Mom's lifeless body.

I gasped as my own father's eyes rolled back in his head and when he stared down at the two of us, they were solid red like a nightmare. He grabbed a scalpel from a nearby tray.

"I give my life for theirs."

And he slashed his arms and throat, dropping on top of our cadavers with a thud. His blood sparked and cracked as it seeped into our skin and clothes.

SNAP! The baby me's eyes popped open and she breathed in life.

As the last vestiges of life left my father, his eyes began to swirl black, like the holes I could see in dead people. Faster and faster it spun until it twisted its way out of his eyes and into mine.

In that moment, my mom of the past, gasped for air underneath my father's dead body.

"That was how you got your power," Mom responded quietly next to me. I could see this memory was the most painful for her to watch. There were tears in her eyes as she saw herself on the gurney screaming at the sight of my father's corpse.

Doctors rushed in, shock on their faces. They quickly removed my father and grabbed the crying baby to make sure I was okay.

The scene froze in an eerie melee of chaos and blood.

"Why didn't you tell me?" So many things were racing through my head. If she knew all along what had happened, why was she just now telling me? And in *this* freaky way, and getting back to the original topic, *how* was she showing me this? What was happening?

"I'm not done."

THUMP!

I really wished the thumping would stop already. I could handle the visions, but the thump, thump, thump, was going to make my head explode, literally. The environment began to transform once again, colors melting into each other like an impressionist painting until our trailer slowly came into view. We were inside and I gasped at what I saw.

We were in the memory of the day when I first used my gift. Bruce threw my mother of the past into the trailer wall. I almost started to panic when I knew that I was about to watch myself kill him. The seven-year-old me was screaming at the top of her lungs and suddenly Bruce was being taken down by the black widow. It was sickening to watch. It was one thing to reflect in a memory, but seeing it in front of me like this, like a voyeur watching some gruesome snuff film, was unbearable.

"Stop it, please," my voice was barely a whisper.

It was as if she hit pause again. She froze the scene just as Bruce dropped to the floor from the spider's poison.

"You knew I brought him back?" I could hardly believe it. My self-imposed prison was all a lie. She knew and let me do it anyway. I felt betrayed and hurt.

"It was necessary." Mom still wouldn't look at me. She just stared at the frozen memory in front of us.

"Necessary?! Why didn't you tell me you knew? You know I have to stay near him, or he'll rot." I still couldn't believe that she truly understood the facts of the situation.

She looked at me, her eyes filled with sadness and regret. "Just trust me, Chelsan. It was necessary."

"Mom. What is going on?" I couldn't take this anymore, and I needed to know what was happening.

THUMP!

"MOM!" I cried out from the pain.

And we were back in her garden in front of the trailer. The green smoke was layered in a thick fog blinding my view of the park. All I could see was my mother on the ground, choking. It was surreal standing next to a ghostly version of her and watching as her body on the ground was writhing in agony.

"I'm dying," she confirmed.

I looked around in panic. "No. I can save you!"

THUMP!

"I can't take that noise anymore! Make it stop!" I screamed.

"It'll stop soon enough. It's what's keeping us linked together right now."

"MOM! I'll go back to the park, I'll save you! Let me go!" I was sobbing now. Keeping us linked in this strange way was stranding me under that damn tree. I could be half way back to the park by now.

"Promise me something, Chelsan." Mom looked at me as seriously as I'd ever seen her.

"Anything, Mom, just let me go help you!"

"Promise me you won't bring me back."

I caught my breath. And I knew then; she was really dying. "The thumping…" my voice broke from emotion.

"It will end soon." She tried to comfort me.

I knew in that instant that the thumping was her heart beat. It was the only thing that would tie us together. No! I could barely keep it together.

She nodded and then smiled through tear-filled eyes. "I love you, Chelsan. Promise me."

I could only nod in response.

"You must keep safe. Your Grandfather will be coming, and he *will* try to kill you. You were meant to die today. He won't stop until we're both dead."

THUMP!

And I was back under the willow tree.

I gasped for breath as I was slammed back into my body. The pain to my head was gone as soon as I returned. And I screamed for it to come back again. The alternative was far more excruciating. She was dead. My mother was truly dead. I could feel it with that last thump of life.

Feeling returned to my body and I ran as fast as I could through the willow branches, across the field of flowers and straight into…

…A nightmare of unimaginable proportions.

The whole park looked as though it had been hit by a tornado. Trailers were smashed, overturned, destroyed beyond recognition. The green smoke was gone, dissipated by the time I got back to the park.

But only *my* eyes could see the most terrifying picture of all. A sea of swirling black holes of people I knew and loved. My heart nearly stopped when I saw *her* just as I left her in the vision, my mother, lying dead amidst her demolished garden. A garden I had kept flourishing and alive for the last ten years. I couldn't bear it. I couldn't stand to see her like that.

I raced past the twisted metal and corpses to reach her side.

All I had to do was reach into her chest and bring her back. She'd be with me, forever. I couldn't live without her. I didn't want to. I needed her.

"I'm sorry, Mom. I have to," I whispered in her ear.

Every part of me fought the compulsion to break my promise and use my gift, but grief does terrible things to people and I couldn't think clearly anymore. In less than an hour I lost everything. She was my everything. I could barely breath. I could barely function. And then I did it.

Mom's eyes fluttered open and she looked at me. There was nothing there, just emptiness.

Her soul was gone.

I had violated her soul.

I immediately dropped my connection with her black hole and she fell to the ground once more. I quickly turned my head and puked all over the smashed petunias. I collapsed in a heap on top of her and something inside of me broke. I couldn't stop crying. My eyes felt like they would swell shut from the amount of tears pouring out of them.

Then I heard a noise that disturbed the agonizing silence. Sirens and the whizzing of hover-cars coming my way. I peered up from Mom's body to see what looked like a swarm of over-sized bees heading straight for the trailer park.

It was the press and emergency crews. I looked down at the crushed flowers and plants of my mother's garden and I knew she wouldn't want anyone to see her pride and joy like this. I concentrated as hard as I could in my heartache and slowly began to repair every inch of Mom's legacy. I made every flower bloom whether it was their season or not, every tomato was the richest red, yellow and orange, every peapod was bursting with marble–sized peas, every tulip, petunia and azalea were the most vibrant colors imaginable. By the time I was finished the garden was more gorgeous that it had ever been.

The onslaught of hover-cars reached their crescendo as they came to a halt a hundred feet outside the park. In a matter of seconds, I was surrounded by reporters, paramedics, firemen and police. Cameras flashed, people's voices melded into one loud shout, the buzz of hover-gurneys moving around from victim to victim. My head was going to explode from the assault on my senses. There were about two hundred camera crews all crowding around the most news worthy sight there.

The lone survivor.

Me.

Fantastic.

The voices slowly started to separate from each other in an annoying attack.

"Were you here when the tornado hit?"

"Is this your trailer?"

"Do you know the woman you're standing over?"

"Are you the only survivor?"

Too much. Too much. I instinctively scooted in closer to Mom as if she could protect me from all this. But I was truly alone.

"She's my mom." I found that when I spoke, every single person in the area quieted down to hear my response. "What tornado?" Mom didn't show me any tornado. It was some kind of green smoke. Tornados didn't give off smoke.

"Clear the way. Clear the way." Two paramedics swooped in and before I could respond they had hovered Mom away in a gurney.

"WAIT! That's my mom!" I cried out. I stood up and tried to take on the crowd full force to get my mother back.

"We'll take good care of her," one of the paramedics called over his shoulder and they were out of my view.

The pack of reporters closed their ranks, making it impossible for me to cut through.

"How sudden was the tornado?"

"Did you hide somewhere?"

I wanted them to all go home and leave me alone. "There wasn't a tornado. Something else killed them. Some kind of green smoke."

There was a roar of chatter almost like a rhythm.

"What kind of green smoke?"

"Are you suggesting that *smoke* caused this kind of damage to these trailers?"

Their voices became a single chatter yet again and I couldn't tell one reporter from the next.

"I don't know… I… my mom…" My head started to spin. Go away! Can I see my mom? Leave me alone! All the things that I wanted to say, but I found that my tongue was locked in place from being overwhelmed.

"Were you close?"

Did he really just ask me that?

"THAT WILL BE ENOUGH!" a voice came roaring from behind the press.

All eyes, including the firemen, policemen and paramedics turned to the largest man I had ever seen. I recognized him right away, the Mayor of Los Angeles Norman Bradfield. Everything about Mayor Bradfield was round: tummy, face (including the three chins he was sporting) arms, legs, fingers, toes, everything! He had a kind and warm face on the holo-tv. He always reminded me of Mel and that made him great in my book, but in person he had a slyness to his gait. He was a shark, I could tell right away.

Everyone moved aside as he walked toward me. All the reporters made room for his eminence. It was as if they all sensed a photo opportunity within their grasp and they drooled in anticipation.

"Leave this poor girl alone," his voice boomed. At least, this, I agreed with. "She just lost her mother!"

Okay. True, but the way he said it made my skin crawl. He had absolutely no *real* emotion behind his words. He said them for affect only, no true sympathy or care about me and how I might feel. I had seen

Jill pull the same kind of manipulative tactics all the time on teachers and other students; a fakeness I had developed a kind of radar for over the last few years. And this guy made Jill look like an amateur.

To prove my point, the Mayor actually leaned in close to me and gave the cameras the cheesiest, most over-the-top look of concern he possibly could. I wanted to vomit again, this time on his perfectly shined shoes.

"Now, now. From the looks of it, this girl was the only one who survived this terrible tragedy." Mayor Bradfield's voice was so loud it carried all the way to the furthest reporter.

"She says it was green smoke."

"She said there was no tornado."

I watched the Mayor's face very carefully to see what his reaction would be, and I wasn't disappointed. There was a brief second of what could only be described as panic. I knew something was going on here, and my mom died before she could tell me everything. She was so focused on letting me know all her secrets (and my own) that she didn't even think I'd want to know how she died in the first place. It was vital that I found out. What if this was a new kind of bio-terrorism, or some kind of natural disaster created by Mother Nature to control the population? What I *did* know for sure was that it wasn't a tornado. I was less than half a mile away. I would have felt it, heard it, seen it, something!

"This girl is obviously confused." Mayor Bradfield recovered with a smile that stretched so far across his face I didn't think he could speak. I was wrong. He must practice. "Were you knocked out in the tornado?" He placed his hand on my shoulder as if to comfort me, but he was squeezing quite a bit of pressure on me to the point of... ow!

I removed his hand with an exerted shove, which caused a slight gasp from the swarm of press. "I was just over that hill and there WASN'T A TORNADO!"

I could barely hear anything from the uproar I caused. The Mayor put his hand back on my shoulder with so much force I was paralyzed where I stood.

"You see! She wasn't even here! How would she have seen..." He leaned down to me so only I could see his face. His eyes were raging at me. "What did you say you saw?"

With every chubby finger clamped down on my shoulder in a vise of warning, I spoke quietly, "Green smoke."

Mayor Bradfield turned to the press with his glorious fake grin on his blobish face. "Aaah, yes, *green smoke*. She was probably seeing the tail end of that tornado!"

I cringed and I could tell from the reporters' reaction that they ate up every word he said. It was so frustrating not having proof. But who was going to believe a trailer girl over the Mayor of Los Angeles? I suddenly had a flash of petty brilliance.

I concentrated as intently as I could, though it was difficult with the Mayor's hand now a permanent clamp on my shoulder.

It was enough. I had been doing this one the longest....

...Bruce walked out of the tangled metal that used to be our trailer.

It was like a lion's roar when the press saw him. This was more excitement than anything so far. Here in front of them was a true witness to what really happened. And lucky for me, I controlled every word that came out of his mouth. I was tempted to bring a few others back too, but that would be too much to take on. Bruce would do just fine.

In all the upheaval Mayor Bradfield's grip loosened and I tugged away from him to run into Bruce's open arms. "Daddy! You're alive!" I made sure my voice carried out to the cameras and press.

It was complete and utter chaos. Camera flashes, screaming voices, and the Mayor like an island in a sea of madness, staring daggers at me.

"Sir, sir, was it a tornado?"

"Did you see anything?"

Bruce stepped forward with his arm wrapped around me. Everyone was silently anticipating what he would say. "I didn't see a tornado. All I saw was green smoke."

Take that Mr. Mayor.

Between the Mayor and I, we were making the Media's day. They acted like they hadn't seen this much excitement in years. And the more I thought about it, the more I remembered a lot of *natural disasters* like these, but they always seemed so straightforward to me, now it made me wonder.

Mayor Bradfield used the bulk of his body to maneuver himself in the spotlight once more. He pulled out a holo-tape. My heart leapt with anticipation. Holo-tapes were small devices that projected holographic images from a satellite. We'd be able to see *exactly* what happened, like a security camera from space. "Let's see the truth for ourselves, shall we?"

He activated the device and a holographic image of the trailer park appeared in front of the watching audience. It was just like before I left it to read under the tree. My eyes welled up with tears when I saw my mother in her garden, not a care in the world, not realizing she was about to die. And then...

A tornado.

An actual tornado touched down in the center of the park. It ripped through the trailers like they were made of paper, smashing them to obliteration. Bodies were flown around and torn apart in a terrifying spectacle of torture and destruction. Just as suddenly the tornado dissipated into nothingness, gone as quickly as it came. The holo-tape ended with an image of me running to my mother's side in the garden and soon after the cavalry arriving. There was no green smoke. There was nothing of what my mother let me see.

And then I noticed something...

The garden in the holo-tape was still ruined and destroyed. I looked behind me at the vibrant, gorgeous garden I had fixed for my mother and then again at the satellite feed. They didn't match.

This was much bigger than a simple tornado. I decided in that moment to shut my mouth. If the Mayor could manipulate a holo-tape then there were bigger players at work here. This had conspiracy written all over it and I intended to figure out what was going on.

"I must have just missed seeing it touch down," I pretended to confess. Then I made Bruce wobble a bit as if he had hit his head a little too hard.

Mayor Bradfield turned to me again so the press couldn't see. "Right decision." Then he whirled around, open arms, open face and with, crinkled-in-concern-eyebrows, motioned to two paramedics. "Help these two out, would you? They've been through quite an ordeal." After posing for one more picture with us, the Mayor started toward the middle of the park. "Come. Let's see the horrendous damage this tragedy has caused."

And the swarm was off, following the Mayor like ants chasing after food.

The paramedics gave us a once over and moved on to their hover-gurneys, lugging the bodies to their vehicles.

I felt a tapping on my shoulder. I turned around and came face to face with…

…Jason Keroff.

Gulp.

He was even more gorgeous in person, but standing in my mother's garden with *zombie* Bruce sitting amongst the flowers I didn't feel anything for my childhood crush. Jason leaned in to me and whispered in my ear. "You're in danger. Take this."

I felt something slip into my hand, it felt like a square piece of metal. "That's my contact info. Call me. Landline only. No cell."

And he was gone. Off to join the rest of the journalists.

After all these years of being infatuated with this man, seeing him only reminded me how much of a fantasy it really was.

My mom was real and the most important person in my life and now she was gone forever. It made meeting Jason hollow and uneventful. I wanted to cry, but I knew that it would immediately become a photo op for the media so I held it in and waited for them to leave.

I didn't have to wait long. With a bigger than life wave to the cameras, Mayor Bradfield entered his hover-limo and whizzed away to wherever Mayors go. The paramedics loaded the last corpse in their hover-trucks and with barely a minute passing, press, paramedics, police and firemen were gone, like they never came. I was completely alone with a drooling Bruce. I rolled my eyes and decided to do a little investigating of my own.

"Hey! Chelsan!" I turned around and nearly burst into tears when I saw Nancy running toward me. Her clothes were dirty and she looked pretty scuffed up. Seeing her made my heart swell with emotion. I didn't realize how much I needed a friendly face until I saw her coming straight toward me. Before I could move to embrace her, she tackled me to the ground in the biggest bear hug I had ever experienced. "Chelsan! You're alive! They've completely closed off the park for miles, but I crawled through the back fence and seriously, I was like a ninja, I stayed as low to the ground as possible, I'm a complete mess, but I got here…" She was rambling and I loved every second of it.

"Nancy, I can't breathe." Her hug had turned into squeezing every last breath out of my lungs.

"Oh, sorry. I'm just so relieved to see you alive! They said on the news there were no survivors when the tornado hit. They did a life scan and everything! How did they miss you?!"

"I wasn't in the park, I was reading under the willow." Uh, oh. If they did a life scan and someone was really paying attention they'd know that Bruce was *really* dead. I couldn't focus on that, yet. If Jason thought I was in trouble then I'd have to keep that piece of information on my "potential danger" list. Now that I knew Vice President Geoffrey Turner was my grandfather and what he was capable of doing to his own family, I had to be on my toes. Mom warned me he'd be after me and now Jason Keroff was cautioning me, too. I needed to be prepared for anything.

"I've always hated that tree! All the bees! But I'm completely grateful for it now!" And then she noticed Bruce. "Oh Bruce! I'm so glad you made it, too!" She turned to me. "So lucky." Her face suddenly went from relief to horror. "Your mom?" Nancy said it so cautiously and carefully it took away some of the pain I felt when she mentioned her.

I simply shook my head and Nancy hugged me again. "I'm so sorry, Chelsan."

I pulled away from her and made a decision in my head. I needed help and Nancy had more than proven she was someone I could trust explicitly. "Look Nancy. It's time we had that talk."

Nancy's eyes widened, but she nodded as if she knew exactly what I was talking about.

"Nancy, Bruce is dead. Really dead, like eleven years dead."

Nancy looked over at Bruce with shock and curiosity. "The frogs were dead, too, right?" I could tell she was already making calculations in her head.

"Yes. I can bring back anything that's died. Like this garden: it was smashed and destroyed when I got here, but it was my mom's and I couldn't let..." I choked. Thinking it and actually saying it aloud became much harder than I thought. I needed to keep my head clear for my mother's sake. She had warned me that my life was in danger and if I fell apart now, I didn't think I could ever recover. I wouldn't care if I lived or died if I let my grief overwhelm me, and my mom wouldn't have wanted that. It was why she showed me what she did. To protect me somehow.

To warn me. And it was up to me to figure all of this out.

Nancy hugged me once more. Despite me telling her that I was a defect that essentially made zombies, even plant zombies, she still wanted to be my friend. She pulled away and looked at Bruce. "So, nothing's going on upstairs? Or is he really alive?"

"No, nothing, I control all of it. That's why I didn't bring back my mom," I lied. I couldn't admit to what I had done. It made me feel dirty thinking about it.

"Good call." We sat there in the garden, facing each other. "I kind of figured it was something like that, but I didn't want to say anything because… well, because if I was wrong you'd think I was a psychopath," she admitted apologetically.

"I didn't tell you for the same reason."

"Ever since the frog thing, I've been doing some research on the subject. There have been more cases than just the Science Journal's report on the Voodoo necromancy. There are Egyptian, Wiccan, Indian, all sorts of places that have spells. Which one do you use?"

"None of them. I was born with it, or re-born, or I don't know. This is going to sound even crazier, but before my mom died, she took me back, back to her memories or something. It's why I know she wasn't killed by a tornado." I was still trying to process all this.

Nancy looked just as interested. Nothing I said seemed to faze her. She had obviously been thinking about this for a long time. Three years, I guess. The frogs made more of an impact than I originally thought.

"What did she show you?"

"My grandparents didn't want my mom and me to live, so they did some ritual so that we'd die when I was born. It worked and my father killed himself over our dead bodies, doing some spell or ritual and boom, we were both alive again and I got my powers." At least that was what it looked like from what my mom showed me. I couldn't be certain that I wasn't completely insane and delusional, but from the look on Nancy's face at least I wasn't the only one.

"Okay. When we get back to my place, you'll have to tell me *every* detail of what you saw. We can look it up and see exactly what spell they used."

A warm glow spread through me. It was like a comfort I had never felt before. Not only did Nancy believe me, she was helping me. It felt really nice knowing someone had my back. Like all this was real instead of the giant secret I'd been keeping my whole life. I felt liberated.

"Okay. That sounds good."

"How does it work, exactly? Your powers, I mean." She was very business-like as if she had an encyclopedia in her brain and she was scrolling down it to find the perfect information to help me.

"I see black swirling holes in dead things and I can connect to them and control them like puppets."

"That's freakin' sweet." Nancy started to laugh and I felt a pang of doubt. Please don't tell me she was placating me this whole time. No, no, no, I couldn't take that. "Did you make that fly attack Jill yesterday? That was classic."

Huge sigh of relief. I even laughed a little myself. "Yeah."

"Nice." Nancy was simply thrilled, and I could tell she was relieved I was finally telling her the truth. She had been waiting for it for a long time. Nancy looked around at the destruction of the park. "We should get out of here. Clean-Up will be here soon."

Clean-Up. An organization "dedicated to cleaning up the World's disasters before you have to!" Once the authorities had left a disaster area, Clean-Up came in and pretty much wiped the vicinity clean and planted trees or fields of flowers, like the one up by my willow tree, which basically meant I was running out of time.

"I have to find out what happened." I couldn't leave yet. There had to be something here to tell me the truth.

"How?" Nancy stood up and helped me to my feet. I kept Bruce sitting in the tulips, slumped over.

I scanned the area and noticed something very interesting. "They're all dead."

"Yeah… these are things we know already." Nancy's voice was laced with concern.

"No, I mean, flies, rats, bees, cockroaches, spiders all of them." This had to have significance.

"Wouldn't a tornado kill everything?" I could tell Nancy was asking to help with the thinking process, not to try and prove me wrong.

"It would definitely kill most of them, but *all*? I just wish I could *see* what happened." So frustrating!

"Can't you use Bruce or something? If you can control his movements why couldn't you see through his eyes or something?" I obviously had a bewildered look on my face because Nancy immediately appeared abashed. "Sorry, I don't know how this whole thing works."

"No, no. I just never thought about doing something like that before," I confessed. My mind raced. Was that possible? Could I actually play back what Bruce saw when he was experiencing *the tornado*? I decided it was worth a try. "I'm going to try it."

Nancy's eyes lit up with excitement. "Cool. Tell me what I should do."

"Just keep an eye out for Clean-Up. This may take a bit. I'm not sure what I'm doing."

Nancy gave a mock salute and her face was filled with anticipation of what would happen next.

I made Bruce stand and walk over to me.

Nancy let out a small gasp of excitement. "Sorry," she mumbled.

I reached up to Bruce's face and placed my hands on his puffy cheeks. I could still see the tiny bits of rotted skin under his stringy hairline from when I had left my four-mile radius and let him die the second time. I needed my mind clear of any distractions, so I closed my eyes and began to concentrate as hard as I could. "Okay, Bruce, show me what you saw."

Nothing.

I tried not to think of what must be going on in Nancy's head right now.

Stop it!

Focus.

Come on, Bruce. I shut everything out, sounds, movement, smells and lastly thoughts…

…a red neon glow filled the inside of my head like a psychedelic balloon bouncing around my eye-sockets. Small pinpoints of light appeared in the far distance. I instinctively moved toward them, or soared toward them would be a better description, until the tiny bits of light began to take form. Suddenly, I stood in my trailer next to Bruce. He sat in his recliner watching the holo-tv and everything was as it was before the destruction.

I did it. I was actually there, or some part of me was there anyway. I looked down at what I thought would be my body, but there were only wispy shreds of the same red glow I saw before. I had no corporeal form. I was simply an observer. It kind of creeped me out, but I didn't want to become distracted and break out of what I was accomplishing. I hurried to the window and then I saw her…

…my mom. She was in her garden watering the roses. She had a sweet smile on her face as if all was right in the world. I wanted to scream and warn her, tell her she was about to die, but I had to remind myself I wasn't really there. This was just Bruce's memory.

Green smoke oozed across the ground of the trailer park like a devouring snake swallowing the life out of everyone there. People coughed and choked, dropping to their knees, falling to their deaths.

Mom saw what was happening and her face crumpled. She looked up at the sky and closed her eyes. I knew she was connecting to me under the willow tree in that moment.

Flashes of yellow moved through the trailers and I squinted through the green fog to see what it was. It didn't take long to recognize a HAZMAT suit and the men inside of them. Strapped to their backs, were two-foot canisters connected to spray nozzles and they were spraying my neighbors and mother with poisonous green toxin.

This wasn't a tornado.

This was an extermination.

I was about to jump out of the memory when the sound of crunching metal tore through my senses threatening to knock me out of my head. A large hovercraft, the size of the park itself was acting like a kind of magnet, collapsing and crunching the trailers like they were crumpling up a wad of fabric. Within seconds the park looked like it did when I found it. As if a tornado had destroyed it.

A large ramp from the hovercraft lowered to the ground and the men in the HAZMAT suits shuffled their way inside.

And then they were gone. The ship moved so fast I could barely see the blur as it zoomed out of sight. The green gas dissipated and I watched me from the past run up to my mother in her garden. I saw myself about to bring my mom back, as I reached inside her body to her black hole, as I grabbed onto her essence and…

I jolted myself out of Bruce's head.

I could barely breathe. Nancy's arms grabbed onto me and held me up for support. Bruce had fallen backwards, crushing the tulips.

"Are you okay?" Nancy's voice was frantic with worry.

"I'm okay. I'm okay." I took in deep breaths, trying to re-gain my bearings. "I saw…everything."

I turned to make eye contact with Nancy. Her demeanor relaxed a bit when she saw that I was coming back to myself. "What did you see? You only had your eyes closed for five seconds."

"Really?" Really? It felt like forever. Or at least as long as the memory lasted, but I still had no idea how this worked, let alone that I could even do something like that. It made me wonder what else I could do?

"Yeah. You got all rigid and then, wham, you were gasping for air. I thought he tried to suck you in, or kill you, or something. It was really freaky looking." Nancy seemed scared.

"It was very weird, but it felt a lot longer for me than that. Look, Nancy we have to get out of here. I'll tell you everything when we get out of this place." I suddenly felt panicked. Whoever these guys were, they could always come back to kill stragglers. Especially a straggler who went on international television claiming this wasn't a tornado, but green smoke! No wonder Jason Keroff said I was in trouble. He knew something about this. I needed to contact him. Maybe he could help me.

"It wasn't a tornado, was it?" Nancy asked in dread.

"No, it wasn't. Nancy, I don't think you should get involved in all this. I think I may be in BIG trouble." I started to really worry for her safety.

"Oh no! You can't tell me in one sentence that you'll spill everything and in the next say you can't tell me anything! That's just cruel. We're going to figure this out *together*. No more keeping stuff in. It's not good for your complexion and don't think I've forgotten about that crater that stayed on your forehead for a week. If you had just confided me in the first place you could have been pimple free." She smiled now and I found it contagious.

"Got it. Acne free life from now on. But seriously…"

Nancy placed her finger to my mouth to shut me up. "I don't want to hear it. Let's get out of here before we end up with a California Oak on our heads."

"Yeah about that… I don't exactly have a place to stay." I was officially homeless and Nancy's house was seven miles away, which was why I had never been there before.

"You'll stay with me, dummy." Nancy started to walk away toward the edge of the park.

It wasn't long before she noticed I hadn't budged.

"Come on, Chelsan. Don't give me the whole 'I can't possibly accept' speech, you're staying with me and that's final."

"Um, Nancy…" I didn't know how to tell her.

"What? Clean-Up will seriously be here any second."

"Bruce." It was all I could sputter.

"Leave him."

"But, I was just on TV, they all think he's alive." I had my one shot to free myself of Bruce once and for all and I blew it for my stupid pride.

"So? Trust me, Chelsan, natural disasters are lame TV, no one will remember."

"But Clean-Up will see the body. They can't re-form an area until it's clean."

"Look, Chelsan, he's a ten-year-old anchor you don't need hanging around your neck. What about the willow? You're never going back there again."

Yeah. She was right. It was time. Time to say good-bye to Bruce. I nodded and made Bruce follow Nancy and me to the flower fields and my willow tree.

Knowing it was the last time I'd ever be here made me sad, but I couldn't say that a part of me wasn't a little relieved at the same time. Bruce would be out of my life forever. I could live my own life now. I wouldn't be tied down to an eternity of puppeteering.

And I didn't want to be in the place that would always remind me of the moment I lost my mother forever.

"Should we just leave him here?" I could tell Nancy was wondering why I wasn't moving.

"Give me a minute."

"Sorry."

I made Bruce sit with his back propped up by the tree trunk. He looked peaceful. I was controlling the bare minimum. Now that I had no one to fool, it felt wrong to make him act *normal*. Like I was abusing him or something. The real Bruce was a vicious monster so I guess we could call it even.

"This may gross you out. You might want to close your eyes or turn your back or something," I warned Nancy.

"I'm good. Do your thing." Nancy looked morbidly curious, but I knew after what she was about to see, she wouldn't be so quick to want to participate anymore.

Okay. Here goes. I reached into Bruce's fiery black hole that I had known so well over the years and…

…disconnected from it.

What happened next was revolting. Bruce's skin looked like a million flesh eating bugs were devouring him in a giant feast. Gooey glumps of blood and tissue slopped to the ground, revealing Bruce's bones underneath. The rest of his flesh oozed off his skeleton to create a chunky indistinguishable pool of blood and skin. But even that began to turn gray, then black, then disappear into the ground all together.

I could hear Nancy gag behind me, but as much as I wanted to do the same, I couldn't keep my eyes off of Bruce.

It all happened within seconds. One minute my stepfather was sitting under a tree, the next a pristine white skeleton. All traces of blood and flesh gone as if they had been consumed whole.

Then we both heard it at the same time.

"Clean-Up," Nancy muttered quietly. She looked dazed at what she just saw.

"We're far enough away. Let's go see." I wanted to get her out of there. I knew her *researching* and her actually *seeing* might make her change her mind about helping me. It made my power more real than anything else so far.

It terrified me, and gave me such a profound sense of guilt. Bruce was such a horrible person before he died. I never even thought about how I was violating him as a human being. I should have just let him die that day.

We walked from out of the willow's protective branches, leaving Bruce behind.

Clean-Up was a group of seven skyscraper-sized hover-trucks. Two of them were storage vehicles, equipped with giant magnets that picked up all the trailers, scraps of metal, anything and everything that was magnetized and stored them inside their steel bellies.

The third truck lowered itself to the ground and hundreds of ten-foot steel blades shredded the dirt below, loosening it for planting.

The fourth, fifth and sixth hover-trucks carried the plants (in this case it was indeed oaks) and dropped each tree to the ground, roots down, until they were shoved deep into the tilled soil.

The last truck carried a mixture of water and fertilizer, which was dumped on the freshly planted trees like a heavy rain, hardening the earth and securing the roots.

Twenty minutes later, Clean-Up had left and a forest of oaks stood in front of us. The trailer park was gone forever, just like Bruce.

Just like my mom.

"The quarantine should be down now." Nancy's voice sounded so quiet after the noise of Clean-Up.

It was like my home had never been. The wafting smell of wet foliage hit my nose as if it had been raining for days.

"Let's get out of here," I said just as quietly. "Are you sure it's okay if I stay with you?"

Nancy nodded. "Don't worry about my parents. They'll want to take care of you."

I had no idea how Nancy's family would really feel about letting a trailer girl stay with them even if it was just for a little while. But the truth of the matter was, I had no idea what I was going to do or where I was going to stay for the long haul. I was essentially homeless with no family, except…

…For some reason it hit me in that moment. Vice President Geoffrey Turner, the guy that my school was named after, the guy that everyone worshiped was my *grandfather* and the killer of my parents and everyone in this park. I didn't know exactly how to feel about that.

"Um, Nancy?" I figured I should tell her everything. We were walking through the newly planted trees, the ground hard and wet. Pieces of clothing and non-magnetic items lay half-buried in the soil. Over time all of these things would deteriorate altogether from weather and abandonment, leaving no trace of their existence.

"Yeah?"

The sound of the Hover-Shuttle whizzed above our heads. The driver would never have to stop here again. I didn't want to think about it.

"Um.." I wasn't sure how to broach the topic.

"You don't have to say anything, Chelsan, you've been through more in the last hour than most people will ever experience in eternity. When we get to my house you can rest and have alone time and then we can talk."

I realized in that moment that Nancy had reached her limit of *new information*. I'd have to tell her about gramps later. And to be honest, I felt like I could sleep for days. "Okay, later."

After about an hour of walking (I was suddenly very impressed with Nancy; she must have ran the entire way through trees, fields and foliage to get to me as fast as she did) we arrived at a Hover-Shuttle station. It was right next to the largest shopping mall in California.

The entire structure was made of multi-colored plexiglass from the walls, to the doors, to the flooring. It consisted of five dome-shaped buildings making the whole place look like rolling hills of stained glass. Built on top of a canyon-sized crater, it was hard not to have a moment of vertigo when looking down through the colored plexiglass floor.

The crater was a mile deep and with all its crags and fissures it was stunning to look at. The mall had been around for over two-hundred years and supposedly was one of the most structurally sound buildings ever made despite the fact that it was basically covering up a large hole in the earth.

There was always a loud humming at the mall from Hover-Service. Since all packaging was banned in 2070, Hover-Service took over everything.

Basically, once you paid for an item (you did this by sticking your thumb on a scanner and typing in your seven digit pin number that was linked to your account), it was then sent in a large hover-box and delivered directly to your house. Hover-Service traveled in a lower air space than regular traffic so whenever you were near a large shopping area there was constantly a mass of metal boxes whizzing twenty feet above your head.

It didn't bother most people, but it still bugged me. I guess I didn't shop enough to make it apart of my "sound" vocabulary.

"Uh, oh." Nancy nudged her head toward the end of the cobble-stoned street.

Jill was there with her cronies. She hadn't seen us yet and I didn't plan on her having the chance. "Let's duck into the mall. I really can't deal with her right now."

"Good idea."

Nancy grabbed my hand and led me through the first door we could find which happened to be a shoe store.

Nancy dropped my hand and her eyes lit up, completely forgetting I was there. Shoes were Nancy's thing. Her solution to everything was pretty much to buy a new pair of shoes. According to her, she had nearly a thousand pairs. I couldn't even imagine how much space that would take up: probably the size of my trailer. Or not anymore… Uugh. I didn't want to think about it.

Fortunately, the colorful melee of the shoe store was a distracting rainbow of eye candy. All the shoes were displayed on the same colored plexiglass that the mall was made from and it made it hard to differentiate between all the different types of footwear.

"Nancy, shoes later. We should get to the other Hover-Station on Fourth Street."

"Right. Completely." She was already focused on a particular pair of sandals. "Just let me check the price real quick."

And before I could utter a word she was making a b-line to the shoes.

"Nancy," I grumbled under my breath and joined her by the sandals. "Really? My mom just died and you want to buy shoes?" I was tired and grumpy and frankly, I needed to bawl my head off.

Nancy's voice was almost shaking and her eyes welled up with tears. "I'm so sorry, Chelsan."

My heart squeezed in pain. I knew Nancy wasn't trying to be insensitive, she simply didn't know how to cope.

"It's okay. I'm still in shock, I think." I nodded to the foot wear. "Go ahead and buy some shoes."

Nancy wiped her eyes and shook her head. "I needed to pretend everything was okay and normal for just a second. But it isn't, is it? Nothing will ever be okay again." Then she hugged me.

I was about to lose it. Pulling away, I took a deep breath to steady myself. "Let's get to the station."

Nancy nodded and motioned to the exit. "Is the coast clear?"

I cautiously looked out the doorway for any signs of Jill. So far, so good.

"Hey."

I turned to the voice and the small tapping on my shoulder.

Oh boy.

There, standing in all his perfect glory was Ryan Vaughn. He combed his hand through his hair in an almost nervous gesture. Was he nervous? In front of me? Considering I still hadn't uttered a word, I realized I was pretty anxious, too. Even after everything that happened today, Ryan still made the butterflies do hang-gliding flips in my stomach. I didn't know what that meant, but it made me nauseous.

"Hey," I replied all cool-like. At least I made something come out of my mouth.

"I saw you on the news. Are you okay? Where's your dad?" I knew people would notice Bruce was gone! "I was really worried. I'm just glad you're okay." Then he touched my hair in an almost unconscious manner. I nearly died. I physically tingled all over. I really was going to vomit now.

He pulled back his hand as if he'd touched a hot burner. "I'm sorry. I didn't mean… I'll leave you alone."

I wish I could control what my face looked like. Why did I always manage to make him think that I thought he was a leper?! It wasn't this hard when he was tutoring me. Probably because I could just ask him questions about the homework and I was content to listen to him speak. We never did get too personal. And why did it always take me so long to respond! If the situation were reversed I would be in excruciating torment right now. Wait a minute, I was.

"No, don't leave." Do something! Grab his hand or arm or something! I fumbled my hand toward his hand and somehow managed to slap his arm. The crater underneath our feet seemed like a really good place to be right now. "Sorry. I'm just still… I don't know." I didn't want to talk about what happened at the trailer park with him or with anyone. It was too painful. And in that moment, I was suddenly very grateful to Ryan. Even if it were for just a few seconds, he made me feel something other than anguish over my losses. At least Ryan torment was torturously good in some ways when I didn't act like a complete moron.

"Well, you didn't need to slap me though I probably deserve it." He was smiling. It was a relieved, endearing smile that made his eyes sparkle. It made my insides rise in temperature about a hundred degrees.

It was infectious. I smiled back. "Sorry."

Ryan placed his hands on my arms to grab my attention and force eye contact. "Do you need a place to stay?"

I was shocked I didn't explode right there.

"Sorry, I.Q. boy, she's staying with me." Nancy chimed in with a knowing smile and a quick look of *good job* to me.

Ryan released his hold on me and actually looked relieved. I wasn't sure if I liked that response or not. Especially the part of him letting me go. "I just thought, well the news said… never mind. Nancy's perfect."

"What did the news say?" Nancy was concerned.

"Nothing. I'm just glad you could take care of her."

He said it so sweetly even Nancy's face fluttered a little. "Of course I'll take care of her. Speaking of which, look at my clothes. I look like I just crawled out of the jungle. I need to change."

"Let's just go somewhere where there aren't any humans."

"Too late." Ryan nodded his head toward a swarm of lights and cameras.

Before I could run in the opposite direction they were on us like the leeches they were.

"Chelsan! Chelsan! Is it true you're staying with the Merryweathers?"

"Is Bill Merryweather your boyfriend?"

"Where is Mr. Merryweather?"

I looked at Ryan and Nancy in shock. Nancy seemed surprised by the onslaught of reporters and their questions, but Ryan appeared more sheepish than caught unawares. He glanced down at me with what could only be described as embarrassment.

Nancy caught on pretty quick as well. "I guess *this* was what was in the news, *Ryan*?"

"I…" Ryan was at a loss for words.

"Coming through," a familiar voice rang through the crowd of press.

And there was Bill, smashing his way forward to get to me, his face wracked with concern and relief at seeing me. He shoved clear of the flock and hugged me fiercely. "You're staying with me," he announced in my ear.

Out of the corner of my eye, I could see Ryan's face fall. And even though I was grateful for Bill's concern and friendship, I suddenly wanted to comfort Ryan and explain to him that Bill and I weren't like that.

I pulled away from Bill. "Bill, thank you so much, but I'm staying with Nancy."

Bill's expression was one of awkwardness and disappointment. "But my parents already announced that you were staying with us."

"She just lost everything she's ever known and you're concerned about what the press might think about *you*?" Ryan stepped forward and grabbed my hand, holding it firmly. There went my knees again, I was shocked I was still standing. Why did I fall apart every time he touched me?

"No. I didn't… you're right, of course, Nancy is a perfect choice." In Bill's effort to hide his horror of what he was accused of, he didn't even notice Ryan's hand holding mine.

The press did though.

"Is *he* your boyfriend?"

"Did you break Bill Merryweather's heart?"

"Bill, I know you didn't mean it that way." I wanted to repair the look of pain in Bill's features.

"You guys better get out of here. Nancy, my hover-limo is out front. I'll stall these guys."

"Thanks, Bill." I smiled as sincerely as I could and Bill tried his best to look reassuring.

"I'll call you later," he said, though there was doubt in his eyes.

"*Come over* later, stupid." Nancy punched his shoulder and shook her head. "Just because she's not staying at your house doesn't mean you can't see her."

This seemed to brighten Bill's mood although at this point he couldn't stop staring at Ryan clasping onto my hand possessively. "Seriously, get out of here. I'll catch up to you later."

"Thanks." And we were off, running for the exit. I could hear Bill's booming voice keeping the press at bay with 'a surprise announcement from Merryweather Corporation,' it was a much juicier news bite than a trailer girl surviving a tornado. I'd have to make up for humiliating him later.

Ryan was still holding my hand and it was starting to feel like the most natural thing in the world. And in my chemistry-induced stupor, I wondered if I could surgically attach my hand to his.

The mall doors practically flew off their hinges from the amount of force Nancy used to open them. She was in protective mode now and wanted to make sure I didn't have to endure any more public scrutiny today. That and she kept muttering 'this is all my fault, stupid mall,' under her breath, which meant she was guilting hardcore. Normally, I'd try and comfort her, but frankly, all I could focus on was Ryan's hand in mine.

"Over here." Nancy spotted the hover-limo first and Ryan and I followed her toward the thirty-foot black stretch monster parked a few yards away.

Jill and her clone Joan stepped in front of the passenger door, blocking our way into the limo.

"This is Bill's limo, if you get in, I'll call the police." Jill's arms were crossed and her face glowed with superiority.

"We have his permission, Jill." Nancy practically spit on Jill's feet.

"We'll just have to wait for him, won't we?" Jill smirked. "Who knew that losing your trailer park would turn you to a life of crime?" Jill laughed, but Joan's eyes widened slightly as if even she was a little surprised at Jill's words.

It was impossible to believe that Jill could actually be that cruel. I underestimated her hatred for me. I could see in her eyes she was enjoying my pain, she was thriving on it.

"Get out of our way," Ryan spoke with such venom that even Nancy and I were taken aback.

"Holding hands, I see. I never took you for a trash lover, Ryan. I'm just glad I never let you kiss me on our *date*," Jill directed the last part at me. And I admit, it stung that Ryan went on a date with *Jill*. "You're just sloppy seconds, trailer girl."

Nancy apparently had had enough. "You heard the man, get out of our way!" She shoved Jill with some force.

Jill fell to the ground in horror and disbelief. Joan helped her to her feet and from the look on her face she wanted to stay out of it.

"Come on." Ryan opened the door of the limo and led me inside.

Nancy scooted inside and slammed the door shut. She turned to the driver. "Take us to my house, Gary."

"Everything okay out there?" Gary asked as he put down his electronic reader and brought the hover-limo to life.

"Yeah. Just get us to my house and away from here." Nancy sank back into the seat next to me and leaned her head against my shoulder in exhaustion. "Sorry I tried to buy shoes."

I laughed. The first real laugh I had since everything happened. My adrenaline was amped up to about a billion and I knew the crash would be coming soon.

Ryan turned to me and put his forehead to mine. He reached up and touched my face with his hand in a protective manner. My heart couldn't take this. I may have been eighteen, but I was going to croak of a heart attack any second now. His eyes were so intense as they met mine. "Jill's the trash, that's why she hates you so much. Don't ever take anything she says seriously, okay?"

I could only nod. My voice box would probably squeak something unintelligible anyway. I wanted him to kiss me so badly in that moment, but I knew I'd probably end up missing his mouth entirely and slobbering on his neck or something. I was such a clueless idiot when it came to boys.

Ryan pulled his hand away and placed his arm around me and included Nancy in the embrace since she was already asleep on my shoulder. We must have looked like quite the threesome to Gary, but he didn't say a word; he just drove the hover-limo towards our destination.

It only took a few minutes for the hover-limo to arrive at Nancy's house. Her street was a typical upper-middle class neighborhood. Perfectly coifed grass separated the parallel lined mansion-sized houses. It used to be cement streets and driveways separating their property over two-hundred years ago, but once hover-cars took over, the need for suburban roads became obsolete and if it wasn't a landmark or shopping center it was replaced with grass. In dry, hot places like California, large water silos were set at each row of houses (covered from view by trees and foliage, of course) and an endless process of water-filtration and recycling took place to constantly keep the grass watered and green. Residents were required to empty their fuel cell tanks from their hover-cars into the silo to keep the water fresh and replenished.

Gary landed the limo with ease on the hover-pad in front of Nancy's house. "Here we are."

"Thanks, Gary." Nancy was alert and awake now as she opened the door of the limo. "Come on, Chelsan, let's go tell my parents you're staying."

"What about Ryan?" I asked, not wanting to part from him yet.

"I live a few houses down across the street. I'll come by later." Ryan pulled his arm out from under me and gently nudged me to the exit.

I couldn't fathom that he was still near me, that he still wanted to have anything to do with me. I kept on waiting for him to laugh hysterically and tell me it was all a big joke. I really barely knew the guy and yet it felt like we'd known each other forever. I wondered if that was how it was for my mom and dad. I'd never know.

All three of us stood outside the limo as Gary lifted the limo up into the air and out of sight.

"Well… I'll see you later," Ryan said quietly. He actually looked shy and insecure. It made me wonder if he had been like this when he was tutoring me and I was just too oblivious to notice.

"Okay. See ya. Thanks for everything." Okay. Awkward. Neither one of us was sure what we should do next. I think he was debating on whether or not to kiss me, but he was obviously going through some kind of battle inside his head because he just stood there. And I just stood there. And Nancy just stood there.

"Yeah, okay, bye Ryan." Nancy had a lot less patience in this matter. "Chelsan, let's get inside before any more reporters show up."

Ryan settled for a wave and a slight nod of his head. "I'll come by tomorrow." And he sauntered off to his house.

I felt Nancy's hand grab mine and pull me toward her front door. "Come on, crazy girl. You'll see him soon enough."

I let Nancy lead me to her abode. The structure itself was one of the most modern I'd ever seen, but I hadn't been able to leave a four-mile radius my whole life, so that wasn't saying much. Her house was essentially three white stucco stories stacked on top of each other like a three-step staircase. Windows lined each wall, promising a bright interior and the glass was already tinted a dark brown to block out the sun for the day, making it impossible to see inside.

I felt a pang of nerves as Nancy opened the steel front door. Most people had steel doors and sometimes steel window shutters, essentially making their entire house a fortress. With Age-pro promising immortality, no one wanted to risk dying from a random crime or natural disaster, so making one's home impenetrable became a priority to the general public. Especially for the rich.

We entered her house and I was amazed at the impeccable décor of the bottom floor. The entry way was painted in soft golden tones to compliment the terracotta tiling beneath us. Directly after the foyer was the living room with a giant life-size holo-TV playing the news. It was like watching a play it was so crisp and life-like. A giant wrap-around black vinyl couch faced the TV and Nancy's parents' backs were to us watching the news cast.

"Mom, Dad," Nancy greeted her folks and I could sense the hesitancy in her voice.

Nancy's parents immediately turned to see the two of us standing in the entryway. I was put at ease right away when the two of them came running up to us, concern oozing off their faces, like true parents.

"Chelsan, are you okay? We heard everything on the news. We saw you too, young lady. Look at you, you look like you went on a safari. Go change your clothes."

This all came out in a worried rush from Nancy's mom, while her father hugged Nancy as if he hadn't seen her in days.

"You went through the blockade, didn't you?" her dad mumbled in her ear. "I'm so proud of you."

And then I was suddenly being slammed with a hug from Nancy's mom. "You poor dear." She held on tight and in that moment I fell apart. It was too close to having my own mom embracing me. I started to cry. And the harder I cried the tighter she held on. "I'm so sorry. We'll take care of you. You stay here as long as you want," she kept reassuring me and it made me feel safe and devastated all at once.

"Give her some air, geez, Mom," came Nancy's voice right next to me.

I relaxed my death grip on Nancy's mom and she pulled away from me, tears of sympathy in her eyes. "George, get us some hankies."

George hurried to the end table next to the couch and grabbed a few handkerchiefs from a small stack and brought them back to the two of us.

"I'm Vianne, by the way, and this is George, but you probably already knew that." She smiled as she wiped away her own tears and blew her nose for measure. "And I mean it. As long as you need or want to, you are welcome here. We've heard so much about you from Nancy. It's just so lovely to finally meet you. I just wish it had been under different circumstances." She kissed my cheek.

It almost made me break again, but I wiped my tears clean from my face. "Thank you. I really appreciate it."

"Your step-father is welcome here as well, where is he?" George was making sure I knew my whole family was wanted. They had obviously seen my fiasco in front of the press with Bruce. My mind went blank. I didn't know what to say.

"He died, Dad. Of complications," Nancy quickly interceded.

Vianne's hand went straight to her mouth to cover her shock. "We didn't know. The news didn't report it. I'm so sorry, Chelsan."

"I think I need to lie down for a while." All I could think about was collapsing and turning my mind off, even if it was for a little while. It was taking too much energy to breathe, let alone carry on a conversation of cover-ups and lies to people who genuinely wanted to help me.

Nancy grabbed my hand. "I'm taking her upstairs to my room."

"Good night. Let us know if you need *anything*," Vianne said over our shoulders.

"Night. Thanks again," I barely called out as Nancy dragged me up a spiraling wrought iron staircase leading to the next floor.

A long hallway greeted us with the same terracotta tiling as the foyer. The walls were Spanish yellow stucco and the doors were darkly stained oak. There were six doors total and they were all closed. Nancy opened the second one on the right and we entered my dream room (which happened to be Nancy's).

First of all, it was huge! At least the size of one of our classrooms at school. Blue seemed to be the color of choice in terms of decoration, from the bed, to the carpeting, to the walls, all different shades of the same deep ocean blue. The entire back wall was lined with shoes. Nancy wasn't kidding; she literally had hundreds of pairs. It was like she had a shoe store in her own room!

And then there were the holographic-pictures, and I had to stifle a laugh. The wall facing her bed was covered with holos of Jason Keroff, all with the same serious expression he always had on his face when reporting. She must have downloaded them from the same place I did, since I was seeing a lot of the same ones that I had.

Wait a minute.

Jason Keroff gave me his contact info.

He told me I was in danger. He knew about the exterminators. Or had suspicions anyway.

"Okay, so I'm obsessed, but so are you, so don't give me that look." Nancy had seen my horrified stare and misinterpreted it as shock from seeing her shrine to Jason.

"No. It just reminded me…" I knew Nancy needed to sit for this, so I led her to the bed and plopped her down. "Nancy, don't freak out, but Jason Keroff was with the press at the trailer park. He told me I was in danger. It was like he knew what really happened. He gave me his contact information."

"Okay, hard not to freak, Jason Keroff, seriously? You've got Ryan and Bill, Jason is mine."

"Focus, here, Nancy. And I don't really have Ryan or Bill."

"What were you saying about focus?" She smiled knowingly at me and then her tone turned serious. "Right. What *really* did happen anyway? You didn't tell me."

Sitting on the bed next to Nancy, it unexpectedly hit me that she knew absolutely nothing. Not who my grandpa really was, not about the green smoke, not about Jason Keroff. I had some explaining to do, so I started at the beginning and told her everything, all the way from the very details of my grandparents' ceremony, to what really happened at the trailer park. Nancy's eyes widened to the size of saucers in a few places and I could tell she was holding her tongue (a mammoth effort for her). When I was all finished I was more exhausted than I thought possible. And even though Nancy was just bursting with questions, she obviously saw this, too.

"You need to sleep," Nancy observed as she squeezed my hand with encouragement. "I'll interrogate you tomorrow." She smiled.

"Sleep sounds really good. Do you have a sleeping bag? I can set up over there." I pointed to a particularly nice corner in her gigantic room. It was a mass of pillows and looked exceedingly inviting.

"Oh no! Are you joking? Do you think I'm Jill or something? My bed is a double King! No way are you staying on the floor, you're sleeping up here in my nice fluffy bed." Nancy seemed almost appalled.

The bed was bigger than my room in the trailer and it felt ridiculously comfortable. "Thanks," was all I had the energy to say. I almost blacked out on impact when I lowered my head to a pillow.

I could barely hear Nancy saying good night as I drifted off to sleep.

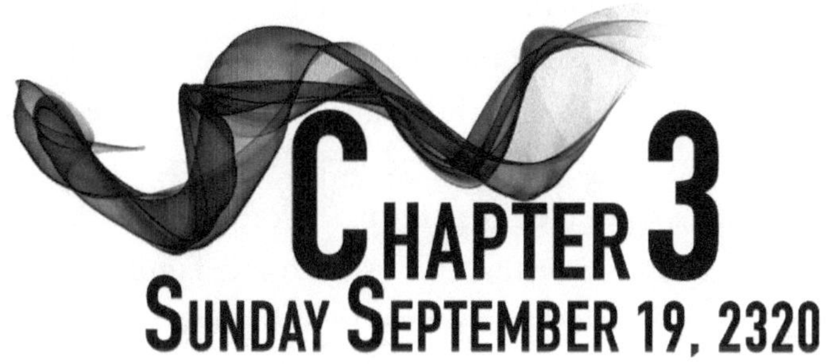

The whole morning was spent answering all of Nancy's questions. She was the most fascinated by the fact that Vice President of Population Control Geoffrey Turner was my grandfather.

"The one time I wish I could flaunt something in Jill's face," Nancy grumbled aloud. "If she knew that her daddy's head honcho was your grandpa! The most powerful man in the *world*! It's too juicy!"

"Not that juicy. He tried to have me killed, remember? And *me* living meant his only son dying."

"Yeah, but Jill doesn't know that!"

"Nancy, telling Jill anything is basically telling Turner." I could see Nancy's gears churning, trying to find a way to rub this in Jill's face, but I had to make sure she kept it between us two.

"Yeah, I guess you're right," Nancy groaned.

We sat in her back yard on a swinging bench secured between two trees. She lazily pushed it with her foot causing it to swing crookedly.

Nancy's property seemed to stretch on forever once you reached the back. There were several trees and lots of foliage in the main yard and in the back was a thick row of forest running down the entire street. I knew this was only an illusion of course. Each block of houses had a line of trees eight to ten rows thick in their back yards to follow with the Environmental Code of Oxygen policy.

The kind of trees also showed how expensive the neighborhood was, the lower middle class, had bamboo, Nancy's was pine, and zones as rich as Bill's were cherry blossoms and bonsais. It was weird how everything was so divided by how much money you had. Trailer parks like mine didn't even have tree policies, we just lived near wild flower and oak disaster zones so it made the planting of forest rows like Nancy's moot.

"What about the ritual? Does it sound familiar to you at all?" I asked, wanting to bring the conversation back to figuring out how I had my gift in the first place.

"I can think of a couple of things. I'll transfer some of the books I found to your reader so we can both get in research mode. I'm more interested in your father's spell. He somehow managed to manipulate Turner's hex and flip it back on himself. Sorry."

She must have seen me cringe when she mentioned my father's death. Up until recently my father was just an imaginative figure that died of natural causes when I was born. Now, not only knowing, but seeing my mother's vision of the way that he died, it was difficult not to be upset. "Don't be sorry. I want to figure this out. I just didn't know how hard it was going to be."

"We'll do this one step at a time. The first thing we need to know is *exactly* what spell Turner used. Then we can deal with… the other stuff."

We searched all morning in our readers. Nancy found some things, but there'd always be one thing different in the ceremony. And it wasn't a simple thing like candle choice or the kind of knife he used, it was sacrificing a goat or severing a limb. So needless to say we'd have to search elsewhere. I asked if Turner could have made up his own spell, and while Nancy thought that might be possible, she still wanted to find the base spell he used.

"This is very powerful mojo we're talking about here, Chelsan. This isn't your run of the mill curse. He *made* you and your mother *die*. That's as serious as it gets." Nancy leaned back on the vinyl sofa. We had moved to the living room once the Recyclers made their rounds on her block. Their machinery was so loud sucking up all the garbage from each house it made it impossible to concentrate. I knew I shouldn't complain, everyone's garbage ended up in Clean-Ups' fertilizer and mulch trucks, but listening to a giant vacuum cleaner sucking up slurpy garbage made me a little queasy.

"Why do I get the feeling that a spell that powerful wouldn't be found in a library download?" I began to feel like this was hopeless.

"I know, right? There has to be some way we can get access to books like that." I could tell Nancy was frustrated as well.

"Maybe I should call Jason?"

"Yes, please." Nancy immediately perked up. "He'd definitely have access to stuff like that."

I smiled at Nancy's enthusiasm for calling Jason Keroff. I almost wanted her to do it. The thought of picking up the phone and dialing his number made my palms sweat. "I'm kind of nervous," I admitted to Nancy.

"Don't be. He asked *you* to call him. It's not like you're some kind of stalker that tracked down his number and are trying to get a date. Your mother and your entire neighborhood were just exterminated and he wants to help you. You are the one in control, okay?"

Nancy's speech gave me some confidence. I had to stop thinking of Jason as someone better than me just because of who he was. I kept reminding myself that when I met him yesterday, I didn't feel anything. I wasn't nervous, I wasn't excited, I was just blank. That was good. I had to pull on that, if I had any chance of making this phone call without barfing.

"Okay. He said no cells, just landlines." I took a deep breath as Nancy practically squealed reaching for the phone receiver. I grabbed it out of her hand and put it against my ear. "I'm so nervous," I blabbered. I couldn't hide it, especially not from Nancy.

"Do you want me to do it?" Nancy was serious and concerned. I could tell she genuinely felt my pain, but as tempting as it was, I knew I had to be the one who called.

"No. Thanks though. I really should do this. Here's the number." I flipped up the metal device Jason gave me and a 3D holograph of his number popped up and rotated slowly like it was on display. Nancy quickly dialed and I held my breath as I could hear his ringer through the receiver. Don't be home, don't be home, don't be home…

"Jason Keroff."

Uggghh. Major butterflies. "Um, hi, this is Chelsan, the girl from the trailer park. You told me to call you." I said this so fast, I wasn't sure if he could understand me.

"Chelsan, hi. Did you call from a landline?" His voice was warm, but had an edge of caution to it as well.

"Yeah, I'm at my friend Nancy's house."

Nancy leaned in to me as close as she could be without toppling me off the couch. Let's face it, Nancy was definitely in swoon city. She could barely contain her sighs and squeals of delight and I had just started the conversation.

"Okay, look. I don't want to talk on the phone. Can you meet me tonight at Alby's Bar and Grill at the Riverside mall? Say, seven o'clock?"

I took the receiver away from my ear and placed my hand over it so Jason couldn't hear me. "He wants to meet at Alby's."

Nancy's eyes bugged out of her head. "Tell him YES! What are you thinking?"

I put the receiver back to my ear. "Yeah, that sounds good. I'll see you then."

"Be careful, Chelsan. I mean it." Jason sounded intense and it made the pit of my stomach sink even further into the terrified zone.

"I will, thanks." And I hung up.

"You didn't say *bye* or anything?" I could tell Nancy was beyond excited and she could care less on how the conversation ended. "I'm going with you by the way."

"Of course." I decided it wasn't worth an argument and besides, I really didn't want to go alone. Jason said to be safe, and being safe meant having back-up.

"When are we meeting him?"

"Seven o'clock."

"That gives us plenty of time to get ready. It's three o'clock now, so maybe we could go shopping." Nancy's head was spinning now.

"Nancy, I don't want to go shopping. I want to find out as much information as we can before we meet Jason." I just couldn't get excited about meeting Jason like Nancy could. Jason equaled facing the fact that I really *was* in danger, and staying here at Nancy's I actually felt safe. I didn't want to lose that feeling.

"Okay, no biggie, I have plenty of stuff here. Let's get back to the readers." Thankfully, Nancy didn't seem upset at all, she was just excited to be meeting Jason.

The thought of the meeting tonight made my belly do flip-flops and not in a good way. I concentrated on my reader. It was an article on a Voodoo ritual involving the slaughtering of a goat. Why goats? What did goats ever do to anyone? I put the reader down. "You're right. Jason would have access to better stuff than this. We should plan our strategy."

Nancy's face lit up as she put her reader down. "Strategy as in what we're wearing or as in what we're saying?"

I rolled my eyes, but smiled. "You, seriously, have a one-track mind."

"I know, I'm sorry." Nancy smiled back.

The doorbell rang.

"Saved by the bell." Nancy jumped up from the couch and made her way to the front door.

I stayed put, but peeked over the couch to see who it was.

And to my shock, Joan, Jill's lackey, stood at Nancy's doorstep.

"And why shouldn't I slam this door in your face?" Nancy looked like she was about to punch Joan right there.

Joan looked over her shoulder constantly. "Could you just let me in, please?"

"Are you insane?" Nancy was in shock. "What would possibly compel me to do that?"

Joan was serious as she stared Nancy in the eye. "Trust me, Chelsan will want to hear this."

Nancy was genuinely taken aback. She glanced over at me for instructions.

"You can let her in," I replied quietly. I was curious as much as I was suspicious.

"Fine, but if this is a trick, I have no qualms about kicking your ass." Nancy threatened and I appreciated her loyalty.

"It's not a trick," Joan responded as she hurriedly walked inside Nancy's house. "Trust me, I don't want to be here either, but I thought you deserved to know what I know, considering what happened to you and your family…" Joan said with genuine sympathy.

"Know what?"

Joan sat down across from me.

Nancy sat next to me so she was facing Joan as well and she could give her dirty looks when needed.

"Okay," Joan began, still glancing over her shoulder as if someone would show up at any minute to catch her in the act of being seen with us. "Okay. About yesterday."

"Yes?" Nancy was more impatient than I was.

Joan was one of those girls who could be physically glued to Jill and no one would notice. It was almost as if she had no personality of her own, she was essentially an extension of the monster. In fact, I think this was the first time I had ever heard her say more than three words aside from her outburst at Mel's when she was trying to have me fired. Why was I listening to her again?

"I don't know if this means anything, but it's been nagging at me and I thought you should know." Joan fidgeted nervously.

I was skeptical at anything Joan told me and wondered if she was nervous because she genuinely had important information or because this was the longest she had been away from Jill.

"Just spill it, geez, Joan, you're acting like a spaz." Nancy was at the end of her patience and frankly, so was I.

"Fine. The reason why Jill was blocking you from Bill's limo was because her dad told her to," Joan confessed quietly.

"What?" Uh, oh. I didn't like where this was going.

"Yeah. She got a call from him at the mall, saying you were there and not to let you out of her sight. He said he had direct orders from Vice President Geoffrey Turner." Joan made another sweep of the room with her eyes as if it was bugged and she'd be arrested on the spot.

Nancy and I exchanged worried glances.

"Say something. You guys look like you knew this was coming. Did you hear what I said? Geoffrey Turner, the most powerful man in the world, wanted Jill to keep an eye on you! That's not a good thing, let me tell you." Joan was apparently disappointed in our lack of reaction, but I didn't want to reveal too much to her in case this was a way of finding out what we knew.

"Thanks for the info, Joan, we'll take it under advisement. Now leave, please." Nancy was on the same page I was.

"I wish I hadn't told you." Joan was livid.

"What do you want from me, Joan? Thank you for telling me the most powerful man in the world is sending orders to his slave's daughter keep an eye on me? Thanks." I really didn't feel like trying to make Joan feel good about her decision to betray Jill. I was glad she did it, but she was still a bully that had been causing me havoc my whole high school career.

"Fine. See if I ever help you again!" Joan stood up and stormed to the front door, slamming it on her way out.

Nancy and I had to laugh at the dramatics.

"She's going to go tell Jill, you know," Nancy declared in a more serious tone.

"Yeah," I agreed with a sigh.

Nancy shook her head, "There's nothing we can do about it now. At least we know more than we did."

"He's probably having your place watched."

"Good to know. We'll have to be extra careful when we sneak out tonight to meet Jason."

"We're going to need a ride. The Hover-Shuttle seems too *public*. He'll have people looking there for sure." I tried to narrow down a plan.

Nancy was almost excited by the prospect. "This is like espionage. We're literally spies working against the government."

"Nancy, seriously, you're way too happy about all this. Hello? My life is in danger."

"I know, but it's still exciting." Nancy went to the window next to her front door and peered out. "Joan's gone. She lives kind of far, I wonder if she had someone bring her here."

"You mean like Jill?" I asked what I thought Nancy was implying.

"She's been Jill's second limb since I've known them. I can't imagine her doing *anything* of her own accord."

"Me, either. Still." I let the thought linger.

"Oh crap!" Nancy leapt back from the window and scurried to the couch.

"What?!"

Nancy smiled, "You'll see in about two seconds."

There was a knocking on the door for the second time today.

"Who is it?" I asked Nancy, since she obviously knew.

"Why don't you get it?" Nancy picked up her reader with a Cheshire cat grin.

"Nancy?"

Knock. Knock. Knock.

"Are you going to get that, or what?" Nancy wasn't budging.

"Fine," I uttered and rolled my eyes for measure.

I stood up and made my way around the couch at a leisurely pace.

"Hurry up. He might leave."

He? Uh, oh. It was either Bill or Ryan, and at this moment I didn't know who I wanted it to be. Bill meant comfort and reassurance. Ryan meant butterflies and hot flashes. Okay, I was leaning towards Bill for the simple reason of keeping the contents of my stomach from making a projectile force out of my mouth.

I reached the door much quicker than I preferred and opened it slowly.

Ryan.

Breathe.

"Oh, hi, Ryan." Wow. That was the coolest I'd sounded yet.

"Hey. How are you?" How was he always cooler? It was as if he was in tune with everything I said and somehow managed to be that much more relaxed and laid back than I could ever be.

"Come on in." I opened the door wider to let him through.

Ryan came in and I shut the door behind him.

"Ryan! Hey, how's it going? Come sit over here with us," Nancy called him over.

She acted way more excited than was necessary. I guess that was what I got for letting her meet the crush of her lifetime tonight.

Ryan made sure that he sat down next to me on the couch, and even though the couch was huge, he sat so our legs were touching. Nancy tried to hide her obvious amusement by handing Ryan a reader.

"We're doing research, dig in and help us, genius."

My eyes met Nancy's with a strike of horror. Ryan didn't know about anything! What was Nancy thinking? My face must have turned dead white because Ryan didn't take the reader he looked at me in sudden concern.

"What's wrong?" The worry in his eyes was enough to make me almost forget Nancy's blunder. Almost.

Nancy figured it out quickly enough. Her face was actually red. She pulled back the reader and turned it off. "I'm sorry. I didn't even think. I forgot he didn't…" Nancy was at a loss for words.

Know was the end of that sentence. Although a part of me agreed with her. It felt like Ryan knew everything already. Like he was in on all the secrets and yet he wasn't.

Ryan glanced back and forth between Nancy and me and he placed his hands up in surrender. "I have no idea what's going on, but this is really weird." He turned to me suddenly upset, "Do you… oh man, I'm so sorry. You don't like me, do you? You must think I'm this clingy jerk. I'm going to go."

Ryan stood up, face flushed, tail tucked between his legs and I nearly had a panic attack.

"Ryan, stop!" I said that a little too loud.

"No, it's okay, Chelsan, I get it. I'm a jerk. Seriously, I get it." Ryan was genuinely hurt, and for no reason. I had to tell him.

"Ryan, sit. Please. I like you, dork." Just the way I always imagined telling him. Ugh.

It was enough for Ryan, he smiled his *heart-wrenching* smile that always gave me goose bumps, and sat down next to me. Even closer than before. "Then what is it?"

"There are some things you need to know about me."

And I told him everything. I didn't mean to. I started out thinking I'd only tell him what he needed to know, but by the end of it I guess he needed to know everything because I hadn't left anything out.

By the end of the conversation, instead of revulsion (as I fully expected), I saw wonder and awe in the way he stared at me. And he was definitely staring. Then his expression turned sad.

"I'm really sorry about your mom. She was a really nice lady," Ryan stated quietly.

At the mention of my mother, that familiar lump of anguish stuck itself in my throat. "Thanks." Then it occurred to me, "You sound like you met her?"

Ryan's face flushed red. "I did. About six months ago," he paused as if unsure if he wanted to finish this story. "I came by your trailer one night to see you. I guess you were at work, but she invited me in and made me a chocolate shake."

I was shocked. A: my mother *never* told me, and B: Ryan came to see me at *my* house! "What?"

"Don't be mad. She promised she wouldn't tell you and by the look on your face, she obviously kept her word. I didn't want to freak you out. I just wanted to apologize for ignoring you all the time. But I wanted it to come from *me* and not second hand from your mom." Then he smiled. "She gave me some really good advice."

I was going to ask him exactly *what* that advice was, but I decided that was between the two of them. No wonder she was so judgmental of Bill. She had obviously picked sides once Ryan had come to see her. He must have been the *other boy* she kept on hinting at. That was so Mom.

"I'm glad you got to meet her."

"Me, too." He smiled, "Do you think you could show me how you bring something back to life?" he asked a little shyly.

"Sorry, no dead things in here." Nancy punched Ryan's shoulder in a joking manner, but there was definitely some protectiveness packed into that punch. It was Nancy's nice way of saying, *'don't make Chelsan perform like a monkey you jerk.'*

"It's okay, Nancy. I would need proof, too, if someone told me all this." I tried to reassure Ryan and Nancy, but Ryan's face fell. He looked like I had kicked him.

He turned to me so we were eye to eye. "I believe you. You don't have to prove anything to me. I was just curious." He turned to Nancy, rubbing his newly smacked arm. "And I deserved that."

"No, really, it's no big deal. Here." I searched the room for anything dead. There was a particularly large cockroach, but I decided to keep insects out of this, Nancy would freak. And then I saw the perfect thing.

A small houseplant that was on its last legs. It was some kind of flower plant, but the petals and leaves were brown and dead. I walked over to the small pot (it was only a few inches high) and brought it over to the couch. I connected to the plant's swirling black hole and brought it back to life. Green leaves and vines grew higher, larger, fuller than this plant had ever dreamed, and white silky flowers bloomed from every corner. When I was done, a two-foot masterpiece stood before us.

Ryan's mouth had dropped and even Nancy was taken aback. I think it was good for her to see me bring life back to something as opposed to the nightmare I had left her with when I disconnected Bruce from his black hole.

"Wow." Ryan had finally spoken.

"Yeah," Nancy chimed in.

"I can put it back the way it was," I volunteered. I started to feel uncomfortable. What would Ryan say if I brought a human back, I mean, hearing about it and actually seeing it were entirely two different things. Nancy had been exposed to Bruce, but I think she was in some kind of denial about that. I didn't want to scare them off. "Guys, *wow* and *yeah*, not very encouraging." I decided to take the honest approach.

Ryan put his arm around me and gave me a little squeeze. "You just became even cooler, and I thought you were just about the coolest person I'd ever met."

"Don't put it back. My mom will love it. This was her favorite, but she over-watered it to death." Nancy took the relaxed approach at this point.

"Okay. Just tell her I gave it to her as a thank-you for letting me stay with you guys." I turned to Ryan, his words hitting me like a ton of bricks. "You thought I was cool?"

"I think you're the *dork*." He smiled at me and then reached over and took my hand.

Somehow *dork* never sounded so good.

"Knock it off," Nancy said with a roll of her eyes, but I could tell she was happy for me. "Don't let Bill see you do that." She threw that in for measure, which made Ryan scoot in closer to me and made my stomach ache.

I still wasn't sure how Bill felt about me, but I wasn't an idiot. I could tell there was definitely more than friendship on his mind. And as much as I really liked Bill, I didn't feel the same kind of excitement and fire for him that I did for Ryan. How could I go from no prospects to two of the most sought after boys in my school liking me? And even after all the attention both of them had been giving me, there was still a part of me that didn't believe they *really* liked me. Like it was some form of "primitive-animal-ape thing," where as soon as one showed interest the other one became all territorial and mistook it for feelings for me. So really neither one of them liked me, they just needed to win the competition over my affection.

And then I was bummed again. That was probably it. I hated my mind sometimes. I always had to make a good situation turn into some logically horrible one. I never could believe that good things could happen to me and I didn't know how to break that.

"I'm seriously impressed. I'm not freaked out or anything." Ryan let go of my hand and put his arm around me and I literally had goose bumps. It was scary how much power he had over my physical being. I had to be careful I didn't let him have that much control over my mind as well or I'd soon become one of those lame girls that did everything their boyfriend did.

I could tell Nancy thought the same thing as she shoved her reader in Ryan's hands. "Do something useful, Ryan. Aren't you supposed to be some kind of genius? We need access to files that we can't download from the public server."

Ryan pulled his arm away from me and held the reader with both hands. "You mean restricted files from that study Mr. Alaster told us about?"

Nancy raised her eyebrow in interest. "That would be a great start. Yes."

"Can you do that?" I asked. My interest was piqued. All Nancy and I could find was the article published in the Scientific Journal and there weren't any details as to how the experiment was performed or any of the trials leading up to the actual resurrection. If we could read the entire report maybe we could get more accurate answers and figure out why I was the way I was.

"Yeah, no problem. What else do you need?" Ryan was eager to impress.

"We're trying to figure out what kind of spell Mr. Vice President used to kill baby Chelsan, but all we're coming up with is the basics."

Nancy was worked up now. If Ryan could do what he said he could we could potentially find out what had happened to me.

"We need to be careful about what we hack into. If Turner is keeping an eye on Chelsan and you then he's keeping an eye on Bill and me as well. We're the only people that have been around you in the last twenty-four hours." Ryan turned to me as if the next thing he was about to say was going to be difficult. "You need to tell Bill everything, too. He's in danger now just by being your friend. And…" He paused and swallowed hard, "He's a good guy."

"Wow." Nancy raised her eyebrow, impressed. "Look at you, all mature." Nancy was serious as she looked at me, "He has a point, Chelsan."

I knew they were right, but I felt like I was starting to lose control over the situation. If I ever had any control at all.

They would help me even if it meant they were in danger.

I couldn't live with that.

And in that second I made a decision.

The only way to protect them was to leave them.

What was I thinking involving people I care about anyway? They could end up dead and it would be my fault. I'd never be able to live with myself. I was so selfish!

"You're right. Why don't you call him and have him come over." Bill *did* have the right to know. He needed a heads up. "Be right back." I stood up.

"Hang on. Your Chuck's are untied." Ryan pointed out and reached down to tie the laces of my shoes.

For some reason it threw me off a bit, it was such a small gesture, but it made my heart skip a beat. I smiled at him and wanted to say good-bye but I walked to the bathroom instead. They couldn't follow me in there and I knew it had a small window leading to the side yard. I would have to do this quick.

I entered the bathroom and took a deep breath. I tried not to panic. I didn't want to be alone. It was terrifying, but I wouldn't be able to live with myself if anything were to happen my friends. I guess Jill was right to a certain degree, I didn't belong with the students of Geoffrey Turner High. I was trouble.

The window was about twenty inches in height and twenty inches wide, so it would be a tight fit, but doable. Unlatching the lock, I slid the window open as quietly as was humanly possible. I squeezed my body through the opening with surprisingly no sound at all and dropped to the soft grass below. Half-crawling, half-running, I hurried out of Nancy's side yard and once I was at a safe distance I ran full force down the grass street. It was still wet from watering and I almost slipped a few times, but I finally made it to a Hover-Shuttle station a few blocks away without any injury.

There were a few others waiting with me, but they didn't pay me any mind. I looked like a local kid waiting for a ride to the mall. Come on! Where was the stupid shuttle! I knew as soon as Nancy and Ryan found out I'd escaped they'd start an all out search for me, and I wanted to be as far away from them as possible. I had to go where they'd never guess I'd be. And I needed to find a phone to call Jason and make a new meeting place otherwise Nancy and Ryan were just going to show up at Alby's and all this would be for nothing.

Finally! The Hover-Shuttle arrived at the station and I clambered inside it as if the police were after me. I sat down on an aisle seat so no one could see me from the window. I wasn't sure where I was going, I just wanted to GO! I knew that if Nancy and Ryan caught up to me, I wouldn't be able to refuse their help. Especially if Ryan worked his Voodoo mojo on me. That was what it felt like anyway. How could one person make my entire body and brain go completely numb! It was a little frustrating to say the least. I knew I wouldn't be able to leave them again. I wasn't strong enough. Jason was my only hope now. Hopefully, he would steer me to…

…to what? What exactly was I expecting from this guy? I was trying to live moment to moment because when I actually sat down and thought about the future I was instantly queasy. What could I possibly do to save myself from the most powerful man in the world? If Turner really wanted me dead, wouldn't I be dead by now? So what was he waiting for? Maybe he was worried someone would find out he was my grandfather and tie him to the murder? Or maybe my dad's death made him change and he really wanted me back in his life? I just didn't know anything. I felt so lost and utterly alone, my choice or not, it sucked.

What if he knew about my power?

The thought had been flitting around my head since my mother's visions, but it finally solidified itself in that moment. He could want me alive to use me, or study me, or I don't know…. My mind was going a mile a minute. I needed to relax, take a deep breath and find a phone. Baby steps. The Hover-Shuttle traveled into downtown Los Angeles. A surge of excitement flowed through me. I had never been to the city, I had never been anywhere because of Bruce. Everything I had ever seen on holo-tv, I could actually see with my own eyes. I felt like a hermit that finally decided to leave the house for the first time.

I peered over the shoulder of the person across from me to see out the shuttle's window at the oncoming skyscrapers in the distance. Downtown Los Angeles. It was the most stunning view I had ever seen. It was an island of steel surrounded by an ocean of trees.

At first glance, the buildings seemed clumped together in what appeared to be a chaotic mess, but upon closer inspection there was meaning to the madness.

The outer circle consisted of water dumping silos for all the hover-vehicles flying into the city to deposit their fuel cell tanks, making it easy to water the surrounding foliage that stretched for miles in every direction. Just past the silos the first set of steel and glass made up the smaller-sized outer ring of buildings that looked like a circle of miss-matched teeth.

There were five other rings of varying sized skyscrapers leading to the center of Los Angeles, a giant, three-hundred foot in diameter, metal cylinder that was at least a thousand feet above all the other buildings. It was used as a hover-pad landing area, but *how* someone was to get down from the twenty-eight-hundred foot tall structure, was a mystery I was about to find out.

The Hover-Shuttle swooped up to the hover pad on top of the cylinder and landed with ease in its designated area. The door clunked open and everyone started to file out. I slowly stood up and walked out of the shuttle last.

I expected huge gusts of wind from the height we were at, but it was completely devoid of any draft or even a breeze. There were Hover-Shuttles and cars landing everywhere in a constant buzzing and whizzing of sound, but it was calm, as if we were in the eye of a storm.

I noticed a slight blurring of sky every time a car or shuttle came in to land and realized it was a kind of force field set in place to protect people and vehicles from weather. I had only read about technology like that in school. I had never seen it in person.

I might never go to class again.

It hit me hard. I hadn't thought about that.

But, if I was supposed to stay hidden, it wasn't like I could go back to school. Great. I was officially a high school drop-out. As much as I used to complain about homework and class, I realized I was actually going to miss it. And even though my motivation to go to one of the best schools in the country was to keep Bruce alive, it still meant something to me that I was accepted into a school like that. Now that was over. No. I couldn't think like that. Maybe when I talked to Jason he'd be able to clear things up for me so I could go back. I didn't know where I'd find the money for tuition, but I'd discover a way somehow.

Focus. I needed to find a phone.

I watched where everyone was headed and saw several hundred mini-platforms all along the outer edge of the circled roof. I saw as someone would stand on the platform and be sucked down the building. It must be some kind of elevator tube. Another thing I had only heard of before, but had never been in.

I took a deep breath, good thing I wasn't scared of heights.

I waited in line for my turn as I watched people pop out of view as soon as they stood on the platform. The lady in front of me wore her screaming daughter like a spider suit, the girl's grip was so tight. I couldn't blame the girl. We were essentially on top of a mountain about to be propelled down to the ground in a tiny vacuum tube. My stomach started to churn. I had to keep reminding myself that people did this everyday and I had never heard of any mishaps. I had seen one of these elevator tubes on holo-tv, but it always looked like fun. Or it was so quick I didn't think much of it at all. But standing in line waiting to be sucked down the abyss, I really wanted to vomit.

The lady and her tormented child stepped onto the platform in front of me and…

WHHOOOMP!

They were gone, crying and all.

Me next.

I swallowed hard and shuffled forward.

"Come on, kid, we don't have all day!" the jerk behind me yelled in my ear.

"You go." I couldn't do it yet.

He shoved past me and with a roll of his eyes…

WHHOOOMP!

He was gone.

"Are you waiting for someone?" the next woman in line asked me.

"No. I'm just… I've never done this before," I confided.

"You want me to go with you? It's better in pairs for your first time." She looked like she was thirty so I knew she wasn't a rich jerk.

"That would be great, thanks," I sputtered.

"Move it, ladies!" The man behind us shouted.

The lady smiled at me, encouraging. "Don't listen to him. Everyone is always in a hurry. Here."

She grabbed my hand and moved me forward. "Gotta do it quick, or you'll never do it."

I nodded and squeezed her hand a little harder than I should have.

She looked at me and gave me a wink of confidence. "One, two, three."

And we stepped on the square platform.

WHHOOOOOSH!

We flew down the tube at a ridiculous speed, but it was completely exhilarating! The wall in front of us was glass and the city whizzed by us in a blur of silver and black. Two seconds later a door slid open and we were street side. A digital clock directly over the door began to count down from five.

"Quickly, unless you want to go back up." The lady pulled me out of the tube and onto the crowded streets of Los Angeles.

"Thanks again," I said to the lady.

She nodded and waved. "Any time, dear."

And she was off, heading up the street, pushing her way through the large throngs of people.

Cities were one of the only areas in the world where they actually kept the old pavement and concrete in tact. There wasn't a lot of concrete in the world anymore. I could feel the heat from the sidewalk through my shoes, which was both comforting and weird, not like the cobblestone in front of Mel's. It was like flooring with grit.

I decided to walk in the same direction as the lady that helped me and scanned the area for a payphone. (They made a big come back fifty years ago!) I didn't have to go far. I found one on the corner of Olive and Sixth Street, right in front of Pershing Square. I had only read about the place, but it was far more impressive in person. Even the holos didn't do it justice.

It was lined with forty-foot pines acting as sentries to Los Angeles' oldest park. It had its own water silo in the North West corner to keep the vegetation vibrant and breathtaking. Roses of every color imaginable, giant seven-foot sunflowers, red-orange hedging, plants and flowers I had never even seen before made up the inner square. In the dead center of the park was a perfectly coiffed square of the brightest green grass I had ever seen.

According to what I'd read, every summer and spring they'd have outdoor concerts and in the winter they'd bring in an ice-rink for skating. It was also the one place I'd seen so far that wasn't entirely packed with bodies. For some reason it seemed like everyone had a quiet respect for the place of beauty and didn't want to see it trampled by foot traffic.

I picked up the phone and was about to place my thumb up to the money scanner when I realized that if Turner *was* looking for me I would be giving him a giant flag as to where I was. I put my thumb down and looked around for a volunteer. The large shuffling crowd of passer-bys looked like the last thing they wanted to do was stop, so I scanned the park. A man sat at a bench, head bent over his electronic reader. I walked over to him with as friendly a smile as I could muster.

"Hi. I don't mean to bother you, but is there any way you could thumbscan the payphone for me? I'm all out of credit and I need to call my dad."

The man sighed heavily as if I was asking him to lift one of the skyscrapers towering above us. "Yeah, fine," he muttered, annoyed, but willing to help.

I'd take it.

He walked over to the payphone and scanned his thumb.

"Thanks," I said, wanting him to leave, but he just continued to stand over me.

"Well, call your dad. I want to make sure this isn't for drugs or some virtual reality bar scam," he sneered at me.

Okay, so he was paranoid. I could understand that, but I hoped Jason would play along.

I pulled out his number and dialed. The man looked at me suspiciously, obviously upset I had to look at a number. I guess he figured if it were my dad I'd have the number memorized. I turned to him, "He just got a new cell phone." I probably shouldn't have tried to over-explain, but I tended to crack under pressure when I lied.

The phone rang once. "Hello?"

"Dad? It's Chelsan." *Please, please, please remember who I am.*

"Smart girl. Is Harry Dalop standing over you?" Jason's voice sounded amused and I was instantly relieved. Jason must have some kind of caller I.D. and the guy next to me, Harry, apparently, showed up on it.

"Yeah, I ran out of credit again. I can't meet you at seven, can we meet at seven-thirty, somewhere closer?"

Evidently, Harry had heard enough of the conversation to feel content with his decision to help me out and went back to his reader on the bench.

"Okay, he's gone," I whispered.

"We have to go on the assumption that Turner has put out a voice recognition alert on your dear old pipes so let's make this quick. Where are you?" Jason was all business, which put me ill at ease. I wanted to be the only person paranoid; I needed an anchor of calm if I were to get through this.

"Downtown. I wanted to keep my friends out of this and they knew where we were meeting."

"Gordo's Virtual Reality Bar off of Pico and Central. Seven-thirty." Click.

The suddenness of Jason hanging up the phone made me jump a little, but I took a sigh of relief. At least, Nancy, Ryan and Bill wouldn't know where I was going. And a virtual reality bar was as seedy and sleazy as they come. The complete opposite of Alby's Bar and Grill at the

Riverside mall. I had an instant pang of fear going to place like Gordo's, but the more I thought about it the safer I felt. It would be the last place Turner or anyone would expect me to go.

I looked at the digital clock on the payphone: six-thirty. I had an hour. I decided to head over to Gordo's to get a feel for the place. I wasn't sure how long it would take me.

Once I started walking off the beaten path, there were fewer and fewer people, only the distant sound of whirling hover cars above to keep me company. The closer I came to Gordo's the dirtier and more rundown the area became. The trailer park looked like the Ritz Carlton compared where I was now. Cluttered metal lay in clumps in alleyways, stacked up to eight feet high. It felt as if I was walking through the dumping ground of Los Angeles. No wonder Jason chose this part of town. Geoffrey Turner wouldn't be caught dead at a place like this.

I turned onto Pico and saw the blazing holographic sign of "Gordo's Virtual Reality Bar," hovering over the square metal building like a cloud. There were no signs of windows anywhere on the structure, only one opened door in the front with an attendant waiting for customers. I couldn't find a clock anywhere so I had no idea what time it was. I figured I'd wait inside. I knew I was early. It felt like a good thirty-minute walk over here, which meant I had a half an hour more before Jason arrived.

I took a deep breath and marched up to the entrance of the bar. The attendant was a guy dressed all in black with a pencil-thin mustache that made him look like something out of a villain encyclopedia. Appearance-wise he was mid-twenties, which, judging by his occupation, put him in the category of black market Age-pro or actually in his mid-twenties, you never knew. He was skinny like his mustache and smiled at my approach.

"We don't get very many pretty ladies that often. What brings you here? Street fight? Mugging?" He paused for emphasis, "Murder?"

"None of those. Just meeting someone here." I tried to sound as casual as possible.

Virtual reality bars were humanities solution to working out all their pent up aggression. When Age-pro hit the market, I guess society used to be full of violence and war, but when given the option of living forever, people didn't want to be killed or locked up in prison where they'd have to live a life without the anti-aging pill. But according to leading scientists in human genetics, humans needed to satisfy their violent tendencies hence the creation of virtual reality bars. A place where you could be anywhere or anyone and kick the crap out of something. Virtual reality technology had been around for over three hundred years and hadn't changed much.

"Are you sure? You look so innocent on the outside, but I'm sure there's a demon ready to jump out of you."

Was that some sort of pick-up line?

"No demons, just meeting someone." I didn't really want to engage in the conversation he thought we were having.

His face fell a little as he smoothed his creepy mustache with his hand. "Go on in. Bar's down the hall to the right."

I moved past him without a glance or a word. I was afraid he'd ask me to thumbprint, and then Turner would know where I was. I figured this was probably the reason why Jason picked this place. It didn't look like they thumbprinted people that often.

Once I entered the building, I had to walk down a long corridor lined with glass doors. It was hard not to peek in at the inhabitants of the padded virtual rooms. It would have almost been comical, if it didn't make my skin crawl. Everyone dressed in the official blue spandex suits made for comfort and flexibility. Each suit was laden with sensors to make the experience as real as possible. To top off the outfit was a black helmet contraption with a visor that made the whole virtual experience happen.

There was an array of padded props in each room, I guess depending on the individual fantasy of the person inside. The first lady I passed was literally strangling a life-size dummy. She pounced and throttled the poor stuffed person like she wanted to rip it into a million pieces. She screamed a triumphant and terrifying screech that chilled me to my bones.

After that, I diverted my eyes from the rest of the rooms. It felt as if I witnessed a crime the way that she strangled the stuffed man. And knowing that to her eyes, she was really killing someone, somehow made the virtual reality experience a little too *real* for me.

I hurried past the rest of the doors and turned right. There was a run down bar waiting for me with exactly zero people in it. Only the bartender was there, wiping down the counter out of what looked like boredom. His face perked up when he saw me. I couldn't tell if he was a letch or if he was just happy to see someone at the bar.

"What can I get you?" he called out to me with a large smile. He was a heavyset man with dark circles under his eyes and a five o'clock shadow. He appeared to be in his early-twenties, another black market Age-pro would be my guess.

"Nothing. I'm just waiting for someone. What time is it anyway?" I asked as I walked over to the bar.

He didn't seem to mind that I wasn't ordering anything, he just looked happy he had company. "It's…" He looked at his watch, "Seven twenty-five. Who ya'll meeting?" His smile hadn't left his face since I had walked in the room and it was beginning to creep me out a little.

"Just a friend." I tried to sound as casual as possible, but I could feel myself sweating slightly. I really wished Nancy were here. She'd have this guy wrapped around her finger and I could just sit back and watch and not have to participate in any kind of social behavior. I wanted to order a water just so I could have something to fidget with, but I couldn't thumbprint, Turner would find me in a second. It was completely awkward sitting there at the bar with absolutely nothing to do but wait.

"Awfully strange place for a rich girl to meet someone," he leered at me. It was so grotesque and repulsive I flinched instinctively.

"I'm really eighteen, I'm not rich." He had assumed I was wealthy because I looked eighteen. And from the expression on his embarrassed face, the thought had never occurred to him that I actually *was* eighteen.

"Whoa," was all he said. He suddenly found that the other side of the bar was where he wanted to be at that moment.

Apparently, my age really freaked him out.

Good. I was thankful that he left me alone.

"Would you like a drink?"

I whirled around to see Jason Keroff smiling an annoyingly cute lopsided smile at me. "Good girl, keeping away from thumbprints. You must be parched."

"Yeah, a little." The butterflies Jason gave me weren't the same as the ones Ryan did. This was more like being nervous because I was about to give an oral report in front of class. I tried to remember yesterday when I was devoid of any emotion whatsoever at seeing him just to remain calm in his presence.

Why was I such a freak?!

Jason motioned to the bartender. "Two waters, please."

The bartender didn't even acknowledge me as he slid the two glasses of water in front of Jason and I.

Jason turned to me, still smiling. "What's up with him?"

"I think my age scared him a bit."

"You told him your age?" Jason's smile faded. He looked worried.

"I didn't tell him my name or anything. He thought I was a richy and hit on me. It was gross," I shared, hoping I hadn't done anything wrong.

"Well..." Jason trailed off as if thinking of some horribly long math problem in his head. "It's probably fine."

"So what *is* going on? I'm not even sure what I'm doing here. I'm freaking out. My mom is dead, my whole trailer park is now an oak forest, my grandpa is Geoffrey Turner..." I began my panicked rant.

"Wait. What was that about Turner?" Jason interrupted me with wide eyes. He searched the surrounding area as if he was expecting an army to suddenly appear from out of the shadows.

"Um..." Oh yeah, I hadn't told him that part of the story yet. "Yeah, he's my grandpa."

"Does he *know* he's your grandpa?" Jason was actually sweating at this point.

"I don't know." And that was the truth. I really didn't know. "What can you tell me about what happened to my mom?"

"First off..." Jason pulled out an object that looked like a stylus and placed it on the bar counter in front of us. He hit an invisible button and the whole thing lit up blue like a glowing mini-cylinder from space. "This is a frequency jammer, just in case someone has this place tapped."

The blue glow lit up Jason's face in an almost eerie way. I felt as if we were in some kind of covert spy mission huddled over the gadget that would turn into a weapon if needed. Unfortunately, reality wasn't that far off from my fantasy. "That thing doesn't blow up, does it?" I couldn't resist asking. No more surprises for me thank you very much.

Jason's eyebrow lifted in what I could only describe as amusement. "No, it doesn't blow up." Jason leaned in close so there was no chance of the bartender overhearing. "Listen, you mentioned the green smoke. Tell me everything you and your step-dad saw. Is he with your friends? Is he safe?"

"No, he's dead." I didn't know how much I could share with Jason yet, but the look on Jason's face went from concerned to panicked in about two seconds.

"They got to him already? You're in more danger than I thought. We have to think about this." Jason shook his head as if he had some kind of tick.

"No. He died eleven years ago." I let that hang there for a second. I wasn't ready to tell Jason my secret yet, but at the same time, I couldn't let him think that my grandpa or the government killed Bruce or whomever else he thought did the deed.

"Wait. What?" Jason was genuinely confused, and a little bit put off, as if he thought I was messing with him.

I needed to show him. It was the only way I could leave no doubt in his head that I was telling the truth. I searched the room.

There was a dead fly a couple of feet away on the bar. "Will that device block any surveillance cameras as well?" I asked, just to be cautious.

Jason's eyebrows crinkled in genuine fascination at this point. "Yes. Why?"

"Just sit tight." I jumped off my stool and grabbed the dead fly, bringing it over to Jason. I plopped back on to my stool and placed the fly in front of the blue glowing device. "Dead, right?"

Jason nodded, his interest apparently piqued from the curious sparkle in his eyes.

I reached into the fly's black swirling center and made it fly around the frequency jammer. It did somersaults, spins, twirls, everything I could think of and then when I was certain I had made my point I let it drop to the bar with a slight thwack.

Jason swallowed hard and was silent for a good two minutes. My palms were definitely sweating. I wanted to say something, but I couldn't think of what to say. I wish I knew what Jason was thinking, but his face was unreadable.

"I brought Bruce out and made him say that about the smoke because the Mayor didn't believe me." There. I broke the oppressive silence.

Jason nodded slowly. "We're so dead."

"Yeah." It was really starting to sink in that I was in way over my head.

"I'll tell you what I know." Jason talked slower as if he was in shock.

Which, let's face it, he probably was. Before he came here, he was most likely thinking he was going to help some poor teenage girl who accidently witnessed something she shouldn't have. He wasn't prepared for the granddaughter of the Vice President of Population Control who could raise the dead. I was shocked myself that he was still here. But he was a reporter and I'm sure the juiciness of the story far outweighed the danger for him.

We'd see, I guess.

"Let's start with the green smoke," he began, "I've been trying to uncover this story for years, fifty to be exact. I've only been a reporter for a little while. I was a lab assistant for forty-five years at the International Laboratory Sciences Institute." Note to self, he was definitely over the age of seventy, Nancy would freak, she thought he was around our age. "Our purpose was to find new ways to help the environment and population problems such as developing hydroponics for crops and finding new chemical treatments for re-generating plants. I was good at my job and moved up through the ranks. The higher up the ladder I went the more disclosure contracts I thumbprinted until I was dealing with chemical solutions that by my calculations would kill effectively and efficiently rather than re-generate life.

"When I started asking questions, I was terminated immediately. Three attempts were made on my life soon after I was fired. That's when I became a reporter, just to put myself in the spotlight so it would be more difficult to kill me without people noticing. I admit, I tried my hardest to become the 'teen idol,' anything that would make me more valuable and harder to kill." He paused, taking a deep breath. "Your... grandpa..." He shook his head and ran his hand through his black wavy hair. "We're so dead."

"So my grandpa is *exterminating* people?" I tried to keep Jason focused. He seemed to do better when he was focused.

"Yes. Your grandpa's definition of population control is literally that… he controls the population by killing off people he feels the public won't miss. He takes run-down areas like trailer parks and comes in with his armies of poisons. Poisons I helped create." Jason couldn't make eye contact with me when he said the last part.

He was ashamed of himself. I could tell immediately. "Hey." I reached over and squeezed his hand supportively. He let his eyes meet mine, but they were full of guilt and horror. "I don't blame you. If not you then someone else. All I know about my grandpa is that he's one stubborn determined guy. If he wants something done, he won't stop until he's succeeded." And in the spirit of the moment, and the glowing blue of safety, I told Jason all about my mother's vision and the ceremonies that led to my unique talent.

Jason responded with a raise of the eyebrow, as if remembering something he had tucked away in the back of his mind. "I know what he did to you…"

Before Jason could finish his sentence the bartender swooped over and smashed Jason's frequency jammer with a baseball bat. It was so sudden and violent Jason and I couldn't move for a good three seconds. Jason was the first to respond with cat like reflexes, grabbing the bartender's bat and yanking it away.

The bartender didn't even struggle. He just placed his hands up in supplication and nodded toward the doorway as if trying to communicate some hidden message to Jason.

And apparently Jason understood this strange language of bats and nodding because he turned to me and grabbed my hand. "Jig's up. Gramps has found you."

This froze my insides as if someone had poured liquid nitrogen down my throat. "He's here?"

Jason carefully led me off the stool and toward the back door of the bar, away from the entrance. "Chances are the big man himself isn't making an appearance, but his extermination squad is here."

"The poisons?" I gulped. I didn't want to die the way my mom did. It was somehow more terrifying than the act of dying itself.

"No, worse: guns." Jason tried the back door, but it was locked. He looked at the bartender for help.

The bartender shrugged almost apologetically and then screamed, "They're in here!"

"Great." Jason took matters into his own hands by letting go of mine and using his strength to slam the bat onto the door handle. It smashed into pieces. He kicked hard and the door's wood splintered enough to fly open.

Gunfire cracked loudly from behind us. A few stray bullets lodged themselves into the wall. Jason took my hand once again and practically threw me into the adjoining room, which happened to be one of the virtual reality padded cells.

The man inside didn't even notice we had interrupted his fantasy. He was throttling a stuffed dummy with every ounce of energy he possessed. Jason pulled me toward the exit, swinging the door open and throwing us both to the ground of the hallway beyond, just as another round of gunfire whizzed overhead. I managed a quick look back just in time to see the poor man in the padded cell turn into Swiss cheese from the onslaught of bullets ripping through his blue spandex suit and the dummy he was strangling. He was dead before he even knew what had happened.

I screamed. I couldn't control myself. I had seen way too much brutality in the last two days and my brain couldn't take it.

Jason pushed me forward. We were half-crouched as we ran through the hallway. More men with guns appeared in front of us and started firing. Jason shoved me into another padded cell with a woman punching the wall in front of her. Glass shattered into a million pieces as the rain of bullets tore through our room, killing the lady in front of us, her black spinning hole already formed before she hit the ground.

Jason searched the room for another exit, but the only door was the one we came in. I could see the poor man riddled with bloody holes across the hall from us, his black chasm swirling madly.

"No way out," Jason said, holding the bat in front of us protectively, then shrugged at the obvious futility of it.

"I can help." I had to try something.

The gunfire had stopped. Orders were barked out to the other soldiers. They thought we were dead and they were coming in to collect the bodies.

Screams from the other inhabitants of the virtual reality bar echoed outside our room. They had obviously heard the gunfire and were running out of the bar for their lives.

I only had a few moments, maybe less before the soldiers turned the corner and saw us huddled in our rattrap. I took a deep breath and connected to the lady's black hole in front of us. Just like Bruce, I kept reminding myself.

Footsteps crunched over the glass…

… almost to our door.

I made the lady run up to the doorway.

Gunfire tore through her, shredding pieces of skin, causing them to slap against the wall and floor. I still couldn't see any of our attackers. I knew as soon as they saw us alive they'd shoot us instantly. They were at close range, but I made the lady move closer to them. And then I heard the distinct call from one of the men.

"Zombie 442! Take proper aim!"

Zombie 442? Apparently this wasn't the first time this gun crew had seen an active dead person.

I angled myself so I could see what I was doing and made the woman grab the gunman's throat that stood closest to her with frightening impact. His face was already turning blue. I could feel her hand squeezing the life out of this soldier and it terrified me, but I couldn't stop either. All I could think about was keeping his gun from blowing us away. Bullets tore into the woman's head from all sides, as if they thought this was the key to finishing her off. In a matter of seconds she was completely headless, just a pulp of cracked neck bone was left. Vomit. Yes, vomiting sounded like the right thing to do at this point, but I had to save Jason and myself first.

I made the woman throw the man she was strangling down the hallway where most of the bullets had come from. There were actual shrieks of panic and a clattering of metal with a resounding thud of men smacking the floor and walls. I must have had her throw him pretty hard. I had never used my power that way before and I had to say it was making me a little dizzy and excited.

Now that all the soldiers were out of view I needed to see what was going on. I was a blind puppet master, and Jason and I wouldn't be safe until we could get out of this building. I took a sneak peek over at Jason, whose eyes were round with fear.

He made quick eye contact with me. "That's way different than a fly," was all he could sputter out.

"I'll get us out of here, I promise," I lied. I had no idea if that was even possible. I started to think this was it for me. I was going to be responsible for killing my celebrity crush. At least I wouldn't have to feel guilty for long.

Then I remembered what I did with Bruce. When I made him show me what really happened at the trailer park, and I thought I could do something similar with the first man they had killed.

I sought out his black hole and linked myself to him.

Okay. Body parts check, now for the hard part.

I put all my energy in trying to focus on his sight.

POP.

Whoa.

I could see through his eyes *and* I could see through mine.

At the same time.

Talk about instant migraine.

I closed my eyes to eliminate any confusion (and headaches).

From his viewpoint, I was in the room we had just abandoned. I was still aware of my own body back with Jason across the hall. It was totally surreal. I made the man stand up and walk to the doorway. Gunfire tore through him as soon as I made him enter into the hallway. They were aiming at his head, so it was like trying to see through a snow storm with all the bullets hitting his face. Damn, they hit his left eye. I had one eye left. I made a quick count. There were four of them and they were all wide-eyed with fear, unloading their guns into both corpses in front of them.

I realized at that moment I was still controlling the woman as well.

I needed the man's functional eye so I made him put his arm out protectively and let them shred his arm until it was just bloody pulp and bone. I didn't care as long as I could see. I focused my attention on the woman, using the man as a lookout and her as my weapon.

I made her headless corpse leap forward, grabbing the first gun she could get her hands on. It was very awkward, using *his* eyes and *her* body, it made my perspective all wonky. But from the looks on these soldier's faces, they were halfway to peeing their pants, so I took full advantage of their freaked-out status. I could feel that she had a good grip on the handgun. I made her rip it from his hand and point it at the four combatants. Their bullets were tearing through what was left of her flesh, and I felt like I was starting to lose control of her.

I made a note that maybe my gift was somehow tied to skin or something, I would need to tell Nancy right away. We could look it up. Then with a pang of anguish, I remembered I would probably never be able to see Nancy again. Maybe Jason would help me if we survived, but my corporeal self couldn't help but feel him cowering next to me like a baby. I couldn't blame him, I guess. This was definitely some gruesome stuff. If I hadn't been keeping a dead man alive for the last eleven years I might not have fared as well either.

I tried to make the woman squeeze the trigger of the gun she was holding, but I couldn't do it. Physically I could, but mentally I wasn't ready to shoot anyone. I logically told myself that if I didn't kill them, they would most definitely kill me, but after killing Bruce when I was seven I just couldn't do it. I wasn't a murderer even if it was self-defense. I was better than that. I had to think.

I made the man leap forward as fast as I could manage (which was ridiculously fast by the way). Controlling him was about ten times easier than controlling the woman since he still had most of his body in tact. I made him snatch another gun from one of the men and bash the soldier over the head with it. He fell into one of the other goons, unconscious. I felt guilty, but at least he was still alive.

"Retreat!" one of the men screamed. His voice was shrill and breathy. As much action as I assumed these men had seen, apparently they hadn't seen this.

I watched from the man's corpse as the soldiers backed away, guns drawn, one of the combatants potato sacking his unconscious team member over his shoulder. And they were gone.

Out the front door.

I made my one-eyed corpse follow them out to make sure they were truly gone. I had him aim his gun at the retreating soldiers as they jumped in their hover-hummer, dumping their fallen compadre in the back and whizzing away out of view.

I instantly dropped my connection with both corpses. My head was spinning. I had never done anything like that before and it literally drained me of most of my energy. I felt like I hadn't slept for ten days straight. I turned to Jason, my eyes drooping. I knew I would crash soon and we needed to get out of there before the soldiers returned with back up to finish us off.

"We have to get out of here," Jason said as if reading my thoughts.

"Yeah. I'm not sure I can stay awake," I managed to slur out.

He nodded and his previously horrified looks had now turned to determination and protectiveness. Jason picked me up like a baby and carried me out of the building and into the abandoned parking lot.

"Great." Jason shook his head in anger.

"What is it?" My mouth felt like it couldn't open properly and no matter how hard I tried I couldn't seem to keep my eyes open.

"They towed my hover. We're going to have to walk. *Can* you walk?" Jason could see that he was asking the impossible. "Of course you can't, you just managed to make two zombies fight Turner's thugs," he mumbled more to himself than to me, but then he smiled his signature roguish smile and looked at me. "Impressive by the way."

I could barely enjoy the compliment, but I managed a weak smile. Or at least I think I did, it was always impossible for me to tell what expression I was making my face accomplish. Especially when I was this tired. "It's….good…" Don't know what that meant, but I was trying.

Then I heard the whirling fan of a hover car. "They….they're… coming…" I tried to make my mouth and voice function normally.

"It's not them. Maybe we can hitch a ride, looks like they're coming to the bar." Jason carried me over to where the hover car landed. "Hey, we need help."

Maybe I was imagining it, but I swore I heard Nancy shriek. I tried to pry my eyes open. I must have been delusional. Wishful thinking. In my tired stupor I really wanted my best friend with me.

"What did you do to her?!" It really did sound like Nancy.

"Nothing. Look, we need a ride. We really need to get out of here, NOW!" Jason was feeling the pressure and the panic as time was slipping away.

"Don't you yell at me! Just because you're some famous reporter doesn't give you the right to use and abuse my best friend!"

It *was* Nancy. Please don't be a dream. Please don't be a dream. Even though I knew now more than ever that having my friends around me was a possible death sentence to them, I couldn't help but be selfish. I needed Nancy. I needed Ryan. And I needed Bill.

"Best friend?" Jason was confused now.

"Nancy?" I managed to squeak out.

And suddenly I was being taken out of Jason's arms, into someone else's. My stomach managed to perform the impossible back flip as I realized Ryan had grabbed me from Jason. His face was worried and flushed. It was like a full on battle with my eyelids to stay open. Ryan was ridiculously gorgeous.

"I knew you'd try something. I managed to put a tracer in your shoes before you took off. It took a while to track you down, with all the crowds and then there was some kind of frequency jammer messing with the signal." I heard about half of that. I couldn't stop staring at his lips moving. I must have looked like an idiot.

"We better get you out of here." It was Bill's voice. Bill had come, too.

"Bill." His name was easier to say being only one syllable.

"Yeah, it's me." Bill's hand touched my hair and I hoped it wasn't my fatigued state, but he looked fine with me being in Ryan's arms.

"In the car. Let's get out of here." Nancy had taken charge like she always did.

"Let her go to sleep. Trust me, she needs it," Jason said to the others.

I felt Ryan's lips touch my forehead and then everything went black.

CHAPTER 4
MONDAY SEPTEMBER 20, 2320

"Chelsan, wake up. It's time for school."

Bruce? Were the last three days all a terrible nightmare? Sure, I'd still have to take care of Bruce the rest of my existence, but that would be paradise compared to what I'd been through. It made sense. I mean, being Vice President Turner's granddaughter? Extermination of trailer parks and zombie fights? Really? It had to be a dream. And best of all that meant my mom was still alive…

"Mom?" I opened up my eyes in expectation of seeing my drab trailer wall.

I was in Nancy's room.

My heart sunk. All of it actually happened. Mom was truly gone. My eyes welled up.

"Hey, you okay?"

That was when I noticed that Ryan was lying next to me!

I was immediately self-conscious. I must have looked like a complete disaster because he kept on staring at me.

"You look beautiful." Ryan brushed his hand against my cheek and smiled.

I decided to throw caution to the wind and I reached up and held his hand in mine. Not as bold as Nancy probably would have been, but I was pretty wimpy when it came to boys I was fast discovering. Ryan didn't seem to mind, he snuggled in closer so we were forehead to forehead.

"Were you here all night?" I asked.

"No. I just snuck in the window this morning. No one knows I'm here, Nancy would freak. I'll climb out when she comes back up," Ryan whispered. His breath was minty fresh and I realized with sudden horror my breath probably smelled like the sewer.

"I think I need a mint." Wow. I amazed myself at what came out of my mouth.

Ryan didn't even blink as he reached down in his jeans pocket and pulled out his personal metal gum container. He took out a piece of gum and placed it in my mouth. This guy really made my mind turn to jelly.

"Better?" he asked with a smile and put his forehead back to mine.

"Better." I needed to get past this "school girl crush mode" that made me paralyzed around him. "Why do you like me?" I blurted out.

And to my surprise, he just smiled. "Anyone would be crazy not to like you."

"Then everyone's been crazy my whole life. You're the first one." Being a leper at school was pretty much common knowledge.

Ryan rolled his eyes. "I know *a lot* of guys who like you, they're just too scared to do anything about it because of Jill."

"Yeah, right." I couldn't believe him. I saw the way people looked at me, like I was going to eat their pets or something. Jill didn't have that kind of power. Did she?

"You don't even know how beautiful you are, do you?" Ryan's hand stroked my cheek again and then he turned serious. "Ever since I tutored you last year I wanted to be with you, but I let my fear of being a social outcast make all my decisions for me."

"But you're so popular. No one would have cared who you dated." I was both excited to hear him say that he liked me since last year and hurt that he didn't like me enough to do anything about it.

He leaned in and kissed me.

Mush. Pure mush. I couldn't think straight. All I could do was kiss him back. I didn't want to stop. The more we kissed the tighter I held onto him.

Eventually he pulled away. His stare was so intense I couldn't keep eye contact with him for very long. It scared me how much I liked him.

"I shouldn't have cared what people thought." Ryan's face was full of hurt and embarrassment. I could tell it was a decision he had struggled with.

"We could have kept it secret." We could have. No one would have needed to know. And I certainly knew how to keep a secret. Until recently anyway.

He held my face with both hands so I had to look him straight in the eye. He was almost angry he was so passionate. He accentuated every word, "I would *never* disrespect you like that."

"It wouldn't have been disrespectful. I get it. People don't like me because I'm trailer trash. I wouldn't expect you to…" I couldn't even finish my sentence. He silenced me with another kiss.

Ryan pulled away. "You are *not* trailer trash. You are the most amazing human being I've ever met. You can do things with your mind that scientists all across the world have been trying to do for centuries. You're the smartest person that I know, *and* you're drop dead gorgeous. And I love it when you make that confused little face of yours. You get this cute little crinkle on your forehead." He was smiling by then and it made my heart spin. "And I'm shocked that you'd even be interested in me. I'm a weak jerk for not telling everyone to *F* themselves when I wanted to ask you out. I treated you like crap and I don't deserve you." He was hurt again.

"Hey." I held his cheeks in my hands like he did to me. "Don't beat yourself up for trying to fit in. If I thought I had a remote chance of having a *normal* high school existence, I wouldn't date you either." I smiled at my own joke, but Ryan wasn't having it.

"Don't brush this off. I was mean." Ryan was more serious than I'd ever seen him.

"Okay. I get it. But that's over now. Everyone pretty much knows we're going out. You made that quite clear last Friday."

"Why are you trying to make *me* feel better for being a dick?"

"Fine. Feel like crap, just don't break up with me." A part of me liked the fact that he was beating himself up about the way he ignored me, but another part of me just wanted him to shut up already and kiss me.

Ryan smiled. "I'm never going to break up with you. In fact, even if *you* break up with me, because you probably will you know, I'm very boring, I'll stalk you forever."

I snuggled in closer. "Boring? Yeah right. You're only the smartest kid alive.

I'm surprised my grandpa hasn't snatched you up to enlist you in his services."

"He's tried." Ryan looked at me cautiously. He wasn't sure how I was going to react and I could tell he was scared.

"What do you mean he's tried?"

"You know how I get recruitment offers on a daily basis?"

"Yeah?" It was crazy how basically the whole *world* wanted a piece of Ryan. When someone tested off the charts like Ryan, it made him a very popular guy. He received job offers from every science research lab in the world. When he was eleven years old he figured out the missing piece of some unsolvable math equation that had stumped mathematicians for centuries. It was no wonder Turner wanted him.

"No. I don't mean he tried to recruit me recently. He tried to recruit me when I was eight. Three years before I solved Trildion's theorem." Ryan paused, "Chelsan, Turner kidnapped me."

I couldn't say I was surprised considering what my mother showed me in her visions. Turner was ruthless and kidnapping kids to serve his interests seemed on par with what I knew about him already.

"He must have had access to my test scores. That was the first time I tested above the genius level. Some men in suits arrived at my house two days after I took the test and told my parents that I was selected for a special government program for the gifted." Ryan paused.

"You don't have to tell me…" I could see how hard it was for him to continue.

"No, it's alright." His face was determined. "Anyway, my parents asked me if I wanted to do the program and I told them 'no.' When they told the men my answer they said it wasn't an option and took me anyway. My mom was screaming, my dad tried to tackle them with a fire poker, but one of the men pulled out a gun and put it to my head. That stopped them in their tracks. I was shoved into their hover-limo and taken away." Ryan swallowed hard.

"I'm so sorry." I did the only thing I could think of to make him feel better, I kissed him gently. "How did you get out?"

Ryan took a moment to re-group then looked me in the eye. "I was taken to some sort of research facility. It was a giant single room with ten-foot ceilings and row upon row of computers and electronics. There were kids my age everywhere either on the computers or strapped into virtual reality gear poking the air in front of them like they were writing on a chalkboard or something.

That's when I met Turner. He came over to me and welcomed me to the facility. He said he'd been watching my test scores for a while and that this would be more of a home to me than with my parents." He paused thinking, "He scared me more than anything, Chelsan. It was like I was talking to the Bogeyman. He looked at me like he was the hunter and I was the prey. My instincts kicked in and I started to cry. I lied and told him that I had cheated on all my tests. I told him how I stole the tests from my teacher's computer and memorized them, that was why I didn't want to come here because I knew they'd find out about me. I couldn't tell if I had convinced him or not, he just stood there staring at me as if judging whether or not I was telling the truth. I told him that I'd study hard and I'd try and prove that I could be smart. If I could memorize the tests then maybe I could actually learn what was on them. I hoped that by pretending that I actually wanted to be there, he'd believe my lies more. After staring at me for what felt like an eternity, he sent me back home. My parents and I were so relieved, and when I told them what happened they said I should mess up my schoolwork to back up my lie. Just to be safe.

"The men in suits came to the first couple of tests, waiting to see my scores. I made sure that I missed half the questions. Eventually, they stopped coming all-together and I felt safe again. I slipped back into my normal behavior and started to forget all about Geoffrey Turner." Ryan took a deep breath.

"About three years later, I was in math class and the teacher put Trildion's theorem on the board. He gave us all a crack at trying to solve it, not expecting any true results since we were all eleven and no one had solved it in three hundred years. But I just saw the answer, you know? That's how things work for me. I see problems and equations and the answers just form in my brain as if they were already written down for me. My teacher flipped out. He called the news. I was the poster child for geniuses. They had a national dinner for me with the President and everything.

"That's when I saw Turner again. He looked at me from across the room with such venom and hatred I nearly pee'd my pants. I was suddenly grateful for my teacher announcing the fact that I solved the theorem to the world. I think Turner would have taken me again if it had been kept quiet. The only interference we've had since is the government telling my parents in no uncertain terms that I was to go to Geoffrey Turner High. To keep an eye on me, I guess. I'm still scared of him. And now knowing what you told me about what happened to you and the exterminations, I don't feel so ashamed about that anymore. Any sane person *should* be afraid of Turner." He stopped and looked at me.

"I'm related to him. The man is a monster and we share the same blood."

"You're nothing like him. I'm telling you, I've looked into his eyes. That guy is as evil as they come." Ryan cupped my face with his hands again and kissed me. "I just wanted you to know my history with him, and a little bit of who I am before you decide I'm a boring idiot." And he smiled his disarmingly charming smile.

I smiled back, then a thought hit me. "What do you think he wants all those kids for?"

Ryan shook his head. "I don't know. I've been trying to block it out of my memory for so long, I never really thought about it."

"We should. I'll tell Jason, maybe he knows something."

Ryan looked away, his face suddenly distant.

"What's wrong?" Oh boy. He thought he could handle Turner being my grandpa, but I bet he couldn't. What happened to him was too traumatic.

"Do you like him?" he asked quietly.

What?

"What?" I had no idea what he was talking about.

"Jason Keroff. I know you had those holo-pictures of him before you actually met him, and he obviously likes you…" Ryan trailed off.

I covered my mouth to hide my laugh.

Ryan didn't find it funny at all. He started to sit up in Nancy's bed, preparing to leave.

I quickly grabbed his arm and pulled him back down so we were forehead to forehead again. "No. I don't like Jason Keroff. I only started liking him to keep my mind off of you."

Ryan eyed me suspiciously, but I could see the relief in his eyes. "Really?"

"Yes, really." I played on his guilt strings for fun. "I mean, after you ignored me as soon as I didn't need tutoring anymore, what was a girl to do?"

Ryan kissed me again. The kind of kiss that made the hair on the back of my neck raise and my toes tingle.

I pulled away. "And how did you know I had holo-pics of Jason anyway?"

Ryan's face turned red. "When I met your mom. I could see inside your bedroom. They were kind of plastered everywhere," he teased.

"Stalker." I smiled.

"You know it." He kissed me again.

We heard a noise outside Nancy's bedroom and he pulled away.

"Better go." Ryan snapped up from bed and headed for the window.

"Nancy won't mind. Stay." My mind was still numb from his kiss and the last thing I wanted him to do was leave.

"She wouldn't, but her parents would. Better to come through the front door." As if he couldn't stop himself, he ran over to me and gave me a quick kiss. Then he leapt to the window, opening it wide.

And he was gone, out the second floor window before I could say good-bye.

I wanted to giggle uncontrollably from the amount of excitement pumping through my veins. Ryan really liked me. For once in my life something was actually going my way.

The door opened and Jason Keroff walked in.

Lame.

Me of three days ago would have killed for this moment, but a lot can happen over a seventy-two hour period, and seeing Jason there was a cruel wake-up call to last night's events.

"School. Come on. You're going." Jason barked out orders with a grin. It was rather irritating.

"School? Are you joking? Where's Nancy?" I groaned and threw back the poofy comforter that was the down fluffiness of perfection.

"I'm right here." Nancy came in like a goddess. Her hair and make-up looked as if she had stepped out of a fashion magazine and her outfit of jeans and a tank fit her like a glove.

When I saw her, I wanted to tell her everything that just happened with Ryan, but Jason was there so it would have to wait. I ran across the room and hugged her as hard as I could. She nearly fell over from the force and smiled.

"Good to see you, too." Then she pushed me away and smacked me on the arm.

"Ow." I massaged the place where she hit me.

Nancy waved her finger in front of my face in a threatening manner. "Don't you EVER try and leave again! I don't care if you think you're saving the world! We are a team! I knew the risks from the beginning and I don't care, got me?!"

"I didn't want any of you to get hurt," I admitted rather sheepishly. I felt as if I was being grounded or something.

Nancy placed her hands on my shoulders, making forced eye contact with me. "Promise me."

A warm feeling of relief and comfort overwhelmed me for a second. Nancy was the very definition of a best friend. And I knew in that moment she'd risk her life for me. Frankly, she already had, just by being near me.

"I promise, Nancy, geez." My lungs were suddenly squeezed of every last drop of breath as Nancy crushed me in one of her bear hugs. She let go and I gasped for air with a genuine laugh.

"We were so worried. You should have seen Ryan, he was a crazy man trying to find you." Nancy rolled her eyes.

Hearing about Ryan made my stomach churn with excitement. I wished he didn't have that kind of control over my mental state of being, but there was nothing I could do about that. I just had to come to terms with the fact that Ryan made my head spin. Waking up next to him was like a dream. He genuinely liked me. Oh boy, there went the stomach again. I had to stop thinking about him.

"And *this* guy." Nancy nodded her head toward Jason who now sat on her bed. "He's a complete waste of time. What was he thinking getting you all shot at like that?" she spoke in an almost flirtatious way.

To my surprise, Jason smiled back at Nancy with just as much *flirt* as she was giving. "I got her out safe, didn't I?" Jason stood up from the bed, eyeing Nancy with interest.

I flipped out. "You got *me* out safe? Me? Was that when you were huddled in a ball? Or when you were sucking your thumb until I made all the men with *guns* go away? Was that when you *saved* me?"

Jason's smile didn't budge. He even looked at me like he was endeared by what I had to say. "I didn't suck my thumb."

"Might as well have," I mumbled angrily under my breath.

Jason scuffed my head like I was a five-year-old. "You saved my life and I thank you very much for it. Are you happy now?"

I remembered what he had started to say before our attack last night: *I know what he did to you....* "You said you knew what Turner did to me last night! Did you mean it? What did he do?" I was charged with excitement.

"Oh yeah that." Jason motioned around the room indicating that it may be bugged. "I can't remember."

My heart sank. I'd have to wait until later, until we could talk in a secured location. It was so strange that people could actually be listening to our every word. And if Nancy's house was bugged, then I had to assume they had heard everything I said to Nancy and Ryan for the last two days, which meant Turner would know about my power. And he'd have heard the conversation Ryan and I just had. I should have known better. I really hoped Jason was wrong.

Jason saw the panic in my eyes and leaned in to whisper. "I have something with me that will let me find the bug. Leave it to me, okay?"

Nancy must not have liked the intimacy of our conversation because she stepped in to say, "Get ready for school, Chelsan. We have to leave in ten minutes."

"I'm not going to school! You're both insane!" I was still a little panicked by the whole situation.

I suddenly noticed all of Nancy's holo-pictures of Jason were mysteriously absent from her wall. "I see you took all of your…"

That was all that came out of my mouth before Nancy shoved her hand over it to shut me up. "Seriously, get ready."

I pried her hand away and crossed my arms in a final attempt to keep my ground.

Nancy shook her head and looked at me seriously. "Chelsan, it's the best place for you. We have to keep you as public as possible. School is the safest place you can be right now."

"Did you guys discuss all this while I was sleeping?" I had to admit it made sense, but for some reason I was grumpy and more than that, I was just plain scared. If it were up to me I'd hide in Nancy's closet all day (probably where she hid all of Jason's holo-pics). *Keep you as public as possible…* It made me think of Ryan and what he told me about staying in the public so Turner couldn't kidnap him. I decided to tell Nancy and Jason everything right there. If my grandpa were listening it wouldn't be anything new.

Nancy seemed way more interested in the fact that Ryan had snuck in to be with me (like a true friend would) but Jason's face scrunched with worry and what was worse… recognition.

"I've heard about those although there's never been any proof. Conspiracy theorists call them *I.Q. Farms*. I'll find out what I can." Jason's brain was already spinning with a plan.

Nancy grabbed my arms and shook me lightly in exaggerated exasperation.

"Now get ready. My mom is making a special breakfast for that loser." Nancy hid a smile.

"And this *loser* is very hungry, so I'll see you two later." Jason winked at Nancy and strode out the door with a confident swagger.

As soon as he was gone, Nancy nearly screeched with excitement. "Did you see that? He totally digs me."

Her excitement was infectious and I cracked a smile. "He definitely perks up when you're around. I think he's scared to death of me. You should have seen how he flipped out when I …" I didn't know if I was ready to tell her what I had done last night. I was suddenly afraid she'd never want to see me anymore.

"He told us everything, dork. You don't have to hide anything from me to protect me. I've told you before, we're in this together, okay?" Nancy gave me a quick hug and a reassuring smile.

"It was pretty crazy." I sighed in relief and made her lean over so I could whisper all the details I could remember about the incident last night, including the fact that the less flesh corpses had, the harder they were to control.

Nancy whispered back, "You should write that down for Jason. Give him something more to go on." Nancy walked over to her closet and tossed a pair of jeans and a t-shirt on her bed. "Wear that. My wardrobe is officially yours. And if you don't tell me every single detail about Ryan showing up in *my* bed, I'm going to have to kill you."

"Thanks." As I changed into the outfit I gave Nancy a play-by-play of this morning. She squealed in all the right places and high fived me when I told her that he liked me ever since he tutored me last year.

Nancy eyed me up and down as if inspecting a piece of meat. "Perfect. Ryan and Bill will be at each others throats by noon." My eyes must have grown round with horror because Nancy shook her head. "I'm kidding! I just meant that you look great."

"I think you should know; Jason is at least seventy-years-old." I wanted to tell her before she started liking him too much. Most people didn't care about age differences since almost everyone looked the same age anyway, but I wanted to give Nancy a heads up just in case it bothered her.

"Actually, he's ninety-five!" From the way her eyes lit up, I guessed Nancy didn't care at all. "It's so romantic. I always wanted to be with an older man and Jason is… well… he's perfect."

"You certainly insult him enough." I smiled at her doe eyes. I'd never witnessed Nancy liking *anyone* before, mainly because no one would go near her on the account of being my friend. Seeing her so fired up about someone was nice. It made me feel like life was normal, even if just for a second.

"We're just flirting. He knows I don't mean it. Besides, I think he likes it. What a freak," she said with a grin that had no signs of leaving her face any time soon.

"All right, crush girl, let's go to school." I smiled.

"Crush girl? You and Ryan are the ones who are finally speaking after a year of pining over each other. At least I'm being bold." Nancy was almost offended, but her grin stayed in tact.

"Fine. I'm crush girl, you're slut girl." I ducked before Nancy could hit my head with a laugh.

Nancy laughed with me and put her arm in mine as we walked to her door. "Hopefully school will be uneventful and boring. I need to have at least one day of relaxation."

Great. Now I knew I was in for trouble. Might as well dare the universe to spit on us. But of all the places I could be right now, school did appear to be the safest. Jill would seem like a good friend compared to what I had been through the last couple of days.

"Can we eat something? I'm starving." I knew we were short on time, but I needed a full stomach to face the day.

"Sure. We can watch my mom fumble over every word with Jason. I swear she's driving him crazy!" Nancy rolled her eyes.

"Unlike you." I couldn't resist.

"I'm driving him crazy in *other* ways." Nancy squeezed my arm with a small laugh.

We walked down the winding stairs and made our way through the house to the kitchen table. Jason was there with George and Vianne fawning over his every word. It was kind of cute. Jason was the oldest by far of the entire group. George and Vianne were only in their forties, though everyone at the table looked eighteen.

Vianne's eyes lit up when she saw us enter. "Girls, sit down. Have a quick bite."

The doorbell rang at that very moment.

George stood up as if being with three girls and Jason put him at his limit of tolerance. "I'll get that," he mumbled under his breath as he hurried to the front door.

Nancy and I sat down across from Jason who was stuffing a cheese omelet in his mouth.

"Jason here, was just telling me how brave you were last night, Chelsan." Vianne smiled from ear-to-ear.

I nearly choked on my toast. Did Jason really tell her what happened? My mind raced. She obviously seemed fine about the whole thing, proud even, but the more people that knew my secret the more danger they would be in. I was about to respond when Jason cut me off.

"If Chelsan hadn't noticed that mugger and called the cops, that poor lady would have been breathing through a tube the rest of her life." Jason smiled eagerly at me.

So proud of himself. What an idiot. Why would he even make that up?

"Anyone would have done the same." I jammed a fork full of scrambled eggs before I was forced to say anything more.

Jason's annoyed eyes met mine. "Vianne was just asking why we came in so late last night. Filling out paper work, giving our statements. It was a good thing Nancy was there for support. I know Chelsan really appreciated it."

Oh. Maybe he wasn't such an idiot.

"Anything for my girl," Nancy said with a grin.

"You guys ready?" Bill's voice came from behind us.

I turned around in my seat. Bill was there with his usual smile to greet me. I felt a rush of emotion when I saw him. Bill had really been there for me from the moment he gave me a brand spanking new electronic reader to picking us up last night at the virtual bar. Nancy and Bill really were my best friends. I never knew how much they cared until my life became the current nightmare I was living. It was hard for me to accept that Bill may have feelings for me other than friendship. I had to admit there were times where I was tempted because of how safe he made me feel, but I truly didn't feel that way for him. I cared about him so much I almost wish I did like him, to spare him any hurt. I didn't want to be the jerk that broke his heart.

Bill grabbed a piece of my toast and shoved it down his throat. "We're going to be late."

"We're coming, we're coming, geez Bill," Nancy teased.

"You guys have your stuff?" George asked from the hallway.

He walked in followed by Ryan.

My heart jumped in my throat and I suppressed the urge to laugh. Ryan didn't miss a beat. Aside from the quick wink, he acted as if he hadn't just spent the morning with me upstairs.

"I was just talking to Ryan here and he was telling me about the new hydro-converters they installed at the school. Pretty state of the art stuff," George said as if he was incredibly impressed by Ryan's knowledge. "I might want to hire you when you graduate." George patted Ryan's shoulder like a proud father.

Nancy guffawed. "You and everyone else on the planet! Dad, Ryan's already had about a million offers from the top science research labs in the world. Get in line. He's the kid who solved Trildion's Theorem. Duh."

"I appreciate the offer, but I'd like to try college first," Ryan added diplomatically.

Regardless of Ryan trying to let George down with grace, he still looked pretty humbled and embarrassed. George probably thought he was being generous, but Ryan's I.Q. put him above and beyond any job George could offer him at the Science Corp. It was basically considered the lower end of the science community, like making hydrogen fuel cells for cars and appliances and such. Good money, but not much respect in the science world.

Ryan walked over to me, his sandy blonde hair ruffled in all the right places, and kissed my forehead. My knees nearly buckled.

"Hey." I tried to hide the shake from my voice. I kept on flashing to this morning when he held my face in his hands…

"Hey," he said in an 'oh so cool' tone. How could he do that so consistently?!

"Seriously, we're late." Bill's voice deflated the mood.

I looked over at him and I could tell he was trying to hide his irritation at my obvious feelings for Ryan. I wanted to make him feel better, but I didn't know how, and I figured the more he saw us together, the easier it would eventually be.

"Okay, I'll get my stuff," I replied as nicely as I could to Bill, which appeared to make a visible improvement in his expression. It went from angry to shaking his head in exasperation.

"Already ahead of you." Nancy walked over to the counter and tossed me a backpack. "Your reader is in there."

Vianne, George and Jason walked the four of us to the front door.

I turned to Jason before we left the house. "Are you going to be here when I get back?"

Jason leaned in to whisper in my ear again, which made both Nancy and Ryan completely annoyed. "I just wanted to make Nancy jealous. Think it's working?"

"Yes. Now answer my question." I couldn't believe I ever had a crush on this man-whore.

"Of course. We're in this together. I'll research as much as I can about Turner *and* about your special gift. When this place is clean, I'll tell you everything I know about the ceremony he performed. We'll figure this out, get you safe. And get me safe while I'm at it." Jason pulled away with a grin.

Ryan grabbed my hand territorially and threw one last look of 'aggressive boy speak' over at Jason. It didn't faze Jason at all. He walked back into the house with Nancy's parents.

As we climbed into Bill's hover-car, Nancy leaned in close to me. "What did he say?"

I sighed. This was going to be a long day.

***

Driving to school was actually nice. I sat there quietly while the three of them filled me in on what our cover story was. It was basically what Jason had told Nancy's parents with a few added details. Bill seemed to have accepted my power with as much enthusiasm as everyone else had. His only issue being that he hadn't seen me do it yet. Ryan told him all about the plant I brought back to life and the two of them actually bonded. Well, if my curse can bring my boyfriend and one of my best friends together then bully for me, I guess. Boyfriend. It had a nice ring to it.

And during the whole ride over, Nancy would always manage to bring the conversation back to the topic of Jason.

I couldn't help but smile. These were the people who were going to stick with me through everything no matter how hard or how ugly. And I suddenly felt extremely lucky. My mom would be so happy for me.

Bill drove his hover-car into the designated parking area for students. It was about half-full.

"I'd prepare myself if I were you, Chelsan. We'll keep you surrounded."

Bill was in strategic mode and I wasn't sure why.

"What do you mean? I thought it was going to be safe at school?" Maybe he was just being cautious.

Bill exited the car and opened the back door where I sat. He leaned in and smiled at me as if I were a naïve idiot. "Chelsan, your whole trailer park was demolished and your mother died, people are going to treat you differently. There may be press as well. This is a big story. Especially since you go to this school, you're the only person of *meager means* to have been accepted. I'm surprised Jason isn't on this."

I stepped out of the car with a grumble. I knew he was right, I hadn't thought about *those* kind of consequences I was so focused on the *someone trying to kill me* part. "This is going to suck."

Nancy came around and gave me a supportive squeeze. "It'll be fine. Mostly people will just stare and feel sorry for you."

"Keep an eye out for Jill. If Joan was right about Turner giving Jill's dad orders, who knows what she'll do to you." Ryan had positioned himself next to me and I felt his hand wrap around mine like I belonged to him. If everyone was going after me today, I wanted his hand permanently attached to mine.

We walked through the school's third floor entrance to a melee of flash photography and screaming reporters.

"Here we go," I mumbled under my breath.

I couldn't believe the amount of people that swarmed around me like locusts. Nancy, Bill and Ryan quickly formed a circle of protection around me acting like my own personal guard dogs.

"CHELSAN! CHELSAN!" The press shouted my name, edging closer. I felt like a celebrity.

Bill leaned down so I could hear him from above all the ruckus. "Reporters aren't allowed in the classrooms. We just need to get you to Mr. Alaster's."

Nancy took the lead and literally shoved anyone who was in our way, including students. Most of the inhabitants of Geoffrey Turner High never gave me a second thought except to spit on me or shove me on Jill's orders, but now they looked at me like stunned deer. I couldn't figure out if this was good or bad. Their expressions certainly didn't give me much help. I was like a slow moving hover accident that they couldn't keep their eyes off of.

We inched our way toward Mr. Alaster's class on the first floor. The whole time questions were shouted from the reporters around us. Mostly, they wanted to know about the tornado and the mysterious green smoke I claimed to have seen. Others asked about Bruce and where he could be located. So far, nothing of real panic. I could ignore them in good conscious. I wished that this story would get old and they'd leave me alone soon.

Just as we were about to enter Mr. Alaster's class, the entire press corps stopped in their tracks as if someone had hit them all with a stun gun. They appeared to be listening to something.

Ryan leaned in with a sigh of relief. "It's their ear pieces. Stopping like that means that they're all getting some breaking news story. This might just be your lucky day. For them all to be silent like that, the news will be pretty big."

I took a deep breath of thankfulness as Nancy reached for the door and started to open it. Hopefully, whatever it was that they were listening to was way more interesting than me.

A slow buzz of excitement started at the end of the hallway and came to a roar in a matter of seconds. But instead of deserting me like I expected them to, they shoved their way closer, eyes alight with the fire of a burning story.

They screamed at me all at once, desperate for me to answer, but I couldn't differentiate what any of them were trying to ask me.

"Come on." Nancy shoved me inside the room with Ryan squeezing my hand harder than before. Bill came in with us even though he had Calculus first period.

And just as Nancy shut the door in the reporters' faces I could hear one reporter above the rest. "What do you think about Vice President of Population Control Geoffrey Turner coming to meet with you today in person?!"

Nancy slammed the door shut and looked at me with horrified eyes.

Gulp. What was that?

My whole body went numb. Turner's coming to meet me? Today?! My mind reeled and I thought my brain was going to explode.

Mr. Alaster was suddenly in my face, full of concern and sympathy. "Let's get you to your seat. I can't believe you actually came to school today. You should take it easy. We can send your work home with Nancy," he uttered this in a rush. Mr. Alaster apparently wasn't used to the news being right outside his door practically salivating through the window. It was like watching cats in front of a mouse hole, waiting for me to come back out so they could pounce.

I let Mr. Alaster lead me to my seat even though it meant parting with Ryan's hand. Ryan didn't even let poor Ernie Gelson have a choice when he made him switch seats so that Ryan could sit next to me. Nancy, of course, sat in her usual seat, on my other side, and Bill stood awkwardly behind me.

Mr. Alaster patted Bill on the shoulder. "You may go to your first period now, Bill. I have things under control here."

Bill gave me a last look of encouragement and then braved his way through the door. Roars of questions greeted him and most likely a team of them would follow Bill all the way to Calculus as well.

I noticed Jill and Joan staring at me from their desks a few seats back. It was hard to say what was going on in their little pea brains, but whatever it was it didn't look favorable to my cause. Jill was downright hostile. Which wasn't exactly new, but the way she looked at me made me worry. She knew something and I wanted to know what it was. Maybe it would help me prepare for Turner's visit today.

I tried to breathe evenly and slowly. Turner wouldn't kill me today, not with all these witnesses. Unless, he made it look like an accident. I could hear the headlines now: "Geoffrey Turner consoles survivor when she accidently falls down a flight of steps…"

Jason said it best: I was *so* dead.

I had to stay ahead of the game. I had to be smarter than him, like my dad when he flipped Turner's spell back on itself and saved my mom and I. I had to keep reminding myself that I had a power that Turner couldn't touch.

I swallowed in dread.

Maybe he could.

I thought about the soldiers yelling "Zombie 442." I thought about the green smoke. I thought about my mother's vision of Turner's arm slicing open and then sealing back up with an ugly white scar…

He had powers. Or access to them.

And they may trump mine.

I just didn't know.

I didn't want to start sweating in a fit of panic in front of everyone in the class so I settled on taking deep breaths. And besides, I couldn't give Jill the satisfaction of seeing me in such distress. She was probably on orders to spy on me and I didn't want to give Turner any indication that I was scared to death of him. And I was.

Mr. Alaster kept on glancing at me but pretending that he wasn't. And although I could tell he was concerned, it made me more nervous.

"Settle down. Settle down. I still have a class to teach despite all the excitement," Mr. Alaster said to an already quiet class. His mind was so focused on the reporters outside he hadn't even noticed that the classroom was silent. "Click your readers to page four-hundred and six." And he delved into a long and boring lecture that no one really paid attention to. Half the time I don't think even he was listening to himself, his eyes kept roaming from me to the frosted glass square of the door and the silhouetted forms of the press on the other side.

The click of the PA system made Mr. Alaster jump slightly.

"Oh! Everyone quiet! An announcement!" Mr. Alaster waved his hands as if we were all screaming loudly.

Again, no one was talking. If I weren't so terrified, I'd actually find his behavior kind of funny.

The Principal's voice crackled through the speaker hanging over the door. "May I have your attention please?" A pause then a deep breath, "It has come to my attention that Vice President of Population Control Geoffrey Turner will be gracing us with his presence at our school today. This will be the first time he's made an appearance here since the grand opening twenty years ago so I expect all of you to be on your best behavior. His sole mission is to express his condolences to one of our very own, Ms. Chelsan Derée after the tragedy that destroyed her home and family. Our hearts go out to you, Ms. Derée. The assembly will be after class. Have a good day and get back to work."

I could feel all eyes on me. I wanted to disappear from sight. I stared at the surface of my desk, hoping Mr. Alaster would break the tension by finishing his boring lecture on the history of paper. Instead I heard the grating voice of my worst enemy a few seats back: Jill.

"Maybe Chelsan would like to share her feelings. Losing your mom must be excruciatingly painful. Why don't you tell us about it?" Jill sneered.

I tried to rationalize how anyone could be that mean. Some kind of trauma? Horrible parents? Massive insecurity? Or just plain evil. All of the above probably.

Ryan turned around in his seat and gave Jill a look that silenced her immediately.

Mr. Alaster stepped forward so he was in direct eye contact with Jill. "If I hear one more crass and vilely inhuman comment out of you again I *will* be requesting your leave from this establishment! My job be damned, I will not tolerate your archaic, bullish behavior in my class again!"

Whoa.

Jill froze. She was completely stunned.

I had never seen Mr. Alaster that angry before. It was one thing to hear Jill say horrible things to me, I was used to that, it went into my 'Jill filter.' But when Mr. Alaster put her comment into perspective on how mean it really was, it suddenly made the loss of my mom too real at that moment. It was like when you're hit in the head by a ball and you're in kind of a shock until everyone comes up to you and asks if you're okay. And the floodgates open. That was exactly what happened. I just started to cry.

Apparently, even Jill didn't have anything snide to say about that which was almost a disappointment. If I could turn my emotion to anger, I could stop crying! This was so embarrassing! I covered my face so no one could see me, but mostly so I couldn't see them staring at me. My mom was everything to me. I still couldn't believe she was gone. With all the danger and excitement of the last few days I was able to shove back most of my anguish over losing her to simply survive. But hearing Jill and Mr. Alaster put it out there, I felt so bare and dirty almost. Like I needed a long shower to wash away my feelings of being exposed to the public about something so personal. It was hard enough that my mom died.

I felt Ryan and Nancy huddle around me like a protective circle of hugs. It felt nice and I began to calm down. "I'm okay." I found myself mumbling through my hands.

"Take your time, Chelsan," came Mr. Alaster's sympathetic voice. He'd probably be fired when Jill's father heard about what he said to his daughter. But I'd always be grateful to him for standing up to her.

I took a deep breath and pulled my hands down away from my face. "I'm good."

Ryan and Nancy tentatively sat back down in their seats, their worried eyes still on me. The class was silent, watching. I looked up at Mr. Alaster imploringly. *Please start talking about something that doesn't involve me,* I begged him in my head.

He seemed to catch my drift because he cleared his throat and continued his lecture on paper. The minutes dragged by painfully. Part of me wanted class to be over so I could run away from *the stares,* and the other part of me didn't want it to end because I'd have to brave the press corps that pawed at the door waiting for me to exit.

The bell finally rang and I felt my heart leap into my throat. I could hear the rustling of reporters outside. Jill stood up first followed closely by Joan. She hadn't said a word since Mr. Alaster basically told her to shut up, and surprisingly didn't appear all that upset by it. This, of course, made me worry. She was up to something. I had known her long enough to know that.

Jill and Joan were out the door and swallowed whole by the crowd of reporters. The rest of the class slowly started to file out as well, leaving me, Nancy, Ryan and Mr. Alaster staring at the doorway with trepidation.

"Assembly time," Mr. Alaster stated what we were all thinking.

"Yup," I agreed as I tried not to make eye contact with any of the screaming news people.

Ryan grabbed my hand and locked his fingers tightly with mine. "We got your back."

Nancy wrapped her arm around my free arm. "We won't let him touch you."

"Chelsan, I'm here if you need me. And if those screaming monsters are too much for you, you can always sneak in here for protection. They can't enter a classroom under any circumstances. Okay?" Mr. Alaster managed a small smile of encouragement.

"Okay, thanks," I replied shyly. Who knew Mr. Alaster could be that cool?

"Yeah, thanks, Mr. Alaster." Nancy was genuinely grateful, too. "Actually, we need a few moments. Before we go out into *that*."

"Of course. I'll leave you three alone." Mr. Alaster didn't even blink. He headed straight for the door. "Move aside! Move aside!" He shoved his way through the press, pushing a little bit harder than he probably should have. He turned around and gave us a quick wink.

Ryan and Nancy both turned to me, game faces on.

"You ready for this?" Ryan asked, though I could ask the same of him. He looked petrified.

"We could always duck out the back," Nancy suggested, but we all knew that was impossible.

"I'm good. Let's do this." I tried to sound as pumped up as possible though it was the complete opposite of what I felt.

"So, no plan?" Nancy crinkled her nose in concern.

"Nope."

And with that, I charged ahead, Ryan holding my right hand, Nancy clinging to my other arm.

I felt as if I could dive on top of the reporters and they'd carry me to the assembly hall like I was at a rock concert it was so crowded. They all screamed at me again.

"Over here!" I heard Bill's voice above the rest and I tried to find him in the crowd.

The sea of people parted before us like a human pair of scissors except instead of blades it was two lines of men in dark suits and sunglasses. The reporters shoved up against the wall of men, but their defenses held strong. At the end of it all was Bill with a silly grin on his face.

He half ran over to us and nodded to the men in suits. "Money comes in handy sometimes. When I told Dad about how the press was hounding you, he sent a whole team of his best body guards over here."

"Wow. This is just what I needed. Thanks, Bill." I let go of Ryan and Nancy and hugged Bill as hard as I could.

The reporters still yelled, but at least they couldn't touch me. The guards barely flinched as the press tried to tear them apart to get to me.

Ryan pulled me away from Bill by clasping my hand in his again. It made my heart pound knowing how jealous he was, but Bill had really pulled through and I wanted him to know how grateful I was.

Bill shrugged at Ryan's obvious territorial behavior and motioned us forward. "They'll get us to the assembly hall."

The men closed ranks forming a twenty-man circle around us and we made our way comfortably toward the assembly hall.

"I didn't want to show you this, but I think you should know." Bill turned to me cautiously.

"Just show us, Bill." Nancy was having none of it. She was in one of her *get to the point* moods.

Bill pulled out his cell phone and popped up a holo-video for us. It was me in Mr. Alaster's class, crying like a baby. Uuuggghh!

"That's why Jill said what she did. She was trying to provoke you for this video." Ryan shook his head angrily.

"Yeah, well, I was dumb enough to fall for it," I groaned.

"Dumb? The most horrible, horrendous thing that can happen to a person happened to you, *two days ago*! I think there would be something wrong with you if you *didn't* cry!" Nancy appeared more outraged at my response than about the video itself.

"Turner probably told her to do it. It's all about the story and spin for him. He'll make sure that everyone knows you're too distraught to be a reliable witness, and with your step-dad gone, no one will believe you about the green smoke. He's just covering his bases," Ryan said and then kissed my cheek. It instantly made me feel better.

We arrived at the assembly hall without incident. The room itself was the biggest in the school. The ceiling was forty feet high and made out of a solar frosted glass that adjusted to the light outside, keeping the assembly hall the same day-like brightness no matter what time of day it was.

Painted yellow walls complimented the dark-stained brown of the stage and fold out chairs were placed in neat rows for all the students. The main focus of the room was the stage that made up the entire back wall and came up about five feet off the ground. Maroon velvet curtains normally framed the theater like a picture, but today they remained closed, probably hiding my grandpa behind them.

The press was only allowed in the back of the room so we were safe as soon as we sat down in our seats. After making sure we were okay, the bodyguards stood against the wall waiting for us to finish so they could keep vigil once more.

Bill and Ryan sat on either side of me while Nancy took the aisle next to Bill.

I could see the holos of me crying on almost everyone's phone. It was completely surreal. The only part of the video I could stand to watch was when Ryan and Nancy hugged me. I gripped Ryan's hand harder and he stroked my hand with his thumb in response. My toes tingled in delight and it made waiting for the assembly to start more bearable.

Bill leaned down to my ear, "My dad said you can have the guards as long as you need them. Turner won't be able to get to you."

I wanted to tell him that if Turner wanted to *get to me* there was absolutely nothing any of us could do about it, but I didn't want to say anything to upset him. Especially since he'd gone through all the trouble to bring his dad's bodyguards here.

Ryan squeezed my hand to reassure me and kissed my shoulder.

"You don't have to prove that you guys are dating. I get it," Bill fumed.

Apparently, he wasn't as cool with Ryan as I had hoped.

"Are you sure about that? You seem pretty set on the fact that you still have a shot with her." Ryan turned to Bill, just as angry.

"Guys, please don't do this." I tried to calm them down, but neither one of them heard me.

"Here we go," I heard Nancy groan. "Boys."

"Well maybe that's because I've been friends with Chelsan *publicly* for three years now! I wasn't the a-hole that was afraid of what people might think!" Bill's nostrils actually flared.

I sat in the middle of the two of them holding my breath.

"You're so rich no one cares what you do!" Ryan's hand squeezed mine to the point of pain.

"Ow," I said, but he couldn't hear me.

"Nancy isn't rich and she didn't care what people thought!" Bill roared.

The people that were already staring, now stared even harder. Even the press tried to take pictures of this feud.

"Don't bring me into this," Nancy chimed in, but she knew it was a futile effort.

But Bill's comment worked like a slap in the face to Ryan. His grip loosened on my hand and his body slumped in defeat. "You're right."

And to my surprise, Bill actually seemed sorry. "Forget it. I'm just jealous."

Neither one of them could look at each other.

Nancy rolled her eyes and crossed her arms. "You two are idiots."

"Can I say something?" I wanted to clear the air.

"No," all three of them spoke in unison, which made them all smile.

"Fine." Maybe letting the two of them have it out was enough. I'd probably make it worse anyway.

Principal Weatherby walked up to the microphone in the center of the stage. He was a bald portly man who had the thickest handlebar mustache I had ever seen. His face was always a rosy pink color, which gave the impression that he was forever embarrassed. Weatherby appeared to be in his late twenties, but everyone knew he was one-hundred and sixty-seven. He helped build this school. It was his pride and joy.

More nervous than usual, Weatherby's shaking hands grabbed the microphone stand in front of him. "Quiet down. Quiet down." He cleared his throat as everyone in the room stopped and gave him their attention. "It is my honor and privilege to introduce the namesake of our school, Vice President of Population Control Geoffrey Turner!" He yelled the last bit since the room had already exploded in applause.

I think we were the only four who didn't move a muscle. We all waited in anticipation of what would happen next.

We didn't have to wait long. The curtains behind Principal Weatherby began to part. I had been right. Turner stood on stage behind the curtains, probably watching me. He walked toward Weatherby with a plastered smile on his face. Some of the students oooh'd and aaahh'd, not just because they were seeing the most powerful man in the world, but because he actually looked old.

Age-pro was invented when Turner was in his fifties and not many people of that era were very public. It was one thing to see the Vice President on the holo-tv, but entirely different to see him in person. He had wrinkles around his eyes and creases on his forehead, his body seemed normal, but his hands had brownish spots and blue veins that you could literally see from where I sat. It was a bit of a shock for everyone. Old was worse than poor for the general public. Being poor myself, I might have had sympathy for the old guy, but I knew what he was capable of. I tried to block out the images of him slicing his arm open or of his wife and the boa constrictor oozing out of her mouth. Aaaah, my grandparents. No wonder I could raise the dead, look at my genes.

Five others followed after him and I craned my neck to get a better look at them…

"I'm dead…" I croaked.

Nancy, Ryan and Bill all looked at me for something more, but I couldn't utter another syllable.

"What's wrong?" Ryan asked anyway.

I was breathless with disbelief.

Standing behind Turner were five people…

…Five *dead* people.

Their black swirling holes mocking me from my seat.

"His staff…" I tried to keep the squeak from my voice.

"What about them?" Nancy talked to me like I was four to try to calm down.

"They're dead. They're all dead." I could literally hear and feel my voice shake.

My three friends had no words. Their eyes opened in amazement and they watched me as if they waited for me to say I was kidding.

I wasn't.

Someone else could do what I could do. Maybe a lot more than someone, maybe lots of someones. My mind whirled and whirled until I thought I was going to puke on Ryan's lap.

"Chelsan!" Ryan turned my head to his with his hand. "They're calling you up to the stage."

Everyone gawked at me. I took a deep breath. I seemed to be taking a lot of those lately. Worst of all, I peered up at Turner, curious and horrified all at the same time. His eyes bore into mine. I could feel the hatred emanating there, boiling, in fact, so much so I had to turn away. I had no doubt in my mind; he knew exactly who I was and he wanted me dead. I tried to rationalize in my head how I could ever escape this mess. There was a count down happening and I had no control over when it was going to hit zero.

I stood up on shaking legs and made my way to the stairs on the side of the stage. The most important thing I could do was to keep a clear mind and try and think of a plan. First things first, if someone was keeping these corpses alive and kicking, I needed to find out if I could take control of them myself? I walked as slowly as I could so I could experiment. I concentrated and tried to link myself to the dead man closest to me who typed something in his reader.

Nothing. He kept typing.

Okay.

Again. Maybe I was nervous. Of course I was nervous! Concentrate.

Nothing.

But I sensed something new this time. It was as if there was an invisible wall completely covering his black hole. It was literally a barrier of some sort and I had no idea how to break through it.

This was not a good sign.

I found myself on stage standing in front of Turner and his zombie staff.

His smile was forced, but no one noticed.

Turner held out his hand for me to shake and I obliged cautiously. His hands were soft but firm in their grip, his eyes found mine, his smile cunning and cruel. My head churned again. I thought I was going to pee my pants in front of the school. (*The world* actually, considering all the cameras were focused on us.) This guy really had a hold on my fear button and he was pressing it over and over. That was when he went in for a hug.

As he tightened his arms around me, he leaned in to my ear. "Hello, Granddaughter."

That could have been a loving moment in life if Geoffrey Turner wasn't completely evil.

Turner pulled away with an even larger grin than before. The roar of the crowd egging him on. I was amazed that I was still conscious.

He turned to the microphone. "It is with great pleasure that I award Chelsan Derée with a full scholarship for the rest of her stay here at Geoffrey Turner High School."

More roars from the crowd.

Turner droned on and on about the tragic events that led to my mother's death and my home being destroyed.

It gave me time to process. Paying my way through school indicated that he wasn't planning on killing me soon. Or maybe it was an alibi. I needed to discuss this with my friends. But in the mean time, I needed to stay on my toes around this guy. And I needed to calm down! I was letting my terror rule me and I wanted to keep my head clear. Think this through, logically and calmly. I could use any dead thing in my near vicinity to hurt him if need be. That was good. Just because these five corpses were out of my control didn't necessarily mean I was screwed. To keep my mind focused I found a dead mouse's black hole inside the assembly hall wall. I attached to him easily, made him run a little, even threw in a jump. Okay, that meant Turner didn't control every dead thing in the surrounding area. Just these five guys.

I glanced back at one of them. A lady with black-rimmed glasses and blonde hair pulled back in a tight bun. She wore a pants suit and held a briefcase. She even fidgeted for goodness sake! Whoever controlled her was really good. A thought hit me. Maybe someone wasn't controlling her. Maybe this was more like the Vodun ritual Mr. Alaster told us about from the Scientific Journal. If that were true how were they controlled? There had to be some way. I needed more information. I tried connecting with her black hole, but she had the same protective wall that the first man had.

Quick test. Yep. They all did. Great.

My mind ripped back into the present moment when I heard Turner say, "I'm going to meet privately with Ms. Derée in Principal Weatherby's office to take care of all her needs. Thanks to the press for coming out here and thank you to Principal Weatherby for such a kind welcome. Good day to you all."

Privately? Uh, oh.

I searched the audience to see Nancy, Ryan and Bill giving me looks of encouragement, but I could tell they were more scared than I was.

I was dizzy with all the deep breaths I was taking, but it somehow calmed my stomach. I barely heard Principal Weatherby excuse the students. Their shuffling out the door was another step closer to me being alone with Gramps.

"Ms. Derée?" Turner held his hand out for me to follow Principal Weatherby.

Weatherby turned to me with an expression of genuine concern. "Don't worry, Chelsan, we've restricted the press access to my office. They won't bother you."

I smiled, but inside I thought that I'd kind of like the reporters around now. Maybe I could convince Principal Weatherby to stay with us. "Principal Weatherby?"

"Yes, Chelsan." I'd never seen him so worried about me. He was usually warning me that if I didn't have the money for this school I was no longer welcome. I guess with everything that had happened to me, he was feeling a little guilty.

I walked up next to him so that Turner and his staff were trailing us by a few feet. I spoke quietly so only Weatherby could hear. "I'd feel more comfortable if you stayed with me. I'm too nervous around the Vice President." I glanced back to make sure Turner didn't hear.

Weatherby placed his hand on my shoulder supportively. "I hear you, Chelsan, but I can't argue with the man. He wants his time alone with you. Don't worry, it won't take long, he has a busy schedule. He just wants to go over some contracts with you so he can set you up financially. Great man, Geoffrey Turner."

Yeah, he's peachy. Oh by the way did I mention he wants to kill me? Okay, thanks for your support. Bleh.

I was on my own. I could deal. Hopefully.

We were at Weatherby's office in no time.

"Thank you, Principal Weatherby, we'll only be a few moments," Turner said with his usual grin.

"I'll just be in the teacher's lounge when you're through." Weatherby shook Turner's hand, gave me an encouraging wink and headed toward the lounge next door.

"After you." Turner held the door for me and I walked through trying not to shake too much.

Turner entered with his staff. One of his men closed the door. When everyone was inside, the five corpses lined up against the wall.

Weatherby's office was pretty large with a six foot oak desk near the back and brown leather furniture. The throne behind the desk (and it seriously looked like a throne, over five feet high, two feet wide, mahogany trim with grommet punched leather) was a statement of how much Weatherby thought of himself. There were holo-pictures everywhere on his wall of Weatherby with some celebrity or political figure. It was almost like a shrine to himself and how many people he'd met over the years.

Turner sat in Weatherby's seat of power and motioned for me to sit across from him in the puny wooden chair reserved for visitors. "Please sit."

"I'll stand." Better to stay on my feet.

"Suit yourself." Turner nodded his head to one of his staff and the woman with the briefcase walked over and laid it on the table. "Thank you, Marion. Could you close the curtains, please?"

Marion didn't say a word as she walked to the large window overlooking the cherry blossomed courtyard and closed the heavy brown curtains. Only the overhead lights from the office gave any illumination to the room.

"So." Turner let that hang in the air for a good two minutes.

"So," I repeated back, trying to figure out what he was going to do next.

"I finally meet the murderer of my only son."

And there it was. He really *did* blame me for my father's death.

"No chance of this being a heartfelt family reunion then?" I figured I'd throw that out there.

"No chance," he replied and my blood temperature dropped forty degrees.

"If you had given your blessings instead of your curses, he'd still be alive." Wow. That was bold. I was really impressed with myself.

Until I saw the look on his face.

I had never seen so much loathing in a person's eyes before. Not even

Jill's and that was saying a lot. Maybe I should have kept my mouth shut. But maybe I shouldn't have. Something about this man made my skin crawl and I realized it wasn't fear, it was a revulsion that spread through me to every fiber of my soul. If he knew who I was then the attack on the trailer park was intentional. It wasn't random, it was purposeful and targeted. He was finishing the job he started eighteen years ago.

"Trash." He said it so quietly and with so much venom I almost flinched instinctively.

Minutes passed with agonizing slowness as we stared at each other from across the room. His dead staff motionless, watching.

Turner focused his attention on the briefcase and opened it as if we were in the middle of a business meeting. He pulled out an electronic reader and he punched up a contract, sliding it to me on the desk.

"Thumbprint, there. It's your money for the rest of the year." I could tell he was detached at this point. Maybe I could get through this meeting alive after all. Come to think of it, it was crazy for me to think he'd try anything in such a public setting. How would he explain my dead body after he just had his *private* meeting with me? I had been so worked up on the possibility of an attack I hadn't stopped to really think about the practicality of it all.

"I'm going to read it first, thank you." My body and mind were starting to relax a bit. He wouldn't hurt me. Not today anyway.

"Be my guest." Turner leaned back in the giant chair folding his hands comfortably over his stomach.

I read the contract fully which didn't take long since it consisted of two paragraphs. Nothing in it suggested anything of foul play, just a brief summary of how much money I was to receive minus the costs of tuition and materials. It was actually a hefty sum; I'd be able to live out the rest of the year in comfort. If I wasn't killed first, and therein lied the rub. I thumbprinted the document and it instantly deposited the cash into a savings account. Sweet.

"Can I go now?" I asked hoping he'd say yes.

"No."

I tensed up. The way he said it chilled me.

Slowly, Turner stood up from his seat and walked over to me. "You'll be leaving, but it won't be alive."

I took my chance.

I whirled around with as much speed as I could muster and bolted for the door. Two of his staff members grabbed me before I even made it a foot. I tried to scream. They covered my mouth, blocking any sound to signal for rescue.

Turner placed a finger on his mouth and smiled wickedly at me. "Are you going to be quiet?"

I nodded my head, knowing no one was outside anyway. Weatherby had made sure that we were to be undisturbed at all costs. That cost was *me* apparently. The man let his hand off my mouth.

"You must be able to tell that my staff here is *special*." Turner mocked.

"You mean dead? Yeah, I noticed." I could feel my eyes roll.

"You'll be like them soon. It's a quick ceremony, and then you'll be under my control," he stated, very pleased with himself.

I hadn't thought about this outcome. Of course. He could kill me and no one would know the difference because everyone would still think I was alive. Everyone except my friends, they'd know, but who cared at that point? How was I going to get out of this? A question I asked myself a lot these days. Stall. Stalling was good, and then maybe I could think of something in the mean time.

"Do you control them?" I asked not expecting a real answer.

Turner laughed. "You sense my little barrier do you? Tell me, do you know *why* you can't break through it?"

Oooooh, so condescending. I hated that I was related to this guy, but what was worse, I knew he knew more about my power than I did and that was just annoying.

"I know more than you think." I said it with as much conviction as I could muster.

And to my surprise, Turner actually paused in doubt. "What do you know?"

Things started to click in my head and I decided to make a gamble. "Everything Jason Keroff knows. He's been staying with me at Nancy's." I fished to see if he had Nancy's house bugged.

And it paid off.

"That boyfriend of yours may have found a way to block our listening devices, but it won't matter in about ten minutes." Turner glared at me.

Ryan. Why didn't he tell me he had blocked Turner's signal? It didn't make sense, but regardless of how the signal was blocked, the end result was Turner hadn't heard anything that happened at Nancy's. And that meant, he only had the virtual reality bar incident for his information on me. Didn't know what that meant yet, but I knew it was important.

"Syringe," Turner spat out. He was really going to do this.

The woman called Marion went to the briefcase and pulled out a syringe full of clear liquid.

"It's a quick poison, you won't feel any pain. Unfortunately." His eyes were actually sparkling with that last statement.

Panic. This was a good time to panic.

She leaned in to inject me with the poison.

Struggling was out of the question I was so paralyzed with fear. I was going to die. I was seriously, unequivocally about to die.

The needle was about to touch my neck when…

…I acted on instinct just as I had when I was seven with Bruce and the spider.

THWUMP!

It felt like a tearing of flesh as I ripped into the black holes of all five of the dead bodies. The invisible barrier that kept me out was obliterated. My whole body flushed with the power of it. I almost wanted to burst out laughing from the rush.

I made Marion pull back the needle.

Turner's face fell in disbelief. "Marion! Inject the girl!"

I reached into the two men holding me and made them grab Turner instead.

Turner was too shocked to react properly. He looked at me with horror in his eyes. "Impossible!"

"Oh, it's possible, Gramps." I gained my footing and for the first time I knew I would survive this round.

I made Marion point the needle at his neck. I had no intention of killing him, but I wanted to escape this office unscathed.

"Stop! I order you to stop!" Turner tried to order the corpses, but I had full control.

"You're going to tell me a few things, or I'm going to have Marion, here, inject you with that poison. Remember, it works both ways. I can bring you back, too and I have no problems with the authorities finding your dead body later in your own bed," I said coldly. I was right, too. I could end this now. He'd never bother anyone else ever again. All I had to do was let

Marion inject him. We could all walk out of there and no one would know the difference.

Except me. I'd know. I just couldn't do it.

I wasn't a killer.

Without warning, Turner's eyes rolled back in his head and the whites turned a deep crimson. He spouted out words that I didn't recognize and the air started to charge with electricity. I began to feel my grip on the corpses' black holes start to wane. I had to think fast. I would lose control over the dead people very soon.

So, I did the only thing I could think to do.

I disconnected their spinning holes from their bodies, like I did with Bruce when I left him under the tree.

I leapt back from the corpses that dropped to the floor like rag dolls.

This jolted Turner back to reality, his eyes normal once more. He glared at me with an almost awestruck expression.

The five people deteriorated to different levels of grossness before our eyes. Marion was still juicy (that was about the nicest way I could describe it). Two of the men quickly turned to skeletons and the last two were a grayish blue color and smelled really bad. And I mean *really bad*.

That was my cue to leave.

Before Turner could perform some crazy mojo on me.

"You explain it," I said and left the room as fast as I could.

I waved at Principal Weatherby as I passed the teacher's lounge and practically ran back to class. I didn't look back once. I didn't have to. I knew Turner had his own mess to clean up.

***

I hurried into Physics and sat down in a seat near the back. My teacher, Ms. Norbert, nodded to me in greeting, but continued with her lecture, not wanting to disturb her lesson plan. Sitting there without Ryan, Nancy or Bill bordered on torture. I wanted to tell them everything that had happened, but most of all I just wanted to be around people who cared about me. My meeting with Turner ran through my mind over and over again. It hadn't sunk in yet how close to dying I had come.

About five minutes later the loud speaker came on. Principal Weatherby's voice sounded shaky and disturbed. "The school is closing for the day… and maybe the week… I…I… please walk to the carpool or parking areas in an orderly fashion. Your parents will be informed when you can… come back… good day."

Everyone gossiped immediately about the strangeness of Weatherby's announcement and the nervous trill of his voice.

"Settle down, class," Ms. Norbert instructed with firmness. "Now form a single file and do as Principal Weatherby says. Read chapters eight and nine in your readers while you have some time off." Students made their way to the door. "I'll be giving you a test on both chapters when you get back so no slacking!" She added with a note of authority and the class groaned in unison.

I made sure I was the last to leave. My heart raced. I would have given anything to have been a fly on the wall when Weatherby walked into his pristine office and found five rotting corpses on the ground. Especially, since they were alive and kicking ten minutes before. I imagined Turner would be making a massive pay-off to Mr. Weatherby's bank account; that, and I was sure a clean-up crew was on its way, hence the shooing of children.

When I reached the door I sighed in relief when I saw Bill and his twenty bodyguards waiting for me. The look on his face was a mixture of relief and worry. "Are you okay? What happened?" Bill went in for a hug and I hugged him back. It felt so reassuring and nice after everything I'd been through I almost wanted to cry.

"I'm okay," my voice sounded muffled as I muttered this directly into his chest.

I pulled away and gave him a reassuring smile. "I only want to tell it once. Let's find Ryan and Nancy and get out of here."

Bill nodded and talked to one of the bodyguards. "We're headed to the parking lot."

***

We made it to the hover-car without a stitch. Ryan and Nancy were waiting for us both with the same look Bill gave me before. Apparently, they were just as worried about me as I was. And rightfully so, it turned out.

When Ryan saw me amidst the circle of guards he pushed through (or I should say he was *let* through, these guys were pretty impenetrable) and held me close. "We were so worried," he whispered in my ear.

"Really, I'm alright. Let's just get in the car," I reassured Ryan, but I didn't want him to let me go. As soon as he pulled away from the hug, I grabbed his hand in mine. Aaaaahhhhh. Everything good now.

Bill sent the guards packing while we all climbed into his hover-car. "We didn't even need them. The press was sent off campus a few minutes before Weatherby's announcement."

Once we were all situated inside (I sat with Ryan in the back seat while Nancy rode shotgun), Nancy turned to me with impatient wide eyes. "Now, spill! What happened once you left the Assembly Hall? Details!"

I told them everything that had happened, from the invisible walls around the staff's black holes, to their rotting corpses on the floor of Weatherby's office. I left nothing out. The three of them sat in stunned silence.

"No wonder Weatherby was freaking." Bill was the first one to speak.

"That's so gross." Nancy was creating the visual in her head.

"It was terrifying. I thought I was going to die." I needed to say that out loud to make it real for me. So far the last few days felt like a nightmare I couldn't wake up from.

Ryan put his arm around me and let me rest my head on his shoulder. "You're with us now."

"You definitely gave Turner something to think about." Bill shook his head in amazement.

"You kicked his ass is what you did," Nancy chimed in, impressed herself.

"It wasn't me, by the way," Ryan said out of nowhere.

"What do you mean it wasn't you?" I asked.

"Blocking off Turner's listening devices at Nancy's. It wasn't me."

"Oh. I kind of knew that, but who did?" I wondered aloud.

"We'll figure it out when we get there. Maybe Jason will know." I couldn't help but notice the slight trill in Nancy's voice when she mentioned Jason.

After a few minutes, Bill pulled up to Nancy's abode and parked his hover-car in the landing zone.

George and Vianne walked out of the house to greet us, their faces wracked with anxiety. As we exited the car George squeezed Nancy with a hug that made her gasp for air.

"Geez, Dad, what's up with you?" Nancy asked as he released her.

Before he could respond both George and Vianne hugged me within an inch of my life.

"We've been sick all day worrying about you four!" Vianne said in her usual *mom* tone. "Get inside. We have a lot to discuss." She looked at me pointedly.

Uh, oh. What did Jason tell them?

Once we were inside we all sat down in the living room. Jason was there with a mug of coffee smiling at all of us like he was in a pleasant mood. "Now don't panic," he started the conversation, "but I told George and Vianne here everything."

My face must have turned two shades whiter because Vianne reached out and grabbed my hand. (The one that wasn't already taken by Ryan.) "It's okay, Chelsan, we know everything and we're not going anywhere, and neither are you. This is your new home now, permanently. No arguments, you hear me?"

She waited for me to nod and I did. I was so surprised I couldn't speak.

"Before you say anything George and I have known about people with your *talents* for ages. Vice President Turner has been developing re-animation rituals for the last two hundred years. Of course, no one knew it was successful. The article in the Science Journal three days ago was the first proof anyone's ever seen, until you." Vianne squeezed my hand for reassurance.

"How did any of this come up today?" I asked, wondering how on earth this could enter into a casual conversation.

Jason grinned, "I was scanning the house for bugs when George caught me. He told me there was no need for that and then he showed me just about the coolest device I'd ever seen, for a reporter anyway." Jason pulled out a glowing red ball the size of a baseball.

Ryan whistled low. "Is that what I think it is?"

George sat up in his seat like a bright-eyed kid being praised for his accomplishments. "What do you think it is?"

"It looks like a SDS device, but on crack. Can I have a look?" Ryan was extremely excited by this SDS device especially when Jason handed it over to him. It was perfectly round and had its own inner glow that pulsed every few seconds or so.

"Is this why Turner couldn't listen in on our conversations?" I asked.

"Precisely." George acted as if we were in a classroom and I gave him the correct answer.

"You have a guarantee that it works?" Jason realized he didn't know what happened today.

I filled them in.

"Oh you poor dear." Vianne patted my hand in concern. "We always knew Geoffrey Turner was up to something. Jason, the only way to protect Chelsan is to get that man behind bars."

"Let's think on this a little more before we go jumping the gun," Jason cautioned. "I don't want to get any of us hurt."

"Shouldn't we do something?" Bill spoke up. "Money isn't an issue and my parents said they'd help."

I think Bill wanted to make it clear that he was important in this equation. I wanted to reassure him that his friendship was all I needed, but being a guy I think he needed to prove his worth in other ways.

"First things first. I found out a few things today." Jason leaned forward. "Most importantly, I'm pretty sure I was right about what ritual Turner and his wife used to kill you and your mother."

As tired as I was, this immediately piqued my interest. "Really?"

"It's called *The Ritual of Vortex*. From the fire, to the picture, to the serrated knife, to the arm slicing, all there. No one has ever proved that it has worked, it's a myth that goes back hundreds of years which was probably why your father was able to reverse it." Jason grew more and more excited as if he had been waiting all day to tell us everything.

"What *did* my dad do to us? Did you find that out?" I asked, as excited as he was.

"That, I'm not clear on, but I think your father made it up. He must have known about the properties of The Ritual of Vortex and figured out a way to reverse it. Brilliant, actually." Jason was impressed. "Except for the dying part, it was almost flawless."

Nancy smacked him on the arm.

Jason's face turned to me apologetically. "I didn't mean…"

I waved my hand for him to stop. "It's okay. Just continue."

Jason cleared his throat from embarrassment. "Sorry." He paused to gather himself, "Anyway, your dad reversed the spell but I'm assuming the mojo involved was still active after he…passed… and what made you and your mother come back to life, also gave you your gift."

The Ritual of Vortex. It sounded like something out of a sci-fi movie.

Magic so powerful it not only killed my mother and I, but also gave me my gift (with my father's interference). "Why me? Why didn't my mom get any powers?"

Jason shrugged. "I don't know. Maybe because you were a baby? It could be anything really. I also found out more about the Science Journal's report. The stuff that they didn't release. A possibility that may explain why you lose some control over corpses with less …flesh." Jason almost sounded queasy at the prospect. "The subjects they used were actually brought back for over three hours. A part of the experiment they didn't report was the fact that they sprayed the bodies with acid over the three-hour period. The more they destroyed their flesh, the less they could control them, until eventually the bodies collapsed."

"That is so disgusting," Nancy said aloud and I had to agree with her.

"It's not definite proof, but it gives you more to go on than before." Jason raised an eyebrow with another thought. "I also found out a few things about I.Q. Farms as well." He looked pointedly at Ryan.

Ryan's hand tightened in mine.

"Most of this is from rumors and my *conspiracy theorist* contacts, but now that we have a living witness sitting in front of us, I tend to believe it. Basically, Turner started these *farms* going on the research of Larotte Fielding in 2133 that believed children's minds, from the ages of seven through ten, were capable of far more than we ever realized. If utilized properly, there was nothing their intellect couldn't solve or discover. Let's just say Mr. Fielding was arrested and sentenced to life without Age-pro when they discovered his research laboratory where he had kidnapped thirty-three kids and performed experiments on their brains. Supposedly, Turner picked up where Fielding left off. No one has ever seen one since, but like I said, there are still people who believe they exist. And now Ryan is an eye-witness."

I looked over at Ryan sympathetically. He tried to hide it, but I could tell he was frightened. The boy who got away.

"What about that thing the soldiers said; zombie 442?" I asked trying to change the subject.

Jason shook his head. "Nothing. Some military code. And if there is actually a *command* in the military to respond to what you did, it means our world just opened up to a whole lot of chaos. It proves that there are more people like you out there, or at least more who can bring back the dead. Your innate gift may be unique to you. I just don't know."

Everyone was quiet after that.

Too much to process.

"I'm really tired," I admitted. Sitting there with everyone hearing about the kind of trouble we were in made me feel guilty beyond words. And the guilt soon became exhaustion.

"Of course, sweetie. Go get some sleep," Vianne comforted.

"Sounds good. See you guys later."

"I'll walk you up." Ryan wasn't about to let me go that easy and I didn't want him to either.

"Okay." I smiled.

Nancy gave me a wink of approval as we made our way upstairs to her room.

When we arrived at the door I turned to Ryan and leaned my head against his chest. "This is my stop."

Ryan reached down and held both my hands in his pressing his forehead onto mine. "You want me to come in with you?"

"Yes, but I want to sleep and if you're there I won't be able to." I knew that for a fact, the boy made me too crazy for sleep.

"Okay, but I'll be downstairs if you need me." He leaned in and kissed me gently on the lips.

"Go, before I change my mind." I disengaged my hands from his and entered Nancy's bedroom. I shut the door behind me before I actually *would* change my mind.

Her bed looked so ridiculously comfortable with the fluffy down comforter of awesomeness. Single-mindedly I walked over to that paradise of cushions ready to drop and sleep for fifteen hours.

I suddenly felt a hand clasp over my mouth.

I tried to struggle, but the person behind me pinned my arms with his free hand. He was so strong. I searched for anything dead in the room to distract him, something, but the room was clean. My hands were quickly tied together with what felt like leather cords.

I stomped my foot on the ground to make some noise, but the carpet muffled all sound.

No. It can't end like this, I kept on repeating in my head until I felt the sharp prick of a needle in my neck and all my surroundings became a blur. *It can't end like this*, I thought one last time before everything went black.

...I slowly came to. My brain was throbbing and I felt like puking. I couldn't clear my head no matter how hard I tried. Whatever was injected in me was still working its drugtastic wonders. I tried to move my hand, but it wouldn't budge. I realized, through my drug-induced stupor, that I was tied to a chair.

I screamed. Well, I wanted to scream, but I think it came out as more of a garble.

A bright glowing ball of light dangled from the ceiling, but I couldn't make out any details. I could only assume it was a light bulb.

Footsteps clacked on what seemed to be a wooden staircase. Okay, good. My head cleared slightly. I needed to concentrate, break out of this fog. Where was I? Who took me? Was it Turner? After the mess I left him in, I wouldn't be surprised. Who else could it be?

I looked through my bleary eyes to see the silhouette of a man walking toward me. I couldn't see his face, my sight was too blurred, and the angle of the light made him look like a walking black shadow of doom coming toward me.

"Hey." I attempted to speak, but my tongue felt like it was made of lead.

"Not time to wake up, my sweet," the silhouette said. His voice was low and terrifying. I couldn't put my finger on it, but every instinct in my body told me I was a dead woman.

I felt the prick of a needle in my arm.

"No." I didn't even know if that came out properly my mind was starting to fuzz up again.

I made one last lame struggle before the blackness overtook me again.

Wednesday September 22, 2320

…W…w…where…?

Thursday September 23, 2320

PRICK!

Ouch. W…w..hat?

I was awake again. I puked all over the floor.

Why was I feeling better?

I glanced over at where I felt the prick and saw through my blurred vision a tube plugged into my arm. An I.V.? How long had I been here? I looked down and noticed he had taken my shoes and socks off and my ankles were tied to the chair as well.

"Sleep, little one, I'm not ready for you," the man's voice was almost a whisper and sounded like the reaper coming to claim another victim. He injected more of the drug into my I.V.

I struggled to fight off the effects, but the need to sleep overwhelmed me. My thoughts were too scattered. I just needed to stay awa…

Friday September 24, 2320

I came to again. I felt slightly better than the last… I couldn't remember how many times I had woken up… I threw-up on top of a puddle of dried puke. Gross.

I knew my captor would be coming down those wooden steps to drug me again any second now. I had to think quickly, but thinking was proving a challenge unto itself. I needed to be sharp and focused so I could figure a way out of this mess, that much my brain acknowledged.

What could I do? Could I use something dead? I searched the area for any spinning black hole I could find. Tons of roaches (eeeewww), a fly and…. Worms? I wiggled my toes on the ground. Dirt. I was in a cellar of some sort. I just needed something to tie off the flow of the I.V. into my veins without him noticing.

The door creaked open and the same slow clacking of footsteps sounded my doom.

My head still wasn't screwed on straight. I needed more time.

Instinctively, I reached out and connected to a dead worm's black center.

My captor's slow methodic pacing down the stairs made my skin crawl with the realization that this man felt very calm about keeping me tied up down here. He neared the bottom of the stairs. I could see his silhouette through my fuzzy eyes.

I made the worm move as fast as I could. I almost wanted to laugh at the absurdity of making an earthworm slither its way to my chair to perform some kind of rescue mission I didn't even know would work yet. It squirmed up the leg of the chair.

The man was within a few steps of me.

I needed to cause a distraction so I could try and make the worm tie off the I.V. tube.

The man was next to me now. He lifted my I.V. to inject it with the drug.

I looked up at him. I couldn't see any of his facial features. He was completely in shadow. "Who are you?" I tried to divert his attention from injecting me.

The worm slowly wrapped itself around the base of the I.V. squeezing off the flow of nutrients to my body.

"Not now, little one." He stroked the top of my head and I wanted to puke again.

I snapped off both ends of the worm (its dead it can't feel anything!) to disguise the cinch from my captor.

He released the toxins into my I.V. "Sleep." He sounded like the wicked witch in *The Wizard of Oz.*

"N…no… please." I tried to slur my words as much as possible so he'd leave. I didn't know how long the worm restraint would last. The liquid drug was shoving up against it, just waiting to enter my blood stream.

I dropped my head as if I was out cold.

I could feel him standing over me, watching. Please don't notice, please don't notice. I breathed slowly trying to convince him that I was properly drugged. What was he looking at? As the minutes passed by and he remained immobile I found it hard to keep up the charade from sheer terror. His presence felt like a pillar of mortifying psychosis that wouldn't leave. Slow deep breaths. Let the sicko watch me. He obviously wasn't looking at my worm ring or he would have done something by now which meant he was staring at me and only me. I couldn't tell you how scary it was being tied to a chair; helpless, knowing some psychopath stood within inches of you, just staring. He could slit my throat, shoot me, anything, and I wouldn't be able to stop him.

LEAVE!!

It took every bit of strength I could assemble to keep my breathing even and normal.

Finally, he walked away. The sensation of relief I felt was so overpowering I wanted to cry. I was still tied to a chair, but having him leave felt like a physical weight being lifted off my body.

He walked up the stairs in the same slow, even pace he had walked down them. When I heard the click of the door shutting closed I wanted to scream with joy, but I knew I had to keep silent.

My mind was almost completely clear of drugs and I wanted to keep it that way. The sensation of feeling almost normal again was a high I couldn't explain. I wanted to get out of there.

I knew I had to be as quiet as possible. I had to assume that he would hear any sound I made. Or maybe see… There could be cameras…

On the chance that I was being watched, I lolled my head back as if I still slept soundly. I peeked through slitted eyes to gain a better view of my surroundings.

The ball of light that illuminated the room was, in fact, the light of a holo-camera. It wasn't hanging as I first thought; it was resting on a six-foot tri-pod. Okay, he could see me *and* hear me. Good to know. The rest of the room was empty. The walls and floor were dirt, a plywood staircase was against the wall to my right, and a few roots dangled from the ceiling. My only concern would be what was beyond the door at the top of the stairs. If I managed to get that far. I couldn't think like that. My shoes!

The realization that Ryan had put a tracer in my shoes hit me hard. The man who kidnapped me must have had some kind of detector device and that was why he removed them. I guess I couldn't expect help from Ryan. Maybe Jason had some way of tracking me? Oh man, I hope they didn't think that I ran away again! Taking off the shoes would be a sure indication that I didn't want them following me! I wanted to throw-up again and not because of the drugs in my system.

I'd have to rely completely on myself. What else was new?

I rolled my head forward feigning sleep for the holo-cam.

First things first, I needed to get this I.V. out of my arm. I made what was left of the worm slowly tug up. The I.V. popped out of my vein and the fluid poured out onto the floor. I tried to keep it situated so it appeared to still be in my arm, but there was no way to tell if I was successful.

No opening of the door, so I was probably okay.

Next, these bonds.

Cockroaches, get ready to eat.

I connected to about a few hundred dead roaches. He must have had an exterminator down here recently because I could sense from the roaches strength that these troopers were freshly killed. Better for me.

I could hear the skittering and clacking of the hard shells making their way toward me over the dirt floor. Thank goodness they were darkly colored, *he* would be hard pressed to see them on the holo-cam. I tried not to think about the fact that I was making hundreds of the most foul disgusting bugs crawl up the back of my chair and behind my ankles. They were chewing within seconds of my connecting to their spinning centers. I could feel their chitinous mandibles gnawing their way through the leather bonds that held me to the chair. Tiny legs tickled my wrists and ankles as I made the roaches bite and chew. Gross.

SNAP!

The leather ties securing my hands dropped to the floor. Since the camera was only pointed at my front there was no way he could see the bonds fall.

SNAP!

My ankles were free now as well.

I stayed put, still pretending to be asleep, still acting as if I were out cold.

I made the cockroaches crawl far away from me. Never wanted to do that again! I thank the little fellows for freeing me, but yuck!

Next step was to stand up out of this chair. I knew as soon as I did my captor would be down here in seconds, so I had to think of an advantage I might have over him. I knew more than I'd known anything in my life that the man that kept me hostage was a killer. And not the military type of killer who attacked Jason and I at the Virtual Reality bar, no, this was a man who *enjoyed* killing. It was like breathing to him. I could still feel him standing next to me, staring for ages. This was nightmare stuff.

There was nothing for it.

I stood up and smashed the holo-cam to the ground, grinding it into the dirt with my bare foot.

The room went black.

The latch sounded and the door swung open in a rush. The faint glow from the doorway was the only source of light anymore, but it was just enough to see my captor's body hit the stairs at a run. At least I managed to make him move at a speed above turtle status.

It was terrifying not being able to see anything and knowing that this person was with me in the dark charging toward me. I moved slowly and cautiously to a corner of the room, the dirt floor hiding the sound of my footsteps.

The man groaned in what I could only describe as ecstasy. He enjoyed this cat and mouse game. Then he pulled out his one advantage.

A flashlight.

Great.

He found me quickly with the glaring light. The brightness nearly blinded me. Like a bull he rushed at me.

I called on my little roach friends once more and made hundreds of them race across the floor and crawl up his legs, chest, arms and face. He screamed. It was the first time I sensed any fear from him, but cockroaches were harmless, he'd realize that soon enough.

I ran past him before he could grab me and practically flew up the wooden staircase. My heart was racing, my head was pounding, I didn't know what I'd find when I ran through the door.

I could feel him brushing off the bothersome roaches. The flashlight flared in my direction as I reached the top of the stairs and ran through the doorway.

He was already on the steps, taking two at a time.

I slammed the door shut and searched for a lock on the knob, the door frame, anywhere!

Nothing.

BOOM!

The door hit me hard against my chest as he slammed it open, flashlight blinding me. I fell on my backside and tried to get back up to run.

"You're a bad little girl," I heard him say and his voice sounded almost pleased by that notion.

I scrambled to my feet and whirled around to run when I realized…

…I was in a small metal hallway with a steel door at the opposite end that was locked shut.

I turned around to face my attacker…

SMACK!

Ouch.

My head.

Everything went black.

Saturday September 25, 2320

"My little bug girl." I awoke to the excited whisper of my kidnapper. "All the roaches fell to the floor when I hit you over the head." He was beside himself with glee.

Fantastic. Now he knew my gift. At least a part of it anyway.

I tried to move, but I was strapped to what felt like a metal slab. I couldn't see my captor. He was behind me and I could hear his heavy breathing as if he were about to burst out into laughter. I wanted to cry in terror, but I knew it wouldn't do any good. I was stuck here with this man and he had me tied up. Again.

The room I was in was metal, no windows, one ventilation grate and no furniture except the table I was on. Florescent lights on the ceiling made the whole room a greenish hue. I barely recognized the faint outline of a door as it blended with the wall so perfectly.

I wasn't drugged. That was an improvement at least, but the bonds that kept me strapped to the table weren't budging. I searched the area quickly for anything dead. Only one cockroach and from its location I knew that my kidnapper was holding it.

"I didn't want you at first. He made me take you, but now you'll be my biggest prize of all." He heaved with joy.

My eyes welled up before I could stop it. I had never been so scared in my life. I saw dead things every day. I thought it would make me tougher than this. I didn't want to let him observe me in this state. Somehow I knew that it would only make him more excited. I tried to focus. If I was going to get out of this I needed as much information as I could from this man.

"Who made you take me?" I asked.

The man finally stepped into the light and I saw my captor for the first time. I was shocked to see how normal he looked. He was average height and weight, blond wavy hair, cut short, aquiline features, wearing a dress shirt and slacks. I would have thought he was a teacher or a businessman if it weren't for his eyes.

They burned with an intensity that made my heart stop. There was no doubt in my mind.

This man was insane.

Which wasn't much of a leap considering my experience with him so far, but still, knowing I was dealing with *Cuckoo* might help me formulate a plan of escape.

"You know who." He smiled manically. "He lets me do my work without interference and I help him take out the filth of this world."

I tried not to show my fear.

Serial killer. The words played in my head like a broken record. Impossible. There hadn't been a serial killer in over a hundred years, or at least none that the public knew about. No one wanted to risk the death sentence or life imprisonment without Age-pro. There were medical facilities for people with these tendencies to go and get help. *He lets me do my work without interference...*

Another form of population control sanctioned by good 'ol Gramps.

Serial killers? How many were out there? How many innocent lives were taken by the man I was related to? Hundreds? Thousands? More like millions. I now knew of two methods he used: extermination with gasses and turning a blind eye to murderers. How many other ways was he taking out the human race while the world went on thinking everyone was going to live forever? How did he keep these deaths so secret? If people knew how easy it was to die on this planet, religion would still be practiced!

A horrible thought hit me.

No one ever saw Christian Coalition towns. They kept themselves segregated from the rest of the world. Turner could have wiped them all out and no one would have ever known. Were there any left? Had he killed all the people that no one would ask about and now had to move on to the general population? Was over-population really that bad? Or was he like the man who held me prisoner, a murderer who enjoyed killing. Probably a bit of both.

The man placed the dead cockroach in my face. "Your little pet, my pet." His creepy grin wouldn't budge. "Bring it back to life."

"Did Turner tell you *why* he wanted you to take me?" I ignored his request to gain more information.

This made the man's smile fade a little as if he were contemplating the matter. "Bring it back to life." He changed the subject back to the roach.

"I'll bring it back if you answer my question." If I remembered my studies about serial killers, most of the battle would be about who was in charge. I already knew he was *forced* to take me as opposed to a victim he would normally choose on his own.

"BRING IT BACK!" his voice boomed angrily.

I shuddered involuntarily.

Okay. He definitely needed to be in charge, and I was too frightened to fight it.

I made the roach crawl gently up his arm and back down again into his hand. His eyes never left mine.

He smiled, "Your eyes dilate when you do that. Did you know that?"

"No," I admitted truthfully.

"I didn't want to take you," he said flatly, and I couldn't sense any emotion from him, good or bad.

"Then let me go." I tried the honest approach.

"No. I don't think I'll do that. He'd take it all away from me if I did that." The killer didn't sound as if he was opposed to the idea of letting me go, only of the fact that he wouldn't be allowed to continue his murdering spree if he did. "Besides. You're too precious a gift to let go. It's in your eyes. They dilate when you bring the bugs to life."

"Yes, you told me that." I stayed as calm as I could, hoping to talk him down.

"Is it just insects you can bring back?" he wondered curiously.

"Yes," I lied. The less he knew the better.

"I wasn't sure what to do with you at first, that's why I kept you in the basement. I only take filthy girls. You didn't seem filthy to me, but you *are*. You're the filthiest of them all, I think." His eyes widened with a thrilled kind of look. "He must have known that. That's why he wanted me to take you." He was talking to himself at this point, as if rationalizing in his head why Turner would want me dead.

"Turner is my grandfather," I said just loud enough to interrupt his thoughts.

It worked. He turned to me a slight raise of his eyebrow. "Sometimes it's hard to rid the world of filth, especially when it's family. I understand now. He wanted it done special. It's your eyes, you know. I take the filthy parts away from the girls so they can be pure again. Don't you worry, I'll make you clean."

And the way he said it made my stomach drop.

He was going to gouge my eyes out.

And who knew what other body parts he had taken from girls like me.

"In time," he said and walked over to the door. He waved his hand over a seemingly blank surface, it lit up green and the door swung outward. Walking through the doorway, he didn't look back at me. He was planning to *cleanse* me forever.

The door clanked shut and I was alone once more. Well, me and the cockroach. I guess he wanted me to have company. I connected briefly to the roach and realized my captor had snapped off its mandible. He didn't want a repeat of my escape from the basement. I released the roach and ran scenarios through my head. He had stripped me of any help I could rely on. Sad that whenever I was in a dangerous situation (which happened a lot these days) my only way out of them was the use of dead things. How pleasant. Well, you work with what you have, right? And right now all I had was Larry. (I decided to name my mutant roach Larry after my first pet goldfish.) Anything to keep my mind straight. If I gave into the terror, I'd be frozen and useless. I needed to do *something* and Larry was the only one who could help.

I tapped into Larry's swirling core, made him skitter off the table and up the wall into the ventilation grate. That was where it became tricky. I needed to see through Larry's eyes like I had with Bruce and the corpses at the Virtual Bar. I hoped bugs weren't any different than humans. I focused all my energy on Larry and his tiny little eyes and...

...I could see. And surprisingly, I could see very well. And whoa! It felt as if I had a billion points of view. When I stared straight ahead I could also see behind me, beside me, above me, below me, all at once. Cockroaches had ridiculous eye-sight, who knew? Viewing my surroundings in Larry's body, I realized there was a light ahead of him at the end of the ventilation shaft. I made him run to the end of the shaft and peer through the second grating.

My captor was there, sitting at a round dining table eating a bowl of cereal. The room was small, sparse and very orderly. No one would ever know that this was a house of a serial killer. From Larry's angle I had to make him climb out of the grate to gain a better view of the door that led to where I was being held. It seemed like an ordinary wooden door from the killer's side. Nothing special about it, one would think it was to a closet or to a bedroom, not to a sealed off sterilized metal prison. There wasn't a phone in sight. I made Larry hurry back to the shaft for fear of the killer noticing him. He seemed very concentrated on his cereal, he chewed each bite over thirty times. Meticulous and methodical, there had to be some kind of advantage I could gather from that.

And then I felt it.

It was strange having to rely on another creature's senses so I wasn't sure I was actually feeling what I was feeling. But through little Larry I swore I could feel at least seven swirling black chasms coming from the killer's back yard. And these were human. Something about these metal walls prevented me from sensing them myself. I tried to probe the bodies as much as I could through Larry, but I could barely pick up their essence as it was. If there were really corpses back there I'd just need to get through the doorway to access them.

It struck me as funny that I could be so analytical about using dead bodies as weapons. The thought never would have occurred to me before until Gramps had actually tried to kill me. If he hadn't gone after me, I never would have discovered everything I had learned about my gift.

I kept Larry stationed at the grate to be my eyes on the killer's movement. I disconnected from him temporarily so I could clear my head and focus on how I was going to convince my kidnapper to let me into that room. Or at least into the doorway.

Four straps pinned me on the metal table: around the chest, abdomen/wrists, knees and ankles. There was a little wiggle room in the head, elbows and stomach. Question was: how heavy was this table? I needed to tip it over. It would hurt like no one's business, but it might loosen me up enough to scooch to the doorway.

It was a gamble I was willing to take. At this point my options were try something or die.

Like a swing I used my body to lean back and forth. The grating sound of metal was loud and I knew my captor would come through the door any minute to check on me.

I connected to Larry's eyes. Bad guy was still eating his Wheaties.

I swung harder and faster.

KA-KLUMP! KA-KLUMP!

So loud! Why couldn't metal be quieter?

My kidnapper heard that last one. He stood up with an expression of pure hatred and anger etched on his face.

Not much time.

KA-KLUMP!

BAM!

The table fell on its side and it jolted the chest strap loose.

Oh man!

The door opened.

I freed my hands.

Like an enraged animal, the killer swooped down and grabbed my arms to re-secure them. He was so much stronger!

I just needed to get to the doorway.

It was open! So close!

I smashed my head against his in the most painful head butt imaginable. I couldn't tell if it hurt me more than him, but it did manage to make him loosen his grip. I punched his face as hard as I could, he reeled back from the shock of it.

I quickly untied the rest of my bonds and tried to make a crawl for the door.

But this guy was pumped full of adrenaline and he tackled me from behind.

I searched for the seven black holes of hope.

Not close enough.

I kicked wildly and managed to connect with his groin area.

He gurgled in anguish, but his grasp was still tight.

I inched closer.

No black holes.

Come on. Just a few more inches.

He started pulling me back into the room. How was he so strong?

My pure animal instincts kicked in and I whirled around and shoved the base of my hand straight into his face. The effect was enough. He reeled back from the instant explosion of blood coming from his nose and his eyes looked at me in shocked anger.

I had simply angered the beast.

I hoped Larry was right, I was betting all of it on the faith that there were seven corpses out there that were raring for a fight.

I leapt through the entryway and shut the door on him before he could pummel his way through. I knew I only had seconds before he simply swiped his hand over the sensor and came after me. He wouldn't hesitate this time. I was a dead woman if I didn't act fast.

Taking a deep breath, I searched for my seven girls and found them instantaneously.

The door burst open.

I grabbed a chair from his dining table and smashed his chest with it as soon as he was visible. He fell back into the room and I slammed the door shut on him again. I knew this wasn't a permanent solution. He'd just open the door again, but maybe this time he'd be more cautious, all

I needed was a little time.

The girls were in varying degrees of decomposition. I know, gross, but as I learned from the virtual bar and Jason, the fresher the better. I squeezed my eyes shut and slammed myself into their swirling black chasms. They were buried, but shallowly. I made them dig as fast as they could. One only had one arm, ewwww. It made me realize what this monster had done to innocent girls and I was filled with such a rage that I wanted to make him suffer like he made these girls suffer before he ended their lives.

And that was my plan.

He was about to have a reunion he'd never forget.

The door creaked open.

I stood aside, second chair in my hands, ready to smash his face in a second time.

The girls were through the dirt and on their way to the house.

I was about to slam the door shut again when he shoved the metal table through the entryway keeping the door open.

I saw him then, his eyes wide with excitement and glee, blood on his nose, lips and chin from where I had hit him. He looked like something out of a nightmare. This man was the physical incarnation of a monster.

And he was coming for me.

The back door was locked. I made the girls shove hard against it to break it down.

This made his head turn from surprise, then he smiled wickedly at me. "Police won't help you, girl. Your grandfather keeps me quite safe."

I held the chair in front of me as a barrier between us. "Not the cops, a-hole."

His only response was a raised eyebrow, but his eyes were still filled with the thrill of the chase. "More bugs?" I could tell he welcomed that idea. He had adapted from the first time I sent the cockroaches after him. He wanted to live the experience again and defeat it. He fed on his own fear.

"Something like that."

BAM! BAM! BAM!

Almost through.

"Big bug." He leapt toward me.

I swung the chair at him, but he caught the leg with his hand.

He managed to yank the chair out of my hands and throw it across the room.

We circled each other. He salivated with delight, ready to pounce. I felt like I was a gazelle cornered by a lion.

BAM! SNAP!

The door flew open.

And in poured the most grotesque vision I'd ever seen in my life.

The seven girls were naked and mangled beyond comprehension.

He had stripped off what made these girls human. One had her lips ripped off and her teeth and jaw were visible beneath. One had no nose. One had her hands removed. One was missing her arm. One had her skin removed as if she had been boiled and peeled. One had no eyes. And the last girl was missing her entire face, just sinew and bone left.

I wanted to scream but I also wanted to cry. These girls had been tortured and murdered in the most horrendous way imaginable. There was no way of telling if he took these parts from their bodies while they were still alive or not. I couldn't imagine the kind of pain and torment they must have gone through before they were finally killed. I stared at the girl whose eyes were ripped out. It would have been me if I didn't have my gift.

The killer had stopped dead in his tracks as he watched the seven girls walk through his back door.

"No," he muttered so quietly I could barely hear him.

"Yes," I said with so much emotion I almost choked it out.

Time to make them talk.

I controlled the eye-less girl first. She walked up to him so they were within inches of each other. He was still paralyzed by the sight of his victims. "What can we collect from you?" I made her say. Her vocal chords were deteriorated from rot so her voice was gravelly and low.

"Impossible." The killer dropped to the floor and held his knees to his chest. All his momentum and fire gone.

I knew it wouldn't last long. I needed to get him tied up.

I made the girl with no face kneel down to his level. "I want my face back," she spoke in the same rough voice as the other girl.

I had the girl with no mouth run into the metal room and grab the fallen straps from the table. Once in hand, I made her come back and place the killer onto one of his dining chairs, tying him in place. He still didn't struggle. His eyes kept moving from one girl to the next as if daring himself to wake up from a terrible dream.

His head was down and he shook it back and forth mumbling, "Impossible. Impossible."

I made all seven girls surround him in a tight circle just in case he came to his senses and managed to break free.

"You keep saying that, but here we are and I want my arm back." I made the armless girl speak.

"I just wanted something to remember you by. It was your wickedness that made me take those things from you. I made you all pure." He sounded like a child trying to explain why he broke his toys.

"Do we look pure now?" I made the skinless girl speak and bend down so close to his face that he actually flinched. Without lips, her words were garbled and lisped.

He rocked the chair violently, screaming in anguish. I realized that this may be too much for his warped mind. He sounded like a rabid dog, barking and yelling, snapping his jaw together and biting the air.

It was so much more frightening than when he was calm. I had provoked the monster within and it was coming out. Suddenly, the seven girls were exactly what they appeared to be, empty shells, nothing more. I felt more exposed and petrified than I did when I was strapped to that table.

His eyes met mine.

"YOU DID THIS!!!!" he howled in excruciating fury.

I backed away unconsciously. I was up against a whole other species of human being here and I was way out of my league. Being clever and wanting to exact revenge on this psycho may have cost me my life.

"MEAT PUPPETS! JUST LIKE THE BUGS!"

The way he said meat puppets made me instinctively gag. What had I been thinking? I should have just ran and left these girls to stall so I could escape. My own sense of self-righteousness had kept me there so I could see this man suffer. Selfish! Egomaniac! Stupid! All these words applied to how I felt about myself in that moment.

I needed to find a phone. If I couldn't call the police I'd call the gang.

Jason could by-pass the police. He was a reporter. He told me that the more public I made things the easier it was to stay alive. Advice I should have remembered earlier.

The killer broke out of the bonds that held him by smashing the wooden chair to the floor. Along with the snapping of wood a very distinct crack came from his body. He had broken something.

Good.

Maybe enough to distract him while I escaped.

I was so shocked by his sudden transformation from crying mess to raging bull I had let the girls go lapse.

Tongue hanging loose and eyes bugging out, the killer came charging at me with a guttural roar.

I acted fast and made all seven girls tackle him to the ground. He struggled as if his limbs were made of chainsaws, tearing and ripping into the corpses. If he broke something his adrenaline and rage prevented him from slowing down on any level.

And then I ran.

Straight out to the backyard.

It was closed off with a six-foot oak fence. I could see over a hundred feet ahead of me the loose dirt where I had made the girls dig their way out to my rescue. I could feel the killer rip through their flesh to get to me. He was pinned down for the moment, but I knew it wouldn't last long.

I ran to the side of the fence and climbed over the top, landing on the neighbor's yard next door. No fences here, so I kept on running, running up the grass street as fast as my legs would carry me. I was instantly tired, days of being locked up and starved were taking its toll, only adrenaline kept me moving.

I was at least a block away, but I didn't want to stop. If I stopped he'd be there like a bad cartoon. All my fears from being locked up in that monster's house were bubbling to the surface in ways I couldn't control.

Tears flowed freely down my face. I could barely move forward as the tears turned to sobs, but I didn't stop. I had to keep going. I choked and bawled and gasped for breath. My run had turned to a sluggish zombie walk. I threw-up all over my clothes, but I kept walking. Nothing could stop me. The farther I moved, the closer I was to freedom. And I still didn't feel free.

I had dropped the connection to the girls without even realizing it. I was so focused on getting out of there I hadn't kept my concentration up. He was probably contacting help to get me back. Turner would appease him instantly. He wouldn't want it to get out that a serial killer still existed in our "perfect utopia" of immortality.

The neighborhood was barely above a trailer park in terms of social status, which meant they were poor, but not the lowest rung of poor. I was scared to knock on anyone's door for fear of them working for my grandpa. I wished there was a payphone I could use, but then again, Turner probably had those tapped in case I escaped. I made a split second decision and turned to the first "normal" looking house I could find. White picket fence, yellow paint, wrap-around porch with a swing set. Please let someone be home.

I was on the verge of collapse as I reached the front door. I tried not to think about the fact that I was covered in vomit, blood and dirt. I must have smelled pretty ripe. I knocked on the door and waited.

A few moments later a plump woman who appeared as if she was in her early thirties opened the door. One look at me and she gasped in horror.

"Please, help," I said through my tears.

"Oh my! What on earth happened to you?! Come in! Come in!" She shooed me inside. "Are you hurt? Of course you're hurt, sit down." She ushered me to her couch and sat down next to me examining each and every wound. Which really wasn't that many considering I managed to get out of there before he could start cutting me up. She had a round and friendly face with a splattering of freckles across her nose. Her hair was dark and pulled back in a messy bun and she wore a worn-in running suit with white socks. She looked like she'd always be in a state of "frazzle" no matter what the circumstances. At this point just seeing a friendly face made me want to collapse from relief.

"I just need to use your phone. I was kidnapped and I escaped, but I think he's looking for me." I wanted to warn her. The last thing I wanted to do was get her killed.

"It's that Brady man, isn't it? I knew it! Here let me get you a phone." The woman quickly snagged a cell phone from the next room and handed it to me. "I've reported him before, but they never do anything. I knew he was up to no good. That man is at least a hundred years old and he looks twenty. What is a richy up to living on our block in that hovel of his? Nothing good, that's what. What did he do to you? You call the police, maybe they'll listen to you," she rambled on and I suddenly understood that if she had her suspicions of the man that took me and called the police…

…Turner would have her phone tapped, or at least re-directed to his people whenever she contacted the police.

She continued her rant, "I've seen him take girls in, but they never come out. One night I had my binoculars and saw him digging in his backyard! The police told me his pet dog died and he was burying him, but unless his dog was a Great Dane, that was a body, I'm sure of it!" She re-focused her attention back on me. "Listen to me ramble on. My name is Doris."

"Chelsan," I said quietly. "Do other people in the neighborhood pay attention to this guy?" I wanted to get a feel for the size of Turner's web on this block.

"They do, but they keep quiet, ever since Franny Lerner walked straight up to his house demanding she see inside. The police came and arrested her and when she came back she was… different." Doris looked like she didn't quite know how to explain herself.

"Different how?" I asked. Though I thought I knew the answer.

"I don't know. Just funny… off. Like she wasn't herself. She said that Brady let her see his house and that everything was fine. He was just a shy, quiet guy. Everyone was a little freaked out by her strangeness and some people said she was replaced by a robot. If you believe such nonsense. Anyway, it scared all of us silly, so after that no one said anything about Brady. *Utopic denial* is what I call it. They'd rather believe everything is just fine than actually have to admit that horrible things still happen in this world. Everyone on the block thinks I'm crazy to keep calling the police like I do, but we all know something is wrong with that man, and I can't just sit by and let him do whatever it is he does in there." She eyed me curiously, "What did he do? Did you see any other girls in there with you?"

"Listen. I need *you* to make this call. I think your phone may be bugged and I don't want whoever is listening knowing that I've escaped. Can you do that for me?" I looked her directly in the eye to make sure she was on the same page as me. And I wasn't ready to answer her questions just yet.

"Will we be able to take that son of a bitch down?" She was very serious.

"Yes, but we have to be careful," I said. "I'll dial the number and you ask to talk to Ryan. Tell him you found his friend's shoes and give him your address so he can pick them up." I hoped Ryan would get the reference to the tracer he planted in my shoes. I wished I could talk to him myself, just to hear his voice. Everything I had been through… seeing him again seemed unimaginable.

Doris was on it. I dialed Ryan's number and handed her the phone.

Doris sounded like a mother when she answered the phone. "Yes, hello dear, is this Ryan? Oh good. Listen, I found your friend's shoes. Yes, yes. Why don't you come here and pick them up. Oh good. My address is 5522 North Glosten Street. Yes. Okay dear, I'll keep them safe until you get here. Bye, bye." Doris patted my hand encouragingly. "He's on his way and he's bringing friends. What a nice young man. He seemed beside himself when I mentioned the shoes. Are you sure they can help?"

"I'm sure. Thank you, Doris."

BAM! BAM! BAM! BAM!

"Is that your friends already?" Doris turned to her front door.

SMASH!

The door shattered as the killer kicked it in.

"Brady!" Doris screamed. "I'm calling the police right now!"

"DO IT, BITCH! *YOU'LL* BE THE ONE IN JAIL!" Brady laughed manically. He was covered in his own blood, his clothes were shredded, his right arm was limp and useless, but he was alert and enraged.

When he saw me he howled like a wolf and charged.

I was so weak. I didn't have much in me to fight back. I tried to connect to any black swirling hole I could find, but I couldn't seem to make anything move. I was completely drained. I wanted to run, but I knew he'd kill Doris. I couldn't leave her alone with this man. I had to make a stand.

I picked up one of Doris' lamps and smashed it onto Brady's broken arm just as he was about to tackle me. He shrieked in agony, but grabbed my throat with his uninjured hand despite the pain he was in. He tried to squeeze the last bit of life I had out of me. It was almost as if I stepped out of my body. I could see the faint stirrings of my own black spinning core growing stronger by the second. I was dying. I took my last bit of strength and clawed my fingers into his arm and tore.

Brady screeched so loudly my ears started to ring.

He let go and I came away with blood and skin in my fingernails.

CRACK!

Brady was silent as he dropped to the floor unconscious.

Behind him was Doris with a five-iron golf club in her hands. She bashed him over the head again for measure as if making sure he was really out. Her hands were shaking and she dropped the club to the floor. Then she ran to me and held me close. "You're okay now. He won't hurt you anymore."

I let her hold me. I was too weak to move, or cry, or anything but lie there.

And to see my captor *Brady* in worse shape than I was didn't give me any satisfaction like I thought it would. I was still scared of him, unmoving, unconscious and all. I think I'd always be scared of him. Forever.

Sirens and hover-fans became almost deafening from outside. Apparently, the cavalry had arrived.

"It's them, Doris." I looked up at her and managed a smile.

"Well, we just took care of ourselves, didn't we?" she chuckled and gave me a warm hug of support.

"Thank you," I said and tears came to my eyes.

"Oh nonsense. I've been wanting that monster out of this neighborhood for years." She tried to make things light for my sake. I could tell. I wanted to do something for Doris, protect her somehow. I knew Jason would have the answer.

My heart leapt.

Ryan came bounding through the door, eyes searching until he found me.

I was never happier to see anyone in my life.

When he saw me his face went from relief to utter worry in about a half a second. He raced to my side on the floor and Doris smiled and moved aside to let him hold me. I clung to him like he was a lifeline. And in that instance, he truly was. He didn't have to say a word, he just held me as if he couldn't believe I was really there. I could barely believe I was alive. And then I realized in horror that I really, truly must stink.

"I'm smelly," I said, my face in his chest.

"I don't care. I'm never letting you out of my sight again." He kissed my forehead.

"Chelsan! Thank goodness!" Nancy's voice rang out like sweet music to my ears.

Nancy and Bill came racing to our side. Doris stood up at that point and sat on her couch.

"Are you okay? What happened?" Nancy glanced at Brady. "Is that the guy that took you? Geez, Chelsan, he looks pretty F'd up." Nancy examined my face and saw the lump forming on my head from where I head-butted Brady. "Uuuck! You seriously stink!"

"Shut up, Nancy." Bill rolled his eyes. "Are you okay? Is this the guy?"

I nodded, not wanting to give Brady any acknowledgment. As if saying anything would wake him up again.

"Guys, this is Doris. She saved my life."

All three of them immediately turned to Doris as if seeing her for the first time. Bill and Nancy practically tackled her in a group hug repeating thank you over and over. Ryan didn't leave my side, but he nodded his thanks.

"Oh, mine just happened to be the door she knocked on. She escaped all on her own." Doris deflected taking any credit.

"Well, the five-iron to his head made sure he didn't finish the job." I wanted to make sure they all knew what a hero she was.

"Sweet. You golf? You now are a standing member of the LA Golf club. I'll send over new clubs, too." Bill obviously felt like he needed to give Doris a reward and I was extremely grateful.

"Oh, my." Doris blushed.

The buzz of hover vehicles and sirens caught my attention once more and I looked over at the shattered doorway.

Nancy followed my gaze. "Jason is out there taking care of the press.

I better give him some details. Do you know anything about this guy? Was he just a thug for Turner?"

The memories were too fresh. I didn't want to talk about it yet, but I knew I had to. To protect Doris and myself. "Guys, he was a serial killer."

"Nuh, uh!" Nancy was in shock.

Ryan held me tighter.

Bill was actually speechless.

"Like a real one?" Nancy apparently couldn't wrap her head around it, and I couldn't blame her.

"Like a real one. Tell Jason he'll find seven dead girls' bodies at this guy's house, and a whole lot of proof," I informed her quietly.

"His name is Brady Johnson and he lives ten houses down on this side of the street." Doris gave the details. "And see if you can wrangle up some police officers to get this *thing* off my floor."

"Will do." Nancy ran out to tell Jason everything.

A roar from the crowd a few minutes later.

"I guess he told them," I said, knowing that I'd be a media frenzy unto myself yet again.

Jason and Nancy ran in after that with two police officers. The officers handcuffed Brady and dragged him out the front door to the onslaught of reporters wanting to get a holo-pic of the first serial killer in over a hundred years. The first one that was caught anyway. How many others were there?

Jason sat on the couch next to Doris. Doris's face had turned bright red at the sight of Jason. Apparently, she was a fan.

"This is Doris. She saved Chelsan's life," Bill told him.

Jason shook Doris's hand. "Then let me save yours. We have to make you as famous as can be. Are you ready for that, Doris?"

"Well, I… uh.. sure." Doris was starting to be overwhelmed by the last twenty minutes of her life.

"Then let's get you out there." Jason turned to me. "Chelsan, you're going to have to talk about *exactly* what happened to you. Do you think you can do that?" He was being gentle with me, but I could tell he'd push the issue if I said no. He was genuinely trying to save our butts.

"I'm ready," I half-lied. I really didn't know if I was or not.

"Are you sure?" Nancy had her hands on her hips. "Don't listen to this creep. If you're not ready, we're not going out there."

"This *creep* knows how to stay alive." Jason rolled his eyes at Nancy.

Apparently, problems had arisen in my absence. This didn't feel like flirting to me.

"Chelsan's been doing a damn good job of keeping alive herself." Ryan held me closer.

"I'm not questioning Chelsan's skill of keeping herself breathing. I don't know *anyone* who could have survived what she has. I'm just thinking of ways to keep Turner from trying to kill her again." Jason was being the level-headed one of the group.

"Vice President Turner?" Doris's gossip button had been pushed. "Is he behind all this?"

I stood up before this became ugly. Ryan stood up with me and held my hand. "I'm going out there. I trust Jason." I wanted to make that clear. If Nancy was having personal issues with him that was one thing, but when it came to the safety of my friends I'd do anything to protect them. Even if it meant re-living the last few days. Or.. wait a minute.... "How long was I gone?"

"Five days," Bill said as if he had counted the minutes.

Whoa. Five days? It felt like two, maybe three, that was almost a whole week! I suddenly felt woozy. I stumbled slightly and Ryan caught me. No wonder I was so weak! "He had me on an I.V. for a while, but I'm feeling pretty tired."

"We'll get you to a hospital as soon as we're done here. Let's do this quick." Jason took me away from Ryan and ushered me to the front door and the awaiting press. "Doris, you too," he called over his shoulder.

Doris stood up from the couch as if she had been poked by a cattle prod. "Coming."

Nancy, Bill and Ryan positioned themselves behind us like bodyguards.

The press corps was about ten times the size of the group that covered the *tornado* at the trailer park. It was like standing in front of an ocean of flashing holo-cams and screaming reporters, there was no end to them, just miles and miles of people and hover-cars.

Jason placed his hands up to quiet the crowd. It was instantly silent. "Chelsan has been through a lot these last five days so we're going to keep it brief people. She needs medical attention so most of your questions will have to be answered after her release from the hospital. That being said, Chelsan will give her statement. Chelsan."

I swallowed hard and fought off the feeling of fainting. "I was kidnapped from my best friend Nancy's house five days ago and taken to that house down there." I pointed to Brady's house, which I now noticed was swarming with police-hovers and officers. "He kept me locked in his basement and drugged so I didn't know how long I had been there…"

I was having trouble talking. I felt detached from my own voice, as if someone else was doing the speaking. I knew I couldn't tell them about how I used my powers on the cockroaches and the girls' corpses, so I had to skip over that part. "I managed to break free and we fought. There were bodies everywhere. I hit him with a chair and tied him up and then I ran. I ran until I decided to get help and knocked on Doris's door. She helped me call my friends and they called the police. Then he broke into her house and Doris knocked him out with a golf club. That's it. That's all I can remember." It sounded so mundane and boring when I said it out loud, nowhere near how horrific it actually was to live it. The press seemed to eat it up though. Especially, when the police took out the body pieces left from the girls.

Jason stepped in and steered Doris to the forefront. "Here's our hero of the day folks. Doris Hornbacher! Without her courageous whack of her five-iron, Chelsan would just be another victim in Brady Johnson's collection. Let's all give a round of applause to Doris!"

The roar of the crowd greeted Doris as she stood red-faced in front of the press. "Well… I…" She adjusted her hair and sweat suit to look more presentable. "It was nothing really. I did what I could for the poor girl." Doris visibly began to relax as she continued. I think she was really starting to dig the attention. "When I saw that man strangling Chelsan I grabbed my golf club and hit him as hard as I could! I barely use my clubs anymore, it's so expensive to play, but this young man," she pulled Bill up next to her, "he offered me a free membership to the LA Golf Club! Sweet young thing." She turned her attention back to the press. "I have been calling the police non-stop for over three years now about Brady, but they did nothing! Nothing! We all knew it! I saw him digging, but they did nothing!

Unfathomable! If Chelsan hadn't escaped, he'd still be on the loose killing young girls and no one would be the wiser! And if you think for one instant that there aren't others like him out there, then you are all delusional! Mark my words, I will find these killers!" She looked directly into the holo-cams for emphasis. "Your days are numbered." Doris had such conviction and intensity in her voice, it gave me goose bumps.

Jason was extremely impressed. I could tell by his lopsided smile. He turned to the press. "We're taking these girls to the hospital. The police will be making a statement at Brady Johnson's house in three minutes."

The mass of reporters moved like a swarm of bees toward Brady's house.

Doris leaned down to my ear. "That's her. That's Franny Lerner. The robot."

I glanced over to the woman Doris pointed to, and sure enough she wasn't a robot. She was dead. Another one of Grandpa's spies. Watching us carefully from afar.

I took my last vestiges of strength, covered in puke and blood and walked over to Franny. She stood there, black hole swirling, staring at me with hatred.

"Turner, if you're listening, you're going to have to do better than that if you want me dead. You lose. Again." I would have kicked the girl except I knew she wouldn't feel anything and neither would he. I just wanted him to think he hadn't broken me down, even though I wasn't sure if that was true.

"We'll see," was all Franny said and then she collapsed in front of me. She began to rot instantaneously as Turner released her body from his power. I knew if I didn't scream people would suspect me of either being crazy or somehow responsible. So I did. I screamed loud enough that half the press came running from Brady's house to my side. Once they saw the rotted mess that was Franny, all holo-cams captured the grotesque scene.

Ryan and the others hurried to my side. I turned to Ryan as he embraced me and whispered in his ear. "Get me out of here."

As soon as we stepped inside the holo-ambulance I lay down

on the bed. My head hit the pillow and all the sounds and chaos disappeared as I passed out.

***

Pitch blackness. It was everywhere. So dark it felt like black fog. Where was I? I was somehow aware that I was dreaming, but no matter how hard I tried I couldn't make myself wake-up. I was stuck in this utter darkness.

"You can't hide from me forever, you know."

I heard a voice from the blackness. It was my grandpa. His voice a nightmare come to life.

"You're just a dream," I said, though I didn't know why. If it really was a dream why was I telling a figment of my imagination that? Something made me unsure of myself. Something in the tone of his voice.

He stepped forward and revealed himself. There was a faint reddish glow around him, emanating power. As if he were trying to intimidate me. "Really? Are you sure?" he replied, as if reading my thoughts.

I wasn't.

I didn't want to say anything.

"I have a friend with me. Would you like to see him?" Turner smiled at me as if anticipating my answer.

"Not really," I said.

"Oh, but he wants to see you. He insisted on it." Turner gestured to his left and Brady appeared next to him.

Dream or not, the memories were too fresh, I jumped back in spite of myself.

Brady didn't move, didn't talk, simply stood there.

"Notice anything special about our friend?" Turner stared at me with a penetrating gaze.

I forced myself to glance at Brady a second time. I noticed a black hole swirling in his chest. He was dead. Which meant Turner had killed him.

Dream. Dream. Dream. I reminded myself, but it was becoming

clear to me that this was something else entirely.

"It will be the trial of the century by the time I'm done with it. Serial killers in this day and age? I was shocked to find out that Brady tapped Ms. Hornbacher's phone so that when she called the police it went directly to his home phone. No wonder LA's finest couldn't catch this monster. The scandal!" Turner snickered with delight. "Isn't that right, Brady?"

Brady's eyes came alive and he laughed evilly. "I killed them all! I just wish that last little morsel hadn't got away." Then his eyes went dead again.

"He'll say whatever I want him to say." Turner's gaze turned hard.

"And then I'll make him say whatever *I* want him to say." I crossed my arms protectively.

"We'll see." Turner repeated Franny's words. He looked neither miffed nor happy at the prospect, just contemplative. "Time to wake up now."

***

I awoke with a start. I was in a hospital bed with an I.V. plugged in my arm. I almost yanked it out on instinct, but I knew I was reacting to my dream. It felt like more. I didn't even know if that was possible. But then again I didn't know half of what Geoffrey Turner did was possible. He was like a giant steel safe with no combination, and it was starting to bug me.

"Oh good, you're up," came Jason's voice from the seat next to me. "Don't worry, your friends are outside. I needed a moment alone with you."

I sighed and ran my hand through my hair. Tangle city. I'd deal with that later. At least I was in a hospital gown and bathed. Small favors. "I should tell everyone what happened all at once." I really didn't want to repeat everything twice.

"That's fine. I want this to be between you and me." Jason was very serious.

"Okay. Weird. What is it?" He was kind of freaking me out.

"I don't know if I can protect you. I'm doing the best I can, but

Turner seems way more determined to kill you than I originally thought. I mean he had a *serial killer* kidnap you! And you're his granddaughter. I can't seem to wrap my mind around that."

"You and me both."

Although I was feeling about a bagillion percent better, Brady lurked in the shadows of my brain like a deadly stalker. And I realized that Jason blamed himself. For everything. "You know, Jason, none of this is your fault."

"Yes, it is. It's *all* my fault. If I wasn't so damned arrogant giving you my contact info at the tornado site you never would have called me and you never would have been at the virtual bar and you never would have…"

"Jason," I interrupted his guilt-ridden rampage. "Once he saw me on holo my fate was sealed. He's not stopping until I'm dead, everyone else that's with me is just in the way in his eyes. Listen, I don't blame you for anything, in fact, I thank you for helping me, anyone else would have ran by now and I really appreciate you sticking around and helping me see this through, okay?" I meant it. Without Jason I would have really been screwed. Then I thought about it a moment and a sudden flash of insight came to me in a rush. This wasn't about me. He just wanted to make sure he knew how I felt about him. "What is this really about anyway?"

Jason's eyes widened as if he weren't expecting me to call him out on his crap. "What do you mean? I…" He placed his hand over his face in exasperation. "Who am I kidding? Nancy hates me and I don't know what to do about it."

I knew something was up with them! "Trust me, she doesn't hate you."

"A lot has happened since you were taken. I think Nancy is with Bill now," he admitted miserably.

I wanted to roll my eyes and slap him silly. "Bill? Really? You're a hundred years old and you still can't tell when a girl is trying to make you jealous, moron!"

"You think? Because if that's the case, it completely worked. I can't see straight I'm so crazy." Jason was as gloomy as I'd ever seen him.

In his moment of vulnerability I remembered why I had a crush on him. He really was cute in a dismal puppy dog kind of way. "Listen, Jason, just tell her exactly what you told me, that you're miserable without her and she'll be yours in a heartbeat."

Jason straightened up in his seat, appalled. "I can't do that. If she knew how I felt she wouldn't be attracted to me anymore. She'd think I was a pathetic loser. Trust me, after a hundred years, this is a universal truth I *know* about women."

"Uuuggghhh! You're such an idiot." I really did roll my eyes then. "Fine. She does hate you, and her and Bill make a great couple, so yaaaay!"

His face fell again in anguish.

Jason was exasperating, and if he didn't have the balls to tell Nancy he liked her, he didn't deserve her.

There was a knock at the door.

"Wait, don't call them in. I need more advice," Jason started.

"COME IN!" I yelled across the room.

Let Jason deal with his issues with Nancy head on. I knew he just wanted me to tell Nancy he liked her anyway. That was the real purpose of our conversation. Jason sure hadn't developed past the grade school level of relationships yet in life.

Nancy, Bill and Ryan came into the room with concerned smiles on their faces. I wanted to jump out of my bed and give them a group hug, but I was still feeling exhausted from my experience with Brady. And the dream made me not want to go back to sleep again, so I was stuck being tired and wanting to stay awake all at the same time.

Nancy barely glanced at Jason as she came to my side. She really was mad at him. Jason tried to hide his disappointment, but now that I knew how he felt it was easier for me to see his despair. Bill seemed indifferent to all of it and kept his eyes on me. His goofy smile made me feel happy he was there.

Ryan was instantly at my side. He pulled up a chair and held my hand. "How are you feeling?"

"Better." And I told them everything that had happened to me. From the drugs, to the worm, to the cockroaches, to Larry, to making Brady's victims attack him. They all sat in stilled silence, listening to me as if they were hearing a campfire story of horror and mayhem and not actually something that *really* happened.

"They didn't find a holo-cam in his basement. That means Turner has it. He'll have his team scour that footage to see everything you did." Jason was the first to break the quiet. "You're an amazing girl." Jason looked at me with awe and I noticed the same look in the eyes of Nancy, Bill and Ryan as well.

"I don't feel amazing." Their attention made me feel awkward. It was pure survival instinct down there and more than that, it was desperation. I was so terrified, in the dark…

"Well, you are, so don't argue." Ryan reached over and kissed my forehead. "Turner isn't going to stop. Making Chelsan famous only gives us a few weeks max. People will forget and when they do, Turner will strike again."

"It's personal now." Bill nodded in agreement with Ryan.

"It was always personal," Nancy said with genuine fear. "He holds you responsible for your father's death, and now you've made a fool of him more than once. Someone like him will *never* let that slide."

She was right. "He wants me dead so he can control me. The public wouldn't know any different. He could attack tomorrow or now and it wouldn't mean anything. Being famous won't protect me. We're not safe." They needed to hear the truth. Jason's bold plan of keeping me in the lime light meant absolutely nothing. Turner could care less if I was dead because then he'd have all the control. It was preferable.

Jason looked miserable.

In fact, all of them had a kind of helplessness about them.

"I don't mean to bring everyone down, but these are the facts. Turner is after me. He wants me to be his corpse puppet. The only way to stop that from happening, is to stop *him*." I realized I was the leader of this pack and I needed to take the reigns of control.

Jason's eyes lit up. "Then that's what we need to do."

CHAPTER 6
SUNDAY SEPTEMBER 26, 2320

We talked out our plan late into the night until we all had to sleep. Everyone crashed at the hospital. I could tell it was because they were worried Turner would try something, but they all said they wanted to get an early start on our mission.

When I woke up it was about seven in the morning and everyone in the room was sleeping and snoring. Bill's parents made sure they all had beds brought in so no one would be sleeping in chairs or on the floor. His parents made large donations to this particular hospital, so the staff was very obliging. Someday, I would finally meet Bill's parents and thank them profusely for everything they had done for me.

I had a moment of serene contentment watching everyone sleep. Up until a couple of weeks ago the only person I was *sure* that loved me was my mom. Nancy and Bill were my close friends before, but now they had proven themselves to be much more than that. And Ryan had a crush on me! Ever since last year! That still made my mind reel. I was so sure he thought I was a freak, but come to find out he felt the same way about me as I did about him. Jason was the biggest surprise. A reporter who was as famous as could be and whose holo-pics I had plastered on my wall ended up being my champion and partner.

This was the gang.

And they would either be in my life forever or I would be the means of their destruction. I hated thinking that way. I already felt responsible for my mother and father's death, I didn't want to be responsible for getting my friends killed as well. I knew it was wrong to keep them involved in all this, but I needed them, selfish as it was, I wasn't willing to let them go. I also knew that if I tried to cut them off again they would just find me and scream at me for trying to. They were here for good. No matter what that meant for their well-being or their safety.

Jason was the first to wake up. I saw him glance over at Nancy briefly. That boy was so far gone it was almost funny, but I knew what it was like to have a crush on someone and live with the possibility that they could care less about you. I was lucky. Ryan turned out to like me back. According to Nancy, more than that actually… Aaack! This was the last thing I should be thinking about! I needed to focus on the task at hand.

We had a plan.

And the plan was simple.

We were going to break into Geoffrey Turner's headquarters.

Even thinking it made my stomach turn.

With the help of Bill and Jason's connections we'd arrive in two groups (we figured two groups were better than one, just in case one of us failed). Bill's group was the "tourists," it consisted of me, Ryan, Bill and Nancy. Like all places of power, there were tours of the facility open to the public daily. Jason would use his *reporter* card and enter the building that way.

Our goal: To find the real footage of what happened at my trailer park. If we could expose the exterminators, maybe we could take Turner down and put him behind bars.

Slowly, everyone started to wake up. Ryan was completely adorable as he yawned and smiled at me. I wanted to crawl up next to him and have him hold me all day.

As if reading my mind, Ryan came over to me and crawled into my bed. "How are you feeling?" he whispered in my ear. I wish he wouldn't do that. It made my brain flutter.

"Better now," I said.

"Except he's lying on your I.V. which can't be good," Bill grunted from the other side of the room.

"Whoa! Sorry!" Ryan immediately jumped out of my bed as if it were on fire.

Ah, man. Bill!

"You have to take it out anyway. I'll get the nurse in here." Nancy punched Bill's arm on the way out and Bill looked slightly ashamed, but not enough for my taste. I'd say the ratio of guilt to satisfaction was a good 2 to 10.

Ryan didn't seem to notice. He was so upset that he might have hurt me. "I didn't give it air bubbles, did I?"

"Don't be paranoid." Jason made a familiar expression on his face. I was beginning to recognize its meaning. It was the, *I'm with a bunch of kids,* expression.

Nancy came back with the Nurse.

"You ready to leave?" The Nurse talked to me as if I was twelve-years-old.

"Yeah," I replied with as little attitude as possible.

The Nurse didn't even care if I had said *yes* or not as she walked over to me and pulled out the I.V.

She handed me a hospital electronic reader. "Thumbprint there and there and you'll be all set."

I thumbprinted in the places she told me to and the screen flashed green.

"Okay. You're good to go. I'll have some nurses take these beds away, don't you worry about it." She directed her *over-kindness* towards Bill who awkwardly smiled at her.

"Thanks," I said, then a thought hit me. "How is Doris Hornbacher?"

"She's just fine. On the news today." The Nurse grabbed a remote and turned on the holo-tv. Doris stood in front of the press, all fire and passion, talking about her mission to take down Brady Johnson. They showed a clip of Brady being taken to prison and my breath caught in my throat. My dream was real. Turner had killed Brady and now he was under his control. Brady's black swirling chasm taunted me through his holographic image.

"Good old, Doris. She's really taking to the limelight." Jason smiled in spite of himself.

Nancy had her arms crossed and purposely ignored him.

The nurse didn't. She smiled the most flirtatious smile she could. "She doesn't look as good as you do, Mr. Keroff."

"You haven't known him long enough," Nancy practically guffawed.

Jason played it as cool as a cat and ignored Nancy's barb. He smiled at the nurse and kissed her hand in farewell. "Thanks for watching."

Vomit.

This was Nancy's cue to roll her eyes at me and we could share a moment of disgust for Jason's cheesiness, but Nancy was livid. Her eyes bulged and she looked like she wanted to punch Jason in the face. She grabbed Bill's hand and dragged him toward the door. "Come on, Bill, let's MAKE OUT!" And they were gone.

The nurse was oblivious to it all, she was still enamored with Jason. "Call me." And she left as well.

Jason's face was riddled with misery and Ryan couldn't hide his enjoyment at the whole situation.

"I don't mean to be the interrupter of high school drama here, but we have another snag." I told Jason and Ryan about my dream with Turner and Brady.

"I've heard about astral projection. Another one of Turner's experiments. From everything I know it should be harmless, just a way of communicating," Jason shared with thoughtfulness. "It works both ways though. If we could get into his dreams… let me research it some more."

"We better find Nancy and Bill," Ryan said through a grin of amusement. "I hope they're not in the supply closet again."

I elbowed Ryan playfully. He was having way too much fun making Jason squirm. He knew as well as I did that nothing was going on between Nancy and Bill, but he liked watching Jason turn into Hamlet every time he mentioned the two of them together.

Nancy told me everything that happened in my absence before we went to bed last night. I guess as soon as they discovered I was gone, Ryan went on a rampage. I was relieved to hear that no one thought I had run away again, but everyone's first thought was that Turner had me somewhere himself. So, unfortunately, all the searching went into

Turner's holdings and properties and where the most likely place he'd take me would be. By the time Ryan remembered my shoes with the tracking device he had implanted inside, Brady had already destroyed them. They were flying blind and completely destitute.

Ryan and Bill went out everyday trying to find any sign of where I might be, but it was like looking for a specific grain of sand on a beach.

Nancy and Jason undertook the other approach of searching the net and following Turner like a hawk to see where he was going at all times. They even checked out a few places they thought might be likely candidates for where he was holding me, but it always ended up being a dead end.

According to Nancy the first few days of working together were *brilliant*. She said Jason was so polite and sweet, he even held her hand. In fact, that was how the whole mess started. When he held her hand, Nancy took that as a cue and tried to kiss him. Jason, apparently, freaked out and said she was far too young for him and that he saw her as a younger sister. Nancy was embarrassed and furious. (I would be too. It was *obvious* to anyone that had eyes that Jason was head over heels for the girl.) So, she decided to test the *little sister* theory and flirted as hard as she could with Bill. (She informed Bill of what she was doing beforehand and he became a willing participant. I think he liked the attention.)

At first, Jason didn't seem bothered by their flirting, but when Nancy planted one on Bill, Jason stood up and left the room. Nancy confided that she felt completely vindicated by his reaction, but when he came back, he acted as if everything was fine and even patted Bill on the back and wished the couple good luck. Good luck? For a hundred year old, he sure was acting like an immature idiot. But then again, he was a lab man for most of his life and being a famous reporter was still fairly new to him. I'd cut him some slack if it wasn't Nancy he was screwing with.

Ryan stayed out of the entire mess according to Nancy. She said he could care less about anything that didn't involve me. Apparently, he even slipped and said he loved me. (This made my heart leap all over again.) Everyone was upset and searching for me like mad, but Ryan was on a whole other level of torture. Since he was the last to see me, he felt as if it was his fault that I was taken. He kept on saying that he should have gone into the room with me and then it never would have happened. I somehow doubted that, and I made sure I told him that I didn't blame him one bit all last night.

So as things stood now, Jason had to live with the torture that Nancy may have moved on, and Nancy had to deal with the torture that… well… that was Jason Keroff. I didn't envy either one of them!

Poor Bill was the pawn in the middle, but he seemed to enjoy being the guy that made Jason jealous. Maybe it was some perverse way of dealing with his own jealously toward Ryan and me.

We left the hospital in two hovers. Nancy, Ryan, Bill and I in Bill's and Jason in his own.

The drive over to Turner's headquarters was uneventful except for the three tirades about Jason and his moronic behavior from Nancy. We just let her vent. I was sure similar conversations were going on in Jason's head.

Turner's headquarters was fifty miles outside of Los Angeles. Its official title was "Population Control Center and Research." I know, very fancy, but the facility was HUGE! As we came within view of the building I realized why there were tours of this place. It was a spectacle unto itself. It looked as if someone took a handful of white crystals and placed them in the middle of a red maple forest. It was truly breathtaking. On closer inspection the building itself was made of a white metal that was shaped in every way imaginable from jagged spirals, to three-hundred foot cylinders, to different sized pyramids, to plain square boxes with no windows or doors to be seen. It was a big jumbly mess of shapes and sizes taking up a good square mile of space and that was just the surface. Jason told us that there was an entire underground department that was twice as big (underground equaled the *research* part of the building).

The ego on my grandpa was just starting to sink in. He really felt like he was untouchable. To have such a fortress that you allowed the general public into everyday was almost like rubbing his power in everyone's faces. And the crazy architecture to boot felt like an extension of Turner's twisted mind.

"The metal is used as a transmitter, look at the four corners of the space, their design is old school. Probably to protect information flow." Ryan pointed to the latticed metal towers at each corner of the building. They looked like mini Eiffel towers, but I had no idea what he was talking about.

"What do you mean?" I asked, genuinely curious.

"The building is used to determine what information goes in and what information goes out, but in the case of your grandpa I'm assuming, it's the *what goes out* that matters to him," Ryan surmised. He was so cute when he was thinking.

"Is that common knowledge, I.Q. boy? Will Jason know?" Nancy asked, a little too pointedly. Jason was obviously still on her mind.

"Probably not. The technology is old, like three-hundred-years-old. It hasn't been used since the early two-thousands. I did a history paper on it sophomore year and Mr. Gratsby thought I made it up. It wouldn't surprise me if Turner took it out of the school curriculum hundreds of years ago so he could hide it in plain sight," Ryan surmised.

"Another point on the agenda of things to check out." Nancy sighed heavily. I could tell she was growing more nervous by the second.

"We'll be okay." Bill tried to soothe all of us as we reached the public parking area of the building. There were hundreds of people coming for the scheduled tours, which made all of us a little less anxious. We could blend in nicely. "You got the thumbprints?" Bill parked and turned around in his chair to see Ryan.

"Yeah." Ryan pulled out a small rectangular metal box and opened it.

Inside were four ultra-thin thumb-shaped sheets of material. Ryan had been experimenting with making false thumbprints for the last five years and today was the day we were going to try them out. He programmed them to be four people that didn't exist which took a lot of time to create their histories and to fake thumbprint records. The only nice thing was that all four of our aliases were seventeen so he didn't have to make too long of history since you couldn't thumbprint until you were fifteen anyway. Genius.

"I just hope they work," Ryan admitted nervously.

"Let's find out." Bill smiled at Ryan supportively.

I still couldn't figure out their friendship. One minute they were at each other's throats, the next they acted like the best of buds.

Ryan offered the box to me first. "Take that one." He pointed to the one farthest to the left.

I picked it up and it felt like really thin rubber. I placed it on my right thumb and it instantly formed to its contours. After a few seconds it blended so perfectly, I couldn't even see the fake thumbprint at all. "Cool."

Everyone took their respective thumbs and put them on.

"Here we go," Nancy said through a nervous smile.

We exited the car and walked over to the admissions *cavern*, is the word I'd use to describe it. It was like the opening to an ice cave with fake stalactites hanging from an arched fifty-foot entryway. Even the surface of the archway looked like ice and rock, all an illusion to distract people's attention to what was really going on inside the building. A metal fence blocked off the opening to the cave, but directed people to a small booth for entrance.

Bill decided he'd be the first to try out the fake thumbprints. If anything went wrong the rest of us could take off, with Bill's money and station, he'd be able to squirm out of trouble easier than we could.

Bill placed his thumbprint on the scanner.

"Thank you, Mr. Jaloux." The attendant smiled at Bill.

Bill walked through and waved. We all followed closely behind. No flags. No problems.

First hurdle: check.

We entered the cavern, which was pretty realistic even up close. It was as if we entered into the abominable snowman's lair with rubber snow and rocky surfaces. Ryan pointed to one of the stalactites. "Cameras. Keep your head down."

We all did as he said, hoping our faces weren't on some recognition program of Turner's. We couldn't rule anything out, but at the same time what could we do? We couldn't go back. Moving forward was the key. The alternatives were too scary to think about.

At the end of the cavern was a rotating glass door, which led to the waiting area. We walked through and entered into a large square room that was completely yellow. The walls, the furniture, the floor were all some shade of yellow. It was as if the sun puked all over this room. The contrast from the blue and gray cavern to this bright explosion of color was made purely for show. The people entering with us were full of ooohhhs and aaaaahhhs and were beyond excited to see the rest of the building.

"Tours over here, please." A petite woman dressed in a gray jumpsuit waved us over to the back of the room. With her blonde hair and make-up perfectly in order, she looked like a living mannequin. And the smile that was permanently plastered to her face indicated that she had been doing this job way too long. "Make sure you stick together, it's a big place in there, we don't want you to get lost." All her words sounded rehearsed.

We made sure we were in the back of the group so it would be easier to slip away. Ryan had memorized the floor plans of the building, but we still had to take in account that Turner's floor plans were probably hiding a few secrets that we'd have to figure out for ourselves. Hopefully, nothing that would sound alarms of any sort, but like I said, we had to keep going. Eventually, Jason would join us, we'd steal the tornado footage, go back to our tour and leave without anyone knowing we were here. Famous last words. I just hoped this time it really would be that easy. For once. Please?

"Through this door, ladies and gentlemen." Our guide pressed a button and a door slid open for us to enter.

There were about thirty other tourists in our group and, in awe, they all walked through the doorway. I pretended to do likewise while at the same time keeping my head down.

The long hallway we walked into was made entirely of black metal and lit with tiny runner lights on the floor and ceiling. It felt like yet another slap to our senses. There had to be some rhyme or reason to all these extreme décor decisions. From what I had learned so far of my grandpa, a lot of research probably went into the psychological effects of color and lighting. I found it interesting, whereas the general public seemed genuinely amazed.

"After this hallway should be the main assembly hall. We can take the south exit to get to the holo vaults," Ryan whispered to me and I nodded.

"Unless Jason gets there first," I reminded him. We might not have to split from the group at all if we received a text from Jason that he already had the footage. We weren't sure if Jason could access the vault. He was going to claim that he needed the holos from his newscast on virtual reality bars and that his news station erased it by accident. (Turner's headquarters had pretty much *all* the holo-footage in existence.)

Supposedly reporters did it all the time, but we weren't sure if the footage we were looking for would even be stored there. If we didn't get Jason's text, we were going to try to get the holo ourselves and wait for Jason there. All good in theory, but we had no idea what security was going to be like. Probably high, but we didn't have any other choice. It was either do something pro-active or wait around for Turner's next attempt on my life. No thank you.

Our hostess turned to the group and began walking backwards while motioning to the strip lighting and metal walls, "This hallway is made with a special type of metal used specifically for transmission waves. All of Population Control's information is sent through hallways like these throughout the entire facility." Then she winked at a little girl as if sharing a joke. "We can't see it, of course, but even as we walk, billions of messages and transmissions are flowing along side us. Think of these hallways as veins and the information traveling through them are the blood cells of life."

Nancy couldn't help but roll her eyes. "Is she for real?"

The door at the end of the hallway slid open on cue and our tour guide didn't even have to turn around. She walked backward with an ease that was actually a little frightening, and waved us into the monstrous assembly hall.

Four walls, a set of ivory pillars and marble staircases lining each. The theme of this room was smooth marble stone. It felt like entering into Ancient Greece but with air-conditioning. There were stone statues and benches throughout the room. It was almost as if we were in an old graveyard. The more I thought about it, there had to be some kind of sense to all this architecture madness, each room so different from the next, but aside from reading Turner's mind, we were only guessing.

Several of the people in our tour were gawking over the statues. Nancy and Bill made some private joke and Ryan carefully examined every inch of the room. He leaned into my ear, "Back there, behind that faun looking thing."

The door.

Our exit.

We were pretty far from our escape, but our tour guide was at least herding us in the right direction. I nodded to Nancy and Bill and they stayed close behind us, letting Ryan take the lead. My grip on Ryan's hand tightened and he squeezed back reassuringly. I was so happy I wasn't alone in this. After my experience with Brady I found that I never wanted to be by myself *ever* again. I knew that would change over time, but honestly, the thought of being alone terrified me at the moment. Although, getting caught in my grandpa's headquarters was quickly rounding off the top of the fear factor list.

"Any word from Jason?" Nancy whispered behind me.

I shook my head.

We were going to do this.

"I hope he's okay," I heard her mumble under her breath.

The guide veered us away from our escape door and on to the next part of the tour.

"Now." Ryan pulled me behind a particularly large statue of a naked guy and Bill and Nancy followed. "Cameras on the left wall." As long as we couldn't see it, it couldn't see us. "Don't run, walk casually as if we were still on tour. We don't want to cause any alarm and running would be an instant red flag."

We all nodded and walked as relaxed as possible to the next statue. One more to go and then our exit.

Last statue. No problem.

Ryan smiled at me, a little excited. I smiled back though the last thing I felt was excitement.

"You guys ready?" I turned to Nancy and Bill.

They held hands as well and nodded.

"Please don't let that door have a siren," Bill said even though Ryan had assured him about fifty times before we even entered the building that according to the plans the door was for maintenance and had no alarms attached to it. I think this was another case of Bill trying to undermine Ryan.

Ryan's response was to ignore him, reach over and open the door.

No alarms.

Ryan raised his eyebrow at Bill triumphantly and held the door for all of us to walk through. Bill tried to appear as innocent as possible to me and I gave him an encouraging nod. He was putting himself on the line for me and any conflict he had with Ryan was between him and

Ryan. I didn't want to have anything to do with it (although according to Nancy the only conflict they had was *me*, but I was ignoring that for the time being).

We walked through and Ryan shut the door behind us.

Finally, this place looked like a regular building! We were in a hallway painted plain white with cheesy holo-pics of daisy fields and sailboats on its walls.

No cameras.

That we could see anyway.

"There should be a door up here to the right." Ryan guided us forward. It amazed me that Ryan memorized the entire floor plan. No wonder Turner wanted his brain. He must have known Ryan's potential and wanted it all for himself. It scared me to think of how many kids were taken by Turner.

Sure enough the door was exactly where Ryan had indicated. He opened it and a gust of hot air blew in our faces. Once we entered the next room we stood on a metal grated walkway of a four-story labyrinth of stairways and platforms. Sporadically, a worker would enter from a doorway, walk up or down a flight of steps and enter another door. It felt almost factory-like with worker bees going to and from their destinations.

"Second doorway down on the opposite side." Ryan led me with his hand and Bill and Nancy followed.

We tried to hide the clank clank clanking of our footsteps, not wanting to draw any unnecessary attention to ourselves. So far no one was paying any attention to us, which didn't exactly put my mind at ease. It felt odd that we were able to walk freely through all these rooms. On one hand, this building was a public building and hundreds of strangers came through here every day, but on the other hand, it was my grandfather's headquarters and I *knew* what kind of a man he was which meant bad things were most likely happening here. Bad things that he wouldn't want the public to know.

We reached the door and Ryan pulled it open.

There were people everywhere!

It reminded me of the hallways at school, hundreds of workers moving in both directions trying to reach their respective destinations.

Ryan took us to the left and we entered the fray as if we belonged there. No one cared. No one noticed. Talk about zombies, but so far no spinning black holes here. Though after seeing that Turner's staff was dead I was expecting a few at least. The thought honestly scared me a bit. After my last encounter with Grandpa's staff, I was worried that I wouldn't be able to break through their wall of protection around their black centers. I did it once, but it was under the threat of death and I wasn't sure if I could do it again.

Another fear was that even if I *was* able to do it again, would Turner be alerted somehow? I just didn't know enough about my power to know any of the consequences of using it. It was all so confusing to me.

We shuffled along until Ryan took us through another door. It was another four-story metal melee of catwalks and staircases.

"We're deep in the underbelly now," Bill said almost to himself. Most of his excitement for adventure had been replaced by stress.

"The holo-footage vault is down three flights. We're almost there." Ryan tried to be re-assuring.

"Has Jason texted you yet?" Nancy asked.

"No," I answered softly. I could tell she was trying not to show how concerned she actually was about Jason. Like it or not, the girl was hooked.

The four of us went down the metal steps and finally arrived at our destination door.

"It's through here. I'm not sure what we're looking for, but we'll have to be quick," Ryan told us all.

"Let's do it," Bill said, followed by a deep breath to steady himself.

Ryan opened the door.

Crap.

The room was shelf upon shelf upon shelf of holo-storage. It was intimidating. Each row was almost five-hundred feet long and had millions, maybe billions, of data slots on each side, and there were hundreds and hundreds of rows. There was *no way* we'd be able to find the holo-footage of my trailer park. I didn't even know where to start.

We entered the room, all of us with the same beleaguered expressions. There was no one to be found anywhere and no cameras. I was beginning to think that if there were holo-cams we just couldn't see them. I couldn't imagine a place like this not having visual security, but maybe Turner was that cocky. I hoped so, but I somehow doubted it.

"Um," I said out loud.

"Yeah, *um*, sums it up." Nancy shook her head. "Please tell me *Genius Boy* has some clue as to how we're going to find this footage."

"Give me a sec. Let me think this through." Ryan let go of my hand and walked over to one of the storage shelves. He ran his hand down the side and examined it every which way.

"You mean this footage?" With an overconfident smirk and holding a small metal chip, Jason stepped out from one of the rows of storage.

When Nancy saw him she forgot all caution and threw her arms around him in a great sigh of relief. "I was so worried, you jerk!" She kissed him quickly on the lips and Jason's arrogant stature turned into dumbstruck slush in about a split second.

"Hi," Jason said lamely.

"Hi." Nancy pulled away and gave him a small smile.

"You found it? In this mess?" I asked. My heart sang with relief.

"I know holo-storage like the back of my hand." Jason was starting to get his swagger back. "But we better get out of here before they realize the footage I took is not the footage I checked out." Jason tucked the metal chip in his shirt pocket. "I can't leave the way I came. They'll scan the chip and I won't be able to leave with it. I hope you have an alternate route?" He raised an eyebrow to Ryan.

"Yeah. Of course." Ryan took us through the door we came in. Hopefully, we could catch up to our tour and no one would ever be the wiser.

"Why didn't you text us if you had the footage?" Nancy, for the moment, was still being nice to Jason though one wrong word from him and he'd be back in the doghouse.

"Like I said, I needed an alternate way out. I knew Ryan would get you guys safely to the storage facility. I just had to wait." Jason tried not to make eye contact with Nancy. He was obviously still struggling with how he felt about her.

Nancy picked up on it immediately. "You're such a baby, really!"

"Guys. Not now." Bill sounded like a dad quieting his rowdy kids.

It worked. Both Nancy and Jason kept their mouths closed as Ryan led us through the grated metal maze.

We were on the bottom floor of the four-story room, making our way up to the top floor.

Nancy pulled me back against the wall. She motioned for the others to follow.

"What?" Ryan whispered.

Nancy pointed upward. "Jill's dad," she answered as quietly as possible.

Oh boy.

Jill's dad, Owen Forester, was Turner's number one man. I had never seen him before and I admit I was curious to see the man who created the monster that was Jill. What kind of a man would take orders from someone like my grandfather and do the things he most likely had to do in his name? I had to see him. It was becoming a craving I couldn't control. It was almost like if I could see Jill's dad, I could see why Jill was the way she was. Just a peek.

I poked my head out slightly to see.

Owen Forester's spinning black chasm almost winked at me in greeting.

Even though I didn't want to, I suddenly felt a pang of sympathy for Jill. How long had her father been dead? Constantly vying for daddy's approval, but never getting it because he wasn't alive anymore. It didn't excuse her being the *nasty* that she was, but it did give some reasoning behind it.

I was about to tell everyone about Mr. Forester's condition when I caught a glimpse of Turner joining him on the causeway.

"Door?" Jason mouthed to Ryan.

Ryan shook his head and pointed up one flight of stairs.

"We're screwed." Nancy leaned against the wall in frustration.

"Of all the staircases in this monstrous building, they had to come to ours," I groaned.

It felt very fishy to me. Especially since it didn't look like they were going anywhere anytime soon. Yet at the same time they made no show of acknowledging our presence. They were just talking, or Turner was anyway, zombie-man was probably just listening to orders.

It made me think of how Turner kept these corpses animated. It was obviously a different process than mine because he looked genuinely shocked when I grabbed control of his staff. Some kind of spell, but what were the results of the spell? Did the dead people retain all their memories and sense of self? Were they simply puppets like mine were? *Or* were they truly back from the dead under Gramps's spell? Whatever it was, it was some serious mojo.

Turner almost gained control back over his corpses by rolling his eyes and spouting out his power words. And what was up with all the eye color changes? First, in my mother's vision with Grandma, then with Grandpa, was that a part of the spell? Brady told me my eyes dilated when I activated the cockroach. Was there some connection there? I had so many questions racing through my brain and the only man who could possibly answer them wanted me dead. Good luck with that.

"Are they going to move, or what?" Bill started to sweat. All the pressure, excitement and fear bubbled over in a whirlwind of panic.

I placed my hand on his arm. "We'll be fine."

Bill's shoulders relaxed visibly at my touch. He nodded.

Ryan squeezed my other hand tightly. I could tell he didn't like me comforting Bill very much, but he didn't say anything because he knew Bill needed it. Extra points in my book.

Before we could react, at least a hundred soldiers stepped out of every door from all four stories. All black spinning holes. An army of dead people. And all of them started marching down toward us.

No wonder Turner had been standing there *forever*. He was waiting for us to try and escape to the door on the second floor. His master plan of having his men enter the room and grab us… not working out so well for him. As usual, his impatience overruled his good judgment. Good. Maybe we could escape from this. I tested the men's black centers and they were just like his staff. Walls of resistance like bulletproof vests.

"Did you really think fake thumbprints would work?" Turner's voice echoed off the metal. He sounded amused.

"What do we do now?" Jason asked Ryan. We weren't near any doors, which was most likely why Turner decided to act impulsively.

"We go down." Ryan nodded to the cement floor about ten feet below us. "There's a vent opening that leads to the lower level of the building."

The first of the dead soldiers jumped down to our platform and grabbed Jason's arm.

I took a deep breath and smashed through the invisible barrier like it was made of glass. It was crazy at how easy it was. I was expecting some kind of opposition, but my mind remembered the sensation of ripping through the protective wall. I made the soldier release his grip on Jason. I slammed through all of the soldiers' invisible barricades and connected to their dark chasms of death. I tried to disconnect them from their black holes, but something was stopping me.

"Not this time, little one," Turner's voice boomed from above.

I looked up and his eyes were the same crimson as they were in Principal Weatherby's office. He had more time to plan this time, to figure out how to prevent me from destroying his minions. And apparently it worked because I couldn't disconnect the corpses from their swirling centers.

I'd have to settle for controlling them.

I made them all stop in their tracks.

I could feel the struggle Turner was experiencing trying to make his soldiers move again.

"Maybe you should have researched that a bit more, huh Gramps?"

Turner fumed. He began chanting loudly.

I could feel my grip on the soldiers lessen. They started to twitch with movement.

"I say we jump," I said to Ryan and the others.

It was the first time I noticed them all staring at me.

I realized they had never really seen me in action aside from a dead plant or small insects. Only Jason was slightly unfazed since he was with me at the virtual reality bar, but even he seemed a little dumbfounded.

"Guys, seriously, he's gaining control of them. I don't know how much longer I can keep them disabled." I needed them to snap out of it.

"Right." Ryan grabbed my hand and we jumped to the floor followed by the others.

Ouch.

And oops.

It was just enough of a distraction for Turner to regain control over his boys. They started dropping like super humans to the floor next to us.

Ryan grabbed the vent grating and flung it open. It was another drop, but only about five feet and it looked like a tunnel entrance to the right. "Everyone in!"

Jason didn't need to be told twice, he was the first to hop down.

Nancy huffed in annoyance at Jason's lack of chivalry. "Typical." And she jumped in as well.

One of the soldiers grabbed Bill and put him in a choke hold.

I connected to the soldier's black hole at about half power. Turner somehow blocked me out of the other half, but it was enough for Bill to fight back. He kicked the soldier back into the others and jumped down the vent.

"You next," I instructed Ryan.

"No way is that *ever* going to happen." Ryan said with so much conviction I almost dropped down the vent.

"I can actually slow these guys down, Ryan," I pleaded.

Ryan reluctantly nodded and jumped down to join the others.

The soldiers came at me. I had enough power over them to make them move in slow motion. It was surreal seeing hundreds of soldiers running toward me at a snail's pace as if I was watching an instant re-play on the holo-tv.

I looked up at Turner and our eyes met. Though they were solid red I could still see something I had never seen before in them.

Glee.

I hopped down and joined the others.

Ryan slammed the grating shut.

"Come on. Through here." Ryan wrapped his arm around me for support.

"I'm only half-controlling them. I can't seem to take them over completely. Turner is too strong and knows *way* more about this stuff than I do," I admitted weakly. Connecting to over a hundred bodies was taking its toll on my brain. "He'll send in live ones soon."

As if in unison to my statement I felt Turner release all his soldiers from their black holes, letting them die for real this time, and essentially making them useless to me. The stink was already wafting through the ventilation shaft's opening.

I finally paid attention to where we were. The shaft we jumped down was huge! I was standing and still had about two feet of headroom. A metal tunnel opened before us... dark and foreboding, but our only way out.

"This leads down four more levels. That's where the main power generators are. If we get that far, there's an elevator shaft we can climb up that leads directly to the front gate," Ryan said as bravely as possible, but I could tell he was as nervous as everyone else.

Nancy pulled out a flashlight from her purse with a shrug. "I was hoping we wouldn't need this, but…" She let that hang in the air, not needing to finish the thought, not wanting to. We were in big trouble and none of us knew how we were going to get out of it.

"One thing at a time." I gave Nancy a reassuring look.

"Right," she said, swallowing her fear, but not masking it completely.

Nancy handed Ryan the flashlight and he took the lead. I had a moment where I felt like Larry the cockroach as we made our way through the giant man-sized shaft. Ryan guided us through the maze of twists and turns with ease. Nancy's small flashlight was the only source of light to show the way. So far, we couldn't hear any signs of pursuit, but we knew it was only a matter of time before we did. Jason took up the rear and Nancy, Bill and I were in the middle. I stayed as close as I could to Ryan for his protection and for mine.

"Why didn't Turner just shoot us?" Bill asked, breaking the intense silence.

I hadn't thought of that.

"It would be definitive proof that he could bring the dead back," Jason pondered as if he *had* been thinking about it the whole time. "If we all came back to our families riddled with bullet holes, but alive and well, there would be questions, investigations, you name it. He can't take that kind of press or attention."

"So we can use that to our advantage. Knowing he can't shoot us, he can only kill us with no marks essentially?" Nancy mused out loud then turned to Jason. "You have family?"

Jason ignored her second question. "Let's not kid ourselves. If we cause him too much trouble, he will take us down anyway he can and spin it so that we were somehow attacked by terrorists or something. For now, he wants Chelsan. *Dead* or *alive*, but luckily for us *dead* means he's not using bullets. As for *us* I'm not sure what he's willing to do." Concerned, Jason glanced briefly at Nancy, but when Nancy returned the gaze he looked away.

She grunted in annoyance.

"No alarms either," Bill observed as if he were running through a check list of possible snags.

"No. Maybe he doesn't want any of the tourists to panic or word to get out," Nancy suggested.

"Or maybe he's so confident he'll get us there's no need for alarms." Bill was spiraling and I needed to snap him out of it.

"Let's just get to the main generator room, okay?" I said, turning to look at him.

He nodded once and averted his eyes. I don't think he wanted me to see him scared.

We moved farther down into the bowels of the Population Control's headquarters. Though I knew it was only four floors it felt as if we had gone miles underground. Still, being that we were already three floors down at the start of our mission, seven floors underground was a bit intimidating.

"Up here," Ryan informed us.

When we turned left we could see light looming in the distance through another grate about a hundred feet away. Ryan motioned us to stay while he checked it out. I watched him move slowly to the vent opening and peer out. Ryan's whole body went slack, arms dropped to his side, not moving, as if something had stunned him.

Danger or no, I ran up to him as fast as my legs would carry me. When I approached him he turned to me and his eyes were so full of terror and anger I nearly flinched at the onslaught of emotion glaring at me.

"What is it?" I asked and touched his arm as if that might help him snap out of the nightmare he was obviously in.

Ryan just nodded toward the grate.

I peered through and I understood immediately.

The vent opening was about eight feet above the ground so the entire room was visible. It was the biggest room I had ever seen. Almost as big as the hangers that held the skyscraper-sized hover-trucks from Clean-Up.

It was exactly as Ryan described to me that morning before school.

This was the place he had been taken all those years ago by Turner.

An I.Q. Farm.

Hundreds of kids at computer stations, virtual reality mats, holo-games, all focused and ignorant to everyone around them. It was a frightening spectacle watching these hunched, hollow-eyed children working on their invisible projects. I pulled Ryan in closer and he hugged me with all of his might. I could feel his emotions pouring into this one embrace. His fear, his sadness, his relief, his anger all jumbled together in a tangled mess. If he hadn't been as quick witted as he was, he would have been one of those kids below.

Ryan pulled away, his eyes clearer. He looked down at the room again. "The main power generators should be at the other end of this room, through that door there."

The others had joined us from behind, not sure of how to react because of Ryan.

"Is this really an I.Q. Farm?" Nancy asked tentatively.

"It's the same one I was taken to. I remember it now," Ryan explained so everyone would know his personal stake in all this.

"Whoa," Bill said softly. I could tell the protective side of him wanted to reach out and give Ryan his support, but the *jealous guy side* of him wouldn't allow it.

Ryan grabbed my hand suddenly.

"What is it?" I asked. His face had gone another shade paler, if that was possible.

"I recognize a few of the kids." Ryan swallowed hard. "They're the same age." Ryan turned to me, eyes wide. "Turner is giving them Age-pro."

We all stood in stunned silence.

Giving Age-pro to kids was an unspeakable act. And it was a double whammy to think that Ryan could have been eight-years-old *forever*. I guess it wasn't a surprise that Turner was capable of such perversion, but it rocked us all just the same.

"They look like they're in comas, it shouldn't be too hard to get past them," Jason observed callously.

Nancy punched him in the arm. "Way to be sensitive, jerk."

"I'm sorry if I don't want to die, but reminiscing on what could have been isn't helping our escape here. Just because there's no alarm doesn't mean they're not after us." Jason rubbed his arm from Nancy's blow.

"He's right," Ryan agreed, though his eyes were still staring at the children below. "This vent is on hinges and swings outward." Ryan reached over and popped the vent opening. "If we move it slowly enough, hopefully no one will see."

I placed both hands on the hinged side of the grate making sure the rate of movement was as slow as possible. Ryan was at the other side and moved the slab of metal as far as he could without falling to the ground below. I clasped my fingers through the metal slats and stopped the grate before it could hit the wall.

None of the kids seemed to notice.

All five of us were now as exposed as could be standing over the entire room like a framed picture.

Jason jumped down first, his patience almost gone. I shouldn't really be surprised. He *did* cry like a baby at the virtual reality bar. Why should being in my grandpa's lair be any different?

Everyone else followed him down, Ryan was the last. It was my turn to be the *comforter* in this relationship and I found that I felt more helpless than I ever did when I was being attacked by Turner's lackeys. What could I possibly do to make Ryan feel better? He was in the very room of his nightmares and it was all because of me. If he had never liked me he would have never had to see or think about this place for the rest of his days. I should have seen this coming. I should have known better. Now Ryan had to face his personal demons, not in a healthy-let's-talk-about-it kind of way, but in an in-your-face-welcome-to-your-own-personal-torture kind of a way.

Yeah. I was a *great* girlfriend.

"The entrance to the generators is on the other side," Ryan informed them quietly and I squeezed his hand supportively. No matter what, I didn't want him to feel alone in all this.

We walked as casually as possible, not wanting any of the children to notice. We didn't even know what they would do if they *did* realize we were there. Would they scream? Would they hit an alarm? Or would they do nothing?

Nothing. It seemed to be the answer for the moment. The kids were so involved in what they were doing I think I could have sat on one of them and they wouldn't care.

Better for us.

Ryan and I in the lead, we were half way across the room when a woman stepped in front of us. She came out of nowhere and I nearly leapt back a few feet from the shock of it. So much so that I didn't even realize who she was until it was too late.

Roberta. My grandma. The Feline.

The last time I saw her was in my mother's vision and a giant snake was coming out of her mouth! If I thought she was scary in a dream, in person she was downright terrifying with her stretched and frozen face. She stared at me with such venom in her eyes I almost expected her to hiss. I wanted to look away. The only reason I didn't was because I was afraid she'd eat me or something. She was taller than I expected, but everything else was the same as Mom's vision. Even her black hair was pulled back in the same tight bun and her skin had that strange plastic shine. Her eyes were so dark and so intense they reminded me of the swirling chasms I saw in the dead.

"Finally! Someone who can help us. We were on our tour and got incredibly lost! Could you tell us how to get back?" Jason came up from the back of the group with a friendly smile, although I could tell seeing a Feline was making him uncomfortable.

I realized then that no one else knew who she was. Only Gramps was on holo-tv. Roberta wouldn't want the world seeing that she was a cat lady. Although, even if she looked like she did when she was twenty, she'd probably still look harsh and nasty. It came from the inside and she didn't even try to disguise it.

Roberta answered Jason in a silent stare that made his smile fade instantaneously.

"We're leaving now," I stated boldly and stepped in front of the group in case she tried anything.

"Oh really?" Roberta smiled wickedly, though nothing else on her face moved. It only added to her creepiness.

"We really did get lost…" Bill tried to back up Jason's story, a little too naïve to realize we faced a foe, and apparently in shock at seeing a Feline in person.

Roberta's eyes turned white as she looked at Bill and he grabbed his throat from pain. Bill bent over coughing uncontrollably, his face turning red, eyes bugging out from lack of breath.

Don't mess with my friends.

I punched her in the nose.

Pretty hard, too, because she actually took a few steps back from the hit.

But it worked.

Bill stopped coughing and rubbed his throat in the aftermath.

They all knew they faced real danger now.

I didn't want to look at them. I didn't want to see the fear in their eyes. I kept my attention on Roberta.

She was livid. She took a step toward me and slapped me hard on the cheek.

That whole side of my face tingled from the blow, but I didn't let my eyes leave hers.

"How dare you!" Roberta hissed at me.

"Get out of our way," I hissed back.

"Just like your mother," she accused malevolently.

"Thank you." I couldn't help but truly hate this woman standing in front of me. How could someone like my father come from two of the most despicable human beings on the planet? There was nothing nice about her. Not even an inkling. Not even a shred.

"Geoffrey told me about you. Told me how much like your mother you were. How stupid and filthy you were. Now I can see you are so much worse," Roberta spat.

"Thank you," I repeated, not wanting to give her an ounce of a response.

Roberta's monstrous face grimaced and she narrowed her eyes. "Geoffrey and I tried for two-hundred years to have a baby and we finally had Franklin, a beautiful, wonderful, brilliant boy. I nearly died during his birth and it scarred me so I couldn't have any more children. He was perfect for a hundred years until he met your mother!"

Roberta's eyes rolled back again, but I was on top of this trick now. I slapped her and her concentration was broken. She shrieked in rage, sounding more animal than human.

"You killed my only son and you *will* die for that," Roberta rasped from being jolted out of her spellcasting.

"Like I told Gramps, *you* killed your own son and took away my only chance at a normal life. So, I'd be watching your back if I were you." I was livid. No matter what I did I couldn't seem to calm down.

Roberta didn't seem to hear, as if what I had to say meant nothing to her. Or everything, and she didn't want to listen.

"These are my children now." Roberta motioned to the room. "Some of them for almost two-hundred years." It was the first time I had seen anything other than loathsome hate from her.

She finally noticed Ryan standing next to me. "Ryan," she said and there was genuine love in her eyes. "You've come back."

Okay. She was nuts. A grotesque caricature of a human being.

Ryan was frozen. I hadn't realized it until now. He recognized her from the start. She must have been involved in his kidnapping and it was all bubbling to the surface upon seeing her.

Roberta turned back to me with malice. "You've taken another one of my children. He'll be mine again soon. The guards are on their way. Ryan will live, the rest of you won't." She said it so matter-of-factly it was worse than when she performed her Voodoo eye stuff.

BAM!

Roberta dropped to the floor with a thud.

Nancy stood behind her with a metal chair in her hands and a look of pure rage. "I was tired of listening to that cat bitch." She turned to Ryan. "Can we get out of here now?"

Ryan broke out of his trance. "Yeah," he spoke quietly and started at a run to the other side of the room. All pretenses were down. No more trying to blend. If the guards were on their way then the kids freaking out wouldn't matter anyway. The creepy part was, the children didn't budge. None of what just happened, the yelling, the whacking, fazed them for a second. They continued their drone-like behavior uninterrupted.

The guards busted through from the side and middle entrances of the room. They carried stun clubs and among the comatose kids we were easy to spot. Not one of them dead. Turner was leading the charge and our eyes met. Then I did what I knew was a horrible thing to do, but I couldn't help myself. I glanced over at the still form of Roberta and then back at him. It worked. He followed my gaze and saw the crumpled form of his wife in the middle of the room. He howled in rage and screamed at his men to capture us at all costs.

We were all at a full sprint now, following Ryan like frenzied rabbits running from the wolves. I hoped he knew where he was going. It would be just my luck if this were the one time he had the directions wrong. Ryan reached the elusive door first and swung it open with his full might. And sure enough the room inside was filled with hundreds of twenty-foot fuel cell generators and a set of elevator doors on the far wall. After everyone was inside, Bill and Nancy slammed the door shut and set the bolt lock.

"That's gonna hold them for about ten seconds." Nancy managed a small worried glance in my direction.

As if hearing Nancy, the pounding on the door began. The hinges were already starting to squeak from the amount of force being applied.

Ryan was halfway across the room, heading for the elevator doors. We all followed in a huddled pack finding it hard to keep up with him. Roberta spooked Ryan more than I realized. Maybe it was because of the way she looked at him after so many years. Whatever it was, Ryan wanted out, and he wanted out *now.*

I reached the elevator doors with the others.

BOOM!

The guards broke down the door and were pouring through in waves of uniformed gray, heading straight for us.

"Get to the other end." Ryan nodded to Bill.

Bill and Ryan pulled open the elevator doors with some exertion. We were going to have to climb, taking the elevator would be too risky. Turner could radio for a shut down and we'd be sitting ducks.

"Move. Move. Move," Bill yelled through gritted teeth.

I didn't need to be told twice let alone three times. I ran through the pried open doors and into the shaft. A security ladder leading all the way to the top was on my right. Just like Ryan had said. Thank goodness for his brain. I made Jason and Nancy start the climb first. I intended to go last.

Bill and Ryan counted to three and leapt inside the elevator shaft.

One of the guards that was way ahead of the others shoved his arm in between the doors, stun club flailing, just before they closed. I knew within seconds they'd have the doors open and we'd be gonners, so I grabbed his club and whacked his arm with it. His hand and arm went limp and Ryan and I stuffed it through the door as the rest of the guards arrived at the scene.

Bill started up the ladder behind Nancy and Jason.

Ryan turned to me. "We're not going to make it."

"Go! I have a plan to stall them. I'll be right behind you!" I said and shoved him toward the ladder. I had no such plan, but I didn't want Ryan to suffer for my sake. All of this was my fault and I couldn't live with myself if anything happened to my friends. Not if I could do something about it.

The guards clasped on to each door, trying to pry the doors open like Ryan and Bill had.

Ryan reluctantly started up the ladder, keeping his eyes on me the entire time.

I glanced at him briefly and smiled. "I'll be okay. Hurry."

Ryan shook his head and stopped mid-rung. "No. I'm not leaving you." He jumped back down and joined my side. "What's the plan?"

"Ryan!" I shouted, not wanting to admit that I, in fact, still did not have a plan.

"If we go down, we go down together. I'm not going to abandon you like I did last year." Ryan kissed me quickly and even with the doors being lodged open to our doom, my stomach still did the proper flip flopping.

"I appreciate you feeling guilty about ignoring me in school, but we could die here." I gave him my serious face though I secretly wanted him to stay right where he was.

The doors were almost open and we could see the hundreds of soldiers ready to pounce on us. Luckily for us the soldiers were trying so hard to get through they were stacked on top of each other making a traffic jam at the doors.

Okay. Maybe we should have tried to make a run for it. I looked up at Nancy, Bill and Jason. They weren't that far away. If I didn't do something fast, we'd all be screwed.

I concentrated. How sad was it that I was wishing and hoping for *any* kind of dead thing in the vicinity?

Relief flooded through me. Rats. Hundreds of dead rats ranging from newly trapped to been-there-a-while rot. All in the walls. Blek.

I'd be revealing to Turner that it wasn't just people I could bring back, but he may have already found that out from Brady anyway. It was worth the risk. It was our only chance. I hoped these soldiers could scare because rats wouldn't cause any lasting damage. I was about to find out.

"Here goes nothing," I said to Ryan and he gently embraced my hand for support. "I hope you're not afraid of rats."

"Oh man." Ryan took a deep breath preparing for what was to come.

I took one of those myself and just as the first soldier had almost wriggled his way through the crowd I slammed into all the rats I could reach.

I would have loved to see the stampede of rodents racing across the floor. A melee of decomposed corpses to freshly killed, all scraggly, all vicious.

And…. Contact.

I made them attack the guards with all their strength. Running up their bodies, biting any piece of flesh I could find, jumping, leaping, snarling, biting monsters.

Screams of terror filled the air and it made my skin crawl, but I didn't break concentration, I kept the battle of the zombie rats going full force.

SHUUUNK!

The elevator doors smashed shut.

We could still hear the cries of terror through the wall.

"I'll keep the rats on them as long as possible. Let's get out of here," I said and found it awkward to walk over to the ladder and control the rats at the same time. I could feel their tiny teeth tear into the fabric of the soldiers' uniforms. I wanted to keep them occupied, but I didn't want to do any serious damage. The soldiers were only doing their jobs even if they were working for pure evil.

Ryan and I started our long climb up, me in front, Ryan in back. After doing the math, we had to climb about ten stories. I hoped I could keep the rodent onslaught going that long.

The elevator whizzed up and down next to us giving a little extra cover just in case the guards decided they wanted to fight with rat corpses as their new uniform.

I tried to pin point Turner's location, give him an extra bite or two in the face (see how he explains that on holo), but I couldn't differentiate between the men down below. I could only see the tiny swirling black masses of the rats. *Just keep them fighting.* It was taking all my energy to climb and control and I was draining fast. We still had eight floors to go and I was breathing heavily like I had already run a marathon.

Up ahead I could barely see Nancy and the others. They were almost to freedom. I needed to give Ryan and I a few more floors before I could let go of my hold on the rats. I just didn't know if I could do it. I had just been released from the hospital! What was I thinking?

"Ryan," I barely croaked out. Wow. I was fading quicker than I thought.

Ryan climbed up beside me faster than I could think. "What is it? Are you okay?" His face was full of concern.

"I'm keeping the connection, but climbing… both… too hard… I don't know if I can make it," I sputtered.

He just nodded. "Climb on my back. You keep the rats up, I'll take *you* up."

I didn't have the strength to argue. I limply crawled onto Ryan, piggy-back style, until I rested comfortably. Much better. It was still a difficult task using all the energy I had left to keep the rodents attacking the soldiers, but manageable. I leaned my head on his shoulder. I knew being six foot three Ryan could easily carry me, but climbing seven more floors with an extra hundred and ten pounds on your back had to take its toll at some point. I did my part. I kept my connection to the rats. And feeling Ryan's muscles expanding and contracting as he climbed up the ladder was somehow more comforting than a hug. Although I could have used one of those, too.

Still no alarms, which I found extremely odd. Turner must truly want to keep everything hidden under the rug. It made me wonder where exactly I was on his priority list. The scope of my grandfather's empire left me breathless. I was just a flea on a Great Dane. How important was I in the grand scheme of things? He could already raise the dead, so aside from a personal vendetta, why did he even care about me? That look in his eyes, in Roberta's eyes. That was my answer, I guess. They were insane with grief and anger and I was the living representation of it all. Although, Roberta looked genuinely crazy, anger or not. Maybe it was her cat-like face, with that frozen rubbery skin. I'm not usually one to judge on how someone looks, but seeing her face up close like that, with the stretching and the shining. Ick.

My eyes felt so heavy... I lost my power over at least half of the rats. I could connect to them, I just couldn't seem to make them move. Hopefully, the little guys I did control could still keep the guards occupied. I glanced up. The others were already on the surface. Ryan was sweating from the exertion of climbing with the weight of two people, but we were only two floors away from freedom.

"Almost there," I heard myself say though it sounded like it came from someone else.

And then my arms slipped from Ryan's neck.

I would have fallen all the way to the bottom if it weren't for Ryan's quick reflexes. He caught my wrist before I plunged to my death.

That woke me up.

I climbed back up to Ryan's back with as much effort as I could muster.

The elevator doors cranked open down below and soldiers began to flow through. They were rodent-free and moving up the ladder faster than I could imagine.

The near fall jolted me out of keeping the rats active, and my exhaustion made me forget to reconnect.

"Don't worry about the rats, just hold on." Ryan began climbing like a mad man.

One more floor.

The first soldier was only two floors away from us. Man they were quick.

I tried to get a good look at the guard closest to us. His clothes were shredded and he was sporting quite a few scratches and bites. He looked severely pissed.

Ryan reached the opened grate. Hands reached down and lifted us to the surface.

"Are you okay?" Nancy was all over me. I must have looked really bad.

I could hear Jason and Bill slamming the grate shut from the outside.

No matter how hard I tried, my eye lids were made of lead. We were on the outskirts of the building about a few hundred feet from the parking lot. "I'm fine. Just tired."

"Not too tired, I hope?"

My eyes flew open from Turner's voice.

We all turned to see my grandpa standing with a few guards. He didn't have one scratch on him! Not even a nibble. He must have escaped as soon as he saw the rats coming. Or something else? I knew so little about my grandpa, his powers, his capabilities, it was frustrating. And worst of all, it was dangerous. Not knowing your opponent could mean fatal consequences.

Turner nodded to one of his soldiers.

The obedient man walked over to the metal grating and opened it for the climbing soldiers to exit. They started to file out one at a time forming a circle around our party. Ryan held me close as if he alone could protect me. The guards from below were shredded from head to toe. Maybe I went a little crazy with the rats. Bill and Nancy on the other hand appeared extremely impressed.

Nancy whispered in my ear with a hint of amazement, "Did you do that?"

I nodded and tried to make myself smile, but it just ended up being some sort of grimace.

Turner walked boldly up to Jason. "Give it to me."

"Give what to you?" Jason smiled that half-smirk that used to be the basis of my crush on him.

"Now." Turner wasn't in the mood for Jason or any of us for that matter.

We weren't going to make it out of here alive.

Jason reached into his shirt pocket and pulled out the holo-chip. He reluctantly handed it over to Turner's aged hands.

"Can't blame a guy for trying," Jason said off-handed.

"Yes, I can." Turner handed the holo-chip to one of his guards. "Search him, make sure he didn't make a switch."

The soldier patted Jason down thoroughly, searching every pocket, nook and cranny on his body. "Nothing."

Turner nodded. "Good. Destroy it."

The guard placed the holo-chip on the ground and used his stun club on it. The holo-chip sparked and fizzled until it went completely dead, a charred black fleck on the cement.

Jason's face stayed in that half-smirk, frozen in time, as if he couldn't decide if it would help or hurt his cause to act scared.

Turner turned to me. "You're free to go."

What?

"What?" I realized I hadn't said that out loud.

"You look exhausted. Get some rest." Turner's face revealed nothing.

What was going on?

"That's it?" I couldn't believe my ears. Maybe I was asleep already and this was all a dream.

"You came here with a mission and you failed. Now go," he stated way too calmly.

We began to walk away toward the parking lot and sure enough the soldiers stepped aside to let us through.

"Wait," came Grandpa's voice from behind.

Here we go.

"You guys get to the car. Don't wait for me," I said and shoved them away.

"Yeah right," Nancy, Bill and Ryan all spoke at once. I did notice that Jason had no arguments.

I turned to face my grandfather.

"Yes?" I asked, waiting for the worst.

"I'll send a car for you tomorrow at Nancy's. Three o'clock. You'll be safe, I assure you. We need to discuss a few… matters." Turner treated me as if we had been colleagues for decades.

And with that, he turned and left with all his guards. They headed toward a private entrance not wanting to draw unnecessary attention to their tattered state. Within seconds Turner was gone. The five of us alone in the parking lot, exactly where we started out at the beginning of this trip.

"Let's get out of here," Jason said with some urgency. I don't think he felt that Turner was on the up and up.

We all walked toward the lot.

"You're not really going to meet him, are you?" Bill asked with a boomingly over-protective tone.

"Yes, I am." I thought I hadn't made up my mind yet, but when asked directly I knew the answer had to be yes. If I didn't settle this with Turner, it would just continue on and on until one or both of us was dead, or worse, someone I cared about. "And don't try and talk me out of it." I knew the protesting would ensue.

"You're way too tired to listen to reason anyway. We'll argue with you tomorrow," Nancy said.

We all arrived at Bill's hover-car.

"Where's your car?" I asked Jason.

"I'm going with you guys. I'll have an intern pick up my car later." Jason replied, and I could tell he was trying to hide some of his fear. "No worries, I'll ride bitch."

No one had the energy to argue. We all piled into the hover-car, Jason sitting between Ryan and I in the back seat. Uggh! I'm sure there was some other way to arrange everyone so we could all be happy, but we were so ready to get out of there no one said anything.

Bill whizzed away from the monstrous structure and it felt as if we were flying away from a funeral. We were all silent. No one wanted to re-live what we had gone through, or maybe they didn't want *me* to have to, and I was grateful. I wanted to lean against Ryan and go to sleep, but Jason separated us. He was fidgeting like a crazy person.

"Would you stop that?" Ryan had apparently had enough of Jason's squirming.

"No. Let's get to Nancy's as fast as this hover-car will hover." Jason's knee wouldn't stop shaking.

Something was up and it wasn't just escaping Turner's grasp. Jason was hiding it from all of us and he wanted to be under the blanket of George's magic-red-orb-of-silence to tell us.

"Sure." Bill read between the same lines I had. We picked up some speed and flew to Nancy's house in no time.

Bill landed the car and George and Vianne came out to greet us.

Jason went straight to George before he could hug his daughter. I stayed close to him, not wanting to miss anything. "Your info-blocker still in tact?"

George was all business. "Had to make a few adjustments, Turner's guys have been trying to break it daily."

Vianne had done all the hugging for George and looked over at Jason and I with curiosity.

"Let's get inside." George nodded to his wife and she nodded back.

We all headed inside Nancy's house.

I grabbed Ryan's hand as we sat down on the couch. I didn't want to be separated from him any longer than I had to. He was becoming a continual source of calm for me lately and I wanted to be the same for him. I could tell seeing those kids really shook him up. His life would have been a comatose state of imprisonment if he hadn't got away. His hand shook slightly and I leaned in close feeling him physically relax. At least I could be some help however small it was.

Jason stayed standing, in fact, he was pacing. This boy needed to calm down!

Bill, Nancy and her parents all took their respective seats and all eyes turned to Jason.

"I have the holo-footage," Jason confessed, his eyes crazed.

"Okay, he's losing it." Nancy was concerned.

"No. I gave Turner a fake holo-chip, well, it wasn't fake, it was some footage I picked up after I stole the tornado footage, but I knew we'd need a decoy, just in case." Jason was babbling out his story now.

"But, they searched you." Bill tried to be the voice of reason to Jason's apparent insanity.

Jason continued to ramble. "They didn't search *inside* of me. I swallowed the chip. It's covering should be enough to protect it from my digestive system, but I need George here to retrieve the data just in case. Nancy's place is the only safe haven we have from Turner, as long as he's in the dark about us having the holo-chip, we could still get it on the air." Jason was excited now.

"You swallowed it?" I asked, as a surge of hope coursed through me. Maybe we could still take Gramps down before he could do any more damage.

"Yup." Jason acted like the cat that ate the canary. And I guess, he actually did.

"So what? You're going to poop it out?" Nancy's face cringed in disgust.

"Well, yeah, but I got it out of top security. Turner was just being lazy, he should have had me scanned but he was too obsessed with Chelsan to be thorough." Jason side-stepped the issue of how the chip was going to re-surface.

"But you're pooping it out?" Nancy wasn't letting it go. "That's disgusting."

"When is it coming out? Are you… regular… or…" Bill suddenly found himself too embarrassed to finish the conversation.

"Would everyone stop obsessing about my bowel movements and start congratulating me on accomplishing our mission. It's not easy shoving a piece of metal down your throat." Jason seemed very put off by the disturbed reaction of the others.

"I think it's brilliant," George beamed. "As soon as it… well… as soon as you clean it up, it'll be no problem retrieving the data. I'll have it transferred on a new chip and read to go… when you are." George apparently didn't want to mention the method of extracting the chip either.

Jason turned to Vianne and held his arm out for her. "Let's make a concoction that will speed this process up, shall we?"

Grinning, Vianne wrapped her arm in Jason's. "I'm sure I can put something together, load you up on fiber."

"This is so gross." Nancy's arms were crossed and she was extremely disgusted by the whole ordeal.

"Hush," Vianne scolded her daughter as she and Jason left for the kitchen.

Once they were gone, George turned to the four of us. "You kids should get some rest, Chelsan looks like she's about to pass out. Bill, Ryan, you better stay here tonight. I'll call your parents and let them know. You all have school in the morning."

Ugggh. School. Did we really have to go to school after everything we'd been through? Apparently, the answer was yes. But George was right about something. I was ready to drop. I only had a few minutes left in me. Just enough time to snuggle up to Ryan before wondrous sleep overtook me.

There were no arguments on anyone's part. We all said our good nights to George and headed up stairs. Bill and Ryan were to sleep in

Nancy's guest bedroom, but there was no way I was letting Ryan out of my sight. Bill obviously didn't want *that* image stuck in his head so he left for the guest room.

Nancy decided to join him, giving me a wink and a nudge toward Ryan. "And besides, it'll make poop boy jealous. Mom and Dad won't care anyway. I think they're secretly hoping I'll marry Bill." And with that she joined Bill in his room.

Ryan and I entered Nancy's room still holding hands. It was like walking into a safe haven of awesomeness. I checked the room once over for anyone lurking about. Once clear, Ryan and I plopped down on Nancy's phenomenal bed of comfort. It was just about the softest most amazing sensation ever.

Ryan and I faced each other forehead to forehead. His hand rested comfortably on my hip while I placed mine on his waist. I was about to nod off into dreamland when Ryan suddenly leaned in and kissed me. It was like an electric charge surged through my system and I kissed him back empowered by this newfound energy.

His lips were tender and firm at the same time and my head went dizzy with the feeling. Kissing him was almost like a drug taking over all my senses to the point of explosion. I couldn't seem to stop. I didn't want to stop. The more we kissed the more I wanted it to keep going. The thought of stopping was actually excruciating to contemplate. His hands pulled me in tighter to his body with just enough force to make the butterflies in my stomach go insane. I held onto him as if he were my salvation from all the craziness. His hand now cradled the small of my back with agonizing tenderness. This boy was going to be the end of me! So much adrenaline, hormones, emotions, everything was becoming too much to bear all at once.

I pulled away breathless.

He was slightly out of breath as well.

"Too much," was all that came out of my mouth.

Ryan nodded, though his hand still cradled my back, which made me want to kiss him all over again.

He was so freakin' hot!

We sat there for about five more seconds before Ryan pulled me in and started to kiss me again.

Oh boy.

It was even more intense than the first time. I found myself wanting more of him. Wanting more than just kissing. I wanted *all* of him. I started to pull off his shirt when he drew back.

His hand cupped my cheek. "We should wait. I want to make this special."

I had to take a minute to calm my brain down from all the excitement. "You're the human equivalent of a brain-fry," I laughed a little.

Ryan smiled back and kissed me gently. "I just want you to know…" Ryan was suddenly very serious.

I had a surge of panic. Was he going to break up with me? Was I terrible? Why was he looking at me like that?

"I love you," he said and there was genuine fear in his eyes.

And I realized the fear was because he didn't know how I felt about him. He was completely putting himself out there and I was officially letting him hang.

"I love *you*." I kissed him again.

We couldn't seem to control ourselves. It was becoming harder and harder to break away. I was filled with a genuine glow of happiness I had never felt before. Ryan loved me. I guess I already knew that from the way he looked at me to his actions over the last week, but to hear him say it made my heart swell uncontrollably. He pushed in closer to me and I was so besieged by this onslaught of sensations I couldn't even keep a coherent thought.

This time I had to rip myself away from him. "Whoa," I said and I felt like laughing again. These past days were filled with one extreme to the next. From the devastating death of my mother, to constantly fighting to stay alive, to the awe-inspiring loyalty of friends, to Ryan. I was shocked that my heart was still beating.

"Yeah, whoa is right," Ryan said with a genuine grin. "I really meant for you to go to sleep," he admitted sheepishly.

"Sure you did, perv." I tickled his side.

Ryan squirmed and laughed, then his eyes met mine, intense. "Everything that we went through today… I just wanted to tell you how I felt… In case…"

"Don't start thinking that way. I'm going to meet with Turner tomorrow, Jason is going to release the holo-footage and everything is going to be fine. I promise." I hoped I wasn't lying.

Ryan held my face in his hands and kissed me lightly. "You're right. Everything will work out. I have complete faith in you." Ryan positioned himself so he could cradle me from behind. He kissed the back of my neck. "Go to sleep. We'll talk more in the morning."

Ryan's arms felt strong and welcoming as they held me close when exhaustion finally claimed me. I was asleep in seconds.

CHAPTER 7
MONDAY SEPTEMBER 27, 2320

I became aware of the fact that I was dreaming when I realized I was flying over Nancy's house. It was strange because I felt completely awake, but I was soaring through the air like a bird. I could even feel the wind on my face and all the sounds of nightlife chirping and hooting as I sped past. I had no control over my destination. It was as if I was a fish on a hook being reeled in.

I was above it all; houses, buildings, hover-cars, almost in the stars themselves. I viewed the city below. Tiny glowing strings of light weaved together like a tapestry of luminosity. One thread radiated brighter than all the rest and I was immediately drawn to it.

When I looked down at my body, I saw that the light was actually connected to my chest and was the source that pulled me forward. Up close the string was bright yellow and seemingly had no substance, it was made up completely of light, and yet it was strong like a rope. It tugged me down toward its end.

Once I gave into the pull, I soared at a thrilling speed to see where this cord of light led. My surroundings whizzed by me lightning fast.

It was such a rush I didn't want to wake up. I could feel my adrenaline course through my body and it was exhilarating.

The roof of an enormous twenty-acre mansion rose up to meet me like a wall of doom and I flinched, ready for impact. Instead, I flew straight through it as if it were made of air. The thread of light was so bright it was almost blinding as I entered a master bedroom the size of Nancy's house and I suddenly stopped, hovering over the source of light. I was drawn to it like a moth to flame. I was connected to it as surely as I was connected to anything. It felt right. It felt warm and inviting.

Through the glow I could tell it was another person who was emanating this cord of light. I squinted to see who I was so drawn to. To see who pulled me out of my body to bring me here? I could barely see their face…

No.

The cat-like features of my grandmother glowed brightly from the string of light that bound us together. I tried to break free. I wanted to wretch from the realization of who was lying in front of me. I could see Turner sleeping soundly next to her then. He just looked like an old man, snoring loudly, thinning hair tousled. Not nearly as scary as when he was awake, but Roberta was just as terrifying asleep, with her pulled back skin and frozen features. Truly a monster in the darkness. I would have thought she was dead if I hadn't seen her chest moving up and down.

The string started to rein me in once more. I tried to put on the brakes. I couldn't believe there had even been a second of comfort from this wicked woman. The last thing I wanted to do was be sucked inside her vortex of evil, but the pull was too strong. I was going inside her head. Just like Turner did to me that night in the hospital. This was the astral projection thingy that Jason talked about. I must have a natural instinct for it. Or, when Turner did it to me, it opened up that part of my brain so I could do it myself. Whatever the reason, I was here in Roberta Turner's bedroom, about to jump inside her brain.

And it suddenly occurred to me: that might not be a bad thing. Maybe I could find some things out. Maybe I could convince her to leave my friends and me alone. It was worth a try.

I closed my eyes and leapt in like I did when I flew through the roof. It was as if her body was insubstantial and only the light was real.

I opened my eyes…

I was alone in total darkness.

I didn't panic like I thought I would. I was actually quite calm considering I was in feline freak's head. Trying to figure out how this whole thing worked was my biggest concern. Do I walk around? Will things just appear in front of me? Is there some version of her in here like when Turner visited me? He was much more experienced than me when it came to this *out of body* ordeal, but so far I'd been figuring this kind of thing out just fine.

"Memories," I said aloud, hoping for some result.

And sure enough a long hallway opened up in front of me with doors on either side. It seemed to stretch out for miles and miles as if there were no end. I walked over to the first door and opened it.

Inside was blurry, like seeing through a pair of someone else's glasses. No matter how much I squinted my eyes to get a clearer picture, it stayed the same fuzziness. From the blurred scene, I could make out a couple. It looked like Turner and Roberta when they were younger, in their twenties, but it was hard to tell for sure. It was outside in a park, Turner kneeled down on one knee, holding Roberta's hand. A proposal no doubt. Blek. I was glad it was blurry. Seeing them happy and in love made me want to puke. I closed the door.

I skipped ahead a few doors and opened a second one. This one was as clear as crystal and I nearly leapt back from the shock of it. It was the actual facial surgery that made Grandma a feline. I could barely watch as they lifted her skin off her skull and began cutting off the excess…

I shut the door as quickly as possible. Gross.

I walked down the endless hallway until I found a door that was partially open. Maybe it was something she wanted me to see? Curiosity got the best of me and I opened it the rest of the way.

It was a birthday party. Streamers, balloons of every color, and a sign that draped over the table that said, "Happy Birthday Franklin." My heart nearly stopped. My dad's birthday! Turner and Roberta came from the other room, looking the age they were today. Roberta carried a cake with two candles spelling out eight-five. I felt a thrill of excitement. I'd get to see my dad again, probably right before he met my mother by the happy expressions on Grams and Gramps's faces (definitely pre-Mom era). They still had that un-tainted pride for their son in this memory. The kind of look I'd seen in parents where they truly believed their kids could do no wrong.

"Franklin! Come blow out your candles! You can play with your toys later!" Roberta called out.

Toys?

I wanted to cry.

My dad ran in the room and he looked eight-years-old.

They gave their own son Age-pro! Eighty-five-years-old and he was still a child! It was grotesque. It was so wrong on so many different levels. My dad was forced to be a kid for almost a century! Maybe longer! This was just one memory and I had no idea how old he was when he died. My head felt as if it was going to explode from a mixture of intense feelings I couldn't even fathom.

And he looked so happy.

That was the hardest thing to watch.

They were a family.

A real honest family. And they loved each other.

I stepped out of the entryway and practically slammed the door.

I didn't want to see that.

I liked thinking of my dad hating his parents as much as I did. They killed my mother, they killed him, they tried to kill me!

So what if they had a few moments of humanity in them! Hello?! He was an eighty-five eight-year-old! I didn't care how cozy they looked, they were still psychotic.

I couldn't seem to shake the sparkling glow of contentment in all of their eyes. It was haunting me worse than anything.

I decided to walk a few doors down. This one was harder to open, but after a large tug it finally gave.

Roberta waited in her gold living room. (I recognized it from my mother's vision.) Her face wasn't as stretched as it was today, but I could definitely tell she had started the madness that ended up being her face. A man entered the room with trepidation. He looked very familiar, but I couldn't quite place where I knew him. He had small furtive features, almost mouse-like, very fitting for the feline standing over him. He seemed to be a doctor of some sort, at least the white lab coat suggested this to be true. His hair was gray and he had crinkles around his pale brown eyes and a large two-inch crease between his eyebrows as if he were perpetually upset.

"John, come in," Roberta said to the man.

John Fortski!

The man who invented Age-pro! Of course, my grandparents knew him. I should have known better.

"Do you have it?" Roberta's eyes were wide with anticipation, and this was quite a feat considering the paralysis drugs injected into her expression lines were doing their job very well.

"Yes, but it's in its very early stages. I can't promise that there won't be side effects." John was down right jumpy as if he knew how Roberta would react.

"I don't care about side effects! Does it work or not?" Roberta went from excited to angry in about a millisecond.

"It should work, yes, but I haven't figured out the proper dosage for the way the drug effects brain chemistry. A couple of the test subjects have had severe brain damage. They've become erratic and even dangerous." John couldn't look Roberta in the eye he was so leery of her response.

"All I care about is the wrinkles, Fortski. Does it stop those?" Roberta seemed unfazed by John's warning.

"It should, yes, but…" John began to argue.

"Give them to me." Roberta was on him, grabbing his lab coat, searching his pockets. John just stood there, frozen, letting her do as she pleased.

"Not yet, my dear." Turner entered the room. He was probably about ten years younger than he looked now.

"Geoffrey, don't start." Roberta let go of Fortski and whirled to face her husband.

"Let's give it a few more tries before we start down that road." Turner was calm and steady as if he'd had these kinds of discussions with Roberta before.

Roberta backed off of Fortski with what I think was a pout (it was so hard to tell from all the injections). "Fine, but if it's not finished within the year, you're buying me another face lift." She shook her finger at Turner.

"Deal, my love, though you hardly need it as beautiful as you are."
Turner reached his hands out and Roberta took them lovingly.

Barf.

I walked out and kicked the door shut on my way down the hallway.

I was getting the hang of this and started to feel more at home inside the head of Grandma. I was sure I could find something that would help save us, if I just picked the right door. I'd stay all night if I had to, and the next night, and the next, I'd know everything about Gramps and Grams and all of their evil plans. I couldn't wait to tell Jason and the others about this, just a few more doors and then I really needed to get some honest to goodness sleep. I was sure this was paying a toll on my psyche and I didn't want to be exhausted in the morn....

I stopped dead in my tracks.

Roberta stood about ten feet in front of me in the hallway.

All the doorways disappeared in wisps of smoke.

Uh oh.

"Well," was all she said, but in that one word *so much* was packed into it and none of it good.

We were in utter darkness, but somehow both of us were visible to each other.

"Well." I tried back, but mine was completely lame. Could I just leave? How did I do that? I was still dreaming, right? My body was back at Nancy's so could she really hurt me?

"You thought you could nose about in my memories, did you?" Roberta wasn't pleased.

"It was sort of by accident. I thought I was dreaming and I saw this giant beam of light and it kind of pulled me in and it was you." I was seriously stalling at this point. I may have been asleep, but she still scared the living crap out of me.

"The unfortunates of being related. We're connected you and I, more than I care to admit," Roberta confessed.

Yuck. I wanted to break that connection more than I'd wanted anything in my life. I couldn't stand thinking of being linked to the woman who was responsible for killing my mother and father.

"You kept my father a child for eighty years." I don't know why that came out, but I was glad it did. Her face winced.

"A hundred to be exact, and he'd still be my child today if it weren't for your mother." Roberta was livid now, but I couldn't help my morbid curiosity. I wanted to know more about my parents and she was my only shot at finding out anything.

"How is that even possible? I saw my mother's vision, Dad was an adult. They met when he was twenty," I repeated what I had been told by Mom.

Roberta laughed which was really grotesque to watch. "Is that what she told you?"

"It's the truth." I did that to provoke her. Mom had obviously fibbed a bit and the only way to get anything out of this feline was to hit her anger buttons. And I was really good at hitting people's anger buttons. I had years of practice with Jill.

Roberta snarled in fury.

Okay, maybe I pressed too hard. I had to remind myself that I wasn't really there. But somewhere deep down I knew that wasn't true. I knew on some basic level of understanding that if I was jolted out of her head, or if I broke the connection between us, I might wake up damaged somehow.

"Lies. Everything that came out of your mother was lies!" Roberta's hands were shaking from the venomous anger coursing through her veins. "Your traitorous mother was our Nanny!"

What?

No, seriously.

What?!

Oh crap.

"When she found out Franklin's true age she kidnapped him and stopped giving him Age-pro! She let him grow up! She kept him from us for ten years! Ten years of not seeing your own flesh and blood! I hadn't been away from Franklin for more than a day in all one-hundred years of his life and then to have him ripped away from me like that!" Roberta said, pain in her voice. I'd almost feel sorry for her, if she wasn't *crazy!* "Geoffrey and I will never forgive your mother for that. For turning our Franklin against us and kidnapping him. Your mother was worse than trash! She fell in love with an eight-year-old!"

My mom would have been about twenty at the time and my dad a hundred, but on some level I was repulsed by the idea myself. This must have been the part that Mom didn't want to tell me. It made more sense why she picked a man like Bruce to be her husband. It wasn't just the guilt of losing my father, it was the guilt of falling in love with a boy who looked eight-years-old. Even logically knowing he was eighty years older than her, the inherent *wrongness* of the situation probably haunted her until the day she was killed.

"Okay. I get it. You're right, it sounds gross, but how is that my fault?" I hoped I could reach her on an emotional level. Even though I wanted to say that I thought it was even more horrifying and repulsive that she kept a human being eight-years-old for a hundred years. But I wanted information and since her *doors of memory* seemed to be out of the question now I needed to nurture her anger for my mother. I went a step further. "Look at my eyes, my lips, they're his, you can see it." I stepped closer to her, trying not to show my fear.

There was a flicker of recognition in her eyes, then it turned to rage. "Get away from me, devil!"

Devil? What on earth was a devil? Some Voodoo thing? Whatever it was, it wasn't good. Even though we weren't *really* facing each other, I was still petrified of what she could do to me in my sleep. Turner and Roberta had already proved their magic was powerful, I didn't need any more examples.

"I said OUT!" she screamed and her whole body glowed a bright green.

My blood froze and I suddenly couldn't take in air no matter how hard I tried. The bright string that kept us bound together flared up between us and…

SNAP!

Severed.

Everything blurred, twisted, exploded until…

SLAM!

I crash landed back into my body like a skydiver without a parachute.

Air came flooding through my lungs and I sucked it up in large gulps.

Instantly, Ryan was awake with his arms wrapped around me. "What happened? Are you okay?" He was all concern.

I fell into him, still breathing in as much air as I could, afraid it would somehow be sucked out of me again.

"I did that thingy," I heaved. "That… astral thingy… get Jason." I could barely speak. I was freezing and shaking uncontrollably. Ryan wrapped the comforter around me tightly before he left to get Jason.

In a few minutes the whole gang (minus George and Vianne; I didn't want to wake them) was in Nancy's bedroom surrounding me like a pack of mother hens.

Jason sat on the edge of the bed and rubbed his hands over my covered arms to generate some heat. I immediately started to feel better.

"You warm yet?" Jason asked.

"Yeah." I took a deep steadying breath.

Ryan crawled on the bed behind me and wrapped his arms around the fluffy blanket that was me. I started to feel down right toasty.

"We have to be quiet, my parents are still sleeping," Nancy whispered.

I told them everything.

Jason seemed the most interested in what I had to say. He asked me the specifics of how everything worked, but I wasn't *sure* how everything worked, so I just told him what I saw.

"This is fascinating," Jason said with animation.

"I was thinking, *terrifying*, but what do I know?" Nancy had her arms crossed and was looking at Jason angrily.

I liked them better when they were in crush-mode instead of this… wait…they were at each other's throats when they liked each other, but I tended to agree more with Nancy on this particular topic.

"In any case, I don't think I can go back, she'll be waiting for me next time," I admitted, hoping to prevent Jason from even broaching that subject.

"I wonder if she ever took the experimental Age-pro. It would explain why she acts like Looney-Mcloon-Pants." Bill seemed the most interested in the fact that Roberta and Turner knew Fortski and were directly involved in the creation of Age-pro.

"When I saw her she was pre-second or third face surgery, so she must have taken it later." I wasn't sure if Bill's suspicions were true.

"Let's assume that both of them took the experimentals, just for the simple fact that it gives us something to work with. If we know were dealing with brain damaged psychosis, we can better prepare for how to act." Jason tried to think strategically. "I should be getting the holo-footage sometime tomorrow, hopefully in the morning."

"Eww," Nancy chimed in.

"*Eww* or not, I can get it on the air and hopefully take Turner down." Jason ignored Nancy's jibes at this point.

"Do you think you can sleep?" Jason turned to me with concern. "It's only one in the morning, you could squeeze out a few more hours of sleep before school."

I couldn't believe it was so early in the night and now that the adrenaline was beginning to wear off, I *was* feeling sleepy again.

"Yeah, that sounds good," I said and opened up the covers for Ryan.

Nancy winked at me in approval and grabbed Bill's hand. "Come on, Bill, let's get back to bed. Night, Jason." She gave Jason a satisfied smirk and left with Bill.

Jason stood up and shook his head. "They make a good couple." His face was crestfallen and hurt.

I rolled my eyes. "You really are an idiot, Jason. Go to bed."

Jason didn't even hear me. He was lost in his own misery. "Night." He left without another word.

Ryan snuggled in close behind me. "He really has no idea she likes him, does he?"

"Not a clue, no matter how many times I re-assure him. He just wants to be miserable." I held onto Ryan's arms and smiled contentedly.

He kissed the back of my head. "Good night."

"Night." I closed my eyes and drifted off into blissful blackness.

***

When I awoke the sun's rays poured into Nancy's room like a friendly visitor. Everything always seemed more positive and hopeful during the day. Then I remembered I was meeting Turner and my good mood was sucked out of me. Not even the sunshine helped.

But…

…Waking up with Ryan next to me was definitely a plus.

Speaking of which… He opened his gorgeous brown eyes and gave me a sleepy smile. "Good morning."

I couldn't resist, I leaned over and kissed him. He gently held the back of my head and pulled me in closer. Here I go again. Breathe. Focus.

I drew back. "Behave."

"You started it," he said, smiling.

I wished he wouldn't do that. He was ridiculously cute when he did that.

I grabbed a tank and jeans from Nancy's closet and went into the bathroom to change. When I came back into the room Ryan was already dressed. (Nancy's dad let Bill and Ryan borrow some of his casual clothes, jeans and t-shirt kind of stuff.) The pants were a little big on Ryan, but he'd look good in a potato sack, so there you go.

We went downstairs and joined George and Vianne for breakfast. Bill and Nancy joined us soon after, followed by a very peppy Jason.

"Morning everyone." Jason exuded cheeriness.

"Did you? I mean, did it?" Vianne was a little leery of the topic of Jason's digestion at the breakfast table.

Jason waved his hand in the negative. "No, not yet, I'm just pumped about what happens when we have it. This could be it. My lifelong dream of taking down Turner could actually happen *today*! I'm just a little excited." Jason was simply beaming.

"Aren't you getting ahead of yourself? What if the chip is broken, we are talking about *your* bowels." Nancy smirked.

"Nancy," George scolded, "Jason is our guest so treat him with some respect," he finished authoritatively.

Nancy shrugged apologetically. "Sorry, just don't want anyone to count their chickens before they're hatched." She eyed Jason with annoyed disdain.

"There's nothing wrong with a positive attitude, you might want to try it sometime," Jason retorted.

Nancy stood up in a huff and left the room. "Bill."

Bill shoveled in the last of his breakfast and followed Nancy out of the room.

Nancy called out from the foyer, "Let's get to school!"

I stuffed my eggs in my mouth. "Great breakfast, Vianne, thanks so much." I stood up to join Nancy when Jason caught my arm.

"This meeting with Turner will be the perfect stall tactic. I need you to keep him busy until I can get the holo-footage on the air. Are you going to be okay with that?" Jason made sure our eyes met.

I nodded. "Yeah. He won't hurt me. He just wants to talk," I said, but didn't believe a word of it. After last nights rendezvous with Roberta I wasn't sure what Turner would do or say at our little meeting today. I tried not to think about it too much, otherwise my imagination would paralyze me.

"I don't want her to go." Ryan stood up beside me and grabbed my hand possessively.

I tried to give Ryan the most reassuring look I could muster. "I have to. I told you yesterday don't try and talk me out of it. I'm going."

"We'll see." Nancy's voice sounded from the other room.

I rolled my eyes and almost laughed. A lioness 'til the end, even if I made it extremely difficult for her.

"I hate to be the bad guy, but you *need* to go. This thing will be ten times easier knowing that Turner will be occupied with you." Jason looked genuinely sorry that he had to be the voice of reason in all this.

"I'm going. Don't worry. Just *do your thing* and then do your thing," I said and Ryan and I left.

George and Vianne walked us out and made sure we were all safe in Bill's car before they went back into the house.

The ride over was somehow comforting. It was nice to be around the three people that I trusted and loved. I didn't want to be all gloom and doom, but my meeting with Turner today was like a black cloud hanging over me and I wasn't sure if I'd ever feel this warm and fuzzy with my friends again. We didn't even talk about anything important. Mainly it was just Nancy trying to fool everyone that she had absolutely no interest in Jason Keroff whatsoever. But in the end even she admitted she was full of crap and then proceeded to ask us all our advice on what she should do.

Bill and Ryan went pretty silent on the topic and I fully admitted to being a complete idiot when it came to boys, so the conversation ended up with Nancy in a huff.

We arrived at school and to my great relief there wasn't hide nor hair of any news reporters.

"Looks like Turner's making things easier on you. Show of good faith maybe?" Ryan sounded hopeful.

"Or he doesn't want anyone watching," Bill said what I was thinking.

"He doesn't trust you." Nancy agreed with Bill.

I always said I wanted honesty, I guess I was getting it in spades now.

"Chelsan!" I heard Jill's voice like fingernails on a chalkboard.

I knew her dad was dead, and I knew she had no clue, but as sad as that was I still couldn't stand her. With her intense, bright green eyes filled with annoyance, she came running up to me in her designer clothes and bouncing black curls.

"Yes?" I greeted her with as little emotion as possible.

"Don't give me attitude, I like this less than you do." Jill smiled at Bill kindly. "Hi, Bill."

"Hey," Bill acknowledged. He reached down and grabbed Nancy's hand. Looked like he wanted to play the same game Nancy was, but instead of trying to make Jill jealous, he was trying to subtly tell her to stay away.

Jill received the message right away. She turned back to me and snarled, "Daddy wants me to take you to Nancy's after school. He says if you don't come with me, Nancy's parents will be charged with a Landscaping Code Violation."

"What?!" Nancy was livid. "Your dad said he cleared that like ten years ago!"

"Well, paperwork gets lost, doesn't it?" Jill was enjoying this.

Before things got out of hand I looked Jill in the eye. "Fine. I'll meet you in the parking lot after class."

Jill's face showed her disappointment at the lack of a true fight, but she shrugged. "Be early. I don't want anyone seeing us together." She whirled around and was gone.

Bill seemed the most upset. "Turner is making sure you go."

"I was always planning on going, it's no big deal." I tried to calm everyone down. I could tell Ryan was livid. I think they were all secretly thinking of a plan to stop me and now it was foiled. Turner really didn't trust me. After everything we'd been through, I couldn't blame him. And he used the one thing he knew I'd never put in danger: my friends. Nancy's parents were practically adopting me and I'd die before I let any harm come to them.

The rest of the day seemed to fly by. I was really hoping I could savor these last few hours of freedom, but as always when you have some horrible thing to do, time goes by too fast.

I probably wasn't walking away from this encounter, but as long as my friends were safe I was okay with that. I couldn't help but think it would have been easier on everyone if Turner had succeeded in his plan that day at the trailer park and killed my mother and I both. But I didn't want to think like that. I was here and I wasn't going to give up. I was learning more and more about my powers each day, which on the one hand made me a force to be reckoned with, but on the other, made me a target. Only time would decide which one I would be today.

The last bell of the day rang like a harbinger of death.

Ryan waited for me outside the classroom. He had that look. That look that said, *I'm not going to argue with you, but I don't like it.* He just took my hand and we walked toward the parking lot.

"I have another job offer from one of the best companies in the world. One that Turner *doesn't* have a stake in." Ryan tried to lighten the mood. "I'm meeting with their VP at Nancy's house. George seemed really excited when I told him, maybe the guy will like George and offer him a job there."

"You did that on purpose, didn't you? For George." I smiled with approval.

"Maybe," Ryan replied slyly. "He deserves it after everything he's done for you. For us."

"Do you think you'll take the job?" I asked. I was secretly hoping we could go to college together. If I made it that long. Ugggh! Stop!

"Naaah, but I always listen to their offers. It'll be pretty boring, but at least I'll get a free meal out of it." He smiled.

"Well… be careful." I couldn't think of anything else to say I was so nervous about what was coming.

Ryan squeezed my hand and pulled it up to his lips, kissing it gently. "Nancy's parents will just have to pay a fine. They'll understand. You shouldn't go."

"I'm going. I'm just a little nervous is all." As much as I wanted to agree with Ryan, I needed to get this over with.

We arrived at the parking lot and Jill was waiting there with her scowl of greeting.

"Let's go." Jill started walking away without waiting to see if I was following.

I turned and kissed Ryan. "Love you."

Ryan kissed me back. "Love you."

I couldn't look at him anymore or I'd chicken out. And where were Bill and Nancy? They were probably tied up in class. I wanted to wait to say goodbye to them, but Jill was almost out of view. I ran after her like an idiot.

I caught up to Jill and walked next to her, hoping we wouldn't have to talk. *Just drop me off at Nancy's and leave me alone.* Maybe I'd see Nancy and Bill before Turner's car came to pick me up.

Jill's hover-car was a top of the line, ridiculously expensive BMW. "Get in," she barked.

I opened the door and slid into the car. I really didn't want to fight with her, and thankfully it appeared she didn't want to either. The interior of the car was to be expected, lots of expensive bells and whistles, including a holo-GPS and auto-pilot.

"Don't touch anything." Jill wanted to make sure I knew my place.

"Jill, just shut-up." I tried to keep quiet, but she was so good at provoking me.

"I'll make you ride in the trunk." Jill's eyes flared angrily.

"I'd like to see you try." I gave her a look that suggested she should back off.

Jill grumbled something under her breath, turned on her car, and took off out of the parking lot. The way she drove we'd be there in no time. Thank goodness.

The holo-GPS projected the three-dimensional map in the middle of the dashboard and led Jill to Nancy's house.

"I could just tell you how to get there," I offered. As soon as I did I knew I shouldn't have.

"Yeah, right. Like I'd take directions from trailer trash. My dad warned me not to listen to anything you say. *Most of all* directions. He said you could lead me into a trap." Jill smirked egotistically.

"A trap? What? Where I beat the crap out of you and steal your car?" Now that I said it, it sounded like a good idea, in dreamland that was. But the more obvious point of Jill's rant was Turner's paranoia that I wouldn't show up for this reunion.

"Exactly. Your seat is rigged to taser by the way, so don't even think about trying anything." Jill actually sounded scared so I wondered at the validity of her threat.

"I'm not going to do anything. Just get me to Nancy's so I can get away from you." I stared out the window trying to ignore her.

"I'm not the freak in this situation, you know." Jill wasn't letting go. It was like now that we were alone she could let out all of her frustration on me. "You're the one who intruded in a life you had no right to. You don't belong with the rich, you belong with your own kind." Jill sounded like she believed the hate she spouted.

I was tempted to destroy her world and tell her about her dad, or worse let him die naturally by disconnecting him from Turner's control, but as annoying and cruel as Jill was, I just couldn't do that to another human being. No matter how tempting.

"Why should you care? What possible difference in your life could it make to have someone who doesn't have any money go to your school? Really? Are you that bigoted?" I sighed, already exhausted from this conversation.

"I am *not* a bigot." Jill seemed horrified by the notion, which was weird because she so obviously *was*.

"What would you call it then? Let me quote: *You don't belong with the rich, you belong with your own kind.* How is that *not* being a bigot?" I stared at her profile as she kept her eyes on the airspace in front of her. I had hit a nerve.

"I hate you," Jill seethed and said nothing more.

Good. Now I could concentrate on… uuuggh… what? How my grandpa was planning on finishing me off? My argument with Jill felt like a vacation compared to what was in store for me.

And then out of the blue Jill said, "I'm sorry I made you cry the other day, when I brought up your mom."

"You have reached your destination," the GPS announced.

I turned to Jill as if my ears had played tricks on me. Was that an apology? She stared straight ahead as if she hadn't said anything, but I could tell there was *actually* some emotion there.

"Look, Jill…" I started.

"Don't," Jill stopped me. "I just need you to be my enemy right now." She still couldn't look at me. "It's the only thing that makes sense to me."

And as weird of a statement as that was, I actually understood it. She needed something stable in her life and I guess her hatred for me was it. Maybe that would change in time. I could only hope. It would make the last year of high school a whole lot easier, but then again I might not make it past the next couple of hours so I simply nodded.

Jill landed the hover-car and opened my door from her side.

"Get out," Jill said quietly.

I exited the car and before I could turn around she had shut the door and lifted off.

So much for Jill Forester.

Almost within seconds a steel box of a hover-truck landed in front of me. It was solid silver like a bar of tin with spinning fans. I couldn't even see where the driver would sit, the metal was so continuous. *Where were the windows?*

"What the…?" My heart sank. This was Turner's "ride."

Two heavy doors swung open and a man dressed in an all white three-piece suit was there with a large grin. "Chelsan, come in." He looked as if he was in his mid-twenties so he either *was* in his mid-twenties or he was middle class and had been Turner's slave for centuries. His hair was short and perfectly in place along with everything else about him. He could have been a doll with his aquiline features and perfectly constructed body.

The inside of the hover-box was as white and sterile as the guy who greeted me. It was devoid of anything except two benches built into the walls facing each other. I sat down on one of them and the spongy white surface wasn't any kind of material I could recognize. I felt way out of my depth in this situation, which was exactly the way Turner wanted me to feel, I guessed. I gritted my teeth in frustration because I was letting it work. I was letting him win even on the smallest of levels and that was unacceptable.

The man in white shut the doors and sat across from me with that same annoying grin. "All set here. Let's go." He seemed to be talking to the air in front of him.

But the hover fans churned in response and we were off. Away from my friends. Away from safety.

What was this place? It was like a quarantine facility… Oh.

It *was* a quarantine facility, and I was the thing that needed to be quarantined. Nothing dead in this spotlessly clean metal box. No swirling black holes here. It was amazing how comforting they had become to me since meeting my grandpa. Something I used to consider a curse ended up being the one thing I could depend on.

"Where are we going?" I asked fruitlessly.

"We'll know when we get there." The man in white said with a smile.

Can we get a little more vague? Probably, so I kept my mouth shut and took deep calming breaths. As we whizzed over Los Angeles I leaned my head back against the wall of the truck and closed my eyes. I knew there was no way I could even guess where we were headed, but since I was stuck here in this sterile box I thought I could try something. I concentrated on the ground below us and sought out any and every black hole I could find. Mostly bugs, ants and houseplants. Okay, that meant we were still in the burbs. That was helpful.

The longer we drove the black holes turned into larger animals, opossums, coyotes, lots more bugs of every variety imaginable (blek), birds, heading over a forest, but which one and where? It was impossible to tell there were so many now because of Population Control's laws. It didn't matter, there were enough animals I could use in my arsenal if I had to. Of course, that was assuming we were going to land sometime soon! Where were we going?! So frustrating!

I was so zoned into all the black swirling chasms, I nearly jumped when they all turned into at least five square miles of giant dead oaks. No dead animal or insect or any kind of corpse that I could sense. Just the blackened roots of lifeless trees.

The hover-truck landed in the center of the dead forest. I couldn't for the life of me remember any place like this. You'd think we'd have learned about places like these in geography class or something, but it must be just another one of Turner's secrets he kept from the people.

The man in white opened the doors of the truck and smiled at me. "Out, please."

I stood up and jumped outside of the metal box.

Burnt, charred earth greeted me like an apocalypse. It made me a little dizzy with the swirling holes of the dead trees and the blackened ground beneath me. The only proof that there had been any kind of life here was *me*.

"This way, please." The man in white was a startling contrast to the darkness of the land.

I followed him around the hover-truck and I gasped.

Turner stood in front of an army of hundreds of soldiers with nothing but scorched earth for miles. It was a surreal moment to see so many men dressed in full army gear, holding automatic weapons, all pointed at me. Turner had a smug look on his face. He was only about twenty feet away, which was way too close for my taste. And *way* too close for those guns to be aimed in my direction. Who did he think I was? Some kind of living bomb? I wish I were at this point. Maybe I could take him down with me. I just hoped Jason would have enough time to get the holo-footage on the air and hopefully save my butt. It didn't look good at this point in time.

The driver of the hover-truck was one of Turner's soldiers and he exited the vehicle with his own gun raised, stepping into line with his fellow combatants.

"Did you enjoy your adventures in my wife's head last night?" Turner had an edge of fury to his voice.

"Yes," I said. A part of me wanted to goad him on. It was like playing Russian Roulette. I felt like I had nothing to lose. If he was going to kill me, there was nothing I could do about it.

"Tell me what you saw?" He took a step closer and something in his eyes warned me that something was off.

"No." I kept my answers as brief as possible and noticed that the less I said the more agitated he grew. I had seen this kind of behavior before. He was stalling. But for what? I needed to find out more. "You brought a firing squad?"

"Possibly, that depends on you. Nothing dead for miles. I wasn't sure how far your reach was, so I made sure five square miles was free of any corpses for you to *surprise* me with." The look on Turner's face was infuriating. He was so proud of himself.

Interesting.

He had no idea I could control dead plant-life.

The dead roots might just become my best friends.

I wasn't sure *what* I could do with them, but it was starting to look like I'd have to figure it out soon.

"Why am I here?" I asked, trying to fish out the truth from him.

"Why indeed," Turner smirked.

He was definitely stalling. It was driving me bonkers and it started to scare me.

The man in white walked over to Turner and whispered something in his ear.

Turner smiled as wide as I'd ever seen.

My heart sank. Something just went his way and anything that went his way was never good.

With a sparkling glint in his eyes, he turned to me. "You, my dear, are no longer useful to me."

Hundreds of guns clicked and clacked in readiness to mow me down.

My whole body shuddered.

I was really going to die if I didn't do something right now.

Now it was my turn to stall.

"Can't you tell me what just happened?" I asked desperately.

Turner laughed at my horror, reveling in it as if I was a swimming pool of retribution. "It will give me great pleasure in telling you how you were duped before I kill you."

Duped?

"You thought you were this special creature that I had an ounce of interest in? I've wanted you dead since you were born. Your mother was very clever in marrying the one man I couldn't track. *Bruce Lenton* one of my first experiments in tracking devices. It was a complete failure and ended up making him and anyone in a two-mile radius of him disappear entirely from the map. Franklin knew about Bruce and must have told your mother before she killed my son. My only tiny bit of satisfaction was knowing that Bruce was a violent man and I hoped that he beat that murderer regularly," he seethed.

Sudden realization brought tears to my eyes. Mom didn't marry Bruce to punish herself, she did it to save me. That day I killed him it wasn't disappointment or judgment in her eyes, it was fear that Turner would find us. A love even deeper than I could ever imagine surged through me. *Everything* Mom did was about saving me.

"When my scientists finally discovered how to find Bruce they were very surprised to find that he was, in fact, dead, and yet living. It wasn't hard to figure out that one of you was keeping him that way," he gloated.

While he rubbed in his superiority, I took the time to connect to every tree root I could underneath him and his army.

"I can do everything you can do with Vodun and Wicca, but what I *can't* do is solve complex formulas and theorems," he said as if revealing something wicked.

What? I can't do that either.

Ryan.

It wasn't me he wanted. It was Ryan.

Duped was an understatement.

I should have realized it when I saw how Roberta was salivating all over him.

The parking lot of the Population Control Headquarters was *way* too public to kidnap Ryan. Turner had to come up with this elaborate ruse just to separate us, knowing I'd never let him take Ryan without a fight.

"Ryan," I whispered in shock.

"He's ours now, I just got word. He should have been ours years ago, but he was more clever than we gave him credit for. He can't replace our Franklin, but it's a start. And we won't have history repeating itself by having his whore take him away from us again." Turner was simply beside himself with happiness. "It's over now. You lost."

He motioned his men to take aim and suddenly all the guns were pointed at me.

"Wait!" I yelped. (Yes, I would actually categorize what came out of my mouth as a yelp; I sounded like a thirteen-year-old boy in puberty.) "I'm about to die anyway, just tell me he'll be okay." I felt the roots of the trees beneath them as if they were an extension of my own limbs, but I needed to trick Turner into giving me some clue as to where Ryan was being held.

Turner actually sighed as if I was an annoying fly he couldn't swat. "Of course he's fine. He'll be treated like a king as he should be. He's ours now."

Ours. Roberta's and his. Replacing Franklin.

Ryan was at their house. I knew it from the depths of my soul. I'd find him there.

"One more thing," I said with confidence this time.

"You're stalling now." Turner's eyes narrowed with sinister glee. "This will be the last thing that comes out of your mouth, so make it good," he almost cackled with triumph.

"It's not just corpses I can bring back, *Gramps.*"

BOOM!

The ground shook as hundreds of thick gnarled roots burst through the ground beneath Turner and his boys. I made them wrap around their bodies like vises. The guns clattered to the dirt as I squeezed the black roots around the soldiers until they couldn't move an inch.

I had fallen from the force of the dead trees bursting through the soil, but stood up and brushed myself off.

I walked up to Turner whose face fumed from betrayal and anger, but his body was ensnared like the others so he couldn't touch me.

I smiled. "I guess you don't know everything about my powers, now do you?"

His eyes flashed with the same curiosity they did in Principal Weatherby's office. I surprised him. *Again.*

I whirled around to see the man in white standing by the hover-truck, terror in his eyes. His hands went up in supplication before any words had come out of my mouth.

"Please, don't kill me," he uttered in panic.

"I didn't kill *him*, why would I kill you?" It was taking most of my energy to keep the roots sturdy and in place, but I tried to sound as strong as possible. "Get the keys."

The man in white practically jumped at the command and hurried over to the ensnared driver, grabbing the keys from his pocket. He ran over to me and handed me the keys. Just to be safe I exerted more of my energy and brought up dead roots to capture him, too. He squealed in fright, and proceeded to whimper once the cage of limbs was in place.

I turned one last time to Turner. "I'm going to get Ryan."

"Good luck with that," he said with such a condescending attitude that I wanted to squeeze the life out of him with one of the roots. It was the second time I had the chance to kill him. It would mean the safety of the people I loved and mine as well. So easy. Thirty seconds ago he was going to kill *me*. His soldiers had been about to mow me down with bullets. Why couldn't I do it? No one would blame me. They'd probably congratulate me.

But I couldn't.

I just couldn't.

It would be the worse mistake of my life. I might regret it later with every fiber of my soul, but right now, I couldn't do it. My grandparents were the only tie I had left with my father and even though that meant nothing to them, it meant something to me. It made me nauseous to admit that, but a part of me wanted Turner and Roberta alive. A very small part, but still. I wasn't ready. Honestly, I hoped I never would be.

But in this case, for Ryan's sake, I did need to bluff.

"Oh, I won't kill you, dear Grandfather, but Grandma is expendable. No one knows she exists anyway the way you keep her ugly cat face out of the media. You killed my mother, I'm killing your wife. Even-steven." And then I grinned in the most vicious way I could contort my face.

It must have worked because Turner looked downright terrified. "You wouldn't."

"Really? Remember, I am *your* granddaughter." And I turned and walked to the hover-truck before he could figure out I was deceiving him.

"NO! I'LL GIVE YOU ANYTHING! ANYTHING! I PROMISE I'LL NEVER TRY AND HURT YOU AGAIN!" Turner screamed and his voice was laced with anguish.

I whirled around before I entered the truck. "We'll see." I threw back his own words in his face and he roared like a caged lion.

I was about to vomit as I sat in the driver's seat. Thank goodness there was auto pilot. I turned on the holo-GPS, gave it Nancy's address and whizzed away from the scene. I knew my connection with the tree roots would end as soon as I hit the four-mile mark, but at least they'd stay in place. I hoped it would take a while for the soldiers to break out of the crusty old branches, but I didn't want to delude myself. It bought me some time.

Hopefully, the team was at Nancy's and we could rescue Ryan together. I needed all the help I could get.

As the car followed the holo-GPS's directions, I tried not to think about what I just went through. I needed to keep focused on saving Ryan. I had absolutely no idea how that was going to happen and frankly, I was secretly hoping that the team would have some suggestions. At full speed the car landed in front of Nancy's house in about twenty minutes.

I flew out of the vehicle and ran to the front door and stopped dead in my tracks.

The steel door was off its hinges and laying inside the house.

This was where they kidnapped Ryan.

I ran inside the house.

"Hello?!" I called out, hoping to hear *anyones* voice.

Silence.

The house looked like it had been hit by a hurricane. The couch was flipped over, glass and wood splinters everywhere.*Please let everyone be okay.* If my adrenaline hadn't been at full throttle I would have broken down right there.

"Hello?! George! Vianne!" I called out again, frantic for any response.

"Chelsan?" It was George and he sounded like he was in the kitchen.

I hurried as fast as I could and practically fell into George on his way out to find me. He embraced me in a desperate hug. "Thanks goodness you're all right. They told us…" His voice started to break up, "They told us you were dead."

I pulled away and wiped the tears from my face I hadn't even noticed were there.

"I almost was," I admitted with a lump in my throat. "What happened? Turner said they took Ryan."

Vianne came hurrying out of the kitchen and nearly toppled me over as she drew me in for another embrace. "Oh Chelsan, we were so worried." She let go of me to inspect me thoroughly. "Any injuries?"

That was when I finally noticed the two of them. They were covered in small cuts and bruises. I held my hand to mouth in shock. "Forget me, are you guys okay?"

Vianne held my hand warmly. "We're fine, dear, nothing that won't heal, but Ryan… he put up such a fight." Tears came to Vianne's eyes. "They took us by surprise. The man who said he was here to offer Ryan a job turned out to be one of Turner's soldiers. He had a whole team with him. We made Jason take Nancy out the back before things got too ugly. He has the tornado footage, Chelsan, he's on his way now to get it on the air. Bill's been hysterical trying to find you, he's pretty beat up as well. You should have seen him trying to protect Ryan…" She trailed off, trying to hide her emotion.

"I need to call Bill." I tried to keep my head clear.

George handed me the phone almost immediately after the words came out of my mouth.

I dialed quickly.

Bill picked up before the first ring had finished its chorus. "George? I'm going to Jill's to see where she dropped Chelsan off." Bill's voice sounded determined through the phone.

"Bill, it's me," I said before he could continue.

"CHELSAN!!! Where are you? Are you okay? Tell me where you are, I'm coming!" Bill went from composed to frantic in about a millisecond.

"Bill, calm down. I'm at Nancy's, come pick me up. We'll go to Jill's together. I think I have a plan." The seeds of an idea were starting to form in my brain.

"Okay, I'm on my way." Bill sounded elated to hear from me.

I hung up the phone and handed it to George. "He's on his way."

"Why Jill? Do you think she knows something?" Vianne asked as she touched up one of George's wounds with a damp cloth.

"No, it's her dad I'm interested in." Man, if this plan was going to work, Jill would hate me forever. But, there was nothing for it.

The whirling fans of Bill's hover-car were louder than normal since the front door no longer existed. I turned to George and Vianne. "Are you guys going to be okay?"

"We're fine, just go. Get Ryan back." Vianne kissed my cheek and sent me on my way.

I ran out to greet Bill and slammed into his six-foot frame like I had smacked into a tree. A tree that grabbed me and squeezed me in a bear hug that nearly popped my lungs. I hugged him back with just as much force; we nearly killed each other from affection.

Bill drew away first and his eyes were watery, but sparkling at seeing me. He kissed my forehead. "We all thought…" He trailed off, not able to finish the sentence that ended with me dead.

His lip was cut pretty badly and his eye was black. "Oh Bill."

He shrugged his wounds off like a badge of courage. "It's nothing."

"It's not nothing. This is all my fault."

"Chelsan, we have to get Ryan back," he said as he took my hand and yanked me to his hover-car.

We were in the air faster than I could think. He kept on glancing over at me, relief etched in every feature. "I tried to stop them, but they eventually had to stun me." I could tell that was hard for Bill to admit.

"Stunners only?" I asked, trying to get a better idea of what we were up against. I just hoped Jason and Nancy's mission would prove successful. It was our only bargaining chip for long-term safety. Without that footage, rescuing Ryan would be a futile effort since they could simply re-take him again. We needed to take Turner out of power or at least bump him down a notch. Enough where it would make it difficult for him to target us. Us. Ryan and me. Somehow we both ended up being Grams and Gramps's obsession. It was difficult enough when they were after *me*, but now they were after my *boyfriend*. In fact, it seemed like they wanted Ryan a lot more than they wanted me. I didn't know if I should be offended or not.

Although after showing Turner that I could control dead plants may have put me back on the top of their list.

"Yeah, just the stunners." Bill answered my previous question. "I don't think they thought we'd fight as hard as we did. If you think *we* look bad." He actually smiled and then it quickly turned to a frown. "When I woke up, Ryan was gone. I'm really sorry, Chelsan. I did everything I could to save him."

"I would *never* blame you for that. Don't ever think that." I wanted to re-assure him.

"You think Jill had something to do with all this? Where did she drop you off anyway?" Bill changed the subject after a moment of quiet.

"She dropped me off at Nancy's. I don't think she knows anything," I said.

"Then why are we going to her house?" Bill asked.

"For her dad."

"Oh boy." Bill swallowed hard figuring out my intent. "Is she going to find out? Or... are you...?" he asked as if wanting to know but not really *wanting* to know.

"Hopefully, she won't know a thing, but Mr. Owen Forester is coming with us. He's our only way in." I tried to muster as much confidence in my plan as possible for Bill's sake, but I secretly worried that making Jill's dad come with us might backfire if Turner warned Roberta that I'd escaped. I was going in blind. I had no idea what to expect of Jill's dad. Did he have thoughts of his own? Was he constantly controlled by Turner and his people? Would they know that I had taken over? I just didn't know, but he was literally *it,* in terms of a plan. I couldn't show up at Roberta's mansion, I'd be taken immediately. Mr. Forester was going in and he was going in alone. Worse case scenario, they break their ties with him and he'd finally die his proper death instead of this half-life he was living. Which was for the best, I knew, but Jill wouldn't see it that way. I'd always be the person who killed her father even though I had nothing to do with it.

"We're here," Bill announced as we landed in front of the most stunning mansion I'd ever seen. Architecture dating back to the early two-thousands, it was made mostly of metal and glass. Five solar panels on the roof were curved like walnut shells reaching up to the sun. They were gigantic, at least two-hundred feet tall and a hundred feet across. The base of the house was bright silver metal and sparkled in the fading daylight. In startling contrast of the metal base, the trim of the house was all colored glass from the doorknobs, to the window frames, to the sculptures on the bright green lawn. It was like a museum or spectacle, I couldn't decide which.

The hover-landing pad was encircled by the most amazing collection of rose bushes I'd ever seen. Every color imaginable in perfect bloom reaching out to greet you as you exited your vehicle. It was extremely unfair that someone like Jill lived in such a castle, but then again Jill had other disadvantages that I didn't envy. Like her dad.

Bill and I left the car and walked up the marble steps that led to the front door.

Jill opened it in a fury. Apparently, she saw us coming. "What on earth are you two doing at *my* house?!" She could barely talk she was so angry.

"Is your dad here?" Bill asked, knowing that anything that came out of my mouth would be met with rage.

"My dad?" This threw Jill off completely. "Why?"

"Is he here or not, Jill?" Bill said brusquely.

"He's here," I confirmed, seeing his swirling black hole in the back of the house. "He's in the back of the house."

"How did you…?" Jill went from fury to shock to suspicion all in a span of a second.

"It doesn't matter, Jill, the less you know the better." I tried to be as nice as was humanly possible.

"GET OFF MY PROPERTY!" Jill slammed the door in our faces.

"That went well." Bill rolled his eyes. "You shouldn't have said anything."

"It doesn't matter. I'll get him myself." I closed my eyes and slammed through the barrier that kept me from Mr. Forester's black hole. He was mine now. And I knew as soon as I connected to him that he was just like anything else dead. Nothing upstairs. Just an empty shell for me to puppeteer. "Just a few seconds." I made him walk to the front door and open it.

Jill was standing next to him, terror, suspicion, fury and sadness all rolled into one heartbreaking expression. She wasn't stupid, she knew something was going on, and she knew I had something to do with it.

I tried to smooth the situation and made her dad speak. "It's okay, Jill, I'm just going to go with your friends for a bit."

And instead of making things better, it seemed to make them a whole lot worse. Jill started to cry hysterically. I made her dad touch her shoulder to comfort her, but she flinched and pulled away, wiping away her tears. She stared at me with resentment and revulsion. "He hasn't spoken to me except to give me orders from the Vice President in three years."

Ooops. And ouch. I couldn't control how awful I actually felt for Jill in that moment.

"I'm sorry, Jill, but Ryan's in trouble." I couldn't begin to explain everything to her now and I didn't know if she was ready yet anyway.

Jill didn't know how to respond, so she fell back to her usual annoying self. "You're an evil disgusting excuse for a human being, Chelsan Derée, and I hope you die. If my father doesn't come back, I'm holding you fully responsible and if you think your life was torture before, you haven't seen anything yet." And with that she stalked off, leaving Bill and I alone with Mr. Forester.

"Bye Jill, see you at school." Bill tried to lighten the moment.

"I don't really care what Jill thinks right now, let's just get Ryan." I made Jill's dad follow us to the hover-car.

I had him sit in back and we were off toward Turner's house. We only had my dream to go by so I made him drive to Nancy's house since that was my starting point in my vision. I closed my eyes and visualized the landscape in front of me and instructed Bill where to go.

"I think we're here. That's got to be it," Bill said.

I opened my eyes and looked down. "That's it." There it was in the flesh. My grandparent's house. The house where my mom rescued my dad, where they came back when she was pregnant with me, where my dad lived for over a hundred years, and where Ryan was now held captive. Hundreds of years of my own family history in *that* house. It almost took my breath away with the enormity of it. The property was ginormous, all twenty acres of it. It was a classic Victorian, brick and wooden trim, ivy growing up the sides. It looked like a mansion version of my high school and Turner's namesake. He must love that era of architecture.

"Park here, away from the house," I told Bill and he quickly landed on a grass street a block away from the house.

I made Mr. Forester step out of the car. "Okay, here comes the hard part. I have to really concentrate here, so keep an eye out for any trouble."

Bill was more than up for the task. His eyes were still filled with wonder as he watched me make Jill's dad move. I kept on forgetting how new my power was to everyone. I held my secret in for so long, and to find out I could have confided in Bill and Nancy from the beginning without judgment, made me wish I'd shared my burden earlier.

I closed my eyes and concentrated…

…And I was in. I was seeing through Mr. Forester's eyes now. I made sure I could move all of his limbs by doing a quick shake down. This made Bill cringe a little, but I couldn't help that now, I needed Mr. Forester to be as fluid as possible when entering the house. I knew that as soon as Roberta saw him the jig was up, but I was more concerned about the guards and making a route for Bill and I to break in.

Through his body, I made my way across the grass-covered road and through someone's lawn to reach my grandparent's house. The gate and fencing surrounding the mansion was black wrought iron and loomed before Mr. Forester like the bars of a prison. Ryan's prison. My father's prison. Soon to be *my* prison if this didn't turn out okay. (That was if I was lucky, knowing Gramps, he was still on his "murder Chelsan" mission.) I erased those thoughts from my mind as they were making it difficult for me to maintain my control over Mr. Forester. Directly to the left of the two-way gate was a small guard station with two men on duty. One sat next to a screen that had hundreds of camera angles from inside the house, while the other leaned against the wall, bored. I made Jill's dad walk up to them.

"Evening. I'm here to see the Vice President. He's expecting me." I tried to sound as monotone as possible taking a few cues from Jill's comment about how her dad had only given her orders over the last two years. If Turner's people were used to Mr. Forester a certain way, I didn't want to act differently than what they expected. I figured *neutral* was my best course of action.

"Of course, Mr. Forester. Word was just sent that he's on his way." The guard sitting at the monitor screen smiled up at him. "I'll let the doorman know."

I tried to keep Mr. Forester's face as cool as possible, but it was a hopeless undertaking. I could never tell what *my* face looked like, so how was I supposed to know *his* looked like? "Sounds good. Tell him I'll wait for him in the study when he arrives." I seriously hoped there was a study in that house.

"Will do. Good day." The guard nodded in a friendly manner.

"We're through," I informed Bill, though my eyes were still closed. I couldn't quite master the art of seeing two different perspectives at once so it was just easier to keep my lids shut. I hoped I would *never* have to do this again! Keeping Bruce alive was one thing, but controlling my enemy's father and sneaking into my grandparent's lair was another.

The guard sitting inside the booth hit the button for the intercom. "Mr. Forester is here to wait for the Vice President."

"Copy. We'll have refreshments ready," came a friendly voice through the speaker above the guard's head.

"Thank you," the guard responded then turned to me. "You're all set, Mr. Forester."

"Thank...." I started to make him say.

BBBBZZZZT!

BBBZZZZTT!

Out of nowhere Bill was there with a stun club and both guards were down.

He turned to Mr. Forester with a smile, but his eyes were full of determination and bravery. "Get your butt up here. We're getting Ryan together."

I opened my eyes and it took me a second to make my own perspective the more dominant one. I couldn't believe Bill! I was shocked, proud, scared and little excited by his aggression. He was right of course; three was better than one dead guy. Once we were in, who knew how many dead servants they employed that I could use to my advantage. Spiders and flies would work too in a pinch.

I followed the same route I made Jill's dad travel and was next to Bill and Mr. Forester within seconds. I disconnected from Mr. Forester's eyes, but remained linked to the rest of his body.

"Get that stun club ready," I advised Bill.

Bill grinned at me.

I looked up at his bruised, cut face and his silly smile and I couldn't help myself. I hugged him. "Thank you, Bill."

Bill gently pushed me off, eyes sparkling, still smiling. "Hug me *after* we pull this off."

"Right," I said and took a deep breath, head back in the game.

I made Jill's dad walk up the long cobblestone footpath that led to the front door. I followed next, with Bill behind, hiding his stun club. As far as I knew our plan was to stun the crap out of everyone until we found Ryan. The more I thought about it, the more nervous I became. This house was HUGE! Too many people, too many rooms. I put out my feelers for any corpses inside.

One.

Okay. Not ideal, but workable. I quickly popped into the dead person's eyes.

My heart skipped about a million beats.

Ryan sat in front of me, chained to a metal chair that was bolted to the floor. The room was a small square of white, walls, linoleum floor and ceiling. No windows and just one single white door. I nearly crumbled when I could see how beat up Ryan was. I thought Nancy's parents and

Bill looked bad, Ryan apparently didn't stop fighting the entire time. Two black eyes, bloody nose, swollen lip, bruises and cuts all over his arms and who knew where else. His worst nightmare came true, he was back with my grandparents and this time it was for keeps.

The body I was in slapped him hard across the face. So much for treating him like a king!

Ryan spit out blood and refused to make eye contact with his tormentor.

And then it occurred to me.

When I connected to this dead person, Turner's usual barrier hadn't been in place. This particular corpse didn't have any defenses against me.

Odd.

Why?

A trick most likely. But what kind of trick?

I immediately took control of the rest of the dead person's limbs. I looked down at the body. A woman. Clothes and skin ragged and dirty. Who was this person?

I made her bend down and whisper in Ryan's ear. "Ryan, it's me, Chelsan, Bill and I are at the house. Sit tight and we'll be up in a few."

Ryan's head whirled around so fast to look in the corpse's eyes it frightened me. "Chelsan, don't! Leave me here, please!"

WHAM!

I was bumped out of the dead woman's body.

"Roberta knows we're here. We have to hurry," I said as my head was spiraling. Why didn't Ryan want us to rescue him? He couldn't possibly want to stay. Maybe they were brainwashing him. I didn't care. I was going after him whether he liked it or not.

Taking full control of Mr. Forester we opened the front door without waiting to knock.

It was empty. The foyer was all dark wood paneling and polished flooring. From the brightness emanating in front of us, I saw the glints of gold from the living room. It was hard to forget the gold gaudiness from my mother's vision and apparently Roberta and Turner hadn't changed their décor in the last twenty years.

The eerie stillness made my mind scream the word *trap* over and over. I finally understood why people in horror movies always *investigated* when every instinct in their bodies told them to run. It was as if someone was controlling me and there was nothing I could do to stop it.

Roberta stepped in front of us out of nowhere with five guards behind her. She smiled her stiff, stretched smile. "Chelsan."

"Roberta." I wondered where on earth this was going. She wasn't having the guards attack. She didn't even look like she was mad that I was there. What was going on?

"Come with me. All of you." Roberta turned and walked up a flight of stairs, her guards following dutifully. "You're outnumbered, dears, please," she called over her shoulder.

"Should we?" Bill asked. I could tell he was thinking the same thing I was.

"Ryan told me to leave," I confided in Bill.

"Maybe we should." Bill was a smart guy. He knew something was wrong, too.

"I just can't, Bill. I can't leave Ryan here. They'll never let him go." Even though I knew I was most likely being an idiot and walking straight into the lion's den. I couldn't abandon Ryan. I'd never be able to live with myself.

"Okay. I'm with you." Bill leveled his stun club, ready to use it despite the odds.

"And besides, there's a dead bee hive on the west wing," I whispered to Bill, sensing it as we followed Roberta and her men up the stairs. I didn't know what I'd do with a bunch of bees, but at least it was something. Other than that, Roberta appeared to have had the house cleansed of anything dead aside from a fly here or there. A rush cleansing job. Which meant Turner must have informed her of my escape and they knew I'd be coming here for Ryan. I kept Mr. Forester with us as well, he was more of a shield now than anything else. Somehow, I didn't think I'd be able to keep Jill's dad safe, but my choices were slim and living was way more important than dying to keep my enemy's *dead* dad in good shape.

Bill and I kept a good distance from the guards just in case they tried anything funny, but they seemed very disinterested in us. Their main concern was my feline grandmother who strode down a long hallway with a slight bounce to her step. The flight of stairs was as tacky as the rest of the house with its gold-inlaid carvings of lion heads on the top and bottom of the railings to the silver and gold Chinese-style runner on the steps. But deep dark brown wood was the main attraction of the upstairs, just like the foyer the walls and floor were the same color. The few pieces of artwork hanging from the walls did little to lighten up the space. There wasn't a window in sight, the only light source being the inset bulbs evenly spaced out on the ceiling.

Roberta stopped at a white door at the end of the hallway and turned to me with a large grin. "Here we are," she practically purred.

I was sure that this was the door Ryan was behind. Sure, because of seeing through the dead woman's eyes and sure, because I knew I was walking into the snappy part of her mousetrap. I looked over at Bill and the expression on his face matched what I was feeling.

Roberta's guards stood next to her like statues, void of showing any emotion whatsoever.

"Shall we go in and see your lover?" Roberta cackled. Like a kid who had a surprise that they couldn't wait to reveal.

"Keys, please. I know he's in chains." I decided that whatever she had planned for me I could handle, I only wanted to free Ryan and get out of there.

Suddenly we heard Ryan scream from behind the door. "CHELSAN! DON'T COME IN! GET OUT OF HERE! PLEASE!"

Hearing his desperate plea made me want to help him even more. I knew this was a mistake, but my heart was stronger than my head at this point. She handed me the keys a little too happily for my taste, but I took them anyway.

I shoved past Roberta and her guards, Mr. Forester in tow, and swung the door open.

There was Ryan just as I had seen him through the corpse's eyes, chained to the metal chair. Tears streamed down his bruised face as he looked at me. He was devastated to see me, as if I had sprung the trap and it was too late. All I saw was him, nothing here that could hurt me.

One step at a time. I ran over to his chains and started to unlock him.

"Chelsan," came a woman's voice from behind me.

Chills ran down my spine and I froze in place. It couldn't be. No. No. No. No.

I looked up at Ryan and his eyes confirmed my worst fear.

"You should have left me here." His face was wracked with sympathy.

I slowly turned my head.

I couldn't breathe.

I couldn't think.

I couldn't react.

Standing in front of me was the corpse I had controlled.

Mommy.

I started to shake violently, dropping the keys to the floor.

Roberta's cackle of delight was the only sound that reverberated off the walls.

Mom.

Mom.

Mom.

No.

She was barely recognizable, she was beaten to pulp, her eyes freshly gouged, her skin left to rot. She looked like a zombie out of horror film. Her black swirling hole was invisible to me. Somehow Roberta had found a way to block me from even seeing if a body was dead or not. This was her trick. This was her plan. She brought my mother here to torture me. To punish me. To watch with utter happiness as I suffered. And it was working like a charm.

I couldn't even cry. I was frozen. Literally frozen.

I hardly noticed Bill as he picked up the keys and continued to unchain Ryan.

My mother walked forward and looked at me with her empty sockets. "Such a failure."

I tried to rationalize that this wasn't my mom, this was Roberta making my mom talk, move, function, but the words were coming out of her mouth, with her voice… even with her torn-out eyes and her rotted skin, she was still Mom.

"Stop," I whispered.

"Stop what? Stop telling you the truth? I can finally tell you what I really thought of you," my mother laughed. And it was her laugh.

Tears flowed freely. My body was shaking so badly I could barely stand.

I tried to find her black hole. To disconnect Roberta from my mother's body. To make her stop myself, but it was as if a real live person stood in front of me. If it weren't for her condition I might think she was actually alive…

"Please," I sputtered.

Mom walked up to me and placed her hand against my cheek lovingly. "You were nothing but a burden to me. You killed your father and forced me to marry Bruce. I'll hate you forever, little one."

Roberta and my mom laughed hysterically at the anguish on my face.

Ryan and Bill were both by my side now.

"Let's get out of here." Ryan tried to lead me out of the room.

Roberta nodded to her guards.

Her men quickly grabbed Ryan and Bill before they could even react. They were both so focused on me they didn't have their defenses up. They both struggled to break free, but they weren't strong enough for the…

…wait a minute…

I could sense something in the guards, something off.

Like flashes of light, it was flashes of dark. They were dead, and their swirling holes were hidden like the one in my mother. My emotions clouded me from seeing it in her, but the guards were another story. Just when I started to gain some kind of stability my mom smiled down at me.

"Every second of my life, I wished you were dead instead of your father. Maybe now I can get my wish." She laughed again.

And then she started to dance. It was grotesque and humiliating.

Roberta stepped forward simply thrilled with the events taking place. "I can make her dance some more." She grinned, looking like the cat she was.

I noticed Roberta's eyes were bright solid green.

"Chelsan, she's not your mother! Your mother died! Don't listen to her!" Ryan screamed.

And I suddenly realized he had been screaming this whole time.

I had blocked him out, I was so focused on my mom and Roberta.

I started to break out of the spell.

Roberta made my mother dance and jerk and slam herself against the wall. How long had she been torturing my mother's body like this? How long had she gotten her kicks out of degrading her and beating her up? Roberta used her corpse as a form a therapy to satisfy her thirst for vengeance on my family.

My mom began to scratch and tear flesh off her arms, laughing manically the entire time, continuing to slam herself into the wall.

It made me enraged beyond anything I had ever felt before. All I could see was red. How dare she? How dare she?

I closed my eyes from the fury. In the depths of my soul a scream started to rumble from the very core of my being. A scream so powerful, I could feel my whole body arch backwards from the force. It poured out of my mouth and filled the room with deafening impact.

I could see then.

Even with my eyes closed, I could see everything.

All the things that Roberta kept hidden.

All the corpses roaming the hallways of this giant mansion.

All of their black raging chasms, welcoming me like their true master.

No more.

I connected to each and every one of them.

I felt their last force of life left to them in this world.

And I obliterated it.

BOOM!!!

The whole house shook from the force.

I opened my eyes and I was covered in blood and chunks of flesh.

What had I done?

Rather than see my mother tortured, I had annihilated her entire body. There was nothing left of her. Nothing. Just blood and pieces of rotted flesh splattered everywhere. I didn't know if I could live with myself after that. It felt like I had killed her, even though I knew that wasn't the truth, it felt true and it was consuming me like a wave of guilt I had no way of surviving.

I realized then that the guards had also exploded.

No more black holes.

No more bodies.

I had destroyed them all.

Roberta's eyes were clear as they stared into mine. She was shocked and scared at first, but when she recognized the shame I felt, it was like I had given her the best prize of all. She started to laugh in triumph again, even covered in her own guards' blood, even knowing she was completely alone against me.

She had won.

And I couldn't take it.

I couldn't take that look of victory in her eyes.

I wanted to rip them out myself.

I wanted her to die.

"See how you like this!" I screamed at her.

I connected to the hundreds of dead bees in their fumigated hive and made them fly through an opened window.

Ryan and Bill stood next to me, holding each of my arms.

"Chelsan. Let's get out of here," Ryan pleaded.

But I didn't want to listen to him.

I wanted to see Roberta suffer.

We heard the buzzing before we saw them.

Roberta's face fell slightly as she recognized the sound.

"Let's see how you handles bees, Grams!" I smiled myself.

The swarm of dead bees entered the room like the cavalry. I made them sting her over and over, just to wipe that triumphant smirk off her face. She screamed in anguish and tried to cover her feline face from the bee blitz.

At that point, Ryan and Bill physically dragged me away.

"Chelsan, come on." Bill's voice was laced with concern.

I followed willingly, but I kept the bees attacking Roberta while we headed toward the front door. With each sting it took away some of my guilt and hatred of myself. It felt like the more I hurt her, the better I would be.

I knew it was wrong.

And yet I didn't stop.

We slipped and slid our way through the blood soaked house. Every servant, guard and maid all appeared to have been dead people that couldn't escape my attack. It made me sick to my stomach. I, literally, made all of these people blow up into a million pieces and now the three of us were covered in it and slipping on all that was left of them. What was I?

The more my head spun with the terror of who I was the more I wanted to punish Roberta. It was her fault! Her fault I was the way I was! They performed the ritual to kill me! They had been trying to kill me non-stop for the last two weeks! They had murdered my mother and my neighbors! They had tried to kill my friends! Neither one of them deserved to breathe! Making each bee sting every part of her I could reach was a small penance to pay for what she'd done.

That woman made the last image of my mother a nightmare! She knew I'd never be able to erase that from my mind. And that was precisely why she did it. She wanted me to remember the rotted, beaten, puppet of my mom forever. And I would. And I hated her for it.

She had fallen to the floor now, the bees too much for her.

I didn't care.

Jill's father.

He had exploded like the rest of them.

I pushed it from my brain. He was already dead. I didn't kill him. But why did it feel like I killed everyone in there?! Roberta made me feel like I murdered my own mother! The hate that seethed through my blood was like an addictive poison I couldn't get rid of and a part of me didn't want to. The hate felt right.

It felt good.

The three of us ran out the front door and we stopped dead in our tracks.

Turner was there with a handful of his armed soldiers.

Turner raced up to me, already knowing what I was doing. "Please, take them off of her. Please!"

I shrugged away from him. "I warned you!" I wanted to set the bees on him as well, but something in his eyes made me pause.

"Please, she's all I have left in this world. You took my son away from me, don't take her away, too. I can't stop them! I tried! Please!" Turner was desperate.

And instead of feeling good (like I thought I would) he was actually making me feel bad.

No.

She deserved it!

And so did he!

They killed my mother.

As if from nowhere an onslaught of Police-hovers and Press-hovers flooded the front of Turner's house and started landing all over his property.

The hover-van nearest to us opened its doors. Jason and Nancy spilled out and hurried over to us.

Nancy's eyes were wide with horror as she saw the three of us covered in blood and people bits. Her hand went to her mouth. "We need paramedics!!" she screamed.

"Nancy, it's not our blood. We're okay," Bill reassured her.

One look at us and Jason approached Turner with a serious and condemning expression. "We have the footage of your exterminators killing Chelsan's trailer park already on the air."

A particularly burly policeman handcuffed Turner and started to drag him away toward his hover.

The press was screaming at Turner and screaming at us. I couldn't concentrate, but I couldn't stop making the bees attack Roberta either.

Turner kept his eyes on me, terrified. "Chelsan, please!"

I could feel that Roberta's body wasn't moving as I made the bees continue to sting her.

Ryan whispered in my ear. "Your father died to save you. He could have killed his parents instead, but he didn't."

My head froze up.

My knees gave way as Ryan caught me.

A wave of reality washed over me.

I dropped the bees.

What was wrong with me?

"Upstairs." I grabbed the first policeman I could find. "Roberta Turner was attacked by bees. She needs medical help."

Nancy embraced me tightly. "We thought you were dead. Again." She pulled away smiling, although she groaned when she realized that she now had blood all over her as well. "Oh great."

I tried to smile back, but it wasn't in me. "Can we just go home?"

She picked up on the mood of the moment and figured out pretty quickly that the last thing anyone of us wanted to do was celebrate.

"Of course." Nancy gave me another hug, stains be damned.

"My car is over one block," Bill said and we started to walk through the throng of reporters and police officers, all asking us why we were blood-soaked.

None of us answered them. What would we say anyway? Jason would think of something, like he always did.

Roberta was taken out of the house by hover-gurney. She was alive. I was surprised at how relieved I was about that. With everything that had happened, I let my rage get the best of me. It made me hate myself all the more.

As Turner was being placed into the police-hover he nodded to me then turned away.

Maybe there could be a truce between us.

I doubted it.

I just hoped they'd be able to keep him in jail.

As we made our way back to Bill's hover-car, Ryan held my hand and squeezed it. "You going to be okay?"

I shrugged.

I honestly didn't know.

The ride back was silent. No one wanted to say anything that might cause anyone any pain.

George and Vianne were waiting for us in the front yard. They freaked out when they saw all the blood, but as soon as they realized it wasn't ours they were all hugs and smiles. Their house was back in order and aside from the front door everything looked like home again.

George gave us all robes to change into while Vianne made us a quick meal. The only thing we washed was our hands, we were too tired and hungry to do a proper job. We all must have looked a fright with our hair and skin covered with dried blood, not to mention the cuts and bruises Ryan and Bill were sporting.

I scarfed down my entire plate and even had seconds.

Nancy did most of the talking, telling us of her and Jason's escapade to air the footage. They managed to sneak into the International News Building and through clever maneuvering, Jason snuck into the main server room and aired the footage on all stations across the globe. Nancy explained that Jason didn't want to risk telling his producers about the chip for fear of them working for Turner. "You can't trust anyone. Jason's right about that." Nancy's eyes fluttered. I guess they had worked things out. But knowing them, that could last all of five minutes.

"Turn on the holo." Jason walked into the kitchen and we all jumped slightly.

"You scared us to death." Nancy stood up and grabbed his arm with a flirty smile. Yup. They were definitely on good terms again.

"Just turn it on." Jason wasn't happy and that made my stomach sink.

Vianne clicked the holo-tv on.

The news anchor was at his desk with footage of Turner behind him at a press conference.

Turner had his usual *public face* on. All concern and heartbreak. "It appalls me that Mayor Bradfield could be responsible for such acts. It is a violation of what Population Control stands for and it a hideously cruel act of murder and man-slaughter. Our hearts go out to the victims of this horrendous crime and Population Control will do everything in its power to make restitution for Mayor Bradfield's actions. I'd especially like to thank Jason Keroff and Chelsan Derée for bringing this footage to light. If not for the heroics of those two individuals, Mayor Bradfield would have succeeded. The city of Los Angeles thanks you, the world thanks you, and I thank you..."

Jason turned the holo off with a grunt. "The bastard got away with it. Every bit of footage, equipment and logs were all under Bradfield's name. We should have known when he let us go so easily at Headquarters. It wouldn't hurt him either way if we actually succeeded!" Jason was fuming now.

I should have been more upset by this news, but somehow it seemed expected.

This was a small respite from my grandfather. I didn't know how, but I just knew it in my heart.

"Make him set up a memorial," I said to Jason, interrupting his rant.

Jason stopped and he nodded. "First thing."

Ryan leaned over and kissed my cheek. It was the first feeling of good that I felt since leaving Turner's.

Jason was already on the phone making demands and it made me smile a little as I looked around the kitchen. My new family. Everyone with a few bumps and bruises but otherwise just fine. I felt my emotions course through me as I realized how much they were a part of my life. As difficult as it was to think of my mother after everything that happened, I knew she'd be happy for me. I couldn't let my grandparents have that kind of power over me. I wouldn't let them destroy the beautiful memories I had of my mom. She loved me with everything that she had. She stayed with a man that beat the crap out of her just to keep me safe. She would always be my hero.

Ryan reached over and wiped the tears from my cheeks. I didn't even know I had been crying. I had been doing a lot of that lately. And probably a lot more in the days to come. I needed to heal from all this and it was going to take time.

Ryan held my face in his hands and kissed me. It was filled with just as much passionate, toe-curling craziness as all of Ryan's kisses, but there was something more to it this time. I wasn't nervous. It felt right. I finally felt like we loved each other equally. I never wanted to be with anyone else and I knew Ryan felt the same way.

"You all need showers," George said with a crinkle of his nose.

It was such an obvious statement that we all laughed. It was good to release the tension. And for once in a very long time I felt like everything was going to be okay.

"I hate to be the bad guy here, but school *is* tomorrow." Vianne gave us a look that made it clear she was just the messenger.

Really?!

I couldn't believe it was only Monday! But the more I thought about it, the more welcoming it sounded. Normal. Calm.

Then I thought of Jill's threat: *If my father doesn't come back, I'm holding you fully responsible and if you think your life was torture before, you haven't seen anything yet.*

Well, at least she wouldn't try and kill me.

Who was I kidding? School was going to suck.

Uuggh!

REAPER
BOOK TWO

I was dreaming.

It was the only way I could explain the darkness.

It felt as if I was standing in outer space where someone forgot to add the stars. It had to be a dream…

…Or maybe something else.

My gut was screaming that this was something more. Something all too familiar.

The last time I had a "dream" like this my friend (and super famous reporter) Jason Keroff told me it was called astral projection. Yeah, sounds pretty weird, but actually it's quite terrifying. It basically means that I've either traveled to someone else's brain or they've traveled to mine.

Either way, not exactly my idea of a fun time.

I might be jaded though. The only three times I've ever experienced astral projection were pretty horrific. The first time was my mother telling me that she was being murdered. The second and third times were with my grandparents. Which I know for a normal eighteen-year-old girl might not be a problem, but for me it was terrifying since my grandparents wanted to kill me.

Yes, I said kill me.

What's crazy is that I didn't even know who my grandparents were two months ago! But suddenly they were in my life and ready to take me down. In fact, they were the ones who murdered my mother in the first place!

My grandfather is Geoffrey Turner, the Vice President of Population Control, which basically makes him the most powerful man on the globe. With the world's population out of control due to a tiny pill called Age-pro, which stops the aging process and makes you young forever, he definitely has his hands full. Before I knew him as Gramps I thought he was a pretty decent guy, but that was before I found out *how* he actually controlled over-population.

Unbeknownst to the public, he exterminates them, and my mom was one of the casualties. He gassed our trailer park and made the world believe it was a tornado. If it weren't for my besties, Nancy, Bill and Jason (and my unbelievably amazingly gorgeous boyfriend, Ryan), the public would never have known about what really happened to my mom. Of course, sneaky man that my grandfather is, he completely framed the Mayor of Los Angeles and got away scot-free. So *my* mission wasn't over. I vowed to expose my grandfather for the mass murderer he was.

I still intend to accomplish this.

The first time Gramps visited my dreams he flaunted the fact that he had Brady, (the serial killer he hired to kill me) under his control. (Yes, he employs serial killers for his methods of "fixing" over-population. Serial killers who were supposed to be extinct for a hundred years!) I could see the black swirling hole spinning in the center of Brady's chest and I knew he was dead, and that my grandfather controlled him.

Did I forget to mention that's how I see dead people?

Actually, anything dead. If it had life, and now it doesn't, I see a black churning hole in its center.

Oh, and I should also probably mention that I can control the dead, too. Like they were puppets. Seriously, I know how it sounds, but it's something I inherited as a baby when my father sacrificed himself to save my mother and me from the deadly curse dear old Grandpa and Grandma placed on us. (Another story for another time. Let's just say that Dad's side of the family has some serious conflict-resolution issues.) Anyway, I quickly found out my grandparents have the same power to control the dead that I have, but they use rituals and Vodun spells to do it. I guess that gives me an advantage because my power over the dead is innate, but not much. Turner still manages to be a step ahead of me at every turn.

The third time I experienced this "dream astral thingy" was with Roberta, my grandmother. She's what society calls a *Feline*. Someone who was around when Age-pro was invented in 2030, and had so many face-lifts they resembled cats. Age-pro "freezes" you at the age you're at when you start taking it, so she was stuck with *stretched frozen face* forever. Turner keeps her out of the public eye since Felines terrify the youthful public. The main difference between my third dream and the earlier ones was the fact that it was actually *me* who traveled to *her* head. I saw all sorts of things in Roberta's twisted brain. The worst being that she and Turner kept my father eight-years-old for a hundred years by giving him Age-pro! So horrific, I still can't stop thinking about it.

So, yeah, astral projection, definitely lame.
I looked around in the darkness, hoping that I wasn't in either grandparent's head. Maybe I lucked out and I was in Ryan's brain.

I immediately wished I hadn't thought that. What if I saw that he didn't like me as much as I liked him? Or he was going to break up with me? Or he secretly liked someone else? I knew I was being paranoid, but I couldn't help it. Ryan was just about the smartest most amazing boyfriend EVER. And I didn't want to find out I was completely delusional in thinking that he actually liked me.

I took a deep breath. I had nothing to worry about. Ryan had proven how much he liked me over and over. I needed to grow some confidence!

A child's voice called out in the darkness. My heart skipped a beat. The voice sounded terrified.

"Hello?" I answered back. The blackness was so complete I couldn't even see my hand in front of me.

Suddenly, I started to glow like my skin was coated with phosphorous. I became the light source in the inky shadows.

That's when a girl about seven years of age stepped into the luminosity my skin radiated. She was stunning to look at, with porcelain skin, bright lavender eyes and long black hair almost as dark as our surroundings. I couldn't stop staring at her eyes. Aside from their over-large kewpie doll size, they were filled with sadness and fear, but mostly hope.

"You are Chelsan, aren't you?" she asked tentatively.

"Yes," I kind of mumbled. I was still trying to figure out why I was in this girl's head or more likely why she was in mine.

"I knew it." The little girl closed her eyes and took a sigh of relief. "I've been searching for you since I first saw you."

"Um…" Wow. I was full of words of wisdom. I couldn't seem to help it. Even though this girl was maybe eight tops, she intimidated the crap out of me. She just held herself in a way that radiated power. I felt out of my depth and I couldn't figure out why.

"I saw you." She stepped forward and her lavender eyes pierced through me.

I felt like I was being probed or something. It scared me enough to take a step back from her.

"Who are you?" I blurted out.

The girl immediately placed her hands up in supplication. "Don't be scared of me. I need your help, and you're the only one with the power to do it."

"Look kid…" I was about to try and break our brain-dream connection. This girl was freaking me out on a core level, even worse than Turner had when I first met him. She was just… well… scary. And I had *zero* reasons to give why. It was just instinctual. Something was very off.

"I'm ninety-eight."

Oh.

Oh man.

Of course. That's what was off. Her eyes were scary because she was almost a hundred years old and stuck in a child's body! She said she had seen me before.

"The I.Q. Farm." I suddenly realized.

"Yes. I saw you use the rats." She looked up at me with desperation. "I saw you bring them to life and attack the guards. You escaped and left us all there." She nearly choked from emotion.

I remembered all too well. When the gang and I snuck into Turner's headquarters I connected to hundreds of dead rats and made them attack Turner's army so we could escape. It was a terrifying experience especially when we stumbled into one of Turner's biggest secrets: I.Q. Farms.

Turner kidnaps kids whose test scores rank above the genius level and brings them to facilities known as I.Q. Farms. The public has no idea these farms even exist, and Turner's goons keep the children's parents silent. The only reason I had even heard of these farms in the first place was because Turner took *Ryan* when he was eight. Ryan pretended he had cheated on his test scores and Turner sent him back home. Three years later my grandparents were furious when they realized that Ryan had tricked them when he solved Trilidon's theorem. (A math problem that hadn't been solved in centuries!) But Ryan never forgot how terrifying the I.Q. Farm had been. And when we discovered one as we were escaping from Gramps's headquarters, Ryan realized that some of the kids were the same age as when he'd left them.

Yet another distortedly repulsive thing my grandfather does. Using Age-pro to keep these kids children forever. I still didn't know why these farms existed, but seeing this girl in front of me and knowing she was eighty years older than me made me want to throw-up a little.

"I'm… I'm sorry." That was all that I could say. The kids had looked like they were in technological comas when we were there, all of them strapped into devices and focused on holo-screens.

But the guilt hit me like a ton of bricks.

I had left hundreds of kids locked in a basement of technology against their will.

I could have done something…

Couldn't I have?

I just didn't know. I was so focused on saving my friends at the time, I hadn't even considered helping the kids.

"Don't be. If you had been captured, you would have been killed. But you can help now." The girl managed a small smile. "My name is Elisha Stearne. I was seven when I was taken. I've been in the main facility ever since." Elisha looked around with sudden paranoia as if someone was about to appear in front of us. "He's coming. I don't have much time.

Turner is monitoring my brain activity. He knows I left..."

"What can I do?" I asked. My guilt made want to do anything I could to help this girl or lady or… gross! I didn't want to think about it too long.

"You need to help me and some others escape." Elisha's eyes were round with fear and determination. "We're guarded by Turner's dead army. You can break through your grandfather's defenses. I need you Chelsan. I have to go."

"Wait!" I didn't want her to leave. I felt like I needed more to go on.

Elisha's beautiful face was contorted with terror. "You only have two days, after that it won't matter."

"Why?" I was already getting in panic mode.

"Turner has scheduled my execution for Thursday morning."

SWOOSH!

Elisha flew out of my sight like a giant vacuum cleaner had sucked her back into the black void she came from.

CHAPTER 1

TUESDAY NOVEMBER 30, 2320

I awoke with a start.

What the...?

It took me a moment to stop my heart from racing. After a few deep calming breaths, (something I'd learned how to do in the last couple of months!) I tried to focus on my surroundings.

I was in my new room at Nancy's house. It was by far the nicest place I'd ever lived. (Although living in a beat-up trailer my whole life, it wasn't exactly hard to top!) But this room was amazing for more reasons than its esthetic. Nancy's parents, George and Vianne, had pretty much adopted me when they found out about my mother's death. And shockingly, they didn't throw me out when I told them about my powers and that Geoffrey Turner was trying to kill me. They were there through it all, and at this point I couldn't imagine my life without them. They helped fill the void of losing my mom without trying to replace her.

Aside from being on Turner's hit list, I was a pretty lucky girl.

I pulled back my fluffy green comforter and slapped my bare feet on the hardwood oak floors. Three windows lined the east wall with a perfect view of Nancy's neighborhood. We were in an upper middle class suburb of Los Angeles, so the trees and grass were green and vibrant. I could barely see the silos at the end of each block used for watering the greens with recycled water from hover-car fuel cells.

Most importantly, just past the first row of houses and all the way to the side I could see the roof of Ryan's house. Nancy gave me this room for that very reason. She joked that I could keep an eye on him that way, and then she'd grumble to herself about keeping an eye on Jason, and then she'd be grumpy for at least an hour. (Their "relationship" was complicated and usually ended up with Nancy in a huff.)

Sometimes, Ryan would sit on his roof so we could see each other, then he'd get impatient and sneak through my window. We had only kissed so far, but that alone made my head explode. I never thought I could be so attached to one human being, but Ryan was seriously beyond amazing. I wondered if it was like that for my parents when they fell in love. I knew they didn't fall in love at first sight since my Feline grandmother informed me that my mother was Dad's nanny. Granted, Dad was a ninety-five-year-old-eight-year-old, but still, eeww. I can only guess that my mom's decision to kidnap Dad was after she realized Roberta and Turner were giving their son Age-pro and that she cared for him deeply as a person. Later, after he grew up, they fell in love. At least, I hoped that was the way it went. I'd never know since both my parents were gone.

I thought about Elisha. So similar to my father. He was almost a hundred when Mom rescued him, now it was my turn to do the same for this poor girl. Or woman. Now I knew how my mom felt. What a horrible feeling talking to a *child* who was decades older than yourself. It really messed with my brain.

TAP. TAP. TAP.

I turned to see Ryan's wonderfully silly grin outside my window. I hurried over and opened it. Being two stories up, I knew he was most likely in a precarious position and the last thing I wanted was my boyfriend to go SPLAT on Nancy's lawn.

"Hey," he said with that lopsided smile that always made my heart squeeze in torture.

Ryan crawled inside the room with the grace of a cat. He pulled me into his arms as soon as his feet hit the floor and kissed me with such intensity it made my knees buckle.

Gulp. Oh boy.

You'd think I'd be able to calm down in his presence by now, but every time Ryan even looked at me my brain fluttered. Which wasn't hard to do considering how utterly gorgeous he was. His short sandy-blonde hair was mussed up in a perfectly saucy kind of way, and his giant brown eyes sparkled when he looked at me. Ryan's face was angular and chiseled like a master sculpture had created his masterpiece and it came to life in the form of my boyfriend.

Why did he like me again?

Uugggh!

I pulled away with a smile, but stayed enclosed in his arms. "Good morning to you, too."

Ryan kissed my forehead. "You ready for school?"

"You know, George and Vianne would probably prefer you come through the front door once in a while." I looked up at him and smiled.

His face suddenly turned serious and he cupped my face with his hands. "What is it? Something's wrong."

Wow.

I couldn't hide anything from him.

"I had a visitation this morning. In my brain." I was still reeling at the fact that Ryan could tell that I was upset even when I had momentarily forgotten what I was upset about. (He had that effect on me.)

His face turned white and he pulled me in closer. "Was it one or both of your grandparents?"

"Neither." I rested my head on his chest and found that if I just stood in that exact spot everything seemed better. "Look, I think I should tell the gang about this. It's big."

I felt him nod and then his lips kissing the top of my head.

I didn't know how I was going to bring up the topic of I.Q. Farms with Ryan alone, so I figured it would be better to tell everyone at once. I had never seen Ryan as upset as he was when he saw the Farm in Gramps's headquarters. That was my fault. I brought him there. I didn't want to see him in that kind of pain *ever* again, but if I was going to help Elisha I'd have to. Ryan would deal. I just didn't want him to have to *deal* quite yet.

"Well, maybe I can keep your mind off of whatever it is," Ryan said as he kissed me passionately.

Sigh.

Ryan led me to my bed since I tended to lose all control of my knees when we kissed. Everything intensified in a matter of seconds as we lay down together. I could feel the strength of his hands pulling me in closer.

Dizzy, party of one.

The more we kissed the more I wanted more. (*More* being the operative word, here.)

Yes, please.

"Oh, sorry." Bill's voice interrupted us like a guillotine.

I pulled away from Ryan to look up and see Bill. He looked devastated and horrified all rolled up into one giant ball of guilt for me.

"Bill, uh, hi," I managed to get out. Could I sound any lamer?

"I… I… sorry…" Bill just kind of stood there awkwardly. Being six-feet tall, with his blue eyes and messy brown hair, he looked particularly adorable today, except for the hurt radiating from his face. Bill was my other best friend. Besides Nancy, Bill was the only other person who didn't treat me like a leper at school before all this craziness happened to me. His parents were the richest humans alive, pretty much, which gave him the social leeway to hang out with anyone he wanted. It wasn't until I started dating Ryan when I realized Bill had feelings for me. It was hard at first with the typical male *territorial ape* crap. I had hoped that, after everything Bill and Ryan went through together to save the world from my Gramps, they had come to an understanding, but seeing Bill's face and the dirty look he had just given Ryan, I could tell there were still some fences to be mended.

"I'll see you guys downstairs." Bill was practically sprinting his way down the hallway.

"I'll go get him," I said as I stood up to go after him.

Ryan drew me back onto the bed and kissed me. "Bill can wait."

I stood up again. "I'm sorry, but he's Bill, and he's hurt."

Ryan rubbed his hand over his face in frustration. "He's got to get over it."

I sat next to Ryan on the bed and placed my hand on his leg. "He will, we just have to give him some time, and some *understanding*." I eyed him knowingly.

Ryan kissed my cheek. "There's a limit to how *understanding* I can be. The guy hasn't let up."

"I know, but let me handle it," I said with as much conviction as possible.

Ryan leaned in and kissed me until I couldn't see straight.

"Seriously?" Nancy's voice interrupted our moment from the doorway.

We both turned to see her with her hands on her hips, rolling her eyes at us. Nancy looked perfectly coifed and gorgeous. Even with a casual tank and jeans she looked like a super model. She was physically the complete opposite of me. Nancy had long blonde locks and giant blue eyes while I had shoulder length chestnut brown hair and boring grey eyes.

"Hey, Nancy." Ryan pulled away from me, (lame) and gently grabbed my hand (better). I guess Bill could wait a little while longer.

"Hey, yourself. It's called the *front door*, genius boy." Nancy walked over to the window and shut it.

"I'm an impatient guy, what can I tell you." Ryan grinned at Nancy.

Nancy shook her head. "Honestly, we should build a staircase for you." Nancy put her hands on her hips again. "Bill looks like he saw his puppy die. I'm assuming he walked in on you two?"

I nodded and she shook her head. "Well, the sooner he gets over this the better." Then she raised her eyebrow with curiosity. "What? You have that look. Is something else wrong?"

Really? I guess I was destined to never win a hand of poker.

Ryan squeezed my hand tighter. "Assemble the gang. Chelsan says it's a biggie."

Nancy gave me a quick hug. "I thought we were done with all the torment and torture."

"You guys are. This is all me. And I just need advice, not help." I wanted to make it clear right away that I was in no way going to involve them in whatever *this* turned out to be. After everything I dragged them through a couple of months ago, I couldn't bear putting them in danger again. (And breaking out ninety-eight-year-old children from an I.Q. Farm wasn't exactly safe.)

Nancy rolled her eyes again and turned to Ryan. "Could you smack some sense into her, please?" She turned to me, "Chelsan, when are you going to get it through your thick head that we're *always* going to help, so just forget about all the arguments and rationalizations you've probably intricately designed in that brain of yours and get over it." Her eyes widened in a sudden thought, "I better call Jason to get his butt over here." Nancy looked down at her outfit. "I can't wear this, I look horrible!" And she was out the door and out of sight.

"She's right, you know. You can't talk us out of it. We're going to help you whether you like it or not." Ryan leaned down and kissed me with an agonizing tenderness that made me wobbly. "You sure you don't want to talk about it now?"

"Yeah. You go downstairs, let me get dressed," I said and squeezed Ryan's hand reassuringly. "I'll tell you guys everything and then you can decide if you really want to get involved. Don't make any decisions until you hear what I have to say." I still wasn't convinced my friends should have anything to do with Elisha, especially Ryan. I.Q. Farms may hit a little too close to home for him and I didn't want him to have to put himself through more torture for some kid he didn't know.

Ryan just shook his head and smiled. "You're crazy you know that?" He kissed my forehead. "I'd do anything for you."

My heart practically flew out of my chest at the sincerity of Ryan's words. "Me too," was all I could utter.

"I love you." Ryan brushed his hand against my cheek and gave me his crooked smile.

"I love you, too," I said, smiling back and punched his arm affectionately. "Now go, I have to get dressed for school. And Ryan?"

"Yes?" he answered affectionately.

"Be nice to Bill," I said as delicately as possible.

Ryan sighed and then nodded. "Yes, ma'am."

He walked toward the door then turned with a sly grin just as he was about to leave. "You sure I couldn't stay? I promise not to look."

I laughed and threw a pillow at him. It hit him square in the chest with a loud thump. "Yeah, right, perv."

Ryan put his hands up in surrender. He quickly grabbed the pillow off the floor and flung it at me.

I ducked and the pillow landed on the floor. "Nice try."

Ryan laughed and shut the door.

Why did I have to have some astral mumbo jumbo ruin everything? Maybe when I sat everyone down and told them about it they'd all agree it was a bad dream and I should ignore it completely.

Yeah, right.

I quickly threw on a fitted T, jeans and my Chucks and headed out the darkly stained oak door.

I hurried across the terracotta tiling of the hallway and barely glanced at the Spanish yellow walls I had grown so used to over the last two months. It had really become home to me. Brushing past the other five oak doors that made up Nancy's second floor, I wondered if Bill was okay.

I walked down the wrought iron staircase and glanced out the window as I made my way to the bottom floor. I could see Bill's hover-car parked in Nancy's landing zone. Poor guy, he probably came by early so he could see me before Ryan did. I didn't know how much clearer I could be with Bill. I pretty much told him there was no way it was going to happen, but he still looked at me in that way... maybe it really was a good thing Bill walked in on Ryan and I, he wouldn't be able to be in denial anymore.

Walking past the living room, I made my way toward the kitchen and heard Bill and Ryan talking. I stopped at the door to listen. They weren't arguing, which was good, but they didn't sound all that cordial either. I wasn't ready to walk in yet. Forget the whole Bill and Ryan thing, I knew I was going to have to talk about this Elisha girl and I.Q. Farms and, frankly, I didn't want to.

"Whatever it is, she looked pretty spooked." I could hear the worry dripping from Ryan's voice.

"Yeah, you looked like you were really concerned about her well-being." Bill's sarcasm was pretty obvious.

"Bill, shut it." I could visualize Nancy rolling her eyes. "And you, calm down." She must have been talking to Ryan.

"Well, don't push her. Let her tell us when she's ready," Vianne scolded everyone in the kitchen. She really was such a mom.

"She can't tell us anyway, Jason isn't here." Leave it to Nancy to bring every conversation back to Jason. I smiled in spite of myself. That girl was really hooked.

"She *so* likes me."

I whirled around to see Jason standing behind me with his signature roguish smile. He was looking pretty gorgeous, I must say, with his messy black hair and bright green eyes. Even his crooked nose looked extra easy on the eyes today. No wonder he was an *International* heartthrob reporter. He used to be the guy I had a crush on to keep my mind off of Ryan. I had no clue that Ryan actually liked me so I needed to focus on someone so I wouldn't become obsessed with a lost cause. And seeing Jason there in front of me I was suddenly filled with a giant balloon of emotion for my friends who had become my family. I threw my arms around him and gave him a giant hug.

"Hi, Jason," I mumbled into his chest.

Jason hugged me back. "Well this is a nice welcome. It must be bad." Jason pulled away and looked me in the eyes. "Yup, definitely bad. You look freaked."

Seriously. Open book.

"Come on. I'll tell you in the kitchen." I grabbed Jason's hand and opened the door.

All eyes turned to us as we entered the room.

Ryan immediately took my hand away from Jason and held it possessively. (It always made my heart skip a beat when he did that.)

Bill tried to ignore Ryan's territorial hand grab and waved a hello to me with an awkward nod. I hated that I made him feel horrible all the time by being with Ryan. I wished I knew some girl I could hook him up with. Nancy was hopelessly in love with Jason and I really didn't know any other girls, least of all anyone that was worthy of Bill. He deserved the best and I just wish I could find her for him.

Vianne came over and kissed my cheek. "Sit down, dear, I made you breakfast."

I sometimes had to remind myself that Vianne, George and Jason were all over a hundred-years-old since everyone in the room looked eighteen thanks to Age-pro.

Vianne was ridiculously cute. She had a short blonde bob that was always flawlessly in place and big blue eyes like her daughter's.

At least four inches shorter than Nancy, Vianne was a petite woman with a slender figure.

"Don't force her if she's not hungry," George said while reading the morning news on his electronic reader. He was six feet tall with short brown hair and dark brown eyes. George wasn't exactly a muscular man, but he wasn't fat either, just soft. Even though his physical age looked eighteen he still seemed like an older man.

"No, it's okay, I'm starving," I said and sat down at the table.

This made everyone visibly relax and soon the whole gang was sitting around the table eating breakfast and… trying to avoid eye contact with me the whole time.

Okay. Here goes.

"I had one of those astral projection thingies." There. I started the conversation.

Jason nodded toward George who produced a red glowing orb. It was a device he invented so that Gramps could never listen in on any of our conversations.

"Turner?" Jason put his fork down and gave me his full attention, as did the others.

"No. A girl named Elisha Stearne. Or, not a girl really… she was from an I.Q. Farm. She's actually ninety-eight," I said the last part very fast. Really just for Ryan's sake, but I knew it disturbed everyone else as well.

"What did she want?" Jason asked.

In the two months since everything happened, Jason had become the resident leader of our little group. Mainly because he was a reporter and had access to information us "regular folk" didn't. It definitely wasn't because of his fighting skills. That boy could scream like a girl when he was in physical danger, but when it came to figuring out a problem, Jason was the man.

"She wants me to help her escape… from the Farm." I was still trying to process what I just went through. "To be honest, I have no idea if that's even possible, but she seemed pretty certain I could do it."

"We *have* to do it," Ryan spoke up and his tone was deadly serious.

I looked up at him. His eyes were determined and there was rage in them as well.

I knew he'd react that way. It was probably why I didn't tell him in my bedroom. I didn't want to see him volunteer for something that may cost him his life.

"Do you know where she is?" Jason took the reigns back in the meeting.

"Headquarters. She saw us there when we escaped."

"Okay. We'll take a few days to try and come up with a plan," Jason offered as he took a bite of his pancake. I could tell his brain was already churning with ideas.

"We have to break her out tomorrow. Turner is going to execute her Thursday morning." I thought I'd throw that out there.

Bill's eyes widened. "Execute?"

Jason nearly choked on his food. "Tomorrow?"

Nancy patted him on the back and turned to me. "Did she say why?"

I shook my head. "No, but he's tried to kill me more times than I can count, so that automatically puts her on our side. Guys, she looked terrified. It was really weird talking to her, I mean she looked like a kid, but she's seven decades older than me. It kind of creeped me out. All I know is, I have to get her out of there. She said there were others that needed help, too. I can't just leave them there to die. I just can't." I didn't realize how emotional I really was about all this. I was still struggling with the guilt of leaving all those kids in Gramps's Farm when I might have had a chance to help them.

"Let's do this." Ryan was in *green light* mode. Rescuing kids from I.Q. Farms would help ease his own feelings of guilt for escaping that fate. And to boot, it had only been a matter of weeks since he had to come face to face with the actual Farm. He told me he was still having nightmares about it. Yet another horrible thing I was responsible for. Traumatizing my boyfriend. Yeah, I'm awesome.

"I have to think this through. I mean this kind of thing takes weeks of planning." Jason was spooked, I could tell. He tended to do that under pressure.

"It only took us one night to figure out how to break in last time." Nancy shrugged.

"Yeah, and if you recall, Turner knew we were there the whole time which was why we were able to get in." Jason shoved a fork full of pancake into his mouth, obviously annoyed at Nancy's comment.

"We still escaped though." Nancy's temper was starting to rise.

"Because he *let* us." Jason wasn't letting it go either.

And that was how Nancy and Jason's relationship had been since the day they met.

"Guys, not now," I spoke up before the argument could escalate into annoying the rest of us. "Jason is right, Nancy: Turner let us in *and* he let us go. If we want any chance of rescuing this girl we have to think of something else."

Nancy looked at me like I had just slapped her in the face. I guess uttering the words, "Jason is right" was not exactly a BFF thing to do, but he *was* right. When we broke in, Turner knew it the whole time. He was just playing with us because it amused him.

"Wipe that triumphant smirk off your face." Nancy glared at Jason.

Jason ignored her and turned to me. "Let me see what I can find out about our new friend Elisha." He focused on Ryan. "If you still have the blueprints memorized that could seriously help us find a way in."

"I remember." Ryan nodded.

Ryan's brilliant brain could memorize anything he looked at. He was the reason we found a way out of Gramps's crazy building.

"I hate to be the bearer of bad news, but if you don't leave now, you'll all be late for school." Vianne brought everyone back to the present moment.

I quickly finished my last bite of pancakes and the four of us stood up to leave.

Jason's phone suddenly made a blipping noise.

"Nice ring tone." Nancy was obviously still mad at Jason.

Jason grabbed his phone with apprehension. "It's not my ring tone. It's an alarm telling me whenever Turner is on the air." Jason stood up. "Let's go into the living room and check it out."

We all made our way into the living room and George and Vianne were the only two to sit down on the large wrap-around black vinyl couch. Jason picked up the remote and turned on the life-size holographic television.

Nancy's holo-tv was one of the best out there. It felt as if the people were actually standing in the room with us the quality was so crisp and clear. Carleton Gordan, the local news anchor (he was incredibly monotone and boring) sat at his desk with holo-video of a burning building behind him.

"Standing by at the site of the terrorist act is Vice President of Population Control, Geoffrey Turner," Carleton said with as little enthusiasm as he could muster.

Vianne's hands went to her mouth in shock. The rest of us felt the same.

There hadn't been any kind of terrorist attack for over two hundred years. My grandpa managed to keep the peace by making people terrified of dying and losing their immortality with Age-pro. If they only knew he was actually mass murdering millions!

If there was an attack, my bet was that Turner was behind it.

Ryan put his arm around me and I snuggled in close. No matter what happened at least I had Ryan at my side. It amazed me at how much a difference that actually made in keeping me sane.

Carleton left the screen and the scene changed to the front of the burning building, where a podium was set up. My breath caught in my throat as my grandpa stepped up to the microphone. I had only seen him twice since he last tried to kill me and both times were on holo. My knees shook. I was still so scared of him, but when someone tries to murder you a bagillion times it was kind of hard not to be. Did I mention he had a serial killer kidnap and torture me?

Ryan held me tighter and I felt a hand on my shoulder. I looked behind me and there was Bill's supportively sweet face, his baby blues full of concern. I touched his hand and squeezed my thanks. Ryan didn't like that, of course, but he didn't say anything.

Turner turned to the holo-cam, which made it look like he was talking directly to us in Nancy's living room. Turner was one of the few public faces that actually looked old. He started taking Age-pro when it was invented over three hundred years ago and he was in his fifties at the time. It was still strange to me so see actual wrinkles and lines on his face. Not many people from that era ever left their houses. They mainly kept to themselves since everyone pretty much gawked at them wherever they went. Seeing someone over the age of forty or fifty was like staring at a hover-car wreck. You just couldn't keep your eyes off them. But power had perks and since Turner was the most powerful man in the world no one ever mentioned his age.

Turner cleared his throat and spoke into the microphone, "I am shocked and devastated to bring you the news of this horrible outrage. Behind me is the Los Angeles Baby Center."

We all gasped, even the normally stoic George couldn't control his surprise.

Someone attacked a Baby Center!

Turner was right. This news was devastating. Baby Centers were all over the world. They were created for the rich so they could have children and not have to stop taking their Age-pro. Age-pro worked in a way that basically stopped the aging process at whatever age you started taking it. So as a result it ended up being the ultimate birth control. If your body stopped growing it meant nothing could grow inside you either. When women realized they had to stop taking Age-pro in order to have kids there was an uproar. (Among the rich anyway, poor people couldn't start taking Age-pro until thirty when the National Health Care kicked in so they could have babies all through their twenties if they wanted.)

Eventually, the solution became Baby Centers. A place where the rich could donate their eggs and sperm and have surrogate mothers inseminated. It was a Win-Win situation for both the women of meager means and rich women. For the poor, if you volunteered to be a surrogate at one of the centers you were allowed to take Age-pro at twenty-three when your contract was up. So from eighteen to twenty-three you were basically pregnant the entire time and treated like a Queen. For the rich, they could have as many babies as they wanted and still be able to take their Age-pro.

The centers had been around for at least a hundred years and pretty much everyone I knew came from the L.A. Baby Center. Except for Bill. His parents were so ridiculously rich they didn't care what people thought of their age so they both stopped taking Age-pro until Bill was born. I met them for the first time a month ago and they looked like they were in their twenties. I admired them for not caring what people thought. Rich people who didn't look eighteen were usually shunned in their community, but when you were as rich as Bill's parents, no one said a word.

Ryan had tensed up at the news. He and Nancy were both conceived and born in that building and to see it burning was obviously upsetting him more than he'd care to admit.

Turner continued, "It saddens my heart to report that all seven-thousand surrogates and their doctors and nurses are unaccounted for and we can only assume that they were incinerated in the fire. There were no survivors. So far we've been able to determine that it was a series of explosives set up by someone from the inside. There will be a full investigation of who is responsible for this heinous crime. In the mean time we've heightened security in all public buildings. We ask that everyone keep an eye out for any suspicious behavior. We don't know if these attacks will continue and we have no way of knowing where they will strike next. As soon as I have more updates I will inform you immediately." And with that my grandfather walked away from the podium and through a swarm of reporters screaming questions at him.

Jason turned the holo off. We sat in stilled silence for a moment.

"Do you think he did it?" I asked the question that was on everyone's minds.

Jason shrugged. "I honestly don't know. It sounds like something he'd do. But if it's not him, then who?"

No one had an answer.

"School." Nancy broke the tension.

Ryan grabbed my hand and we followed Nancy and Bill out of Nancy's house. George, Vianne and Jason trailed behind, seeing us to Bill's hover-car.

"Be careful." Vianne hugged her daughter a little harder than usual.

"They're not going to blow up the school, Mom." Nancy rolled her eyes in mock exasperation, but I could tell she was more than a little worried.

"I'll have my dad send someone over to check the school for explosives," Bill announced. Apparently, he was freaking out about the whole thing, too. "Look, if it is Turner, what better way to get rid of you than to blame it on a bunch of terrorists attacks? And if it's not Turner what better way to send a message to the big guy than to blow up a school with his namesake?"

I guess Bill really *had* thought about it.

"What? Did it take you all of the last forty seconds to think of that one, Mr. Paranoid?" Nancy smiled, trying to lighten the mood.

"Bill's right," Ryan chimed in. "I'd feel safer if the place was scoped out before we let Chelsan step a foot in there." I guess the one thing they could agree on this morning was my safety. At least it was something!

"I'm glad somebody cares about somebody's girlfriend." Nancy directed her comment toward Jason, but he ignored it as usual.

"I'm the one who thought of it, not Ryan," Bill kind of grumbled under his breath.

"Thanks Bill, and thank your dad for me," I said gratefully. He was going above and beyond and I wanted him to know that I noticed.

"You're welcome," Bill responded with an embarrassed smile. I don't think he thought I'd heard that.

Ryan gave me a look. A bad look. Oh man. It made my heart sink. "What?" I asked.

"Nothing. I'm just glad Bill can keep us all safe." Ryan smirked with annoyance.

"Ryan?" I questioned him. He hadn't acted like that toward Bill in quite a while. I guess this morning stirred up a lot of emotions.

Ryan squeezed my hand and kissed the top of my head. "Sorry, just a little on edge," he said, but I could tell he wasn't quite over it yet. I figured there was nothing I could say, so I left it at that.

"I'll call him now." Bill stepped a few feet away and made the call as Ryan and I sat in the backseat of the hover, while Nancy slid into the front.

Bill hung up his phone and waved to Vianne, George and Jason. "All set. Dad's sending a team right now. It'll be inspected before we even get there."

Vianne pulled Bill in for a monster hug and I could see his face turning pink. "Thank you, Bill." Vianne's eyes were watery.

"No problem." Bill smiled awkwardly as he walked away and sat in the driver's seat.

Once inside the car, Nancy turned to face Ryan and me. "I can't believe someone would blow up a Baby Center. It's unreal." She shook her head in thought.

"It has to be Gramps. It's so his M.O," I said. But a part of me didn't really believe it. I knew Turner was capable of mass murder, but for some reason I just didn't think he did it. I couldn't explain it, but somehow I knew he wasn't responsible.

"I don't know, maybe, but I feel like he's more subtle than that," Ryan mused aloud as if reading my mind. "I mean according to Jason, Turner's been researching gases and toxins for hundreds of years to exterminate people, if he just wanted to blow them up he could have done that all along."

"Yeah, I think I have to agree with brain boy here, which would mean a *new* enemy we have to worry about." Nancy turned back around with a large groan.

"You guys don't think this Elisha girl has anything to do with it, do you?" Bill asked quietly.

With the news of the Baby Center attack I had completely forgotten about Elisha. Was it too much of a coincidence? Did she know something about the attack? Was this why she was being executed? Too many questions and no way to answer any of them. It was so frustrating!

"I guess we'll just have to see what Jason comes up with," Nancy said as she stared out the window.

Poor thing. I could tell she was thinking about Jason again and my heart hurt for her. I knew how hard it was to like someone and not really know if they liked you back. When Ryan tutored me my Junior year my whole "crush" thing started, but afterwards he ignored me completely. I tried to block him out of my brain, but it was no good. Every time I saw him my heart did the proper pitter-pattering and I was helpless against it. When I finally found out he liked me my brain nearly exploded. Nancy knew on some level Jason had feelings for her, but Jason couldn't get over their age difference so he kept her at a distance. I shuddered to think if Ryan ever did that to me. I rested my head on his shoulder and he unconsciously stroked my hair.

My mind was still reeling as I watched the oak forests beneath us whizz by. I remembered living near one of the giant forests and getting lost in their enormous shadows. I used to love wandering off and be alone with my thoughts. To simply escape among the trees and just *be*. I felt a pang of anger towards my grandfather. He stole that part of me two months ago by making me terrified. I knew I was still recovering. I knew it would take time. I was just an impatient person and I desperately wanted not to be so scared all the time. I still had nightmares about Brady, the serial killer. He'd kept me locked in his basement for days and was supposed to kill me, but he failed because I had used my power to control Brady's victims to fight my way out…

I blinked away rising tears. I didn't want anyone to notice. I had to stay strong. And at this point, if anyone said anything to me their kindness would probably make me bawl my eyes out. That would make everything worse. I needed to keep it together.

"Chelsan?"

I wasn't in the car anymore.

I was in the darkness again.

I reached out for Ryan anyway, but I was alone.

Elisha stepped out in front of me, her violet eyes watching me carefully.

"Chelsan, can you hear me?" she asked as she took a step closer to me.

"Yes. I can hear you," I answered and wished we weren't in this utter blackness.

As if hearing my thoughts, the scenery started to swirl around the two of us like we were in the eye of a storm made of color and light. When it finally settled we stood in a field of wild flowers stretching for miles and miles. It was stunning, with thousands of different varieties of flowers in every color imaginable and a blue sky like none I'd ever seen.

"Where are we?" I asked in awe.

"You tell me. You brought us here." Elisha was just as amazed as I was. "Is that tree familiar?" Elisha pointed behind me.

I whirled around to see a giant weeping willow.

And I knew where we were.

We were at my tree.

My tree near the trailer park where I'd go to read and get away.

Where I lay stranded while my mother was being poisoned to death.

Where I let my stepfather, Bruce, finally die when I stopped controlling him and let his corpse turn to bone.

I turned back to Elisha and she was looking at me with curiosity. "You know this place?" she asked.

"What are you doing in my brain?" I decided to get to the point. I didn't like the way she was looking at me. Her eyes were so creepy.

"Are you coming to rescue us?" she asked unbothered by my directness.

"Yes. We're just trying to figure out how. It's not easy to break in to Geoffrey Turner's headquarters, you know." Why was I giving this poor girl so much attitude? I couldn't seem to help myself.

"I know how," Elisha said with conviction. "It's why I risked coming to you like this. I wanted you to meet the boys and see for yourself why helping us is so important."

Elisha squeezed her eyes shut as if she were concentrating really hard.

The air started to crackle and then…

SNAP!

Two young boys stood before me. They were identical twins. Their faces were oval with long straight noses and short brown hair. They were holding hands and staring straight ahead. Their milky white eyes told me they were blind, but it was the swirling black holes that disturbed me the most. Disturbing because the holes weren't in their chests, they were in their brains. These boys were completely brain dead.

"You can see it, can't you?" Elisha asked.

"What happened to them?" was all I could utter.

Elisha forced a smile as she looked at the boys with motherly worry. "Chelsan, meet John and Samuel Dane. They were the only two survivors of Larotte Fielding's research in 2133. They were a part of the very first I.Q. Farm. Almost two hundred years of experimentation has left them brain dead." Elisha started to tear up. "I can't leave them here, Chelsan. I just can't."

I reached out and touched her shoulder to comfort her. I felt just as bad for John and Samuel as she did. It was hard not to when I thought of everything these two little boys went through. And knowing that they were really almost two hundred years old just made it that much worse. It made me shudder to think how messed up my grandfather really was. How could he do something like that?

Elisha turned around as if someone were about to run in the field of flowers and chop her head off.

"He's coming. I've got to go." She turned to me. "You don't even have to be in the building. You have a radius, right? A radius that your power works within?"

It was kind of scary how much she knew about my power, but I answered her anyway. "Four miles."

She smiled. "You see? You could help us from a few miles away in the red forest." Elisha's smile faded as she looked behind her again. "Oh God, it's *her*." Elisha's eyes met mine and I could see the genuine terror in her face. Whoever "she" was, Elisha was petrified of her. "Tomorrow."

Must be Grams. She scared the crap out me, too.

POOF.

They were all gone.

I was standing in the ocean of flowers alone.

Okay.

Now what?

"Chelsan! Chelsan! Wake up!"

I opened my eyes to see Ryan's face within inches of mine, full of worry and fear.

"I'm awake. I'm here," I mumbled and realized we were already parked in the school lot.

Ryan visibly relaxed and kissed me in relief.

I should black out more often. This was nice.

"What happened? Are you okay?" Nancy had climbed to the back seat and I was suddenly realizing how cramped we all were back here, since Bill had opened my door and was also crammed next to me.

"Guys, I'm fine, maybe a little claustrophobic though. Geez, how did you all fit back here?" I tried smiling this off, but it was no good. They were officially the Worry Wart clan.

Bill backed out and Nancy climbed over the front seat letting herself out of the car.

Ryan held my face in his hands. "You sure you're okay?"

"Give her some air." I could hear Bill's irritation at Ryan.

Ryan gave him a quick predatory glare, but I made him look back at me. "Don't start, he's just worried and I'm fine. Let's get out of here," I said, pulling him out of the car by the hand.

When we were all gathered around Bill's hover, I told them everything that happened, hoping it would make the boys re-focus on the task at hand instead of starting some sort of fight.

"Larotte Fielding? That's the guy Jason told us about, remember?" Nancy said, still a little dazed by what I told her.

Trying to think it through as well, I added, "I guess Turner took John and Samuel before the authorities got there."

"Well, if we can come up with a plan to help them escape, she's right, you could do it from a mile or two away. Turner wouldn't even know you were there," Bill said.

"I don't like how she can make you black out like that." Ryan wasn't letting the incident go. "I mean it's one thing when you're asleep, but to do it to you while you're awake? We've got to find a way to stop her from doing that."

"Which means finding out more about that astral thing." Bill nodded in agreement.

I hated to admit it, but they were right. The more I thought about it, Elisha being able to render me unconscious whenever she wanted to was actually petrifying. That's a lot of power. "Well, after we rescue them, she won't need to communicate with me anymore, so we won't have to worry about it much longer," I said, more to placate myself than my friends. I couldn't think about it. I had to stay focused on getting Elisha and the twins out of there.

"Let's get inside." Bill gave me a reassuring smile. "While you were out, Dad's guys checked out the school and said it's safe." I could tell he knew I wanted to stop talking about how Elisha could mind-smack me anytime she wanted.

"Thanks, Bill," I said as the four of us walked toward the entrance.

There was something very comforting about Geoffrey Turner High. (The name excluded, obviously!) The structure itself was early 1800s in design, with brick walls, iron-wrought gates and green ivy growing up the sides. Oak arches framed the entryways, making it feel like you were walking into an old photo where tea and scones awaited. We were entering at the top of the three-story building since the hover lot was above the school. The middle story was the hover carpool lane where most of the students were dropped off by their parents or nannies. And the bottom floor was my favorite. That was where the courtyard was, with its cherry blossom trees and quaint benches. It was a great place to escape whenever I needed a moment to myself.

I used to stress about tuition and worked at an ice cream shop to cover what scholarships couldn't, but I've rested easier ever since dear old Gramps added a lump of cash in my bank account when he was pretending to care about my mother's murder in front of the press. Of course, he tried to kill me right after he made the deposit, but he failed, as usual. Now I had enough money to graduate. No day jobs for me anymore. So, too bad for him.

We entered the bustling hallways and had to push and shove our way to our lockers. I could barely see the marble floors that lined the hallways, but the deep red mahogany lockers always grabbed the eye. Everything about this school was extravagant, including the students. I was literally the only poor person there and up until two months ago I was treated like a leper because of it. But things changed…

I opened my locker, pulled out my reader and sweater, and turned to Bill. "See you after class?"

"With bells on." Bill smiled and started toward his first period class, but not without an annoyed glance at Ryan. Whatever was brewing between these two was only at a simmer, I just hoped it wasn't going to turn into a boil any time soon. That was the last thing I needed.

Ryan held onto my hand as the three of us headed to history class.

We entered the freezing classroom and I put on my sweater. Why did Mr. Alaster like it so cold? The classroom was almost full and I tried not to stare at Jill Forester sitting alone in the back of the room. In the past her long locks of shiny black hair would somehow defy physics and always be perfectly styled, but nowadays she just pulled it back in a sloppy ponytail, her green eyes avoiding everyone, her head down.

She was my mortal enemy pretty much the entire time I resided at Geoffrey Turner High. Jill used to make my life torture and everyone at school followed her lead in fear of her father's power. He was second in command to my grandpa, which made him the second most powerful man in the world. Unfortunately for Jill, her dad had been dead for a few years without anyone knowing it. Turner controlled him the way I controlled dead things. It made me feel sorry for her for about a half a second, then she'd open her mouth and all sympathy went out the door. She was so mean! But maybe I would be too if I was living with a zombie. Okay, my stepfather Bruce was dead since I was seven. But it was different with Bruce, I knew he was dead, I controlled him. But with Jill… she must have thought he didn't care. That he had no interest in her whatsoever. That had to sting.

And I admit, I was fighting a bit of guilt regarding Jill's dad.

I kind of blew him up.

I really didn't mean to. Basically, my grandmother, Roberta, had kidnapped Ryan. Bill and I used Jill's dead dad to break into my grandparent's house to rescue him. When we found Ryan chained to a chair we realized he wasn't alone.

My dead mother was there, controlled by Roberta. She made Mom say horrible things to me, and dance around like a crazy puppet. There was nothing I could do. Roberta had used her powers to stop me from connecting to my mother's black swirling hole. Seeing my mom like that… something inside of me snapped. I screamed from the depths of my soul and somehow managed to make every dead thing within fifty feet of me explode.

And sadly that included Jill's dad.

The day after it happened I thought Jill would destroy me at school. I was expecting her to do her worst, but when she tried to send her lackeys after me they all turned on her. I guess they didn't like her very much either and now that she couldn't use her daddy to control them, they made her the new "leper" of the school. It was kind of sad, actually, watching the social demise of Jill Forester. She was in utter shock at first and tried to lash out at everyone that she felt betrayed her (especially her supposed best friend Joan), but in the end she couldn't really do anything except make a lot of noise. After a week or two she just dropped off the radar and stayed to herself mostly. Joan took her place as Queen Bee of the school and was surprisingly nice to the four of us. It was almost as if Joan wanted to rub it in Jill's face. She knew how much Jill hated me, so she did the worst thing she could think of to Jill. She made me popular.

I hated it almost as much as I hated being an outcast. It was so fake. And it was killing Jill. I knew I shouldn't care. I should write it off as Karma (Nancy certainly did and I loved her for it), but I *had* made her dad blow up like a bomb.

And I mean, BOOM!

Jill probably didn't even know that he died that way, just that he died. I couldn't relish seeing her hurt, especially since, as far as she knew, the father she lost had died only two months ago, not years ago. She must have so many questions and… Okay!! I admit it! I felt sorry for her! There I said it. I felt like crap because I could help her with some of those questions. I could tell her that her dad was pretty much a zombie for who knew how long and I finally let him rest in peace. But Jill's hatred for me was as strong as ever and I didn't know how to break the ice even if I wanted to.

Uggh.

I decided not to make eye contact with her, and I sat in my usual seat near the front with Nancy on my left, Ryan on my right.

Mr. Alaster gave me a slight nod. We had bonded when the press made a field day out of me after my trailer park was demolished. Being a trailer park kid himself, he didn't start taking Age-pro until he was thirty like my mom. He really looked out for me and I appreciated it. Mr. Alaster was wearing his usual cardigan sweater with round suede elbow patches, button up shirt and khakis. He was skinny as a rail with brown curly hair and wire framed glasses.

"Okay class, simmer down," Mr. Alaster said with a sparkle in his eye. "I have something very exciting planned for today." Whenever he was this enthusiastic it usually meant we were in store for something good. "We're going to find out who our ancestors are, dating back at least twenty generations!"

Wait. What?

"How?" I blurted out before I could stop myself. If it ever came out that Geoffrey Turner was my grandfather…

…I didn't want to think about it. Turner would be on a fast track to kill me for sure.

Mr. Alaster didn't even care that I interrupted, he just acted like I was a part of his announcement. "Genetic testing! The big man himself has brought in his people to perform the tests. You'll all be able to find out where you came from and who your family is. What trials they went through, maybe you're from royalty, or maybe from a family of convicts! The sky's the limit, folks!"

Gulp.

And Gulp.

The big man? When anyone at this school referred to the "the big man" they meant Turner! Why would he want these tests? Surely, he knew it would expose his relationship to me. Did he want that? What could it possibly gain him? Or maybe he planned on hiding the fact that we were related, but needed my blood for some horrible spell? I really wished I could read minds!

Nancy's eyes were as round as mine as she started to put the pieces together and Ryan's hand was already squeezing mine in support.

"Maybe this is a good thing," he suggested, but I could tell he was just as freaked as I was.

"Let's give them a big welcome." A group of four men and women in lab coats entered the classroom and the class applauded their arrival.

And one of them was dead.

Great.

It was one of the women, her black spinning chasm practically winking at me as she stood in front of the class with the others.

The leader of their group was a man who looked like he was fifteen. (You'd think the rich people that started taking Age-pro at eighteen who still looked so young would wait a few years, but everyone was about status!) He carried a large metal case. "Hello, everyone. I'm Dr. Grun and these are my associates. If you could just stand in line on this side of the room we'll start taking your blood samples. Thank you."

Students started filing in line against the wall, talking to each other with some excitement. Finding out about relatives that actually *died* was a fascinating topic that even kids who weren't interested in history still wanted to know about. I admit, if I didn't know Turner was my grandfather, and there wasn't a dead woman being controlled by him issuing the test, this would be really cool. Ha!

Out of the corner of my eye, I could see Jill's green eyes staring at me with curiosity. (And hatred, she looked like she was in a constant state of *I want to kill Chelsan.*) I pretended like I didn't notice and took my place in line with Nancy and Ryan.

"Why is Jill staring?" Nancy obviously saw the same thing I did.

"Who knows? I really don't want to guess," I said, hoping Jill would stop with the glaring. I wasn't sure if I should tell them about the dead assistant yet. Honestly, I think Jill saw my reaction and was trying to figure out why I was wigging out. If I told Nancy and Ryan they'd start wigging out and Jill would *definitely* know something was up. Not that I should care what Jill thought, but in her hey-day she was a dangerous enemy and I still couldn't be sure she wasn't planning my demise.

"She's been doing that a lot lately," Ryan said to my surprise.

"She has?" I asked. I hadn't noticed, but now that Ryan said it out loud, maybe I had and was just ignoring it.

"Yeah. I'll keep an eye on her, make sure she stays out of trouble." Ryan put his arm around my waist protectively.

And then a thought hit me.

"Uh guys," I barely croaked out. "What if my blood is different because of my power? What if Turner is doing this so they'll take me in? Like I'm an alien or something!" I gulped.

"You're fine. Don't worry. Jason can get you out of anywhere if it comes to that." Nancy reassured, but I didn't have her confidence.

"But that lab assistant is dead." Oops. I shouldn't have said that.

It was my turn next.

I left Nancy and Ryan with shocked looks on their faces. No doubt Jill was taking notes.

I walked straight up to the dead assistant. "You're not taking any blood from me," I whispered in her ear.

She leaned in close so only I could hear, "I know you have no reason to trust me, but this is necessary. I'm not here to kill you, I promise."

"Sorry. Not good enough," I said and began to walk away. I tried not to sweat as I was fully expecting her to grab my arm and forcefully take my blood. I was even ready for it. Ready to smash through the flimsy magical barrier surrounding her black hole to stop her. My grandparents placed the barriers in all their zombies trying to keep others from taking control of their slaves. I had plenty of experience obliterating this particular defense and I was raring to do it.

But the dead woman didn't even flinch. I heard her voice behind me, "Thank you for the sample, Ms. Derée."

I sat down at my desk and kept my back to the testing. What was going on? Could this day get any weirder?

And, as if in answer to that very question Jason popped his head into the classroom and made eye contact with Mr. Alaster. "I need to see Chelsan Derée immediately." Jason had his serious face on and my stomach did flip-flops.

The girls in the class giggled uncontrollably at the sight of Jason which made Nancy huff in an annoyed, jealous way.

Mr. Alaster looked at me for approval and I nodded. "Go ahead," he said, waving me to leave.

I gave a quick glance to Ryan as the dead lady took a sample of his blood. He shot me a supportive grin, but I could tell he was preoccupied with the fact that the assistant was dead. Besides, he knew I'd be safe with Jason.

Although Jason coming to school was a first. Must be something big.

I walked over to Jason and we left the classroom.

The hallway outside was stark and empty. I could practically see my reflection on the marble floor, it was so clean and polished.

"What is it?" I decided to get right to the point.

"Um, how do I explain this?" Jason paused.

"Spill. You're giving me a heart attack," I said and meant it. Jason at a loss for words was an event I had never seen before, and it made me more nervous than I thought possible.

"Well… The good news is they figured out who bombed the Baby Center." Jason half-smiled as if this bit of information was about to cushion what was to follow.

"Okay. Is it Turner?" I thought I'd guess.

"Nope, it wasn't Turner. It was Roland Light," Jason said with trepidation.

"The Christian Coalition minister?" I could feel my face scrunching in confusion. I admit, it was shocking news that the Christian Coalition was behind the explosion. For the last three hundred years they'd pretty much kept to themselves. It was only in the last month that this Roland Light guy showed his face publicly. He had been all over the news talking about religious rights and bringing the atrocities of this world to justice. Secretly, I kind of hoped the guy would take on Gramps. If Roland only knew what Turner did, he'd be all over him. I actually kind of liked the guy, mainly due to the fact that my new friend, Doris Hornbacher, was his champion. She helped me escape from the serial killer by whacking him with her golf club. She had taken to the limelight and in only two months had become quite a vocal figure in bringing to light some horrible things our society hides. Maybe Doris was the reason Jason was freaking out?

"Why are you freaking out?" If I didn't prod Jason it would take him forever to tell me whatever it was he wanted to tell me.

"His mother's name wasn't Light, it was Stearne." Jason let that hang there for a second.

Stearne?

Elisha Stearne.

Um, she was seven when Turner took her. How could she have a baby?

"NO! Not that!" Jason reared back in disgust, apparently my face was expressing the extreme grossness I was feeling about what I thought he was implying. "Elisha's *sister*! Roland is Elisha's sister's son. Elisha has a twin sister, but this girl actually shows her age. You had that look on your face."

It made sense now, why Elisha was so desperate to help John and Samuel escape. She was a twin too, but she was separated from her sister at age seven. It must have been devastating.

Jason checked his phone for a second and then focused back on me. "If Roland blew up the Baby Center, maybe that's why Elisha is being executed. I mean she visited you probably right after the explosion. We didn't get the news until later this morning. It can't be a coincidence."

My mind was racing.

Roland Light, evangelist, and now, a murderer. He was Elisha's nephew? Why would he kill all those people? Did he even know about his aunt? Was Turner executing Elisha to punish Roland Light? I couldn't seem to wrap my brain around any plausible explanations. Nothing seemed to make sense. There was no clickage in the puzzle solving part of my mind.

"Wow," was all I could say.

"Yeah." Jason nodded and placed a hand on my shoulder.

I heard a muffled barrage of giggles behind a couple of classroom doors.

Jason shrugged. "Part of the gig."

"You love it," I said, managing to give him a half-hearted smile. "What do I do now?"

"We have to wait for the live broadcast. Roland is giving a statement."

"Isn't he in jail by now?" I was incredulous that he'd even be allowed to make a statement in the first place.

Jason shook his head. "He's protected under Coalition law. As long as he stays in his town the authorities can't touch him. You're taking history and you haven't gone into Christian Coalition law?"

"Just tell me, show off, some of us aren't as old as dirt," I grumbled.

Jason just smiled. He really did love being insulted. "Basically, when Age-pro became the norm, the Coalition separated from society and built up towns. They negotiated with the government to secede from the country and essentially were given the authority to make their own laws. As a result they're considered separate countries and have their own extradition laws. They're not going to hand Roland over, so unless he leaves the sanctity of the Coalition he's safe from us."

"Do you really think that Elisha contacting me and Roland blowing up the center are connected?" I genuinely needed Jason's opinion.

"I don't believe in coincidences. Look, there's going to be a holo update projected in every classroom in about five minutes. I just wanted to give you the scoop. Give you a heads up for once, right?" He bent down and kissed my cheek.

A flurry of exclamations, gasps and giggles from prying eyes behind closed doors.

I rolled my eyes. "Nancy's going to kill you, you big ham."

Jason's face went white. "You're not going to tell her."

"But *they* are, idiot." I nodded toward Mr. Alaster's classroom at the girls peeking through the small square window.

"Well, she needs to move on anyway," Jason said miserably.

Such a moron. "She has, didn't she tell you?"

"What?" Jason was horrified.

"You're such a jerk. Why don't you get over yourself and just be with her?" I punched his arm lightly for emphasis.

Jason slumped in defeat. "I gotta go. I'll meet you back at Nancy's."

I grabbed his arm before he could leave. "One more thing, broody boy. Turner is having all students give blood samples for genetic testing and "historical research." There's a dead assistant in there who told me I should trust her, but when I wouldn't give her my blood she thanked me for it anyway. What do you think that's about?"

Jason's mood immediately perked from the intrigue. "Turner brought in a dead one?" Jason tiptoed to see over the girls' heads and into Mr. Alaster's room. "Weird." He turned back to me, "I'll see what I can find, but if he sent a corpse, then it's a safe bet he wanted to send you a message."

Great. I secretly hoped my grandparents were out of my life forever, but it was becoming more and more obvious that my period of solace was soon coming to an end. If I thought chanting *Please don't kill me* over and over in my head would help, I'd be doing it all day. Most people dread seeing their grandparents because they were boring or over-affectionate, they didn't have to worry about Gramps and Grams sending zombie soldiers over to murder them. I figured I'd have to keep my guard up even more than usual. It was bad enough that I was going into the lair tomorrow to rescue more of Turner's prey. I seriously hoped he wasn't wise to my plan. I reassured myself with the fact that he probably would have had *dead girl* threaten me or something if he knew anything.

"I just hope the message isn't, 'Surprise, you're dead!'" I groaned in frustration.

We both heard the clacking of footsteps on the marble floor and turned to see Principal Weatherby coming toward us. I shuddered in guilt as Weatherby's swirling black hole spun like an over-sized top inside his chest. During one of Turner's many attempts on my life I managed to get away by releasing his zombie staff from their black holes. As a result, they decayed to the exact time of their deaths (i.e. very gross stuff, ranging from juicy to bones). I left Turner with the cleanup and the task of explaining how his staff walked into Weatherby's office alive, but when Weatherby walked in he was confronted with five smelly cadavers. Leave it to my grandpa to decide that it was just easier to kill Weatherby and control him. No witness, no questions, no problems.

I never really liked Weatherby that much before: but now that he was dead, it was just depressing.

Jason and I made eye contact. We both knew that Weatherby was now going to be Turner's message bearer since I'd left the dead assistant inside the classroom.

Weatherby arrived with a blank expression. Turner wasn't even bothering to animate him for our sake. I kind of appreciated it in some weird way. Like he was showing an inkling of remorse for what he did. Yeah, right. A girl can dream. The Principal looked like he was in his late twenties (he was actually a hundred and sixty-seven) and was bald and chubby. He used to have a handle bar mustache, but the upkeep must have been too much of a nuisance, so he was clean-shaven now. Another reminder, besides the black tornado in his chest, that he was truly gone.

His round pink face turned to me, "Get inside the classroom. You have to see the holo announcement."

"What's going on?" I asked, hoping for an answer, but not expecting one.

"At some point you're going to have to trust me to a certain extent. I've left you alone for two months now. I could have killed you at any point," Weatherby said in such a monotone voice that it made my skin crawl. Turner was talking through him, which meant he was controlling Weatherby directly.

"Give me one good reason why I should trust you?"

"I just told you why," Weatherby said. There was actually a bit of attitude in the way he said it. Or maybe I was just imagining the way my grandfather meant it.

"Like I told your lackey in there, not good enough. And what exactly are you trusting me with? Why do you even need my trust? You just come in here out of the blue and say *Trust me* and I don't even know what that means!" I was getting angry and frustrated.

The girls who were watching Jason now ducked out of sight completely. Seeing me arguing with the Principal probably just made me Page One news of the gossip column today, but I didn't care. Turner was fishing for something, needed me, but he was being vague as usual. Although I liked this better than fighting for my life, it was somehow just as maddening.

"Well now if I told you, *Granddaughter,* I wouldn't need the trust, would I? Just go in and listen to the broadcast. I'm worried about a potential problem that I will be disposing of Thursday morning, but this

Roland Light may have something up his sleeve," Weatherby said.

So… Turner was worried about Roland breaking Elisha out. And by the way he was talking to me I was as sure as I could be that my grandfather had no clue I was the one planning the deed. The only question was, "And what exactly does this have to do with me?"

Weatherby stopped and stared at the wall for a second. I was afraid he was about to drool from inactivity. "If my suspicions are correct, *everything*."

Huh?

"Go in and see for yourself. I'll be in contact." Weatherby walked away and out of sight.

Jason turned to me and shook his head. "Everything, huh? Maybe we should re-think this breakout scenario."

"No, we'll get them out and deal with the consequences later," I responded, still trying to think of how we were actually going to accomplish this alleged breakout.

"And we still don't know how many I.Q. Farm kids Elisha wants us to help," Jason added.

Oh yeah.

I told Jason what happened with Elisha during our last "meeting."

Jason was stunned. "She can do that to you? Just render you unconscious?"

Great. Make me paranoid all over again.

"I'm working on it," I lied, but hoped it to be true.

"You better, because if *she* can do it, anyone with that kind of power can, too." Jason shook his head, troubled by the news.

"Okay, I got it. There's nothing we can do about it now, geez. But our real problem right now is not letting Turner kill Elisha when her only crime is being locked up in an I.Q. Farm for ninety years! Once we have her, we'll figure out what Gramps meant. If anything, it's this Roland guy we should watch out for. He's the mass murderer," I said as I reached for the doorknob.

Jason sighed. "You sure have a knack for getting involved with the crazies."

"Tell me about it."

I opened the door and the two of us walked in just as Mr. Alaster was rolling out a cart with a holo-tv on top. It was a much smaller TV than Nancy's, the rectangular platform only fifteen by ten inches, but the figures were solid and clear as Mr. Alaster turned it on and Roland Light stood in front of a crowd of pregnant women.

Interesting.

Joan and her new cronies whispered and giggled as they stared at Jason and I in the back of the room. They obviously could care less about any announcement from Roland Light.

Nancy and Ryan left their seats to stand next to us. Ryan took my hand then leaned down, kissing my cheek. "Everything good?"

"Yeah. I'll tell you later." I watched as Roland Light cleared his throat.

He was an older man, like my grandfather: maybe a little younger, but late forties at least. He was lean and tall with a full head of white hair cut short. His face was long, its deep lines making him appear ominous.

Roland spoke through thin, pursed lips, "Fellow citizens. As you can see from these women behind me, I have killed no one on this day. My fellow Christians and I do not believe in the murder of *innocent* lives. These women and their doctors were taken out of the *breeding farm* because they are victims of a heinous crime. The women will stay with us in Havenville until further notice, the doctors will be returned home immediately. I *am* guilty of destroying the monstrosity that you sinners call a *Baby Center*. This is a travesty in the eyes of the Lord and I will not rest until these Centers are wiped off the face of this planet. Using women to carry your life so you can stay unnaturally young forever? This goes beyond any kind of evil imaginable. Your world is spinning out of control. It is becoming Hell on earth, and you are all embracing it like moths to flame. But it's the Devil's fire and I am here to cleanse you. I will be your savior in this madness."

He sounded like the serial killer Brady. Brady used to talk about *cleansing* too. Even though I was relieved to hear that no one was killed, Roland was off-kilter. Maybe it ran in the family, but my gut was telling me that there was something not quite right with the minister.

Roland continued his speech, "These women will deliver their babies here in Havenville. The babies will not be returned to the donors. They will be a new generation, a generation where the new world embraces the old world. It is time, people. You will not be warned again."

The holo-tv feed went to wavy lines.

A holo of Carleton Gordon sprang into quick focus. He actually looked stunned. "Now a word from our sponsor."

Mr. Alaster turned the holo-tv off with a kind of dazed expression.

No one spoke.

The babies will not be returned to the donors? Over seven thousand babies would never know their real parents. They'd be raised by their surrogates, or worse… by Roland Light and his followers. There had to be something someone could do. This was the biggest kidnapping *ever!* And what was he going to do? Blow up all the Baby Centers? It certainly seemed so.

And if Roland knew about the I.Q. Farms, there was no way he wasn't going to go after those, too. I mean Baby Centers were one thing, but making children take Age-pro and experimenting on their brains was another. If he really was planning on rescuing Elisha, then it also meant that he planned on exposing the I.Q. Farms. Most likely, he wasn't sure if anyone would believe him without proof. Bring him proof and I.Q. Farms would be sought out and shut down.

As crazy as I thought this guy was, I was starting to see our paths colliding. No matter how justified Turner thought he was in keeping these Farms, they had to be stopped, and if this Roland Light guy could do it, then… well… I didn't know. I didn't trust him, pure and simple. Elisha was the key. She still scared the bageezies out of me, but one look at her and the public would be outraged.

Something was definitely brewing and somehow I was creeping toward the middle of it yet again.

I still didn't know why Turner was convinced that I had anything to do with anything. He had no idea I was planning to break out Elisha and the boys, so why would he think this Roland guy even knew who I was? But Turner said (or Weatherby said) that this whole thing had *everything* to do with me. So what was I missing?

I needed answers and I clearly wasn't going to get any.

The shock of Roland Light's statement started to wear off and the class sounded abuzz with chatter.

Joan and her girls began their stare down of Jason, and flirting smiles and giggles followed. Jason was a sucker for it as usual and waved back, giving a slight wink to Joan. This sent a flurry of whispers and excited noise around the classroom.

I smacked Jason in the chest while Nancy crossed her arms in a fury.

PUNCH!

Ouch!

I fell on my butt before I realized it was Jill's fist that landed me there.

"You know something!" Jill yelled at me with anger.

Jason's fans and Jill's punch were apparently too much for Nancy to handle: she tackled Jill to the ground before I could utter the word, "Ow."

"Girl fight!" one of the students yelled as Nancy and Jill wrestled each other on the ground. Their bodies were smacking into desks as they clawed at each other.

The crowd that formed around them was so thick that Mr. Alaster couldn't break through to stop the fight.

I tried to get up, but I had to sit immediately because I was so dizzy.

Jill and Nancy were in the hair-pulling stage of the fight and it was starting to get nasty.

Jason flipped out and was about to jump in to stop them when Joan and her girls forced him back into the crowd, where five big thugs held him back.

"Let them fight it out," Joan said with an evil grin.

I started to stand again, but I couldn't seem to focus on anything.

Ryan tried to help me up. "She's in trouble. I gotta stop this."

And suddenly the weirdest thing happened.

I could see millions of tiny swirling black holes.

They were everywhere, floating around like dust…

…wait a minute.

It was dust.

Dust consisted of dead skin cells so it made sense, but why didn't I ever see them before? I could hardly see anything. Even Ryan was barely visible. He didn't leave my side to help Nancy, I could tell he was too worried about me. I tried to turn it off. I didn't want to go through the rest of my life like this. It was like walking through billions of floating black crap that everyone, including myself, breathed in and out and walked through and it moved and spun and swirled… It was giving me a headache.

I shut my eyes and concentrated. When I opened them again, I managed to tune out the dust and then made it come back into focus. I did this a few times until I got the hang of it. It almost felt like I was switching between two dimensions, one normal and one with black snow.

I connected to several thousand of the swirling black cores of dust like I do when I connect to anything dead. It was a strange sensation since I hardly had anything to work with. Normally, the things I linked to were big enough to really grab a hold of, like a person, or even insects, because they had more substance and working parts. Dust was just… well… dust.

It was almost calming as I made the dust swirl and sway like I was bonding with the wind itself.

Jill was on top of Nancy and strangling her at this point.

Nancy's face was starting to turn blue and no one was doing a thing, they just watched like it was paid entertainment.

I couldn't let Jill hurt Nancy, so I acted on instinct.

I made millions of particles of dust fly straight up Jill's nose and down into her lungs.

She went into a sneezing fit and started hacking up a storm. She immediately let go of Nancy and fell back on the ground, clutching her throat. Before I could stop what I was doing, Jill's face was beet red and she collapsed on the floor, unconscious.

I made the dust leave her body as fast as I could and then disconnected from it.

Fear raced through my veins. Did I kill her?

The classroom went still with shock and confusion at what just happened.

Mr. Alaster was able to break through the crowd and he knelt down to Jill.

Jill took a huge gulp of air.

I leaned into Ryan with relief, but I was shaking from what I had just done.

Jason raced to Nancy's side as Joan's thugs no longer held him back.

Nancy's mood brightened considerably though her hair was a mess and her shirt was ripped.

Jill had regained her composure and stood up with anger. "You did that!" Jill turned to me, her eyes alight with renewed anger. "Don't bother denying it! I'm on to you!" Jill was in tears now.

"What a freak." Joan laughed, and her lackeys echoed the sentiment.

Jill turned to Joan with venom. "What are you laughing at, fatty?"

That actually shut Joan up. Who knew *fatty* would pack such a punch? Especially since Joan was as skinny as a rail.

Before I could even utter a response, Jill whirled around and stormed out of the classroom.

"You all right, Chelsan? Nancy?" Mr. Alaster asked the both of us.

I nodded. Nancy echoed the sentiment.

"All right class, relax! Fun's over! Finish up your blood tests so these nice lab people can leave." Mr. Alaster was so done. He went to his desk and started reading his electronic reader.

People began to re-form the line and the lab assistants (living and dead) began testing once more.

Joan and her gang huddled in a corner far away from us to gossip about the fight and Jill's strange coughing fit. Not to mention keeping a flirty eye on Jason.

Ryan held me close and checked my nose. "No blood. Good thing she's a weakling." He smiled.

"She just wants answers," I said quietly. I really did feel sorry for her.

"Weakling? I have a few bruises that say otherwise," I heard Nancy grumble under her breath. "Are you seriously all right?" she asked me, still scowling from her wrestling match, although she lightened up considerably when Jason started examining her for injuries.

"I'm all right. Are you?" I asked, just as upset.

"I'm fine. It was pretty lucky she had that coughing fit when she did." Nancy looked over at me with eyes that said she agreed with Jill that I had done the deed.

"I just need to sit down for a sec," I said as we returned to our desks.

Jason stood behind Nancy completely ignoring the admiring fans in the room now. I was actually proud of him, his attention was entirely focused on Nancy for once as if seeing her in a fist-fight brought out his love for her. Such a weirdo. But it made Nancy happy and that was all I cared about.

Nancy mouthed, "Did you do that, with the coughing?"

I nodded, feeling a little guilty.

They all had serious expressions on their faces.

"What did you do exactly?" Nancy asked.

"Dust. When she hit me it made me see it everywhere. Tiny microscopic black holes. I never noticed it before probably because it was too small."

"Dead skin cells, makes sense," Ryan said coming to the same conclusion I had. I knew his brain needed to give a scientific explanation of what happened to make it easier to cope.

Jason suddenly smiled. "I think I have an idea of how we're going to do that *thing* tomorrow."

"Well, do tell," Nancy said impatiently.

Jason nodded over to dead girl in the far corner. "I don't know how good her hearing is. Let's save it for home. See you guys there." Jason left without another word.

Nancy smiled at me. "He said *home*. He meant my house, you know." She had a renewed pep to her tone despite her torn t-shirt.

"Yes, Nancy." I rolled my eyes with a grin. We sat through history class with a snore.

The rest of the day was pretty uneventful. Honestly, I couldn't wait to get out of school so we could sit down and make a plan of attack. I was in my last period, which happened to be English. Ms. Knudson, a pointy faced woman who looked about twenty, was spouting on and on about comma placement. Nancy, Bill and Ryan weren't in this class, unfortunately, so I had to suffer my last minutes of school alone.

Jill sat two rows over and one seat back. She had been staring at me the entire period. I made sure I kept my eye on her this time. I didn't want a repeat of Mr. Alaster's class. I knew at one point we'd need to have some kind of confrontation. I actually welcomed it. It was tempting to think about telling her the truth. Maybe it would make her change and she wouldn't be so horrible. I somehow doubted it, but still… Blew up her dad. Kind of owed her.

The bell rang and I practically sprung for the door.

"Chelsan, stop for a sec," Jill's voice sounded behind me like a harbinger of doom.

I froze in my tracks and turned around slowly to face her.

People shuffled around us, trying not to stare, but word of Jill's punch had been circulating all day and it looked like the crowd was raring for another fight.

Jill gave them her typical, *Get out of my face* look and they all left the classroom.

It was just the two of us, even Ms. Knudson had left.

"I don't want to fight you," I said, keeping at least a few feet of space between us.

"I'm not going to punch you, if that's what you think." Jill acted as if the idea was preposterous.

She took a step forward and I took a step back.

"Just stay where you're at. What is it?" That came out a lot colder than I meant it to, but no matter how much my guilt button was pressed, I still despised Jill.

Jill rolled her eyes and crossed her arms. "You owe me an explanation," she replied very quietly, almost as if she were convincing herself that it was true.

"After everything you've put me through in the last three years, why on earth would I tell you anything?" I uttered angrily. Wow. I was madder than I thought.

"So there *is* something to tell?" Jill deduced.

"Of course, Jill, what did you think, Geoffrey Turner asked your dad to have you spy on me because I was poor?" I shook my head. "I'm sorry your dad is dead, but it's not my fault."

Jill stood there for a second and I couldn't for the life of me tell what was going on in that brain of hers.

"I'm not stupid, you know," Jill said softly.

"I never said you were." I tried to be as gentle as I could. I really didn't want her to snap again.

"You have some kind of power." Jill stared straight at me and I felt the intensity of her glare like a stab in the brain.

Did she know something? I didn't want to say anything for fear of… I didn't even know what I was afraid of. What could Jill Forester possible say or do that would hurt me?

"Um, Jill." That was intelligent.

"*Um, Chelsan.*" Jill mocked me like her true, nasty self.

"I'm leaving," I said, turning toward the door.

I felt her hand grab my arm and I immediately shrugged it off, whirling around to face her. I was ready for a fight. I was ready to scream at her. I was ready for anything.

Except for those eyes.

Those large green eyes were filled with so much pain it almost made me cry.

"I'm sorry, okay?" Jill's voice was so sincere it was heartbreaking. "About everything." Jill rushed past me and almost made it through the door when I stopped her with five words.

"I do have a power."

Oh boy. Did that really come out of my mouth?

Jill turned slowly and with purpose. For the first time since I had known her she looked at me with genuine curiosity instead of her normal *I hate you* glare.

"It's something to do with dead things, isn't it?" Jill asked cautiously.

I could tell she still wasn't sure what her boundaries were with me. We had been enemies for so long it was awkward to have any kind of meaningful discussion. Jill had obviously been thinking about this for a while now, and I was pretty impressed that she had guessed that much.

"Yeah, something like that," I said and I motioned for her to sit.

We both sat down at desks across from each other. I knew this was it. I was going to tell her about her dad, about my power, and about how she had been living with a zombie for years.

Jill closed her eyes for a second, and then opened them slowly. "I'm not sure I'm ready to hear any of this," she said as if she already knew what I was going to say.

"I'm not sure if I'm ready to tell it, but you deserve to know." I paused, unsure of how to proceed. How do you tell a girl her dad was a walking, talking corpse? And that I blew him to smithereens? I braced myself for another punch in the face. "Jill, I control dead things, and I mean anything dead, from plants, to animals… to people." I let that sit for a while so she could connect the dots herself.

She was silent again, staring at the surface of the desk, no longer able to make eye contact with me. "He was dead already?" she whispered. Her voice was shaking, I could tell she was about to cry.

I didn't want to embarrass her so I continued, "Yeah. Turner must have killed him years ago. He can control dead things too, but he has to use spells and rituals, my power is innate." I tried to keep it informative.

"Three years." Jill suddenly looked at me. Her eyes piercing and filled with torment. "That's when it happened. He went to work in the morning and he came back… different. He never spoke to my mom and I after that, only to give us orders." Jill wiped away her freshly fallen tears and regained some of her composure. "What happened to him that day you took him away? Turner's men said he died in the line of fire."

Yeeeek.

Here we go.

"Turner and his wife were holding Ryan hostage and were keeping my mother on their puppet strings. They tortured her body, gouged her eyes out, and made her say terrible things to me." I found that I was choking up myself at the memory. I never wanted to remember my mother like that and it was for that precise reason Roberta did it. I also didn't want to tell Jill that the Turner's were my grandparents. Not yet. If her hatred shifted from me to Gramps, I didn't want her know we were related. "I just wanted it to stop. I couldn't stand the sight of her, eyeless, beaten, dancing around like a crazed toy. So I screamed. And it must have tapped into some part of my power that I wasn't aware of because everything dead that was near me exploded." I left it at that. I really didn't want to elaborate and I wasn't sure how she was going to react.

Jill stared at me with hollow eyes, then slowly started to nod. "So you blew him up?"

Uh.

"Yeah."

"You couldn't have kept him alive long enough to say good-bye to me?" Jill asked and I could tell she was starting to get angry again.

"It doesn't work that way, Jill. He wasn't really alive. He was just an empty shell…" I started to explain.

"Forget it." Jill stood up and before I could stop her she was out the door.

Well, that sucked.

I slowly stood up and opened the freshly slammed door.

Ryan was there to greet me with that ridiculously adorable smile of his. "I was starting to get worried, especially when she-bitch stormed out before you."

"Don't call her that," I said, mildly defensive.

Ryan raised his eyebrow in slight surprise. "What's wrong?"

"I told her about her dad… and what I can do," I admitted the last part quietly. I was the only one who thought it was a good idea to tell Jill what happened. Everyone (including Ryan) thought it was dangerous and had pretty much thought they had talked me out of it.

I looked Ryan in the eye, awaiting the lecture that was sure to come. I wasn't disappointed. I could tell he was surprised and a little angry, but in a matter of milliseconds it was replaced with a shake of his head. "You did what you thought was best. I trust you." He leaned down and kissed me until my toes curled. He pulled away. "Let's get to Bill's car. We have a big night ahead of us."

I nodded as Ryan took my hand and we plowed our way through the crowded hallways.

We ran into Bill and Nancy as soon as we exited onto the hover parking lot. Nancy wore a cardigan to cover up her ripped shirt, but otherwise she was unscathed by her fight this morning.

I told them both about Jill immediately. I wanted to do it quickly. I was pleasantly surprised by both their reactions.

Bill shrugged and I could tell that a part of him was relieved, while Nancy just guffawed and mumbled that Jill would have found out eventually anyway.

"I didn't tell her Turner was my grandpa, though. Gramps would kill me if that got out. *Literally*," I said as we reached Bill's car.

Nancy noticed something. "She's not going to be happy about that." She nodded to a few cars down.

And there was Jill's BMW hover. Completely vandalized. There were scratches, sprayed-on profanity, bird crap, you name it, it was on her car. Even I didn't get attacked like that. (Although I didn't own anything to damage, but still.) Knowing that Jill had just found out about her dad and then would come out to see that…

Bill unlocked the doors for us, then a strange look crossed his face. "Be right back."

Bill hurried over to Jill's car and it was then that we all noticed she was sitting inside. Crying.

We all watched as Bill knocked gently on her window. They had a brief exchange and then Bill came back to us. "I know she probably deserves it for how she's treated you and everyone else over the years, but she's in pretty bad shape," Bill said as he opened his door and sat inside.

Everyone followed suit and soon we were in the car, flying away toward Nancy's house. No one spoke. What was there to say?

Except one thing.

"It was nice of you to check on her," I said to Bill. He really did hate seeing people treated badly. It was the reason we were friends in the first place. Bill Merryweather *Defender of All.*

Bill didn't respond. He looked conflicted.

Nancy brought us all back to reality. "Well, we have much more to worry about than Jill Forester. We have to break into a high security I.Q. Farm in about ten hours and we still have no plan."

"Jason said he had an idea," I reminded them.

"What does he know?" Nancy grumbled.

Guess she was back to being annoyed with him. I couldn't keep track.

Bill landed his hover on the landing area in front of Nancy's place and we all piled inside the house.

George sat on the couch with Jason watching the news on the holo-tv. They both turned when we entered.

"Oh good you're here." Jason smiled then he yelled, "Vianne! Get your butt in here!"

Vianne came in from the kitchen. The smell of roast beef and potatoes wafted in with her and my stomach began to growl. "I'm here. Now what's going on?" she asked, wiping her hands with a dishtowel.

"Everyone sit. I'm going to tell you how we're going to break out Elisha and the twins," Jason replied with a grin.

My stomach growled again, but this time it was because I felt like vomiting.

"Chelsan?"

Great. I recognized that voice. Elisha was in my head yet again.

At least I was sleeping. It was much better when she visited me when I was already unconscious.

I opened my eyes within the dream and Elisha stood in front of me. We were in the red maple forest surrounding Turner's headquarters. Dark thick trunks surrounded us and their long branches sprouted out about ten feet up the long boles. The bright red leaves of fall had now turned into the deep red buds of winter. I could barely see the flashes of white coming from the spectacle of a building. I could still remember driving up in Bill's hover two months earlier and seeing the monstrosity for the first time. It looked like hundreds of twisting and spiraling crystals made of white metal reaching into the sky. Even through the trees it was breathtaking.

"Hey," I said lamely. I still wasn't comfortable with *astral* conversations.

Elisha smiled warmly, which put me more at ease. "I just wanted you to see the rendezvous point. When I get out with the boys we'll meet here. See the odd tree there?" She pointed to one of the maples next to me and it had a large crack in the bark making it stand out from the rest.

"Yeah," I said and tried to memorize where I was standing.

Then a thought suddenly occurred to me. "Where am I going to take you?" I was so focused on planning out the escape that I'd completely forgot about what I was going to do with them once they were in my custody. It wasn't like I could stash them at Nancy's. Maybe Bill's? Turner would never think to look there and Bill's parents had a lot of social clout.

"Don't worry about that," Elisha answered with authority. "Someone you know will meet us here and take us to safety. I just need you to get me out of the building." It still creeped me out, the contrast between how old she sounded with how young she looked.

Wait a minute.

"Someone I know?" I asked.

"Oh my," a woman's voice sounded from behind me and my heart sung.

"Doris?" I whirled around to see Doris Hornbacher standing in front of me looking frazzled as usual. Her face was round with freckles dotting her button nose and her dark hair lay in sleepy tangles on her shoulders. She was in her pajamas and quite frankly had a confused kind of expression on her face. Somehow I doubted she knew what was going on and assumed she was having a very odd dream. I didn't care either way, she was a friendly face in an awkward situation, so I immediately gave her a welcoming hug.

"Chelsan, dear, it's been way too long. I haven't seen you since that horrible night with Brady. Is this real?" Doris spoke almost too fast to understand.

"Yes, it's real. *She* brought you here." I nodded toward Elisha, who stood next to the marked tree silently watching us with her violet eyes. I felt so bad being so freaked out by a little girl, but I couldn't help it. She was just weird in that *Make me uncomfortable* kind of way. And she wasn't a little girl, I had to keep reminding myself.

"Oh my," Doris repeated herself and looked over at Elisha with motherly worry. She turned back to me, "Roland is just beside himself with worry."

I flinched instinctively. "Roland Light?"

"Now don't look at me like that. Roland is just doing what he thinks is right."

I couldn't believe I was hearing this from Doris. I thought when she found out he kidnapped thousands of pregnant women she'd be done with him for sure. But I guess she wouldn't be here in my head if that were true. I just couldn't accept it. I needed to know why.

"Doris, those children will grow up without ever meeting their parents. You have to know that's wrong." I tried not to sound condescending.

Doris's eyes suddenly welled up with tears. "Now, you just don't know a thing about it, do you?" She turned away with a sniff.

I couldn't figure out why she'd be so emotional about it, so I pushed a little further. "I'm just calling it like I see it. Doris, Roland isn't right in the head. Empty or not he blew up that building."

Doris whirled back to face me. I was shocked to see the anger raging in her eyes. "I blew it up!"

I turned to Elisha, angry now myself. "This isn't Doris." Not the Doris I knew anyway. "Why are you showing me this?"

Elisha stared at me with her penetrating purple eyes. "I promise you: this is Doris Hornbacher."

I felt the fake Doris put her hand on my shoulder. "I'm afraid so, dear."

I turned back to Doris, not wanting to believe it was true. "No. You wouldn't do something like that." But I could tell from the tears in her eyes that not only was she the real Doris, but that she had truly blown up the Baby Center.

"Why?" I could barely croak out.

Doris took her hand away. "Chelsan, this isn't easy to explain."

"Well, try," I said a little more abrasively than I intended.

"I was a surrogate, Chelsan." Doris's eyes filled with tears again.

Oh man.

I had never met a surrogate before.

"Okay," I replied not sure of what to say.

Doris reached over and took my hands in hers. "You have no idea what it's like to give birth to six babies and have them taken away from you. I know, I volunteered, and yes, I know it was out of vanity so I could take Age-pro at twenty-three but, Chelsan, it doesn't make a lick of difference. I still had six children, they may not have been technically mine, but I carried them for nine months! I gave birth to them! They felt like mine. They *were* mine," she trailed off, holding back emotion. She regained her composure and squeezed my hands tighter. "Having so many children… There were complications in my last pregnancy. The baby came early and I barely survived… I can no longer have children."

Doris looked me in the eye with an intensity that made me physically shiver. "Do you know what it's like to have six children and never see them again? They're it. They're all I'm ever going to have and I can never see them! Chelsan, it's just torture. I didn't even take Age-pro after I left the Baby Center. I didn't care about anything except my four girls and two boys that I'd never see. And I'm not the only one. Over half of the girls can never have children after their term of service. We're not meant to have that many children that fast. A third of the girls commit suicide because they can't handle the separation. Chelsan, Baby Centers are evil. I made sure it was empty, but you're damn right I blew up that Baby Center. It was the place that nearly destroyed me. And I promise you, I intend to destroy every last one of them." Doris finished with her eyes aflame with renewed anger.

I never thought about Baby Centers like that before. I never thought about them period. It was just *normal.* Nancy and Ryan were born at that Center. It made me wonder. What if Doris was one of their surrogates? What if she was the one who carried either of the two people I loved the most to term? It made my head spin. Being poor, Baby Centers weren't even an option. I was born the old-fashioned way. But if I had been born in a Baby Center would I ever wonder who my surrogate was? Did Nancy? Did Ryan?

Doris let go of my hands and waited for my response.

"I'm still not sure about blowing up buildings. You could have killed someone walking by, did you ever think about that?" I wasn't going to let Doris off the hook for basically being a terrorist.

"I made sure the area was clear. The *whole* area. You know I'd never kill anyone." She thought a moment. "Except for Brady that is, but I think we can both agree he deserved the clocking I gave him."

I gave her a small reassuring smile. "Yes, Brady definitely needed the golf club to the head, but you didn't kill him."

"I know. I'm still working on sending him to prison for life without Age-pro," Doris replied.

"Oh no, Doris; he's dead. You just didn't kill him," I said.

Doris's face scrunched in confusion.

And it suddenly occurred to me.

Doris had no idea about my power.

"Doris, I'm the one who is going to break Elisha and the boys out. Now it's your turn to listen."

Then I told her I could control the dead and how I escaped Brady's clutches. I couldn't tell her Geoffrey Turner was my grandfather, though. My gut was screaming at me not to, so I listened. It wasn't that I didn't trust Doris, it was just that the less she knew the better. But I did tell her that Turner could control the dead like me. That he, in fact, controlled Brady, and that he had him killed already.

"Well, my, my…" Doris looked flustered. "You used his victims to escape?" she repeated as if trying to understand what I told her.

"Yeah."

Doris hugged me spontaneously. "I'm so sorry you had to go through that."

"She's coming," Elisha spoke.

I had almost forgotten Elisha was there. We both turned to her.

"Who's coming?" I asked.

Elisha was trying to hide her fear. "Roberta."

Grandma. Of course. Who else had the super power of slamming into other people's brains?!

Elisha said quickly, "I'm sending the both of you back. It's going to hurt, but she can't know who I'm talking to. This is the place. We'll rendezvous here. We good?" Elisha waited until the both of us nodded. "See you in a few hours."

***

I awoke and grabbed my throat. I felt like I had swallowed a bucket of ice cubes. I couldn't breathe at first, all the air sucked out of my lungs. Elisha wasn't kidding, that freakin' hurt!

Ryan's arms were immediately wrapped around me to try and

calm me down. "Chelsan! What's wrong?!" his voice was wracked with concern. I so loved that! I also loved the fact that George and Vianne had no arguments about Ryan staying in my bed. Apparently, breaking out I.Q. kids afforded special privileges.

I took a few moments to steady myself. Eventually I started to feel normal again. "I'm okay," I said finally and was surprised to hear the gravel in my voice. It sounded as if I had been screaming for hours. "Was I screaming?" I asked out of curiosity.

"No, you just woke up gasping. What happened? Was it that Elisha girl?" Ryan moved the hair out of my eyes with his hand in an agonizingly gentle way. I wished he wouldn't do that! Wait a minute. Scratch that. More please.

I told him everything.

He leaned in and kissed me. "Are you sure you still want to go through with this?"

"Ryan, Elisha will be executed if I don't. Do you really want to live with that on your conscience when you know we can save her?"

"You know I want to save all of them. It could have been me in there. I just care about you more than I care about saving Elisha. I'm sorry, but it's true," Ryan said, kissing me again.

I lay down on his chest and he wrapped his arms around me.

"Don't be sorry," I said. "I wouldn't have been able to survive the last two months of my life without you." And that was the truth. Ryan stuck by me when most boys would have run screaming. He had been willing to be Turner and Roberta's *slave pet* just so I wouldn't have to see my mother in zombie form. I'd never forget that. Not ever. He was definitely a keeper. I just worried about putting him in danger. And the more I thought about it… "I'm going alone."

Ryan shifted himself so we could make eye contact. "No. Nancy and Bill can stay home or at school or whatever, but not me. I'm not letting you out of my sight again. I mean it."

And the thing is, I knew he meant it, and I knew he wanted to come, but that stubborn part of me didn't want to let him. I was always walking around with this constant rock of guilt smashing me to the ground. And a part of that guilt was continuously putting my loved ones in danger. I had such a knack for it I could literally make it a career.

"Ryan," I said and couldn't find the words to let him down.

"You can say whatever you want. I'm coming. If you try and give me the slip I'll follow you, so don't even think about finishing that sentence." Ryan had *serious face* and I knew I couldn't argue. Then he nailed me in the coffin of acceptance. "You know this is personal for me."

"All right, but just you, and I'm going to need your help convincing Bill and Nancy to stay at school. They're not going to take it very well." I snuggled back into Ryan's firm chest and I suddenly realized how exhausted I was. "What time is it anyway?"

"It's 2:00AM. You should get some rest." Ryan kissed my forehead and we both sank into the comfiness of the bed.

I couldn't wait to for this whole Elisha debacle to be over and done with so I could get a solid eight hours of sleep. This whole astral projection thing was tiring and I was glad I wouldn't have to put up with it for much longer. I closed my eyes, exhausted. The last thing I remember was Ryan's arms pulling me in tight against him.

***

WHACK!

I felt the poof of a pillow hitting my face.

"Get up, sleepy, we only have an hour before Turner's headquarters opens to the public, so we have to move." Nancy's voice cut through my dazed state of sleepiness.

"Nancy, you and Bill aren't coming," I said groggily.

"WHAT?! Nuh, uh! You have no say in the matter. Now get up. We're all going. Bill's downstairs." And with a very audible huff, Nancy was out of the room.

"That went well." Ryan scratched his head as he rolled out of bed. In just a t-shirt and boxers that boy was gorgeous.

"The pillow threw me off." I got out of bed and quickly dressed. Ryan did the same until we were both ready to go.

Ryan opened the door for me. "Shall we?"

I nodded. "Get ready for a blow out."

Ryan smiled at me and we both headed downstairs.

It wasn't a complete blow out, but it was pretty close. After a good twenty minutes of grade school arguing Nancy and Bill were finally convinced to go to school. It was actually Jason who made them see the light. He said he'd monitor the news channels while Nancy and Bill would play the decoys. It would be pretty suspicious if all four of us didn't show up to school, but if just Ryan and I ditched, no one would even flinch. It was pretty common for couples to skip school together for… well… for obvious reasons. Bill stopped arguing somewhere in the middle of Jason's reasoning and was in serious pout mode, not to mention the daggers he was throwing with his eyes at Ryan. It really *did* seem like he was jealous and it made me feel like crap. Nancy picked up on it and tried to veer the conversation in a different way by suggesting that Bill keep an eye on Jill to make sure she didn't poke her nose where it didn't belong. Jill was definitely suspicious and today was not the day we needed her calling any attention to our absence. Bill seemed to perk up at that. I hoped that his anger and frustration was just about not feeling useful and not about me. Fingers crossed.

"It's time," Jason said with a finality like death itself.

George and Vianne saw us to the door. Nancy and Bill reluctantly left in Bill's hover to school. Jason took off to the news station and was going to do his best to steer the news clear from Turner's headquarters. Ryan and I said goodbye to George and Vianne, then made our way to the Hover-Shuttle waiting area. We figured if we took the shuttle there would be no way Turner could catch us on satellite. This way we could hand over Elisha and the twins to Doris and take the shuttle back. No one would ever be the wiser. At least I hoped so.

There was no one else waiting for the shuttle when we arrived so we sat on the bench and waited.

"I never thought I'd be taking a Hover-Shuttle to break someone out of a high security prison," Ryan said with a slight laugh.

"I never thought I'd be breaking someone out of a high security prison *period*." I marveled at the strangeness my life had become.

"True, but a part of me always hoped I would help the I.Q. Farm kids escape." Ryan leaned forward and rubbed his hands over his face. "Listen to me. *Kids*. Most of them are over a hundred. It's just weird, you know? It's hard not to think that it could have been me."

I knew he was holding in some emotion to stay strong. I took his hand and kissed the back of it. "Maybe helping Elisha will finally bring an end to I.Q. Farms," I said, trying to make him feel better.

"Yeah," Ryan responded, though his voice was distant. I didn't want to interrupt his thoughts so I just held his hand so he'd know I was there for him.

The whirling of fans greeted us as the Hover-Shuttle landed at the waiting area. Being at an upper middle class station this shuttle was about a million times nicer than the one I used to take to school from the trailer park. It was essentially a large shiny silver box with rounded windows framed in black trim. The small set of metal stairs lowered in front of us and we walked up and entered inside. Ryan had placed a fake thumbprint on his thumb so we could pay with a false identity. It was one of his little inventions that he perfected since the last time we used them. The first time was when we broke into Turner's headquarters and unfortunately Turner had seen right through them. But, Ryan said he had figured out the problem and this was the perfect time to try it out.

Ryan placed his thumb on the credit machine: it flashed green indicating that the Hover-Shuttle was happy to welcome "Fred Tilly and friend." Ryan gave me a quick smile and I smiled back. Inside, there were two rows of two seaters lining each wall. They were plush red vinyl and were ridiculously comfortable as we plopped down on the nearest seats. The shuttle was empty except for the driver, which made me a little nervous. I hoped we'd pick up more passengers as we went. It would be much easier to remember two kids all alone than a shuttle full of people.

As we drove closer to our destination, more passengers filled up the shuttle and I started to relax a little. Ryan was quiet. I guess I was, too. There really wasn't much to say. We were both just trying to get through it. I was so grateful Ryan had convinced me to let him come. Doing this alone would have been torture. Besides, Jason had the winning argument in favor of Ryan coming: Ryan knew the blueprints. I was going to need that information if this plan was going to work.

"Next stop, National Red Forest," the driver announced in a monotone voice.

I squeezed Ryan's hand.

The hover landed at the entrance to the maple forest surrounding Turner's headquarters. It was surreal exiting the shuttle and seeing the forest again, this time fully awake. I somehow knew exactly how to get to the marked tree as if Elisha had planted the directions in my head. I suddenly shuddered as I realized she probably did.

Ryan and I separated from the crowd, who were there to take a tour of the maples. We veered east toward the marked tree. No one saw us go and it didn't look like anyone would care anyway.

Walking for about an hour, we finally reached the marked tree. It looked exactly as it had when Elisha brought me there last night.

"Everything's going to be okay," Ryan soothed. He leaned down to kiss me. It made most of my brain turn to mush, but I was still freaked.

I needed to calm down if I was going to do this. I still wasn't even sure if it was going to work…

"I know." My voice was shaking a bit. "We better start."

Ryan's hands were immediately framing my face. "I'm serious. You don't have to do this."

I gently pulled his hands away and tried to smile as bravely as I could. "Yes, I do."

Ryan nodded and kissed my forehead. "Just tell me everything you see and I'll lead you to the Farm."

"Okay." I turned toward the building. "Here goes."

I closed my eyes and searched the building for a dead body. It wasn't hard: there were about a hundred people in there with swirling black holes. I searched for the twins' black spinning heads and couldn't find them. Had Turner moved Elisha and the boys? Were they even in the building? I quickly calmed myself and concentrated on the task at hand. I'd try and find Elisha first, then go from there.

I connected to the dead body closest to the basement where Elisha was being held. Of course, Turner had all one hundred dead people protected by the invisible barrier he placed up with his voodoo rituals, but I had long since been able to break through them like they were nothing more than a hiccup.

Having my own eyes closed made the whole experience easier as I made myself see through the corpse's eyes. I looked down at the body I was using and made note of the fact that I was a slightly overweight male. He was sitting at his desk staring at a holo-monitor displaying 3-D charts and graphs of something or other. I still didn't know how my grandfather used his dead servants. It seemed like they still worked and functioned without his constant attention. I honestly couldn't imagine that. Keeping my stepfather animated for ten years took at least some kind of concentration even if I was on auto-pilot for a lot of the time. But the amount of people that were dead under Turner's spell? That would drain me to the point of knocking me out cold. How did he do it? Another question I hoped I'd find the answer to, but somehow I doubted I'd know anytime soon.

This guy was mine now. And that was all that mattered at the moment.

His office was small and sparse with generic holo-paintings of grass fields and sailboats mounted on the wall. The desk was clean and free of any kind of personal kitsch, just a computer and an electronic reader. I made him stand up and walk out of the small room to the hallway beyond.

"I'm on a floor near the bottom of the building in the hallway," I told Ryan, still keeping my eyes closed.

I could feel him clasp my hand tighter in support. "Are you nearer to the north side or the south side?" he asked.

"Somewhere in the middle." I gauged.

"Face south and there should be a door up on your left in about twenty feet," Ryan voiced from memory.

Sure enough, the door was there just like he said. It was hard not to be impressed with Ryan's brain. To have memorized the entire schematics of a building a mile wide and who knows how far down was truly mind boggling. But once something was in Ryan's brain, it was in there forever. It was probably as much of a burden to him as it was a gift. Like my power. We never really talked about it, but I made a mental note to broach the subject when this was all over.

"Okay, I'm through," I said as I made the man open the door.

I was on familiar ground now. This was the same stairwell where we escaped from Turner's dead army two months ago. It was four levels of grated walkways and staircases like a jumbly mess of metal. I could see I was on the third floor down: only one floor away from the entrance to the ventilation shaft that would lead me to the Farm.

"Recognize it?" Ryan answered my thoughts.

"Yeah," I replied and made the corpse walk down the stairs and jump to the bottom floor. "Just through the grate, right?" I asked, making sure I was in the right place.

"Yeah. Once you're in I'll lead you through." I could tell Ryan was trying not to sound nervous.

I made the man open the grating on the floor and dropped him down to the ventilation tunnel below. The shaft was at least a foot higher than the body I was in, so I didn't have to make him duck. Ryan guided me down four more levels of metal hallways and tubes until we reached the giant grate that led to the I.Q. Farm. So far, so good. I was surprised that Turner hadn't locked down all entrances to the Farm since our last break-in, but the more I thought about it the less strange it seemed. My grandpa didn't see me as a threat and never would. He probably figured if I was even going to attempt anything like this he'd have ample warning. Well, his mistake was my advantage.

I tried to sense the twins' swirling black heads, but I still couldn't see them. I didn't know how I was going to find Elisha without using them as a compass, but I made the corpse open the grate just the same. I quickly had him jump down.

And then I surveyed the horror that was an I.Q. Farm before me.

Hundreds of children filled the room, oblivious to everyone around them. Some were hooked up to machines, some were in virtual reality suits jumping and kicking at unknown objects, some were at computer stations typing a mile a minute. But all of them had the same dark circles under their eyes and the same comatose expressions on their faces. It was a terrifying spectacle. I felt relief that Ryan wasn't there to see it.

"Okay, I'm in the main room. Where do you think Elisha is being held?" I asked, hoping that no one with authority was in the vicinity to see the man whose body I was controlling. I didn't sense any dead guards, which was both good and bad. Good because maybe there weren't any guards down here and bad because if there were guards I'd prefer it be with people I could control.

"There are two doors on the east wall," Ryan directed. "If she's down there she'll be behind one of them. Those doors are the only exits, and the rooms are small. Like prisons." I could feel the sweat on his hand as he squeezed mine. Although maybe that was my sweat. I couldn't tell I was so nervous.

"Which way's east?" I asked, slightly embarrassed. I had no sense of direction down there and I didn't want it to be the reason we failed.

"If you're standing with your back to the vent opening the doors will be on the left wall," Ryan said without a hint of condescension in his tone. (One of the many reasons why I loved him.)

I made the man walk toward the doors and past the section of comatose children strapped into machines with strange looking wires and suction cups attached to their heads. Their hair was shaved: they almost looked like aliens with the spider-like wires seemingly growing out of their brains connecting to some unknown source above. I really didn't want to know what was happening to them. It was sickening to watch.

Making the corpse look around, I still didn't see any signs of guards. If Elisha was set for execution tomorrow morning wouldn't she be under heavy guard?

Unless she wasn't here.

I made the man open the first door.

Inside was a small room about eight feet by eight feet. About three feet in front of me was a plexiglass wall with no door or opening to speak of. But huddled in a ball in the corner I could see Elisha with her head down.

Great.

I found her, but how was I supposed to get through what looked like four inches of plexiglass?

"Elisha," I made the corpse say.

She lifted her head and a huge smile spread across her face when she saw the man in front of her. "Chelsan?" she asked.

"Yeah, how do I get you out?" I made him ask.

"Turner just put in the plexi wall this morning." Elisha was cut off by a sudden blaring screech filling the air.

The alarm.

Fantastic.

"Chelsan, I'm going to need you to concentrate." Elisha was standing in front of the man I was controlling now. Only the plexiglass between us.

I could hear the thumping of guards running toward us and their clacking of guns.

"Hang on. Let me take care of them first," I made him say and I put Jason and my plan into play.

I made the corpse open the door to see the oncoming guards running toward him.

Then I connected to the millions of pieces of dust in the room. Like a swarm of gnats, I made the dust fly up their noses and slammed it into their lungs.

Just like I had with Jill.

The result was just the same. They all grabbed their throats gasping for air. Their effort was futile as I kept the dust in their lungs. After a few seconds they dropped to the ground unconscious. I quickly removed the dust from their lungs and knew I only had minutes before they awoke.

I made the man turn back to Elisha. "What do I do?"

Elisha's purple eyes were intense but calm in a way I envied at the moment. "Chelsan, I'm going to ask you to do something to your vessel you probably haven't done before, but it's the only way I can think of to get out."

I knew we were cutting it close on time so I just wanted her to spit it out. "Tell me."

"You're going to have to make his blood boil," she said.

What?

"What?" I made him say out loud.

"Plexiglass becomes malleable at a hundred degrees Celsius and blood boils at the same temperature. If you can make your vessel's blood boil there's a good chance you'll simply be able to maneuver an opening for me," Elisha said as if I were an idiot and should have known better.

"But…" How was I supposed to do that?

"The vessel you're controlling is completely under your power which means you can do anything to it," she said as if coaching a student.

And then I remembered.

I had made my mother explode. And Jill's dad. And all those other corpses. Granted, I was in a state of shock and reacted on impulse, but still. I did make their bodies go boom.

"Is everything okay?" I heard Ryan say out loud.

I was so enwrapped in what was going on, I almost forgot I wasn't actually in the building itself. I squeezed Ryan's hand and he squeezed mine back. I needed him to be my lifeline. "No matter what, don't let go of me," I said to him.

"Never." He held my hand tighter.

I focused all my attention on the dead man I controlled. I visualized heat warming up his blood. Gross. I had no way of telling if it was working or not.

"Put your hands to the plexiglass," Elisha instructed me.

I did as she said and made the corpse put his hands flat on the smooth surface. I nearly pulled them away when I noticed the color of his skin had changed drastically. It was white and puckery like boiled chicken skin. Eeeww. And then I felt it.

It was the strangest sensation I'd ever experienced.

Inside the corpse it felt like a million bubbles popping continuously. I swallowed hard and nearly cut off the circulation to Ryan's hand, but he didn't say a word.

I was making this man's blood boil.

Elisha's eyes were round with anticipation and excitement. Disturbing.

But I couldn't think of that now. The guards were going to wake up soon and the alarm was still blazing, which meant more troops on the way. I made the man's hands push into the plexiglass. I was amazed at how he was able to push through the plastic like it was made of thick custard. It was such a strange sensation, it was almost cool, but I had only a matter of minutes so I couldn't let myself enjoy the moment. And besides, the bubbling blood inside the corpse was so distracting it was literally making me sick.

I pulled down with his hands, opening the plexiglass by the handful. I made him pull and swipe until he had created a small two-foot by one-foot hole. Elisha was on it. She squirmed her way through until she was out.

"We have to get John and Samuel," Elisha replied.

"I didn't sense them in here," I made the man say. "Maybe Turner had them moved?"

"No. They're in the next room," Elisha said and left the room we were in.

I made the corpse follow and stopped his blood from boiling. This was a much easier task, since all I had to do was stop concentrating on heat. But as soon as I did, the skin from his forearms slopped off. I guess the skin couldn't handle the continuous heat and now it was dropping off him one section at a time.

"Elisha!" I made him call out.

Elisha was opening the second door and turned around to see my problem. Her face was more irritated than anything else. "Anything else you can connect to?"

I felt around, but all the dead people were at least four floors up.

Wait a second…

Oh crap.

"Elisha. Turner's dead army is coming," I made the man say just as his jaw fell to the floor. Yuck.

I guess Turner's soldiers were a part of the hundred dead people I sensed in the beginning. I was losing control of the man I was in. The more skin he lost, the less power I had over him.

"In here, quickly." Elisha held the door open for the man and I made him shamble through.

Inside was a metal wall with a metal door.

"They're in there," she said with authority.

"But I can't see their black holes," I made him say, though it came out more as a garble due to his lack of jaw.

"That's because of the metal. It's designed to keep people with your gift out," Elisha informed me.

What?

Oh.

The room that Brady the serial killer had kept me in.

It must have been made of the same metal. I hadn't been able sense anything dead outside of the room. It wasn't until I had used Larry the dead cockroach that I discovered Brady's victims buried in his backyard. I had to clear the doorway before I could connect with them and use them to escape. Turner must have had it installed for him knowing that people like me would be rendered useless. More questions were running through my head about a mile a minute, but I had to focus on the present.

The dead army was one floor up and making their way down.

Both of my corpse's thighs slid to the ground.

"Ryan this is so gross," I said to Ryan in the forest. My eyes were still shut and I desperately wanted to open them to see him. I felt that just one look from his big brown eyes would make the nightmare I was experiencing in the building all better. But I needed to keep my concentration at full power if I were to help Elisha and the twins escape.

"I'm right here. If you want to leave now, I'm with you." Ryan tried to calm me.

"No. I'm good, just more typical *me* stuff." I kept it vague. Ryan's over-protectiveness would probably make him force me to stop.

Ryan let go of my hand to wrap his arms around me from behind. He kissed the top of my head and I immediately relaxed into his chest.

Since the man's face was starting to melt off, I knew I had to find another black hole fast.

I was tempted to tap into the oncoming dead army, but I knew I needed to save my strength for that. And besides, I wasn't even sure I could. I really didn't know if Turner had found a new way to block me from his corpses. What if he used this metal somehow? It obviously worked on me…

I'd find out soon, I guess.

Before I lost sight completely, I connected to a dead fly on the ground. I really wished I hadn't. It was like seeing the same image through eight hundred points of view. So, watching the bloody pulp of a corpse I was just controlling slop to the floor in gumpy mess like it was on a thousand holo-tvs: not good.

I made the fly buzz in front of Elisha hoping she'd understand that it was me controlling the insect. I wasn't disappointed.

"You'll be able to connect to the boys soon. I can pick this lock." Elisha made quick work of the locked door with the use of a stylus she found in the corpes's bloody pocket. She apparently wasn't fazed at all by the pile of guts at her feet, which made me wonder what she'd been through over the last hundred years to desensitize her.

The door swung open and John and Samuel stood there just like in my vision that Elisha sent me last night. They were holding hands while their milky blue eyes stared straight ahead at nothing. I still couldn't see their swirling heads yet, but when Elisha led them out of the metal room the black masses spun wildly.

"Connect to them," she ordered. I shuddered from the look in her eye. From the hundreds of violet eyes giving me the same expression. It was almost like a challenge. Like she wanted to see what would happen if I did. I felt Ryan hold me tighter. He obviously didn't like my reaction.

He leaned down and whispered in my ear, "I'm here. You're okay."

I was instantly more at ease, but my doubts about Elisha were growing by the second. I was almost tempted to leave her there and run away with Ryan as far as I possibly could. But there was something about the boys that made me stay. They were so helpless. So vulnerable. The fact that they were brain dead because of my grandfather… It was too much to bear. I just couldn't leave them there.

And I couldn't leave Elisha to die. If I abandoned her now it would feel like I pulled the trigger myself. If Turner was going to execute her, I needed to give her a fighting chance. I didn't have to trust her, I just had to help her.

She was right though: the boys would be easier to connect to than the fly.

I slammed myself into their swirling black holes.

FLASH!

The light was so intense it was like stepping into the center of the sun. I couldn't see anything, just the glaring light all around me.

I jumped out of them and reconnected to the fly.

I was still in shock at what just happened. I was suddenly afraid I would open my eyes in the forest and I'd be blind myself. What was *that*? I knew in that instant that yet again there was way more to this than I originally thought. Again, my instincts were to run. But my stubbornness won out as usual.

Elisha's face couldn't hide her disappointment. "Didn't work, huh? Follow me. I know the way out."

And she was off with John and Samuel in tow. It was the oddest train of three children I had ever seen, with Elisha in the lead holding John's hand and John holding Samuel's. They headed toward the back of the giant room to another ventilation grate. It was very strange following them as a fly and I knew I'd need to connect to a body soon to be of any real help.

The alarms blazed like a constant reminder of our doom and I felt the dead soldiers enter the I.Q. Farm.

Elisha removed the grating and helped John and Samuel into the ventilation tunnel, which was barely two feet tall and maybe three feet wide max. They'd have to crawl. I noticed that the boys were having no trouble guiding themselves. Even though they had no sight, it was like they could still see. And come to think of it, as they were crawling ahead through the shaft, it made me wonder how dead their brains really were. They seemed to be thinking for themselves just fine. Maybe they were acting on instinct? This whole situation was getting more and more crazy.

As the first soldiers came within twenty feet of us I concentrated as hard as I could and slammed through their barriers and straight into their swirling black holes. I only connected to the first five, but it was enough for the moment. I made them turn around and block the other twenty from coming closer.

The remaining men opened fire at my five guys tearing their bodies to shreds. Three were pretty much rendered useless so I disconnected them from their black holes. They rotted to bones within seconds. I guess they had been dead a while.

I made one soldier stand in front of the other and fire at the twenty guards while I built up the energy to connect to the remaining army.

The I.Q. kids all around us didn't even flinch or look at the mayhem going on around them. Their brains must have been so far disconnected from reality that nothing could faze them.

It took all of my strength to take control of Turner's men, but I managed to do it without passing out. Ryan didn't know it, but he was holding me up at this point. I was ready to collapse. I could immediately feel Turner trying to gain back control over his men, so I tried to disconnect them from their black holes as well.

But I couldn't.

No matter how hard I tried, Turner was gaining the upper hand and I was losing my grip on his men.

Only in this building did he have that kind of power. It was hard to come to grips with the fact that Turner knew so much more than I did about my own power. Pretty soon I probably wouldn't even be able to connect to the dead people under his control. He'd find some new way of keeping me out for good.

I was losing them, one at a time, as Turner took back his power over them.

And just when I was about to abandon the last man standing, one of Turner's dead stepped forward. "Chelsan? Is that you?"

Um.

I turned around to see how Elisha and the boys were progressing and I was relieved to see the grated cover now sealed back in place. Maybe I could give them enough time to make it. Or hopefully Turner thought they were still back in their prison. I just needed more time for them to make their escape.

"Yes. It's me," I made the soldier say.

"You fool!" the soldier in front of me screamed. "Is she gone? Did you help her?" He practically spat at the man's feet.

"You were going to execute her!" I defended myself with the corpse. I couldn't figure out why I needed to explain myself to Turner, but I couldn't seem to stop myself.

"With good reason!" the soldier Turner was puppeteering screamed.

"Were you going to execute those poor helpless boys, too?!" I made the man scream back. I didn't like being scolded, especially from a man who continually tried to kill me.

The soldier's face that Turner was controlling suddenly went slack. "You freed the twins?" his voice was so low and so quiet I almost didn't hear him.

"They didn't deserve this life. No child does." I made the corpse say. It scared me more than I cared to admit at how quiet Turner's corpse was.

"What have you done?" Turner's soldier said as he and all the other soldiers dropped to the floor.

Turner had released them from their black holes and now their bodies were decaying to the state at which they died. It happened so quick I hardly had time to react. Not that there was much to react to. I was now standing in front of a pile of dead men ranging from bones to freshly killed.

I didn't know what to do.

I just stood there inhabiting the last man, staring at the mess in front of me.

What *had* I done? Turner's accusation played over and over in my brain.

"Chelsan, they're here," Ryan's voice sounded in my ear.

I disconnected from the soldier and opened my eyes.

Everything was too bright.

I bent over from the shock of it.

Ryan was immediately supporting me.

"Quickly, dear. The alarms just sounded outside." I could hear Doris's voice from beside me.

I used Ryan to stand up straight and regain my bearings. I blinked in the light and found I was able to see once more.

Doris was there with Elisha and the twins. John and Samuel were comatose once more, holding hands, staring into nothing. Doris's hovercar was parked a few feet behind them. She was already ushering the twins into the car.

Elisha came up to me and for the life of me I couldn't read her expression. She was trying to look grateful, I think, but it was coming across as blankness. "Chelsan, thank you. I am in your debt," she said.

"Um, sure," I said not exactly *sure* at all. (And very smooth by the way, I was such a wordsmith!)

"Listen, you know so little about your power," Elisha said with some authority.

Ouch.

But she was right.

"She saved your ass," Ryan retorted, his defensiveness kicking in.

"I didn't mean to offend her," Elisha addressed Ryan with an almost flirtatious smile.

Eeeww.

She's ninety-eight, she's ninety-eight. I had to keep reminding myself. But still.

Eeeww.

I could tell Ryan was taken aback because he didn't say a word.

Elisha continued but this time she turned to me, "I just meant that there are things I can teach you about them. When things die down, I'll find you and we can talk. It would help me if I knew how you received your powers in the first place?"

"My dad did a spell to save my mom and I," I said not knowing why I answered her. But just the slim chance of an opportunity to learn more about my powers made me blabber. If I could just get the upper hand on Turner…

"Interesting," was all she uttered.

"Elisha, we have to go." Doris was beside her now.

"Go," I urged and before I could move, Doris had her arms around me in a bear hug.

"Good luck, dear, and thank you," Doris whispered in my ear.

"Be careful, Doris." As I said it I found that I was suddenly very worried for her.

"I will, dear, and same goes for you," she responded as she pulled away. She reached over and scuffed Ryan's hair. "Take care of this girl."

Ryan grabbed my hand in response. "I will, Doris. Watch yourself and *her*." Ryan stared straight at Elisha, not bothering to disguise his hostility.

I was shocked and worried. Ryan definitely didn't like her and I was afraid to admit that I agreed with him.

Doris didn't seem to notice she was so frazzled and ready to get out of there.

But Elisha did and her response was a simple smile.

The two of them hurried into the hover-car and the whirling of the hover fans soon became a distant sound until it disappeared altogether.

The sirens blared from the headquarter building and hundreds of hover-cars were leaving in droves. I couldn't tell if they were Turner's soldiers or regular people evacuating because of the alarms. Either way we needed to leave fast.

"Let's get to the Hover-Shuttle station," Ryan said quietly and led me away from the marked maple tree and back the way we came.

"You don't trust her?" I asked aloud as we made our way through the giant trunks.

"No," Ryan responded and squeezed my hand tighter.

"I don't either," I admitted. I wasn't sure how I felt about that, either. I mean, I'd just helped her escape after all. Turner's shock and his warnings still echoed in my head. I told Ryan everything that happened.

Ryan's response was simple, "Turner is just as untrustworthy. You did what you thought was best."

"I guess. But Ryan, I have to tell you, I can't shake this feeling like I did something horrible." I was in full confession mode now.

Ryan stopped me and made me face him. "She was going to be executed. Now, I might not trust her, and you might not trust her, but she didn't deserve to be killed. Saving her was the right thing to do. Period. Okay?"

I nodded. I knew he was right, but I still worried…

"At least we know my Kryptonite now," I said, changing the subject.

We started walking again.

"We have to figure out exactly what the *magic* ingredient is. Maybe it's not the metal, but something he mixes into the metal, you know? Whatever it is it could be a diluted version of it in all of his dead minions and that's what causes the barrier," Ryan mused out loud.

"And if I can break through the barriers…" I started.

"You can find a way to break through whatever it is in higher doses," he finished.

"It makes sense. It's probably the way they hid my mom and all those corpses from me that day." Everything seemed to be clicking into place.

"If we could get our hands on some of that metal, I could figure it out," Ryan said with confidence.

And I knew he could. It was such a great relief having a super genius for a boyfriend. But where could we get a sample? I wasn't about to attempt to go back into Turner's headquarters again.

"We could get some at Brady's," Ryan replied softly. "You wouldn't have to go. Bill and I could do it," he finished quickly.

I tried to hide my fear, but it was useless in front of Ryan. Even the thought of going back to Brady's made my skin crawl and my stomach churn. Being tied up in his basement, in the dirt, in the dark, with that monster… I didn't think I'd ever get over it.

But I also knew Bill and Ryan wouldn't know where to look or which room to take the metal from. Unfortunately, Brady had two separate metal rooms and I only knew for sure that one of them was made from the "Kryptonite." If we were really going to figure this one out, I needed to go with them.

"I'll go. You need me to tell you which room," I replied with as much confidence as I could muster. "We should go today. Get it done."

"I'm not letting you go," Ryan insisted.

"You don't have a choice. Besides, I'll be okay if the whole gang goes. Really." I looked up at him as we walked and smiled.

He tentatively smiled back, but his eyes were brimming with distress. "We'll be in and out. Just point to the room and I'll take you out right after."

"Deal," I agreed, then leaned my head against his arm.

We walked in comfortable silence until we reached the Hover-Shuttle platform. Hover-cars were still whizzing by, but the alarms had stopped blazing in the hour it took us to get there. I guess Turner would continue his search in secret. He worked better that way anyway. I just hoped he wouldn't find Elisha and the boys before they made it to safety. If their destination was a Christian Coalition town, Turner wouldn't be able to touch them.

The Hover-Shuttle arrived promptly and we made our way inside. It was packed, buzzing with people trying to figure out what had happened. Apparently it was all over the news that someone had broken into the high security section of "Population Control Center and Research" (as Turner's headquarters was known to the public). Ryan and I pretended to feign interest as complete strangers questioned us about the alarms since we had just left the scene. We played dumb and acted like two teenagers who had played hooky for the day to get lost in the red maple forest. So far, nothing of importance had leaked to the public. I probably had Jason *and* Turner to thank for that. My whole life felt like a cover-up lately.

It didn't take long before we were exiting the Hover-Shuttle and making our way to Nancy's house. School wasn't going to be out for another couple of hours, but we decided to hang out with George and Vianne until the rest of the gang arrived.

I unlocked the door and we let ourselves in. George and Vianne were beyond relieved to see us. When they heard about the alarms, they had assumed the worst.

We all sat on the couch and Ryan had his arm around me in an "oh so comforting" way.

I told them everything that happened.

"Those poor boys." George shook his head.

"Those poor *kids*," Vianne added. "I just wish there was a way to free them all."

"Yeah," I responded, but at this point I was happy to be away from the Population Center and everyone inside. I didn't like the way I was getting used to the events that occurred in my life.

"I'm with you two," George replied after taking a moment to think. "I'm not trusting this Elisha girl."

"Well, there's nothing we can do about it now. At least she won't be popping in my head any time soon," I said and I was very glad of that.

"We hope." Ryan held me tighter.

And from the looks on their three faces I could tell that they didn't think Elisha bumping into my head again was out of the realm of possibility. I hoped they were wrong, but now that I flitted with the idea in my head, I wasn't so sure. Great.

Vianne made us some lunch and food never tasted so good. She made my favorite: a grilled blue cheese sandwich with sweet potato fries and ranch dressing, yum.

The sound of Nancy's voice made me jump to my feet. She came rushing into the kitchen with Bill in tow.

"Oh thank goodness!" she practically yelped and gave me a tight hug.

"We heard about the sirens, but no one knows what happened," Bill said as he gave me a warm hug as well. "What happened?" he asked.

"Don't start without me." Jason walked in with a serious expression on his face. He had obviously let himself in. George and Vianne had pretty much given everyone a key since they considered us all family now.

I told them everything that went down and Nancy made the most noise in response to some of the near escapes.

"I'm with genius boy, here. I think Elisha will pop into your head anytime she feels like it." Nancy shook her head, uneasy.

I was afraid someone else would think that.

"Well, I'm not going to flip out about something I can't control,"

I said. "Besides, we better get to Brady's before it gets too late." I didn't really want to go, but needed to change the subject.

Bill stepped over to me and placed his hand on my shoulder in a comforting way. "Are you sure you need to come with us? We can get the metal on our own."

Ryan apparently didn't like seeing Bill's hand on my shoulder because he reached over and grabbed my hand.

Bill rolled his eyes. "Insecure much?"

"Maybe if *someone* wasn't always fawning over my girlfriend," Ryan's voice was low and angry.

Uh, oh.

"Guys… please don't." I tried to intercede, but they weren't even listening.

"Fawning? Are you serious? Chelsan and I were friends before you even cared to know she existed." Bill pulled his arm back from my shoulder while Ryan's hand squeezed mine more intensely. Ouch.

"Oh, here we go again with the 'I've known Chelsan longer, so I know her better' speech. Guess what? She knew you longer, but she still didn't want you." Ryan knew it would sting.

And it did.

Bill's face turned red from anger. "You don't know that."

"I don't?" Ryan turned to me, "Chelsan, once and for all, please tell Bill you never had feelings for him."

Both their eyes were on me.

Gulp.

"Shut it, both of you!" Nancy earned her best friend card in that moment. They were about to be cut to size. Ryan first. "You! For the smartest person on the planet, you're a complete idiot. She's loves you, stop being so possessive." Bill next, "And you! She picked Ryan, okay? Get over it! This pining from a distance is driving us all crazy!"

"You should talk," Bill mumbled under his breath, obviously referring to her crush on Jason.

"Okay, enough teen angst," Jason interceded. "Brady's place, remember?"

"I'll drive." Bill's arms were crossed, but I could tell he was trying to calm himself down.

"Are we all okay?" I asked, seriously not needing this particular headache, and thanking my lucky stars Nancy pulled me out of having to answer whether or not I ever had feelings for Bill. Truth was, I didn't know if I had or hadn't because the thought never entered my mind back then.

"Yeah," Bill tried to smile, but it was weak.

"Of course," Ryan kissed me briefly on the lips and I couldn't help but think he was trying to prove something to Bill again. Ugh.

Saved by the doorbell.

"Expecting anyone?" Vianne asked with a slight edge to her voice. Vianne and George never interrupted our arguments preferring us to work out our issues on our own, but I could tell it bothered them to see us at odds.

We looked at each other and shook our heads in the negative.

"Let me get it." Nancy was out of the kitchen and answering the front door before any of us had even budged.

Jason couldn't help himself and started to peek through the kitchen door to see who it was.

WHAM!

The door swung in his face before he could move out of the way.

I would have laughed hysterically if it wasn't for who walked in beside Nancy.

Jill Forester.

No one spoke. Everyone was unsure how to react.

Including Jill.

She just stood there with a mixture of uncomfortable defensiveness.

"Yes?" I couldn't seem to stop the attitude from my voice. Old habits die hard, and I was still trying to calm myself from the previous tension so I took it out on Jill.

"Forget it," she mumbled and turned to leave.

Nancy was going to let her go, but Bill gently touched Jill's arm to stop her.

Jill looked up at him with a kind of insecurity I almost found heartbreaking simply because I could relate to it. I used to look at Ryan like that before I knew he liked me. I tried to read Bill's face to see if he returned the affection, but he was a brick wall.

Bill's tone was comforting and kind, as he said, "Jill, what is it?"

Jill turned away from him and her eyes met mine. There was still some hostility there, but there was also something a lot more prominent: fear.

"After yesterday… " Jill began with trepidation. It must have been quite intimidating with seven people you barely knew and quite frankly hated up until…(well still probably hated), staring at you. "I started thinking about… my dad."

Everyone was silent during her pause so she could gather herself together. No one wanted to say or do anything that would either make her angry or, well… make her cry.

Jill took a deep breath. "If he was killed like you said, then there had to be a reason for it." Jill pulled out a holo-chip (which was a small circular device that records footage and information).

Jason's eyes immediately lit up. And it was in that moment that I realized how alike Jason and Jill looked. Their black hair and green eyes could have made them brother and sister. I wondered how I never noticed it before. Weird. I noticed that Nancy was making the same connection I had, but I could tell she thought it made them a good-looking couple instead. I just hoped Nancy's temper wasn't going to boil over.

"I remembered the last day I saw my dad… alive. He gave me a locket and told me it was a family heirloom. About a year ago I found the exact same necklace in the Tiffany's holo-logue, but I just figured he had bought it for me and didn't want me to know how much he paid. I know you probably won't believe this, but my family, especially my dad, was very humble and didn't want me to ever brag about how much money we had."

"Ha!" Nancy couldn't help herself. We're talking a lot of years of Jill rubbing her riches and power in all of our faces and to hear that her dad tried to teach her how to behave the exact opposite was a little hard to take.

Jill immediately crossed her arms defensively. "I don't have to tell you anything, so be quiet, Nancy!"

"You're giving me orders in *my* house?!" Nancy's fists were actually starting to clench so I stepped in.

"Nancy, just let Jill finish." I gave her *the look. The look* that only best friends can give each other. It's the, "*I'm with ya, but this is important*" look.

Nancy nodded, but didn't look happy.

I looked over at Bill and nodded him toward Jill. Bill immediately took the cue and placed his hand on her arm supportively.

I shouldn't say I was surprised at the way Jill leaned into him. I knew that she'd had a crush on Bill for as long as anyone could remember. But what did take me aback was how much Bill actually seemed to enjoy it. I wouldn't really describe my emotion as jealous, but I admit it did make me feel a little betrayed. It's not like I wanted Bill for myself, but… well… I didn't really want him with Jill. As much as she was trying to be helpful, I still harbored a ton of resentment for her. She had made my life torture since I'd known her and two months of exile from her throne of power just wasn't enough punishment for all the pain she caused most humans.

"Anyway. It got me thinking and I broke open the locket and found this." She handed the holo-chip over to Jason's greedy hands.

"Do you know what's on it?" Jason asked completely oblivious to the tension between Jill and everyone else in the room. Who was I kidding? Jason probably did notice, but when it came to juicy news, he just didn't care.

"It was encrypted. I thought maybe you guys would be able to crack it." Jill leaned in closer to Bill and he didn't push her away.

Lame.

But still…

"Thanks, Jill. I know how hard it must have been to come over here," I managed to say. As much as I despised the girl in the past, it really did take a lot in coming over to your worst enemy's abode and handing over the reason behind your father's death.

"Yeah, well… anyway, I should go." Jill pulled away from Bill and reached for the exit door. "You'll let me know what's on it," she said it as a statement rather than a question.

"Of course." Jason pushed past her with a grin, out the door and most likely headed for George's holo-computer to try to de-code the chip.

"He's charming," Jill said sarcastically and opened the door herself.

"He's also the one who's going to find out why your dad was killed, so a little more gratitude, thank you very much!" Nancy was full of piss and vinegar again. And besides, in Nancy's book no one could mess with Jason except her.

Jill stopped in the doorway and instead of anger, she turned to Nancy, her eyes starting to tear up. "You're right. I'm sorry. Just call me when you find something."

Jill was through the door before she went into full "bawl" mode. Vianne gave Nancy a look that instantly made her cringe with guilt. "Go after her, you little brat." Vianne nudged Nancy forward.

Nancy sighed and followed after Jill.

"I'm going, too," I said, but when Bill and Ryan moved to come with me, I put my hand out to stop them. "This is a girl thing."

I left the kitchen and wondered why I'd said that. It wasn't really a *girl* thing, I just didn't want to see Bill comforting Jill. What's my problem? I really didn't want Bill to have feelings for Jill. I was such a jerk! He deserved to be happy. But with Jill? I wasn't ready for that.

And another reason I didn't want them to come was because after Ryan and Bill's confrontation I wanted them to be stuck with each other for a little while. Maybe come to some sort of happy ground again. Was I delusional these last couple of months when I thought they were becoming close? No. They'd probably be best friends if it weren't for me. My fault again, what a shock.

I caught up to Jill and Nancy near the front door in the foyer.

Jill was wiping away fresh tears and Nancy was awkwardly standing in front of her. "Look, Jill, we have a lot of history. Bad history. I'm really sorry." Nancy sounded genuine.

"Don't apologize. I get it. I should just go." Jill tried to make it to the front door, but I grabbed her by the arm.

"Jill, stop. You shouldn't drive home like this. You could get into an accident," I said before I knew what was coming out of my mouth. Was I actually asking Jill to stay? With us? In the same house? For more than five minutes? The lack of sleep from Elisha tromping in my brain must be frying my synapses.

Jill was like waterworks now. What did I say?

Jill turned to me almost angrily, "Why are you always so nice?! It's infuriating!"

It was such a strange accusation, Nancy and I actually laughed. After a second or two Jill started to smile through her tears.

"You think I'm nuts," Jill said, but there was no anger behind it.

"A little. But I also think you've been hurting for a very long time, and that would make anyone crazy." I tried to break her out of her downward spiral. "Why don't you stay here with Nancy's parents and Jason for a while. Get yourself together and maybe Jason will be able to figure out what's on that holo-chip," I suggested.

"Where are you guys going?" Jill wiped her face clean.

"Somewhere that isn't safe. But we won't be long." I hoped she'd drop it. Yeah right.

"What do you mean it isn't safe?" Jill was curious now.

Great.

"I mean: you should stay here. None of us really wants to go, but we have to," I stated very clearly. I really didn't want Jill near me when going to Brady's. It was going to be hard enough as it was.

"Can I come?" Jill asked as if she didn't hear a word I just said.

"No, Jill. I'm serious, it's too dangerous." I tried to be firm.

"Is it something to do with Vice President Turner? Chelsan, he killed my dad, I want to know everything. Please." Jill's eyes were desperate. She was looking for answers I couldn't give her. I was tempted to tell her Turner was my grandfather, but I was still unsure how she'd take it. Our relationship was about as fragile as you could get and anything could send her over the top.

Nancy turned to me. "Maybe she should see first-hand what he did to you." She had a defiant kind of gleam in her eye, almost like she was proud at how I escaped Brady and wanted to brag to Jill about it.

"Take me with you. Please," Jill pleaded and her voice was quavering.

Why was I such a softy? I used to think this girl was evil and now I actually felt sorry for her. Maybe it would be a good idea for her to see Brady's. To see how insane Gramps really was and show her what I had gone through on top of the way she treated me at school. Seriously, serial killer.

"Okay, but no crap from you. I'm not kidding." I wanted to make it clear.

Jill nodded, her green eyes determined. "I promise."

Bill and Ryan had come up behind us without me noticing. Ryan wrapped his arms around me from behind and leaned down to rest his chin on my shoulder. "Let's go."

"Shotgun." Nancy claimed not giving Jill any special privileges, which meant Jill was going to be in the back with Ryan and myself.

Why did I agree to this again?

George and Vianne saw us off and we were in the air before we knew it.

I sat in the middle and leaned in close to Ryan on my left. Jill sat on my right and stared out the window, not saying a word. I tried not to stare out the window myself as we flew closer and closer to our destination. The trees were the only way to tell we were headed to the poorer parts of town. The richer the neighborhood, the more expensive the trees. Bill's, being the richest, was full of perfectly coifed bonsais and cherry blossoms while Nancy's upper middle class was pine. Brady's neighborhood was lower middle class, which mainly consisted of bamboo trees. The lowest of the low was where I grew up. We hardly had any trees, just fields and fields of wild flowers. I felt a pang of emotion at the thought. It wasn't that long ago that I'd sit under my favorite willow tree amongst the flowers and just chill. It wasn't that long ago that my mother was still alive. It wasn't that long ago that I was locked in Brady's basement with only dead roaches to save me…

I shuddered despite myself. The memories were fresher than I'd like and as we approached our destination my fear was starting to grow.

It was then that I noticed Jill staring at me. "Where exactly are we going?" she asked. "You look petrified."

"I can open that door and let you off here if you don't keep your mouth shut." Ryan apparently didn't like Jill's accusation.

"Calm down, Ryan," Bill defended Jill. Her face lit up and I couldn't be mad at Bill, I just didn't want Ryan to argue back.

I squeezed Ryan's hand to let him know I was okay and to ignore Bill. I looked back at Jill. "I *am* petrified."

"That story about the serial killer. That was true, wasn't it? That's where we're going." Jill didn't react to Ryan's threat she was so pleased with Bill defending her. She actually seemed upset. For me. It was very surreal.

"Yeah. Turner hired him to kill me," I answered quietly.

"What an a-hole," Jill said in a near whisper and went back to staring out the window.

I smiled briefly. Quite honestly it was the nicest thing Jill had ever said to me.

Bill landed in front of Brady's house.

"You need a sec?" Ryan asked me gently. "You can wait in the car."

"No. I need to tell you which room." I practically crawled over him to get out of the car.

Ryan got the hint and exited quickly so he could help me the rest of the way out.

And there it was.

My former prison.

My former nightmare.

Scratch that. My *recurring* nightmare.

I never really saw it from the front before. Brady had knocked me out to bring me here. And when I escaped, I ran out through the back.

It was a simple house, white with brown trim, a wrap around porch and a solid black door. The grass was as fresh as ever from the automatic sprinklers, but it was like a jungle of green since no one had cut it since Brady's arrest. The holo-line surrounding the house, flashed the words, "Do Not Enter! Crime Scene!"

"Won't that set off an alarm if we cross it?" Jill asked. She was taking this all in and I could tell she was making an effort not to be too intrusive.

"I got it," Ryan answered as he made his way to a small rectangular floating device that was the source of the holo-line. It took him a few minutes of tinkering, but in the end the holo-line shut off and no alarms were sounded. "Let's get this over with."

Bill went to his trunk and pulled out what looked like a metal laser gun. George had given it to us so we could cut off a piece of the metal to bring home.

"Are you sure you know how to use that?" Nancy asked Bill.

"We'll find out." Bill shrugged and led the group inside.

I was the last to enter, with Ryan leading me by the hand.

The smell made me gasp for air. I hadn't even thought about it when I was making my escape, but now that I was back just the smell of the place rocked my insides. It wasn't even abnormal, just a little musty, but it brought me back to that week of my life. I had never been so scared. So alone.

Everything was how I left it: the smashed chair, the round wooden table and the orderly sparse furniture that made up Brady's home. Only the bodies were gone. Brady's victims. That I used to attack him…

"Behind that door. The metal walls." I nodded to the door that was almost off its hinges from the amount of times Brady and I fought to keep it open and shut.

Bill was already through the doorway. A moment later I could hear the sound of the laser carving its way through the metal.

Why did I come here?

I could have easily told them where the room was.

It wasn't exactly brain surgery.

I guess I thought that if I came back maybe I could finally be done with this fear.

Sometimes I found it almost funny how, out of everything that had happened to me, *this* experience terrified me the most. Even over everything Turner put me through, from fighting off his dead armies, to almost being executed by him in the Principal's office, Brady was different. He was born to kill. Born to terrify. I loathed the fact that he had that much power over me.

And Brady wasn't even alive anymore.

But the real fear came from knowing that there were others like him. Others that Turner sanctioned to "control" the population. What if Gramps sent another one of these monsters after me again? What if he surrounded me with this metal and I couldn't use my gift to save myself the next time?

I felt naked and helpless.

I turned to see Jill looking at me with more sympathy than I ever thought her capable of. I knew in that moment that she got it. Even just seeing the remnants of the aftermath was enough for her. And there was more to her expression than just sympathy. There was guilt. Guilt and an overwhelming sense of responsibility. She was speechless, but her eyes were speaking volumes.

"Thanks," I said and then everything went black.

***

Oh man.

I was in the utter darkness again.

I searched for Elisha, assuming she had gone inside my head once more. It made me furious. Furious at her for her disrespect of my privacy and furious at me for not knowing how to stop her.

"Elisha! Show yourself! This has got to stop! I mean it!" I screamed in the blackness.

"How dare you!"

That wasn't Elisha.

I whirled around and suddenly I was in a bright grey room facing…

Roberta. My grandmother.

Really?

She was grotesque with her stretched skin and frozen features. Roberta was the quintessential *Feline*.

And though Roberta's face could barely make an expression, I could tell she was furious.

"What are you doing here?" I asked feebly, but tried to sound brave. Knowing that my body was vulnerable and stuck in Brady's house while my mind was facing Roberta made my insides shake.

"You stupid child! How could you help her escape?! How could you?!" Roberta was breathing through her nostrils like an enraged bull.

"She was going to be executed! By you! I'm glad I did it!" I screamed. I may have had my pangs of indecision about helping Elisha, but I wasn't about to let Roberta know that.

"Trust me, fool, you should have let us kill her. And taking the twins? Congratulations, *Granddaughter,* you may have successfully ended the entire world." Roberta's tone was angry, but more importantly she was dead serious.

How could two brain-dead kids end the world?

I was about to ask this when suddenly Roberta's face was directly in front of me.

I screamed in spite of myself.

"Let's see what kind of memories you've got for me, and I might just be able to save you from your own idiocy." Roberta grabbed my head and I felt a sudden pulsing like a migraine in every part of my brain.

I cried out from the pain. "Stop!"

Roberta pulled her hands away, her eyes flared with anger. "Up to even more trouble? A holo-chip, huh? Only Jill can decrypt that chip and only Geoffrey and I know how she can do it," Roberta smiled wickedly, "Well, Owen could too, but you blew him up now, didn't you?" Her feline eyes narrowed, "But I'm not going to give you and your gang the chance to figure it out. Say good-bye to Jill Forester, sweetheart." Roberta's face was frozen and icy, "And don't let Elisha in your head! She's after your memories now, you stupid twat!"

***

"Chelsan?!"

Ryan's worried face greeted me in Bill's hover-car.

We were in the air and on our way back to Nancy's. Jill was beside me as well, trying not to stare, but I could tell she was freaked out.

Nancy was turned toward me from the front seat. "What happened? Was it Elisha?"

"Roberta," I grumbled and started massaging my aching temples. Between Elisha and Roberta I wasn't sure how much more I could take of this. It was really starting to take its toll on me.

"Geoffrey Turner's wife? Bill explained this astral thingy, but I didn't know anyone could just jump in like that." Jill looked like she was trying to make sense of the last few hours of her life and wasn't having much success.

"Jill you're in trouble." As the words left my mouth the glass next to Jill's head shattered into a million pieces.

Jill screamed. A bullet shot through her window and straight into her arm.

Bill swerved from the shock of its impact. Thank goodness he did as another bullet whizzed through the open window and out the other side shattering Ryan's window now.

"LAND! LAND! LAND!" I screamed. Staying in the air was a death sentence to Jill.

It was very obvious that the shooter was only after Jill. In fact, it was disgusting that my grandparents were being so precise. It meant that they needed me for something and it also meant that in their evil distorted brains, they actually thought they were being nice by not killing Ryan, Bill and Nancy. Gee thanks!

But there was no way I was going to let them kill Jill.

Bill was on the ground before we knew it and I saw the hover-car with the shooter. It was a small, black two-door hover with the sniper in the back. I couldn't even see his head, just the long tip of the silencer on his rifle. The hover-car swung down from traffic to get a better aim.

Bill had landed on a grass field just outside of the upper middle class zone. There was no one around, which meant it was probably about to get wet very soon. As if on cue the sprinklers shot out around Bill's car. The hover's broken windows let all the water inside and we were immediately soaked to the bone.

Jill clutched her arm in pain, but I was surprised and impressed at how calm she was. "Where?" she asked of her assassin.

The black two-door hovered a hundred feet above us. I could see the gun leveling to take aim.

I didn't know what to do.

Ordering Bill to land, I had just made us sitting ducks.

If he had kept driving, maybe we could have lost them.

But I knew that wasn't true.

Jill would have been dead already if we had kept going. At least down here there might be something I could use.

I searched the area for anything dead.

Worms, flies, spiders… come on….

POP!

The gun fired.

I was too late.

No wait.

I slammed into the black swirling hole of a dead raven and made it fly in front of Jill's head at lightning speed. It looked like a black blur across Jill's face. The bullet tore straight into the bird, preventing it from hitting Jill.

Jill's eyes were wide with a mixture of terror, curiosity, and gratitude.

I knew it wasn't over yet.

Before another shot could be aimed, I found other dead birds within my four-mile control radius and made them all fly directly at the hover-car.

The driver tried to swerve out of the way, but I made the birds attack and attack until the car crashed to the ground a few hundred feet away. There was no movement from the car, but I knew they were still alive since I couldn't see any black holes in their bodies.

"Go, Bill! Get us to Nancy's!" I screamed.

Bill didn't need to be told twice. He was in the air in seconds, racing back to Nancy's.

I kept the two men trapped in their car with the birds until we were out of my control radius.

I knew the assassins were just the first of many.

Now Jill was a target.

Uugh.

"She's losing a lot of blood." Ryan took off his t-shirt and tied it around Jill's arm as a temporary tourniquet.

"We have to take her to a hospital!" Bill was frantic.

"I'm with Bill here, Chelsan." Nancy was scared.

"Turner and Roberta are trying to kill her. They'll have someone waiting at the hospital. Bill can you call your parents? Isn't your mom a doctor?" I pleaded. I knew if we took one step in a hospital Jill was a goner.

That seemed to calm down Bill. "Yeah, yeah. We'll go to my house. Turner won't attack my parents' house, they're too prominent. Okay. Good. Let's do that." Bill was breathing deep and talking himself down.

Bill was right. His house was the best place to be. Turner might be willing to risk taking another crack at Jill at Nancy's house, but not Bill's. His parents were too well connected. They came from old money, and old money was the most respected and the most revered.

"Do I have a say in this?" Jill's voice was weak.

"Jill, you're going to have to trust us. Roberta knows about the holo-chip and she said you're the only one who can decrypt it. She's going to try and kill you before you can. You understand?" I told her what I had learned and hoped she'd listen.

To my relief Jill nodded.

Twenty minutes later we landed on Bill's hover-field. His house was huge. I had only been there once before to meet his parents and have dinner, but his home still made an impact on me. Its design was simple and elegant, like one large rectangle with five dark brown sloping rooftops sectioning off each wing. Its body was painted a deep golden yellow, with masses of burgundy bougainvillea growing up the outer surface making the mansion bright and vibrant. Arched window looked out at us like friendly eyes welcoming strangers inside. The house was surrounded by grass and an outer circle of cherry blossom trees, which were bare from the oncoming winter. And as intimidating and gigantic as Bill's house was, it still managed to feel cozy and warm because of the people in it.

Bill's parents came running toward us. They were extremely alarmed since they had obviously seen the hover's smashed windows and knew something was wrong.

Bill picked up Jill and carried her in his arms, holding her like a baby.

"She's been shot," Bill said and he couldn't hide the worry in his voice.

"Let me take her." Bill's dad, Gordan, took Jill from his son's arms. He looked like a slightly older version of Bill, but not as muscular.

Bill's mom, Frances, was tall and beautiful. She looked like she was in her mid-twenties, (she had Bill naturally, so she didn't start taking Age-pro until she was twenty-four) with long sandy blonde hair, delicate features and large blue eyes. She made a quick exam of Jill's arm, "The bullet passed clean through, she should be fine. Come on in and tell us everything," she said. She held onto Bill's arm and we followed them inside.

The foyer itself was almost the size of Nancy's entire house. The floor was a bright blond-colored wood and the walls were painted a dark coral, holo-paintings hung on all the walls. The sitting room was visible in the distance. Soft, plushy, pleather seats, awaited us.

"Bill go get your friends some dry clothes," Bill's dad said gently.

Bill hurried off and soon returned with a pile of the warmest most comfiest looking sweats I'd ever seen. We all took turns dressing and then plopped down on the poofy chairs. Gordan got the sum-up of what happened, then left to see if his wife needed help with Jill's bullet wound.

None of us could speak. There was nothing to say. Jill was shot.

Ryan leaned in close and kissed my cheek, trying to make me feel better.

After an hour of waiting, Frances came out to give us the skinny.

"She'll be fine. She's going to rest here the night. I've called her mother already." Frances's face was warm and calming, but there was a slight edge to her voice. "Bill, you should take them home. It's late. Good night." Frances left without another word and I felt like we had made her upset.

Let's face it. Bill's mom held me responsible for being a constant source of danger in her son's life, and rightfully so. She was just too nice to yell at me for it. Bill probably made her swear not to say anything mean to me. I was such a jerk.

"I'm really sorry, Bill. Tell your parents I'm really sorry." I didn't know what else to say.

"It's not your fault. Let's just get you back to Nancy's." Bill seemed distracted, not mad, just distracted. I didn't want to push it, so I just left it at that.

The ride back to Nancy's was silent and windy.

After we landed, Bill handed me the small sample of metal taken from Brady's. "See you tomorrow at school."

"Yeah. Thanks, Bill, for everything," I said, giving him hug.

He hugged me back, but it was brief. Before I knew it he was in his hover and gone.

Ryan took my hand and we shared a look of exhaustion. "Sleep?" he asked.

"Oh man, like a hundred years worth!" Nancy groaned.

"Yes, please." I couldn't wait until my head hit the pillow.

CHAPTER 3
THURSDAY DECEMBER 2, 2320

"**D**ON'T YOU DARE! YOU STUPID CHILD!"

I awoke with a start.

What?

That was definitely Roberta's voice. Was that just a nightmare or was she just yelling at me at random now?

"You okay?" Ryan was instantly holding me.

"I think my grandparents' new plan to destroy me is to keep me from getting a good night's sleep. I can't take much more of this." I collapsed into his embrace, completely exhausted.

Six straight hours of sleep; that's all I needed. Just six. Please?! I was lucky if I was able to have two, what with Elisha and now Roberta going into my brain at all hours of the day. Seriously, what was going on?

"Roberta again? Not Elisha?" Ryan asked and kissed my head. I loved it when he did that.

I just nodded into his chest.

"What is she up to?" he wondered aloud.

"I don't know." I was thinking the same thing. "I really don't care. I just wish I could sleep without being interrupted."

"Go back to bed. We don't have to be up for another couple of hours." Ryan scooted down so we were both lying flat now. I snuggled in close.

"Sleep. Yum," I think I muttered as I drifted off once more.

***

"Am I going to have to do this all day, too?" Roberta's voice scolded me.

I opened my eyes and I was standing in my old trailer park. I was taken aback when I noticed that I was in the middle of one of my memories. It was the day that Larry the goldfish died and I saw my first swirling black hole. A three-year-old version of me stood next to a glass fish bowl where poor old Larry floated at the top.

My heart nearly stopped when I saw my mother kneeling next to me. Her silky brown hair tied in a ponytail and her hazel eyes twinkling at the three-year-old me. It made me choke up instantly. The last time I saw her she was a walking zombie with gouged out eyes and rotted, torn skin. The reality of it hit me hard. Seeing her so beautiful and so full of life and so full of love, made me want to scream in anguish. I missed her so much.

"Calm down, it's just a memory," Roberta's voice came from behind me.

I whirled around to face Grams, her stretched, frozen face greeting me like a nightmare.

"Why are you doing this?" I asked, hoping beyond reason that she might actually tell me.

She guffawed as if I was the stupidest human being she'd ever met. "Trust me, I'd rather be anywhere but here, but you did this to yourself! You have no one else to blame."

"You're just going to torture me forever. Is that it?" I almost screamed at Roberta, livid at her constant intrusions.

Roberta rolled her eyes and actually looked more exasperated than her normal evil self. "You've got to learn to keep people out of your head, for your own sake. And for the world's. You've really messed up this time."

The memory of my mother popped out of existence and we were suddenly in the dark. I turned around in vain for one last glimpse of Mom, but the image was gone. It hurt worse than if I had never seen it. I wished I could erase it from my brain, just to make my stomach stop hurting.

I turned to Roberta to confront her and was shocked to see fear in her eyes. "She's gaining in strength. I don't know how long I can keep her out."

"Who? Elisha?" I asked. Seeing Roberta scared was actually terrifying.

"Yes, Elisha. You stupid girl," Roberta snarled at me. "I have to clean up your mess now."

***

I was startled awake for the second time that evening, gasping for air. I clung onto Ryan like he was an oxygen tank. He was instantly awake and holding me tight.

"Again?" he asked incredulously.

"Roberta said something about Elisha getting stronger like she was keeping Elisha out of my head," I said. I pulled my hair back behind my ear and realized it was wet with sweat. My body felt like I had just ran three marathons and hadn't slept for a year.

"Do you think Elisha is trying to warn you of something? I mean we are talking about your grandparents here," Ryan asked quietly in my ear while stroking my hair.

"That makes sense." That had to be it.

Turner and Roberta had been trying to kill me since they found me. Not to mention their attempt on Jill this evening. If Elisha was trying to warn me about something, their first line of attack would be to keep her out of my head so I'd be in the dark. As much as I didn't trust Elisha, I trusted my grandparents less. "We'll have to wait and see, I guess."

"In the meantime you don't get any rest." Ryan sounded irked that this was happening to me. "I hate to be the bearer of bad news, but it's time to get up for school."

I groaned. I wanted to lay my head on the puffy goodness that was my pillow and sleep for at least another five hours.

"Maybe you should call in sick," Ryan suggested.

"We called in sick yesterday. No, I'm getting up." I made myself slap my feet on the oak floor. It was cold and unwelcoming and made me miss the days when I shared a room with Nancy for her plushy carpet.

"You sure?" Ryan asked and stood up next to me, cradling my face in his hands.

I smiled up at him and was about to respond when…

"She's sure. You *both* have to go to school today. Turner's making an appearance." Jason had entered the room with Nancy close behind.

What?

"What?" I was incredulous.

Oh man. Roberta now him? Turner was going to kill me for breaking out Elisha, I just knew it.

"Well, then I definitely can't go, right?" Right? Please tell me that it would be insane to go into the lion's den with a rabid lion waiting for me.

"Don't worry, it's going to be very public. He announced to the press that he intends on speaking directly to *you*." Jason was obviously intrigued and excited by the news while I was halfway between hiding under my bed and jumping out the window screaming.

"I'm glad you're so amused by this whole thing, but I have some news myself that may change your mind," I said and told them about both of my visits from Roberta.

Jason didn't seem fazed at all. In fact, he seemed even more excited. "Interesting."

Jason stepped forward and placed both his hands on my arms, I think in an attempt to steady me. "Chelsan, we have to know what he wants and why he wants to see you. Rule number one: *Know your enemy*."

"Whose rules are those exactly, yours?" Nancy said angrily. "Did you just make that up now? We were just shot at last night, if your tiny little brain can wrap around that, and Turner was the one who sanctioned it!" Nancy was apparently annoyed at Jason this morning, and I had to say, I agreed with her.

"Listen," Jason ignored Nancy's tirade (as usual) and focused on me, "I don't want you to get hurt any more than you do, but when Turner tells the world that he wants to see *you* and he doesn't say why? You have to see him."

And the weird part was, I kind of wanted to. I didn't know what was wrong with me, but the thought of possibly getting some answers from the man himself was intriguing. More than that, I wanted to know why Roberta and Turner were so upset about Elisha and the twins. And I had a gut feeling that Gramps was going to tell me.

I slowly nodded.

Jason clapped his hands in relief. "Get ready. I'll take you to school."

"What about Bill?" I asked, not wanting to offend Jason, but I really only wanted Bill to take us.

Jason shrugged. "He called this morning: he's taking Jill to school." And with that Jason left the room.

I felt a pang of… I didn't even know what, it just hurt. Was I jealous? Was I feeling guilty? Was I scared that Bill hated me now? That maybe his differences with Ryan would somehow transfer to me? Was I scared that Jill would poison his mind against me? She had a genuine case for it now! All of it, I guess. The whole thing made my stomach twist.

Nancy and I shared a look. I could tell she was experiencing the same doubt. Bill was as reliable as they come, and for him not to come over to the house worried me more than I thought it could. I just wanted to see him and tell him again how sorry I was for getting him involved in all my problems.

I shook the horrible thoughts from my brain. It was just a ride! Geez! Bill's good nature didn't want Jill going to school alone, and with a bullet wound for goodness sake! A bullet wound that I was responsible for.

"This should be an interesting ride." Nancy crossed her arms and rolled her eyes.

"You guys fighting again?" I asked, knowing I was about to get an earful.

"When *aren't* we fighting?" Nancy grumbled. "I just wish he'd get over this whole age thing. No one cares, why should he?"

"He'll get over it. He already is, really, he's just too stubborn to admit it." I tried to make her feel better. The sad thing was I was right. Jason really was head over heels in love with Nancy, but he had made such a stink over their age difference, he couldn't seem to let go of it.

"I'm going to go home and shower." Ryan kissed me and headed for the window.

Nancy tried to stop him. "My parents know you're here, you can leave out the front door."

Ryan smiled his roguish smile. "This way's faster. I'll be back." He opened the window and gracefully climbed down to the grass below.

Sigh.

Nancy walked over and nudged me with a grin. "Come on, get ready. He'll be back in a few."

Nancy left and I quickly showered and got dressed. I wore a tank top, jeans and cap-sleeved cardigan with my Chuck Taylor's. I was ready to face the day. Nancy and I wolfed down our breakfast while Jason theorized about what Turner could possibly announce. George and Vianne chimed in their opinions as well, but we were all pretty much guessing. With Gramps, there was just no way of knowing what his next move would be.

Ryan met up with us just as we were filing into the car. Nancy sat up front and Ryan sat in back with me. It felt weird having Jason drive us. Even though he looked like he was our age, he was over eighty years older, and sometimes it felt that way. I knew most people didn't care about age differences since everyone appeared to be the same age, but for me it was hard not to think of everyone twenty years and older as an adult. I would always be the perpetual child in my brain. Ryan reached over and held my hand as we made our way through hover traffic toward school. All seven levels of hover space were crammed in the same direction. Apparently, Jason wasn't the only one who was excited to see what Turner had to say. The more crowded the road space became the more nervous I got.

After another twenty minutes of Nancy and Jason unifyingly agreeing about the lameness of traffic, we finally landed at school.

Bill was there to greet us with five of his dad's bodyguards. There was press everywhere. I hadn't seen it this crowded since, well… since the last time Turner came to school to talk to me… or kill me… I really hoped he wasn't here to kill me. A part of me wished we were past that part of our relationship. Ha!

The press was thankfully roped off at the doorways so students and teachers could land and enter the school without interference. I wished I could just hang out in the parking lot all day, at least I'd have some peace.

That was when I noticed Jill. She wore one of Bill's hoodies and I could see the bulge of her bandage through the sleeve. She stood next to him like a feral cat behind its mommy. Her eyes met mine and there was actual kindness behind them. "Hey," she said quietly.

"Hey," I responded. "How's the arm?" I asked lamely.

"It's good. Bill's mom took good care of me," Jill answered in the same quiet voice.

It was like she was a totally different person. Broken, shy, humble. Words I never thought I'd use to describe Jill Forester.

"Listen, Chelsan," she paused as if unsure how to continue, "Bill told me everything... I'm really sorry for everything I did to you."

Her apology was so genuine I almost didn't have time to panic that she knew Turner was my grandfather. Almost.

"I was going to tell you..." I started, but Bill interrupted me.

"Can I talk to you a sec in private?" he asked.

"Sure." I was a little weary at his abrupt tone.

Bill pulled me away from the others, his expression serious. "I didn't tell her Turner's your grandpa."

I was relieved and disappointed all at once. I was kind of hoping everything was out in the open and I wouldn't have to stress about her reaction. Our budding relationship was tentative as it was (plus, arm, bullet, yeah) and now Turner was becoming her focus of hatred. Deservedly so, but if she knew I was related to him? I just didn't want to take the risk.

"Okay, Bill, thanks for the heads up," I said and he smiled awkwardly. "Is everything okay?" I asked. Was he starting to hate me like I thought? My heart hurt just thinking of it.

"Yeah, just tired." He was definitely being distant.

"I'm really sorry about everything," I blurted out. I felt a kind of desperation rising up inside me. I was losing him.

"I know." He sighed. After a few moments of silent torture Bill squeezed my arm affectionately and I went in for the hug. I really needed a Bill hug right then. Bill held me a little tighter than I expected, but it felt nice all the same. The thought of losing him was excruciating.

I pulled away first. "We good?" I asked.

"We're good." He grinned.

Phew! I hadn't lost him... yet. But I knew if this tension between him and Ryan didn't resolve itself I might lose Bill forever.

"If happy time is over, I'd like to get in there." Jason was clearly impatient to find out Turner's announcement.

Nancy whacked him in the arm appropriately, but he was right.

Ryan quickly grabbed my hand as soon as I was in proximity and I gladly took it. I was going to need every ounce of support I could get.

Nancy walked ahead of Ryan, Bill and myself with Jill. I heard her soft but threatening voice tell Jill, "After everything you did to *all* of us, but especially to Chelsan, you're on probation, but let's be clear: if you go back to your old ways you're done, gunshot or not. We'll keep you safe, of course, until this whole *kill Jill* thing is over, but it doesn't mean it has to be pleasant if you cross us. Are we clear?"

Jill surprised us all by simply nodding. She then turned to Jason, "Any luck on the holo-chip?"

"Not yet, but Roberta telling us that you're the key helps limit our search. Once we find out what kind of a crack it needs, like a password or a decryption code, we'll try and figure out how you play into the deciphering." Jason tried to be reassuring.

"Okay," Jill replied quietly and rubbed her arm as if she was soothing the pain of her wound.

Bill's bodyguards stuck close to us as we entered the school and the fray of press.

Jill's eyes darted around like mad. I wouldn't pull it past Turner to hire another assassin here at school. Although, considering his announcement was the focus of today, I somehow doubted he'd want a "teenage murder" to outrank his news. My heart told me Jill was safe for the moment. I wanted to reassure her, but I really didn't know how. It was an odd feeling, wanting to comfort my worst enemy. But in a matter of a day she had gone from nemesis to… I didn't know what. Friend? Too soon, I think. For both of us. How do you erase years of constant hatred? Time. Hopefully, we'd both have some of it.

Snaking our way through the screaming press, we made our way to the assembly hall. When we entered it was packed. There were thousands of chairs for all the students, which were mostly filled by now. The press stood at any free space they could find, holo-cams in place and ready to shoot. The hall itself was huge! Forty foot ceilings made of solar frosted glass that kept the room lit at all times of day. Yellow walls and deep brown floors, with a five-foot stage stood in the front of the room. The maroon curtains that normally framed the stage were open and a single microphone rested in the dead center in anticipation of Gramps's *big news.*

Bill, Nancy, Jill, Ryan and I sat in the student section near the back while Jason joined his news crew already set up for the announcement.

Before Jason left he placed his hand on my shoulder. "No matter what he says, don't let him get you alone. We can't protect you when you're alone."

It was jarring, but true. I waited with the rest of the crowd to hear what Turner had to say.

Ryan's hand was like a vise, a very comfortable vise, one that I didn't really want to be released from. He leaned in close, "I'll come up with you. What can he do?" he offered as if reading my mind.

But I didn't want him to be in any more danger than… well, than normal. "No, stay here. I can take care of Turner."

"He should go with you," Jill stated.

I was surprised to hear her say anything and even more surprised to hear the protective tone coming out of her mouth.

"Seriously. Turner's a psychopath that killed your mom and my dad. Don't let him get the upper hand." Jill's eyes were intense with a burning anger for Turner.

I leaned over Bill so only Jill could hear. "I don't want Ryan to get hurt."

Nancy sat on the other side of Jill so she heard, too. She placed a hand on Jill's arm. "Chelsan can handle this. She's done it before."

And I had. An assembly just like this where Turner came to give his condolences to me for the loss of my mother and home. Little did everyone know he was the one who killed her. After the assembly he had cornered me in Principal Weatherby's office and tried to kill me and turn me into one of his dead puppets. No. There was no way I was letting him have a chance like that again.

Jill didn't respond she just looked worried. I couldn't tell if it was for me or for herself. Not many people are shot at, and not many people have to face the person who ordered the gunman. Looking at her was making me more nervous so I just focused on Ryan's hand.

Joan shot us a look from a few rows up and her eyebrows lifted at seeing Jill amongst our group. Definitely not pleased. Good. Make her wonder a bit.

Principal Weatherby walked on stage, his swirling black hole a constant reminder of my grandfather's cruelty. Turner had him well animated today with a large grin framing his round face. "Welcome students and press. It is with great honor that I introduce Vice President of Population Control, Geoffrey Turner!"

The applause and cheering was deafening. In fact, I'm pretty sure us five were the only ones not clapping. It was only a glare from Jason that made us pretend to be excited. I guess since the announcement somehow involved me the press' eyes were glued to my seat. Jason obviously didn't want any trouble. Any *visible* trouble anyway.

I could see Jill stiffen out of the corner of my eye as Turner walked out on stage. He was alone. None of his staff (dead or living) to accompany him. He still made my skin crawl, and seeing him in the flesh only amplified the feeling. Even this far back he was an intimidating figure, wrinkles and all.

Weatherby shook his hand as he reached the microphone. "Thank you Principal Weatherby for the kind welcome." The dead Weatherby smiled profusely and left the stage to watch from the sidelines.

Turner turned to the crowd of onlookers and smiled warmly, "Chelsan Derée, will you please come up here and join me?"

All eyes and cameras were instantly on me. I forced a smile and stood up. Ryan reluctantly let go of my hand, but his eyes screamed that he'd jump on stage to protect me if he had to. I tried to give him as reassuring look as I possibly could, but I think it just came out as resigned fear. I turned away before I chickened out and made my way to the stage.

I noticed how quiet the room was. No one was talking. No one was even whispering. They were all just watching me walk up to join Turner on stage. I could hear the hum of the holo-cams and the slight shuffling of feet from the people trying to get a better view. I swallowed hard and wished I hadn't sat so far back! I hurried my steps and thought about running the rest of the way, but I'd probably trip and make an idiot of myself.

After an excruciating minute of silent walking I finally stood next to

Turner onstage. I didn't like being this close to him. He smelled like mint. *At least he wouldn't have bad breath*, I thought randomly.

Gramps smiled down at me, then placed his hand on my shoulder. He really did look old as I stared into eyes that were the same shape as mine.

"Chelsan, as you know, Geoffrey Turner High took blood samples of every one of its students as a part of a national study on genetics."

Oh crap! He wasn't… They didn't even get a sample of my blood… Did it matter? The results would be conclusive.

"And to my surprise, we had some very interesting results," Turner said with a smile, but his eyes were telling me something completely different. It was that same expression on his dead minions faces, *Trust me*, it screamed.

No. No. No.

Why?

What possible reason?

"You and I, my dear, are related," he announced as he faced the gasping crowd, "Gentlemen, Ladies, Chelsan Derée is my granddaughter!"

The audience went nuts. The press was screaming out questions. Students were shocked and gossiping amongst themselves. And Turner just let them all go wild.

I stood there, with his hand on my shoulder, in total shock.

By telling everyone, surely this would make him expedite his death sentence on me. There was no way he could let me be in the public eye as his granddaughter without muzzling me by becoming one of his dead slaves. This was just a public way to tell me he was going to try again.

The truce was over.

He was coming for me.

I couldn't breathe.

I couldn't speak.

But I didn't have to.

"I can tell that you're just as surprised as I was, little one, but it is with one hundred percent certainty that you are indeed my granddaughter." He turned back to the press, game face on, "You see, my son went missing when he was just eighteen and after years of searching we never saw him again." He paused to sound choked up. Lame. "From the research I found after hearing these surprising test results, it appears as if he married Chelsan's mother, Janet Derée and died when Chelsan was just a baby." He turned back to me and actually faked a tear. Vomit. "I just wish I would have been able to meet your mother. A woman who could win the heart of my boy must have been an amazing person indeed."

I wanted to kick him right there and push him off the stage, but the room was loving every second of this unfolding drama.

Turner wiped the fake tears from his face, "After thinking I had no family left on this earth, I have a granddaughter."

He reached down and hugged me tight. It took everything I had to force myself to pretend to hug him back.

I whispered in his ear, "I don't know what you're playing at, but I'm not going to die that easy."

"I need to talk to you in private," he whispered back.

"Not going to happen," I whispered harshly in his ear.

Turner pulled away and returned to the microphone, his arm wrapped around me like a prison. "I will answer all questions later, but for now I need to spend some time with my new family."

Oh no.

I stepped away from his embrace and turned to the crowd with as much dramatics and tears as I could muster, "I… I need to be alone… to think about this… I…" And I ran offstage like I was overwhelmed with the shock of the news. I covered my face with my hands to make it look like I was crying, and raced toward Jason and the gang at the back of the room. Two could play the sympathy card, jerk.

In a completely out of character move, Jason stepped forward to meet me halfway and embraced me in a hug. Students and press alike were eating it up, but I was surprised at how much safer I felt wrapped in a trusted friend's arms.

Jason whispered, "That's my girl, quick thinking. Let's get you out of here before he forces the issue."

I nodded into his chest and we walked to the back of the assembly hall with the gang close behind.

Mr. Alaster met us at the door and nodded toward the hallway. "You can hide out in my room. The press can't legally go in."

I smiled my thanks and we all were quickly inside the safety of Mr. Alaster's classroom.

Jill came up to me directly, "He has to be lying. Don't worry we'll get the proof that he isn't your grandfather." Then she stopped and really looked at me.

There goes my "open book" face again.

"You already knew," she said in shock. Jill searched everyone's eyes for some invisible proof that she wasn't the only one who didn't know. She didn't find it. "You all knew."

"Jill, I…" I started to explain, but Jill put her hand up to stop me.

"Don't," she said quietly as she put her hand down. In a matter of seconds her eyes met mine and they were full of anger and worse… betrayal. "I should have known. You're just like him, you know. A conniving liar. No wonder why I hated you for so many years, you have *his* blood pumping through your veins."

That was too much for Nancy. She pushed Jill toward the door. "You may be upset, but Chelsan is the one who has been hunted down by her own family! You wouldn't even be alive if it weren't for her!"

Jill turned to Nancy, furious. "Wrong again, idiot. If it weren't for Chelsan and that stupid mind-meld thing Turner wouldn't even *know* about the holo-chip and I wouldn't be running for my life." She turned to me, "Is that how Mrs. Turner can jump in your brain like that, because she's your grandmother?"

I felt for Jill in that moment, and I wished I had told her about Turner right away. Although her reaction would have undoubtedly been the same, at least she wouldn't have brought over the holo-chip.

Because she was right about that. It was my fault Turner wanted her dead. It would have been better for her if I had just kept my mouth shut and left her in the dark about her dad. Hating me would have been paradise compared to what she had already gone through for trusting me.

Jill rubbed her wounded arm and tears came to her eyes.

Before I could stop her, Jill was out the door and halfway down the hall.

And then to everyone's surprise Bill wheeled on Nancy. "Look in the mirror, Nancy, you're acting just as bad as Jill ever was. Can't you cut her a break for once? She's alone and being hunted by *her* grandfather, show a little sympathy."

Ouch. *Her?* He couldn't even say my name?

Nancy looked like she had been slapped, "Bill… I…"

Bill's face was immediately crestfallen. He looked so conflicted in that moment, I just wanted to give him a big hug to comfort him, but instead I took a deep breath and said, "She's not safe alone."

Bill nodded and went after her quicker than I expected. He was developing some kind of bond with Jill, and as much as it was hurting me to see him so angry at Nancy and me, I was glad. Jill needed someone reliable and trustworthy and that was basically Bill in a nutshell.

Nancy's fury started to rage at Bill's quick-step out the door. "See?! She's turning Bill against us! She's evil! Blaming you and accusing you and… ugh… I could kill her myself!"

"Nancy, it's cool. We should have told her. She's just freaking out." I wanted to keep her calm.

"Bull! She's still a spoiled little brat! And Bill! Did you hear what he said to me? He said I was just like her! How dare he!" Nancy fumed.

"Okay, Nancy, relax," Jason cut in. "She's gone and will probably be assassinated in the next few hours, so you won't have to think about her much longer." Jason was done with Nancy's tirade and the severity of what he said hit Nancy like a ton of bricks.

Her eyes welled up, "I don't want her to die, I just…" Nancy couldn't continue.

Jason walked over to her and did something that shocked everyone in the room. He kissed her. It wasn't an all out passionate kiss, but it was full of a sweet tenderness that was normally lacking in Jason. He pulled away. "None of us do. Bill will take care of her, and nothing she says will turn him against you. I'd bet my life on it, and you know how much of a wimp I am." Jason smiled warmly at Nancy.

Nancy smiled back and I knew in that moment that Jason was over the age thing. His whole demeanor changed. I think he was just tired of holding back how he really felt and needed to show Nancy he was ready. Nancy's previous anger melted completely away. "Can we do that again?" she asked with a contented sigh.

"Later." Jason winked. So smarmy! But so Jason, and Nancy loved it.

What timing this guy had! Turner was in the school and my little *crying fit* wasn't going to hold him up all day.

Ryan seemed to be thinking along the same lines, "Can we get out of here now?"

"My thoughts exactly," Jason said as he looked out the small window on the door to see if the coast was clear, "Damn. Is there a back exit? How far up are we?"

I raced to the door and my heart sank.

Turner was leading the pack of reporters straight to Mr. Alaster's room. I could hear Mr. Alaster screaming about how he'd sue and that going into his room was illegal, but we were talking about Gramps here. He was definitely above the law, and entering a classroom was the least of his offenses.

"Too late," I said and felt Ryan's protective hand in mine.

Nancy took my other hand and we looked like we were bracing ourselves for a hurricane.

Jason made us back up and for once he stood as front man. I guess he thought this was his territory, or maybe it was his newfound confidence from kissing Nancy, either way, I was kind of proud of him.

The door swung open to loud shouts from the press and Mr. Alaster, but my eyes were only focused on the calm, solitary figure of my grandfather as he stepped into the room. He turned to the gathering, "That will be all. I need a few words with my granddaughter alone. Stay away from the door." Turner shut the door behind him and waited until the crowd was out of view before turning his attention to us.

It was just him.

Alone.

With the four of us.

Didn't he know he was way outnumbered?

We all stood there in silence like we were in some kind of western showdown waiting for the other one to draw their weapon first.

I searched the room for anything dead, knowing that he could do the same, but also knowing my power was innate and his had to be performed by a spell.

Nothing. Only some flies. But dust could work in a pinch, too, I'd learned.

"If I can't speak to you in private, I'll speak to you in front of your cronies," Turner's agitated voice broke the tense quiet.

"We're not her *cronies* we're her first line of defense." Jason stood his ground and I felt an excited squeeze from Nancy at his braveness.

Turner's eyes turned red and he canted a few words to send Jason's body flying across the room, slamming into Mr. Alasater's desk.

"Good defense," Turner snickered.

I reacted out of instinct and made five dead flies on the windowsill fly straight up Turner's nose and down his throat until he was hacking fly carcasses on the floor.

"All right. Enough games!" Turner yelled after he'd regurgitated his last dead fly.

Nancy rushed to Jason's side and helped him to his feet. No damage it seemed. Lucky for Gramps.

"What do you want?" I asked coldly.

"What do *I* want? What I want is for you to grow a brain! Do you really think I'd come all this way and announce that you're my granddaughter just to kill you? Are you that stupid? Don't answer, I already know you are." Turner brushed himself off. "Now listen, you little brat, I tried to be reasonable with you. I even tried to help you: I was going to announce our relationship all along. Why do you think I had my scientists come here and take blood samples of every flippin' student in here?!" Turner took a deep, steadying breath. "No one's been able to get under my skin like you. I'm not used to losing my temper like this."

"I find that hard to believe." I decided not to budge an inch. Gramps was obviously angered, but I still had the sense that he was going to tell me something very important no matter what I said to him. If he were willing to risk himself being alone with me and my friends, then he definitely had something to say.

"Well, it's true." He looked at me with a frustrated expression. "When I told you I thought you were pivotal to Roland Light and his plans to break out a mysterious someone which now I realize you were already planning on breaking out yourself... I meant that Elisha..." he began, but I never got to hear the rest of his sentence.

BOOM!

The whole school shook to its foundation.

Immediately, twelve bodyguards rushed in and surrounded Turner.

"Wait!" Turner screamed at his bodyguards. "I'm not finished."

BOOM!

This time we all fell to our knees from the impact.

"What was that?!" Nancy had to yell over all the commotion from the screaming reporters and students all rushing down the hallways outside.

"Explosions. The school was just bombed." One of Turner's guards announced and started pushing Turner out the door.

Explosions?

Please tell me Roland and Doris weren't behind this!

"I said I wasn't finished!" Turner's livid expression was palpable.

"Standard protocol, sir. We have to remove you from the premises," the same guard said and all twelve men encircled Turner and led him to the door.

Turner turned to me and our eyes met. His face was angry, but more than that… pleading. "Chelsan. The boys. They're the key to everything! They're not brain dead!"

And he was gone.

Out the door and into the chaos of the hallways.

"We have to get out of here." Ryan took my hand.

Nancy became our leader since she remembered a shortcut out of the school to the courtyard below. I let Ryan lead me, my mind spinning a mile a minute. The enormity of Turner's announcement was only felt by me.

If John and Samuel weren't brain dead, then why were their heads swirling black holes? And why, when I connected to them, did I almost go blind from light? Why were they the key to everything? I felt like throwing up. Elisha had used me to help her break them out. It wasn't because she felt sorry for them, it was because she needed them for some reason. But what? What? What? What was I missing?

Smoke filled the hallways and the jam-packed crowd screamed and coughed in alarm. I could feel the heat from the fire that the two explosions caused, but I still couldn't see where exactly the school was hit. I searched the school for dead bodies, in the fear that I might find some, but I was relieved to only pick up on Principal Weatherby's months old corpse. The bombs didn't appear to have killed anyone.

Which meant they were designed for something else.

Bill's head bobbed up a few hundred feet ahead of us. When he saw me he waved for us to come to him.

We shoved our way through the thick throng of scared people until we reached his side. Jill was there and she wasn't making eye contact with any of us. I'd have to deal with her later.

"Come on. We can get to the hover lot through here. The cars weren't touched. It was just the courtyard," Bill told us. He appeared to be his old self again, apparently hoping we'd all forget his little tirade at Nancy.

But the news that the bombs had hit the courtyard made my heart skip. That was exactly where we had been headed, but also the one place that was always empty. I felt a pang of sadness. That courtyard had been a sanctuary for me when I had to deal with Jill's torment. It was by far the most beautiful part of Geoffrey Turner High.

It wasn't a stretch to think Roland Light was behind this attack, blowing up buildings without actually hurting anyone was kind of becoming his signature move. That meant that Doris and Elisha were definitely involved. But why? Surely, if their target had been Turner they would have attacked his hover-limo when he landed. But even as we reached the hover-car landing area I could see Turner's limo flying safely away, and leaving me with his last words, *They're not brain dead.*

"Chelsan! Over here!" I heard Doris's voice over the crowd.

Well, that solved that one.

Giant clouds of smoke were stretching up into the sky as far as I could see. Hover vehicles were evacuating the school in a mayhem of alarm, but so far no swirling black holes which meant no accidents. I could hear the sound of police and fire hovers drawing closer.

I saw Doris first. She was hiding behind a large hover-van that could easily sit twelve people.

"It's Doris, let's go," I said to the others and we made our way to her.

I stopped in my tracks when I saw Elisha looking at me through the back window. Even Ryan paused.

Bill and Jason turned back to us.

Bill's face was confused, "What's wrong? Doris will get us home. Jason and I can pick up our cars later."

As if in unison with Bill's thought process, another explosion shook us all to our knees.

"Hurry, kids, there's one more explosion coming." Doris's face was wracked with worry and I suddenly felt the urge to punch her.

How dare she put all these lives in danger?

Even Bill stopped at that. "How would you know that unless…" Bill figured it out and his face went from welcoming to furious in about a second. "We'll get our own ride home, thanks."

Elisha stepped out of the van.

Jason, Bill, Nancy and Jill had never seen her before and their eyes were immediately glued to her striking figure. The child with violet eyes, long black hair and porcelain features was a stunning contrast to the smoke-filled sky. It was like seeing a human china doll in the midst of an apocalypse. Jill was the first to start backing up. Elisha obviously creeped her out.

"Why did you do this?" I found myself asking.

All of us rooted in place, our instincts screaming at us not to go forward.

Elisha stepped forward to stare me straight in the eye. She was only ten feet away, but it felt like we were nose to nose, she was so intense. "We came for you, Chelsan. Turner was going to kill you and your friends. We couldn't let that happen." She paused and nodded toward the demolished courtyard. "You can sense it yourself. No one has died. We were careful. Just like the Baby Center."

"You blew up the Baby Center?" Jill looked like her old self for a brief moment as she viewed Elisha and Doris with disgust. "Are you with that Roland Light guy?" She turned to Bill, "These guys are psychos, Bill. Can you take me home now?"

Elisha moved her gaze to Jill and Jill moved behind Bill instinctually. "You're number one on Turner's hit list, Jill Forester, Chelsan a close second, but don't you doubt it for a second, if we hadn't come here to get you, you'd already be dead," she said it with such intensity that no one could really argue.

"I hate to be a pest, but we have about ten seconds before the last one blows and we're not in the most ideal location," Doris announced and waved her hands trying to usher us into the hover-van.

Jason was the first to move. "We'll talk about this later. Let's just get in." Apparently, coming face-to-face with the people responsible for the attacks on the Baby Center and now the high school was too juicy a story for Jason to pass up. He grabbed Nancy by the hand and pretty much made her come with him.

It was better to stay together and I was pretty sure I could take Elisha and Doris if I had to. We all piled into the van: there were sixteen seats, eight on each side of the van's wall across from each other. They were leather and plushy and under normal circumstances pretty cool, but considering the fact that in about five seconds another explosion was about to go off, I just wanted to get out of there. Ryan, me, Nancy and Jason sat on one side while Elisha, Doris, Bill and Jill sat across from us.

As soon as we reached the sky the last bomb went off. I could see it this time, coming from the same general area of the courtyard. A ball of red, orange and yellow rolled up to turn into a black cloud of smoke. I searched with my power to make sure that no one was killed and to my relief I still couldn't see any black holes, human anyway, though the courtyard was a giant mass of spinning chasms from all the plant life that was obliterated.

No one said anything as we entered the throng of craziness that was the hover lanes. Ryan placed his arm around me for comfort and I leaned into him. He was a beacon of feel-betterness at the moment. I didn't even want to look at Doris and Elisha. Frankly, they both made me sick to my stomach. And I really didn't want to have anything to do with either one of them, truth be told.

Jason on the other hand…

"Do you think I can have an exclusive interview with the two of you?" he asked with no qualms whatsoever.

Nancy elbowed him, making Jason grunt from the force of it.

What surprised me more was the prompt answer from Elisha. "Of course. Anything to get the truth out there."

Jill made a noise that sounded like, "Hurrumph."

I agreed with Jill on this one.

Elisha appeared to sense the beaming distrust and anger towards her because she leaned in close to me. "Chelsan, all I'm trying to do is save your life. You rescued me and I honestly just want to return the favor."

I turned away from Elisha without giving her a response and leaned into Ryan.

Jill and I made eye contact and I felt like we were on the same page. I knew she was still upset with me, but I also knew she could see that circumstances had changed and we'd be better off sticking together. At least, I hope that was what I saw. It was hard to tell with Jill.

"We'll be at Havenville in less than an hour," Doris informed us.

Excuse me?

"Havenville?" Ryan piped up with shock in his voice.

"Oh no! You're not taking us there!" Nancy was actually livid. "You're taking us to my house, right NOW!" She was having none of it.

"I'm afraid not, dears," Doris said with an apologetic expression.

"Doris, we're not going to Havenville and Roland Light. We can't." I tried to reason with her.

"It's the only place we can protect you from Turner. He can't reach you or Jill there." Doris tried to soothe the escalating situation.

"Besides, there's really nothing you can do to stop us, now is there?" Elisha's expression was frank and annoying.

"We'll just leave when we get there," Ryan stated, not keeping his eyes off Elisha.

"Your choice. But for now we're going to keep you safe whether you like it or not," Elisha's voice was cold and to the point. It was very creepy to watch this child's face talk like an adult. I had to keep reminding myself that she was eighty years older than me.

KER-KLUMP!

Our hover-van stopped with a violent jolt.

"What the..?" I gasped.

With a loud CLANK the hover-van started to fly straight up at a sickening speed.

Elisha swung open the cover to the hover-van's skylight just in time to see the roof of the car smack directly into a giant electromagnet.

"Clean-Up," Elisha muttered under breath.

As I looked out the window I saw exactly what she was talking about.

A giant skyscraper sized hover-truck held us within its magnetized belly. Clean-Up. Normally, they were in groups of seven, two for picking up metal from a disaster area, one for tilling the damaged earth, three to plant whatever trees they wanted for the new area and the last truck to water and fertilize the freshly planted foliage. When my trailer park was destroyed within the hour an oak forest had taken its place.

Above us was only one Clean-Up truck and it was the magnetized kind. Looked like Gramps wasn't letting us get away that easily.

The Clean-Up hover-truck was now on the move taking us with it toward whatever destination Turner ordered. For all I knew, he was sitting next to the driver.

We all sat in stunned silence.

"What do we do now?" Doris turned to Elisha for instructions.

Elisha's purple eyes met mine. "Chelsan saves us."

I looked behind me as if there were another Chelsan in the van sitting behind me… in the sky… or behind the chair… or… yeah.

I didn't want Elisha to say another word. I knew she had some crazy scheme in mind that would somehow involve my powers, but I didn't want to have anything to do with it. I almost wanted Gramps to bring us back to headquarters and take her away. Something about Elisha just rubbed my instincts the wrong way. But I was probably being too judgmental. She was a victim. A victim that was going to be executed unless I got us out of this mess.

"I don't see anything dead I can use," I informed her just in case that was her plan.

"Chelsan, come here with me." Elisha sat crosslegged on the floor of the carpeted van.

Ryan's hand held me back. "Don't."

"I have to. He'll kill Jill and Elisha if I don't." I kissed him on the cheek and sat across from Elisha on the floor. "What do you want me to do?" I asked without actually wanting to know. Last time I listened to her advice I boiled some corpse's blood and his skin slopped to the floor.

"I'm not certain if this will work, but it's the only thing I can think of." Elisha reached over and took her hands in mine, and from the gleam in her eyes I could tell she was lying. I just wasn't sure what she was lying about. Was it the fact that she knew whatever she was about to tell me was actually going to work or that it was the only thing she could think of? Either way, it made me nervous. But one look at the terror in Jill's face and I knew I had to try. "I want you to concentrate on the magnet."

I looked up through the open sunroof and stared at the slab of metal linking us to its surface. But that was it: nothing dead, no black swirling holes.

"I don't see anything," I admitted.

"Try to see the dust around it and in the van," Elisha's voice was calm and commanding.

I could feel our speed start to slow down. We were coming close to our destination. As if in unison to my thoughts I heard Bill say, "Population Research Center up ahead."

"Don't listen to him, listen to me. Can you see the dust?" Elisha brought me back to the task at hand.

SWOOSH!

I saw tiny black swirling holes everywhere, like thick black snow. "Yes, I see the dust."

"Good, now I want you to look even closer than that, but inside the magnet itself. Smaller than the dust: millions of times smaller. Can you do that?" Elisha couldn't hide the excitement in her voice. Just like with the boiling blood guy. Like my powers were some kind of thrill for her, but I did as she asked.

Nothing.

"I can only see the dust in the van's cabin." I tried to calm my nerves as I felt the Clean-Up truck slowing down even more. We were getting close.

"Concentrate. You can see this, Chelsan, I know it. Just focus on the magnet and look for the black holes. They'll be so tiny you might just miss them, but focus." Elisha tried to hide the condescending tone from her voice, but I could hear it loud and clear. I certainly had heard enough of it from Jill over the past four years. *If it's so easy you do it*, I wanted to say, but I knew for all our sakes I needed to do as she asked.

I concentrated as hard as I possibly could on the magnet.

I stared at it so intensely that everything around me started to disappear. What was I supposed to be seeing? What's smaller than dust? Cells? Molecules? Atoms? Seriously?

VOOMPSH!

Black.

So black, nothing could penetrate it. And yet it was moving. Like a hurricane of utter darkness. "I'm blind," I managed to sputter out.

Elisha's voice was somehow reassuring now as she whispered in my ear, "Can you see the way it's spinning?"

I don't think anyone heard me. I WAS BLIND. Completely blind!

"Don't panic, Chelsan. We need you. Can you see the way it's spinning?" Elisha repeated.

I tried to focus on the movement of the blackness. It appeared as if the swirling darkness was going every which way, but when I calmed myself down, I could sense more than see the direction it was going. "I see it," I said not sure even then what I could do about that information or what exactly it would mean for our escape.

"Good. That's good, Chelsan. Now I'm going to need you to make the blackness spin in the opposite direction. Can you do that?" Elisha's voice was my only anchor in the darkness.

I was focusing so hard on the spinning black that my head started to ache uncontrollably. I knew I needed to make this happen so I pushed aside the pain and with all my might I concentrated on making the black fog swirl in the other direction. Slow at first, then faster and faster, I made the blackness spin in the opposite direction.

KER-KLUMP!

"We're free, you did it!" I heard Elisha say and felt our hover-van speed off.

My heart started to race. It was still dark. I was going to be stuck in this blindness forever. I felt Ryan's arms pull me up into him and I grabbed onto him for dear life. "I can't see!" I cried out into his chest.

I felt Elisha's tiny hand touch my arm. "Disconnect from the blackness, just like you trained yourself to do with the dust. It's the same process," her voice was soothing and I calmed down.

I made myself visually zoom out of the dark space, like I did with the dust.

I could see again, though black swirling dust still surrounded me like a rain storm.

One more zoom.

I re-focused again.

The dust was gone.

I could see normal once again.

Everyone was staring at me with concern.

Even Jill.

"I'm okay, guys," I told them though no one looked convinced.

I could see out the window that we were moving faster than I'd ever gone in a hover-car. We weren't even in a sanctioned lane: the driver obviously didn't want a repeat of what just happened, so he was driving above the seventh lane. I guess Havenville was next on our stop. No one argued against it this time.

Gramps almost had me. Again. And I wasn't exactly sure how I even got us out of there. It terrified me at how little I knew about my gift. But it terrified me more at how much Elisha seemed to know.

"What did you make me do?" I asked her directly.

Elisha was still next to me, but she sat back in her seat across from me with a smile. "You reversed the polarity of the magnet."

I what?

"I'll explain everything to you once we're in Havenville." She pointed up toward the sunroof. "You never know who might be listening."

She was right. That was exactly the sort of thing Turner would do. If we did somehow manage to break free, he'd definitely try and plant something behind to listen to our every word. Once we landed, they could get rid of the van and we could talk freely.

Elisha's words repeated over and over in my head. *Reversed the polarity*. Whoa. That was like… whoa. I was stunned. I'd written myself off as zombie girl, but now the scope of my powers was becoming a little overwhelming for my taste.

"We'll be there in about ten minutes," Doris broke the silence with a half-hearted grin. She was obviously still frazzled at being magnetized to a Clean-Up truck, then freed by a circus freak like me. Seeing her so stressed out took the edge off of my anger toward her and Elisha for blowing up my school. Well, maybe not. I wanted to confront them both about their behavior, but felt muzzled by the possibility Gramps might be listening in.

No one spoke after that.

Ryan leaned his head on mine while he held me and I clung to him for support. In all this craziness it was a relief to have someone I could count on unconditionally. My head still throbbed, but being next to him somehow stemmed the pain.

I didn't like the way Elisha kept on staring at him though.

Really gross and disturbing.

Ryan just ignored her, but I couldn't keep my eyes off of Elisha.

We landed a few minutes later in a large grass field overlooking the small Christian Coalition town of Havenville. After exiting the car, I admit that the scene looked like it was out of a fairy tale. Standing on rolling hills of bright green grass, below us were ten rows of clay-shingled houses made of zigzag patterned brick with arched windows lining every wall. The houses were almost identical in three specific designs from what I could tell. Havenville was only a few square miles in size, and it was crowded. I could see the inhabitants bustling about, going in and out of their houses and near the middle of town, which looked like a shopping area.

But it was the dead center of town that was the crowning jewel. There stood by far the most stunning building I'd ever seen in my life. I could only guess that the building itself was made entirely of stone because of its grey color, but the intricacies built into the walls were breathtaking. The base was a large rectangle, but as the walls grew up they all ended in triangular spires that stretched to the sky. Even the arched windows were a sight to behold with the stained glass and stone carvings intricately patterned. In fact, the masonry was so detailed that the whole building looked like stoned lace. Only at the very top spire, towering above the rest, was there anything simple: a metal cross. If we were going to stay in this town that was the first building I wanted to check out. I truly had never seen anything like it.

"A cathedral, am I right?" Ryan asked Elisha and Doris.

Elisha responded with a smile. "That's right. It came from Italy."

I looked at Ryan for more and he smiled at me. "About two hundred years ago when the religious sects branched off from the rest of the public, they wanted to bring their places of worship with them. The Christians and the Catholics decided amongst their organizations which building would go to who. Then they dismantled them brick by brick and had them reassembled in their respective towns. These buildings, they're called "Cathedrals." They used to be all over Europe and there were even some in the States, but they have been rebuilt in the Christian and Catholic towns across the world."

I didn't even know Catholics had towns of their own, or that any other religion did, either. Or to be perfectly honest, I didn't really know what exactly a Catholic was. I only knew about Christian Coalition towns. I guess because they were the ones that made the segregating legal and formed their own nation.

I probably should have been impressed by Ryan's knowledge of all this stuff, but it didn't surprise me. Ryan's brain pretty much retained everything that went into it. If he casually read about something four years ago he could recite it back as if he had just finished reading it two seconds ago. It was one of the reasons why Turner wanted Ryan so badly.

"Are we all agreed that you'll be staying awhile?" Doris asked tentatively.

We all exchanged glances and nodded in agreement. "Yes," I spoke for everyone.

"Oh good, I'll show you to your houses then." Doris appeared visibly relieved. I think she was expecting another fight. At the moment, though, none of us had any fight to give. After our school exploding and escaping the magnet clutches of Gramps, all we wanted to do was collapse into blissful rest.

Doris spoke up again, "Don't worry, we'll contact your parents and let them know you'll be here for a while. For your own safety."

I was glad to hear that (if it were true: the jury was still out on Doris and Elisha) but if the 'rents were worried at least they'd know where we were and not have to wonder if we'd died in the school explosions.

We made our way into the town proper and I could see that almost every other person in the town was pregnant. It was a very surreal feeling, walking amongst a bunch of women pregnant with essentially kidnapped babies. I was probably the only one of our group who had actually seen a pregnant woman in person before now. Living in a trailer park, women had babies all the time. But my rich friends, whose parents and friends all went to the Baby Center, they had never been exposed to the sight.

Nancy seemed the most fascinated. She outright stared at most of the women walking by.

Then I nearly stopped in my tracks.

I suddenly noticed that a handful of these people were old.

And I mean *old*.

Their faces were crinkled and wrinkled and sagged.

It was terrifying.

I thought Gramps looked old, but by comparison to these people he was a young man.

Everyone else had stopped as well.

Jill looked like she was going to vomit and Nancy clung to Jason's arm as if he'd protect her from the wrinkled monsters.

I knew I shouldn't be thinking that way, but it was hard not to.

Their shrunken, bent bodies looked grotesque in person. I had only seen pictures before, but nothing like this. The media obviously hid the true reality of age from the general public, and I suddenly felt very grateful.

"Oh goodness, they're younger than Jason. Show some respect." Doris sounded angry at our obvious discomfort in the presence of the elderly.

"I'd look older than *that*?" Jason blurted out and it took Nancy a good few seconds before she elbowed him accordingly. She had obviously been thinking the same thing.

"Sorry." Bill seemed embarrassed and guilty for all of us.

"Let's just get to our rooms," I said, knowing that Doris was right.

It was rude to stare in horror at anyone, and I should know. People used to do it all the time to me just for existing at Geoffrey Turner High and it made my life miserable. I didn't want to do the same to these people. I had to keep reminding myself that they chose this life on purpose. They didn't want to take Age-pro and they seemed very happy by their decision.

I focused on the town itself to try and keep my mind and my *eyes* off the people in it.

The roads themselves were made of cobblestone and reminded me of the streets outside of my old job, Mel's Ice Cream and Soda. The stones ranged in all shades of grey giving the streets a faded salt and pepper pattern. Most of the buildings were indeed houses, but, like I thought before, as we reached the center of town the buildings that surrounded the cathedral were all shops. From what I could see, though, there were no pay stations, so I could only assume that everyone shared their goods here. It was actually quite nice.

"Elisha?" A gravelly voice sounded from the steps of the cathedral.

An elderly woman, shrunken with time and age, walked toward us with the support of a wooden cane. It wasn't until she came within a few feet of us that I noticed her violet eyes staring at Elisha with tears.

Her twin sister.

But she actually looked their age.

Elisha choked back tears as she embraced the old woman. "Beth."

The two sisters held each other, crying into each other's shoulders. Elisha's small child's frame was almost the same height as Beth's shrunken aged one. But through all the wrinkles; their noses, lips, eyes, face structure were identical.

"I thought I'd never see you again," Beth said as tears streamed down her face.

Elisha's own tears flowed freely as she clung onto her sister. "Me, too."

Yet another moment of clarity for me as I watched the two of them reunite: Turner had managed to destroy another family for his own selfish reasons. I suddenly felt very glad that I'd helped Elisha escape just so she could see her sister again. As much as I distrusted her, I had to remind myself that it was probably the fact that Elisha wasn't really a child. She was the same age as this woman in front of us.

And, like the other old people in this town, I still found it hard to look at Beth. I knew it was wrong, but when you live your whole life and the oldest person is thirty, seeing a ninety-eight year old is really disturbing. I tried to imagine what the world was like before Age-pro. There were probably millions of old people walking around with everyone else back then, and most likely no one even gave it a second thought.

Weird.

I looked around at everyone else and they were all looking at Beth and Elisha with sympathy.

But it was Jill's reaction that was slightly different from the rest. While everyone was focused on the sisters' reunion, Jill was completely focused on Elisha.

Only Elisha.

The more I observed Jill, the more I realized that it wasn't sympathy on her face, it was suspicion and maybe a little bit of fear mixed in.

Jill turned to me, apparently feeling me stare at her. And instead of the nasty glare I expected, she gave me a look that clearly said, *We have to stick together on this.*

I was a bit taken aback since I usually only get those looks from Nancy, but I knew I wasn't mistaken. Jill was keeping on her toes.

I needed to do the same.

Elisha pulled away first, and I noticed her eyes glance at all of us briefly. So quick no one caught it, but I did and I didn't like what I saw. Elisha was gauging what our reactions were. Like this was a set up. Like she wanted us to see this reunion so we'd feel for her. And if it hadn't been for Jill, I would have missed it.

I gave Jill an almost imperceptible nod in acknowledgment of her warning look. She nodded back and I felt a strange sensation in my belly. Did Jill Forester actually have my back? I shook my head in disbelief. I must be in Bizarro world. But at this point I didn't want to jinx it.

Doris wiped away her own tears, completely engrossed in the drama of the two sisters seeing each other again. "Come on, kids. Just over here."

Elisha kissed Beth's cheek. "I'll see you in a few minutes. I'm just going to take them to the guest quarters."

Beth nodded and pulled out a hankie, wiping away her own tears.

As we walked away I glanced back at Beth and I couldn't see any duplicity in her expression. Their reunion was real, and to her it was heart-felt, but to Elisha it was a manipulative act for our benefit. Of that I was sure.

It wasn't far until we were past the town square and down one of the side roads reaching our destination. Standing in front of us was a two-level house made of the same zigzag patterned brick like all the others, with clay tiles on top. Up close it was an odd combination, like Victorian meets Adobe, but I had to admit it looked pretty cozy at the moment. I was physically exhausted and could barely think. With our escape and all the astral head butting of the last couple of days, sleep was becoming a prize I constantly fell short of winning.

Ryan and I led the pack toward the heavy iron wrought door.

"Hold on, there. This is the girl's house. Boy's house is next door," Doris admonished from behind.

What?

Seriously?

"Why?" is what came out.

"Because this is a religious town and boys and girls do not sleep in the same bed until they're married." Doris's chest seemed to puff out at this like she was on the band wagon with this one.

"Respect where you are, Chelsan." Elisha's eyes met mine and there was a slight triumphant glint to them.

I was about to argue when Ryan leaned in and kissed me gently. "It's fine. I'll see you tomorrow morning." Then he hugged me and whispered in my ear so only I could hear, "Security doesn't look all that tight. I'll sneak into your room later tonight." He pulled away and tried to act as disappointed as possible.

I could hardly contain my happiness at the news, but I didn't want Elisha to suspect anything, so I played the role of annoyed girlfriend.

Nancy reached up to kiss Jason, but he turned away and kissed her on the cheek instead. It was the equivalent of a slap in the face to Nancy. She tried to hide her shock and pulled away from him, stomping past me and through the front door.

Jill hugged Bill before he could even react and raced after Nancy in seeming embarrassment.

The boys waved their good-byes to me and followed Doris to the next house over.

I turned to Elisha before I went through the door. "You'll tell me everything tomorrow."

"I promise," Elisha conceded, but there was so much going on behind her eyes I couldn't begin to guess what she was thinking.

Before she could say or do anything else I walked into the house and closed the door behind me. Inside, the house was pristine to the point of uncomfortableness. The first floor consisted of a living room to the right and a dining room to the left. There was a door in the back next to the staircase that I assumed led to the kitchen. The staircase was at the center right when I opened the door and led to the upstairs bedrooms. The couch and recliner in the living room were wrapped in plastic making the place feel like a museum. The décor was old-fashioned: dark stained floors and floral print furniture. I didn't want to touch anything for fear of alarms going off.

Nancy and Jill were making their own assumptions, but from the looks on their faces we all felt uncomfortable at our surroundings.

"Let's just go to bed." Nancy had had enough and tromped up the wooden staircase like she was ready to collapse.

Jill went after her and I followed close behind. Through the arched windows I could see the sun starting to set so I knew it was only about five o'clock, but I just wanted to crawl in bed and fall asleep.

Upstairs there was a narrow hallway with two doors. Nancy opened the closest one to us and we were relieved to see four twin beds lined up against the far wall. Other than the beds, though, the room was empty. And I mean empty. There was no other furniture to speak of, just the four beds in a perfect row with sheets and top blanket tucked pristinely into place. To my relief there were three arched windows that I'd be able to let Ryan through if he couldn't sneak in by the front door. I knew he thought security was lax, but I wasn't so sure.

Jill plopped down on the bed farthest to the right.

"I'm freaking out right now! Did you see how Jason dodged me?" Nancy was pacing.

Oh boy.

"You know Jason, he's just in *reporter* mode right now." I tried to make her feel better.

No such luck.

"Did I imagine the whole thing? Did he or did he not kiss me in Mr. Alasater's classroom?" Nancy fumed.

"Yes, I definitely saw him kiss you." I didn't know what she wanted me to say, but I figured just backing her up was the best way to go.

"I didn't see him kiss you," Jill piped in.

Why? Why? Why?

Nancy whirled on her like a viper. "I don't care about anything you have to say, Jill Forester so shut it!"

But instead of getting angry, Jill rolled her eyes, "Nancy, just chill for one second and let me finish. What I was going to say was, any idiot can see that the guy is madly in love with you. And that's coming from a former enemy."

That stopped Nancy in her tracks. "Well… You… Former? Not so sure about that," she huffed.

"Yes, *former*." Jill shook her head. "I'm sorry I blew up at you two. I was just thrown off by Turner's news about being your granddaddy and all and when I saw that you already knew… well, I was angry."

I knew how hard that was for Jill, and I also knew that she had already forgiven me because of our non-verbal exchange earlier, but Nancy hadn't and I could tell she was starting to soften.

Nancy walked over and sat next to Jill. "Look, Jill, I'm not promising anything, but at least while we're here I say we call *truce*. Deal?"

Jill practically laughed, "Of course it's a deal, what did you think I'd say? We're kind of all imprisoned here in *freaky town*."

"Agreed, and agreed." I sat down on the bed across from them. "Something is going on here and it's more than just *saving our lives*. Elisha wanted me here, and I guarantee she blew up the school just to do it." I tried to think things through.

"Are you sure that's why she blew up the school?" Jill asked thoughtfully.

"What do you mean?" Nancy was curious now, too. "You think she did it just for kicks?"

"No," Jill mused aloud, "but it does seem like quite a coincidence that, right after Turner tells the world you're his granddaughter, Elisha comes with the cavalry."

Jill was hitting some invisible chord with me. I could feel that she was on the right track, but I couldn't figure out what train I was on. "Yeah, but the damage was done. Why would Elisha need me if Turner already told everyone?"

"Maybe it wasn't what he told the press. Maybe it was something he needed to tell you," Nancy mused. "I mean he was going to tell you something, remember? And all he managed to get out was that the twins weren't brain dead. What does he mean by that anyway?"

"I don't know. Their heads are just swirling black holes to me. I mean, what else can they be but brain dead?" I flopped back on the bed in frustration. "I just don't know. Everything's a guess at this point."

"Well, let's sleep on it, we're all exhausted." Nancy stood up and lay down on the other bed next to mine.

"Ryan said he was going to try and sneak over later, maybe he'll bring the boys." I tried to cheer them up.

I was happy to see the both of them grin in the same goofy way. At least some things could be normal in my life! "Good night, guys," I said and before I could even hear a response I fell fast asleep.

CHAPTER 4
FRIDAY DECEMBER 3, 2320

"**I** know what you think of me," Roberta's soft voice called out to me.

I knew I was still sleeping, and if I could groan in my sleep I would have. But something in Roberta's tone made me pause. She sounded almost… defeated.

I opened my eyes in the dream. Roberta sat in a rocking chair in what looked like a nursery next to a wooden slatted crib underneath a large square window. The room was decorated in all shades of blue, from the carpet to the walls to the perfectly polka-dotted curtains framing the crib. A changing area and small wooden dresser were the only other pieces of furniture in the room. I was sure this was my dad's nursery.

"I think you've made it quite clear that you don't care what I think of you." I wondered why she'd brought me to this place.

Roberta barely looked up, her stretched and frozen face impossible to read. She looked calmer than usual… well… less hostile anyway. "I'm beginning to feel something for you," she admitted with a matter-of-fact tone.

I didn't know how to respond to that, not verbally, nor mentally.

"Okay." So eloquent.

Roberta looked up at me then and actually smiled. (Or as much as her face could manage anyway.) "Franklin was supposed to be the very first baby from the very first Baby Center. Did you know that?"

I just shook my head. I didn't know much about my father.

Roberta nodded, "Geoffrey and I tried for years and years to have a baby," she pointed to her grotesque face, "hence the state of my *Felineness*." She paused, "Even though my heart's desire was to be young forever, I wanted a baby even more, so I put off taking Age-pro until I could get pregnant." Her eyes were distant.

What was going on? Was this some kind of heart to heart with psychopath Grams? I didn't even want to be standing there with the woman who made my mother's corpse dance like crazed puppet for her own amusement.

But...

At the same time, I wanted to know more about my dad, and Geoffrey and Roberta Turner were the only two alive who could do that for me. I'd take what I could get, even if it was from cuckoo head.

"I had seventeen miscarriages. Do you know what that can do to a person?" she asked, but I got the feeling she wasn't waiting for an answer so I simply shook my head. "As you can imagine, it was devastating." Roberta paused again, rocking in the chair staring at the wall as if she were having this conversation by herself. "There were no other options for me. I had to find a surrogate. Surrogates existed in my day, but nothing as big as the Baby Centers. Back then, we would have been crucified for even thinking of starting a center like that. But over time, as the young ones started taking Age-pro and realized they'd have to age if they wanted children, a Baby Center seemed like an Godsend." Her frozen face appeared to be smiling at the memory although it came off more as a smirk. "I only had ten eggs left. Just ten. If one of the eggs wouldn't fertilize, Geoffrey and I would never be able to have children of our own."

Roberta looked at me and there was actually full on emotion behind her icy face. I was still in mute shock. It was as if I didn't belong there and she was confusing me with someone else. I just stood there waiting for her to continue afraid that anything I might say would make her flip out and turn back into raging-witch-Grams.

"The last egg. Franklin was conceived in the very last egg. He was our little miracle." Roberta stared at nothing once again, lost in the past. "We planned on implanting a surrogate and launching the first Baby Center, but I just couldn't. I had to carry him myself. I just had to. Even with all the miscarriages, I knew it would work this time... and it did." She smiled, then paused, continuing, "I can't tell you why we kept him a child for all those years, but trust me, it was necessary." Her eyes hardened. "And when your mother took him from us, all our plans for him were destroyed. We were trying to keep him safe! We thought helping a poor girl like your mother would gain us loyalty, not betrayal." Roberta was getting riled up, I could tell.

"Why *can't* you tell me why you kept him a child?" I asked quickly to put her back on focus. I really didn't want another Roberta tirade right now. I wanted information.

Roberta stood up, calm once more. She walked over to me and, in a very creepy moment, touched my cheek in what I can only describe as lovingly. "Because this will be a fresh memory for you. Geoffrey and I can't tell you everything because Elisha keeps scanning your mind for a very specific memory. You obviously can't keep her out, you don't even know she's in here half the time. I've been keeping her away from the memory she wants, but I can't keep her out from everything. So, there's my dilemma."

Elisha had been in my head without me even knowing it? I wanted to think Roberta was telling me this to scare me, but my gut told me she was right. Which meant...

"If she's seen all my new memories, then she knows..." I trailed off in a big gulp.

Roberta smiled as she held my face, "That's right. She's seen all these new memories with Goeffrey and me. She knows you don't trust her, and she knows Geoffrey told you about the boys. The question is: What are you going to do about it?"

I didn't know what to say.

I didn't know what to do.

I didn't even know how much trouble I was actually in.

How can you get scared about something when you don't even really know what that something is?

Roberta pulled away and looked around the room with a grunt. "She's prying again. I'll keep the memory she's looking for safe, but be a dear and try and figure out how to stop her from getting in."

***

"You're so full of yourself , Vaughn!" Bill's angry voice woke me up with a jolt.

Vaughn? Was he really referring to Ryan by his last name? Bill was a pretty mellow guy and if he was in "last name mode" it meant he was pretty angry. I'd only heard him do that once before when he referred to Jill as *Forester* after she secretly fixed it for him to be Homecoming King.

"Maybe if you stopped drooling all over my girlfriend!" Ryan yelled back.

PUNCH!

Uh, oh.

"Did someone just hit someone?" Nancy's voice cut through the silence.

"We better get down there," Jill said, scuffling out of bed.

The three of us raced down the stairs and out the front door in seconds. I almost fell over from the head rush of getting up so fast, but my fear of Bill and Ryan fist-fighting made me push through it.

The two of them were rolling on the ground in between our two houses wrestling like a pair of idiots.

Seriously?

I ran up and tried to grab Ryan's arm, but it was like trying to reach into a cyclone. I couldn't even get near them without dodging a fist or a kicking foot.

It was eerie to hear them grunting and fighting in the near silence of Havenville. I wondered if someone would come out and we'd get in trouble for disrupting the peace.

Jason was just standing off to the side with his arms crossed, apparently fed up with us teenagers.

"Are you going to help me or what?" I whispered harshly to him.

Jason shook his head with exasperation and the two of us dove into the flailing arms of Bill and Ryan.

"Knock it off!" I screamed in their ears.

Ryan kicked Bill in the stomach to push away from him and stand next to me. We all could hear the air physically leave Bill's lungs as he gasped from the blow. Bill was still on the ground trying to catch his breath, looking like he was about to make a running tackle toward Ryan, but I stood in front of Ryan to block Bill's bull run.

"I said knock it off! Elisha could order security in a heart beat if she hasn't already and I don't want to give her any excuses to lock us up!" I warned the both of them, at first to scare them into stopping, but then as I said it I realized that it might actually be true.

Bill stood up, still breathing heavily, but they both appeared to be listening to me, for once.

"He started it!" Ryan accused lamely.

"I did not! You're just too freaking sensitive! All I said was that I should check on Chelsan, she is my best friend, you know." Bill eyed Ryan with venom.

"Yeah, you said *I should check on Chelsan* like Jason and I didn't matter or care if Chelsan was okay." Ryan turned to me with almost desperate eyes. "Chelsan, you have no idea what Bill is like when you're not around. He acts like he owns you or something. Like, just because he was friends with you for three years, he's closer to you and the rest of us are just acquaintances," Ryan fumed.

I had no idea what to say to that.

"Ryan, you know the sitch," Nancy spoke up tentatively.

"If you're trying to tell me I have to put up with Bill's annoying possessiveness because he's in love with Chelsan, I'm going to puke. I'm sick of it!" Ryan turned to Bill, furious, "Get over it! She doesn't love you!"

Bill just stood there. He looked so hurt, it made me want to cry.

"Ryan, you're way out of line," I managed to say.

Ryan looked at me with the worst look I'd ever seen in his eyes. Betrayal.

Great. I'd managed to hurt two of the most important people in my life.

"I'm out of line?" Ryan repeated as if he couldn't quite believe I had said it.

It gave Bill back his confidence, which wasn't a good thing. He strode up to Ryan with an almost triumphant grin. "You heard her."

"Bill, shut up." I didn't want him to use this situation to hurt Ryan more.

But it was too late.

Ryan shook his head and looked at me with more pain than I could ever have imagined. "I need to take a walk."

And he turned his back on me and started to walk away.

"Ryan, don't," I called out to him, but he just kept walking.

I moved to go after him, but Nancy grabbed my arm. "Give him a chance to cool down. You can talk to him in the morning."

I knew she was right, but I couldn't let him leave like that. I gently shrugged her off and ran after him. "Ryan wait." I caught up to him, but he wouldn't look at me.

"You always take his side," Ryan's voice was small and wounded.

"I don't, but he *is* one of my best friends. You don't think it was mean to say that to him?" I tried to reason with him.

Ryan stopped and turned to me with frustration. "He's worse to me when you're not around. He rubs his friendship with you in my face any chance he gets. I don't care if he's in love with you. *I'm* in love with you! And I feel like you're split between the two of us. I think you're lying to yourself if you say you don't love him." There were tears forming in Ryan's eyes.

I was shocked. I didn't love Bill. I loved Ryan.

"That's not true," was all I could say.

"Maybe, maybe not, but it feels true. Look, I just need to think." Ryan started to turn away.

"Think about what?" I was terrified of his answer. "Are you going to break up with me?" My voice cracked.

Ryan wheeled around and kissed me desperately. "Never." He pulled away and his eyes were distant. "I need to figure out how to deal. Bill's not going anywhere and neither am I. I guess one of us needs to be the better man. I just didn't want it to have to be me." And he gave me a little smile at that last part. "I'll talk to you in the morning."

Ryan left before I could argue with him again. I watched him go and knew I'd be counting down the seconds for morning to come and everything would be back to normal again.

Famous last words.

***

I awoke with the sun streaming in through the large window above me like an annoying alarm of light. It was morning already and no Ryan. I tried not to be disappointed. I'd see him soon and everything would be okay again. Nothing a good breakfast couldn't fix. Nancy and Jill were still fast asleep and I wondered what time it was. Knowing how tired I was, it was probably pretty early.

I wondered suddenly if Elisha was poking around in my head. I tried to concentrate and focus only on her, but I felt the same as I always did. If Elisha was in there she was doing a great job of keeping herself hidden. Speaking of which: where was Ryan? I hoped he wasn't still mad. I hoped Bill wasn't still mad. I had enough to worry about without the two of them at each other's throats. But what worried me the most was that Ryan wasn't here already and what did that mean? Did he finally see the light and want nothing to do with me? He told me he'd never break up with me, but maybe after his walk Ryan decided I was more trouble than I was worth. My mind couldn't stop thinking the horrible. I wished I had a button I could switch to make me calm down.

I decided to go exploring on my own while the girls were sleeping. I stood up, shrugged at the fact that I was wearing the same outfit as yesterday, and went downstairs. It was just as quiet as it had been last night in this town. I never realized how loud life really was, with its constant hum of hover-cars and hover-delivery and just the sheer noise of people constantly buzzing about. It was like a tomb here. I couldn't hear anything outside, not a peep. There must be some kind of air-restriction laws or something. And for some reason that made my stomach turn a little. I felt like a city girl that was just thrown in the middle of the woods. I never realized how the sounds of over-population were actually so much of a comfort to me. It made me feel protected somehow, like help was only a scream away. I guess I was developing *issues* after everything that'd happened to me. So far my traumatic experiences in life had all been when I was isolated and alone. Turner would never try and kill me in public.

But, my concern wasn't Turner at the moment, for better or worse, Roberta's recent visit made me calm down on the grandparent front. Though I knew I could never truly trust them, (for the time being at least) they were being civil. And at least they couldn't make an attempt on Jill's life while we were in Havenville. At least I hoped not.

I walked to the front door and found myself opening it very slowly as if I was expecting to wake up the whole town. I just wasn't used to this amount of quiet, I guess. I stepped out onto the front porch and breathed in the fresh air. It was a cool crisp morning and the slight breeze felt amazing on my face. The brick houses seemed like the walls of a prison, though, and kind of took the joy out of the moment. I walked across the bright green lawn to the boys' abode next door, the soft grass squishing underneath my bare feet. I hadn't felt like putting on my shoes, though now I wish I had, just in case I had to run.

Wow.

Why did my mind think like that? It didn't used to. Lame.

I reached the heavy oak door of the boys' house and knocked softly.

Within a few seconds Jason's smiling face was there to greet me. "Alone?" he asked as he let me in.

"They're still sleeping," I said, stepping in.

Their house was nearly identical to ours on the inside, from the furnishings to the paint on the walls. It was creepy actually. Why did everything have to be the same? "Where's Ryan?" I asked, a little more impatient than even I thought I was.

Jason's face scrunched in confusion. "I thought he was with you."

Wait.

What?

"Why? Isn't he here?" I could feel panic rising in my chest all the way to my throat in a matter of milliseconds. "I thought he came back here after…"

"After the five-year-old temper tantrum fight? No, we just thought he went back to you afterward." Jason wasn't bothering to hide his disdain for Bill and Ryan's altercation. I didn't blame him.

Bill walked down the stairs and upon seeing the look on my face came running down two steps at a time. "What is it?"

"Ryan's not here, and he's not at Chelsan's either." Jason eyed Bill like it was his fault.

"Let's make sure." Bill ran back upstairs to search the house guilt written all over his face. I knew he shouldn't feel guilty, but for some reason it made me feel strangely satisfied that he was.

Jason and I checked the downstairs.

Nothing.

Ryan. He left me.

"Maybe he's at your house and you guys missed each other." Bill tried to smile at me reassuringly as he rejoined us from upstairs. I felt a surge of anger toward Bill when he smiled. I was being stupid, but I couldn't help it. How dare he smile when Ryan was missing!

I nodded instead, but my gut knew Ryan wasn't there.

It was becoming harder and harder to breathe.

Bill started to put his arm around me and I shrugged him off. He recoiled like I had hit him. I immediately felt bad. "I'm sorry, I'm just freaked out right now."

Bill nodded, but he was upset. I had hurt him again, lovely person that I was.

Jason took me by the hand and we all walked over to where the girls and I stayed last night.

Once inside I yelled louder than I anticipated, "RYAN!"

I was in full freak-out mode now. I ran up the stairs ignoring the complaining grumbles of Nancy and Jill as I searched every nook and cranny of the upstairs. Somehow I doubted Ryan was in the medicine cabinet, but I checked anyway. I could hear Bill and Jason downstairs calling out Ryan's name as well.

But there was no answer.

Ryan wasn't there.

He was gone.

"What's going on?" Nancy was up and next to me in a matter of seconds from the expression on my face.

"Ryan. He's gone," I said and plopped down on one of the twin beds.

"What do you mean gone?" Jill asked with folded arms. "Couldn't he just be checking this place out? You know, looking for something incriminating against Elisha? Isn't that like your boy?"

I impulsively stood up and hugged Jill.

She had to be right. That *was* just like Ryan. He probably went on his walk and discovered some kind of intel that he needed to scope out before coming back. I pulled away from Jill and tried not to notice the awkward expression on her face. Hugging was apparently the last thing she expected from me, but I couldn't help it, she gave me hope, and I really wanted to believe that Jill was right. I put on my Chuck Taylors with renewed vigor. That had to be it.

Bill and Jason joined us from downstairs.

"He's not here," Jason said with worry.

"Jill thinks he might be doing a re-con mission," Nancy reported as perkily as possible to put everyone at ease.

Even as she said it, my heart began to sink all over again.

Ryan wouldn't go anywhere without me. Unless he was afraid I'd get hurt. But he promised to come back to me in the morning. He promised he wouldn't leave me.

On some subconscious level, I knew something was wrong.

My gut was screaming at me that Elisha had Ryan.

"I hope you're right, but I just have this horrible feeling."

"Me, too," Jason echoed my thoughts.

Nancy elbowed him with a disapproving glare, then turned to me with a supportive smile. "He's fine. You're just being paranoid because we're in *Freaky Town*."

There was a knock on the door.

Relief flooded through me.

Ryan.

I raced down the stairs and opened the door to see...

Elisha.

Her creepy seven-year-old face made me want to puke. "Where's Ryan?" I asked abrasively. I was tired of playing nice with the ninety-eight-year-old brat. I may not like Roberta, but I knew she was right about Elisha poking inside my head without permission.

"He's safe." Elisha's purple eyes seemed to smile at me.

My stomach churned in response. She didn't even deny having him. She didn't even make up a lie about him being off exploring or something like that. Just: *He's safe.*

"We'd like to see him *now*," Bill ordered. He and the others had joined me without my noticing, I was so frozen with shock and indecision. Bill obviously was feeling responsible about Ryan's disappearance. But it was my fault. I should have never let him walk away from me.

"Later. Trust me, he's fine. We just had some questions about how he solved Trilidon's Theorem all those years back. Nothing to worry about, I assure you," Elisha's child-like voice tried to sound reassuring.

But I wasn't biting.

"No. I'd like to see him now." I crossed my arms in defiance.

"I didn't want to say anything, but now that you've forced my hand… Ryan doesn't want to see you right now. I gave him private quarters," Elisha said soothingly.

My eyes instantly welled up. She's lying. She's lying. I repeated over and over in my brain. I knew it to my core. I hated Elisha for trying to manipulate me like that, even while the insecure part of me wondered if she was actually telling the truth.

I almost decked Elisha right there and if it wasn't for Jill gently holding my arm back, I would have. I whirled on Jill, but her expression made me pause. Her eyes very distinctly told me, *Not now*. And, being that it was so out of my "normal" zone to have Jill Forester actually warning me, I turned back to Elisha. "Fine, but he better be here for lunch."

"That'll be up to him," Elisha replied so condescendingly I instinctively looked for anything dead to annoy her with.

And that was when I noticed…

Whoa.

Nothing dead.

Anywhere.

But how?

Christian Coalition towns bury their dead. There should be hundreds and thousands of dead bodies buried somewhere near. And what about insects? Or dead plants? Or anything?

Something was definitely off. Or definitely prepped for me coming here.

Which meant Doris, Elisha and Roland Light had prepared this place for me.

Prepared it so I couldn't use my powers.

Gulp. And gulp.

We were walking into a snake pit, I could feel it, and yet I couldn't walk away. My feet just seemed to go wherever Elisha told me, and I couldn't stop myself.

"Come on, one stop and then I'll take you to breakfast." Elisha began to walk away and we all followed.

See?

What was my problem?

Whoa.

As soon as I left the doorway…

Boom.

Thousands of black swirling holes on the nearby hillside. The graveyard no doubt. Not to mention the usuals all back: dead bugs, grass, plants. The house was hiding my ability to see dead things.

I walked close to Jason and whispered so only he could hear. "Whatever is in the metal at Brady's that blocks my powers is in the walls of the house."

Jason's nod was barely perceptible as we followed Elisha toward the cathedral in the center of town. The cobblestone felt wobbly under my shoes, or maybe I was concentrating so hard not to fall over from nerves I was a little oversensitive.

The cathedral's intricate carvings of complexity and design were just as breathtaking the next morning. A loud bell rang and people started filing out of the church in droves. No wonder it had been so quiet, they were all inside, what? Hanging out? What exactly do people do in cathedrals? Pray, according to Ryan, but to themselves? Out loud? I had to admit the whole thing was kind of fascinating.

I found it hard not to stare at the older members of the community, although today they seemed more sweet than scary. So fragile. I instinctively wanted to help an old man that was using some kind of metal cage on wheels to walk. But I was too shy, and it looked like he had plenty of help from his neighbors. Everyone seemed so friendly, waving to us as they passed, and nodding their hellos. I would have almost felt comfortable if it wasn't for the hundreds of pregnant women in the crowd reminding me that this was the biggest kidnapping in recorded history.

That and creepy Elisha standing in front of me.

"You know, I rescued you," I said a little snarkily.

Elisha turned to me with that same icky grin she'd been using since I first laid eyes on her. "Yes, and I thanked you for it."

"I just want to see Ryan and see if he's okay," I sputtered in annoyance.

"He's fine. He doesn't want to see you, so drop it." Elisha turned away from us and started walking up the steps of the cathedral. "I want you to meet someone. Come with me."

Why was I following her again? And yet, there I went, following Elisha right into the maw of the church. Maybe Ryan really didn't want to see me… Stop it! I couldn't let Elisha wheedle into my paranoia like that. If I could just see Ryan, I could make everything right.

We all trudged up the twenty or so stairs to the pointed arched doorway and walked through into the most beautiful room I'd ever seen. First off, it was huge! The masonry on the inside was just as delicately ornate as the outside, with stone flowers, vines and swirlies all over the place. Light poured in from the stained glass windows surrounding the entire room with one large shaft of light the main focus. It came from the largest stained glass window that framed the back of the room in the same kind of pointed arch like the doorway and it lit a single podium on a wooden stage.

That was where I saw Roland Light.

His tall, lean form was hunched over the podium, peering at his electronic reader as if its contents were sacred. Roland looked up at the sound of us walking on the slate flooring as we came closer, passing by row upon row of long wooden benches. His short white hair looked like plastic perfection and his long face smiled at our approach making the deep creases in his cheeks appear even larger and more menacing.

Roland stepped down from the podium and off the wooden platform to greet us. He leaned down and hugged Elisha first. "Aunt Elisha, it's still a miracle that I could finally see you." He turned to me. "And I have you to thank for it." Roland hugged me so fiercely I could barely breathe. I didn't want to hug back so I sort of just stood there limply, letting him squeeze the air out of my lungs.

He finally pulled away and I forced a kind of half-smile.

"You're welcome," I muttered.

Roland laughed out loud and it was actually warm and inviting.

No.

I had to remind myself that I needed to be suspicious of Roland, he could be dangerous. If Roland could make me drop my guard that easily I needed to be more alert.

"I thought you could join us for breakfast, Roland," Elisha said with a childish grin.

I hated it when she did that. No acting like a kid!

"Where are the twins?" I decided to ask suddenly. I didn't know why I said it just then, but I wasn't disappointed by their responses.

Both Elisha and Roland were completely taken aback. They weren't expecting me to mention the twins.

Roland recovered first. "They're safe. Resting, I presume." He didn't look as happy to see me anymore.

Good. I'd rather have him annoyed than super nice. It helped keep my brain clear.

"*Safe.* Seems to be the standard answer for anyone that's missing," Jason chimed in and typed something in his electronic writing pad.

"What are you writing there?" Roland went from friendly to territorial in about two seconds.

"Just some notes." Jason smiled, then tucked away the pad in his interior jacket pocket. "And Doris, where's she? Let me guess. She's safe?"

I loved him so much in that moment. Good old Jason, making them sweat.

"Everyone welcomed into Havenville is safe. You think I'm the bad guy, I can see it in your souls." Roland smiled warmly. "I'll just have to prove you wrong. It wouldn't be the first time." Then he laughed and slapped Jason on the back like an old friend. "Come on. Let's grab that bite."

See it in our souls, huh? I really didn't like this guy.

And I suddenly felt a wave of massive disappointment in myself. Why *did* we come here? Why didn't we insist that we be taken home? Why did I help us escape from the Clean-Up truck? It was scary that I was now trusting Turner more than these two. And now that Ryan was missing, I felt helpless. There was no way I'd leave now. Not without him. And I guess they knew that. That was probably the very reason they separated us in the first place. I just hoped he was okay.

I didn't say anything after that. I just followed Roland and Elisha out of the cathedral, the gang surrounding me like bodyguards. (Even Jill seemed over protective of me.)

Our small procession made its way through the cobblestone streets, past townsfolk and pregnant ladies, all happy, all smiles. Were we in "Stepford" country or something? I just focused on the shoes on my feet and tried not to think about how deep I was in this mess. I sussed out all the dead things I could see and confirmed that the hundreds of swirling holes on the hill was indeed the Havenville graveyard. Well, as long as I was outside, I had an army that could protect us. Small comfort. And gross, too. The rest of the villagers were so nice, how horrible of a person would I be if I brought back the rotting corpses of their loved ones for my protection? Pretty horrible. But still, if I had to, I would.

After a brief walk we entered another house that looked like all the others. The inside matched that of the boys' living quarters exactly. I did a quick dead things check and sure enough, I couldn't sense any black holes. Whatever they did to the houses completely blocked me from using my powers. I wished that we had had a little more time to figure out what the magic ingredient was in Brady's metal, but the sample was at Nancy's house and we weren't. I just hoped we could get Ryan and get out of Havenville before whatever nasty proverbial shoe dropped on my face.

Why were we here again?

Uggh.

The smells of eggs and bacon filled my nostrils with a kind of culinary bliss.

"Man that smells good," Bill echoed my thoughts and I had to smile at his simpleness.

"It'll be better than anything you've ever tasted. All our food is grown and raised here in Havenville. There are miles of farmland surrounding this town and everything is chemical-free. Trust me, you'll taste the difference." Roland was smiling as he motioned for us to sit at a large dining table. It sat twelve normally, so the seven of us fit perfectly. Especially since I could distance myself from our hosts by sitting across from Elisha and a chair away from Roland, who settled in at the head of the table. Nancy and Jill sat across from me, but also kept a chair between themselves and Elisha, while Bill sat on my right with Jason next to him.

A few moments later a couple of servants appeared with plates full of everything you'd ever want in a breakfast: pancakes, bacon, eggs, toast, even a couple links of sausage. There was no way I could finish a plate that huge, but I was going to try. After we were all served, no one really spoke, we just ravenously dug into the mound of deliciousness in front of us. I didn't know if it tasted any different from the food I normally ate, but it did taste amazing.

There was a knock on the front door followed by a clunking and a shuffling of feet. Elisha immediately rose from her seat when we all saw Beth walking toward us, using her cane for support.

"Am I too late?" Beth asked with a smile.

It was such a strange sensation watching her walk toward the table. She was exactly identical to Elisha, but old. And sweet. Beth wasn't faking that. She was genuinely a kind person, some things you just can't pretend.

"Of course not, sit down next to me." Elisha made room so that Beth would be between her and Roland.

"Mother. Always good to see you." Roland stood up and pulled the chair out for Beth to sit.

I noticed a strange expression on Beth's face, but it was gone before I could even form an opinion. File that away for later discussions with the gang. Thinking about the gang, I felt a sudden pang for Ryan and my palms began to sweat. I really didn't like not knowing where he was and my gut was screaming at me that he was in danger.

"Good to be seen, Roland." Beth smiled and kissed his cheek lovingly. "Though probably not for much longer, I'm getting old." Beth winked at us in friendly way, but all our faces dropped.

How could she talk about death so casually? She'd said it with a smile and a wink? What was up with that? It scared me. But I had to remind myself that these towns thought differently about death. Purposely not taking Age-pro because they believed in their religion so much was a concept that eluded me.

"Why so grim?" Beth seemed genuinely bothered as she sat down. "I'm not dying *today*. At least I hope not." She turned to Elisha and patted her sister's child hand lovingly, "Not when I've just reunited with my sister."

A servant brought in a plate for Beth and she began to eat with the rest of us.

"So what do you plan on doing with all those pregnant women?" Jason apparently had enough of small talk.

Roland didn't even skip a beat, as if he was expecting any and all questions. "I plan on keeping them here and raising them in our faith."

"The children too, or just the women?" Jason appeared casual, but I could tell he knew he had the news exclusive of a lifetime and he was probably doing everything in his power not to salivate on the table.

"Both. I believe the children being carried in these women are theirs. Science is the devil's work." Roland acted serious, but I could tell it was an act. Everything about him was an act.

"Who's the devil? Is he some kind of scientist or something?" Nancy asked thinking she was making the conversation lighter.

"Well, I'll teach you all about the devil, though the minute you start taking Age-pro you've already given into his temptations." Roland nodded his head toward Nancy as if this confusing sentence said it all.

"Okay." Nancy had *attitude face* which made me smile.

"There's nothing funny about Satan." Elisha's eyes scolded me.

"If I knew who that was, I might agree with you." I was tired of faking my complacent attitude with Elisha. "But I'm assuming by the sudden change in both of your attitudes and the seriousness of your tones that these guys Devil and Satan are bad dudes. I just know the difference between good and evil, and frankly I'm not so sure about you two."

I stood up as if everything I had been through was about to boil over in an explosion all over the table.

Roland stood up with me, his hand waving a placating gesture. "Please, I don't wish you any harm. Sit. We'll talk this out."

"Talk what out? How you've kidnapped my boyfriend and refuse to let me see him? Or that you've kidnapped 7,000 babies from their real parents? Or that you haven't made one peep about I.Q. Farms since I helped Elisha escape? You were supposed to expose them or shut them down or something: what happened to that? Or that you and Elisha are planning something and keeping us here against our will."

Then I turned to Elisha, and with as much confidence and viciousness as I could muster, I said, "Or the fact that you've been poking around in my brain since Tuesday!"

Elisha stood up then, angry herself. "Well, I wouldn't have to if you had just been honest with me!"

The others at the table were keeping silent, not sure where this confrontation was going. I wasn't so sure myself, but now that I was airing everything out…

"Honest?! That's a joke! Why did Turner tell me that Samuel and John weren't brain dead?" I said this more to see Elisha and Roland's expressions and less for any kind of truthful answer.

"Samuel and John have nothing to do with this," Roland said a little too quickly. "And I have no idea what goes on in the head of that psychopath, Geoffrey Turner. He probably said it just so you'd distrust us. He doesn't want us to join forces. He's terrified of that."

I slowly sat down as if their words were sinking in, but honestly it was because I was afraid if I pushed them too far I would put my friends in more danger than they already were.

Roland and Elisha took this as a victory and sat down as well, their expressions relieved.

Elisha tried to re-iterate Roland's point. "Your grandfather has been trying to kill you since he knew you existed. Why would you start trusting him now?"

I threw them a bone. "Maybe."

What I wanted to say was that I didn't trust Turner or *them*. One was that Devil guy and the other was that Satan dude. "Honest about what?" I asked as calmly as I could. Maybe I could suss out what Elisha was doing in my head in the first place.

"Honest about your grandmother and your distrust for me. If you had talked to me about this, Chelsan, your imagination may not have gotten the best of you." Elisha was acting like I was her two-year old child who had just acted up. Like I was supposed to feel stupid for even having my doubts about her.

"Listen. We've obviously started out on the wrong foot." Roland's cheeky grin was back. "Why don't I tell you all a little bit about Havenville and our beliefs, so you can see where we're coming from. Sound good?" he asked.

We all nodded, though I didn't think anyone was all that enthused to hear a speech from Roland. We'd heard enough of him on television and, frankly, he was way too over the top for me. He started rambling on about his religion, and how there was something called a heaven and hell, which apparently the hell part was where this devil guy lived. I guess the devil and Satan were the same thing, oops, my bad. There were all kinds of invisible protectors called angels, while the devil guy had demons. It was all pretty elaborate and frankly, a little scary, but, just like one of Mr. Alaster's lectures, I eventually tuned out.

What surprised me most was the fact that Roland and the people of Havenville were so dedicated to these stories that they refused to take Age-pro. They really believed that when you die you went somewhere else! And depending on how you lived your life, it would determine whether or not you'd go to heaven or hell. Just from what I'd seen so far, Roland and Elisha were definitely going down. Beth on the other hand... I truly wished there was a heaven for her sake. She really seemed so nice. It made me feel better about being related to my grandparents. If she could be genuinely good and still be related to those two, maybe I could, too.

All this new vocabulary was making my head spin, but it reminded me of some of the things Roberta had said to me before. I wondered if she had ever been religious at any point in her life.

I didn't know whether to be impressed with these people because they were willing to literally die for what they believed or sorry for them because they could be wrong and it was all for nothing.

Roland went on for at least an hour without interruption. Aside from the fire and brimstone talk, I was bored to tears. The last thing I had expected that morning was a lecture about Christian Coalition towns and their belief system. I envied Ryan at the moment, but he probably knew about all this already. He seemed to know everything. And thinking of him...

I needed to stay focused. No matter what Roland or Elisha said, I was going to find Ryan as soon as we left this house.

I looked over at Jill and Nancy and they looked like they were about to doze off. Beth listened with a glowingly, proud expression. Elisha looked just as bored as I was. Bill was playing with his fork next to me and Jason was fully enwrapped in every word Roland said at the end of the table. Such a reporter.

"Well, I can see I've lost the youth." Roland smiled and he stood up. "I hope you understand us a little better now?" He directed his eyes to me.

"Uh, yeah, thanks," I said and turned to my crew. "We'd like to take a look around for ourselves, if you don't mind?"

"Of course. This town is yours for the time being. Just try not to upset the locals with blasphemy." Roland reached down and kissed Elisha's cheek, followed by Beth's, "If you'll excuse me," and he walked out of the house.

I didn't really know what blasphemy meant, but I assumed he didn't want us dogging his beliefs to the Havenvill*ers*. I was pretty sure that never would have entered any of our minds, but I guess I understood why he said it.

A servant walked in from the kitchen. "Ms. Stearne, you're needed in Building Sixty."

Elisha's eyes flickered in my direction, but she nodded to the servant. "Thank you, I'm on my way." Elisha stood up and gave her sister a hug. "I'll visit with you later."

"Bye, bye, sweetie." Beth's whole face crinkled into a smile.

Elisha gave me one last glance as if she wasn't sure she wanted to leave her sister with us, but then left quickly without a word.

"Well, I should be on my way, too. It was lovely to have breakfast with all of you. I hope to do it again soon." Beth took some time to stand, using her cane to help her up.

"We're going, too. We'll walk with you a bit, if you don't mind?" I wanted to figure out what those strange looks at Roland were about.

"That sounds nice," Beth answered and we all started walking her to the door.

As we left the house and began to stroll down the cobblestone streets I made sure I was next to Beth. "So Beth, what's it like seeing your sister again?"

Beth beamed. "It's a dream come true. It really is. Our whole lives we wondered what happened to her and now she's back and home safe."

"Our?" Jason asked from behind.

For a brief second Beth's face looked like she was the cat who ate the canary, but she recovered and smiled back at Jason a moment later. "Me and our parents, of course. They died years ago. I'm just sorry they never found out what happened to Elisha." Beth turned to me and kissed my cheek. "This is my stop. Have fun, dears." Before we could respond Beth hobbled hurriedly into her house as if we were the plague.

We all watched her go inside and then resumed our walk.

"She knows something," Jason mused aloud.

"You think?" Jill responded sarcastically.

Nancy looked like she wanted to smack Jill, but per usual Jason didn't respond to the snideness.

"It's just a matter of tricking her into spilling. A gift of mine. I'll work on her at lunch." Jason's brain was already churning.

I looked around, making sure we were out of earshot from passers-by. "Look for Ryan?" I whispered to the gang.

"Elisha said he doesn't want to see you right now," Bill piped up and he might as well have punched me.

His face immediately retreated guiltily, but I could feel my nostrils starting to flare.

"No thanks to you!" I hadn't realized how loud it came out until I saw some Havenville heads down the street turn toward me.

"Quiet down," Jason urged.

"I don't care if he doesn't want to see me, I *need* to see him." I didn't want to give into my insecurities, but hearing Bill say that Ryan didn't want to see me somehow made the whole notion real. And if Ryan didn't want to see me… I couldn't think about that.

"Let's start with this Building Sixty, shall we?" Jason held his arm out for me and I took it with a relieved grin.

"We should split up," Jill suddenly announced.

I stopped, making Jason follow suit. "Don't you think we should stick together?"

Jill searched the area for unwanted ears and made us all gather in close. "I think Elisha wants you to go to Building Sixty and I think she's trying to set you up for something."

Bill, Nancy and Jason all exchanged glances that pretty much radiated that they hadn't thought of that, but they agreed wholeheartedly.

Then Jill paused as if what she was about to say was going to be painful. "Chelsan and I should check out the building and you three should find out what you can from some of those pregnant girls. Maybe even that Doris lady that's always on the news. And definitely find out what Beth knows."

"I like this girl." Jason raised his eyebrows in approval while Nancy gave him a look that could kill.

"I don't," Nancy grumbled. "Why you? Maybe Chelsan should take Bill?"

"Yeah, I'll go with you," Bill said a little too eagerly for Jill's taste. (And for mine.)

"I don't want to go anywhere with Bill," I said more harshly than I intended.

Bill's face fell instantly and I immediately regretted it.

Jill rolled her eyes and acted as if she were talking to children. "*I* should go because I'm the most manipulative and beautiful person here and we can use it to our advantage. Trust me, there's not a guy I can't flirt with. And if my radar is accurate, these old dudes are salivating for me." She turned to Nancy. "You just don't have that kind of confidence, and your crush on *him* will hold you back." Jill eyed Jason knowingly.

Nancy clenched her fist and was about to attack Jill, when Jason grabbed her.

"She may be a little crass, but she's right." Nancy whirled on him with fury and hurt, but Jason held her face to calm her. "She's just saying in a really nasty way that you're sweet and you like me."

Nancy was appalled and embarrassed. "Not anymore!"

Before Nancy could go on another Jason-hating tirade, Jason leaned in and kissed her. When he pulled away he looked serious. "It's okay, Nancy. I like you, too, probably a lot more than you like me. Actually, I'm sure I do. You're all I think about, and you make me crazy."

Nancy sighed in what I can only describe as blissful relief. She kissed him back and for once in a really long time I felt happy. Happy for my best friend who finally broke down the impenetrable Jason

Keroff and got him to admit his feelings for her.

But then they were just kissing and time was ticking.

And Bill looked like an abused dog, just standing there, not saying anything.

"Guys, I hate to break this up, but…" I said, really hoping Nancy wouldn't be mad.

She wasn't of course. She was grinning from ear-to-ear.

Jason casually reached over and held Nancy's hand, which made her physically shiver. The girl was happy.

Nancy turned to me, her eyes now alight with excitement. (I figured in that moment, she could probably care less about Jill and her comments, or let's face it, she could care less about *me* for that matter.) "We'll find out what we can, but you two be careful. You got any dead things you can use?"

"So far, all the buildings seem to have me blocked, but I have access to the whole graveyard when I'm outside," I said, then realized I had only told Jason about the blockage. So I filled them in. I also decided that, while I was spilling, I'd tell them about my strange encounter with Roberta as well.

Nancy was appropriately annoyed. "So that's what Elisha was talking about when she said you didn't trust her. That's hypocritical seeing as she's stalking your brain without your permission."

Jill was the most visibly upset by the news. "You're not becoming friends with your grandparents are you? Because they killed your mom and my dad."

"You don't have to remind me, Jill. And, no: the last thing I'd ever feel for them is friendship. I'm in information-gathering mode here and they have information. All we know is that both Elisha and Turner want those twins. Let's find out why."

Jill's arms were crossed. I could tell she didn't believe my answer but seriously: didn't care. In fact, the only thing I wanted to think about was finding Ryan. I honestly didn't really even care about Samuel and John. I was kind of tired of being pulled into messes that weren't mine. I just wanted my boyfriend back. Was that too much to ask?

"Let's do this," Nancy said, breaking the tension. "Just try and keep one foot outside if you can." She turned to Jill, "If Chelsan gets hurt in any way…"

Jill rolled her eyes. "Yeah, yeah, you'll kick my ass. I know. Can we go now?"

Jill. Jill. Jill.

Such a pleasant human being.

Nancy hugged me while Jason gave me a small salute and recaptured Nancy's hand. I really hoped he wouldn't change his mind again, for all our sakes!

Bill awkwardly hovered near me, waiting for a hug as well. I reached up and pulled him close whispering in his ear, "I'm sorry, Bill."

"Me, too," he whispered back.

When he pulled away we were both grinning uncomfortably at each other until Bill, Nancy and Jason all went back toward the center of town.

Jill turned to me. "I hate to rain on our parade, but where do you think Building Sixty is?"

Oh yeah.

Good question.

"Let's go exploring," I offered, and Jill shrugged in response.

We walked down the cobblestone street toward the back of town, looking for any kind of numbering system. There was nothing of course, but the farther we went the more stares we were getting, so we figured we were probably on track.

"What about that guy?" I asked, nodding toward a man who looked like he was in his thirties standing in front of one of the identical brick houses. He was wearing a kind of uniform that had a badge on his chest and a billy club holstered around his waist. "Some kind of security?"

"I got this," Jill said with an air of confidence and I had to admit that the way she flipped her long locks of wavy black hair was pretty impressive.

I sort of waddled behind her like an ugly duckling that was way out of its depth. Sometimes it was such a relief that the love of my life actually liked me already. I really hated the whole game of flirting and wondering and flirting some more and then wondering some more. It was way too stressful and I was glad that that part of my relationship with

Ryan was stabilized. I didn't think I could handle going through that all over again with someone new!

But Jill was definitely in her element. I had witnessed her flirting techniques at school whenever she'd want something. What was funny was that her power made people do whatever she wanted more than her good looks, but it didn't stop her from using both. Even Ryan went on a date with her for crying out loud. Eeew. Didn't want to think about that.

Jill walked up to the security guy, batted her eyelashes and looked at him with her bright green eyes in a way that made her look absolutely stunning. Her perfect body accentuated by her tight t-shirt and jeans was already making this guy's head spin. "Could you help us?" she asked in the nicest voice I'd ever heard from her.

"You're the visitors from Los Angeles, aren't you?" the security man kind of sputtered out. Jill was definitely making this guy nervous. He was cute in his own way, though he was at least thirty-six. His balding dark hair was shaved with a little stubble grown out and his face was very structured with a slightly crooked nose like Jason's. He looked like he kept in shape since I couldn't see an ounce of body fat on him. He was all muscle.

Just for safety's sake I sought out the closest dead thing I could find, which happened to be a dead dog buried behind the house next door. Must have been someone's pet, but if things got hairy I wanted something to fight with.

Jill laughed and touched his arm, which made this guy immediately melt. "Yes, we are…" She paused for his name.

"Frank," he said, his face turning a little red.

"I'm Jill and this is Chelsan." Jill half-waved to me behind her as if I hardly mattered. She was probably afraid I'd mess up her flirt, and let's face it, that wasn't out of the realm of possibility. I tended to put my foot in my mouth when trying to be sneaky.

"You folks need to turn around. In about a hundred feet you're headed into *off limits* territory," Frank said and I could tell he was hoping we'd comply happily. This guy didn't want any trouble.

Oh well, too bad for him.

"Oooo! Off limits, huh? That sounds like fun. We'd be safe with you, wouldn't we?" Jill went straight for the jugular. This girl wasn't messing around and I had to admire her for that.

"Well, I… *she*… uhh." Frank started to sweat.

Apparently, Jill had broken him.

Jill grabbed his arm and made a pouty face that even I would have found hard to resist. "Please? We're so bored. And you're so *cute*." She touched Frank's nose with her finger for emphasis.

His face went about five shades redder. "Oh.. well… it's just… off limits…restricted… Chelsan… can't."

Jill snuggled in closer so her face was inches from Frank's. He swallowed hard and his eyes were kind of bugging out. I don't think he'd ever had this kind of attention from a girl that looked as young and beautiful as Jill. "You're not honestly going to say 'no,' are you? Don't you want to have a little fun? How much trouble could two little girls cause?"

Frank was literally dripping sweat. I couldn't tell if he was so nervous because he was afraid of getting in trouble or because of Jill's attentions. Probably both. I just stayed out of it because the guy looked like he was about to crack.

"I guess… if we just stick to the street," Frank sputtered.

Jill made an excited squeal and kissed his cheek. "Thank you, thank you, thank you. We're going to have so much fun!"

Frank nearly fainted from the kiss, but quickly recovered, excited now himself. Jill stayed glued to his arm, and Frank led us toward the area he referred to as "restricted."

I stayed a step behind them, not wanting to ruin the magic hold Jill had on the poor sap. One thing that stood out from their conversation though was the fact that Frank knew me by name. He stuttered it out as if it was a name he was told to memorize and keep away from all things restricted. I just hoped that meant we'd find Ryan.

Frank appeared to relax slightly as we walked down the aisle of identical houses. I really didn't see what made this particular stretch of the town "restricted" as compared to the others, but I guess it was what was going on *inside* the houses that mattered.

Oh man.

Just had a pang of fear for Ryan.

Jill seemed to have read my mind because she leaned in close to Frank's ear, which made his face burn red again. "This place looks pretty boring to me. Where's the danger? I thought it was restricted?" Jill started to pout.

She really was good. I could never make my bottom lip do that.

Frank was flustered again, but tried to stay cool. "Oh it is dangerous, but I can't show you anything. I'm under orders."

"You're such a tease." Jill pulled away just enough so that she was still holding onto his arm.

"I'm not, I swear. I'd get fired." Frank's face was as conflicted as could be. Boys were such slaves to a girl's attentions.

"Fired? It's not like you get paid, am I right? I didn't see any pay centers in the stores. You all just live here and share, right?" Jill leaned back in, to Frank's relief.

Wow. She noticed that, too. I was curious as to his response.

"Yes, but there are certain responsibilities we uphold and now, what with the pregnant women and *her*," he nodded back to me, "we have to keep security tight. I'm the best." Frank puffed up proudly.

Interesting. I'm definitely on the top of their *Danger* list.

Jill smiled seductively at him. "Oh, I'm sure you are, which means you can take us to all the really exciting places, right?"

Frank's eyes said he wanted to run because he knew that on some level she was manipulating him, but his face and body were screaming that he wanted Jill in the worst way.

"I… I'm not sure I…" Frank was back to stammering again.

Jill stopped suddenly and leaned in so her lips were barely touching his. "Let's cut to the chase, shall we? You know we need to see her boyfriend. So, just take us to where he is and I promise you won't regret it." Jill ran her hand over his stubbled head and Frank's eyelids fluttered.

"I can't… express orders…" Frank was terrified.

Jill kissed him and I had to give it to her. She really took one for the team.

Frank's knees were actually, visibly shaking. I almost wanted to laugh, poor guy.

Jill pulled away so their faces were still only inches from each other. "She just wants to say 'Hi.' You understand, right? And when they're alone…" Jill brushed his cheek with her hand, "We can be alone."

That did it.

"Well, I can't see how a little hello could hurt. Ms. Elisha was just having him over for breakfast after all. He's probably set to go back to his quarters soon anyway." Frank seemed to be convincing himself rather than explaining the situation to us.

Jill stayed locked to his arm, but she looked back at me and winked.

I smiled my thanks and felt a surge of relief. I remembered the way Elisha eyed Ryan: she probably just wanted alone time with him. My imagination was far more active than it should be, but I also wanted to stay focused, just in case.

We walked for what seemed to be another half mile. The rows of houses had turned into rows of warehouses. Large rectangular blocks of grey with no windows and very few doors.

Why would Elisha have breakfast with Ryan in one of these monstrosities?

Anything dead?

Closer to the graveyard.

Just yards away behind the warehouses.

Jill would have to be my spy while I stayed outside. If the houses carried whatever ingredient that blocked my power in them, then the warehouses would most certainly contain it as well.

We reached a warehouse somewhere in the middle of the pack and Frank turned expectantly to Jill. "He's in there. Better let me go in first, to make sure we're in the clear."

Frank went through the single metal door.

Jill turned to me and shook her head. "Gross. You owe me big time. Especially, if he really was just eating breakfast." Jill had already crossed her arms defensively.

"I totally owe you. Thanks," I said as sincerely as I could.

Jill shrugged. "I just hope Elisha's not in there ready to eat us."

I laughed softly, but I kind of agreed. *Little Violet Eyes*, scared the crap out of me, too.

It was then that I noticed under the hanging light attached to the warehouse wall there was a number.

Sixty.

I pointed to it. "Well, trap or not, at least we're at the right building."

"Oh boy." Jill took a calming breath.

Frank came out with a smile. "He's in here. Quick." He waved us to come.

I whispered to Jill, "When you get to the door, let me know if you can see Ryan. If he's in trouble, I'm going to bring back some corpses."

Jill's nod was barely perceptible, but she was on it.

She ran forward with a smile and rushed into Frank's arms, allowing me to arrive at the door much more slowly.

Jill was halfway through the doorway, searching inside, looking over Frank's shoulder. She turned to me and shrugged.

She didn't see him.

Frank twirled her around and turned to me. "He's in the private study. This way."

Jill and I both gave each other a look that screamed, *What are we doing?* Every fiber of my instinct was telling me to run, but every fiber of my soul was telling me that I needed to see Ryan. And there was no doubt in my mind: Ryan was in there. I just didn't know if he was in trouble or not. And if he was, I wouldn't be able to help him the second I entered the building.

But I wouldn't be able to help Ryan at all unless he was out of the building anyway, so I determined myself to run in there, get him (whether he was in trouble or not) and get him outside. Then I could use the whole damn graveyard to attack if I had to.

Jill and Frank were in.

I closed my eyes to gather myself and stepped in.

Okay, powers off. No swirling black holes.

But, so far, no people either. So maybe we were in the clear.

We entered a large, white hallway with hanging lamps on the ceiling. I could see another metal door at the end of it, just like the one we'd entered. Jill glanced back at me and both our freak-out senses were on overload. I almost ran back the way we came, but that round metal doorknob was calling out to me. If Ryan was in here, I couldn't leave him.

Frank turned the knob and swung the door open for me and Jill to go first.

I somehow knew he wasn't being gentlemanly, but at the same time I couldn't stop myself.

And then I did.

I stopped and it made Jill stop.

"What?" she asked, ignoring Frank completely.

"I just…"

I somehow knew, just like all the other times, that Elisha was pulling my strings. She could make me do things. She was in my head and knew exactly which brain synapses to tap into to make me act against my better judgment. I was sure of it. So sure, that I recognized the battle in my brain to move forward was a battle with Elisha and not my curiosity, as I'd been rationalizing these past few days.

Elisha was manipulating me on the largest scale imaginable. She was using my own brain against me. And even though I had been warned by my grandparents, and even by myself, I kept on taking her subliminal orders. I felt so foolish.

And yet…

Ryan was still in that room.

And I still had to save him.

"Chelsan, run!" Jill yelled quickly.

I didn't know what prompted it, but apparently she saw something in my face, something that told Jill that if *I* couldn't trust my instincts, she would do it for me.

Frank heard enough. He gripped Jill's arm tighter and grabbed mine with his free hand. "Sorry, girls," he said not sounding sorry at all.

Then Frank flung us through the doorway and slammed it behind us.

I nearly lost my breath as I looked up and saw quite possibly the worst thing I could ever imagine.

Ryan…

…suspended in the air with thousands of wires attached to his head.

His eyes were staring ahead at nothing. Body limp. Mouth slack.

The wires were plugged into an entire row of holo-screens, all displaying various images of numbers and calculations.

And I screamed.

I ran up to Ryan, ready to start ripping out the wires when a pair of forceful hands pulled me back.

I couldn't even see who had me, I was in such a blind rage.

I looked for anything dead, anything! In my fury, I was vaguely able to see the swirling holes on the hillside, even through the building's protective barrier. I connected to the strongest one I could find, making the corpse smash through their coffin and claw their way to the surface. I refused to acknowledge the fact that I had somehow broken through the building's defenses of my power for fear I'd lose control of the dead body. The corpse was almost to the surface…

WHACK!

***

I awoke with a splitting headache, tied to a chair.

The chair was positioned a few feet away from Ryan, so I could see his comatose face staring at empty space. I struggled against my bonds, but they were way too tight. I could barely move a quarter of an inch without feeling the burn of the ropes against my hands and feet, and my arms were already sore from being stretched behind me.

My head dropped and I closed my eyes, trying to reconnect with the corpse outside.

Nothing.

I couldn't sense a single dead thing.

The barrier seemed to be working its mojo again and I had no idea how I'd by-passed it last time. Maybe if I could get myself worked up again…

"It won't work this time," Elisha's voice interrupted my thoughts like a dagger.

I whirled my head around to see what I had failed to see when I came to. I was so worried about Ryan I didn't even notice that Jill, Nancy, Jason and Bill were all tied up next to me.

Fantastic.

Elisha and Roland stood to my right while the others were spread out in a line to my left. There was no one else in the room, apparently Frank had been sent away. My friends were all awake and trying to avoid looking at Ryan.

Except for Bill.

Bill couldn't stop staring at Ryan.

I had never seen Bill look so devastated. *Ever.* I could tell he fully blamed himself for Ryan's capture.

I wanted to comfort Bill, to tell him that it was all my fault, not his. But I didn't even know how to articulate anything at the moment. I wanted to cry seeing Ryan strung up like a lab animal. Blank face. Blank eyes.

Why didn't I stop Ryan last night? If I had just convinced him to stay with me, none of this would have happened!

But I knew that wasn't true either.

Elisha would have taken Ryan no matter what. He was just as valuable to her as I was. Maybe even more. Who knew what she had planned for him? *Oh Ryan, I'm so sorry for ever getting you involved in all this!*

The others looked more concerned for me than they did for themselves. I guess they had been afraid that I wasn't going to wake up. Before I uttered a response to Elisha, I took in my surroundings, hoping I could figure out some kind of escape plan.

The room we were in was smaller than I'd expected. I just figured being in a warehouse, well... that it would look like a warehouse. I never would have known that it had low ceilings lit with rows of track lighting, walls nicely painted with a golden hue, a long oak desk positioned against a wall holding the row of holo-computers, and dark brown leather furniture set out like a living room behind us. In fact, if it weren't for Ryan being suspended in air, plugged into some kind of monster computer, and the five of us tied to wooden chairs, the place would have been cozy. It made me think that this contraption they had Ryan hooked up to was recent. That these warehouses were probably used as simple offices for the folk in Havenville. It wasn't until I helped the *monster* escape that it turned into some kind of crazy lab, trying to crack into Ryan's super mega-brain.

I looked at the figures and numbers moving a mile-a-minute on the holo-displays and had a whole new respect and awe for Ryan. His brain was doing that. He was calculating problems *he* didn't even know he could solve. Ryan had always kept that side of himself private, figuring he'd bore me with it. But I found it fascinating. If it wouldn't make Elisha so happy, I would have started crying. Seeing Ryan like he was, was killing me in ways I never thought possible. His worst nightmare was being sent back to an I.Q. Farm, and now, because of me, here he was.

"How could you do that to him?" I asked Elisha incredulously. After years of being in a farm herself, I couldn't fathom how she would do it to someone else.

And I said this as me and my friends were tied to chairs.

Elisha's face was expressionless, but her eyes were smiling. "It's necessary. Ryan is perhaps the smartest person to be born in over three centuries. I'm a close second, but even with all the tools Turner gave me at my Farm, I couldn't solve Trilidon's Theorem." She moved up to within inches of my face, eyes lit up. "Think of what we can extract from him. The science world will be at our fingertips. And with the twins, so will the military."

Military? Us?

"So they're a weapon?" I asked aloud. How could two spinning-black-hole-headed-boys be a weapon? Did they have some kind of power like mine? More powerful, I'd say, if the grandparents kept them locked up for so many years. They never even thought about doing that to *me*. They just wanted me dead. Ergo: Me not as powerful.

Elisha laughed softly. "Look at your pea little brain trying to work things out. It's cute. I should be grateful you're so stupid. It made it so easy to pop inside your head anytime I wanted."

"*You're* stupid!" Nancy said in my defense. And if we weren't in perilous danger I would have smiled at her loyalty.

But, yeah.

Tied up and all, I decided to swallow my witty comebacks. "I guess I have to be grateful to Grams, then, since she's blocking what you want to see." I had no idea what memory Grams was protecting, but maybe if Elisha thought I did, she'd let her guard down and give me some clue as to what she was looking for.

To my surprise Roland angrily stepped forward. "You'll show her, or you'll die, you little vixen."

"Roland, calm down." Elisha put her small delicate hand up to placate him. "She's just trying to rile us up." Then she focused on me. "She can stay nestled in that brain of yours, but I'll get to that memory, don't doubt that for a second."

Wow.

As I sat there, losing circulation in my wrists and ankles and seeing my boyfriend in a computer coma, I suddenly realized how *un*shocked I was at this turn of events. If I was so unsurprised at Elisha and Roland being this insane, why in the world did I get in the van with Elisha and Doris? I let her control me. I let her inside my mind and make decisions for me when I knew what she was. From breaking her out of the Farm to helping her escape to Havenville, I let Elisha use me. And as a result, I put all my loved ones in danger. And Jill, too. (Okay, that was mean: Jill had more than proved herself. Old habits died hard.)

I had to get us out of there. I never thought I'd hear myself say it, but maybe I could get Turner and Roberta to help. I was so busy distrusting them (and rightfully so) I ended up walking into an even bigger pit of evil.

"You can rot in your hell place with that Satan dude," I said, knowing that it would sting, and secretly hoping I didn't sound like an idiot.

It worked.

Roland actually stepped forward and slapped me hard in the face. "Don't blaspheme!"

Ouch. There was that "blaspheme" word again and I guess I accomplished it. Good.

Wait.

Did I just see Ryan's eyes look at me?

I tried not to stare too hard for fear of Elisha and Roland seeing, but when I glanced back at him, Ryan's face was blank like before.

Had I imagined it? Probably. But I decided to keep a careful eye out in case Ryan was somehow, some way, awake and trying to send me a message.

Bill nearly fell out of his seat trying to break free to defend my honor, but I knew it wouldn't do any good. I gave him a look that said I was okay and thanks for trying. I could see in Bill's face how much he was full of rage and fury at our situation and it broke my heart. I needed to get us out of there, now!

If I connected to that corpse on the hillside before, I should be able to do it again.

I concentrated as hard as I could, but…

Nothing.

I tried not to cry from frustration.

I needed to find out everything I could. Any information could be the difference between freedom and death.

"Let them go. I'll tell you whatever you need to know." I tried the martyr tactic. At this point I'd rather die than put my friends in danger and I hoped that whatever it was Elisha wanted from me was more important than keeping my friend's hostage.

Elisha laughed. "You wouldn't be able to tell me. The memory is too far back. I need you to kick Roberta out of your head so I can get into that memory. If you do that, I'll send your friends back to their homes, no questions asked."

The weird thing was: she was telling the truth.

Jason didn't believe her, though. "You're telling us that you'd let us go, with all the information we know about you? I doubt that." Jason paused, curiosity flitted across his face. "Why *didn't* you come forward about the I.Q. Farms? It seems like a perfect match to your religious *coming out* party. What better way to get people on your side than liberating a Farm of Age-pro'd children?"

Elisha turned to Jason, expressionless. (*Expressionless* I'd learned with Elisha meant she was trying to hide something.) "Roland and I didn't come forward about the I.Q. Farms because we don't care. We're perfectly safe here. We don't care about some over-aged runts that Turner has hooked up to his machines. And we certainly don't care about the famous reporter Jason Keroff. You're a joke just like the rest of your gang. We'll have everything soon, and you are just fleas in my way. Only Chelsan and Ryan matter. I could care less about you lot."

I remembered my accusation that morning about the I.Q. Farms. Why hadn't they come forward and freed all the other kids? Elisha could have been a hero: the poster child for sympathy and the horrors of Age-pro. I suddenly had a very bad feeling. This was far bigger and far deeper than my *pea brain* had fathomed.

Elisha and Roland were out for power.

They had a plan and, somehow, Ryan and I were a part of it. Ryan I understood, he was crazy brilliant. But *me*? Did Elisha think I'd use my powers for her? Or that she could control me enough to use them herself? If she had that kind of power she would have done it already. And what memory was so far back that I wouldn't remember it? And why would Elisha need it so bad?

Oh.

Crap.

"You're after my powers," I said quietly, realizing, "You want the spell that my dad used." I was a baby when it happened and well… dead. There was no way I could remember the details of that spell. But my mind did. And if Elisha had access to that memory she could perform the same spell on herself. According to Jason, my dad had made it up. I guess Dad used elements of the spell that my grandparents used to kill my mom, called The Ritual of Vortex. But no one knew for sure. Only my brain was witness.

"Very good, Chelsan. I knew there was some kind of brain in there." Elisha smiled wickedly. And let me tell you when a kid with purple eyes smiles at you wickedly, it was disturbing.

"Fine. Just send them to Nancy's house first and I'll kick Roberta out," I offered and literally had no idea if I could *actually* do that. I just wanted my friends out of there and safe.

"Um, no way," Nancy retorted, staring daggers at me. "We're not leaving you."

"Yeah, that's not happening." Bill's nostrils flared in determined agreement. "And we're not leaving Ryan, either," his voice cracked.

"Do I have a say about that?" Jason asked with his usual yellow-belly tone.

"NO!" Nancy and Bill answered in unison.

Jill stayed quiet, but she looked at me, and another one of our *mutual understanding moments* passed between us. She knew, like I did, that the only way to help Ryan and me was to get out of Dodge. Four extra bodies meant four extra prisoners that needed to escape, something that was near impossible in a town like this. I gave Jill one last pleading look and hoped Elisha wouldn't notice.

"Get them out of here and I'll give you what you want," I said to Elisha.

Elisha stared at me for a good minute…

She decided I was telling the truth. "You got it."

Elisha hit a button on a nearby console and the low ceiling suddenly opened like a giant sliding glass door. Apparently the roofs were removable. Interesting. Elisha talked into a small round device next to the console. "Hover-Five to Building Sixty."

A man's voice responded and within minutes a large hover-van like the one we came in whirled above our heads and landed on the roof next to the ceiling's opening. A retractable metal ladder slid down to the slate flooring, followed by five burly men with guns climbing down to join us. They cut the ropes binding my friends, then manhandled them toward the ladder. Only Nancy and Bill were fighting back, struggling to free themselves and somehow help me and Ryan escape…

But these men were professionals.

One of them simply put a gun to Jason's head. "Up the ladder or he dies."

"Let's not be hasty. I'm cooperating here." Then Jason looked angrily at Nancy and Bill for fighting against the guards. "Would you guys knock it off?"

Nancy gave me a desperate look of anguish. This was killing her.

Nancy and Bill stopped their struggle.

"Nancy, it's okay. It's for the best. But guys, please, watch out for Jill. Turner will want that chip and he'll kill her so we can't access it. All he wants is that chip, he doesn't care who he hurts. So just give it to him, okay? It's not worth Jill's life." I knew I was being cryptic. But I hoped one of them would realize I was telling them to give Turner the chip in exchange for help. I knew Elisha had been in my brain, so she knew all about the chip. I was counting on the fact that she expected me to be worried about my friends, so a message like that wouldn't trigger any red flags for her.

Nancy started to cry and I hoped it was her way of hiding from Elisha that she was trying to sort out what I had told her. Nancy had known me long enough to realize that I was trying to give her a message. She could talk about it with the gang once they were safely inside Nancy's house and protected by George's red orb of radio silence.

Bill looked utterly devastated by his helplessness. He tried to offer me a look that would give me some kind of hope, but he just ended up looking like a lost child.

Jason had no problem climbing up the ladder and away from the gun aimed at his head. Aside from being threatened, he knew the advantage of leaving, even if the others were being emotional about it. Jason was a reporter and a survivor. He knew when to get out.

Jill was the last to go. She gave me a small supportive nod, then followed the others up.

I turned to Elisha. "I'm not giving you anything until I have confirmation that they're at Nancy's."

Elisha didn't seem fazed by this at all. "Of course."

Roland stood behind her with his arms crossed, watching me with disdain, but he didn't argue.

The hover-van whizzed away and we sat in silence, waiting. Elisha focused on the holo-displays of Ryan's computations and made small "Ooooos" and "Aaaaaahhhs" while Roland just stared at me, fury in his eyes.

I really hated him.

After about forty-five minutes of my wrists seriously starting to hurt from the ropes, the hover-van's driver sounded on the speaker. "We're here."

"I want to speak to Nancy," I said.

Elisha nodded as if this were par for the course and gestured for me to speak.

"Nancy? Are you guys safe?" I asked aloud.

Nancy's voice sounded raw from crying and I nearly broke my composure. "We're good. They let Bill contact his dad and we've got about thirty bodyguards surrounding the house."

I could hear Vianne in the background, "Is that Chelsan? Chelsan? Are you okay?"

"I'm fine. Don't worry about me, just worry about Jill and that chip," I said in my last attempt at giving them a plan of attack.

"We got it, Chelsan. The chip isn't worth a life," Jason's voice echoed over the speaker, and I was instantly relieved. I could tell from his tone that Jason knew *exactly* what I was trying to say. Jill wouldn't be happy about it, mainly because she wouldn't want *any* help from Turner if she could avoid it, but staying alive meant more, so I knew in the end Jill would comply. I just hoped it would be in time.

"Good?" Elisha turned to me for approval.

I nodded. "Good."

Elisha smiled into the intercom. "I hope you enjoyed your stay in Havenville."

Just as Nancy's voice started to say something nasty, Elisha broke off communication and turned to me. "See? All safe. Now are you ready to kick cat lady out?"

"Here goes." I squeezed my eyes pretending to concentrate and then opened them, breathing heavily as if exhausted. "Okay, she's gone. Go on in." I hoped I knew what I was doing.

I had just the hints of sensing Elisha in my brain before and I was counting on a full attack once she was inside. I had no idea what exactly that meant, but I wasn't going to take Ryan hanging from the ceiling and living out his worst nightmare lying down.

Elisha sat down on the couch and closed her eyes.

And there she was.

I could feel her like a cloud swimming through my brain.

How could I not have felt this before?

She was going directly to the barrier that Roberta had set up like a high security prison. A part of Roberta was there. I could feel her, too. But it felt more like some kind of magic essence of her, probably some kind of spell or voodoo to protect the memory. Even if I wanted to I don't think I could have broken that kind of mojo. I had to give props to the Grams, she was a seriously powerful woman.

I closed my eyes and decided to delve in full throttle.

I was immediately next to Elisha, in a long hallway with millions of doors on either side of us. It looked just like when I visited Roberta's memories. It must be the same for everyone, or this was just how I processed seeing memory banks. Upon closer inspection there were a few doors with a translucent bubble surrounding them.

Grandma's mojo.

Elisha turned to me with fury. "Break it down. It's this door." She pointed at the door next to us on the right.

"Okay," I said and then turned to her, angry. "Oh, wait. No."

"No?" Elisha didn't bat an eye. "I can still kill your boyfriend, you know?"

"But you won't because you need him for his brains." I was definitely scared that she'd kill him anyway.

Elisha crossed her arms. "Why don't you want me to see? What do you care if I have the same power as you?"

"Why do you want it?" I asked, trying to get some kind of information out of her.

Elisha waved her hand and two armchairs appeared facing each other in the hallway. "Sit."

I sat down. Elisha sat across from me. To my surprise, she did not seem angry. "Chelsan, this is going to sound very strange to you since you were never raised with any kind of religious background, but I am a part of a prophecy."

"You mean like a fantasy novel thing?" I could tell this was going to get crazy.

"For you, I suppose, yes. But for people who believe in something beyond them, prophecies are very important."

Elisha sat forward and held my hands in hers. Awkward. But I didn't take them away. "In the Bible the *man* named Elisha was the prophet Elijah's successor and a prophet himself. He was said to capture the spirit of Elijah and all of Elijah's power were transferred into him." Elisha stared at me with her cold violet eyes, "Chelsan, Elijah could bring back the dead. According to a vision that came to Roland, I'm meant to have this power for our church. It's my namesake, and rightfully mine."

She was serious.

And what was I supposed to do with this information? Not let her get into that memory, that was for sure. Elisha was trying to convince me that this was a part of her destiny, but in the last few days, (actually, more like the last few hours) I knew Elisha wanted these powers for something else. Something far more dangerous than a simple *I was named after the guy that could bring back the dead.* Elisha thought she was doing a damned good job at manipulating me, too.

"You're full of crap," I said out loud.

I regretted it immediately.

The chairs disappeared and Elisha's hand reached up, grabbing my throat. "I can kill you right here. Astral projection is much deadlier than you know."

I couldn't breathe. Even though I knew I was just an image of myself in my own brain, I still couldn't breathe. I was choking to death.

"You keep yourself in the dark and don't bother to learn anything about your powers. Even when two people are walking into your brain like a revolving door you *still* don't do anything about it. Your grandmother tells you to learn to control it, someone who's tried to kill you, and you just sit there and let us in anyway. You are quite possibly the stupidest girl I've ever met. You don't deserve your power."

As I tried to claw her child's hand off my throat, I realized Elisha was absolutely right.

I was in complete denial. Of everything. And my way of dealing with it was ignoring it until I couldn't anymore. And it may have cost me and Ryan our lives.

No.

I reached down and grabbed Elisha's throat with all my might. The two of us stood there, choking, strangling the life out of our ethereal forms.

One thing I got out of her little speech? If she could hurt me, I could hurt her.

And I was bigger.

I threw her body like a rag doll and Elisha slammed against a door.

But before I could gain my bearings, she instantly materialized in front of me and pushed me down the hallway about forty feet.

I guess she was stronger in ghost form.

I had to stop thinking like I was a person in a hallway. I had to think of myself as a ghost myself and if I was a ghost I could…

…I made myself materialize behind Elisha just as fast as she had. Before she could react I grabbed her arm and smashed her body against the wall.

Elisha screamed in rage more than pain.

"OUT!" I yelled from the depths of my soul.

My eyes opened.

I was back in the warehouse, still tied to the chair.

Elisha jumped up from the couch and punched me in the face.

I barely noticed as I smiled back at her.

I had kicked her out of my brain.

I still hadn't figured out how to *keep* her out, but it was a good start.

Luckily, a seven-year-old punch wasn't as powerful as her ethereal form punch.

"You'll show me that memory if I have to torture you to do it!" Elisha's violet eyes were livid.

Roland was quickly by her side and ready to hit me when she said hit me. Wow. Such a great minister. Religion was awesome.

"Torture me all you want. You must have seen all my *other* memories. I've been through everything imaginable *including* blowing up my mother! What do you honestly think you could do that would be worse than that?" Take that. Serial killers, zombie attacks, guns, and grandparents. Nothing would make me show her that memory.

Elisha paused and she was calm again. "Now, you were right about something. I can't kill Ryan, I need him too much. But I can do something else."

I struggled to break free out of instinct. Not Ryan. Please not Ryan. "What are you going to do to him?"

"Well, well, now that I've got your interest." Elisha looked up at Ryan's comatose face and touched his cheek lovingly. Then she turned back to me. "I'm not going to hurt him, silly. I'm going to make him better."

"What do you mean *better*?" I asked. I was so helpless tied to this chair! Concentrate! I was almost starting to sense the black swirling holes on the hillside. Concentrate. Concentrate.

"Oh simple, really." Elisha smiled and leaned in to my face. "I'm going to erase all his memories of you."

Um.

Could she do that?

"No," I said and I could hear the shake in my voice.

Elisha smiled. "Aaww, does that upset you?"

Unbidden tears started to flow down my cheeks. Ryan wouldn't even know who I was. He wouldn't know I loved him. And he wouldn't know he loved me. We'd be strangers. It was worse than death. To have his mind stripped of everything we had been through...

I couldn't even speak.

Elisha smiled triumphantly. "Give me that memory and I'll let him keep his."

And even though the thought of Ryan never knowing who I was or how we felt was excruciating, I knew I could never let Elisha see the spell that would give her my power.

"No." I said it with as much confidence and attitude as I could muster. "Never going to happen." I followed it up.

Elisha was so angry she even screamed a little, which inspired Roland to step forward and slap me.

Elisha put her hand up to stop him and steadied herself, her eyes alight with rage. "I'm going to wipe his brain anyway, just to spite you. And in the end it won't matter anyway because I'll break down Roberta's magic bubble and see that memory. You saying 'no' to me will all be for nothing."

Elisha motioned to Roland. He started to untie me.

Huh? Was she letting me go?

Elisha's expression was amused. "There's one torture I don't think you've experienced yet." Elisha hit a button on the console.

Frank and another guard walked in carrying a large metal box about six feet long and three feet wide. It looked an awful lot like…

Oh crap.

A coffin.

Elisha laughed as she saw the recognition in my eyes.

She turned to Frank with a smile. "Bury her."

I felt a small prick in the back of my neck and I could barely focus enough to see Roland pulling away a needle. The last thing I remember seeing were Ryan's eyes, fully aware, looking at me with desperation.

Ryan…

Then everything went black.

CHAPTER 5
SATURDAY DECEMBER 4, 2320

"Don't panic," Roberta's voice called out in the darkness of my dreams.

Panic about what? I couldn't seem to open my eyes. I was in that comforting half-sleep mode where I didn't want to wake up yet, and no matter how hard I tried, I couldn't quite think clearly. My head started to hurt and wait a minute…

…Why was I lying on the ground?

I opened my eyes.

It wasn't ground. It was metal.

A metal coffin.

Short quick gasps. That was all I could get into my lungs. It wasn't enough. My head started spinning. It felt like I stood up too fast, but I was lying down. Breathe. Breathe. I couldn't. I couldn't!

I flailed my arms in the darkness only to hit the coffin's metal roof and walls. I kicked my legs only to smash my knees on the ceiling. I tried to sit up only to whack my head.

Breathe. Breathe. Breathe.

No air was reaching my lungs.

I...
I...
I...
Blackness.

***

"I told you not to panic," Roberta's voice cut through the darkness again.

All of a sudden an oak forest materialized around me. It was the oak forest near my trailer park. One of the places I would go to read a book or just be by myself. I was instantly calm as I looked down at my hands and legs and stretched them in the crisp autumn air.

Roberta appeared in front of me. At least it looked like Roberta. Roberta of the past before all her surgeries and injections. She was actually quite beautiful. Like a pretty version of my father. Her black hair was pulled back in a loose ponytail and her midnight color eyes didn't hold the same kind of cruelty they normally did. It was strange and comforting seeing Roberta like this. Like a human being.

"I'm taking this form to keep your heart rate down, and besides..." Roberta primped herself, "This is how I looked when I was young and beautiful. If I could look like *this* forever..." Her eyes stared off in to the distance, sad. Then she re-focused back on me. "Never mind all that. Now, I know you hate me, but I'm going to get you through this. Do you understand?"

Through what? I was in my old oak forest. This was great. Why would I want to leave here? "What do you mean?" I asked.

"Oh boy." Roberta walked over and studied my face for a moment. "Denial, I see." She sighed. "Well, it's better this than putting yourself into a coma. It's a start."

Huh?

"But I'm home," I stated in confusion. What was she talking about, *denial?*

Wait.

How did I get here?

I wasn't really here.

It came back to me in a flood.

Tied up. Ryan's eyes. Metal coffin.

Buried alive.

I started to hyperventilate.

"Okay. Calm down." Roberta placed her hand on my back. I shrugged her away.

The last thing I wanted was comfort from the woman who killed my mother, and laughed at me when I was in pain, and…

"Get away from me," I practically snarled.

Roberta stepped back. "Your basic instincts are kicking in. You could tolerate me before because you thought you were safe. Now that you realize you're locked in a box… well… Despite what you might think, I'm here to help you."

No. "I said get away from me!" I screamed.

***

My eyes opened.

Blackness. Metal walls. No air.

My heart raced. Too fast. Too fast.

No air. No air!

Can't breathe!

I screamed and screamed until my voice was cracked and hoarse.

I felt like I had ants crawling in every part of my body and that my brain was going to explode.

Why? Why? Why?

Breathe. Breathe.

I can't. I can't… get… enough… air!

I cried and gasped at the same time.

Mom…

Dizziness.

I was going to pass out again.

Good.

No air…

***

"You really need to get a grip on yourself." Roberta was in front of me and we were back in the oak forest, and she was her young, beautiful self. I hated to admit the fact that I found having *anyone* there comforting. I wished it was Ryan, or Nancy, or let's face it Jill would be better than psycho Grams, but, even knowing that Roberta and my surroundings weren't real, it calmed me down immensely. I never thought I'd be grateful for the whole astral projection thingy.

"I'm going to run out of air, aren't I?" I said, trying not to go to pieces.

"No. Elisha fitted the coffin with an oxygen tank and a feeding tube. You could stay down here for months." Roberta's voice was calm and collected. I could tell she was trying to keep me from a full-blown nervous breakdown, even in my unconsciousness, and I grudgingly appreciated it. "When you wake up the next time, try to figure out everything you can about where you are. Geoffrey put a tracer on your shoulder at the school assembly, but we can't find you anywhere on our radar."

"Maybe Elisha found it and destroyed it," I suggested, not knowing why I wasn't screaming at her for Gramps planting a tracking device on me. I knew why. Because it was my only hope at being found at this moment and the grandparents actually seemed like they were trying to save me. Wonders never ceased.

Roberta shook her head. "This device is undetectable: it crawls into the skin and attaches itself to blood cells. Elisha would have had to dissect you to find it."

"Are you joking?" I said a little too sharply. "I have a tracking device in my blood?!" I was angry now.

"Calm down. It was for your own good. We needed to keep an eye on you and apparently, we were right to do so." Roberta crossed her arms for emphasis.

I lay back on the ground in exasperation. "So what would cause your device to malfunction?"

Roberta was quiet. She looked nervous.

"What? Is it bad?" I asked, sitting up with a surge of dread rising up to my throat.

"You need to relax." Roberta sat crosslegged in front of me.

I took her advice and tried to slow down my heart rate. "Just tell me."

"I'm going to tell you, but you have to promise not to be alarmed.

Can you do that?" Roberta talked to me like I was a bomb about to go off.

"Yes! Tell me!" My patience was gone.

Roberta took a deep breath. "The only way we wouldn't be able to read the location of the tracer would be if it were too far away to track."

"What does that mean? I'm not in Havenville anymore? I'm in another country or something?" I was trying not to freak, but failing miserably.

"No, we'd be able to track you anywhere in the world. We just can't track *down*." Roberta looked at me like I was supposed to guess the rest.

"Down?" Where was she going with this… "Oh, down."

Roberta nodded her head slowly. "Elisha has buried you so deep, we can't find you."

I stood up and started pacing.

Oh man. Oh man.

Roberta was up next to me in milliseconds. "It's far worse for you to panic while you're unconscious. I debated whether or not even visiting you, but when we couldn't find you with the device, I knew I had to. But, Chelsan, listen to me." Roberta grabbed my shoulders and made me look directly into her midnight colored eyes. "In your unconscious state your body is calm and rested. If you keep your heart rate pumping this fast for too long, it could cause you to have a heart attack. I need you to wake up and figure out where you are."

I nodded, trying to breathe, knowing that whatever I was doing here in my head, I was doing to my body. "Okay." Deep breath. "I'll try and find something dead to help me." Deep breath. "Okay." Deep breath. "I think I'm good."

Roberta's face didn't seem to agree as she let go of my shoulders. "Chelsan, I think the metal she buried you in contains a compound that prevents you from connecting to the dead."

"What?" Oh man. That stupid crap!

"It's not that bad." Roberta tried to sound soothing. "You've been able to break through it before. It's the same ingredient we inject into our corpses so people like you can't take over their bodies."

"But I do take over your bodies."

Roberta actually smiled, and, seeing her without her frozen stretched features, it was actually the first *normal* moment of our insane relationship. "Yes, you do. Which is why I know, if you concentrate hard enough, you'll be able to break through past the coffin to help yourself. Elisha will have put a high concentration of the compound in the metal to prevent that from happening, but at this point it's your only hope of escaping. We'll continue our search for your tracer, but…" Roberta let the sentence hang and for the first time I felt something other than loathing hatred for her. And, frankly, I was too scared to feel guilty about it. She was really trying to save me and not kill me. It was kind of nice as messed up as that sounded.

"What exactly *is* this compound?" I decided I'd ask.

"Do you really want the details? I promise you won't know what I'm talking about." Roberta didn't come across as patronizing. She honestly believed it was something way over my head.

"Try me," I answered. Even if I didn't know what she was talking about, I could tell Ryan and he most definitely would.

Ryan.

He was conscious and aware, strapped into Elisha's brain contraption.

Unless I was imagining it.

I honestly didn't know for sure.

But it helped me to believe Ryan was fighting Elisha. And I hoped her attempt to erase his mind of all our memories together would fail.

"It's a form of anti-matter," Roberta's voice cut through my thoughts. "I really don't know the science of it. I've always been a bit more of a black arts kind of girl myself if you haven't noticed." Before I could respond to that, Roberta said, "Your powers are a mixture of both…"

***

SPLASH!

I was startled awake by the liquid slop pouring on my face. It made me choke uncontrollably not to mention the parts of slop that actually entered my mouth were disgusting. Like liquefied wheat barley. Not that I'd had a lot of wheat barley in my life, but… Yeah, gross. I moved my head out of the way as the rest of the liquid food splattered to the bottom of the coffin. In the darkness I could hear it draining into the ground below.

Listening, I was calm enough to hear the hissing of the oxygen tank

Roberta had told me was there.

Okay. I wouldn't run out of air or food. That was something.

But the darkness.

The enclosed space.

Breathe.

It was really hard to.

No matter how much my brain was telling me to calm down, my body just wouldn't listen. I could already feel my heart pounding in my chest and my palms sweated.

If I could just see!

I reached up to feel how tall the metal box was and to my surprise it was higher than I expected. At least two feet. Enough so that I could sit crosslegged with my back hunched over, which I did immediately. Somehow sitting made me feel slightly better. I felt around for the feeding tube opening: it was a few inches from the front edge of the box. I made a complete inspection of my coffin with my hands, confirming that the only openings in the box were for the oxygen, food and drainage.

I decided to take Roberta's advice to try and sense anything dead outside the box. I concentrated as hard as I could, but whatever this *anti-matter* was, it was doing its job pretty well. I guess we were right when we thought that whatever protected the corpses' black holes was the same stuff in the metal at Brady's place. Small comfort, but still, it was good to know from Grams that it was a singular ingredient. It gave me hope that I would be able to break through it and get out of wherever I was buried.

Regardless of how I felt about my grandparents, for whatever reason, they wanted me to escape, of that I was certain. And even if their motivations were evil, (of which I assumed was the case) their advice would probably be sound.

So.

Black swirling holes.

Where are you?

I decided to lie back down, to really focus.

But once I was on my back, my stomach felt like it was on fire. I sat up too fast and hit my head on the ceiling. I flipped myself over so I was on all fours. I was going to vomit, I could feel it. And at this point, I felt like it would have been a relief. My nerves were getting to me and my body was losing control of itself. I needed to calm down, but the fear was just too strong to ignore.

I was buried in a metal box underground.

I couldn't see.

I couldn't do ANYTHING!

Tears streamed down my face and I felt like I was going to lose my mind.

I pounded my fists on the ground and screamed as loud as I could.

I started to cry uncontrollably again.

No matter how hard I tried I just couldn't seem to keep it together.

Maybe because I was buried alive!

Breathe.

I had to break through this metal. I'd make bugs work. Or maybe I could figure out where I was based on what was around me. Then Gramps could find me. And…

And… Kill me?

What was I thinking?

Did I really think Turner would save me?

After everything?

Yes.

I couldn't explain it, but I knew he would.

Maybe it was desperation.

At this point I didn't care. It was something.

It wasn't that I didn't have faith in Nancy, Jason and Bill to find me, it was that I knew they didn't have the resources Turner did. Maybe Jason got in contact with Turner. Maybe Roberta told them I was buried alive. Nancy and Bill wouldn't be able to rest until they rescued me. For better or worse it was the truth.

And Ryan.

If he even remembered me. He wouldn't let me rot down here.

I had plenty of highly intelligent people trying to rescue me. I just needed to calm down and get them the information they needed to find me. I just wished that Nancy could do the whole astral projection thing. It would be so much more reassuring to visit her in my unconsciousness instead of Roberta. Though Roberta was definitely on her best behavior and her best appearance, it was still hard to be civil to her after what she did to my mother. I couldn't think about that. It wasn't helping me.

Then I thought about what Roberta had said just before I was awoken by slop. *Your powers are a mixture of both...* Science and black magic. She definitely knew more about my gift than I originally thought. I wanted to ask Roberta a slew of questions, but for the time being that would have to wait.

Okay.

Calmer now.

Breathe.

So what if it was dark?

So what if I was miles underground?

Panic. Panic.

Breathe.

Start with dark.

Darkness was okay.

Oxygen flowing.

Gross slop food aplenty.

Calm.

Good.

Okay, now think.

Elisha was keeping me here for a while (at least she hoped so). Until I let her into the memory of my father's death. Not going to happen. Okay. So. Escape.

I closed my eyes.

Now, first things first. I'd defeated whatever this *anti-matter compound* was before, just in smaller doses. Good. So I needed to tap into the same jolt I felt when I broke through Turner's corpses. It was hard to figure out the exact reason I moved past the barrier, I really didn't even know what I was doing. Ever since I did it the first time, my brain seemed to remember the sensation of slamming through a wall, and I'd been able to do it ever since. But why? Or more importantly, how?

I tried recreating the sensation I'd feel when I'd broken through the corpse's protective barrier.

...Something...

A thrill of excitement coursed through me. I definitely felt something. Of course, my excitement completely threw me out of concentration mode, but it gave me hope. And that was what I needed at the moment.

I tried a second time.

SLAM!

***

"Not going to happen, little one," Elisha said in the darkness.

Great.

I had lost consciousness again.

I was in my head.

In the *other* darkness.

Colors swirled around me like mixing taffy until I was standing in a grass field on a sunny day. Elisha stood in front of me, her expression only slightly amused. The sunlight, fake as it might be, hurt my eyes from the suddenness of the exposure. I was amazed I wasn't completely insane from the constant visits from Elisha and Roberta, mixed in with… I don't know…

…BEING BURIED ALIVE!

I'd say I was doing pretty well as far as the sanity department went. I just wished Elisha was really in front of me so I could strangle her.

"Get out!" I screamed, trying to repeat my previous performance of kicking Elisha out of my brain.

Elisha crossed her arms. "You caught me off guard before, but I won't be pushed out a second time. I've been using astral projection for fifty years, what have you got? Two months? You can't stop me, Chelsan, so just let me see the memory."

"She can't stop you, but *I* can." Roberta suddenly appeared behind Elisha.

Elisha's face went from triumphant smirk to real fear in about a millisecond. She tried to leap away from Roberta, but Roberta grabbed Elisha's seven-year-old neck from behind and held her up like a mamma cat holds her young.

"You'll be leaving us now," Roberta's voice was fierce and commanding, and I was extremely relieved she wasn't talking to me this time.

Elisha's violet eyes went wide as Grams squeezed her neck so hard that she literally popped Elisha's head off like a dandelion.

Elisha's body disappeared entirely and Roberta and I were plunged into darkness.

"Hang on," Roberta spoke calmly. Almost instantly we were back in the oak forest. "Better?"

"Better," I said, still reeling at what just happened. "Is she…"

"Dead?" Grams finished my thought and I nodded. "No, I'm afraid not, just booted."

Roberta was in her younger form, which I was growing used to. I never wanted to see her again in person since her Feline form was so terrifying. It was almost as if the woman standing before me was an entirely different person from the killer I knew. I could almost pretend… almost.

"I'll get you out, I promise." Roberta tried to comfort me.

"I was close to breaking through the metal, wasn't I? That's why she rendered me unconscious." I mused out loud, my brain back on escaping.

Roberta smiled and sat down on the ground, motioning me to sit as well. "You might as well make yourself comfortable. She really did a number on your brain. You won't wake up for hours."

I sat down across from Roberta and decided to enjoy the feeling of being outdoors in my favorite forest. I was fully aware it wasn't real, but it felt real, and that was all that mattered at the moment. "I could almost sense something…"

"Oh yes. The next time you regain consciousness you will be able to work your powers." Roberta's eyes were actually glowing with… pride? "You almost had it, just a few more minutes and nothing would have been able to stop you. Very good."

I kind of half-smiled back, still unsure how nice I wanted to be to Roberta. "And as soon as I came close, Elisha felt like she needed to jump in. That tells me there's something in my powers I can use to escape. Maybe she buried me in the graveyard?" I was thinking aloud, more for myself than for any kind of pow wow with Grams, but she *did* just kick Elisha's ass, so maybe hearing her opinion might be a good thing.

Roberta nodded. "Maybe. Or maybe something else. Hold on, I'm telling Geoffrey and your friends now that you may be in the graveyard and to use the tracking surveyors to search there first."

My heart leapt and squeezed at the same time. Friends: yay! Working with Turner: terror. "He didn't kill Jill, did he?" I didn't want to ask it, but I had to.

Roberta looked at me like I was insane. "Of course not. They figured out your little message and contacted us. We have a temporary truce until we can recover you safely."

"Don't look at me like I'm crazy for asking. You said you were going to kill her, and you didn't seem all that apt to changing your mind about it." Then I leaned forward with as much threat and menace as I could muster. "If you lay one hand on *any* of my friends, I swear I will take you down or die trying."

Roberta groaned as if dealing with an annoying fly. "Yes, yes. Threaten away. Are you quite done?"

I didn't know how to answer that because I just couldn't seem to shake the feeling that I was playing with evil. "Yeah, I guess," I said. Oooo, very menacing. Then I smelled something horrible. "What's that smell?"

***

I awoke to the horrendous smell of ammonia.

Guess Elisha didn't want me talking to Grams.

I stuck my nose up to the oxygen release valve, trying to clear my nostrils of the awful smell. I quickly realized that Elisha was pumping the ammonia smell through the same tube so I ended up with an extra dose of it, making me queasy beyond words.

Maybe this was my chance. While Elisha was off guard. I needed to see if I could use my powers and get out of there!

I took a deep disgusting breath and tried to see past the metal walls of my coffin.

Nothing.

Really?

I tried again, recreating the feeling I had before.

Nothing. Not even a *something*.

I guess Roberta's faith in me was seriously misplaced. It took me a moment to realize that disappointing her actually upset me. I grunted in frustration which then turned into a full-out scream.

I was seriously going crazy.

I had no concept of time or space or anything. The ammonia smell had at least dissipated which cleared my head a little, but my brain felt like it was about to explode.

"I'm sending food down. This time I expect you to eat it," Elisha's voice came out of some kind of speaker.

And as evil as the girl was, and being fully aware of the fact that Elisha was the one who put me down here, just having a voice say *anything* was a small comfort.

This time I could hear the slop making its way down the long tube. As gross as it was, I cupped my hands and tried to catch as much of the food as I could. I was starving and even crappy food was something. The chunky mixture plunked into my hands and I almost gagged from the sensation. I never thought I'd prefer Brady's intravenous feeding method: it was far less smelly and messy. I ate everything I caught in my hands and tried not to throw it all back up. It was beyond disgusting. I had no idea what the chunks were made of and I really didn't want to. It stopped my stomach from growling and that was enough for me.

"Sooner or later, your grandmother won't be there to protect you and you're going to have to let me into your memories again," Elisha's voice sounded like she was scolding a misbehaved dog. "You can't escape. Only I can let you out," she said it with such confidence, I almost lost hope. "Even if you could get past the metal barrier to use your powers, there's nothing dead around you for ten miles. I made sure of that."

A dead zone.

That was something.

Something I could tell Roberta and my friends to help find me.

But also…

Lame.

There were probably thousands of dead zones all over the world. Elisha could have me buried anywhere!

Maybe, like Turner, Elisha forgot about dead plants, or trees. I could make dead tree roots lift me straight to the surface. I needed to ignore her and just focus on breaking through the barrier first. Then I'd figure out what to do.

Or truthfully what I *could* do. If I could do anything at all.

"No dead roots or anything like that either," Elisha said with what I could imagine was a smirk. "I may not be able to get inside your head at the moment, but I know how you think. And I want you to know that you have *nothing* to connect to."

Of course she knew about me being able to connect to dead plants and roots. Not only was she on a Chelsan-brain-jamboree for the last couple of days, but Elisha knew more about my powers than I did, from the prison break and boiling that corpse's blood, to making me connect to the teeniest, tiniest dead particle that released us from the giant electromagnet.

I had been so distracted by everything that had been happening that I forgot about the magnet. Elisha had said I *reversed the polarity*. Whatever that meant. Roberta said my power was a combination of science and black magic.

Did that mean I was connecting to atoms?

And did that mean they were dead?

I didn't know enough about science to know if that was even possible, but my gut told me it was something like that. Something Ryan would know. My eyes welled up with frustration. Ryan was living his worst nightmare and everything I thought of was completely a guess. I was so helpless.

"Why are you holding onto this memory so tightly?" she asked. "I'm not taking your power away from you, I just want the spell to have the power myself. Did you ever wonder *why* your grandparents don't want me to see it? It's not to protect you: it's to stop me. They don't care about you, Chelsan: they're just protecting their own power and interests. The sooner you accept that the better." Elisha's voice was as genuine as she was capable of.

A part of her argument made sense. Why was I keeping this memory from her? What did I care if Elisha had my powers? Like she said, I wouldn't be losing my own powers, (though sometimes I wished I could get rid of them and live a normal life) I just wanted out of here! It would be so simple. Just let Elisha in and let her see that memory, then she'd let me go and I could be free.

What was I saying? There was no guarantee that she'd let me go. Why would she? She could find out the spell and leave me here to die.

Stop the oxygen.

Stop the feeding tubes.

I started hyperventilating again.

Breathe.

I screamed in the darkness.

The only sound: a hissing from the oxygen tank.

Elisha was a nut job. And nut jobs with powers equaled dangerous. Look at my grandparents. Elisha couldn't have my memory. It would mean I'd die, of that I was certain.

I wasn't ready to die just yet.

"Um... No." I wasn't sure if Elisha could even hear me, so I felt stupid talking to a speaker.

"I see," she responded.

Okay. She definitely could hear me. Good to know.

"You can't hurt me," I said with a confidence I wasn't feeling.

"Well, let's see how you like it without any oxygen," Elisha sighed with resignation.

The hissing stopped.

"You can't kill me! You'll never get the memory!" I screamed desperately.

"I'm not going to kill you. I'm going to break you." She paused letting that little gem sink in. "You'll do your part. Eventually everyone does what I tell them, even if they don't realize it," Elisha's voice echoed in the darkness.

The air was thin.

I started to gasp.

Running out...

No.

I probably had hours of time left. I was just freaking out.

I tried to breathe.

I tried to calm down.

But the more I thought about calming down, the faster my heart raced.

She can't win.

My breathing was short.

I couldn't get enough air.

In the blackness…

I couldn't tell if I was seeing a swirling black hole forming in my chest. Was I dying? Elisha said she wasn't going to kill me. Maybe she didn't know that the lack of air this far down would kill me? Maybe there was some sort of carbon monoxide air pocket in the earth and I was being poisoned? Maybe…

My brain couldn't stop racing around in circles.

Breathe.

Can't.

***

"The air is back on, in case you're wondering." Young Roberta sat across from me in the oak forest.

I was lying on the ground staring up at the low winding branches and the thousands of multi-pointed leaves above me. Even though I knew it was impossible, I actually felt groggy. I slowly sat up and faced my grandmother.

"I'm exhausted," I admitted. "And I'm starving." My stomach was growling like crazy, even through my unconsciousness I could feel it. I groaned. "How can I be hungry? I just ate a ton of that slop crap."

"That was two days ago," Roberta told me cautiously.

I was alert now. "Two days?!"

Roberta took a deep exaggerated breath. "Breathe."

I followed her advice and it made me feel a little better.

"Your body and mind must have needed the rest. I've been keeping a protective barrier around you so Elisha couldn't get her grubby paws in here."

I started to cry. It was too much. Knowing I was underground in a steel box and now sitting across from Roberta, a woman I loathed, but at the same time I didn't. Seeing Roberta's feelings for me grow was too conflicting. Too overwhelming.

Roberta leaned forward and wrapped her arms around me.

I wanted to scream. To push her away. To kick her. To hit her.

But I just let her hold me. The hardest part about it was the fact that I knew she meant it. There wasn't any manipulation or ulterior motive.

My grandmother was holding me because I was in pain and she wanted to help.

No. No. No.

I pulled away. "I can't. Not with you," I said as I wiped away tears.

Roberta nodded, but there were tears in her eyes as well. "I understand, of course."

"I wasn't able to break through the barrier."

I needed to change the subject. I needed to calm down. I was also afraid of the disappointment I was sure to see in Roberta's eyes at my failure. I kicked myself for even caring, but it was instinctual, no matter how hard I pretended it wasn't.

To my surprise she didn't look disappointed at all. She simply raised her eyebrow in thought. "You're trying too hard. I need to help you relax… and I also need to teach you how to keep people out of your head, including me." She smiled at that end part.

"That sounds good." I smiled back. It was a start, and it was neutral. I needed to learn how to stop everyone from brain-knapping me.

"Now, one thing I've learned about you is that when your back is up against the wall, you tend to make your powers do what you want. We need you to accomplish that all on your own, *without* being threatened," Roberta coached.

She was right, though I didn't know why exactly. It seemed like I could do some pretty crazy things when I was running on instinct. Sure, I had always thought about learning how to control my power and the things I knew I was capable of, but I never seemed to have enough time to do it.

Apparently being buried alive was just the kind of time I needed. Ha, ha.

"If you break it down, it's all about thought. As strange as this may sound, you have to use your imagination for this to work. You have to physically see yourself building a wall around your brain. It can be that easy. That's what you're doing when you're tapping into your power. You're *seeing* what you want to happen and your power does the rest. I have to rely on spells and black magic to control the dead, but the astral projection I can do without them. Anyone can do it if they know how." Roberta sounded like Mr. Alaster giving one of his lectures, but this time

I was all ears. "Geoffrey opened your mind to astral projection when he visited you after the Brady incident."

"The *Brady incident*?" Roberta's casual reference to one of the most traumatic moments of my life brought me straight back to my anger towards my grandparents. "I wouldn't call hiring a serial killer to murder me an *incident*. And it was my mother who introduced me to the astral thingy, thank you very much, just before you had your men exterminate her!" I fumed.

"Calm down," Roberta scolded. "Things are different now. We wouldn't send you to… well… to someone like Brady, again. And, I'm pleased to hear your mother taught you some things before she passed. It made you stronger."

"I'm completely reassured." I hoped I said that with as much sarcasm as I felt. "And *never* talk about my mother again."

"My point being that once Geoffrey or *your mother* entered into your mind, your natural instinct was to do it yourself. The very next night after Geoffrey visited you, you traveled into my memories. Let me tell you: *no one* has ever been able to do that. Elisha is the most powerful astral projectionist I've ever know and she's *never* been able to break down my defenses." Roberta actually smiled at me as if she was proud. "But *you*, a complete novice, jumped right past my barriers and straight into my memories."

"I really don't know how I did that," I admitted honestly.

"Because you are a remarkable young woman." Roberta smiled at me.

What was going on?

She was looking at me like… well… like a grandmother looks at their granddaughter. I was used to the Murderess-Death-Stare she usually gave me. This was freaking me out a little too much.

"I, seriously, can't do this," I said and stood up. "Why are you being so nice to me? It's repulsive."

Roberta stood up as well, her expression serious. "I know I've been horrible to you." She stopped herself and I could see that even she knew how much of an understatement that was. "More than horrible. I was evil. I blamed you and your mother for Franklin's death and I wanted you to suffer for it. I wanted you dead."

Roberta took a moment to gather herself, then continued, "When you miscarry as many times as I have and then you finally have a healthy child, it does something to you. It makes your mothering instincts distortedly strong. We killed your mother because we trusted her and she betrayed us. She put my son in far more danger than even she knew. Did you ever think there was a reason why we kept your father a child? Did you honestly believe it was because we were deranged lunatics that wanted to torture our only child?" She took a step closer to me. "Everything that Geoffrey and I do is for the greater good, I promise you that."

"Killing my mom was for the *greater good*? Trying to kill me a bagillion times was for the *greater good*? We obviously have very different views of what's good and what isn't." I crossed my arms defensively. I didn't like hearing her speak, it was making my skin crawl. I didn't want to know the reasoning behind every evil that she'd done. I just wanted to hate her.

"I admit, killing your mother was pure vengeance. But trying to kill you *was* for the greater good…" Roberta started.

"No. I don't want to hear anymore," I interrupted.

Roberta placed her hands on my arms forcing eye contact. "You have to. Chelsan, this is very important. We tried to kill you because…" She couldn't seem to continue.

After a moment she exhaled deeply, "Chelsan, the reason why I've been keeping Elisha away from that memory isn't because I'm afraid she'll see the spell that gave you your power." She paused again.

"What do you mean?" My curiosity was overpowering my anger and hatred. This whole time Elisha has been after the spell to give her powers like mine. What was more dangerous than psycho girl being able to control the dead? "If it's not to hide the spell that gave me my power, then what is it?"

Roberta calmed herself. "Chelsan, there was a second spell. Franklin's first spell gave you and your mother life, but the second didn't give you your power: it *transferred* Franklin's power *to* you."

Whoa.

My mind froze and went into overdrive all at once.

My dad had my powers?

A lot of things started to make more sense in the deep recesses of my subconscious. Things I hadn't thought about or even recognized before. All those times when Turner seemed so surprised at what I could do with my powers. All those times when he seemed to know so much more about my powers than I did. When he said there are others like me and he wasn't intimidated.

"I can do things that Dad couldn't though. That's why Turner and you were always so shocked when I did something new with my powers." I couldn't stop staring into Roberta's midnight colored eyes.

Her smile was small. "It meant either Franklin didn't tell us everything or he didn't know how far he could take his gift. Either way, it just made us hate you more. To see you alive with his gift, when he was dead. It was too much." She dropped her hands from my arms. "But that's all different now. You're all we have left of Franklin. And you're so much like him in so many ways: your spirit, your kindness, your insatiable gift for survival. You're *ours*."

I really didn't like the way she said that. Why did I get the feeling that my grandmother's obsession for her son was turning into an obsession for me? I couldn't figure out which was worse: evil psychopath grandma, or just insane stalker grandma? Both weren't looking so good right now.

"That still doesn't explain why you kept Dad a kid," I blurted out.

"To protect him. When we discovered what he could do, we knew the world would make him a human lab experiment. We told everyone that our child had died and we kept Franklin a secret from everyone. We learned so much from him, from his gifts…"

"Wait a second," I interrupted Roberta again. "You can do all your voodoo dead controlling thing because you turned *your own son* into a lab rabbit yourself. You didn't want 'the world' to have him because he was more valuable to you and your cause. You used him for your own gain." Tears welled up from my disgust. "You repulse me."

Roberta didn't even look offended, she just said calmly, "I know you see it that way, but we did do it for Franklin. To protect him."

"Yeah, right." I didn't want to give her an inch. I didn't want to give her a millimeter. I just wanted to punch her face. But I knew she wasn't really there. That it wouldn't do any good. "Stop making me see you all nice and pretty. I want to see you as your Feline self. I want to see the woman who tortured my mother's dead body!" My anger boiled to the surface and before my eyes, Roberta changed back to her stretched, frozen face.

That was her. The woman I hated. The woman I wanted dead!

And, to my surprise, she smiled. A grotesque, stiff smile. "*You* did that."

"Did what?!" I couldn't seem to calm down.

"You changed me back to this form, all on your own. You imagined it and it came to pass. *This* is how you can keep people out as well." Roberta seemed pleased by my progress.

And it was enough to make me pause. It really was that simple. I thought it, and it happened. I knew in that moment I could kick the all-powerful Roberta straight out of my head, but something held me back.

As much as I was angry and hated her, I found myself comforted by her as well. Maybe it was because I was buried alive and she was my only connection to reality. Or maybe a part of me wanted to believe she was sincere…

I sat down once more in an exhausted heap. "So, Elisha having access to my memory would allow her to steal my powers. Maybe she should just have them. I'm tired of all this." I lay back on the ground and stared at the twisting branches of the oak. I almost wanted to stay here forever. I could feel my brain starting to shut down. I didn't want to *feel* anymore at all. I just wanted to lie there and stare at the branches for all eternity.

"It's not that simple." Roberta sat down next to me. "Your father sliced himself with a knife to revive your mother, that was the first spell, but that's not what killed him. It was the second spell. When Franklin transferred his powers to you. That's what killed him. If Elisha performs the ritual, transferring your powers to herself, you would die."

That woke me up.

The oaks didn't seem all that interesting anymore.

Did Roberta just tell me that *I* killed my father?

My mind froze.

I started to cry.

Roberta was shocked. I could tell she didn't know what to do. She reached her hand forward to comfort me, but I shrugged her away.

"What is it, Chelsan?" Roberta really did seem clueless.

"You're saying *I* killed him, just so I could have this stupid gift!" I croaked out.

Roberta's frozen face actually moved. Her eyes flashed guilt, and I could see she genuinely felt for me. "No, Chelsan, I don't think your father knew what he was doing. He knew the spell would kill him, but I think he thought he was destroying the power forever. I don't believe he knew he'd transferred his gift to you. He wouldn't do that to his child, knowing what a burden it was for him. Dying was worth it to him to rid himself of his gift forever. He thought Geoffrey and I would leave you and your mother alone if he died. He knew about Bruce and he told your mother to find him. I don't think he ever wanted her to marry him, but your mother was a survivor, like you. She did what she had to do to keep you protected. If I hadn't been so crazed with anger, I might have admired that in her."

"Shut up!" I screamed. "I told you, you don't get to talk about my mother!" I stood up, angry.

Roberta was on her feet next to me in seconds. "Listen to me. Chelsan, listen to me."

I stood there trying to compose myself, but just ended up cry-breathing.

"You're missing the bigger picture, here. I'm letting go of the past and you need to also, or Elisha will win." Roberta's feline face was concentrated. "Do you understand?"

I nodded.

"Good. I need you to keep Elisha out of your head and we need to find you and get you as far away from her as possible. Now that I've told you everything, if she gets inside for long enough, she'll know the truth." Roberta was talking to me like I was a mental patient (which I felt like I *was* at the moment).

I took a few moments to breathe and it calmed me down. I knew I needed to keep it together, but Roberta throwing me these zingers wasn't helping. But she was right, I needed to push away my hatred of my grandparents. At least until I could escape. Assuming I would escape.

And Ryan.

I still had to save Ryan.

I sat back down and Roberta joined me. "Elisha thinks gaining my power is some sort of prophecy. She won't care about killing me."

"I know. The only reason why she's kept you alive this long is to see that memory. Once she has it, she'll perform the ritual and have no problems taking your life. She's never had that problem. She's murdered over twenty I.Q. Farm kids over the years," Roberta said it almost lazily, as if killing the I.Q. kids was normal.

"You and your little 'Farms' have turned innocent children into psychopaths. You know that, right? Don't you feel any guilt or responsibility?" I was upset by Roberta's relaxed tone about the subject.

Roberta's cat-like face actually laughed. "We didn't turn her into a psychopath. We picked Elisha because she already was one. A sociopath to be more precise. Geoffrey and I only take children with these tendencies. Once their high test scores have been flagged, we send observers. If a child shows any signs of sociopathic behavior, we take them to the Farm. Trust me, Chelsan, if we didn't take them, they would commit far worse crimes. We can at least use their intelligence for something useful to this world."

"But Ryan isn't a sociopath," I said and was suddenly very scared. Could he have fooled me this whole time? My experience with Brady was clouding my judgment.

"Oh, no. Ryan was a mistake. It happens from time to time. Did you really think Geoffrey would let an I.Q. kid go simply because he made up a fib? We took Ryan because his dog was missing. In most cases, the I.Q. kids start out by killing their pets. It's one of the first signs. About twenty minutes after Ryan arrived, Geoffrey got word that Ryan's dog had been found by a neighbor. When Ryan told Geoffrey his lie about cheating on his tests, Ryan's face was so earnest and sweet, Geoffrey knew he didn't belong at the Farm. I admit, I wanted to keep him. He reminded me so much of Franklin... It wasn't until Ryan solved Trilidon's theorem that we had any real regret about releasing him. We wouldn't have kept him in the Farm with the others, but we could have kept him ourselves," Roberta said with a far off look, then she realized how that last part would effect me and said, "But everything worked out, didn't it? What are the odds that you and Ryan would find each other? Everything happens for a reason."

I was fast learning that this was Roberta's way of backpedaling, but I really wasn't as upset as I thought I should be. I felt guilty for even having a pang of doubt about Ryan. Then Roberta's words sank in.

I.Q. Farms weren't a bunch of innocent kids that were taken from their families and strapped to machines for experiments.

They were potential serial killers.

Suddenly I didn't feel so guilty about how two months ago I didn't even think to help those kids escape the I.Q. Farm. My instincts must have warned me on a subconscious level. No wonder Elisha didn't want to take down the I.Q. Farms. She didn't want a bunch of psychopaths on the loose, or more probably she didn't want the world to know *she* was a psychopath.

Then it made me think of something. "Why wasn't Brady brought in as a child?"

Roberta answered, "Brady is the worst kind of psycho. The dumb kind. We allow a few hundred to live under our protection throughout the world." Her eyes pleaded for understanding. "This world will strangle itself if the population isn't kept to a certain amount. I know this is a bit overwhelming, but we are doing this to protect human survival."

I shook my head. "Those girls in Brady's backyard didn't deserve to die, and I saw the way you looked at the I.Q. Farm kids. You looked at them like they were your children. With love." Takes a sociopath to love a sociopath.

Roberta nodded not bothering to deny it. "Yes, I do love them. Geoffrey and I have made them better people. Their brilliance is responsible for almost every single advancement we've had in the last two hundred years. Keeping them at the age range of seven to ten allows their brains to calculate fifteen billion times faster than an adults. They're essential to the growth of technology and our survival. I admit it, I'm proud of them."

Gross. She actually believed what she was shoveling.

"What about the twins? Are they sociopaths as well?" I asked.

"They were the only survivors. Geoffrey and I kept them safe," Roberta admitted quietly.

She was being vague, and didn't really answer the question. "Well, when I connected to their swirling black brains, I almost went blind."

Roberta's eyes widened. "You did? Are you sure?"

I was a little taken aback by her intensity. "Yeah, it was nothing but white light."

Roberta stood up. "But you connected to them?"

I nodded.

"Chelsan, I have to go. You've been able to kick me out of your head since you made me look like *this*. You know that, right?"

I was surprised she knew that, but I nodded anyway.

"Good. Don't let Elisha in. She can't have access to the conversation we just had, or everything will be lost." She looked at me sincerely. "We'll find you, I promise, but I have to tell Geoffrey about what you did and saw."

"Wait. Why is connecting to them or seeing light important?" I asked desperately. As much pain as Grams was causing me, I didn't want to be alone again. In the dark. Underground. "Don't leave."

Roberta touched my cheek, and I let her. "I won't be gone long, but in the mean time, tell Elisha you're hungry and eat. And practice breaking past the metal. Maybe there's something you can still use. Something a dead zone has that Elisha isn't aware of. You've surprised us before." Roberta's pulled back face didn't look as monstrous as it normally did. "Time to wake up."

***

My eyes opened to darkness.

Back in the coffin.

And I really was starving.

"Food," my voice was gravelly and full of morning phlegm. I didn't even know if it was morning. I had no idea what time or day it was. I just knew that two days had gone by, and I was starving. I couldn't remember being this hungry. I almost didn't want to eat, the growling in my stomach was so painful it kept my mind off of the fact that I was in a metal box.

"You're awake," Elisha's voice sounded overly loud through the speakers.

"Food," was all I could say.

It took a few moments before I heard the sloshing of slop coming my way. I sat crosslegged and held my hands out. They were shaking. I wasn't in good shape. My head was cloudy, my body was weak, and I was freezing. I guess being in a metal box for two days wasn't good for your health.

The down pouring of sludge splashed into my cupped hands. As soon as they were full I ravaged every drop of the disgusting mixture. I even licked my fingers. I ate so fast I immediately wanted to throw-up, but I calmed myself enough to keep it down. The last thing I wanted was the smell of vomit in such tight quarters.

I could hear the last of the liquid drain out of the coffin into the dirt below. I stretched my legs and arms as much as I could in the small space. My body was cramped from the cold and the disuse.

I wanted to scream from frustration, but I knew it would make Elisha feel like she was winning. No. I needed to get out of here.

Now.

I lay back down on my back and closed my eyes to concentrate.

"What are you doing?" Elisha's voice broke the silence.

I debated whether or not to answer her and decided not to.

"Your grandmother may be able to keep me out, but she can't keep it up forever." Elisha had a sneer to her voice.

"She's not keeping you out, *I* am." I couldn't resist.

Elisha sounded so condescending I wanted her to know that I could protect myself against her. Of course, now that she knew the big guns weren't in my head anymore she might try to jump on in full throttle. I decided I needed to let her try. Otherwise I'd never know if I could really keep her out myself.

Whoa.

I almost smiled.

I could literally feel Elisha trying to butt back into my brain. It was a very strange sensation. Like a small wind trying to push through my skull. And I could recognize Elisha's stench like a signature. The more I pictured Elisha trying to nestle her way in, the easier it was to keep her out. The brick wall I imagined became stronger and stronger the harder she tried to weasel in.

I wanted to laugh. It felt so good to finally be in control of something. I didn't realize how being shut down here was not only killing me physically, but mentally as well. Roberta was right. I just needed to imagine the barrier and believe in its power. It was becoming easy to cut

Elisha out. So easy, I couldn't fathom not being able to do it before. I could even file it away knowing she'd never break in.

But, Elisha didn't need to know how easy it was.

I needed her to think I was using all my concentration on keeping her out so I could really focus on getting *me* out!

I made some grunting noises and a couple of gasps followed by some panting.

I could hear Elisha snicker through the speaker.

Good.

Now to really get down to business.

Okay, Roberta, let's put your advice to use.

I imagined seeing outside the metal of the coffin. As if it was made of glass. I tried to picture swirling black holes that were just waiting for me to control. All the while, I continued my grunting and guffawing.

"Just let me in," Elisha cooed through the speakers.

I rolled my eyes in the darkness. She was really getting on my nerves.

Glass. Glass. Glass.

See past the metal.

No blockage.

I repeated these things over and over in my mind.

And that's when I saw that same old *something* I saw before.

A thrilling sensation surged up my spine.

I was actually *doing* it.

Just a little more.

And even in the darkness, I saw it.

I could physically see this anti-matter that Roberta talked about. It was swimming in the walls of the metal like millions of tiny snakes. And I could see past them. They weren't solid. They never were. Just like Turner's corpses when push-came-to-shove I could see through the barrier and connect to their black spinning chasms.

So that was what I did.

I looked through the slithering material, and it *worked!*

I could see past the metal.

It was like looking through a glass wall with opaque maggots crawling on its surface.

Eeww.

I searched for anything dead.

Anything.

This really was a dead zone, and by dead zone I mean nothing in it was actually dead. Live zone was more like it.

Then I saw that *something*. It was much clearer now that I could see past the metal. It was right at the border of my four-mile radius, so it was a bit hard to distinguish. (Although I was seriously impressed with myself that I'd even sensed it before!) What was it?

There were two swirling black holes. I was sure of it. But what were they? Dead bodies? Animals? Plants? I couldn't tell. They were just two spinning holes and I couldn't sense anything else about them.

Maybe if I could make whatever they were move, then I might have a better sense of what was rotting four miles away and see if it could help me in the least.

For Elisha's listening ears, I made another grunting sound.

"No oxygen for you," Elisha's voice was irritated. She still hadn't entered my brain, so she was starting to get the hint that I might be up to something. At least that was how I rationalized her taking away the oxygen.

I tried not to get flustered.

She wouldn't let me die, I knew that from before, but I also didn't want to pass out for another two days. Not before I figured out what those two dead things were.

The hissing of oxygen stopped and I connected to the black spinning holes.

FLASH!

Bright white light nearly blinded me.

I disconnected immediately.

The twins.

They were buried alive, too.

Elisha knew my grandparents wouldn't be able to find them, so she stuck them in…

…wait a minute.

They were in a metal box like mine. I could see the swimming wormy anti-matter in their coffin walls.

My heart went out for John and Samuel. I could imagine their blind eyes staring in the darkness while the two of them held hands. Okay. They still creeped me out a bit. And Roberta's vagueness on whether or not they were sociopaths put me on edge, too, but I decided I wouldn't judge until the three of us escaped.

I needed to use them to help us, but how? Why did I see light when I connected to them? Was that why they were blind? What did it mean? I needed to think. They had to be powerful, otherwise Turner and Elisha wouldn't covet them like they did. And Elisha must have thought she buried them out of my radius since it was so close to the four-mile marker, which meant she was afraid of me connecting to them.

Light.

And my mind immediately went to the hover-van, when Elisha had me connect to the tiny dead particles. All I saw was black. Utter black. Void black. So maybe…

John and Samuel were the opposite?

But what did that mean?

What did that mean?! If that was true, it would mean they could connect to anything alive!

I was frozen with fear.

The implications were terrifying.

Before I let my brain fry with worry, I decided to test out my theory first. No sense freaking out for nothing. But my gut told me I was right. And the reason they had black swirling heads was because Turner needed to control them. He had probably found a way to kill something around the brain so he could keep them under his power.

Stop.

I needed to try and connect to them again.

Without going blind.

The air grew more and more stuffy by the minute, but I tried to push that out of my thoughts.

"Eating every two days isn't good for anyone." Elisha's voice was laced with amusement.

I guess she knew exactly how much oxygen to deprive me of to keep me out cold for forty-eight hours. I wouldn't even dignify Elisha with a verbal response. I needed all the air I could get. I took small breaths to conserve what little air I had left.

I closed my eyes and connected to the boys.

The light was so intense I almost pulled out instantaneously, but I searched for any darker space. I found some immediately. It was the outer edge of their brains, like a shadowed film surrounding the entire surface. As soon as I made my target the outer edge, everything came into focus.

I was in *over-exposed* land. Everything was so bright that the details faded into the light.

I was in one of their memories.

The boys stood in the basement of some kind of house. There were other children around, though it was difficult to make out their faces since the light was so blinding. The silhouette of a man walked down the stairs to join the children. All the kids ran up to him like he was their father.

Except for John and Samuel.

They just held each other's hands and kept their distance.

The man was the only dark thing in the basement. My skin was chilled when I looked at him. He was like Brady, I knew it instantly.

"He was our first owner," John said as the two of them stared at the man.

I noticed that the two of them weren't blind in here. I guess that was how they kept sane and connected. Just the fact that they were always together, even in astral projection land, was serious mojo. Or serious brain connection.

"Who is he?" I asked.

"Larotte Fielding. He made us like this," Samuel answered, though if I hadn't been staring at them I wouldn't have been able to tell which one said it, since the two of them sounded exactly the same.

Larotte Fielding. The founder of I.Q. Farms. Jason had told us how Fielding started taking kids and experimenting on them in his basement. He was arrested in 2133 and supposedly all the children were returned home. Apparently, there were two exceptions.

I knew we were in Fielding's basement, but why?

"Why stay *here*?" I asked. "Isn't there somewhere else you'd like to be? Like *anywhere*?"

John and Samuel both looked at me directly and I stepped back from the creepiness of it. I was instantly ashamed, because I could see the fear and sadness pouring out of their eyes.

"This is the only place we can remember," John answered quietly.

Oh man.

"When he made us discover our powers, we went blind," Samuel said. He seemed the braver of the two. "We don't remember anything before the basement."

"But what about Turner and Roberta? Don't they let you see things?" I asked with a slight hope that these boys would paint a nicer picture of my grandparents.

"No," they said in unison.

"We have been in the metal room since we were brought there," Samuel said.

Of course. Why should I have thought any different?

"Geoffrey deadened the cells surrounding our brains so we couldn't kill anymore," John spoke with such a deadpan voice it made my skin crawl.

"We like to kill," Samuel offered with little emotion.

Wait. Fantastic. Roberta's vagueness equaled crazy-ass-twin-freaks!

But her words were as clear as a bell. They picked sociopaths for the I.Q. Farms. Why *would* these two boys be any different? I was stupid to think there was a chance they were actually sane.

"What exactly is your power?" I decided to keep them thinking I was their friend and hoped they wouldn't try and kill me.

"We connect to everything that has life," John stated.

"Down to atoms," Samuel finished with almost a smile.

"We can't get past the metal barriers, though." John looked sad.

"Right when we discovered what our powers were, Geoffrey and Roberta collared us with the metal that stops us."

Go team grandparents.

"Did you ever use your powers?" I asked, scared to hear their response.

"Oh yes, we killed Larotte and the other kids in the basement," John admitted with a proud grin.

"Just by a single thought," Samuel agreed.

"That's when Geoffrey came in with the collars," John said quietly. "We thought we'd killed Roberta, but she lived somehow."

"She's powerful," Samuel cooed.

"We don't know how she survived," John finished Samuel's thought.

"Geoffrey knew about Larotte the whole time and was watching," Samuel added.

"The metal and the dead cells keep us imprisoned." John stared at me like I was supposed to help him or something when I was never so grateful for my crazy grandfather in my life.

If they could kill with a single thought, and they could connect to atoms, they could destroy life as we know it in an instant.

I wondered suddenly if they had the same four-mile restriction that I did? I certainly hoped so for humanity's sake. If they were to get free…

Yet somehow Roberta survived their attack.

Probably through some kind of voodoo mojo, I couldn't be sure, but that was her usual modus operandi. I was never an advocate for killing, but I couldn't fathom why Turner would keep them alive. It was too dangerous! I never thought I'd even think such a thing, but these kids were the most dangerous human beings on the planet. Gramps probably thought his brain deadening thing and the metal room were enough to keep them safely contained. And he was right.

Until I broke them out.

Even Elisha buried them so deep that no one could find them. She wanted my power so she could use the twins. She could kill all her enemies in a single thought. Not even Turner tried that. (Or at least, I don't think he did. I just figured he would have tried to use them on me a couple of months ago.) No, I think Turner was as scared of these boys as I was, and for the first time in my life, I trusted his decisions pertaining to them. Maybe killing John and Samuel would unleash their power? Or, maybe he wanted to transfer their power to someone more stable? After all he was a power-hungry tyrant who wanted to dominate the world!

Wait a minute.

I could totally use the twins, and they couldn't do anything about it.

They couldn't get past the metal, but I could. And I could control their brains by controlling the dead brain cells.

"I'll get us out," I said and forced a smile. I still wanted them to believe I was on their side. "I'm going to have to use your powers though. You ready?" I tried to look as nice as possible.

The twins nodded vigorously.

"Okay. Here goes." I closed my eyes to shut myself out of their little basement setting.

I focused on the black swirls around their heads, separating myself from their astral connection. (The less I was in their brains the better.) And…

FLASH!

There was that bright light again.

I really didn't want to go blind, but I didn't want to be stuck underground either, since I was running out of time and air.

I sucked it up and tried to keep my eyes shielded.

Man. They were right. When I really concentrated on the details of the light, I realized that it was actually a billion tiny lights. Molecules? Atoms? No, they were too big.

Soil!

I was seeing dirt!

And it was alive!

If no one could find me to dig me out, then I'd dig myself out.

I concentrated on the dirt around my metal box and through the boys I connected to it like I connect to dead things. The weird part was, it felt *exactly* the same. I made the dirt push and pull the coffin up.

My body felt the movement of the box and I nearly lost my connection from the excitement.

"What's going on!" Elisha's voice crackled through the speakers. The movement of the coffin was causing the sound system to break.

The dirt was so bright, I knew I couldn't stay connected for much longer or I really would be blind. I made the dirt move me up as fast as I could. How far down was I?! Almost there! I could see the surface drawing closer because it was slightly darker. Not as much life in the air as in the ground, I guess. It was like a beacon to me. My heart leapt that I was finally going to be free.

In a dead zone.

What if Elisha was on her way?

Couldn't think about that.

Just needed to free myself.

I almost felt bad that I had zero intention of rescuing the boys, and there was nothing they could do about it. I was using them like everyone else had in their lives.

For their power.

And it was intoxicating.

To feel every atom of life...

I tried to see if they had the same four-mile restriction I did, but there was no way of telling. It was too bright. It felt like I was connecting to all of it. Everywhere. The light was so beautiful.

The box pushed out of the ground and I disconnected from the dirt. But I couldn't seem to disconnect from the boys. The light. Life. It felt so right.

"OUT!" Roberta's voice jolted my connection to the twins.

I was so focused on my connection and keeping Elisha out, Roberta had managed to sneak back inside my head.

I immediately disconnected from the boys.

What had I been thinking?

I could see the trails of light even in the darkness of the coffin. Was I blind? Did I stay connected to them too long? I was so ashamed I let their power engross me like that. If it hadn't been for Roberta!

I lay back down and used both my legs to kick open the lid.

I had to cover my eyes from the onslaught of sun that attacked my eyes. I wanted to cry and scream at the same time. Cry because I was free and scream because I was so angry at myself for losing control with the twins' powers.

I blinked my eyes really fast so I could adjust to the light. At least I wasn't blind.

"We've got your signal. We're on our way," Roberta's voice sounded in my head and despite the relieving news, I kicked her out.

No one in my head again without my permission.

That was a violation I never wanted to experience again.

My eyes slowly adjusted to the light, though I knew that after two days confined in darkness it was going to take longer than a few minutes for my sight to be normal again.

I stood up and stepped out of my prison. My legs were shaky and I found it hard to stand. I looked at the metal box in front of me. If I could burn metal I would have. I never wanted to see a coffin or a man-sized box again!

The oxygen tank was bolted to the side. The sound system I had smashed when I flipped the lid off since that was where it was attached and the feeding tube was bent and broken from its way up to the surface. Dang, that feeding tube was long. Just the parts that were still intact were sticking up at least forty feet high. I must have been more than a mile deep.

Which meant the twins were that far down as well. I tried not to care, but I couldn't help it. Being buried alive was not something you'd wish on your worst enemy, and I'd used them to escape that fate. I just couldn't help them. They were too dangerous. I'd tell Turner where to dig and he could deal with them. I couldn't believe I was even thinking that, but the reality was that John and Samuel were killers who *wanted* to kill. I couldn't let that happen. Even if it meant trusting my grandfather to keep the twins prisoners for eternity. And I couldn't pass judgment on his reasons for not killing them. It still struck me as odd since he didn't seem to have a problem murdering a third of our populous, but that was another issue entirely.

I took in the view before me. Miles and miles of dirt. No trees, no flowers, no grass. Nothing grows, nothing dies. Just the dirt. I was amazed that there weren't even any dead insects or worms, or anything. The land must be treated with some kind of insecticide or repellant or something. It amazed me that these zones even existed. Because it meant that they *existed* specifically for people like me.

I heard the whirling of hover-cars in the distance.

Question was: was it Elisha or Turner?

I couldn't believe that the day had actually come when I wished it was Gramps.

I felt around for anything dead, but aside from the twins, there was nothing. I was tempted to use their powers again, but I knew I'd be asking for trouble. I couldn't allow myself to connect to John and Samuel anymore. I couldn't take the chance of losing myself like that again. With a little more time, I honestly didn't know what I would have done with their powers.

To connect to every atom of life like that…

It was more than an adrenaline rush. It was unreal. And terrifying.

I wanted no part of it.

It suddenly occurred to me what Roberta was talking about when she said she and Turner had tried to kill me for the *greater good*. They had no idea of my character and were afraid of what I'd do with the twins' powers if I ever got hold of them. If I had been a psycho I could have killed *everything*. Scary.

The hover-cars were government town-hovers, so I knew it was Turner. There were seven of them and as they drew nearer I realized there were at least twenty dead people inside.

I had a moment of fear as I suddenly thought Turner was going to try and take me out, but he had to know I could easily break through his barriers and control his dead. In fact, Roberta must have told him that the compound no longer held me back. I could see right through it. I tried not to jump to conclusions, but it was hard not to with our history.

All seven of the black hovers landed.

The door of the town-hover closest to me opened up and I nearly cried when Nancy came flying out, racing toward me as fast as her legs could carry her. I was in her bear hug before I could utter a word and I clung onto her just as tightly. I started to cry before I could stop myself. I never thought I'd see anyone ever again, and to have Nancy with me, hugging me, it was overwhelming.

"We couldn't find you anywhere! Your grandparents said they put a tracer in your blood. Gross. But honestly, Chelsan, they didn't give up. They really did seem sincere. It was so weird. Jill's been an inconsolable bitch ever since they showed up, but she'll come around," Nancy babbled the last few days of events in my ear.

"It's good to see you, too, Nancy," I interrupted her with a grin.

I pulled away, so happy to see her, but I felt for Jill. And I was having the same issues. "Turner killed her dad, Nancy. I don't expect her to ever get over that."

"I know, but all I cared about was getting you back, so Jill was annoying." Nancy shook her head as if the last couple of days were pure torture for her.

Turner joined us.

I didn't exactly know how to feel.

There he was.

Normally, we'd be facing off in a death match when talking in person, but this time, it was just… uncomfortable. Should I say thanks? Should I tell him to go away? Should I… I was at a complete loss.

"Where are the twins?" Turner asked.

"I'll show you," I said.

Okay.

Brief. Business. To the point. That was how it was going to be.

We walked back toward the front town-hover.

"Where's Jason and Bill?" I asked Nancy.

"They're with Roberta at my house. They didn't trust Turner so they're using her as collateral," Nancy whispered in my ear. I got the feeling she didn't want to make Turner angry.

"Why all the dead people?" I asked Turner.

"In case we need them," Turner answered as we entered the town-hover.

I felt it then.

John and Samuel's spinning black heads were moving.

Up.

"She's digging them up!" I said trying not to freak out, but failing miserably.

Turner nodded to the driver: all seven cars were up in the air in seconds.

"Where?" he asked.

"Four miles that way." I pointed.

We could already see the silhouette of the skyscraper sized Clean-Up hover in the distance. Elisha was using the same kind of magnetized vehicle to dig up the twins that Turner had used on our hover-van when we were escaping the school.

She knew I could reverse the magnet, so why would she try and free John and Samuel this way? My instincts said it was one of her sneaky traps, but maybe she just needed to get them up fast, so Turner would have no shot at recapturing the boys.

Turner turned to me, his expression agitated. "She wants you to reverse the polarity of the magnet again. What's she up to?"

I shrugged, but I was relieved to know I wasn't the only one who suspected that Elisha had ulterior motives. "I don't know, but John and Samuel will be gone in about twenty seconds if I don't do that thing I did with the magnet."

Our hover-car reached the Clean-Up hover a few seconds later. I could see the dirt rumbling below where it was pulling out the twins' metal box.

I closed my eyes, connecting to the tiny particles of the magnet like I did before. It was much easier this second time, which was a relief, since the first time had been such a struggle. Everything was instantly black, like a void of darkness. I could see the swirl of the tiniest particles turning the same direction.

I could hear Turner's voice. "I'll send out the army. Kill them all."

Nancy's voice was frantic, "You can't kill them! Those are the townspeople! They don't even have weapons!"

"I need those twins back, little girl! I don't care if you're Chelsan's friend, shut up and let me do my job!" Turner's voice was angry.

"Chelsan!" Nancy screamed in my ear. "You have to stop him! Elisha brought the townspeople! Turner's going to kill them!"

I used all of my energy to reverse the circular motion of the tiny particles.

THUMP!

I opened my eyes just in time to see John and Samuel's coffin smash onto the grass from ten feet in the air.

Ouch.

I hoped they were okay, but a part of me wished they weren't. I know I was terrible, but they were capable of killing every living thing so I was a little jaded.

Nancy pulled me to her so we were face to face. "Stop him!" She was frantic.

Turner was gone. He was outside with his dead army about to attack fifty some-odd townspeople that had made a protective ring around the twins' metal box. Roland stood on the coffin like the preacher he was.

Elisha was nowhere in sight.

Not good.

"I won't let Turner hurt anyone, but we have to get the twins," I said to Nancy.

She nodded vigorously.

"We'll push our way through, just don't let him kill anyone!" Nancy was close to frantic.

"I won't," I said.

Turner signaled the attack and his dead army swarmed toward the townspeople, guns raised.

They were about to fire.

I slammed into all their swirling black holes, freezing them in mid-action and nearly fainted from the exertion. After connecting to the magnet and now this, I was losing strength fast. (Not to mention the lack of food and lying in a coffin for three days!)

I could hear Turner scream from outside, "Stop fighting me!"

I ignored him and made all the dead soldiers drop their guns, but as I did, I could feel their need to pick the guns back up. Turner was trying to regain control of his army. It was taking every ounce of strength I had just to keep the men in one place. If Turner and I didn't work together, the dead army would just stand there, and we needed to get the twins.

I walked out of the car. My legs were even more shaky and I couldn't walk in a straight line. I was fading fast. I reached Gramps's side with Nancy's help. "Make them attack, just don't kill anyone. These people are innocent," I tried to say without passing out.

Turner was annoyed but he listened to me by making the men charge forward, fists only. Some townsfolk would get hurt, but no one would die. I could barely hang on to consciousness, but I didn't want to give in until I knew we had the twins safely in our possession.

Oh no.

Elisha's presence slithered its way inside my head.

And I was so weak I couldn't stop her.

I could hear her inside me, "You're too predictable, Chelsan. I knew you couldn't resist reversing the magnet, and I knew you wouldn't let your grandfather use his army to kill the good folk of Havenville, making you weak enough to let me in. I've seen the memory now, and I know what I must do. It's my destiny to kill you, Chelsan. Your powers will be mine, just like my namesake took Elijah's powers, I shall take yours. No one can..."

With the last shred of strength I had left, I shoved her out of my head. I couldn't bear to hear her monologuing. But it was too late. She had taken advantage of my weakness. I really was too predictable. All that effort to keep her away from the memory of my father's death was for nothing. Now she knew how to steal my power and she was coming after me.

Turner's screams at his men were a distant echo as I tried to keep my eyes open. We had lost the twins. Roland and some of his men had loaded the coffin inside the truck by hand and the truck had taken off toward Havenville where we couldn't touch them. I felt Nancy's arms trying to hold me up and crying out my name, but I couldn't find the energy to answer her.

Dirt.

My face hit the dirt and it felt soft.

Can't stay awake…

"Well, what do you want me to do? She's been sleeping for a whole day! That isn't natural. We need to take her to a hospital," Nancy's voice was flustered. I would have grinned, but I was way too exhausted.

I slowly opened my eyes to find myself in my soft cozy bed at Nancy's house. I had never been so comfy in my entire life. After lying on cold metal for days, being immersed in soft fluffiness, felt amazing.

"She's awake!" Bill's voice sounded from my left.

As I shifted myself up to sitting position, (this was quite a feat, believe me) I saw Nancy, Bill and Jason crowding around me. Bill sat on the side of the bed to my left. Nancy hovered over my head on the right, and Jason casually sat on a wooden chair at the foot of the bed. They all had overly worried expressions on their faces and I wanted to hug all of them. No matter what, they always came through for me.

Then it hit me.

"Ryan?" I asked, hoping beyond hope that they'd rescued him while I was asleep.

Nancy shook her head. No words were necessary. Elisha still had him.

I started to get out of bed. "We have to get him back," I said, fighting off the wooziness I felt.

Nancy could see right through me. "Slowly, Chelsan, slowly." She sat next to me on the edge of the bed.

Bill and Jason came around to stand in front of me.

"We're going to get him back, don't worry," Bill stated with a determination that made me shudder. He was definitely taking Ryan's capture to heart.

"You don't understand, Elisha took away his memories of me." It nearly killed me to say it.

"She can do that?" Nancy asked horrified.

I nodded. "With that machine he was hooked up to."

"Maybe it won't work," Nancy suggested hopefully, but I could tell she didn't believe it.

Bill looked like his brain was computing a mile-a-minute.

"Well, we can't worry about that right now. We need to focus on getting Ryan out of there." Jason brought us back on target. "And we need to be careful, Chelsan. Doris is dead."

Huh?

"What do you mean?" I choked out.

"She supposedly died in a hover-car accident." Jason showed real grief and I felt the same.

Doris had saved my life, and now she was dead.

We may not have seen eye-to-eye, but her heart was in the right place, and now Elisha had killed her. Yet another person who would still be alive today if they hadn't met me. My stomach turned painfully.

"We're going after Ryan, but you may need to prepare yourself…" Jason started a sentence there was no way I was going to let him finish.

"No. Don't even think it. We're getting him back. Now what's the plan?" my voice cracked.

Nancy decided to shoo everyone out of the room and give me the scoop of everything that happened while I was gone. Apparently, after they left me, Elisha really did drop them off at Nancy's and leave them alone. Jason immediately contacted Turner and set up a meeting to exchange Jill's chip for my grandparent's help. Jill was the only one who was completely against it. After all, there was no guarantee Turner wouldn't just take the chip and kill her anyway. But, according to Nancy, (after hours of Bill calming her down) Jill finally agreed.

Nancy said there was mayhem as soon as they arrived. Jill pounced on Turner and Bill and Jason had to pull her off of him. Turner almost ordered his men to kill her, but Nancy reminded him that they still had the chip and that I needed their help. Jason managed to convince Turner to let Jill hold onto the chip as collateral since they had zero reason to trust the grandparents. Nancy kept on referring to Roberta as *Cat Lady*, but she admitted that Grams was the more decent of the two. Roberta stayed in my room the entire time I was buried so she could be inside my head and protect me. Nancy told me how she'd come in every once in a while to see how I was and Roberta would politely tell her everything that was going on with me. Nancy seemed a lot more comfortable with Roberta's new attitude adjustment than I did, but Grams really saved my butt *and* my sanity when I was down there. Something I was still struggling with.

Apparently, Bill was taking Ryan's kidnapping the hardest. Nancy said he wouldn't eat or talk about anything else but getting me and Ryan back. I was right, Bill completely blamed himself for the whole ordeal.

I asked Nancy about her and Jason and she sighed contentedly. Apparently, Jason was officially *courting* her. That was what he called it anyway which ended up being a fancy term for dating. George and Vianne were thrilled. Nancy rolled her eyes in fondness of her parents and said that they had been secretly hoping Jason would screw his head on straight and ask Nancy out. Nancy was a little frustrated that the two of them hadn't had any real time to be alone together, but rescuing me and Ryan was obviously a higher priority.

"It's your Grandpa that's been the real annoying one." Nancy finished up. "He's a hard one to read. I can't tell if he's going to turn on us and try and kill us, or not. It's been a very weird couple of days." Nancy pulled me up off the edge of the bed. "Get dressed."

I went to the closet and pulled on a thermal and jeans.

We were just about to leave when Nancy gave me *serious face.*

"What?" I asked, not ever liking to see *serious face.*

"You should talk to Bill," Nancy said with a grunt.

"Is he okay?"

"That's a matter of opinion." Nancy seemed down right annoyed.

"He has to stop blaming himself," I said thoughtfully.

"It's not that, it's something else," Nancy grumbled.

"Nancy, what's going on? Tell me." She was killing me here!

"I'll let him do the honors." Nancy was actually angry.

"Nancy, you're seriously freaking me out right now," I said, seriously freaking out.

Nancy opened the door, and to my surprise Bill was standing right there. Nancy rolled her eyes and crossed her arms, looking at him with mild annoyance. "What a shock. Listening in, were we?"

Bill looked away, slightly ashamed and embarrassed. "Things have changed now, Nancy."

Nancy reared back in confusion. "What do you mean? You finally came to your senses?"

"Fate may have stepped in." Bill was being cryptic.

I had had enough.

"Would someone please tell me what is going on?" This felt like a break-up of some sort and my heart was already squeezing with terror and pain. "Are you… Are you leaving me?" I asked Bill, and found that I was choking back unwanted tears. Maybe the fighting between him and Ryan was too much to take and he didn't think I was worth it.

Bill immediately rushed forward and touched my arm. "No, of course not. I just need to talk to you about something." Bill caught Nancy's eyes rolling, "Something different, not what you think anymore."

Nancy guffawed and gave Bill a knowing look. "Whatever. I'll leave you two alone." And she stormed off down the hallway.

I motioned for Bill to come in and it felt like I was never going to leave this room. My mind was racing. What was it? Was he dating Jill and afraid I'd be upset? I really wouldn't, they'd make a good couple. I secretly hoped that this was it. It would explain why Nancy was upset. I didn't think Nancy would ever approve of Jill. And it would mean that Bill had moved on. That we could all be friends again. Even him and Ryan…

We both sat at the foot of the bed. "What is it, Bill?"

"Now, just hear me out before you say anything." Bill reached forward and held my hands.

What was going on? "Just spill. You're killing me here."

"Well, Jill and I hooked up," Bill began. I was elated! Yay!

"Bill, that's awesome. You guys are great together." I really didn't know if they *were* great together, I just wanted them to be.

"Things have changed," Bill started awkwardly.

"What's changed? You don't like her anymore?" I really wished he'd say more than five words at a time.

"It's just that… It's… How do I say this without sounding like a jerk?" Bill was obviously conflicted.

"Just say it." I was feeling annoyed like Nancy now.

"Okay, jeez." Bill held my hands tighter as if what he was about to say would make me run or something. "It's just… Now that Ryan's memories are gone… you should let him go… for his sake… for his safety," Bill spilled out in a jumbled heap.

What?

"Don't freak out." Bill inched closer and gripped my hands like a vise. "I'm just thinking that when we rescue Ryan… and we *will* rescue Ryan… he'd be better off and safer if he never knew…" He paused.

"Me," I finished for him.

"Well, yeah." Bill looked away, but still kept his grip on my hands.

Let Ryan go.

My heart started to constrict like it was being strangled by a noose. No. I needed Ryan. I needed him. I needed him. I needed him.

One of Bill's hands came up to touch my face. "You're freaking out, I can tell, but you're freaking out because deep down you know it's the right thing to do."

No.

Ryan.

Bill's words were pounding on my soul.

Ryan would be safe.

He would be better off never knowing me. He could live his life in peace.

I started to cry and I couldn't stop. What was my problem? I didn't have to listen to Bill. I didn't have to give up Ryan. We could start from scratch. Our feelings went beyond memories. We'd create new ones…

Selfish.

I was a horrible person.

I wanted to be furious at Bill for even suggesting it. Wasn't he pummeling the crap out of Ryan just a few days ago? Sneaky. Sneaky. But that wasn't a word to describe Bill. I knew in my heart of hearts Bill actually *was* thinking about Ryan's safety.

"You wish you never got involved with me, don't you?" I asked my worst fear, that my friends secretly wished they never knew me, that their lives would have been normal and safe without me in them.

Bill pulled me in for a hug and I collapsed into his chest. His arms felt safe and nice like he could protect me from anything. He whispered in my ear. "I'll never regret being your friend. Ever. I love you, Chelsan."

I kept crying into his t-shirt. "I love you, too, Bill." I clung to him like he was my lifeline to sanity.

I felt him kiss the top of my head lingeringly and my body froze.

Did he mean he loved me, or that he *loved* me?

"Um, Bill." I pulled away and looked into his eyes.

Yep.

He was looking at me the way Ryan did. Oh man. I didn't want to hurt him. I didn't even want to go near this kind of conversation with Bill. Not after everything I had just gone through. Not with Ryan being held captive by Elisha. I thought I had been clear that night when the two of them fought! I thought Bill had moved on to Jill. I thought…

"It's never crossed your mind? Ever?" Bill asked tentatively.

"Bill." Why? Why did he need to discuss this? Hadn't I told him already that I just wanted to be his friend? Hadn't he figured out that my heart belonged to Ryan?

I closed my eyes. Yes. Bill knew all those things. But with Ryan potentially not being in the picture things could be different for him. At least that was what he was thinking. Jill must really hate me right now.

I opened my eyes. "We can't."

"Why not? We've been best friends for three years. I love you, Chelsan, and I always have." Bill's face was so raw and vulnerable I almost wanted to say yes just to spare him the pain I was about to give him.

"I don't feel that way about you," I said quietly, secretly hoping he wouldn't hear because I knew how it would hurt.

"That's a lie." Bill didn't even flinch, he was still as eager as ever to prove his point to me. "I know you felt the same as I did before Ryan came into the picture. Don't deny it. I won't believe you. Now's our chance. We'll save Ryan and you'll let him go so he can live his life safely without you in it."

That shouldn't have stung, but it did. And it made me mad. I stood up and Bill stood up with me, his expression immediately troubled. My face was still pretty readable, I guess.

"You know what, Bill? Not buying it," I said as I crossed my arms. I was feeling a rant coming on. "You didn't like me *until* Ryan liked me, and not before. Otherwise, in our three year friendship, you would have asked me out on a date. I'm sorry if me being with Ryan stirred up feelings for you that weren't there before, but that's the point, *they weren't there before.* Now you've just convinced yourself that you're in love with me because boys always want what they can't have. And Jill! She finally gets you and the second you think you have a chance with me you dump her?! You *are* a jerk!"

"You finished?" Bill asked.

"Yes," I practically harrumphed.

"It's true, it may seem like I only started liking you when Ryan did. But, Chelsan, I've liked you since the day you ran into me and knocked me on my butt in the hallway. I just never thought you thought of me that way, and to be honest, I thought you'd think it was kind of creepy that the *rich guy* was hitting on you, and when I was finally getting enough courage to ask you out, Ryan freakin' Vaughn kisses you in front of everyone, and you kissed him back!" Bill was rambling and starting to get angry at that last part. "So yeah, little frustrating. And Jill and I kissed once. Once! Not enough to call it a relationship, so don't call me a jerk."

"Bill." I didn't know what to say other than that.

"Do you know how annoying it is to watch some stranger come in from the middle of nowhere and swoop you off your feet when I'm the one who's been there from the beginning? I'm the one who should be your rock. I'm the one whose shoulder you should cry on. *I'm* the one, Chelsan. Not Ryan. And the universe has made it easy on us. It's giving us the opportunity to be together like we should have been from the beginning. It's giving me the shot I was too scared to take the first time."

Bill placed his hands on my arms and looked at me intensely. "Chelsan, you know I'm right. Regardless of how you feel about me right now, in time, after you've let Ryan go, after you've had time to heal… we can start with a date. That's all. I promise."

"You know what, Bill? Gross." I shoved his hands away. "Ryan is being tortured by a seven-year-old psychopath and you want a date. I'm getting Ryan back, and I may or may not let him go, but either way, I'm *never* dating you!" I screamed and ran out of the room. I was so mad at Bill! How dare he?! How low?! How?!

I barely made it out the door when I collapsed to the hallway floor and started to cry. I couldn't take any of this right now. I just wanted to crawl into a ball and shut out the rest of the world. I felt Bill's arms wrap around me and I didn't have the strength to fight him off.

"I'm so sorry, Chelsan. I'm so sorry. I'm a complete a-hole. We'll get Ryan back. I promise, it's all my fault, it's all my fault," Bill whispered over and over in my ear. He was devastated and my anger for him melted. Bill couldn't help how he felt. No more than I could.

"What did you do?!" Nancy's mother bear voice rang shrilly from the top of the stairs. "Get away from her, you dolt!" I could feel Nancy prying Bill's arms off of me as she lifted me to my feet. I let her support most of my weight while I gathered myself together.

"I'm all right, Nancy," I said weakly and briefly looked at Bill.

His face was wracked with guilt.

"I hate Jill, too, but it's not worth crying over," Nancy said warily.

I shook my head, "He wants me to let Ryan go. He won't remember me anyway," I croaked out.

Nancy's face paled, "You're not going to, are you?"

She wanted an answer. She wanted to know if I would do it. Truth was, as mad as I got with Bill, it didn't change the fact that letting Ryan go might be the best thing for him.

The pause had been too long. I felt Nancy's nervousness emanating from her pores.

"I'm not sure yet, Nancy. I need to think about it." I left it at that and that seemed to be enough for her.

"So you're not with Jill anymore?" Nancy asked Bill.

"No," he answered in a low voice.

Nancy's nostrils flared in anger, "Making Chelsan dump Ryan? That was your idea? I can't even stand Jill and I feel sorry for her!" Nancy whacked Bill in the chest.

"I didn't mean…" Bill was heartbroken.

"*Didn't mean*, my ass…" Nancy was about to rip Bill a new one.

"Nancy," I interrupted, "I already put him through the ringer. Let's just drop it, okay?"

Nancy huffed, but kept quiet.

Bill looked at me with anguished eyes. "Please tell me we're okay?"

I nodded. "We're okay." I made him keep eye contact with me. "I *never* want to talk about the issue we discussed *ever* again. Okay?"

Bill nodded and it looked like I had kicked his family jewels. I didn't care. I couldn't even entertain the thought of having a conversation like that one again. Not until Ryan was safe. When Ryan was with me again, I'd know what to do. I made a pact with myself in that moment to not make any decisions until we were *all* back safe and sound at Nancy's.

"We're meeting downstairs. Turner wants to rescue Ryan today." Nancy looked at me like she was trying to figure out if I was sturdy enough to function.

"I'm okay, Nancy. Let's get downstairs." I walked toward the stairwell. I didn't wait for Nancy or Bill, I just wanted to go downstairs, listen to plans and immerse myself into finding a way to save Ryan. It was the only thing keeping me sane at the moment.

Rounding the corner to the living room I saw that the rest of the gang was there plus Turner and Roberta. They sat next to each other on the far end of the couch while everyone else kept their distance at the other end. Vianne stood up from sitting on the arm of the couch and rushed over to me, embracing me tightly.

"Thank goodness we got you back! How are you feeling?" she asked me with relief in her voice. Vianne and George felt like an extra set of parents and having her hug me made me feel safe.

The news played softly on the holo-tv like surreal extras in a movie trying to break up the obvious tension between *us* and *them* (*them* being my grandparents). A reporter was interviewing one of the moms whose surrogate was now with Roland Light. Her eyes were swollen and red from days of crying and my heart immediately broke for her. I still had no idea why Roland and Elisha had kidnapped the surrogates, but I knew it had to be something diabolical. Vianne must have realized how the holo-tv was distracting me because she turned it off and gave me a gentle squeeze of support.

Jason and George turned their heads toward me with smiles of welcome while Jill stood as far away as she could from my grandparents and still be in the room. Only two days ago they had sent assassins to kill her, after all. I was actually getting used to my grandparent's fickleness (and by fickleness I mean psychotic behavior). I didn't want to figure them out. I just wanted to use them to get Ryan back and then be done with them forever. I wanted them out of my life.

"Sit down," Jason called out to me and motioned for me to sit next to him.

I quickly obliged, taking a place in the middle of the couch between the two parties.

Nancy and Bill stood like sentries behind me.

I looked over at Jill. She watched me like a hawk, probably wondering how I was going to treat Turner. Most likely hoping I'd tell him to get lost. Sorry Jill, but we needed his help. I couldn't worry about her reaction right now.

Ryan's safety was more important.

"So what do we do?" I asked, starting the meeting.

Turner sat forward and gave his attention only to me. I could tell he didn't like being around my peeps, probably because they all wanted him in jail or dead, but mainly because he thought he was above us. To Gramps, my friends were the annoying bugs he had to work with because of me. I hated him so much in that moment that I wanted to scream, but I held back for Ryan.

"Ryan's being held in the same facility you left him. They haven't moved him," Turner reported dryly. "Elisha only had enough time to set up one machine and the man-power that's involved would make it very difficult to move him easily. It's the reason why we've kept the same location of the I.Q. Farms for so many years. The twins are another story, Elisha hasn't re-buried them, so we know they're in a building four blocks over from Ryan. We'll have to split up. I'll get the twins and you and your *crew* will get your boyfriend."

Split up? I both liked and disliked the notion. Liked because it was physically difficult for me to even be in the same vicinity as my grandparents. Disliked because I didn't trust them: they could just abandon us there. I was about to say something when Jill took a step forward.

"I can't believe you're actually going to work with *him*." Jill practically spat from across the room.

"Here we go." Turner rolled his eyes. "Are you sure I can't just kill her?" He turned to Jill, "I let you keep your damn chip, didn't I?"

"Only because we can't crack it!" Jill focused her attention to me. "Chelsan, you can't honestly tell me you trust him. Please don't be that stupid."

"Jill, we don't have a lot of options here. We can't exactly take Bill's hover and stroll back into Havenville. We need the resources Turner can provide." I tried to sound as calm as I possibly could. I actually agreed with her, but I cared about Ryan more, so I was willing to give my grandparents a shot. The mere thought of the twins and their power in the hands of Elisha… not that Turner was much better, but at least he had a track record of almost two-hundred years of keeping the boys in check, which made me feel safer about Turner having custody over them.

"What are *they* getting out of all this? Ever wonder that?" Jill wasn't letting this go.

"The twins, Jill." I looked at Turner and he nodded in agreement. "That's why you're helping us."

Roberta sat forward, smiling at me. "And we're doing this for you, too."

"Can I vomit now?" Jill rolled her eyes.

"Jill, this is hard enough…" Nancy started.

"No!" Jill interrupted, "You have no idea how hard this is, Nancy! *He* didn't kill your dad!" Jill's eyes started to well up.

"We could rescue your boyfriend if you'd just let me kill her." Turner leaned back into the couch rubbing his face with his hand in frustration.

I stood up at that. "Stop threatening my friends. It's not funny."

"I wasn't joking." Turner's eyes were deadly serious. "Your silly little friend is overreacting like she's been doing since we arrived."

"Overreacting?" I was incredulous. "You murdered her dad and then kept him as your personal puppet for years! How do you expect her to feel about you?!"

"I didn't keep him animated just for myself you know, I do have a heart." Turner crossed his arms in anger.

"Of course you did it for yourself. You needed her dad to do everything you said and you knew he was going to turn you in." I was livid now.

"No. I *killed* him because he was going to turn me in, I kept him *alive* for that little brat." Turner glanced over at Jill.

"You let a child grow up with a zombie dad for *her*? Are you joking?" I asked and then realized that no one else was piping in. Everyone seemed to want to give Turner and me the space to hash this one out.

"It felt like the right thing to do, yes." Turner's eyes bore into me. "We're not that different, Granddaughter. You did the exact same thing with your stepfather for your mother."

I sat there stunned.

He was right.

I did do that for Mom. I kept Bruce's dead body going so she wouldn't be devastated. I didn't realize at the ripe age of seven that Mom only wanted him alive because his mere presence protected us from Turner, but either way the intention was the same. I'd kept a dead man animated for the love of my mother. I was just like him and that thought killed me. I wanted to hope for the best, that maybe Gramps really did feel for Jill and kept Mr. Forester *alive* for her sake, but after everything Turner had done, it was hard for me to think better of him. Not to mention it was always difficult to see what was truth and what was manipulation with Gramps. Either way it made me feel like a horrible human being.

"It would have been better if you'd let my father be dead," Jill admitted so quietly I barely heard her.

Turner sighed like he'd been forced to eat worms. "I'm sorry for that, but I thought I was doing the right thing."

Jill left the room.

I knew how she felt. She had no energy to argue. She just wanted to be left alone. I'd been her last shred of hope to throw Turner out on his heels and now she had to deal with the fact that I was just like him. A sicko.

"Are we done?" Gramps brought us all back to reality.

"Tell me what you've got in mind." I wanted to change the subject as well. Turner knew he'd won that argument. Thankfully, he wasn't gloating.

We talked through the afternoon, going over the plan to rescue Ryan and the twins. It was a simple snatch and grab, but we had to make sure no one would get hurt. Turner didn't care much about that point, but I made him promise he wouldn't hurt anyone. Roberta backed me up and this seemed to make Gramps reluctantly agree. I was finding the whole conversation surreal. Just two months ago my friends and I were sitting around discussing plans to break into Turner's headquarters! Now we were all in the same room, having a civil discussion and working together. It was making me nauseous. I couldn't stop wondering what my mother would have thought of all this. Would she hate me right now? Tears sprung up before I could stop them.

"We've got a plan. I'm going to rest before we go." I stood up before anyone could see me cry.

"I'll go with you." I heard Nancy call from behind as I walked toward the staircase.

"No, it's cool. I really just want to crash for a while," I said over my shoulder, hoping Nancy would oblige without an argument.

"Jason and I will just go over the details then." Nancy's voice was unsure, but I couldn't look back at her. If I saw her concerned eyes I'd break down right then and there. I had to keep moving toward my bed and the safety of my pillow that I intended to bawl my head off into.

"Cool. I'll only be an hour or so," I called out as I took the stairs two at a time and practically fell over my feet to reach my room.

I opened the door and to my surprise, Jill was there in my bed lying on her side. She was alone, her eyes bright red from crying. When she saw me she immediately sat up and wiped the wetness from her cheeks. "Sorry. I'll go somewhere else."

Our eyes met. Our pain linked us in that second. An understanding that only the two of us could share. Turner took my mother and her father. We'd never get them back.

We both started to cry. Jill jumped up from the bed and embraced me like we were sisters. We held onto one another like we could suck the poison out of each other by just this embrace.

Jill pulled away first and started to laugh through her tears. "We're quite a pair, aren't we?"

I had to laugh myself and soon the both of us were laughing uncontrollably. Pain is a funny thing. Sometimes when it's too much to bear you find yourself going a little mad and laughter is the only cure, like some kind of emotional protection. We both plopped down on the bed then became very quiet. We were drained. There was nothing left to emote.

"I'm sorry I put you on the spot down there," Jill confessed with sincerity.

"I'm sorry we have to work with that murderer."

"It really is the only way to rescue Ryan," Jill whispered. I realized the effort it took for her to say that. She was trying to make me feel better about my decision to use Turner and Roberta.

"Did you ever think three months ago that we'd be where we are now?" I asked with a pained smile.

Jill smiled back, thoughtful. "No. I never thought in a million years I'd be nice to you." She paused. "But I just want you to know that I consider you a friend now, even though I don't act like it. You're the only friend I've ever really had. I'm just sorry I was… well… you know. I just really hated you."

"Why?" I couldn't believe I was actually having this conversation with Jill Forester. I'd always wondered why she was so mean to me and to finally have the chance to find out… It was kind of liberating.

"At first it was because of Bill." Jill shrugged. "He liked you before you had your little run-in. I still think he planned the whole thing." She laughed, "The only way that shy boy could introduce himself was to smack right into you."

"That was my fault," I said. There was no way Bill devised something like that. I was so klutzy and I wasn't paying attention to where I was going.

"You really think that, don't you?" Jill shook her head as if she were incredulous at my ignorance. "Bill had been eyeing you for months before. And if you haven't figured it out, I kind of like him. I couldn't understand why he'd want you when he could have me. No offense."

"None taken." At least not verbally. She really was full of herself, but I let it slide.

"I mean, look at you, you're poor. How could he like a *poor* girl? How could he like such a freak?" Jill lay back on the bed with exasperation. "That's how I felt anyway, and the more I was cruel to you, the better I felt. It took away the pain of my dad, and of Bill not giving me the time of day. I know this is going to sound horrible, but it felt good to see you suffer. I can't explain it, but it made me feel good," Jill's voice was laced with emotion. "I know, I'm a horrible person. I don't feel that way anymore. I was just really screwed up. I just *am* really screwed up." Jill sat up again and looked me in the eye. "And now, I was so close to having Bill, we even kissed, and it was… amazing. But as soon as he found out that Ryan lost all his memories, all Bill wants is for you to give up on Ryan and be with him. Bill and I have spent so much time together lately, and I really thought…"

She shook her head. "It doesn't even matter. Just a shred of a chance with you and Bill's completely lost interest in me. I'll always be second choice, if he ever chooses me at all."

"But, Jill, I love Ryan, not Bill," I said, hoping this would make her feel better. It didn't.

"Duh. But it doesn't matter. Bill still holds some crazy torch for you. He'll always be waiting for you, I think." Jill closed her eyes with a pained expression.

I wanted to comfort her in some way, but I knew anything I said would upset her more. "I didn't ask for any of this." My voice was barely a whisper.

"I know. But it doesn't change the fact that it's true." Jill opened her eyes and forced a smile. "I'll try and keep my temper, I promise. Let's just get your boy back. Sound good?"

"Yeah." I took Jill's cue to change the subject. It was too hurtful for her to talk about Bill and I didn't want to be the jerk who kept bringing it up. I could only imagine if Ryan was in love with someone else and how that would devastate me. I didn't envy Jill's position. I was just sorry I was the reason she was in it in the first place. "How's your arm?" I asked, just now remembering her bullet wound, which she seemed to be hiding very well.

Jill rubbed her arm in response. "Good. Roberta injected it with some kind of drug that made it heal up in a day. Look." Jill pulled up her sleeve: the wound was already healed, with a fading scar as if she had been shot months ago.

"Weird." I examining the arm. I didn't like the thought of Grams injecting anyone with anything, but at least Jill wasn't injured anymore and it was another nice thing to chalk up for the grandparents. I hated that.

"I figured it out by the way," Jill said without making eye contact with me. She actually looked scared.

"Figured what out?" I asked, hoping she wasn't about to hit me with some kind of emotional-accusation-bomb.

"The holo-chip." Her eyes met mine and there was real fear there. "I haven't told anyone, and I wasn't even going to tell you, but... well... I needed to, I guess."

My heart stopped. The holo-chip. "How?"

"When Roberta told you that I was the only one who could decode it, I started thinking that there had to be some kind of genetic lock. I researched for hours on anything and everything I could find on the subject. There are literally hundreds of genetic locks and I tried every one of them until the files decrypted. There was a false covering on the chip with a tiny concave slot in the center. I put a drop of my blood inside, closed the covering and plugged it into my computer. And there it was."

Jill's eyes widened from the memory. "Turner has killed millions of innocent people. Millions, Chelsan. All under the guise of *population control.* My father must have spent years collecting all the proof... and it's there, on the chip. Everything we need to put your grandfather away forever."

My heart sang and squeezed in terror all at once. "Jill, you can't tell anyone. If Turner knows you have access to those files, he *will* kill you. Where is it now?" I was frightened for Jill.

"My house. I hid it where no one will find it." Jill was just as scared as me, but she looked slightly relieved to have shared this burden with someone else. After everything I'd put her through, I was glad to oblige.

"Okay, good. After Turner helps us rescue Ryan and the twins we'll give it to Jason and take good old Gramps down." I managed a shocked smile at that. We could really put him away. As much as he'd been helping me, Turner still deserved to pay for everything that he'd done.

Jill smiled back, then she reached over and squeezed my hand. "I'm in."

I sighed with a crazed kind of laugh. "For your dad."

Jill nodded, determined. "And your mom."

I nodded back. "First things first, let's go save Ryan."

Jill put her sleeve back down, covering up her scar. "When do we leave?"

"Two hours."

***

I sat at the window of Turner's hover-van watching the California oaks below fly past at frightening speed. Nancy, Bill, Jason, Jill and I were in one of Gramps's *test vehicles,* while Turner and his mini-army were in another traveling beside us, which basically meant the vehicles had their own flight lane and traveled very fast. He also said they had a kind of cloaking device, but I could see the hover-shuttle Turner and his men were in flying next to us pretty clearly as I looked out the window. Turner called it *dimension displacement,* but the more he tried to explain it the more I didn't care. I just hoped Elisha wouldn't be able to see us coming. Since Gramps didn't seem worried about it, I wouldn't be either. I just wanted to get in there, grab Ryan, and get out. I really hoped it would be that simple.

Yeah, right.

With Gramps and his men going after the twins, it would be up to me to defend my rescue team. I opted against using any of Turner's men: it was literally just the five of us and our driver. Well, the five of us and whatever dead things I could muster up. The hope was that all of Elisha's forces would be protecting John and Samuel, so that breaking Ryan out would be the easier of the two tasks. We were assuming a lot, I know, but at this point, I was blinded by my obsession to have Ryan back with me, and everyone else seemed to be indulging me.

I could see Havenville and its stunning Cathedral in the distance. My heart started beating faster. I tried to stuff down the terror I was feeling. My last memory of Havenville was being drugged and put into a coffin, so yeah, not pleasant.

We were moving so fast I couldn't tell if anyone down below could see us, but Gramps seemed to be right: no crowds of people looking up or hovercrafts sent to stop us. This *displacement* thing appeared to be doing its job.

Our hover-van started to slow down as we approached Building Sixty, the warehouse of doom, but also the place where Ryan was strapped into the brain-sucking machine. Turner's craft zoomed past us. I could just see it in the distance, about ten warehouses further than ours. At least he was still close enough I could keep an eye on him. I just hoped he wouldn't break his promise to not kill the villagers. If push came to shove, I feared that he'd start slaughtering anyone in his way to get to the twins. I honestly hoped his rescue mission would be easier than ours so he wouldn't have to go back on his word, but it was a pretty slim hope. Elisha wanted Samuel and John more than she wanted me, and definitely more than she wanted Ryan. If she could tap into their power, Elisha could literally rule the world. I shook my head. I didn't want to think about that.

Focus.

Ryan.

The hover-van came to a stop and it was the first time that I realized none of us had spoken a word the entire trip. It was as if we were all mentally preparing ourselves for what we had to do. I didn't really want any of them to go with me, they were just more bodies I'd have to look out for. But I knew there was no way I could talk them out of it, so I hadn't even wasted my breath. Even Jason insisted that he go along, and that was saying a lot seeing as he was normally the first one to run from danger.

Now that I was able to use my powers *through* the special compound metal or whatever it was, I'd be able to use anything dead inside or outside of Building Sixty, including the entire graveyard of Havenville. I could sense from the van that a lot of the corpses were almost completely decomposed, which meant my control over them would be less powerful. Still, there were just as many fresh ones as well. Gross. I hated having to think tactically about dead bodies and their levels of decomposition. Seriously messed up.

Our driver turned to me, "I'm going to shift the van back so you can exit, but I'll be cloaking myself until you've obtained your target. Just signal me with *this* when you're ready to leave." He handed me a small round device with a diameter of about a half an inch. "Just press it into your palm." Apparently, I was eyeing the thing with confusion. "Vice President Turner's diversion is scheduled to start in two minutes."

I nodded, wondering what Turner had planned. He hadn't told me any details and I really hoped it wouldn't involve hurting anyone. There was no controlling him, and I had to keep reminding myself that Turner would have gone after the twins with or without me. Small comfort, but I couldn't feel responsible for everything bad Gramps did. It would kill me, I think.

The same buzzing sound that we heard when we first entered the hover-van sounded again. This must be the displacement thing at work, but to us nothing visually changed, I just opened the door and stepped out of the vehicle with the others. When we were all out the buzz sounded again. This time my mouth dropped in shock.

The hover-van was gone. As in, not there anymore.

I reached out to see if it was just invisible, but there was nothing there. I guess displacement meant exactly that, it could *displace* itself from where we were. *Dimensions*, Turner had said. Too much for my brain to handle at that moment, so I tucked the circular device in my jeans pocket and hoped that when the time came, the ship would re-appear when I activated it.

"Shouldn't you get some dead thing wrangled up before we go in there?" Nancy asked as she looked at the doorway to the building.

"Is it weird that there aren't any guards, anywhere?" Bill searched the empty street carefully.

"Yeah, I was thinking the same thing. Maybe they're all protecting the twins." It was eerie. Like we had stepped into a ghost town. When Jill and I had been here before there were at least a couple of random guards strolling the perimeter, but now... trap? Probably.

BOOM!

A large explosion sounded in the distance. That must be the diversion. I put my feelers out for any new dead bodies, but so far Gramps had kept his promise. The explosion hadn't killed anyone.

"Let's go." I swung the door open to Building Sixty. I led the pack and raced down the hallway towards the door that would lead me to where Ryan was held.

Still no guards.

I stopped.

Everyone clambered up behind me, almost tackling me to the floor.

"What is it?" Nancy asked as she and the others regained their bearings.

"I'm not going to run in there blindly. We need a guinea pig," I said.

The others nodded their approval.

"Anyone in particular?" Jason asked.

"Any of the dead villagers will do." I connected to the freshest corpse I could find in the graveyard behind the warehouses. Making the body dig its way up from its grave sent shivers down my spine since the memory of being buried alive was still fresh in my mind. But there was no time for my problems. I concentrated, and after a few minutes the corpse was running at full speed toward our location.

For the sake of their own sanity, I seriously hoped no one who knew the dead person saw it running down the street.

I made the body open the door to the building and a dirty, grey-skinned, old woman stood before us.

Not just any old woman…

"Beth," Nancy exclaimed in shock.

I nearly lost my hold on Beth as I recognized Elisha's twin sister. They killed her. They killed Beth! Why? I knew Elisha's *reunion tears* was an act, but enough to kill? I could tell Beth had been beyond happy to see Elisha, but the next day at breakfast… something had seemed off between Beth and the Elisha/Roland team.

"I knew something was wrong," Jason practically spat. I had never seen him so mad. "When we split up, Nancy, Bill and I went back and talked to Beth. She seemed scared, but we couldn't get anything out of her."

"Then we were ushered here to the warehouse," Nancy said and I could tell she was upset as well. "She was so nice."

"And Roland's her son. How could he kill his mother?! He's supposed to be a minister," Bill piped in.

I couldn't fathom the reason why either, but I also knew we were running out of time. I would've taken control of another body, but we didn't have the time to spare. And the horrible part of me that I was ashamed to admit existed secretly knew that Beth would be a valuable tool in throwing Elisha and Roland off their game.

"I'm sending her in," I told them.

That quieted everyone.

I made Beth enter the next room, then I closed my eyes so I could see through hers without the headache.

About twenty armed guards surrounded Ryan in a tight circle. Elisha was there as well, monitoring the read-outs of Ryan's brain activity.

No sign of Roland, he was probably protecting Samuel and John.

Almost as soon as Beth entered the room, the guards all pointed their guns at her.

"Freeze or we'll shoot," one of the guards yelled.

Just for Elisha's sake I made Beth talk. "Go ahead. Sister, what do you think about that?" I cringed at the sound, and in that moment I loathed Elisha more than I ever had before. Beth's voice was grated and crackled like she had been screaming when she died. How could anyone do that to someone they loved? I guess being a sociopath gave you the ability to feel nothing. Or at least not let feelings get in the way of your *psychoness*.

"STOP!" Elisha screamed to the guards. Her face was wracked with terror and fury all balled up into one. "Don't shoot her! Shoot the people behind that door! You'll pay for this, Chelsan Derée!"

Gigs up, and I only had Beth to block. "Get back outside! They have guns! I'll bring in more corpses, you come back in with them and try to free Ryan while I take care of Elisha," I instructed very quickly.

"We'll keep the exit open in case you can't make Beth fend them off," Bill said as they all followed my orders and ran out the hallway to the exit door.

I concentrated on seeing through Beth's eyes.

Inside the room, the soldiers ran toward her, but not shooting, per Elisha's command.

I puppeteered Beth to block the doorway and then made the ninety-seven-year-old kick some serious butt while I slammed into about thirty black swirling holes in the graveyard outside. It was making me dizzy, having thirty corpses claw their way up through the ground while super-grandma was punching and kicking Elisha's guards, but the No Kill order was keeping her intact at least, and by default keeping the goons away from me. None of them had reached the door yet.

I backed up to the exit just in case. I really didn't want to be shot today.

Elisha's men were shoving past Beth, twenty against one, and even at super-strength I couldn't make her corpse fight that many off. The thirty corpses finally broke ground and I made them run towards the entrance as fast as I could make their dead legs move. Some bodies were more decomposed than others, so they lagged behind, but a good twenty were strong and fresh. Ewww. I'm glad I wasn't there to see my friends' faces as these decaying corpses came running at them full speed, but they knew the score, and they knew it was necessary.

Beth was finally knocked aside. I opened my eyes to see the first guard fly around the corner to the doorway and aim his gun at me. I dove through the exit as bullets flew over my head. More men filed into the hallway, guns blazing, just as I made all thirty dead bodies enter the hallway in front of me. Bullets shredded their already rotted skin and I heard some of the soldiers scream in terror. As a town that had never taken Age-pro and lived by their religious beliefs, seeing their dead family members come back to life to attack them was too much to handle.

The bullets stopped. I heard the clacking of guns falling to the ground. There were cries of horror and recognition.

I knew this: once the soldiers realized that their friends and family were nothing but zombies, they'd be furious at the girl who brought them back, namely me. We only had a few minutes to rescue Ryan and get out before the guards came to their senses and wanted revenge.

Wait a minute.

I suddenly felt at least a hundred more corpses digging their way up from their graves and I wasn't the one controlling them.

Turner.

I guess he was using the same tactic I had, and apparently he needed a lot more bodies to get the job done. I was relieved he was using corpses as opposed to having his men mow down the townspeople, but I knew I needed to keep an eye on those dead bodies just in case he decided to do anything drastic.

I made the thirty corpses I controlled mob their way into the guards. The screaming and the crying weren't stopping. I felt bad for putting these poor citizens of Havenville through that kind of torture. I knew what it felt like having a decrepit version of someone you love attack you. It happened to me, and now I was doing it to these innocent people. I knew I was just defending myself and trying to save Ryan, but it still felt evil.

I followed my mob of corpses with the gang surrounding me like a circle of guards. Even Jill had a protective stance like she wouldn't let anyone hurt me.

As we entered the room with Ryan, Elisha's men were hysterical. They completely abandoned their posts, despite Elisha screaming for them to attack. I watched in pleased shock as all of her soldiers shoved their way through the throng of zombies and ran out the door, eyes wide with terror. They'd never be the same again. I knew how they felt.

Only Elisha stood between me and Ryan. Her face was scared, no false bravado. An army of dead people behind me, she better be scared. I could tell she was furious as well. "How dare you bring Beth to me," Elisha seethed.

"How dare you kill her! How dare you bury me alive! How dare you strap Ryan up to those machines! Bringing Beth back only makes you face what you did!" I screamed. I was tired of people telling me what I did wrong.

Elisha was completely taken aback. "I didn't kill Beth. Why would you think that?"

"Oh gee, I don't know, let me think on that one: because you're a psycho!" I said and realized how hypocritical that sounded with Beth on my right and thirty rotting corpses behind me.

Elisha's eyes filled with tears. "Beth killed herself."

"Is that why her throat is raw from screaming? Yeah, right, sell it to someone else." I didn't believe Elisha's act for one second.

"Her throat is raw from crying. She was inconsolable. I left her alone, thinking she'd cry herself to sleep and be better by morning, but she drowned herself in the bathtub. You really are an evil thing, you know that?" Elisha wiped away tears.

My friends shifted uncomfortably. I felt a giant weight fall on my shoulders. I couldn't think about this right now. If Beth killed herself and I brought her back, by accident or not, it was cruel to flaunt her in Elisha's face. As loathsome as I thought Elisha was, I just didn't have it in me to be that mean.

I made a decision then. It might the end of me, but my conscience wouldn't let me do anything else. I made all the corpses, including Beth, leave the building, return to the graveyard, and dig their way back underground. I couldn't be sure they were in the right graves, but at least the townspeople wouldn't be forced to bury their dead a second time. I just couldn't live with myself if I didn't do something to fix what I'd just done. I'd have to do the same with the people Turner brought up as well, but I'd wait until he had the twins safely away.

Now it was just Elisha, Ryan strapped to the machine, and the gang standing on both sides of me.

"I'm sorry about Beth," I said before I could stop myself. Why was I treating Elisha like a person?! She was evil! I had to keep reminding myself. I can't tell you how hard it is to stay in hatred-mode while facing a seven-year-old child with giant, tear-filled violet eyes.

"You have me outnumbered, you can have your boyfriend back, but please, Chelsan, listen to me, you can't let Turner take the boys," Elisha pleaded.

She was serious.

"It's too late for that. He's already breaking them out." I wasn't going to budge on this one. The twins were too dangerous for anyone but my grandfather to have. Like I said, he'd proved himself by keeping them under lock and key for the last two-hundred years.

"Did you ever wonder why Turner didn't just kill Samuel and John when he knows how dangerous their powers are? Why risk them being alive?" Elisha asked.

Yes, of course I wondered that very thing, but I wasn't going to let myself be manipulated by her. "Bill, Jason, get Ryan down from there." I didn't bother to answer her question.

"Chelsan, listen to me: I wanted you to break me out of the I.Q. Farm because Turner was about to use the twins for his own gain. I had to get them out of there!" Her eyes were desperate for me to listen to her.

I really hated this yo-yoing, Elisha and my grandparents were doing to me. They both made sense in their own ways and it was driving me crazy because I didn't know which one to believe. Elisha was a sociopath, but my grandparents were too.

Bill and Jason carefully unstrapped Ryan from all the tubing connected to his head and chest. He looked so pale and fragile as his body slumped into Bill's like he was a rag doll. *This* is what Elisha was capable of.

Elisha's eyes were pleading. "Think about it, why would I let you take Ryan? Why wouldn't I be with Roland protecting the boys if I didn't think you'd listen to reason?"

I shook my head. "Um, the first words out of your mouth after you saw Beth were to kill me in the hallway, so yeah, you're full of crap."

Then I threw caution to the wind and ran over to Ryan's unconscious body. I knew I shouldn't keep my eyes off Elisha in case she tried to stage another attack, but I couldn't stand to be away from him for one second longer. I was terrified he wouldn't remember me, but a part of me would be fine with that as long as he was okay. I could see Bill's face looking down at me with his fatherly glare, whispering wordlessly that I should let Ryan go for his own sake. I didn't want to concede.

"He won't remember you, you know." Elisha almost grinned when she said this, and that was when I knew everything out of her mouth was a manipulation of the truth. She wanted to see me suffer and she wanted my power for herself. Elisha saw how I could control the twins and she was salivating for it.

I entertained the thought of bringing Beth back to torture her, but I respected Beth too much to do that. She couldn't help that she was related to a psychopath anymore than I could.

Ryan was barely conscious. He had to use Bill and I as crutches to keep himself upright. I couldn't bring myself to look into his eyes. I didn't want to see the blankness I knew would be waiting for me. After everything that had happened, it just wasn't something I was ready for.

A voice sounded on Elisha's intercom. It was Roland. "Elisha! Elisha! Come in! Turner is using the corpses to kill our soldiers! We need more men. Now!"

Elisha's face went pale, then she was out the back door and running before anyone could move to stop her.

My mind went blank from dread.

I had been so focused on blocking out Elisha's words and freeing Ryan that I had lost track of the dead bodies Turner raised from their graves. I nearly choked from tears as I realized he had used the corpses to kill at least forty more people. Their swirling holes were screaming at me that I had let them be murdered. How could he? He promised! Then it hit me. His promise was that he wouldn't use any of *his* men to kill villagers. In his twistedly warped mind, he had kept his promise. Technically, they had killed each other. He didn't even need to use his men, he could just use the freshly killed guards and make them kill more guards. This was going to stop right now.

I slammed myself into every single black hole in Turner's vicinity and made every corpse stand still. Gramps couldn't break through my powers. He was trying, I could feel it, but I was stronger. There was no way I was letting him kill another innocent person. Not when I could stop him.

"Let's get in the van," I said weakly.

It was taking all of my strength to keep Turner from gaining back control of the townsfolk.

Jill took my place and supported Ryan, while Nancy in turn supported me. They could see I was about to drop and I was grateful they were there. As we stumbled out of the building, I took the circular device out of my pocket and pressed down. The hover-van immediately popped into view and we hurried inside.

I collapsed on one of the chairs next to Ryan's half-conscious body. I could feel Bill's eyes on me, pleading for me to keep my distance from Ryan.

To let him go.

I wanted to spit on Bill, but I knew that was my own frustration coming out. He was doing what he thought was right, I just couldn't see it that way yet.

I wasn't ready to lose Ryan. The thought of him not being in my life was too excruciating to bear.

On the pilot's intercom I could hear Turner's voice, "We have the twins. Drop your passengers off at the girl's house and report back to headquarters. Tell my granddaughter she can release her hold on the corpses, we're at a safe distance."

I wanted to take a hammer to both the intercom and Turner's stupid smug face. I should be happy he had the boys, but at what cost? He'd murdered innocent people! And what if Elisha was right and he planned on using Samuel and John for some dark deed. What if he planned on using them to slaughter millions? I made a vow to myself I wasn't going to let that happen. I seemed to be the only one who could control them and I intended to keep it that way.

I felt Roberta trying to push inside my brain, but I didn't want to talk to her. I didn't want to have anything to do with her. She was probably going to give me some lame excuse about why Turner did what he did, but I was tired of the lies. I was tired of it all. I dropped my link to the corpses. I didn't have the energy to put them back in their graves. I couldn't even tell which ones were the older bodies and which ones were recently killed by Gramps. Our van was moving too fast anyway and before I knew it we were at the four-mile mark and my powers were useless. I lay my head on Ryan's shoulder and tried to keep the tears reined in.

Nancy and Jill were looking at me with such sympathy I had to shut my eyes. Don't look at me like that! Like I just lost the love of my life. Like their hearts were aching for me and what I had to do. It made it too real. Ryan had lost me and he didn't even know it. I just wanted to pretend for a little while that things were okay. That Ryan was Ryan and we'd be together forever. So, I kept my eyes closed and my head on his shoulder. He was asleep anyway, so I could pretend he was still mine.

We were back at Nancy's in no time and my heart dropped. This was it. When Ryan had a clean bill of health, he'd be gone. Back to his house and out of my life forever. I tried to choke back my tears, but I wasn't fooling anyone. The driver barked for us to get out of the vehicle. Bill and Jason peeled my head away from Ryan's shoulder, carrying him out and away from my frozen body. I couldn't move. I didn't want to walk out to a future without Ryan.

Nancy and Jill each took one of my arms and lifted me to my feet.

"You don't have to let him go, Chelsan," Nancy said. There wasn't much conviction to her tone. As much as she wanted me to be happy, even Nancy felt that it was selfish to keep Ryan a part of the gang when he could be free and safe.

"Just get me inside," I answered quietly. I didn't have the strength to say anything else.

As soon as our feet hit the ground, the van shifted to its invisibility mode, and was gone.

I barely heard anything that was going on as Nancy and Jill led me inside the house. George and Vianne introduced me to the doctor that Turner had sent over to make sure Ryan would be okay. All I could do was grunt a hello.

Nancy and Jill ushered me upstairs with the doctor and the four of us arrived at my room, where Ryan was already lying down in bed. Jason gave me a small supportive smile. Bill couldn't even look me in the eye. A part of me was so angry at Bill! He was the one who came up with the idea to set Ryan free! I wondered if the idea would have even occurred to me if Bill hadn't brought it up. Probably not. I was kind of blind when it came to Ryan, and the thought of him not being in my life would never have entered my mind.

The doctor checked Ryan thoroughly, then nodded to me when he was done.

"Guys, I'd like to be alone with Ryan." I shrugged off Nancy and Jill's support to sit on the edge of the bed next to his sleeping figure.

No one argued. They all left without a word. There was nothing to say. What had to be done, had to be done.

I watched him sleep. Maybe it was creepy, but I didn't care. It was the last time I'd ever be this close to him and I was going to savor every second. An hour passed. I barely moved. His chest moved up and down in peaceful slumber. I was glad of that. He'd probably have nightmares for the rest of his life, but at least for the moment, he was calm and steady.

My heart leapt in my throat as Ryan suddenly stirred. His eyes opened and immediately found mine.

"Where am I?" he asked. And his eyes were empty of any recognition.

I would have cried right then and there if I didn't think it would upset him. "You're a few houses down from your place. You hit your head so we brought you in here to rest," I lied. I figured it would explain what would probably be the worst headache of his life with all the probing Elisha did.

"Who are you?" Ryan asked kindly and it made my heart wring in misery.

"Just a concerned neighbor. You should rest for a while before you go home. The doctor doesn't want you to move around for a few hours." I was finding it harder and harder to hold in my tears.

The love of my life didn't even know who I was.

I didn't know how to handle it, so I just sat there and tried to look as "normal" as possible. Like I wasn't about to bawl like a baby in front of the neighbor that "hit his head."

Then his lips turned into a sly smile. "I can't believe you were going to dump me."

What?

I mean, what?

Before I could speak or move Ryan pulled me in close and kissed me.

I lost it.

I literally lost it.

Tears streamed down my face as I kissed Ryan with everything that I had.

I pulled away to look at him, to see if this wasn't a mirage or a figment of my imagination. But there he was with his silly little grin looking at me with his sparkling eyes.

"You remember me?" I asked. (Or sort of choked from emotion.)

Ryan smiled at me and pulled me in for another kiss. My toes and fingers tingled in response, and my head felt like it was going to implode with relief and happiness. Ryan's memories weren't wiped. I could hardly believe it.

"No... freaking... seven-year-old... head case... could take away... my memories of you," Ryan said through his kisses. I pulled away, grinning from ear-to-ear, his smile just as big. "I'm way smarter than her."

"I thought... I mean... I was ready to..." I kissed him again. "I never thought I'd be able to do this again." And I kissed him again just in case he lost his memory suddenly.

Ryan kissed me more passionately than ever. "Why would you send me away? You're everything to me." His face was hurt and wracked with pain.

I didn't know how to respond. It wasn't as if I'd wanted to let him go. I just wanted him to be safe, and that meant me being out of his life. "You're safer without me," I mumbled quickly.

Ryan reached up to touch my cheek. "I don't care about being safe. I'd strap myself into the brain machine a hundred times over to be with you. Promise me, you'll never even consider leaving me, no matter what happens." His eyes were pleading and determined.

"I… I promise. I thought I was saving you," I confessed.

Ryan kissed me lightly on the lips and pulled away with a serious expression. "I know you felt like you were doing the right thing, but splitting us up is *never* an option. Okay?"

I nodded and collapsed into his chest. I just wanted to stay cuddled up to him forever. His arms wrapped around me and I nearly giggled from contentment. Ryan kissed the top of my head and I felt his chest move, laughing himself.

"What?" I asked and started to laugh, too.

"I don't know," Ryan laughed even harder.

It was officially contagious and the two of us couldn't stop laughing. It was as if all the pain and torture we'd both gone through in the last couple of days all disappeared because we were together again. Like we had defied death and won.

We both let the laughter die out as Ryan slowly sat up, rubbing his head. "Man, my head hurts."

I sat on my knees next to him and kissed his forehead. "We'll get you something for the pain."

"Did I hear laughing?" Nancy entered the room with a half-worried, half-hopeful look on her face.

I smiled at her and she could see the truth from my expression.

"So brain boy outsmarted the seven-year-old." And then she was racing over to Ryan and giving him a giant hug. I didn't think I'd ever seen Nancy hug Ryan before, but apparently the relief of him being all right was incentive.

"Speaking of which, you should bring in the gang. I've got a lot to tell," Ryan said. "And by *gang* I mean just the good guys, no Turners."

"No worries about that, they went back to headquarters after they rescued the twins," I informed him. None of us had talked about it, but the underlying feeling was leeriness and distrust. I was furious at the way the rescue went down.

Maybe Ryan had some more insight. He certainly seemed to be chomping at the bit to tell us whatever it was he was going to tell us.

Nancy picked up on this, too. She immediately walked to the door saying, "I'll go get everyone."

After a few minutes Jason, Bill, Nancy and Jill all sat around Ryan and I on the bed. If Bill couldn't make eye contact with me before, well, now it was ten times worse. He looked genuinely ashamed. I made a promise to make him feel better about the whole *Ryan* situation. It was funny: now that I knew Ryan's memory was intact, I could care less about Bill's advice to let Ryan go. Obviously, Bill thought I was going to be angry with him, so I forced eye contact with him and smiled. Bill's eyes widened, then he gave me an awkward smile back, but it was a good first step towards "the mending." Jill watched the whole exchange and she looked decidedly happy that I had forgiven Bill and that Ryan was in full form. She really did like Bill.

"I'm sorry about the fight," Bill sputtered out. I realized that he wasn't just feeling bad about me, he still felt responsible for Ryan's whole kidnapping.

Ryan nodded. "Forget it."

And that seemed to be it. For now, anyway. Boys.

Nancy and Jason were holding hands and looking a lot more comfortable with the whole *relationship* thing, which made me happy.

I helped prop up Ryan into a sitting position and everyone stared at him as if waiting for a bomb to drop. "It took me a while to figure out how the machine that Elisha strapped me into worked, but, once I did, I was able to control the results of every test she performed on me." He smiled. "Her results state that I'm of mild intelligence and highly overrated in the academic field. It's why she allowed you to take me. I made her believe I was of no use to her."

"What if she'd killed you?" I asked, my voice laced with the tone of *what if.*

"I knew she was going to use me as leverage and I knew you'd rescue me," Ryan said with his adorably roguish grin, but I wasn't having it.

"Ryan, she's psycho, you could have died." I couldn't believe he risked his life by making Elisha believe he wasn't as smart as she thought he was. I couldn't believe he believed in me enough to entrust his survival on the mere chance that I'd break him out. The whole thing made me anxious.

Ryan reached out and held my hand, which calmed me down. "I'm safe now, you can't think about what could have happened. Now let me tell you what I know," Ryan said softly.

I nodded knowing he was right, but my mind still reeled over the fact that Elisha could have snuffed him out on a whim.

When Ryan was sure I was okay, he continued, "I witnessed a lot of really horrible things when I was in there. The story Elisha told you about her sister committing suicide was a lie. Elisha tortured Beth for two days before she finally killed her. It was brutal. She took an axe and smashed it into Beth's chest. Elisha made up that story about suicide and wouldn't let anyone see the body, including Roland. He really believes his mother killed herself."

It was hard to feel sorry for Roland Light, but I started to get the feeling that he was just as used by Elisha in this whole situation. If Elisha lied to him about Beth's death, then she was afraid of his reaction, which meant they weren't on the same page about certain things. Maybe we could use that to our advantage.

"That's so messed up," Bill said as if not fully accepting the truth.

I guess I would have been more shocked if I hadn't learned from Roberta that all the I.Q. kids were sociopaths. I realized then that I hadn't told anyone that little tidbit of information. I immediately told them everything, from Roberta's helping me, to connecting to the twins, to the way Turner chooses I.Q. kids.

"So my seven-year-old manipulation skills weren't as fantastic as I thought they were." Ryan was trying to make light of the situation, but I could tell he was a little frazzled by everything I just laid on him.

I leaned down and kissed his cheek. "It wasn't until you solved Trilidon's Theorem that Turner regretted not keeping you. But you were too old by then."

Jason mused out loud, "You must be connected to those twins by more than just their powers, if they were both able to bring you into their memories and thoughts. I've just never heard of that."

It really *was* strange that two separate people, twins or not, were able to bring me into their... what? They had two separate brains, so how could I be in both? I could connect to their swirling black holes, yes, but their memories? As one? Jason was right, my connection with Samuel and John had to be deeper than just having opposite powers.

"Unfortunately, most of their plans were spoken in rooms I wasn't in. Roland and Elisha aren't much for using computers to map out their strategy. But I have some things that could help." Ryan looked at Jason. "I can show you later, nothing to bore everyone else with."

Ryan's eyes started to droop from exhaustion.

"We should let you rest." Nancy stood up, bringing Jason with her.

Bill and Jill followed suit, but I stayed where I was. There was no way I was going to leave his side. Besides, I needed sleep myself.

No one argued, not even Bill. They all left the room in silence, but just before Nancy left she smiled and gave me a thumbs up. I smiled back, then snuggled up next to Ryan as she shut the door.

Ryan wrapped his arms around me. I lay my head against his chest and was so contented I wanted to burst. I had my Ryan back.

Ryan situated himself so we were forehead to forehead. "The only thing that kept me going was that you would come for me," he said, kissing me lightly on the mouth. "I could hear your voice when Elisha would talk to you underground. It nearly killed me to hear how scared you were." Ryan kissed me again, this time more passionately.

"It was terrifying, but I knew I had to get free and save you. It's my fault you were there in the first place." I still reeled from guilt, and there was a teeny tiny part of me that almost wished he could forget everything.

Ryan cradled my face in his hand and stared at me intensely. "I don't blame you for anything. You know that, right?" He waited until I nodded. "Turner found me long before I ever knew you. I solved Trilidon's Theorem long before I knew you. Elisha targeted me long before I knew you. We're in this together, okay?"

I simply nodded. I wasn't going to argue with him how Turner had left him alone before he met me or how I was the one who helped Elisha escape or how she never would have had the chance to capture him if it weren't for me. I decided I was just going to be happy. Period. I deserved it.

So I kissed Ryan with everything I had and he responded in turn. Kissing him was somehow different now. More intense. More emotional. We had been through the ringer and survived yet again and it only made our bond stronger. Neither one of us was able to stop. It felt like kissing him was giving me oxygen. I still felt all the butterflies and the tingling, but this time it was more powerful. Like if we let go of each other we'd wither and die.

We both knew where this was headed. I never wanted anything more in my life. My mind went numb with bliss as Ryan and I made love.

Chapter 7
Thursday December 9, 2320

I was still reeling from being with Ryan in a way I can't even describe. I felt like I was surrounded by this bubble of joy that would pop at any second, so I clung to that feeling of pure happiness like it was a life vest.

Wait a minute.

I was asleep.

I'd had so many astral experiences in the last week that it took me a minute to realize I was in the blackness of my own mind. I imagined myself in a field of flowers with a bright blue sky and I was instantly there. I felt Roberta tap-tap-tapping to come inside my brain and I decided to let her in.

Roberta popped into existence in front of me and took in her surroundings. "Nice." She smiled her frozen smile. Her hair was tied in a loose ponytail for once instead of the usual tight bun she preferred. She looked more relaxed than I'd seen her before.

"What do you want?" I demanded. I was still angry at Turner's betrayal when he killed the innocent townsfolk.

Roberta sighed at my attitude. "I want you to know, that Geoffrey had no choice. He had to kill those people. The twins could not be allowed to stay in Elisha's hands. You must know that." Roberta's eyes were penetrating and I could tell she truly meant what she was saying.

Maybe it was for the greater good, but I'd never be able to accept killing innocent people. Ever.

"Elisha said you were going to use the twins for something. She said she had me rescue them because she was protecting them from you guys." I honestly didn't believe a word of what Elisha said, but I wanted to see how Roberta would respond.

I wasn't disappointed.

Roberta shifted from foot to foot in a nervous fashion. "Well, you needn't worry about Samuel and John. Turner felt you were right about them being a threat and he had them killed."

"She's lying." John popped into the field of flowers with Samuel next to him. They were holding hands and their milky white eyes stared at me with eerie stillness.

I looked at them and then at Roberta for her reaction, but there was none.

"She can't see us," Samuel snickered with delight.

"Only you can," John snickered in unison with his brother.

This went far beyond creepy. First off, they had managed to break past my barrier without me detecting it. Second off, they were kids with blind eyes and black swirling heads. Vomit.

"What are you looking at?" Roberta's eyebrow raised in curiosity and suspicion.

"You said he killed them?" I asked her, daring her to tell the truth.

Roberta paused like a kid deciding to commit to the lie or tell the truth before the lie gets out of hand. "Yes, of course, they're dead, Chelsan. Why would I lie?"

I prodded even more. "You saw their bodies?" I needed to know if she genuinely didn't know.

"Yes, I saw the bodies myself. We had them incinerated." Roberta looked me straight in the eye and if the twins hadn't been standing right in front of me, I would have believed her.

Samuel and John continued to snicker at the situation.

"We're in a chamber beneath Turner's headquarters," John said.

"You must save us," Samuel finished.

"You know they're here, right?" I decided to call Roberta out.

All the color drained from Roberta's face. "What do you mean, they're here?"

"The twins. They're standing right next to you. They told me where you're keeping them." I looked at her waiting for her to explain herself.

"I forgot," Roberta said almost to herself.

"Forgot what?" I asked wanting to squeeze as much information as I could from her.

"Nothing," she said, her focus was fully on me. "Don't let them in your head, kick them out! Yes, I lied, but it was for your own good. They're the reason you have your power…"

Whoosh!

Roberta was gone.

And in mid-sentence.

"We don't like the nasty cat lady." Samuel looked angry.

"We made her go away." John's smile was wicked.

They made her go away. In *my* head! Only I should be able to do that!

"I think I've had enough of all of you," I said and imagined myself slamming a wall down in my head to keep everyone out.

The twins disappeared.

I was alone in the field of flowers.

Time to wake up.

***

I awoke to the warm rays of sunlight on my cheek. I didn't know what to do. Roberta lied about the twins, which made me think Turner did have plans for them. And, maybe, if I helped put Turner away with Jill's holo-chip those boys would starve to death. I couldn't believe I was thinking that, but I'd had my own experience with Brady the serial-killer-sociopath, and people like him and the twins were born to inflict pain and cruelty on innocents, and they didn't feel a thing. Samuel and John could end the world. Maybe letting them go was the best possible scenario, but as long as Turner was in power, they'd be a potential threat to everyone's very existence. I hated that I wanted them dead. Who was I becoming?

I looked over at Ryan sleeping soundly next to me and my heart felt a sigh of contentment. I'd have to talk to the gang about all this to see what they thought.

I slowly reached over and kissed Ryan on the cheek. He stirred awake, then laid his eyes on me and grinned. "Morning, beautiful." He pulled me in for a kiss.

"Morning," I mumbled through kisses.

I pulled away smiling. "I had another one of those dreams."

Ryan turned serious. "More bad?"

"Afraid so. I think it's time for Jill to get that chip."

"I thought it didn't work. Did you guys crack it while I was gone?" Ryan sat up, alert now.

"No one else knows, but Jill told me she figured it out. She said she's hidden it in a safe place. I think I should go with her to get it." I reluctantly slid out of bed and started to dress.

Ryan followed suit, pulling on a t-shirt and jeans. "Sounds like a plan. You want me to come?"

"Yes, but I think Jill would feel safer it was just me. Don't tell her I told you about the chip." I walked over to Ryan and kissed him again.

Ryan gently brushed the hair out of my face and kissed my forehead. "I won't say anything, but be careful. If your grandparents figure out what you're doing, they'll kill you guys."

I fell into his chest. "I know, but am I crazy to think that they won't?" I really wanted to believe that we had come to some sort of truce, albeit a thin one since I still thought they deserved to spend the rest of their lives in jail, but still.

"You're not crazy, Chelsan, but you can't trust them. If it came down to their safety and killing you, they'd kill you in a heartbeat. Don't doubt that for a second. If I'm wrong then great, but if I'm not, and you put your guard down…" He left the thought unfinished, but I knew the rest of it: if I put my guard down, I could die.

"You're right. It's just been a rough week," I mumbled into his chest.

"I know." Ryan held me closer and it felt so wonderful. More please. "But some pretty amazing things happened too." Ryan looked at me with expectant eyes.

"Very true," I agreed, then I reached up, pulled his head down to mine, and we started kissing again. Everything melted away in a large tidal wave of goodness. Ryan and I somehow found our way to the bed and I was about to pull off his shirt when…

"Um, guys, discretion please?" Nancy's voice was laced with happiness.

We pulled away from each other (and believe me this was a feat of its own) to see Nancy standing there shaking her head with a grin.

"Sorry," I said, but no apologies were needed: Nancy was totally on team Hook-up. "You better get Jill. I've got a mission that involves her, and the sooner we do this, the sooner I won't chicken out."

Nancy's eyebrow rose in curiosity, but she headed off to find Jill.

"Are you sure you want to go after Turner right now?" Ryan asked. "I mean, we might need him to take down Elisha."

I was thinking the same thing, but I couldn't live with myself if I didn't keep my promise to at least try. Turner was a mass murderer and needed to be stopped. I'd take care of Elisha myself. She had no powers and she'd lost the twins so maybe Elisha would no longer be a real threat. What could she possibly do? Her biggest leverage left was the seven thousand surrogates, but I could let the government take care of that. How would I be able to make seven thousand women leave Havenville against their will? My first priority was to keep everyone safe, and that meant finally putting Gramps away.

Jill was by my side in no time and we made eye contact. No words needed to be said. I was keeping my promise to her.

"Ready?" she asked with a look of determination.

"Ready." I nodded.

"Alone?" Nancy chimed in with annoyance. "No way! I'm not letting you out of my sight again! And what's this about anyway? Where are you two going?" Admittedly, she sounded a little jealous.

I turned to Nancy. "Nancy, alone. Holo-chip, remember?"

"I thought that was here. We haven't even cracked it…" Realization washed over Nancy's face. "Oh! Oh man, okay, wow, we're really doing this, aren't we?"

I nodded. "We good?"

A few seconds of unhappy groaning. "Fine," Nancy conceded, then stuck her finger in Jill's face, "If anything happens to her…"

Jill whacked Nancy's hand away from her face like it was a bothersome fly. "She'll be protecting me in this situation, so get your finger away from my face."

"We'll be fine," I said with as much confidence as I could muster. "Jill, let's go." I turned to Nancy, "Tell Bill and Jason, but under no circumstances are they to follow, got me?"

"Yeah, yeah, just be back soon, and I'll have Jason ready to transmit the chip." Nancy shook her head as if she wasn't expecting the excitement to start this early in the day.

I gave her a quick hug and Ryan a kiss, then Jill and I were off.

We took Jill's hover-BMW and I had to say, compared to most vehicles it was out of this world. The seats were like cushy paradise with ergonomic back and head rests. Jill drove the car with ease and thirty minutes later we were landing at her stunning mansion. The house was made of metal and glass topped by five solar panels on the roof. The window frames and doorknobs were all colored glass, making the house look like it belonged in a children's book.

We exited the car and I barely had time to notice the gorgeous rose bushes encircling the hover-pad. There was a hover-Mercedes already parked nearby.

"Mom's home. I'll tell her I'm spending the night at Nancy's again," Jill said as she opened her front door and we entered inside.

"Does she mind you spending so much time over there?" I asked, always wondering how Bill and Ryan managed to explain all their time spent away from home to their parents.

"She really doesn't care," was all Jill answered, and I could tell from her tone that she didn't want to elaborate. With a zombie dad and a mom that didn't seem to care too much about her whereabouts, it seemed like a pretty lonely life. "The chip's in a secret compartment in my dad's study." Jill took the lead, guiding me through her monstrous house.

Every hallway was painted pristine white, holo-paintings perfectly lining each wall. I felt like I was in a museum. It was lovely, but very cold.

"Up here." Jill led the way up a small wooden staircase.

We entered a large room that was extremely high-tech looking. Glass and metal was the décor, from the huge desk lining a corner of the room, to the end tables, lamps and furniture. Who would want to sit on a metal chair I had no idea, but it did look cool. There were about ten holo-screen bases that were all turned off. Sunlight poured in through the ten-foot windows forming the North wall, and the room almost sparkled from all the reflections going on.

"There's a safe in the floor." Jill pointed, hurriedly walking over to a seemingly normal looking square of slate that made up the office flooring.

"Jill?! What are you doing?" Jill's mom's voice sounded like she was coming up to the office.

"Nothing Mom, just getting a few things for Nancy's," Jill yelled over her shoulder and pulled out the square piece of slate, revealing a safe underneath. Jill typed in the code to unlock it.

"Jill, I need to talk to you. Are you alone?" Jill's mom was getting closer. She was just down the hallway.

Jill was so focused on the safe and retrieving the holo-chip, she didn't make eye contact with me. I was starting to worry. What would we possibly say to her mom to explain why we were in her late husband's office breaking into his safe? I started to sweat.

"Jill, we should go. Hurry!" I urged.

The safe beeped twice and the heavy metal door popped open. Jill reached down inside and her face went white.

"It's gone," Jill could barely get the words out.

Of course it was.

Why me?

I was seriously an idiot to think it would still be there, and now we were going to get in trouble from Jill's mom.

Fantastic.

"Jill, are you in your father's office?" Her mom was right outside the door.

Jill motioned for me to hide behind the door as she slammed the safe door closed and replaced the slate to its natural resting place.

The door opened. I leaned against the wall so it wouldn't hit me.

"Mom! I just wanted a few minutes of alone time in here." Jill turned to her mother.

"I see." Her mom sounded off-kilter.

I couldn't put my finger on it, but something was wrong. I peeked through the crack of the door to get a better view of Jill's mother. I could barely see her head, but even from that angle it was remarkable how much Jill looked like her. From the black wavy hair to the delicately stunning face, they were definitely related.

Then I saw it.

And I reacted on instinct.

I jumped from behind the door and threw Jill to the ground.

Just in time.

Jill's mom had nearly sliced Jill's throat with a butcher knife.

"Jill, she's dead!" I cried before Jill could react to my sudden tackle and her mother's attack.

Jill was speechless. She looked dazed. I knew I'd have to do all the maneuvering and thinking in this situation.

The black swirling hole spinning in her mother's chest was just another horrible reminder that my grandparents hadn't changed. I suddenly remembered Jill's *miraculous* recovery from her bullet wound and realized they must have injected her with a tracer. It would have been so easy, follow Jill back to the house, find out where she hid the holo-chip, take it, kill her mom…

Next time Jill comes home, dead.

But they hadn't counted on me going home with her.

Just as Jill's mom tried to take another swing I slammed through the barrier that blocked me from her black chasm and connected to it with ease. It was an awkward moment, I didn't want to make Jill's mom do or say anything, so I just let her stand there.

Jill pushed me off as she gained her senses and stood in front of her vacant mother. Tears fell heavily down her cheeks, though she didn't seem aware of them. Jill couldn't stop staring at her mother's eyes, as if daring her to say something. To come back to life. Anything. My heart broke for her. I knew how Jill felt. I'd felt the same way only a couple months before, when Turner had murdered my mother.

"Jill, you should leave the room. I'll let her go." I tried to make my voice as steady as possible for Jill's sake.

"Let her go? What does that mean?" Jill's voice shook, but was strangely calm at the same time.

I reached out and grabbed Jill's hands, turning her to look me in the eye. "She's dead already. I'm going to let her rest, okay? Turner turned her into a puppet and right now I'm controlling her. I don't want to do that anymore, so I'm going to make it impossible for anyone like me or Turner to ever control her again. Does that make sense?" I felt like I was talking to a brick wall. Jill's lights were on, but there was no one inside. She was in shock, barely holding on by a thread. I needed to get her back to Nancy's before Turner realized he needed to finish the job.

After a moment's pause, Jill moved her head slightly in what I assumed was a nod.

"Just wait for me in the hallway. We're going to walk out together in case Turner sent others. Okay?" Her eyes distant. I was losing her again. "Okay, Jill? Just a few seconds?"

"Yeah… yeah… okay." Jill stepped around her mom like she was a fragile egg, but in the end Jill was out of the office and standing in the hallway.

I made her mom walk further into the room and sit on one of the metal chairs. I wasn't sure how long Jill's mom had been dead, so disconnecting her from her black hole could prove messy. There was nothing I could do about that, I couldn't let her be used again. For Jill's sake. Once she was seated I disconnected her body from its swirling black hole.

Jill's mom's skin barely turned gray. Turner must have killed her only a couple of days ago. Like I thought, right after Jill hid the holochip. What a guy. My brain still couldn't fathom how he could be such a maniac. I felt dirty for ever having anything to do with him. I abhorred the fact that I'd been grateful for Roberta helping me through Elisha's torments. Why did I ever consider trusting them?

Jill and I were now bonded by the worst possible experience anyone could ever go through. Our parents were gone, and it was Turner's fault.

I hurried out of the room and joined Jill's stick-still figure in the hallway.

Gently taking her hand, I said with urgency, "Let's get out of here."

I moved ahead, but Jill wasn't budging.

"I'm all alone now," Jill's voice was quiet, but her words felt like a scream.

"You've got me. Now I mean it, let's get out of here." I wished Jill could have time to let out everything that was going on in her brain, right here and now, and have a good cry, but I knew we weren't out of danger. Turner would have back-up. Of that I was certain.

I practically pulled Jill through her house and towards the front door. I put out my feelers to see if there were any more dead people Turner may have stationed around the place, but I couldn't sense anything. I mentally kicked myself for not recognizing Jill's mom's black hole when we entered the house, but with those stupid barriers the grandparents put into their corpses, my mind didn't pick it up right away.

Since I was leading, I had a hard time remembering the way out of Jill's monstrous house, but after a few wrong turns we finally arrived at the front door. I peeked out the window to see if anyone was out there.

What?

Standing in front of Jill's hover-BMW was none other than Turner himself.

I was frozen.

Do I go out there?

Was he here to finish us both off?

What was going on?

I took another peek. No one else around.

"Chelsan, come out here," Turner's voice sounded mildly annoyed. "I see you peeking out that window. I'm not going to kill either of you."

Yeah, right.

Then, before I could stop her, Jill flew out of the house and straight for Gramps.

Oh boy.

Jill jumped Turner and had him pinned on the ground before I could even make my way out the front door. She punched him in the face while screaming at the top of her lungs. It would've almost been funny if I didn't expect fifty of Turner's soldiers to suddenly show up and kill her. But no soldiers. So far.

"Get your dog off of me!" Turner yelled in annoyance. "Trust me, you need to hear what I have to say." He grunted.

I ran up to them just as Gramps threw Jill off. She landed with a thump a few feet from her car. Before she could launch herself at him again I grabbed her arm.

"Jill, stop," I said, though I didn't really want her to. I liked seeing

Turner's butt being kicked by Jill, but I also knew that, if he came here alone, what he'd have to say would be pretty important.

Jill angrily whirled on me. "Don't you dare defend him!"

"I'm not, but he's here alone. Us against him. Let's hear what he has to say," I pleaded with her.

Jill shrugged me off and stormed toward her car. "I'm tired of listening! I'm tired of *him* trying to kill me! And I'm tired of you!" Jill opened her car and sat down inside, slamming the door shut. She didn't take off, though, so I knew she was going to let me talk to Turner first. It was scary that I was actually able to understand "Jill Forester fits," but she deserved to act out towards me and especially towards Turner.

Gramps and I walked a few feet away from the car. I crossed my arms and stared at him with as much anger as I could muster. "Speak," I more or less snarled.

Turner glanced briefly behind him to make sure Jill couldn't hear. "I didn't know you were coming with her."

"So, if I wasn't here it would have been okay to kill her?" Unbelievable!

"Maybe not okay by your standards, but easier to deal with, yes." Turner had that annoyed expression on his face again. "I'm not here to be judged. I'm here to ask for your help."

It took me a few seconds to really hear that. Gramps was asking for my help. Sure, I'd helped him recently, but that was more of a mutual need situation. But now he was actually *asking*. It was probably the hardest thing he'd ever done.

Good.

It was nice to see him squirm, and he was definitely squirming.

"I know you know the twins are still alive. Roberta told me they came to you when she was inside your mind. I need to know if you let them in, or if they just appeared." Turner was eyeing me like a hawk.

I could tell this information was vital somehow and it immediately scared me. Mainly because I *hadn't* let them in. They came in on their own and I had no defenses against them. And if they could do it, maybe Elisha would find a way back in as well. The thought paralyzed me with fear. "They just came in on their own," I mumbled. I could hear the shake in my own voice and the look on Turner's face didn't exactly ease my mind.

"I know you think I should just kill them, but I can't." Turner confessed quietly. "Chelsan…" his voice actually cracked.

Seriously, major crackage.

It froze me. I'd never seen any kind of emotion from this psychopath I called Gramps. To hear his voice laced with emotion while saying my name actually had me stumped. I looked over at Jill's figure sitting in the driver's seat of her BMW and even from this distance, the slump of her shoulders, the lowering of her head, her pain was obvious. And it was all *this* man's fault. Everything that had caused me anguish over the last two months was *his* fault. I would never have even known Elisha if it weren't for Turner. I never would have seen an I.Q. Farm. It would have just been a nightmare Ryan told me about his past that we could have forgotten about because our lives would have been safe and normal and wonderful. Why did just hearing the slight quaver in Turner's voice make me feel for him? Why was I so conflicted over a psychopath? Grams, too. They both managed to make me feel *something* for them. It was making me sick to my stomach.

"Just tell me."

"I'm afraid if I kill them Roberta will die." Turner's voice was quiet. And something more… Frightened. "And possibly you," he said as an afterthought.

Thanks.

"Okay, you can knock off the *mock concern* for me, it's insulting. Why would killing the twins kill Roberta?"

"It's not mock concern, it's just… well… originally it was Franklin we were worried about. Now that you have his powers, well… you may be in danger as well," he explained. "When the twins killed everyone in the first I.Q. Farm, Roberta was there. She was pregnant with your father. She was the only one who survived and we don't know why. We can only speculate that it had something to do with her pregnancy. We were too scared to kill John and Samuel for fear that she and Franklin were linked to them somehow. If we killed them, it might kill her and our only son."

"That's impossible. My dad was a hundred and ten when he died, if Roberta was pregnant with him in 2133 that would have made him…" I quickly tried to do the math in my head, but I sucked at math, "well older anyway."

"A hundred and sixty-nine. Franklin was a hundred and sixty-nine when he died."

"See? Wait." I rolled my eyes. "Let me guess, you lied to him about his age."

"We had to. Franklin found out about the twins and he was a smart boy, we knew he'd make the connection of his birth and his powers. We were afraid of what would happen. If he started to control the twins... You of all people know the intoxication of it. We didn't know if we could stop Franklin if he combined his powers with theirs... If that was even possible! It was too much of a risk. That's why we kept him a child, so he'd never know the origin of his power, or his true age. We celebrated his birthday every year until he was thirty-eight, then every other year after that. Sometimes even I forgot how old he was. When you lie to yourself enough it starts to become truth." Turner was in full confession mode now. "But now we know that you're strong enough to control them. The fact that you were able to disconnect from their powers, despite the temptation... We could use that to our advantage."

What was I supposed to say to that? It was too much to take in at once, so I just stood there staring at Turner.

"Those twins could destroy life as we know it," I said out loud. If those boys were to die, Roberta and I could die, too. But if it meant saving the world... What kind of a person would I be if I didn't at least consider the option... I didn't want to die, I didn't want Roberta to die but...

I vomited.

Right on Gramps's shoes.

Turner took a step back and shook off the chunky contents of my breakfast. Surprisingly, he didn't look mad or upset, he just looked... worried.

Grrr. I wanted him to be evil. It was so much easier that way.

"We think the twins have the same four-mile restriction you do, but yes, they could wipe out every living thing in that vicinity." I think he was trying to comfort me, but it didn't change the fact that Turner didn't really know that for sure, and I certainty didn't want to test it.

"How can I keep them out of my head?" I asked, desperate for an answer. I didn't like it that I was intricately tied to these monsters. It was bad enough having Elisha and Roberta popping inside my head anytime they wanted, but I'd learned how to kick them out, maybe I could learn to do the same with the twins.

"Roberta will teach you how. I'm sure she can find a way." I could see that Gramps wasn't exactly convinced of that. "Listen, Chelsan, I know you're scared about John and Samuel, but we may need them. Right now they're in a cell two hundred feet beneath Population Control Center. Elisha can't reach them. To be honest only you can." He paused as if thinking of how to proceed. "Roland Light and Elisha are going after the Baby Center Headquarters in Arizona. Our sources say they're going to kidnap all fifty thousand surrogate mothers and blow up the building. I can't let that happen. I know you don't trust me, I know you don't agree with my methods, but if Roland and Elisha take those women, there will be thousands of devastated parents who *will* fight back. Chelsan, we're talking about a possible war."

War?

A topic I had only read about. Masses of people killing each other for whatever reason suited them at the time. Age-pro pretty much took the fight out of people since they could live forever. Was that Roland and Elisha's goal from the start?

"What can I do?" Seriously, what could I possibly do that Turner couldn't do himself? He could control the dead, he could control the living, why did he need me?

"I need you to use John and Samuel's power. If I could I would, but you're the only one we know of who can do it." Turner was serious.

"No way." The words came out of my mouth before I even had time to think of a proper answer. I guess my body and mind were speaking for me at the moment.

"We would hover John and Samuel out and all we'll need you to do is use their power to control the surrogates. If we can get them away from the center and into a more defensible area, Roland and Elisha won't be able to take them to Havenville." Turner kept talking as if I hadn't said a thing. "It's the only way to keep everyone alive. My sources tell me that a large majority of the surrogates at the Baby Centers are riled up from what happened at the LA branch. They *want* to leave. They want to have these babies and raise them on their own. If I didn't have my security teams on every single one of the Baby Centers we'd already have millions of surrogates breaking out to find the first Christian Coalition town they could find. If I don't have you, I'd have to attack Roland's men, and there would be casualties. There really would be a war then, and there wouldn't be any way to stop it. But if we remove the problem by keeping the surrogate mothers safely with their donors, under my *protection* no one will have cause to fight just yet."

"What about the seven thousand Roland already has?" Was I really having this conversation? I thought I'd just said *no way*.

"Well, we could rescue them the same way."

My mind was spinning a mile a minute. Use the twins to take control of living beings? Not only living beings but pregnant women? It seemed so wrong. So violating, for me and for the women. It was one thing controlling dead things, but making people do things against their will? It was revolting. It was wrong on so many different levels I couldn't keep track. But on the other side of the coin, there were thousands of parents out there wondering if their unborn children were safe. If they'd ever see them again. Completely helpless. How would I feel if someone stole my unborn baby? It was making my head churn with confusion. And what if I *couldn't* disconnect from the twins? It scared me, but I also knew I was the only one who could help so…

"Okay."

"Okay?" Turner asked with a raise of his eyebrow.

"Okay," I repeated and found that the word stuck in my throat a bit. "When?"

"They're planning on kidnapping the surrogates tonight." Turner's face was full of relief.

"We better get going then."

***

Wow. Phoenix, Arizona was quite possibly the ugliest city I had ever seen. Granted, I'd only seen Los Angeles in my lifetime, but wow, seriously, all strip malls and cactuses. And I guess Joshua trees counted for the tree law (the International Law that passed in 2142 where it was required to plant a tree every twenty feet for oxygen levels) because there was one almost every seven feet or so lining the gravel streets below.

Ryan sat next to me in the giant hummer-hover as we stared down at the desert abyss that was Arizona. I couldn't wait to get this over with and head back to California where I belonged. The rest of the gang was there, too. It had taken some convincing to get everyone on board with the crazy plan, especially Jill, who was sitting in the corner by herself with her arms crossed. I really wished she'd come around, but I didn't want to push her. She had lost both her parents in the last two months and she needed to deal with it in her own way. If that meant me being her punching bag then so be it. I was just glad Jill was here. I was glad they all came though I knew it was wrong. They should be at Nancy's where they'd be safe, but I'd learned over the last two months there was no arguing with any of them, so I decided to just be happy that my friends were here. My human security blankets.

Bill sat behind me, with Nancy and Jason, but he was definitely the odd man out as Nancy and Jason held hands and talked in whispers. I felt a pang of sympathy for Bill as he sat there, expressionless, but still willing to put his life on the line to help. He deserved better. They all did.

Roberta and Turner were in a separate room of the hummer-hover. The vehicle itself was a beauty to behold, with four rooms in total all black leather and tinted windows. Behind us flew the biggest hover vehicle I'd ever seen and that was saying a lot, considering the fact that Clean-Up's hovers were the size of sky scrapers. This was at least twice that size. Turner claimed it carried up to two hundred thousand people. Why a hover monstrosity like that was ever made, I had no idea, but in our case it would be vital to making this a quick trip. I just had to control the surrogates long enough to walk them into the ship, and Turner would take them somewhere safe where the parents of the unborn babies were waiting.

Ryan squeezed my hand to get my attention. I looked up at him and smiled. He leaned down, kissing me gently. "You ready for this?"

I nodded, afraid to talk. I could see the spinning holes of John and Samuel's heads in the back room. Turner's scientists had led the twins into the hover, their faces blank, their eyes milky white, holding hands as they walked in unison. Part of me still wanted to see them as innocents, but the brief contact I'd had with them was enough to know that they were quite possibly more evil than even Elisha.

I tried not to show Ryan the worry I was feeling. The thought of connecting to the twins was giving me heart palpitations. I wasn't convinced that I wouldn't go blind, and that was the least of my concerns by far.

I mean, I was about to connect to thousands of human beings and make them my puppets essentially. It appalled me.

I understood that it needed to be done, but I felt like I was playing at some kind of power trip that made my skin crawl. Who did I think I was, treating people like sheep? Dead things were one thing, they were well… dead. But a person? What if Turner had that kind of power? He probably would have taken control of my body and made me kill my mom or visa versa. I made a vow to myself: I'd connect to John and Samuel, get the girls out of Arizona, then out of Havenville, and, boom, no more contact with the twins. Not ever. Having to do two trips sucked, but I'd deal.

I also vowed to let Roberta teach me how to keep them out of my head. I didn't know if she could, but I had try something. Now that they could enter into my brain at will, I was sure they'd make me go insane. Or worse, they'd figure out how to make me use their powers without me being able to stop them.

That was the real fear, I guess.

What if they found a way to do that?

I never thought I'd wish anyone dead. Even two months ago when I almost let those dead bees kill Grandma, in the end I couldn't do it. And that was something I was proud of. I didn't want anyone to die at my hand. I knew what that felt like and I never wanted to feel it again. And if John and Samuel could make me…

I took a deep breath.

I couldn't think that way. What ifs would kill me if I let them.

Ryan wrapped his arm around me and held me close. "You're doing the right thing," he said as if reading my thoughts.

"Thanks," I said in response.

I *really* didn't want to connect to the twins.

REALLY didn't.

Roberta walked into our room with her feline face and hair stretched back into her usual tight black bun. "We're almost there, you'd better prepare." She made eye contact with me alone.

I nodded and stood up, Ryan next to me. I kissed him gently. "I need to do this alone… Or with her… you know what I mean."

Ryan smiled and kissed me back. "Yeah, I know. You know where we are if you need us."

Bill had stood up as well and reached down to hug me before I could react. I hugged him back, knowing how hard the last day had been for him. He whispered in my ear, "I'm really sorry."

I whispered, "It's okay, Bill. I'm sorry, too."

Bill pulled away and we exchanged awkward but *back to normal* smiles.

Nancy and Jason as a team hugged me as well. Nancy's face was full of worry and unspoken lectures on how dangerous this whole thing was, while Jason just looked excited for a good story.

Jill didn't move from her chair, but we made momentary eye contact. It was enough for me.

"Let's do this," I said to Roberta.

Roberta walked to the back door that would lead us to the twins' room. I took a deep calming breath (really didn't help) and followed after her. She was just about to type in the code on the keypad to open the door when our vehicle made a sudden lurch and wheeled itself all the way around, speeding in the opposite direction. We were going back to California. What was going on?

Roberta's frozen features barely moved, but from my time spent with her when I was buried alive I could tell she was surprised.

We both turned at the same time to see Gramps run into the room. That action alone was freaking me out. I'd never seen the man walk faster than a turtle. He'd usually just stand there and be menacing, not exactly a mover.

"What is it, Geoffrey?" Roberta asked, real fear tightening her voice.

"It was a set up. Elisha set us up!" Turner yelled across the room.

It was frightening to see Turner lose it like that. He was always so composed, no matter how many wrenches one threw into his plans. (And trust me, as one that threw a lot of those wrenches, I knew what I was talking about.)

"What do you mean a set up?" I found that I was the one who was speaking. My blood had turned cold. What had Elisha done now?

"The surrogates are already gone, taken to Havenville. My sources lied to me, they're working for Roland." Turner was pacing, fuming, livid.

"So we'll get them at Havenville, it'll save us two trips," Nancy suggested, trying to put a positive spin on the current events.

And as much as I dreaded doing this mission in the first place, she had a point. It would be a lot better, mentally, if I only had to use the twins once and not twice like we planned.

"You stupid girl! They have the surrogates, yes, but luring us out to Arizona was the set up!" Turner raced across the room to Roberta and held on to her tight. Roberta fell into his arms like a wilted flower. It would have been sweet if it weren't *them*.

"Geoffrey, what did she do, just tell us?" Roberta actually had tears streaming down her cheeks. Apparently, Gramps's erratic behavior scared Roberta a lot more than any of us.

"She broke out the I.Q. Farm." Geoffrey's words made everyone in the room go completely still.

Oh man.

"She what?" My voice sounded strange in the silence.

Geoffrey pulled away from Roberta to focus on me. "She knew we were the only ones capable of stopping her, so she made sure we were both out of the way. And just to rub it in our faces, she took the surrogates before we even left the city."

"So we're talking about an army of sociopaths?" Jill's voice cut through the tension only to cause more tension.

"Army?" Nancy questioned. She obviously hadn't thought that far ahead.

"We're talking about a group of the most brilliant minds in existence, present company excluded." Turner nodded to Ryan. "And, yes, they're sociopaths which makes them far more dangerous than any soldier. They have no conscience. They feel *nothing*."

"So they're like you then?" Jill piped in again. As much as I completely agreed with her, it wasn't helping. I could see the terror in Nancy, Jason and Bill's faces and I wanted to say something that would make them feel better.

Only Ryan appeared calm, probably because he was trying to keep me calm as well. He reached down and held my hand, squeezing it to let me know he was with me no matter what.

I realized in that moment that I needed to do something. I needed to be the strong one, the one that would somehow save the day and make everything okay again. It was funny that as I looked back it was much easier when I was just dealing with the grandparents. Our battle was with each other, not with thousands of pregnant women in a Christian Coalition town and an army of Age-pro'd super geniuses that were psycho enough to do *anything*. It was amazing how perspective could change. It was time for me to step up.

Again.

"We're going to Havenville," I said with as much confidence as I could fake. "I'm using the twins to get the surrogates *and* the I.Q. kids out of there. We're taking Elisha and Roland down at whatever cost, and we're doing it *now*."

I could see that even Turner and Roberta were nodding their heads in agreement.

I had no idea *how* I would stop Elisha and Roland, and I didn't really care, I just knew I had to try. I was going to have to use John and Samuel's powers, but at least I'd only have to do it once, Nancy was right about that.

"How are you going to tell the difference between the surrogates and the townspeople that are pregnant? And how will you know the I.Q. kids? Elisha will have them blend in with the other kids," Bill said as if thinking out loud. I really hated it when he did that, it kind of took away from the momentum. But he was right.

I couldn't let us be defeated. "I'm taking them all, we'll sort out the townspeople from the others once we have them in the giant hover behind us."

Jill whacked Bill in the chest with a roll of the eyes. "No more questions. Let's get this done." Surprisingly, Bill took the whack with dignity and even gave Jill a smile. He got it. We couldn't afford to voice any more doubts. We had to try.

"I'll make the arrangements," Turner said and he and Roberta left the room.

We all just stared at each other after they left. No words needed to be said. This was it. Elisha would win or we would.

At the moment my bet was on Elisha.

Uggh.

It was another hour before we reached Havenville. Elisha's soldiers were in hover-trucks surrounding the town in a tight circle. Turner's enormous people carrier was almost as big as the town itself and I must admit it probably looked quite intimidating landing on the outskirts of town. Not like it had any weapons, but still, any kind of edge was helpful. I wished we were in one of Turner's stealth hover thingies, but we didn't have any time to go get them. The sooner we nabbed the surrogates and psycho kids, the better.

Ryan's hand was glued to mine and I wanted it there. In the original plan, I was going to use the twins' power with Roberta by my side, but now I needed Ryan's strength to help me through as well. If I could just keep myself physically tied to him I knew I could get through this. At least I hoped so.

The rest of the gang was going to help get the surrogate mothers and kids situated inside the people-hover. I knew I could control them long enough to herd them inside, but to make them sit or stand was not something I was sure I was up to. It was going to be hard enough connecting through the twins to over fifty thousand pregnant women, not to mention, the couple thousand kids.

Ryan and I walked into the room housing the twins followed by Roberta. Turner was trying to find out what building Elisha and Roland were in so I could try and control them too. We walked into the back room of the hummer-hover to see John and Samuel sitting politely on a pair of black leather seats. They were holding hands as usual, their milky blue eyes eerily staring up at me. For blind kids it certainly felt like they could see just fine, but I was probably being paranoid.

Roberta shut the door so it was just the five of us in the room.

I clasped Ryan's hand harder and he kissed my cheek in response. "You can do this," he encouraged.

Roberta stepped forward and grabbed my other hand. "You're going to need my strength. If you feel like it's too much, disconnect, take a breather, and re-connect. Do you understand?" she asked in her *kind* voice.

I simply nodded.

I didn't want to think about it anymore.

I just wanted to get it over with.

I closed my eyes and slammed myself into the black swirling heads of the twins.

The bright light engulfed me at once and I almost jumped out of them on instinct. I could feel Ryan and Roberta's hands tighten as they sensed my trepidation, or maybe it was the small gasp I just realized I let out. Either way, I found the comfort I needed from them, then I concentrated hard enough so that I could see everything in *over-exposed* view rather than *blinding sun* view.

Instead of black swirling holes, I saw only swirling light in almost everything around me and in the town. I steadied my thoughts to concentrate on isolating the white swirling light in only the people. It was hard because, just like with my own power, if I thought hard enough about it I could see the tiniest dead molecule, it was the same with the twins, to the tiniest atom. It was much harder controlling life than death. There was a lot more of it, first off, and John and Samuel's power was brand new to me. I didn't have the years of experience I had from using my own power, so isolating just people took a lot of deep breathing and focusing, but after a few moments...

"Okay, I can see the people," I said aloud, giving Ryan and Roberta a play-by-play of what was going on.

It was actually a beautiful sight. In the midst of all this terror and mayhem, seeing every single person's glowing bright light was stunning. I noticed two other things as well. One: the swirling white lights were in the chest, just like the black holes in the dead. Two: the twins did indeed have the same four-mile restriction I did. Good to know. It was a conflicting sensation seeing such beauty and at the same time ticking off stratagems for using the twins' powers.

Then I saw something that took my breath away.

All the pregnant women. Their swirling white holes were brighter than the rest, but what was truly stunning was the almost blinding white lights swirling in their bellies. The babies. I almost cried at the sight, it was so beautiful!

"Pretty babies. We can't kill those, they're too bright," Samuel said in his oh-so-creepy voice in my head.

Shut up! I wanted to scream. At the same time I needed to file that information away. It was one more detail about how Roberta and my father survived their first attack, and any information could be helpful later on.

I tried not to think about the fact that John and Samuel could see what I saw, but I wasn't surprised by it either. I had to block them out if I was to stay concentrated.

I focused back on the women and then tried to seek out the I.Q. kids.

Nothing.

I couldn't sense anyone under five feet tall. I knew I might have to control some short adults and then release them later, but there weren't any short adults, either. Maybe Elisha didn't bring them here? Maybe they were somewhere else entirely.

"I don't see any kids," I said more to Roberta than Ryan. She'd need to tell Turner that we may have to look elsewhere.

I kept my concentration on the surrogates, but I could hear Roberta report my lack of findings to Turner.

"The I.Q. kids are with Elisha in Building Sixty," Turner's voice came through Roberta's speaker phone.

I immediately put my feelers out near the vicinity of Building Sixty, but I only saw one man's spinning white hole. "I only see one guy, probably Roland."

Turner responded, "She must have found some way to mask them. Just get the surrogates into the containment-hover and then come over here as soon as you're done."

"What about the twins?" I asked, hoping he'd say to send them as far away from this town as possible once I was finished.

"Keep them with you, Elisha can't use them, and if we figure out how to break her camouflage of the I.Q. kids we may need you to use John and Samuel again to control her," Turner said through the speaker and I tried not to let my skin crawl. He was right though whether I liked it or not, I'd have to connect ot the twins a second time.

I slammed myself into every spinning white hole of every pregnant woman in Havenville. I vomited immediately.

"What's happening? Are you okay?" Ryan's voice was hurried and panicked in my ear.

The twins giggled in amusement.

"She'll be fine. Connecting to the light takes far more stamina and mental agility than connecting to the dead. Let her be," Roberta's voice was calming and she sounded so sure of herself. It made me gain a little bit more of my bearings.

"Chelsan, you can stop. I don't want you to get hurt." Ryan completely ignored Roberta, his only concern was for my safety.

"No, I'm good. I'm connected to them all. It's just… overwhelming." Every fiber of my being felt like it was spinning with energy. If I thought connecting to the dirt was a trip, this was like being filled up with a giant shaft of light, beaming life into every cell of my body. It was incredible. And I knew in that moment I had to stop. If I didn't I'd be lost to it.

Just get them in the ship.

I had to repeat it over and over in my head.

I tried with all my might to ignore the exhilaration thrusting through me.

I was controlling life.

Life.

These were human beings that I made walk through town toward the giant transport ship waiting to take them back to the babies' birth parents. I could hear the screams from the town. I was causing chaos and terror as I made thousands of women leave town against their will. The light surged through my veins. I felt all powerful. I *was* all powerful. I could make atoms move.

Focus.

Focus.

Just get them into the ship.

It was the longest twenty minutes of my life. It was the most elating. It was the most terrifying. I could feel Ryan and Roberta's light like they were stars bursting into existence. I hardly noticed the twins. I was draining them so utterly, I was barely aware of the small whimpering sounds they started to make.

"They're all in. They're all in," Nancy's voice sounded through Roberta's speaker phone.

"Disconnect, Chelsan," Ryan said in my ear loudly. I was vaguely aware of the fact that it was the fifth time he had said it.

The light was enthralling, I didn't want to disconnect from the twins at all. I wanted to bask in this light. The spinning white holes were so much purer than the darkness I was bound to. I was tired of death. Of using death. Of seeing death everywhere in everything. It was an anchor.

A curse. The light was healing and invigorating. It was alive.

"Chelsan, stop. You're killing them," Ryan pleaded.

That was when I noticed the black spinning chasms starting to grow in the center of John and Samuel.

I disconnected and fell into Ryan's arms. My sight back to normal. No more bright light. No more over-exposure. My eyes still needed to adjust, it was like I had walked into a dark cave from a bright sunny day.

The twins still stood, but they whimpered like injured dogs.

I did that to them.

I couldn't look at them.

I closed my eyes and took comfort in Ryan's hand stroking my hair.

Turner's voice interrupted the moment, an unpleasant reminder that we weren't done yet, "Get to Building Sixty. We need to take the kids back to the Farm."

Roberta grabbed my arm to jolt me out of my stupor. "You two can hug later, let's get over to Geoffrey."

Ryan removed Roberta's hand from my arm with an angry shove. Roberta looked like she was on the verge of some kind of attack so I stood up and calmed her down with a look. "I'm ready."

Roberta walked over to John and Samuel and forced John to take her hand. She led the way, and with the twins in tow, we exited the vehicle, jogging toward Building Sixty. The town was in turmoil, everyone running around like they were under attack, but no one was shooting. They ignored us completely and before we knew it we stood in front of the giant warehouse.

I was no longer connected to the twins so I couldn't test the theory of whether or not the I.Q. kids were really inside, but I was going to take Turner's word for it. Gramps came to greet us with fifteen of his soldiers behind him.

"My scouts say that Elisha and Roland are in there with the kids," Turner informed us.

"They don't have super strength or anything do they?" I asked wanting no surprises.

"No, they should pretty much be comatose, and they are in children's bodies so they're weak," Turner responded.

Comforting. And it suddenly occurred to me this was another

reason Turner kept the I.Q. kids *kids*. It must drive the sociopaths crazy not being able to have the physical strength to hurt anyone.

"Once we're in there, I'll connect with the twins again and we'll get those kids into the transport. Just keep Elisha and Roland busy," I said as I led the charge inside.

I opened the door and hurried down the corridor to the main entrance. I could feel rather than see the entourage of people behind me. My back-up: crazy grandparents, psycho twins, and fifteen soldiers who had probably tried to take me out at one time or another in the last couple of months. Ryan was the only one I could truly trust, which was why my hand was pretty much glued to his.

"Are you going to open it?" Turner hissed with impatience.

I opened the door.

We entered into a room that looked like a recreation of Turner's I.Q. Farm. Most of the kids were connected to the same kind of brain machines Ryan had been wired in to, but a few others were standing against the wall behind Elisha and Roland, holding hands, staring at seemingly nothing. To say it was scary would be an understatement.

Elisha and Roland watched us all come in with a calmness that suggested they were expecting us.

Uh-oh.

I suddenly didn't care too much about the I.Q. kids, I just wanted to get out of there.

"Chelsan, do your thing." Turner smiled triumphantly at Elisha, but she stared back at him with such confidence that I seriously wanted to run away screaming.

I figured I'd just get this over with: one way or another, I wasn't going to let Elisha use her army of crazies.

I slammed into John and Samuel's black swirling heads once again.

I was accustomed to it this time. I immediately shifted focus to keep everything in over-exposed vision. No more blinding light. I was about to connect to all the I.Q. kids when I realized…

I still couldn't see their spinning white centers. I could see Elisha and Roland's and all of my gang, but not theirs.

Wait.

There were three others I could see just out of view behind one of the consoles. They must be lying down and they were…

Pregnant.

Elisha still had three pregnant women.

"Now!" Elisha screamed.

Now what?

SLAM!

I lost all sight. All I could see were the white spinning holes against complete darkness. I gasped for air. I tried to connect to Elisha to stop her from whatever she was doing to me, but…

I couldn't.

I physically couldn't connect to any of the white holes.

And then I saw them. All of them. All of the I.Q. kids like a swarm of fireflies surrounding my head.

It wasn't their physical bodies, it was their life sources. Elisha had managed to use the machines to separate them from their physical forms and essentially render me useless.

I tried disconnecting from the twins, but the I.Q. *collective* stopped me from doing that as well. It was worse than being buried alive. I was trapped inside my own head. Inside my own power. Inside John and Samuel's power.

Ryan's light was brighter than it had ever been, standing next to me, squeezing my hand, knowing something was terribly wrong. He was trying to push me out of the building, but Turner's men wouldn't let him. I could hear Turner and Roberta telling him that the only way to break Elisha's hold was to keep me there and fight.

"Ryan, trust us. We can break her hold, but not without Chelsan here," Roberta pleaded with him.

I wanted to speak, but even speech was taken away from me. I was more helpless than I'd ever been. My only ray of light was literally Ryan standing next to me, not letting go.

I could hear Roberta and Turner chanting. They were about to do some major mojo.

SLAM!

The swarm of lights made me connect to Ryan, my grandparents and their men, stopping them from helping me in any way. The I.Q. kids forced me to keep Ryan and the soldiers and, more importantly, my grandparents, completely still.

I suddenly knew how John and Samuel felt when I'd used them to get the surrogates into the transport hover. It was horrifying and draining. The harder I concentrated the tighter the swarm of lights closed in on my head. I needed to break out of their hold…

…But I didn't even know where to start.

"Bring out the vessels." I saw Roland's white swirling hole walk toward the three pregnant women. From the way their lights moved I could tell they were on hover-gurneys. Their lights and the lights of their babies floated toward me until there were six glowing spheres right in front of me in the darkness.

I really wished I could see normally. Even if it was only out of the corner of my eye, just to see Ryan. I felt so alone. I could still feel his hand in mine, but neither one of us could squeeze or hold on tight. We were just locked together that way because it happened to be the position we were in when the I.Q. swarm took over my body.

"Ready?" Elisha asked.

"Yes," the collective swarm of I.Q. kids answered in unison.

SLAM!

Oh no.

No.

No.

They made me connect to the white swirling lights of the mothers and their babies and disconnect them from it. The same way I disconnected the black holes from dead things so that they were dead forever, so that no one else could control them. Elisha and her army were making me kill these three surrogate mothers and their babies.

And I couldn't stop them.

In seconds I had done it. I had disconnected them from their light.

But…

They weren't dead.

Their lights were spinning as bright as ever.

Oh man.

Just like Roberta when she was pregnant with Franklin.

And it hit me.

Elisha just made me do what the twins did to Roberta and my father.

I'd just created three babies who would have powers like mine.

I wanted to ask a million questions, but the I.Q. kids held me under their power with an iron grip.

"Did it work?" Elisha's voice sounded in the darkness.

"Yes. They're all alive," Roland's voice answered with some excitement.

"Wonderful." Elisha was obviously thrilled by this. "Get the ritual prepared for Chelsan."

"Of course." I could hear Roland clinking around in front of me.

The ritual. The ritual to take my powers and kill me in the process. I couldn't let that happen. If Elisha had my powers she would be able to connect to the twins and pretty much kill anything she wanted within a four-mile radius. And I was relatively sure that was exactly what she would do, starting with all of us.

But…

A part of me knew this couldn't be true otherwise she would have done it already. She just had me disconnect the pregnant women from their lights, so why didn't she have me do the same to my posse? Too difficult maybe? I didn't know, but I filed it away as a possible weakness I could hopefully exploit.

I needed to stall her while I tried to break through this I.Q.-craptasic-wonder-prison she'd managed to snare me in before she'd make me do something like… kill Ryan. I erased that thought from my brain. It made me lose focus. I concentrated as hard as I could and it took every ounce of strength I had to mutter the word, "Gramps."

I wasn't sure why I chose that particular word, but I was sure it would make Elisha say or do something. She hated Turner as much as I did. Maybe more. I hoped it would distract her for a minute or two while I figured a way out of this mess.

I wasn't disappointed.

"All that energy expended and you call out to *him* for help?" Elisha snarled. "Tell me Chelsan, did you ever ask yourself *why* I was to be executed?"

My plan was to completely ignore Elisha to stay focused, but now that she said it out loud, I realized that after I'd helped her escape I never did find out the reason why she was to be executed. I just assumed it was because… well… because it was her.

"Why?" I managed to squeeze out. This was good. The more I pushed, the more words I could form. I was still in the darkness, but maybe I could break out of this trap after all.

"She's regaining speech, tighten your hold," Elisha ordered, her voice carrying an edge of hysteria to it.

Good: it worried her. I was on the right track.

Bad: I immediately felt the circle of I.Q. kids' light tighten around my throat. I almost choked from the pressure of it.

"Good," Elisha crooned. "Your grandfather was going to kill me because I was working on a very special project for him. In fact, you're witnessing his project right now. I was told to come up with a way to control you, Chelsan."

"He *what*?" Wow. That came out despite the choke hold. I had no idea how I was breaking through their grasp, so I had no idea how to expand on it. I tried to move any body part, a finger, toe, eyebrow, anything. But I couldn't budge a muscle.

"I said tighter!" Elisha screamed. She was not liking this a bit. Nice. Let her think I was stronger than I was, maybe I could use it to my advantage. The grip of the lights grew tighter: I didn't know how much longer I could breathe through the pinhole of air I had left in my throat.

"Yes! I figured out a way to use the machines to unite the farm children and to take control of your body, but Turner wanted my invention for himself. He knew I'd use it against him. Do you hear me, Chelsan? He was going to keep you in the farm as a comatose puppet and use your power for his own purposes. He'd have the gift of life and death. Now that power will be mine."

Chelsan, can you hear me? Ryan's voice popped into my head.

My heart surged with excitement. I almost thought I was imagining the whole thing out of false hope until he said into my thoughts, *Can you connect to me and make me move?*

Elisha was still ranting about Gramps. I tuned her out, positive she had no idea Ryan and I were communicating.

I'm connected to you now, but Elisha stopped me from controlling anyone, I said in my head and hoped he'd hear me. His light was still the brightest in the darkness. *I'll try and break through.* I seriously crossed my fingers that I was actually communicating to him. The swarm of lights were closing in like a noose, but I concentrated as hard as I possibly could to slither my way through to Ryan's limbs.

Nothing.

I needed a different tactic.

So far the only way I was able to break through anything was by tapping into my anger for my grandfather. So... emotions. Maybe if I thought about everything that Ryan meant to me...

A flood of images raced through my brain. Our first kiss, holding hands, his arms around me, his smile, his laugh, making love...

SLAM!

Got it, I said in my thoughts and knew Ryan heard me.

I was in his head, and in full control of his body!

But more importantly, I could see.

I was seeing through Ryan's eyes. It was like seeing double, like when I took over a corpse. I could still see the shadow of darkness with the bright lights from my eyes, but I could also see everything else with Ryan's sight.

The pregnant women were in front of us on the hover-gurneys. They appeared to be asleep and had IVs strapped to their arms. Elisha was ranting, while Roland watched her with moonbeams in his eyes as he prepared for the ritual. The I.Q. kids were all still, motionless as if in some sort of coma, controlling my mind and body. My grandparents and their men stood behind us like statues.

So far, no one knew I had control over Ryan.

I need to plug into one of the machines, Ryan's voice sounded in my head.

What? No. Why? I thought nervously. There was no way I wanted Ryan to strap himself into that machine again.

Just trust me. All you'll need to do is make my right arm reach over to the right, see? I only need to attach one node to my head. Don't worry, they suction on, Ryan's voice in my brain was calm and reassuring.

Ryan, don't risk yourself, I think I can break out of this. I didn't really know if I could or not, but I was terrified Ryan would get hurt.

Chelsan, you have to trust me. Make me grab the node. Ryan was firm and commanding. He was right: I needed to trust his judgment. I hoped he knew what he was doing.

Here goes, I thought to him.

I made Ryan move as slowly as I possibly could for fear of Elisha noticing. I carefully had him grab a node from the spider-like tubes attached to the holo-computer stations and place the suction cup on his forehead.

SWOOSH!

Our surroundings blurred into a billion threads of light. It felt like we were flying at light speed down a tunnel of colors and lines.

What's happening? I could barely think.

We're in the machine, Ryan's voice was cool and composed it made my heart slow down a few notches. *I had a few days to explore the ins and outs of this place. Hold on tight,* Ryan said as we raced through the inside of the machine.

I couldn't believe how fast we were moving. Everything was still a blur, but the more I looked around, the more I could see little details here and there. It was like we were flying over a city made of holo-chips and tubes. It was very disorienting and exhilarating at the same time.

Suddenly, up ahead, there was a line of the brightest lights I'd ever seen. As we flew closer to them I recognized them immediately: the swarm of I.Q. kids, their life sources joined as one in the machine.

And we were headed right for them.

This may hurt a little, Ryan's voice echoed in my head.

If I could have closed my eyes I would have, but since I was in Ryan's brain I was forced to watch as we slammed into the line of lights like a bowling ball. The lights scattered like roaches, but re-formed quickly as one.

We zigged and zagged through the electronic ether, hitting balls of light that came hurtling towards us. It was surreal to think that we were actually attacking the I.Q. kids, but when I realized I could wiggle my hand, I knew it was working.

I can move, I told Ryan in his head.

I vaguely heard Elisha screaming commands, and could feel my body moving from being pulled. She screamed "Ritual" so I knew she was about to try and steal my powers and kill me once and for all. She knew something was happening, but by the sheer alarm in her voice I could tell she had no idea what.

My hand was ripped from Ryan's, but I was still connected to him.

Keep fighting them, I have to jump out, I said inside his head as I started to gain control over my body again.

Will do, Ryan replied back.

I ripped myself away from Ryan's head and came back to myself. I could see again with my own eyes. The I.Q. kids' hold over me was weakening from Ryan's attack. I still couldn't control my grandparents and their men, but I kept a part of my brain dedicated to the task.

I had control over myself and I knew I had to stall Elisha.

I pulled away from Roland with as much power as I could. He leapt back in shock.

I turned to Elisha with a wicked grin. "Guess, you underestimated my boyfriend."

Elisha's eyes went wide with shock and horror. "He's… he can't be… it's impossible."

"He's in your little machine and he's taken over." I knew this wasn't completely true, but I liked seeing Elisha sweat like that. It was the first time *ever*.

"No one can control the machine. Not even I can." Elisha whirled around to the holo-stations, frantically studying the readings, but there was nothing out of the ordinary. Ryan was hiding everything from her.

"You're not Ryan," I said, rubbing it in as much as I could.

"But his test results… they said he was just above par… nothing special…He shouldn't even remember who you are." Elisha was seriously at a loss. I don't think she'd ever been duped before and it was freaking her out.

"Guess you're not as smart as you think, Elisha." I smiled. "Ryan spent the whole time you had him prisoner and wired-in studying your little apparatus there, and sending you falsified information, and now he's going to destroy your little army." I really hoped I was right about that. I could move around freely now, but I still had no control over the lights.

"Get her! Let's do this!" Elisha hysterically commanded Roland. Then she yelled at the I.Q. kids. "Make Chelsan kill them all! The sinners must die!"

I braced myself for the moment I dreaded: making me use Samuel and John to kill Ryan and the others… but nothing happened.

I smiled at Elisha triumphantly.

"Looks like your little experiment is broken." I even tried making the pouty lip thing that Jill did so well in mockery of Elisha.

She screamed in rage.

Roland tried to grab my arm, but I stepped away from him and looked him in the eyes with as much emotion as I could muster. "Elisha tortured and murdered Beth, are you really going to follow her? You call yourself a holy man, but look what she's making you do." I was desperate. I needed to delay them.

Roland was immediately choked up. "Beth committed suicide, you heathen, how dare you make up a story like that!"

"I'm not making it up. Ryan saw the whole thing. Why would you trust an aunt you've never even met!" I tried to appeal to Roland's rational side, because maybe he really didn't know how psycho Elisha was. (Though she did just order the kids to make me kill everyone in here. Still, in his warped mind Roland probably thought it was justice.)

"He'll never listen to you, Chelsan. He knows the difference between lies and truth." Elisha was confident when she said this, so confident it made me wonder…

"Listen, Roland, you don't live in the real world. You live in this town where people age and grow old and die. You live peacefully. I know you thought taking the surrogates was the right thing to do, but do you really want to start a war? Because that's what's going to happen if you keep listening to what Elisha says. She killed your mother. Did you ever check the body?" I was grasping at straws, I knew, but I was starting to feel a tingling sensation in my head. I could feel just the outsides of the swirling white holes.

"Elisha told me: Beth killed herself… it was all too much for her." Roland looked like he was starting to doubt. I needed to take advantage of that.

"Enough! Ready her for the ritual!" Elisha screamed at Roland.

"Roland, think about it: Beth wouldn't want this. Elisha killed her because Elisha *likes to kill.* It's why she was chosen for the I.Q. Farm. They only take sociopaths, Roland. Elisha doesn't care about you. She doesn't even know you."

Roland's eyes flared with anger. "Stop saying that! I know Elisha, I knew her from the day she was born, they were my little angels…"

"STOP!" Elisha screamed.

But it was enough.

I hoped my face wasn't showing my shock, but I knew Elisha read it there.

Roland wasn't Elisha's uncle, he was her father.

But he…

…And I understood. Roland had been taking Age-pro probably since Elisha was taken by the government. He'd been lying to his community. He'd duped them all just to save his daughter.

"I just wanted them to know how it feels to have your baby taken away from you." Roland was broken.

He'd taken all those surrogate mothers because he was a dad whose daughter had been ripped away from him. He didn't care about any of the consequences. Elisha knew that. She took advantage of his love for her so she could start a war and recreate the act that gave my dad his power. The unborn babies in front of me were going to be born with my powers, and Elisha would have mine as well. They would be indestructible.

"Why these three?" I asked her, trying to sound as defeated as possible. I could almost control the lights.

"I looked for genetic markers similar to mine. The first batch of surrogates didn't have any, but in the second there were three." Elisha was coming back to herself. She was in gloat mode.

"Genetic markers for what?" I asked.

Roland stared at Elisha in confusion. I hoped he was puzzling out the whole Elisha-is-a-psychopath in his brain.

"The same genetic markers your grandfather uses to find I.Q. kids," Elisha said with a grin.

Great, more sociopaths.

With my powers.

Four against one.

Oh crap.

"You killed Beth," Roland said as if waking up from a cruel nightmare.

Elisha turned to him with a sadistic expression. "Yes, Father."

SWIPE!

Before I could even move or react, Elisha had grabbed the ritual knife off the table and sliced Roland's throat.

I gasped.

It was so shocking, I nearly passed out.

Roland held his neck like he was trying to keep the blood inside his body. And then it was over: he dropped to the floor, unmoving, his black swirling hole telling me he was dead.

Elisha giggled. "I've been wanting to do that for a long time now." She turned to me holding the knife in her child hands, "Get on the table."

"Um, no," I said as I kicked Elisha in the chest as hard as I could.

Her little body flailed backwards and hit the console behind her.

Cool.

All the I.Q. kids dropped to the floor unconscious.

CLAP!

Powers back.

Oh yeah.

Thanks, Ryan.

I disconnected from the twins instantly. It was just now that I realized they had been whimpering the whole time. I hadn't drained them as badly as before, but they looked like they were about to collapse.

"NOW!" Elisha screamed and at least forty armed men ran into the building. "Get the mothers out of here!" Elisha commanded the men closest to her.

Five or six of the men started pushing the hover-gurneys out the back.

Roberta and Turner began chanting again, and I did the only thing I could think of.

Sorry twins.

I slammed back into their swirling black heads, then made Elisha and all of her men freeze.

Without the I.Q. kids controlling me I could feel John and Samuel's power surging through me once more.

Turner and Roberta stopped chanting and stood beside me.

"Can you control her back onto the ship?" Turner asked.

I nodded my head.

Whoa.

I nearly fell from something draining my energy fast.

Ryan was there in an instant to catch me.

"What's wrong?" he whispered in my ear.

"I don't know," I answered honestly. My legs were shaking, I could barely stand up. It was like I had been running on batteries and someone just pulled them out.

My eyes wouldn't stay open.

I was losing my grip on the twins.

I looked over at them with hooded eyes.

And they were smiling.

The black swirling holes in their heads were growing fainter and fainter.

"Turner!" I gasped. "John and Samuel… they're healing…" was all I could sputter out.

Turner and Roberta looked at each other with horror.

"The connection with the I.Q. collective. They figured out how to regenerate the dead cells," even Turner's voice sounded pale from what that meant.

I was fading fast.

Elisha and her men were squirming loose.

John and Samuel giggled as they slowly started to take control. They were chomping at the bit to use their powers once again.

We'd all be dead soon.

"Geoffrey we have to," Roberta's voice sounded determined.

"NO! You'll die!" Turner was crazy with terror.

"We have no choice!" Roberta pleaded.

I tried to push myself up.

Ryan kept me clasped in his arms. "Don't. I'm getting you out of here."

"No… I… have… to … help…" I gasped.

My vision was blurring.

John and Samuel's black holes were almost dissipated.

Turner and Elisha's men were dropping like flies as the twins disconnected them from their spinning white holes. It took all of my being to stop them from killing Ryan, Turner, Roberta and myself. Elisha was up now, taking the three surrogates, and steering their hover-gurneys out of the building.

No.

I could see Roberta run to the boys.

Turner grabbed for her, but she was faster. He was screaming.

I kept Roberta protected.

The boys were desperately trying to kill her.

I was fading fast. I didn't know how much longer I could hold on.

SLICE. SLICE.

John and Samuel dropped to the floor like Roland, their necks slashed, their black holes now spinning in their chests instead of their heads.

Turner caught Roberta just before she hit the floor.

The last thing I saw was the black swirling chasm raging in Roberta's chest, her dead body clutched in the arms of my grandfather…

***

I awoke next to Ryan, in my own bed at Nancy's house.

I leapt out of it like it was on fire. Ryan was immediately up with me and put his arms around me protectively. "It's okay. You're home now."

I fell into his chest and started to cry. I couldn't seem to stop. Everything that happened was too much. Roberta was dead. Elisha was…

"Elisha?" I asked.

Ryan held me tighter. "Gone. She escaped with the three surrogates. Turner said they were dead like Roberta, but the babies might have survived."

I shook my head. "They'll be like me."

Ryan cupped my face with his hands. "You need some rest."

"I don't want to." I tried to stop the tears from falling down my face.

Ryan leaned close and kissed me.

"Can I come in?" Nancy popped her head through the door. Her face somber.

I raced over to Nancy and hugged her tightly.

The whole gang followed behind, Bill, Jason and… Jill. We all sat down on the bed, silent for a good few minutes, no one sure what to say.

Jason was the first, "The surrogates were reunited with the babies' parents. Turner took care of all that."

"How is he?" I asked and found that the lump in my throat was making it hard to swallow.

"I don't know. He was pretty quiet for most of the trip. He only talked shop before he dropped us off," Jason answered.

I couldn't help but feel for Turner. I knew I should feel like he finally got what he deserved, but I didn't. No one should have to lose someone they love. No one.

"He told us to be ready," Bill said, a little bit of fear in his eyes.

"Ready for what?"

"Everyone is in an uproar." Jason sighed as if the next sentence was difficult to say. "From the attacks on the Baby Centers and the bombings at the school…"

"A war," I said guessing at his next sentence.

"Not just a war, Chelsan. A holy war," Jason's voice was quiet with fear.

A holy war?

I looked at everyone and they all looked at me. We were all in shock. No one spoke. There hadn't been a war on this planet in three hundred years, and somehow I felt as if I was the one that started it.

Oh man.

I leaned into Ryan and wished it would all go away.

Yeah, right.

Here we go.

RIPPER
BOOK THREE

Chapter 0
Year: 2321

Are those coffins?

I couldn't quite make out the boxy silhouettes before me.

I must have fallen asleep doing my homework again. This was starting to become a habit with me. But I couldn't help it! Two chapters of Biochemistry and I was out cold.

I tried to get a better look at my surroundings to determine if this was really a *dream* or *astral projection*.

When it comes to my brain, it could be either.

Roberta stepped out in front of me.

Definitely a dream, considering Roberta died five months ago. And besides, this Roberta was young, about twenty or so. The Roberta I knew was a Feline. Felines were people who lived before the invention of the drug Age-pro and they had used multiple surgeries to keep their youthful appearance. The only problem was that after so many face-stretching surgeries they ended up looking like cats. With the immortality of Age-pro, they ended up looking like cats *forever*.

Roberta was my grandmother and she was by far the worst offender.

I was relieved, then, to be dreaming of Roberta in her twenty-year-old form. Back when she was alive, seeing her all stretched and frozen was like coming face to face with a monster. (Of course, it didn't help that she actually *was* a monster!) Let's just say I have a history with my grandparents and the bottom line is: they're psychopaths.

Still. Roberta had helped me out. She even saved my life a couple of times when she wasn't trying to kill me. (I know, sounds like I'm contradicting myself, but you *really* have to know my grandparents to understand.)

Even though I hated to admit it, I really *was* sad when Roberta died.

After all, she killed herself to save my friends and me.

I still couldn't believe she sacrificed herself like that. Selflessness was not one of Roberta's traits.

But she did.

And I was grateful.

I suppose I was dreaming about her because a part of me missed her.

When she wasn't trying to kill me, I almost liked her.

In fact, when Elisha (an age-pro'd-seven-year-old-ninety-eight-year-old-sociopath-I.Q.-Farm-kid, long story!) buried me alive, Roberta had been my only lifeline. She visited me through astral projection so I wouldn't go insane. That was how I knew what she looked like at twenty. Roberta appeared to me in the form of her younger self when I was trapped in that metal coffin…

Even though the boxes were in silhouette, I was sure they were coffins now.

I must be having some kind of nightmare dealing with… umm gee, let's think… BEING BURIED ALIVE!

Did I mention that? Thank you very much.

I thought I was over it, but I guess it was the kind of thing you never get over.

"Chelsan." Roberta brought my focus back to my dream.

That was new.

This wasn't the first time I'd dreamt of dear old Grams in the last five months. But it was the first time she spoke. Normally, she'd just look at me like she was trying to talk, but wasn't capable of it. Even now, the way Roberta looked at me, made me pause. It was hard to believe that this was coming from my imagination. She looked real and her eyes were so intense.

I wasn't sure if I should respond. It felt weird, like I was talking to myself, which I guess I was since this was a dream.

"This isn't a dream," Roberta shook her head.

Okay…

Now my brain was really trying to mess with me. I felt like a schizophrenic. Was I really going to have a conversation with myself in the form of my dead grandmother whom I hated 98% of the time and kind of liked 2% of the time?

"Can you hear me?" Roberta sounded agitated.

Apparently I was going to do exactly that.

"Yes," I answered reluctantly. I really hated giving into my inner crazy.

"Chelsan, you're not talking to yourself. I'm actually here," Roberta's younger self spoke rather convincingly.

So convincingly, it made me pause. I knew she was dead, I saw her die myself, but what if she was a ghost? Roberta's mojo was insanely powerful. It wouldn't surprise me at all if she could somehow have become a spirit and was now trying to communicate with me.

But then again, maybe this was all guilt. A part of me desperately didn't want to be responsible for her death. I knew it wasn't really my fault, but unfortunately the human brain didn't work that way. Roberta killed the twins and died as a result.

I couldn't stop remembering those twins, John and Samuel, especially the creepy way they always held hands and stared at me with their blind eyes… the way I took control over their power…

I shuddered.

Sure, I can control the dead, but the twins… they could control life itself.

My grandfather had deadened the cells surrounding John and Samuel's brains, allowing someone like me to control the twins by using their dead brain cells. Weird, but effective. Roberta and Turner could control the dead too, but not innately like me. They had to use spells and black magic to do it.

I still couldn't believe the things I'd done and seen over the last year.

I had sort of slipped into the lull of "normalcy" these last five months, but when I was asleep I couldn't hide from my past.

From who I was.

I was the girl who sees swirling black holes in dead things and could make them do whatever I wanted.

And the twins were the reason I had my power.

Over two hundred years ago they killed everyone in the original I.Q. Farm by detaching the living from their spinning white holes. (That was how they saw life, as a spinning white hole of energy.) One of those victims was Roberta, but for some unknown reason, because she was pregnant, she lived, and as a result my father was born with the power I have today. When Roberta and Turner tried to use a powerful curse to kill my mom and me when I was just a baby, Dad performed a spell and sacrificed himself to save us. Unbeknownst to him, he transferred his power to control the dead over to me.

Warped as they were together, my grandparents truly loved one another. Turner and Roberta kept John and Samuel locked up because Turner was afraid that if he killed them, Roberta would die. He was right. Elisha used the collective minds of the I.Q. Farm kids and temporarily turned me into her puppet, making me use the twins' power to kill everyone in the warehouse that night. Elisha almost succeeded. I almost killed everyone I loved. But Roberta, knowing full well that if she killed John and Samuel she'd die herself, forced herself to walk over to them and slit their throats. She died instantly.

Elisha escaped with her three pregnant hostages (she made me use the twins to detach the spinning light from their bodies so the babies would have the same powers as mine) and none of us had heard from Elisha since. We had no idea if she performed the ritual on one of the babies to gain their power to control the dead for herself.

Elisha had disappeared off the face of the planet.

Which was actually a lot more terrifying than I cared to admit.

"I'm not a ghost," Roberta said as if reading my mind.

This only confirmed that my brain had made Roberta up, otherwise she wouldn't know what I was thinking...

Ugh.

I was over-thinking again. I was supposed to be relaxed and sleeping, not playing mind games…with *myself!*

"I'm sorry for what happened," I began. I figured if this was a guilt dream, I might as well say what I felt, therapy-style.

Roberta rolled her eyes, annoyed. "Would you listen to me? I don't have much time."

"Fine. What?" I figured my subconscious wanted to tell me something. I might as well give it free reign.

"Elisha is awake now," Roberta announced.

Huh?

This dream was getting weirder and weirder.

"Was Elisha asleep?" Why was I giving into my insanity?

Roberta's image flickered, as if she were a bad holo-image about to go off the air.

"Cocooning is more like it." Roberta seemed disgusted. "Pay attention, keep your eyes open. She has spies everywhere and they're watching you." Roberta pointed her finger at me for emphasis.

"Kay," I said, thinking this whole dream was becoming one big paranoid delusion.

"Chelsan, you're not taking me seriously. I can see it in your eyes."

Roberta stepped forward and touched my cheek.

Whoa.

I felt a chill run up and down my spine as if I were fully awake.

Roberta's touch was real.

Real.

This wasn't a dream.

"You're dead," I said to reassure myself that Roberta was truly gone.

"Yes, but not quite, I can't explain here. It takes too much energy and I don't have a lot of it." Roberta's image flickered once more.

"Then you are a ghost," I needed to know what was going on.

"Not quite that either." Roberta popped out of the dream.

I was still in the room with dozens of silhouetted coffin-sized boxes.

Roberta's image faded in again, but she was transparent now.

"Look inside." Her voice sounded as if she were talking to me over a great chasm.

I peered inside the boxes.

Every single one had a body inside.

Not just any body, but the *same* body.

Roberta's.

A room full of sleeping bodies, all with the face of my grandmother in her youthful appearance.

"Clones," she whispered.

CHAPTER 1
MONDAY APRIL 4, 2321

I awoke in my bed with sweat dripping down my face.

I gasped for air, not seeming to breathe in enough of the stuff.

Ryan's arms held me in a protective embrace. "What is it? Are you okay?" he asked gently.

I melted into him, immediately feeling more relaxed. I managed to catch my breath and steady my heart beat as Ryan held me.

"Nightmare," I mumbled into his chest.

Then I told him about the dream.

Ryan pulled me in tighter and kissed my forehead. "It's over now," he whispered softly.

Man, could this boy make my toes curl.

I could see daylight peeking through the curtains of my room and I knew it was close enough to "wake-up" time to get up for school.

"George and Vianne don't know you spent the night," I said with disappointment. I didn't want Ryan to leave, but I also didn't want to disrespect George and Vianne either. Not that they'd really care if Ryan spent the night but, since they were my official guardians as of three months ago, I didn't want them to feel like they weren't in charge. They were the only parents I had left and I'd do anything for them. But Ryan was my weakness and I was grateful he had snuck inside my room last night. It was almost as if he knew I'd have this terrible nightmare and made sure he would be there when I woke up.

"I'm going, I'm going." Ryan pulled away with a smile and I couldn't resist.

I kissed his perfectly perfect lips and then realized, "I know I have bad breath." I was suddenly horrified at the thought of how disgusting my morning breath probably smelled.

"I don't care." Ryan kissed me back. "Mine's worse."

I didn't even notice.

Ryan was just about the most beautiful specimen I'd ever laid eyes on. With his sandy-blonde hair, light brown eyes and chiseled features, sometimes it was hard for me to believe he was actually attracted to *me*. I always thought I was so boring to look at. Brown hair, grey eyes, boring face. Although Ryan and Nancy would kill me for being so down on myself, sometimes it was hard for me to see myself as anything but ordinary looking. I always wanted to be beautiful like Nancy with her golden locks, perfect little nose and gorgeous blue eyes. I definitely felt like the ugly duckling of the group, despite how Ryan always told me how beautiful he thought I was. Someday I'd work on my self-esteem, but for now, I just wanted to stay in Ryan's arms and forget about my crazy dream.

Ryan abruptly pulled away and flinched in pain.

"What is it?" I asked.

Ryan massaged the temple of his head. "Same. I'm all right." Ryan brushed my concern away, obviously not wanting to worry me.

"You should have Turner's doctor look at you," I tentatively suggested. I hadn't heard from Gramps in five months except for the occasional update report, but Ryan's experience with the I.Q. Farm kids in Havenville had left him with killer migraines. Not surprising when you think that he literally plugged himself into a computer that connected all the kids' brains together. When Elisha made me use the twins' powers to kill everyone in the room, that meant all the I.Q. kids, too. Which meant that they died while inside Ryan's brain. No one knew what the ramifications would be. So far it was just headaches.

Really terrible headaches.

I reached up and took over massaging his temples. Ryan relaxed into me, physically melting at my touch. At least I could do something to help him.

Ryan gently pulled my hands away and kissed them. "I better go. I'll see you in a bit."

"You sure you're okay? George and Vianne probably wouldn't mind that you snuck in." I didn't really want to him to leave while his head was hurting so badly.

"I'm fine. Don't worry about me." Ryan kissed me lingeringly.

Before I could argue any more, Ryan was climbing out the window and running up the street toward his house.

I watched him go.

"You two are not fooling anyone, you know."

I turned around to see my best friend in the whole world, Nancy, standing in the doorway in her pajamas. She had her arms crossed and a smile on her face.

"Yeah, I know, but I don't want your parents to be upset," I reasoned.

Nancy guffawed, "You obviously don't know my parents. They'd give Ryan permission to stay here permanently if you two just asked."

"I wouldn't feel right asking if my boyfriend can live with me in their house. I'd be mortified."

Nancy just laughed at that. "But he practically does already, dork."

"I guess," I admitted, seeing her logic. Suddenly I felt like a total hypocrite. Somehow keeping all parties in ignorance had felt like the right thing to do at the time.

Nancy's best-friend-radar was always on. "You look spooked," she said, suddenly serious.

I told her about my dream.

"You think we should tell the rest of the gang?" Nancy asked after I finished recounting the nightmare.

"Maybe… What do you think?" I genuinely wasn't sure if I was just having residual guilt dreams or if Roberta's ghost or clone or whatever had visited me in my head or not. Not exactly a *normal* thing to think, but then again my life was far from normal.

"I think, with you, we should assume the worst and prepare for it. After you tell everyone, then we can all keep our eyes open. I mean even if it's your subconscious, you basically told yourself to watch out for Elisha and possible spies for Elisha. Sounds like playing it smart to me," Nancy rationalized.

I nodded in agreement. "Better call Jason. Bill will be here in a few and I'll tell Jill at school."

"Weird that Jill is a part of the gang. Never thought that would happen in a million years," Nancy sighed. "Still, she has been useful these last few months."

I had to agree. Jill had been my mortal enemy at the beginning of the school year and now I considered her family. We all went through a lot together and Jill had come out the other side a better person. Sure she could still be a raging bitch, but at least it wasn't directed at us anymore.

Mostly, anyway.

"I'm going to jump in the shower." I suddenly felt like the soothing hot water would improve my mood.

"I'll assemble the troops." Nancy left with a slight bounce to her step. Calling her boyfriend Jason always put her in a good mood. Although they usually ended up in an argument, Nancy and Jason belonged together and were madly in love. It was a long road coming though. Jason felt he was too old for Nancy at first, being eighty years her senior thanks to Age-pro, but in this day and age everyone looked eighteen, so it hardly mattered to Nancy. Eventually, Jason's feelings for Nancy overpowered any doubts he had about their age difference and they finally hooked up. And I was happy to say they'd been together ever since.

I was about to head into the shower when something caught my eye.

Or more precisely, someone.

At the Hover-Shuttle station just up the road was a kid from my school, Max Grunter. Max and his sister Eva just transferred from New York about three months ago. The two of them were total opposites. Everyone assumed they were adopted, since Max was black and Eva was as pale as anyone I'd ever met.

Max was tall and lanky, like he'd just grown six inches in the last month and his body hadn't caught up yet. He had a shaved head, full lips and dark eyes that always seemed to be contemplating something deep.

I had to admit, Max was a very good-looking guy. (Sorry, Ryan, love you always, but I still have eyes!) Jill thought so too, though she was keeping her cool about the whole thing. After everything that went down with Bill, I guess Jill decided she didn't want to be second fiddle to anyone (me being the *anyone*, Bill had professed his love to me while he and Jill were dating!).

And, besides, Bill had now shifted his interest to Max's sister Eva.

Eva was quite beautiful with long auburn hair and bright green eyes. Well, beautiful except for the burns. Only her face was unmarred by the long streaks of scarring covering her entire body. Neither Max nor Eva ever talked about how Eva received her burn marks, but they looked excruciatingly painful.

I had never seen Max at the Hover-Shuttle station before. I didn't even think he lived around here.

Max's eyes suddenly looked at mine with purpose.

I froze.

He was trying to tell me something.

And I mean literally.

I could feel him tapping at my head.

My Grams, Roberta, had taught me how to keep people like Elisha out of my brain, since astral projection was not only a real thing but also a dangerous thing. I shuddered thinking about how Elisha had made me go against my basic instincts by crawling inside my head and influencing me to do stupid things I wouldn't normally do. Teaching me how to resist Elisha's brain invasion was another thing I was grateful to Roberta for. Once I knew how to keep Elisha's meddling creepiness out of my head, I was able to keep anyone out.

But Max?

Did he even know what he was doing?

Most people had no idea that they were capable of astral projection. It was like when someone says something that you were just thinking. Either you or the other person had popped into each other's head and most of the time no one was the wiser.

Except me.

I could tell.

And Max was trying to get in.

I almost let him, just to see what on earth he wanted to say or what he was thinking. But I trusted my instincts and kept him out.

Max looked away as the Hover-Shuttle arrived. He stepped onto the shuttle without another glance in my direction.

Bizarre.

I shook the thought of Max from my brain and took a quick shower.

I put on a pair of jeans, my favorite blue T and my black high top Chucks. I was ready for the world or, at least, school, which sometimes felt like the world. I couldn't believed we only had two months left of school and we'd all be graduating. With the craziness my life had been this last year, I hadn't even thought about real life. Or normal stuff anyway. Prom, graduation, homework, boys: they were all things that most teenagers stressed about. I had to think about psycho grandparents, sociopathic seven-year-olds and learning as much as I could about my power to control dead things.

Lucky me.

Grabbing the electronic reader from my bedside, I hurried out of my room, to the terracotta-tiled hallway and down the spiral staircase to the living room. The life-sized holo-TV was on, but no one was watching it. I barely glanced at the newscaster giving her report as I pushed open the door to the kitchen.

The gang was all there waiting for me.

Ryan stood against the wall and immediately grabbed my hand when I walked in. He kissed me softly with a grinning, "Good morning, beautiful," as if he hadn't seen me already this morning.

"Morning," I said back, giving him a slight roll of my eyes at his attempt at subterfuge.

"Hey." Bill nodded in greeting. His brown hair was perfectly messy and his big blue eyes sparkled with a hello. Even after all the rejection I'd put him through, Bill still wanted to be my friend. I considered myself very lucky. Bill was such a good human being it made my brain hurt.

"Clones, seriously?" Jason was already there sitting at the kitchen table with Nancy at his side. His curly black hair mussed as usual and his green eyes looking up at me with an amused twinkle.

Apparently, Nancy had given them the scoop.

George and Vianne sat across from Nancy and Jason. Vianne waved a hello. "Sit down and have some breakfast, Chelsan."

George, Vianne, Nancy and Jason all had a bowl of cereal in front of them and I had a pang of disappointment. I would've killed for pancakes. Bad dreams always brought out my comfort-food cravings. But cereal would do just fine as long as it was full of sugar. I let go of Ryan's hand and pulled down a box of rainbow colored nuggets with pastel-colored marshmallows and knew I had selected a breakfast of champions.

Pouring ample milk on my brightly colored food, I sat at the head of the table. "It could have just been a nightmare."

Armed with a spoon of his own, Ryan sat down next to me and snuck a couple of bites of cereal from my bowl.

"With you, we can't be sure. Cloning though… Unless your grandparents have the secret of all secrets, there has never been a successful case of cloning," Jason mused.

"But I thought they'd been cloning things for years?" Nancy asked in confusion.

I had to agree with her. Everything we'd read in school said scientists had been cloning for over three hundred years.

"*Successful* cloning, cutie," Jason said to Nancy, reaching over to kiss her cheek.

Nancy turned pink as usual and that led to the inevitable silly grin, which would be stuck to her face until Jason pissed her off.

"What's the difference between successful cloning and just plain cloning?" I asked, not as amused as Nancy with his answer.

"When I was working as a lab technician I read a report on the first attempt at human cloning," Jason began. I sometimes had to remind myself that before Jason Keroff was the most famous reporter in the world, he was a lowly lab technician in my grandfather's empire. He used to help develop toxic gases that Gramps would use to exterminate the populous making it look like they'd died from a natural disaster or whatever he'd make up. (That was how Turner murdered my mother and everyone else in my trailer park!)

Jason continued, "But every time they cloned a test subject, they'd turn out… wrong."

"Wrong?" George inquired. George was a science nut himself. Mention any access to secret government experiments, he was all ears.

"Even though everything down to the cell was identical, the clones wouldn't be all there." Jason tapped his head for emphasis.

"They were crazy?" I asked.

"Crazy, mute, comatose, spastic, you name it. None of them were matches to the original test subject. And none of them were normal. None of them were even coherent. Supposedly, all experimentation stopped two-hundred years ago."

Bill was incredulous. "And you'd really be surprised if Turner had kept the experiments going?"

"Not at all, but I'd be very surprised if he was successful." Jason seemed convinced of this.

"Well, Roberta said clones, and how else can we explain why she was twenty-something?" I wondered aloud.

Jason pushed the idea further. "Assuming it was real and not a dream, how is Roberta alive? If she's just a clone, she'd have no memory of you. She'd be a lab baby. And lab babies only know what you teach them. It's not like a clone is suddenly born with all the knowledge of their donors. They'd still be babies that grow up to adulthood. Just genetically and physically identical people to the person they're cloned after."

"Anyway, it was just weird," I mumbled through a particularly large bite of sugary goodness.

"More importantly, your dream told you to watch out for Elisha's spies." Nancy brought the conversation back to the very thing that disturbed me the most about my nightmare.

Bill answered quickly, "We can spot a seven-year-old a mile away, and if she's gained your powers, it's not like you won't be able to see a dead person spying on you as well." He had obviously been thinking this one through.

Ryan interjected, "True, but maybe she's using people from Havenville. People we'd never even know are working for her."

And I thought of Max.

Max and Eva, they were new. Maybe they didn't come from New York. Maybe they came from Havenville and were spying for Elisha.

I told the others about Max trying to butt his way inside my head.

Nancy was all over it. "You should let him in next time. I mean, Max could be trying to warn you. Or if he doesn't know he's doing it, you could search his brain or something, find out if he works for Elisha."

Bill interjected defensively, "Max, fine, but Eva has been through enough."

"Here we go." Ryan rolled his eyes.

"What's that supposed to mean?" Bill made forced eye contact with Ryan.

Bill was angry.

What a shock.

Ugh.

"It just means you've moved on to the next wounded bird." Ryan was obviously annoyed.

"Ryan…" I wanted to stop this fight before it got out of hand.

"Excuse me if I have compassion." Bill crossed his arms.

Ryan put down his spoon and stood up to face Bill. "I don't mind you having compassion. I *do* mind you turning a blind eye when this Eva could be dangerous. You don't want to even consider the possibility that she could be working with Elisha and that puts Chelsan in danger. So, yeah, I have a problem with your compassion."

"Eva is not working for Elisha!" Bill exclaimed defiantly. "I'd know."

Pin drop.

"Are you dating her?" Nancy broke the silence.

"Not that it's any of your business, but yes." Bill looked at me to gauge my reaction. When I obviously didn't give him the expression that he'd hoped for, his face turned from defensive to angry.

"Has she ever asked about Chelsan?" Jason asked, stepping in before the situation became too uncomfortable.

"Not exactly." Bill started to squirm.

"Spill." Nancy gestured with her hand for Bill to confess everything.

"Nothing. We just talked about past relationships and stuff. Your name came up. It was nothing." Bill looked uncomfortable. He was embarrassed and I didn't want to make it worse.

"Why would Chelsan's name come up in a 'past relationship' conversation? You two never dated."

Ryan.

I could kill him.

Bill's stance grew rigid, like he was about to deck Ryan. "Of course

Chelsan came up in a past relationship conversation: I was in love with her, she was in love with you, it sucked. End of story. Eva is cool, she's not with Elisha. Can we drop it?"

"It's dropped." Ryan put his hands up in surrender. I could tell that he felt bad. "Sorry," he kind of half-mumbled under his breath.

"What was that, genius boy?" Nancy couldn't resist teasing Ryan.

Ryan turned to Bill. "I'm sorry," he said sincerely, "I'm a dick."

"Duh," Bill responded, but like the true sweetheart he was, he slowly smiled. "Just think before you talk next time."

Ryan saluted and that was that.

I didn't move for a good few seconds, waiting for the two of them to start up again.

But both of them seemed totally over it.

Boys.

Until the next fight.

"I'll talk to Max and see what he has to say for himself." I wanted to steer the subject away from Eva, but if Max was working for Elisha, then Eva most undoubtedly was, too. Still, I didn't want to push Bill. He genuinely seemed happy about Eva. I didn't want to ruin that for what might turn out to be no reason at all.

Besides, if I was right and Jill was into Max, I didn't want to ruin that, either.

I never thought there'd be a day where I actually cared about Jill Forester's feelings!

"Let's get to school," Bill suggested.

I could tell he wanted to get out of there.

Before long we were all headed toward the front door and to Bill's hover-car outside.

The news was still playing on the holo-TV. I barely heard Carleton Gordan (anchorman extraordinaire and by extraordinaire I mean monotone boringness!) talking about the still-missing John Fortski as we left the house. It was kind of odd that the inventor of Age-pro was kidnapped three months ago and his family had still received no word from the kidnappers. I was starting to wonder if the guy hadn't just left town on his own volition.

Still. It always struck me as peculiar. I couldn't quite put my finger on it, but somehow I knew Fortski's disappearance had something to do with either Turner or Elisha. I even asked Gramps about it a couple of months ago, but he never responded.

I hated that my life consisted of every little thing being a possible threat. I felt like a paranoid freak sometimes.

Better safe than sorry, I guess. I really didn't want to be taken by surprise again. I'd had enough surprises.

Why would anyone want John Fortski? Sure he invented Age-pro, but the guy had pretty much stayed off the radar since then. According to Fortski, once he invented immortality he wanted to enjoy it.

No one heard much from Fortski over the last three hundred years, until three months ago. Fortski's holo-call to the police went viral within seconds of it happening. There was Fortski, wide-eyed and freaked, simply saying, "They're coming for me." Then fuzz. His home showed no signs of forced entry, but there was evidence of a struggle in his living room where the holo-call was made. The investigation was still open, but I got the impression that everyone had pretty much given up on the guy.

Except me.

Something was off and I'd figure it out sooner or later.

I'd only told Jason about my suspicions and he agreed to look into it. So far he was coming up blank as well. At some point I planned to interrogate my grandpa about the whole ordeal, but for now I let it go.

We piled into Bill's hover-car and in seconds it was up in the air, zooming towards school on hover-level five. There were seven hover lanes to keep traffic to a minimum. In an overpopulated world, traffic could be a real problem. Luckily, all hover vehicles ran on hydrogen fuel cells, so the only waste they excreted was purified water. There were water dumping stations all over the planet that used the water for pretty much everything from watering lawns to drinking water. It was a very recycled world, but it worked.

No one had said much on the ride over. Bill and Ryan hardly fought anymore, they hardly spoke, but they had at least been civil. But the fight this morning must have caused more of a rift than was already there. Ryan had held my hand in the car, but he stared out the window the entire time, his mind on other things. At one point I thought they would be close, but when Bill had decided that Ryan was the enemy (and his one roadblock to me), it turned into a fistfight. Of course, Bill immediately regretted his actions towards Ryan when we realized that Ryan had been kidnapped by Elisha and hooked up to an I.Q. Farm computer like a comatose lab rat. But Ryan only saw Bill's jealousy and I guess he felt defensive and insecure.

In the distance I could see Geoffrey Turner High II. Dear Elisha had blown up the first school of the same name five months ago. The new one was temporary. Basically, the new building was an old abandoned elementary school from a hundred years ago, kind of dingy, but I didn't mind. I grew up in a trailer park, I was used to dingy. But Geoffrey Turner High was made up of all the rich kids in the Los Angeles area and they complained daily at the conditions they had to endure by being forced into the "old cobweb-infested building."

The school looked like a giant rectangle from above. It was one level with over two hundred classrooms inside. Surrounded by a forest of California Oak, the building itself looked like an unwrapped present with green leafy wrapping strewn around it. Off to the side was a small clearing of dirt that served as the school's hover-lot.

Bill landed on the dirt floor and we all exited his car.

"Over here!" Jill's voice came from over at the door to the school.

We all turned and started walking toward her.

To say Jill Forester was beautiful was an understatement. She was one of those girls with the perfect figure, face and hair. From her giant green eyes to her long wavy black hair, she was pretty much Snow White in person.

When we arrived at her side, she grabbed Nancy's arm, "Joan says you aren't going to bring Jason to the prom and that *she* is."

Nancy's face went from neutral to furious in about a millisecond. "Is she an idiot?!"

"That's what I thought… at first." Jill looked at Nancy meaningfully.

Nancy swallowed in horror. "What do you mean *at first?*"

"I started thinking about your boy and how he tends to do stupid things like agreeing to go to a dance for an interview with the daughter of Population Control's new advisor per se?" Jill raised an eyebrow.

"He wouldn't." Jill's face had gone white.

Jill was right. He would. It was just the kind of thing Jason would do.

The boy was clueless when it came to women, and extra so when it came to Nancy. If he thought he could get an "exclusive" he'd do anything to get it. And Joan's dad had just come into his new position at Population Control, so Jason would be chomping at the bit to interview him.

Joan was the number one bully at Geoffrey Turner High, although before Jill and I were friends Joan was just Jill's lackey. Jill was queen of all bullies back then, pretty much getting away with anything because her dad was Turner's number two and that meant her family had a lot of power and sway. But after I kind of blew Jill's dad up (literally), Jill became the lowest rung on the totem pole and took over my old role as school leper. That was when Joan became the new Jill. She was horrible! But now that Jill was with me and everyone knew Turner was my grandpa, Joan was fast becoming the new outcast.

I hated school politics. I left those completely up to Jill and tried to stay out of it as much as I possibly could. I just hoped Jill was wrong about Jason, not only for Nancy's sake but for Jason's sake as well.

"I'll kill him," Nancy grumbled.

"I'll help," Jill agreed. She linked her arm through Nancy's and they led the way into the school building.

I had to smile as the rest of us followed them inside, though I shook my head in disbelief. Jill was one of us now. I guess that was what happened when you almost died with someone. It brought you closer together. I never thought I'd say it, but I knew that Jill Forester actually had my back and I had hers.

Strange.

The new/old school was the complete opposite of the previous Geoffrey Turner High. Whereas our last school looked like an 1800s Ivy League College campus, this one looked like an over-sized trailer. The floors consisted of cream-colored linoleum squares that were stained and streaked with black dirt. There weren't any lockers to speak of so everyone had to carry their things with them. (Not really that big of a deal since the only required item any student needed was an electronic reader.) Every door had a small rectangular window at eye-level and all seven hallways looked identical. It took me a while to adjust without becoming completely lost. I literally had to follow the numbers on the doors to find all my classes. But I didn't mind, the school felt cozy.

Ryan still held my hand, but he hadn't said a word.

Neither had Bill.

Bill suddenly turned to us and waved briefly, "See you guys later," and he was off. I glanced in the direction he was headed and quickly saw the auburn tresses of Eva over the sea of crowded heads. I was happy that Bill had finally found someone, I just didn't want to celebrate too early in case Eva turned out to be a spy.

And besides, there was something about that girl I didn't like. She was cold or distant, or something I couldn't quite describe. It was just a feeling. Maybe I was jealous. Not that I liked Bill like that, but having Bill love me for so long and then lose interest entirely… maybe it was a shock to my system. I didn't know. But since I knew I'd never feel anything but friendship for Bill, I figured I'd get over it. It would just take time.

On the plus side, Jill appeared completely over Bill, which lightened my spirits a bit. Bill had been so flakey with her, I didn't want her to get her heart broken. More importantly, I didn't want to admit to myself that my friendship with Jill might be more fragile than I thought. Bill could have been detrimental to our budding bond if he had chosen to stay interested in me and not her.

But from the look in Jill's eyes when Max Grunter walked up to her, I could tell she was smitten. "Stalker much?" Jill turned her nose up.

This was her way of saying that she liked him. (I know her social skills were still in bitch-mode.)

Max didn't even seem phased by her response. In fact, he didn't seem to have any emotion at all. He kind of just stood there looking like a model, all intense and smoldering. "Lunch today?" he asked Jill as if they were old friends.

Jill was so taken aback, she actually turned shy. It was pretty amusing. "Um, sure."

Max nodded once and walked away. As he passed me our eyes met.

Tap. Tap. Tap.

He was trying to get in my head again.

I kept him out, but I took a step back in spite of myself.

What did he want? I was a little freaked.

"I need to go to the nurse," Ryan's voice jolted me out of my reverie.

"Why? Are you okay?" Nancy beat me to the punch.

Ryan massaged his head, "Yeah, just need something for this headache. I'll see you in class." Ryan kissed me and left without waiting for my response.

Nancy and Jill both turned to me, concerned.

"His headaches are getting worse. I have to call Turner," I said in answer to their unasked question.

Jill smiled encouragingly, "He'll be all right."

"I hope so." I watched Ryan disappear down the hall. Then I turned to Jill. "Max may be working for Elisha, so be careful."

"What?!" Jill's eyes widened.

I told her about my dream and Max's strange attempts to jump into my head.

Jill shook her head in annoyance. "Just my luck. I start to like someone again, and he's probably a Coalition freak working for Elisha." She sighed deeply. "Let's just get to Mr. Alaster's class. I can already tell today is going to be jam-packed with craziness."

I had to agree with her. It certainly felt that way.

Jill linked arms with Nancy and I and we plowed down the hallway. "Why do I get the feeling we're headed for trouble, drama girl?"

Nancy grumbled under her breath, "I'm seriously going to kill him."

Jill and I laughed. Nancy hadn't heard a word anyone said since Jill told her about Joan's claim on Jason. She seriously had a one-track mind when it came to that boy.

"What? I am," Nancy said defensively.

"We know," Jill cooed and winked at me.

But Jill's prediction for today still echoed in my head. I didn't want to be *drama girl*, but inevitably I always ended up in that role.

Oh well.

Let's see what Mr. Alaster's history class had in store.

***

Apparently, Mr. Alaster had nothing in store for us. He just told us to read chapters twenty through twenty-three for the whole class. As the bell rang end-of-period, my heart squeezed in worry: Ryan had never showed up in class.

Screw it.

As the students shuffled toward the door I pulled out my cell phone and dialed.

It was Turner's machine.

Shocker.

He never answered his phone. In fact, most of our conversations were through phone tag. I didn't care. I just hoped he'd check his messages today.

The beep sounded. "Um, hi, it's Chelsan. Ryan's headaches are getting worse… um…so you need to send someone… now. Okay, bye." I hung up.

That was smooth.

Answering machines made me nervous. Especially when you were asking the most powerful man in the world for a favor. Not only that, but he was my grandfather. Not only that, but he tried to kill me about a hundred times. Not only that but he killed my mother. Not only that but he may blame me for his wife's death. I could go on, but it just made my stomach hurt.

I hurried to the nurse's office and found Ryan walking out holding an icepack to his temple. His smile when he saw me made my heart flutter.

"Hey you," he said as if everything were perfectly normal.

"Hey yourself, what did the nurse say?" I asked in-between Ryan kissing me.

Yum.

Ryan shrugged. "She just gave me some pain killers. Somehow I don't think the school nurse can help me with a bunch of kids dying in my brain." Ryan tossed the icepack back into the nurse's office and grabbed my hand.

His hand was cold from the ice, but I didn't care. Just having him next to me made me feel less worried. He genuinely looked better and hopefully Turner would send one of his specialists.

If he checked his messages.

If he even cared.

Ugh.

I vowed that if Turner wouldn't help me, I'd find another way to fix

Ryan's ailment. Whatever it was.

"Are you going to class or are you going home?" I wanted to make sure he wasn't staying at school just for me.

"Class." Ryan turned me around so that we were facing each other. He cupped my face in his hands and kissed me gently. Toes. Curling. Seriously. "I'm fine. I promise you. I just needed to lie down for a bit. Now that I have, I feel tip top. Okay?"

"Okay," I said reluctantly. I didn't believe him for a second. "But if it gets too bad, promise me you'll let me know. Don't hide it because you don't want me to worry."

"I promise." Ryan kissed me one more time, then grinned. "You better get to class. I'll meet you at lunch."

Ryan kissed my hand in parting and he was off to Physics. Not that he needed to take a class in Physics, he knew more than the teacher did. Ryan was just about the smartest person on the planet. And I wasn't saying that because he was my boyfriend. He really was. Something that annoyed Elisha to no end, and I was pretty proud of that. Ryan beat her intellectually and I didn't think she'd ever forgive him for that.

But that was also what scared me the most. I feared that maybe she was causing Ryan's headaches. It wasn't beyond the realm of possibility. She was really skilled at popping into people's heads.

Ryan gave me permission a few months back to go inside his head to check and see if Elisha was messing with him. I didn't see anything out of the ordinary. I didn't want to stay in his head for too long, because I was terrified to see what Ryan thought of me. Yes, he said he loved me, and I believed him, but jumping inside someone's head and seeing their thoughts and memories?

It scared me.

What if his feelings were changing for me?

What if he didn't like me as much as I liked him?

Paranoid I know.

I scoped his head for Elisha and when she wasn't there I jumped back out immediately.

A part of me wondered if I had jumped out too early. That was what nagged at me. My own insecurities may have prevented me from really making sure Elisha wasn't attacking him.

I shook the thought from my head and walked toward Biochemistry. Students were thinning out as they filed into their respective classes, and I hurried my steps to make it in time. I started to become nervous as I was suddenly the last person in the hallway. I really hated being late to Biochem, Ms. Floster always made an example out of anyone who was even five seconds late. Today really wasn't my day.

WHAM!

The wind flew out my lungs with sudden impact.

I barely saw the fist that had just punched me in the gut as my attacker quickly disappeared behind me, grabbing my throat with one hand and pulling me into an empty classroom with the other.

I clutched at the hand and tried to pry it loose, but the grip was strong and tight.

I started to choke.

The door shut and I knew we were completely cut off from the rest of the school. The one thing this building was good for was sound control. You literally couldn't hear through the walls of the next classroom.

I searched for anything dead around me to distract whoever was assaulting me. When I couldn't find anything, I knew dust would have to do. I realized recently that I could connect to dust since in actuality dust was mostly made up of dead skin cells. It didn't do a lot of damage, but when I controlled it to fly into a person's lungs, it could at least knock them out.

I could barely breathe.

I concentrated and had the dust under my control in seconds. I puppeteered the dust where I assumed the nose of my attacker was behind me, and slammed it down their throat. I heard coughing and the hand released my neck.

I whirled around to see…

…Eva.

Oh boy.

She kept coughing but when she looked up at me her eyes were so full of rage and hate I nearly flinched.

I quickly pulled out the dust and Eva started to catch her breath.

Eva charged.

BAM!

She tackled me to the floor.

If I hadn't been in so much shock I'd have fought back, but the mere idea of Eva attacking me like this was insane.

I mustered all my strength and shoved her off.

"What is your problem?" I screamed at her.

"You," she said with a glint of crazy in her eyes.

Eva charged at me a second time, but this time I was more prepared. I sidestepped just in time and Eva fell to her hands and knees.

"You're working for Elisha," I accused her. I figured at least I'd see what her reaction was.

Eva flipped herself up to standing like a graceful ninja. "Who?"

Nothing.

There was nothing in her eyes.

Unless she was an award-winning actress, Eva had no idea who Elisha was.

"Why do you have a problem with me?" I asked as I backed up, anticipating another attack.

"Because you're an evil bitch that likes messing with Bill's head," Eva snarled in response.

"This is about Bill?" I asked incredulously. What did he tell her?

"What else would it be about?!" Eva was revving up for another assault.

"That's enough." Max entered the classroom.

His dark eyes met Eva's and she immediately went still.

"Max, stay out of this," Eva pleaded, anger-eyes still held on me.

"Eva," was all Max said.

It was enough.

I didn't know what kind of relationship they had, but apparently Max was in charge.

Eva was obviously annoyed, but she didn't argue back. She wore a long sleeve thermal to cover up her burn marks, but as she reached up to pull her hair back I could see the long striations growing up her wrists like angry pink vines. Only her face was unmarked from scars, the veiny-like marks crawling all the way up her neck to frame her perfect features. Eva had a light sprinkling of freckles across her nose and cheekbones and her giant eyes almost looked like emeralds, they were so green.

It was hard to believe that anything Bill may have said about me could make Eva this angry, but maybe I underestimated how he really felt about me.

"Look, Eva, I don't know what Bill told you…" I tried to explain.

Eva cut me off, "He told me the truth, that he poured his heart out to you and you treated him like an annoying puppy."

First off, puppies aren't annoying, and second off, "I love Bill as a friend. That's all I told him. I can't help how I feel." I was more defensive than I thought.

Max stepped in. "It doesn't matter. Eva had no right to attack you. Did you Eva?"

Again with the control.

Although, looking at Max and how calm and reassuring he was, I'd do what he said too.

Max was the kind of guy that has such a presence that you couldn't help but be enthralled by him. Kind of like a president or a king, Max just carried himself with a strength and power that was more than a little intimidating.

"No," Eva admitted grudgingly.

"I apologize for my sister's behavior," Max said to me with a gentleness that instantly made me shy.

"Um, no problem," I replied. No problem? I could still feel the marks where her fingers strangled my throat. What was going on? I immediately felt inside my head for intruders. Maybe Max had just made a sneak attack like Elisha had before and was influencing my responses?

Nope.

All clear.

I was just a bumbling idiot all on my own.

Eva strode over to Max, slightly shoving me as she passed by. Before she left the classroom she turned to me with venom, "Just stay away from Bill."

Before I could respond, Eva stormed out of the room and slammed the door behind her.

All that was left was Max and I.

"I better get to class," I said, heading for the door.

Max stepped in front of me, preventing my exit.

"You keep blocking me out," Max accused. He didn't say it like he was angry, just that he was surprised that I would do such a thing.

"I don't let people into my head anymore." I tried to keep it light, though having a conversation about brain-jumping was anything but light.

"We need to talk." Max looked into my eyes with a seriousness that scared me a little.

"We're talking." I didn't know what else to say. This was getting freaky fast.

"Not here. Tonight. Outside your house. I'll wait for you at the Hover-Shuttle station," Max said as if we were spies arranging a secret rendezvous.

"What's this about Max?" I asked.

"John Fortski."

Um.

"Um." Good one.

But it caught me off guard. Why would Max want to talk to me about John Fortski? I didn't know the guy. Why me?

"Really?"

"It's important, Chelsan. If you think about it long enough, it'll start to make sense." Max's dark eyes bore into me like they were trying to read my soul.

There went the intimidation button again.

"Cryptic," I finally responded.

"I won't talk about it here, okay?" Max was dead serious.

"Okay," I said, because I found the whole conversation odd. Seriously, what did John Fortski have to do with me?

"Good." And then Max smiled. When he did, it made his whole persona change. His perfectly white teeth were a startling contrast to his ebony skin. There was no getting around it: Max was stunning.

No wonder Jill liked him.

Max was gone before I could utter another lame response. I sighed a giant sigh of relief and checked the hallway for insane-o-Eva before I felt like the coast was clear and made my way to Biochem.

After receiving the expected earful from Ms. Floster about being ten minutes late, I shuffled myself lamely to the back of the room. I hoped she wouldn't keep picking on me throughout the rest of class like she normally did to latecomers. To my shock, Ms. Floster was so enthralled by the latest news on Biochem, she appeared to be ignoring me completely. I crossed my fingers it would stay that way.

I spaced out thinking about all the events that had already happened today. From my Roberta nightmare to the freaky violent confrontation with Eva to the promised conversation with Max. Something big was afoot, I was sure of it. I just didn't know what and that was never a good thing.

Then it hit me.

I was in Biochem.

What better place to research John Fortski than in the class that was his area of expertise.

"Ms. Floster?"

I really just said that.

I had completely interrupted her.

There was an audible gasp from the room. No one interrupted Ms. Floster. At least not without consequences.

She looked pissed. Ms. Floster wasn't exactly the prettiest bird in the flock, but she was downright ugly when she was angry. It looked like she started taking Age-pro in her early thirties from the slight crows feet around her eyes that were now squinting in annoyance at me. She was about five foot two with a dark brown bob, long crooked nose and brown beady little eyes. And right now those beady eyes were staring daggers at me.

"Yes, Ms. Derée?" Ms. Floster hissed.

"Sorry, I… uh… just had a question."

"A question that apparently was more important than my lecture." The way she said it indicated that no question would be more important than her lecture.

How do I get out of this one?

I figured at that point I'd go for it. She'd either kick me out or actually answer the question.

"Why do you think John Fortski was kidnapped?"

Silence.

Silence from the class.

Strangest of all, silence from Ms. Floster.

Her face kind of scrunched up as if she was fighting some inner battle within herself. I could tell right away that she had a theory that she was dying to share, but by sharing it she'd be admitting to me and the class that my question was better than her lecture.

I prodded. "I just thought, of all people, you'd have a theory." I hoped stroking her ego might work.

"I do, in fact," Ms. Floster lifted her crooked nose high, "not that I should be placating your bad behavior, mind you."

Another silence.

Another inner battle.

But her desire to impress us with her theories won out.

"I'll indulge you this once, only because it's relevant to your next assignment." Ms. Floster straightened her blue polyester pants suit and sat down on the edge of her desk. "Dr. John Fortski, as you all know, is the inventor of Age-pro." She paused as if telling a good horror story. "What you may not know is that Dr. Fortski was also the inventor of a number of experimental drugs that never made it into the market. My father worked for Dr. Fortski back in the 1990's, in fact, the reason I look like I'm in my thirties is not because I'm poor, but because I was thirty-five when Age-pro was invented!" Ms. Floster revealed.

Everyone was speechless.

It was very rare to meet people who were around when Age-pro was invented. Unless you were young, being aged was considered grotesque in modern day society. Only religious nuts didn't take Age-pro and let themselves age naturally until they died really young, like ninety or a hundred. I shuddered to think of only living that long. It was quite a shock when we were stuck in the Christian Coalition town of Havenville five months back and I saw some of the old people there. At first it was like a nightmare, they were wrinkled and hunched, like monsters. But after a while, they were so sweet, the old folks actually looked cute, like critters.

My grandpa was the only public figure that was around at the time of Age-pro. He was in his fifties and that was considered ancient. Not even lower income families had to age that long. National healthcare kicked in at thirty, so most poor people looked around thirty-something.

We all assumed Ms. Floster was one of those. I had no idea she was over three hundred years old!

Ms. Floster continued her story. "My father said that Dr. Fortski was working on more than just a drug that would stop people from aging. His goal was to invent a pill that would heal any wound. If you were stabbed, shot or even had a simple paper cut, all you would have to do was take the pill and it would heal instantly. Coupled with Age-pro, it could make humans truly immortal.

"Of course the flaw would be that, if you were outright killed, it couldn't bring you back from the dead. But, according to my father, the drug was being designed so that you could be mortally wounded and still heal as if you were never injured. I believe Dr. Fortski was kidnapped to start his research once more and invent this drug." Ms. Floster was alight with passion.

Gulp.

A drug that heals wounds?

Elisha.

She had Fortski.

I knew it with every fiber of my soul.

Elisha wanted to be invulnerable.

This was big. Bigger than me. I hated to admit it, but I really needed Gramps about now.

But what did Max know about all this?

Did he think I'd come to this on my own? Did this have anything to do with what he wanted me to piece together? Or did I still have to *"think about it long enough"* and I'd come up with some other realization?

"Did Dr. Fortski invent anything else?" I asked before I could stop myself.

Wow. I'd just made Ms. Floster even madder than before.

"Immortality isn't good enough for you, Ms. Derée?" Ms. Floster glared at me. I shrank in my seat.

"No... I just... you said he invented a number of experimental drugs... I just thought..." Please, someone else, help me out here.

"Yeah, what else did he invent?" Drea Noville asked, practically salivating from the new topic.

Ms. Floster apparently liked Drea's response more than mine as she pointedly ignored me and turned all her attention to Drea.

At that point Ms. Floster went into a ramble about all of the scary drugs Fortski experimented with. She even told a story about how, in the beginning stages of Age-pro research several of the lab rats died from aging too fast. It seemed Fortski didn't have a handle on the aging process for quite a while. It made me think of the time I astral projected into Roberta's head and saw the memory of Fortski telling her he was close to finding the cure for aging. She had wanted to take the experimental drug, but Turner wouldn't let her. She chose face-stretching surgery to tide her over, yuck.

The only thing that stuck out was the "healing" drug. I'd have to put Jason on researching that. I hoped he'd be able to find all sorts of stuff on the topic.

I was starting to look forward to meeting Max. I wondered what he was going to tell me about Fortski. Maybe Max knew where he was? I just didn't know.

The bell rang. Everyone started shuffling out of the room. I hurried to the exit so that Ms. Floster wouldn't try and punish me for my tardiness and outbursts in class.

"Ms. Derée, would you come here a moment?"

No such luck.

People were giving me sympathy looks as I made my way past them towards Ms. Floster.

I stood before her, keeping my eyes down, trying to look sorry for all I did.

I could feel Ms. Floster's eyes boring into me. She was waiting for me to look at her.

"Don't think you've learned anything I didn't want you to learn," she said loudly.

I looked up.

What?

Ms. Floster grabbed my arms and pulled me close so that our noses were practically touching. I was too dumbfounded to move. Ms. Floster was annoying and occasionally angry, but grabbing me like this was way out of her normal behavior. I finally looked into her eyes, and instead of the fury I thought I'd see due to her… um… attacking me!

I only saw blankness.

Don't think you've learned anything I didn't want you to learn.

Elisha.

She was controlling Ms. Floster.

And I was talking to her directly.

Elisha had brain-knapped poor Ms. Floster and was using her as a telephone. I needed to take advantage of the fact that after five months I could get information out of my enemy.

I decided to go for logic. "If that were true, then why are you telling me?"

Ms. Floster's blank face was creepy. I was used to this in corpses, but not living people.

Her grip tightened around my arms. I briefly thought about fighting back, but I knew I'd end up hurting Ms. Floster rather than her puppet master, Elisha. My teacher was an innocent victim in all this.

"If Ms. Floster hadn't slipped up a bit, you wouldn't bother talking to me, you'd just let me gather my info and know that I was barking up the wrong tree."

"You still think you're clever, don't you? I hate to be the bearer of bad news, but you're an idiot."

Yup.

Definitely Elisha.

"*Idiot*" being her favorite word to call me.

I responded, "You obviously need me for something, or you wouldn't bother with me. You'd be building your super-army and taking over the world or something. I'm assuming you have my power by now."

Which was true. I may not know about her plans, but I was sure Elisha would have performed the ceremony that gave her the power to control the dead. I shuddered to think of Elisha killing an innocent baby…

But I also knew how the ritual worked. Elisha made me use the twins' power to disconnect the lights from the three pregnant mothers so that their babies would be born with a power like mine. I knew she'd re-create my father's spell to gain the power for herself. The result: the baby would have to die. Of course, when my father sacrificed himself he thought he was ridding himself of this power forever. He had no idea his spell would transfer the gift to me. But it did: I ended up seeing black swirling holes and controlling the dead just like he had been able to do.

"Of course I have your power, and I'm awake now, so I'll be focusing all my attention on you," Ms. Floster/Elisha said.

Then I thought of something.

Elisha wasn't the only one who could brain-knap.

Sorry Ms. Floster, but there's about to be a party in your head.

I concentrated as hard as could, which was quite a struggle since Ms. Floster's hands were clinging so tightly to my arms, but within seconds I flew inside her head.

Blackness.

Okay. Gain my bearings.

"Chelsan?"

The light turned on. And I was suddenly in…

…Ms. Floster's classroom.

Uh.

Weird.

Being physically in the classroom *and* mentally in the classroom inside Ms. Floster's head was very surreal.

I turned around to see Ms. Floster with a terrified look on her face. "No matter what I do," she cried breathlessly, "I can't seem to leave this room! If I try to walk out the door or the window or the ceiling, I end up back here! We're stuck!"

She was starting to become unhinged and I couldn't blame her. Elisha had apparently trapped Ms. Floster inside her own head, and what was worse, she made Ms. Floster think she was forever trapped within her own classroom.

I went over to Ms. Floster and tried to give her a reassuring look. "I'm going to get us out of here, but you have to tell me everything you remember."

"You're such a fool," I heard Elisha's voice coming through the classroom's overhead speaker like she was the principal making an announcement. "You really think you can catch me in here? I'm so much better at this than you," she giggled.

Her voice sounded different, deeper…

"Who is that? Is she the one keeping me here?!" Ms. Floster seemed just about ready to scream.

I placed my finger over my mouth to motion for her silence, then nodded to tell her that Elisha was definitely the culprit. Then I whispered, "I'll take care of her."

Ms. Floster had no reason to trust me, but she nodded her acquiesce all the same.

Little did Elisha know…

…I had been practicing.

Elisha had been in my head so many times that I knew her signature like I knew my own. I could see and feel her presence jumping around Ms. Floster's head like a bouncing ball. I was assuming that this was Elisha's way of preventing herself from being tracked, but it didn't fool me.

I closed my eyes.

I stood under the Eiffel Tower. The courtyard was empty with the giant latticed structure looming over my head.

NOW!

I screamed in my head.

WHOOSH!

Standing in front of me was Elisha, her eyes wide with disbelief.

"How did you…?" she stammered.

"I'm better than you think." I tried not to relish in the genuine surprise on her face.

Elisha was still stunning to look at. Aside from her outfit of t-shirt and jeans she was like a porcelain doll reincarnate, with pale ivory skin, giant purple eyes and long black hair. Elisha looked about seven years old, but I knew she was almost a hundred. The girl was seriously creepy.

Elisha was still spooked until she looked down at herself. A slow smile spread across her delicate features. "I see you remember me with fondness."

I had no idea what she meant. She looked just like she always did. A sociopathic child.

"One of your many faults," Elisha sneered.

Before she could get the upper hand I reached out and grabbed Elisha's hair.

Yes, very "cat fight" of me, but you gotta do what you gotta do.

And more importantly, it kept her there with me, as opposed to disappearing somewhere into my Biochem teacher's head!

I pulled her head back by tugging on her hair.

Elisha smiled at me.

She was amused by all this. It meant she knew something I didn't.

I hated that.

"You're going to leave Ms. Floster's head as soon as you tell me what you're up to," I said with as much intensity as I could. "What did you mean, you just woke up?" One question at a time.

Elisha didn't even look fazed by my grip on her hair. She raised her eyebrow and stared at me with her violet eyes. "It means, I just woke up, and to be honest, I could use another nap after this." She grinned at me triumphantly.

I wanted to punch her scrawny little face, but I also knew that neither one of us were really here under the Eiffel Tower and that if anyone walked in to Biochem, they'd be looking at two comatose people staring at each other. One: Ms. Floster, grabbing her student: me.

Yeah, not good.

"I'm going to figure out what you're up to, and if I can't, Ryan will. Remember the boy who outsmarted the supposedly brilliant Elisha Stearne? He played you like a fiddle and he'll do it again." I tried to press any button I could to get Elisha to slip up.

It worked.

Elisha was pissed.

"I won't be fooled again by your boyfriend," she snarled.

Then Elisha smiled once more.

Again with the knowledge, and me not knowing it.

"How are his little headaches anyway? Getting worse?" Elisha snickered.

That did it.

I snapped her neck.

Elisha disappeared instantly.

I remembered from Grams that when you killed someone in astral form it bumped them out of whoever's brain they were in. At the time it had been *my* head, but Ms. Floster needed to be rid of the brain tumor known as Elisha.

I jumped out of Ms. Floster's head.

And I was back in the classroom.

Ms. Floster still had her hands clasped to my arms, but her eyes suddenly cleared and she looked extremely confused.

"Chelsan?" she asked groggily.

"You should sit down. You don't look so good." I ushered her to the chair behind her desk.

Ms. Floster didn't argue. She allowed me to lead her to a sitting position. "What happened? Where's the class?"

"Class is over, Ms. Floster."

I could see alarm rising up in her eyes, so I quickly tried to make light of the situation.

"I bet you were sleep walking. My stepfather used to do that all the time. You wouldn't even know he was sleeping." Or dead, since I was the one controlling his corpse my entire childhood, but she didn't have to know that.

"Sleep walking?" Ms. Floster was still out of it. "I haven't done that in years."

"Well, you gave a whole lecture on John Fortski. You said your dad used to work for him and that he had been working on some kind of healing drug." I wanted to see if Elisha had jumped in at the end of the lecture or was responsible for the whole thing. I still believed that Elisha was worried that Ms. Floster said something she didn't want me to hear. Maybe if I prodded a little more…

"I said all that?" Ms. Floster rubbed her face as if this would wake her up.

"Was it true? Or were you just dreaming and making it up?" I asked.

"Oh no, it's true. I remember finishing the whole lecture, then right before the bell rang… nothing." Ms. Floster took a deep breath, finally waking out of her grogginess. "Oh my, Chelsan, thank you for helping me. I feel so foolish. I guess it's time to see a doctor."

Okay. Ms. Floster had given the entire lecture, which meant Elisha hadn't jumped into her head until after. So, Ms. Floster obviously said something that Elisha didn't want me to hear. I wished I had recorded class! Jason and I could have picked it apart.

Ms. Floster patted my hand affectionately.

Which was really weird. Ms. Floster was the opposite of a warm fuzzy.

Awkward.

I knew she didn't actually need to see a doctor so I said, "Or maybe you just need to rest."

"Yes, good call." Ms. Floster stood up. "I'm going to go home." She grabbed her purse from underneath her desk. "I didn't assign any homework did I?"

"Nope," I answered cheerfully. If Elisha had been thinking about it she could have been particularly cruel and assigned us a bunch of homework, but luckily she was too focused on me.

"Well, that's good at least." Ms. Floster turned to me as if just now realizing she'd been so casually nice to a student. She cleared her throat as she glanced up at the clock. "Ms. Derée, you're going to be late for your next class."

I smiled and she smiled back.

"Are you sure you don't need anything?" Like a pill that blocks seven-year-old psychos from entering your brain!

"No, I'm fine, thank you," she answered kindly. "Now off to class."

I didn't argue. I hurried out the door and into the empty hallway.

I kept my eyes open this time, though. I didn't want to get side-swiped by Eva again.

I made it to Calculus and couldn't pay attention to a word Mr. Gray said. I played over everything I could remember Ms. Floster saying during Biochem. I really wished I had paid more attention. I felt like, whether or not the healing drugs were real, Elisha didn't care one iota if I knew about them or not. That didn't necessarily mean she wasn't trying to get Fortski to invent them, but it wasn't what she was worried about me knowing.

One thing I was almost a hundred percent certain of: Elisha was behind the John Fortski kidnapping.

There was no other explanation.

Before I knew it, the bell had rung and it was lunchtime.

The rest of the day went off without a hitch, aside from receiving an earful from Jill on how Max stood her up at lunch. I tried not to make eye contact with her, as I was pretty sure that I was the reason for Max's absence. Bill ate lunch with Eva, far away from us and I came very close to going over to their table and telling him what a loony she was. But, no, I figured I'd take the high road and find out first what Max had to say when we met after school.

Ryan seemed to be in better spirits as the day went on. No sign of any headaches, which was a huge sigh of relief. Elisha definitely knew about Ryan's predicament, though, and I was terrified she was responsible for it. I just hoped Turner would send one of his specialist doctors over soon so we could figure out how to help Ryan.

After my last class, I headed for the hover-car parking lot. The halls were packed and I could barely move forward. The last school was crowded enough, but this new building was ten times worse. I literally shuffled toward the exit, trying not to feel claustrophobic. I never used to feel that way but, ever since my buried alive ordeal, I tended to get a little panicky when I felt closed in. More psychological issues for me. Yay.

I tried not to focus on the fact that I was stuck in this pack of people. It was hard to breathe. I started to grow a little light-headed. I practiced some breathing methods I'd learned from Jill of all people. She apparently had been dealing with anxiety attacks since her father died. Of course, she didn't actually know he died the first time since my grandfather puppeteer'd him. All Jill knew was that she woke up one day and her dad was different. He was. He was dead. But she didn't know that then. And it scarred her, making her highly anxious. Jill had all sorts of tricks for me, like breathing methods, distraction techniques, and pacing.

Unfortunately, my brain was getting the best of me and the breathing tricks weren't working.

I needed to move away from this crowd. I shoved my way through a lot of "HEYS!" and "WATCH ITS!" until I managed to escape into an empty classroom. I took a few deep breaths and paced a little, calming myself.

It kind of annoyed me that I could handle almost being murdered (a million times), but I couldn't handle a crowded hallway at school. My fight or flight mode was all off whack.

That wasn't all that was off whack.

One of the wood beams on the ceiling was amassing a cluster of swirling black holes that were moving.

And I wasn't controlling them.

What the…?

SNAP!

The beam suddenly broke and swung at my head with frightening speed.

I dove to the ground, smacking my forehead on a desk, but the wooden beam missed me.

Did I do that?

And ouch.

I slowly rose to my feet and examined the black swirling holes on the fallen beam. Dead termites. They weren't moving anymore. They were just dead again.

Could Elisha be here? At school?

I ran outside the room to see if I could catch a glimpse of her, if she was here.

The halls were still crowded, but thinning out.

No Elisha.

But…

Eva was at the end of the hallway.

She turned to me and smiled.

Did Eva have the same power as me?

I couldn't quite wrap my head around that. No. I was being paranoid.

But if not Eva, then who? It had to be her.

I needed to talk to the gang without Bill. He'd just be defensive. Besides, if I was wrong I'd look like a jerk. I still wasn't even sure if I was going to tell him about Eva attacking me. I hadn't told Nancy or Ryan yet. I figured they'd go straight for Eva's jugular and I didn't want to do that to Bill. I could care less about Eva, but Bill didn't deserve to be hurt.

I had the sinking feeling that no matter how hard I tried to spare Bill's feelings, they were going to get demolished. I had to be honest with myself, something was seriously off with Eva and I needed to figure out exactly what it was.

Making my way out to the parking lot, Ryan grabbed me from behind and pulled me around for a kiss.

"Hello, my lovely," he whispered in my ear.

Sigh.

"You're feeling better." I smiled up at his stunningly gorgeous face.

"Whatever the nurse gave me seemed to do the trick," Ryan said, clasping my hand and heading me over toward Bill's hover.

We had a moment alone. I was about to tell him about my encounter with Eva and then with Elisha and then again with Eva, but Bill arrived with Eva on his arm.

Bill smiled sloppily like he'd just eaten all the cookies in the cookie jar. From the slight remnants of lipstick on his mouth, I could only guess that the two of them had been making out.

Eew.

"You think Eva can squish in the back with you guys?" Bill asked, though he wasn't really asking, he was telling us that Eva was coming whether we wanted her to or not.

"You know what? We'll take the shuttle," I said before I could stop myself.

My polite nature normally would have me saying, "sure, no problem" despite the giant neon sign above Eva's head that said "BAD GUY!" But this time my instincts had won out and my mouth followed.

Ryan looked more taken aback than Bill did, but not by much.

Eva pretended to be hurt. (And I know she was pretending, because I could tell by her stupid face.)

Okay, that was caddy, but the girl had tackled me! And I was pretty darn sure she had somehow controlled those dead termites and almost tried to kill me!

Paranoid much?

Probably, but I didn't care.

Eva was trouble. I wasn't about to be sandwiched between Eva and Ryan in Bill's car.

"Your choice," Bill said nastily and he put his arm around Eva protectively.

That did it.

"Yeah, it is my choice! But it wasn't my choice to have your girlfriend attack me in the hallway and try to beat the crap out of me!" Wow. I was seriously mad. I actually yelled that.

Bill immediately pulled away from Eva and looked at her questioningly.

Eva looked properly shocked and appalled. "I would never…" She started to cry. "She's just making that up because she's jealous that we're a couple."

Bill actually looked conflicted.

Really?

The fact that he was considering that Eva might be telling the truth was beyond annoying. It was offensive.

Ryan apparently agreed, "You're really going to buy that Bill?"

"Why would I hurt her? She's your best friend," Eva said between sobs.

"She's lying to you."

We all turned around to see Max.

He held his hand out for Eva to take. "That's enough, Eva."

Eva's tears stopped instantly. She looked at Max like she was going to tear his head off.

But she did as he said all the same, taking his hand, despite how angry she appeared.

"Apologize to Chelsan," Max instructed.

Eva looked like a punished five-year-old, shuffling her feet, avoiding eye contact, "Sorry."

"Have a nice night," Max said and his eyes briefly met mine.

We'll talk about it later.

Max had succeeded in jumping in my brain.

How did he do that?

I didn't even sense it.

I swallowed hard and nodded my agreement.

This was one of those rare occasions where I felt the loss of Roberta. She'd be able to help me keep Max out. Or even how to sense that he had somehow managed to sneak past my protective barriers like a brain ninja. I was hoping it was because I was a little mentally lax after my ordeal in Ms. Floster's head with Elisha. Either way it disturbed me greatly.

And then Eva and Max were gone.

Bill stood there in shock.

"I…" he started, then he turned to me, regret screaming in his eyes, "Are you okay?"

"A little late for that, bro," Ryan accused.

"You were actually going to believe her, weren't you?" I asked, still upset that Bill could think I'd lie about something like that.

Bill shrugged, which was as close to a "yes" as I was going to get. "I liked her."

At least he made it past tense.

"Well, she's psycho, and I think she has the same power as me." Oops. I wasn't planning on telling them that.

"Who has *what?*" Nancy said as she and Jill came up from behind.

I told them everything that just happened.

"You were going to take the shuttle instead of asking me for a ride?" Jill was appalled. Her giant green eyes actually looked offended.

"Really? That's all you got from that conversation?" Having Jill take the nightmare that was my day and make it about her, made me happy for some reason.

"And Max! I'm mad at him. He totally stood me up at lunch," Jill ranted on in irritation.

"I guess he had other things on his mind, like his sister attacking Chelsan." Nancy rolled her eyes, but I could tell Jill's self-centeredness amused her as well. Nancy turned to me, "Why do you think it was Eva that made those dead bugs eat the beam?"

"Just a feeling. Look, I'm not so sure about that part, but something's up with Max and Eva."

I didn't want to rub Eva's creepiness in Bill's face.

And I didn't want to tell any of them I was meeting with Max later. I wasn't exactly sure why, but until I got my answers from Max, I didn't want anyone to worry.

"Maybe Eva has a good explanation for what she did," Bill mused. "Besides, you said yourself you're not sure who controlled those termites. It might not be her." Bill was already starting to be defensive, so I decided to drop it.

"Let's just get to Nancy's," I said. The others took my cue and nodded.

"See you guys tomorrow." Jill waved as she walked toward her car.

The rest of us piled into Bill's hover and rode to Nancy's in silence. No one wanted to say a thing. At least Eva wasn't crammed next to me. But seeing the pain oozing from Bill's boyish features, almost made me wish she was. Almost.

As Bill landed on Nancy's hover pad, Jason came out to greet us.

Nancy huffed, still annoyed by Jill's announcement this morning that Jason may or may not be taking Joan to prom.

"You!" Nancy exited Bill's hover, pointing her finger at Jason.

"Me." Jason had a calm sort of expression on his face, as if he knew what was coming.

"Please tell me Joan is full of crap and that you are not taking her to prom." Nancy crossed her arms, standing in front of Jason, daring him to deny it.

Jason gently held Nancy's chin. "Joan's father is the new advisor to Turner. We need all the ins we can get."

Nancy shoved his hand away. It almost looked as if she was going to slap him. "Fine! Date her then, because we're so done!" She practically knocked Jason over as she stormed into the house, slamming the door behind her.

Jason was flabbergasted. "Did she just break up with me?"

I patted him on the arm. "You're an idiot, Jason."

Bill mumbled from his car. "I'm taking off. You don't need me for anything, do you?"

Before I could answer Bill was taking off in his hover-car.

"Nah, see you tomorrow," I said to the empty air where he'd been and waved as his hover-car zoomed away.

"He'll get over it." Ryan kissed my hand that was still entwined with his.

"Maybe Eva is just a jealous freak and not a supernatural freak," I hoped out loud.

Jason shook himself out of his break-up gloom. "Supernatural... wha...?"

I told him everything.

"Let's research this mysterious brother and sister duo, more importantly, Elisha is back. That can't be a good thing. Tell me everything you can remember from Ms. Floster's lecture and we'll try and figure out what she didn't want you to know. Healing drugs are too obvious, it had to be something she wasn't expecting Ms. Floster to tell you." Jason was obviously thinking aloud, trying to rationalize and make connections.

"You better get inside and talk to Nancy," Ryan spoke up. "And tell her you're taking her to prom."

"But I…" Jason began.

I cut him right off, "Do it, and tell her Joan is nasty and ugly and that you're glad you don't have to take her anymore."

Jason was on the verge of argument, but then nodded his head in agreement. "Prom, seriously? I'm too old for this."

We all walked in the house and Jason scurried off toward the stairs to Nancy's room.

Vianne was in the kitchen preparing dinner, which smelled ridiculously good. George would be home in a few hours, so Ryan and I had to entertain ourselves.

Not hard.

We went to my room and before I could even close the door, Ryan's hands pulled me in for a mind-blowing kiss. I barely managed to kick the door shut as our lips couldn't seem to get enough of each other. Chemistry is a fascinating thing, it literally made my whole body tingle like I was about to have some kind of euphoric seizure. You'd think after being with each other for over six months that something like kissing would somehow not be as exciting as it was back before I thought Ryan didn't know I existed.

It was still ridiculous.

I led Ryan to my bed, where the two of us fell into the fluffy comforter of softness.

I could feel Ryan's grip on my t-shirt tighten like he couldn't be close enough to me.

I knew exactly how he felt.

His other hand held my face like it was the most precious thing in the world to him.

Ryan's kisses became more intense as he slid on top of me. He separated from me only for a second as he pulled off his shirt.

Holy crap this boy worked out.

It was hard not to gape at my own boyfriend.

As I reached up and pulled him in closer to me I could feel his back muscles tighten.

Then suddenly Ryan reared back with a gasp of pain. He grabbed his head and almost fell off the bed from the shock of it.

I immediately reached out and held him close.

"Ryan! I'm calling an ambulance." I started to leave the bed, but Ryan grabbed me.

"Don't leave. I'll be okay." Ryan fell into me, resting his head on my lap. "It's already passing."

I felt a lump in my throat as I stroked his hair. What was wrong with him? I was terrified that this was something unfixable.

"I need to get you help, Ryan." I heard the choke in my voice and knew that Ryan heard it too.

He sat up and, despite his own pain, gathered me in his lap so that he was comforting me. "I'm going to be fine. It's probably just my brain purging the I.Q. kids or something. Sounds weird, doesn't it?"

I nodded and kissed him gently. "What if it's not? What if it's worse? I know you're going to kill me, but I called Turner for help."

"I'll take it." Ryan kissed me back.

No argument. No anger.

He must really be in agony.

My heart hurt and I wanted to cry.

"This is all my fault," I whispered in shame. If Ryan hadn't met me he'd be a healthy super-genius with no worries in the world. Now he was having migraines because of a hundred dead I.Q. kids floating around in his brain. Yay me.

Ryan smiled and kissed the top of my head. "I love you, Chelsan Derée, and if headaches are the price I pay to be with you, then I'll have a headache every minute of every day. I don't care. You're worth it."

I didn't feel worth it.

"I love you," I said, trying to mask my tears.

I looked up at Ryan and his eyes were starting to droop.

"You should sleep."

"Maybe just a little nap." He was already half asleep.

I gently shifted my weight so Ryan could rest and I could leave him be. I stood up and watched him sleep. His forehead crinkled slightly. He was obviously in pain, even in slumber.

I hoped Gramps would send someone over, but I wasn't holding my breath. I hadn't heard from him in months, why would he care what happened to Ryan?

I walked over to the window.

Max was standing at the Hover-Shuttle stop staring straight at me.

I had almost forgotten about our meeting.

I wondered how long he'd been standing there.

Tap. Tap. Tap.

Knock it off. I said in his head.

Wow. I was getting good at this. He nodded and turned away to wait for me to come down. I was kind of proud of myself. Roberta said I had a special gift for the whole "astral projection" thing, but talking to Max had been as simple as… talking to Max. Just as if he were standing in front of me.

I leaned down and kissed Ryan's forehead, hoping I could take away some of his pain. Then I hurried from the room and out of the house to meet Max.

I made sure no one saw me go. I didn't want to explain why I was having secret meetings with Max. Maybe if he told me something important. Otherwise, I planned on keeping this rendezvous to myself. If Jill heard about it, she'd probably think I was trying to steal another guy she liked.

Max turned to me as I arrived.

"Hey," I said lamely. Hey? Really?

"Sit." Max motioned to the Hover-Shuttle bench.

We both sat down.

Why did I always do exactly what he said? He was such a commanding force, I couldn't seem to control myself.

Head check.

Nope.

All alone in here.

"What about John Forstski?" I asked more forcefully than I intended.

"You haven't figured it out yet?" Max didn't sound condescending. I could tell he genuinely thought I would have figured out whatever it was on my own.

"Nope. Not as smart as you think I am apparently." Snarky! Why was I being such a jerk?

Because Max might be working with Elisha. I needed to remind myself of that every second.

Eva had my powers I was sure of it. And if Eva worked for Elisha…

Wait.

Oh crap.

Oh crap.

Oh crap.

I stood up. Eyes wide.

Max smiled softly. "Light bulb."

"You two…" I was in shock. I couldn't think straight.

"Us two," Max nodded.

"You're the babies from Havenville. The babies that Elisha stole. The babies that I gave my powers to when Elisha made me use the twins. You're them." I stumbled over every word.

John Fortski invented Age-pro to stop the aging process, but his trials… his mistakes… before he found the cure for aging… he caused the aging process to speed up. That was the part that slipped from Ms. Floster. Aging. Some of the volunteers aged fifty years in four days. If given to a baby…

Max and Eva were about five months old, but their bodies looked seventeen.

Eva's burns.

They weren't burns.

They were stretch marks.

"Eva was the first one Elisha tried the aging drugs on," Max said as if reading my thoughts. "Fortski figured out the proper doses after Eva. Elisha didn't want to be scarred. She's obsessed with being perfect."

Elisha wasn't in a child's body anymore. She was an adult.

No wonder she looked scared to see me in Ms. Floster's head. I saw her the way I remembered her. That was why she said I was an idiot because I could have seen her the way she looked now, but all I saw was the creepy little girl.

I looked for genetic markers similar to mine… The same genetic markers your grandfather uses to find I.Q. kids…

Elisha's words echoed in my head over and over.

Sociopaths.

I instinctively took a few steps back from Max.

"Before you jump to the conclusions I already see you jumping to,

Ryan has the same genetic markers as we do. And you know he's not evil. I'm like Ryan, I swear." Max's eyes were pleading.

Wouldn't a psychopath try to convince me he wasn't a psychopath?

But why would Max reveal Elisha's secret? Elisha was so relieved when I saw her as a kid in Ms. Floster's head. She didn't want me knowing about Eva and Max or herself. Elisha had placed them in my high school to infiltrate my group.

And Eva had succeeded with Bill.

And Max with Jill.

I didn't know what to do. Or what to think.

"Max…I…" I really wanted to believe he was good, but too many people had betrayed me, and knowing he was working with Elisha…

Then my curiosity kicked in.

"How can you speak? I mean, you're like five months old. How do you know so much?" Whenever things became too much for me, my mind went towards the mundane and simple.

"The computer," Max answered simply.

Aahh.

The super computer that was killing my boyfriend. A brain-sucking machine that all the I.Q. kids would get hooked up to so Turner could analyze their thoughts.

"Elisha reversed its flow and fed our brains with anything on the computer, wireless, in the ether. It was all crammed in our heads like an over-stuffed sausage. I didn't even know who I was or what I was for three weeks. We only had two weeks to acclimate until Elisha threw us into your school. After that she went to sleep for three months. Fortski told her that it was the only way to be sure the aging would work perfectly. I think he wanted time to try and escape, to get Elisha out of the picture. But her security is too tight. He's with her now." Max was sharing with me. He was tortured and he finally had someone who wasn't psychotic that would listen.

I felt sorry for him.

"What about the third baby?" I asked already knowing the answer.

"She was killed. Elisha performed the ritual that gave her our power."

Our power.

"So you can…?" I started.

Max nodded.

"Elisha will kill me if she knows I've talked to you," Max's voice was barely a whisper.

At that moment I knew Max was good. It was hard to explain, but I felt it in my core. He was just like me, but stuck in Elisha's web of evil. Max lost his mother, had a power he knew hardly anything about, and now was being forced to do the bidding of the girl that was responsible for all of it. I still needed to be cautious, but I gave him the benefit of the doubt. For now.

"Eva and Elisha are the same?" I asked tentatively. I could tell that Max cared for Eva. Now that I knew who they were, I knew that Eva would have been an I.Q. Farm abductee for sure. That girl had no conscience.

Max didn't say anything. His face couldn't hide the hurt he felt.

After a few moments of awkward silence, Max finally spoke up, "Eva can be fixed. She's just confused. We both are."

Oh Max.

He was truly alone amongst a sea of piranhas.

"Look, Max..." I began.

But he cut me off. "Just don't. I know how to handle Eva. Let's just leave it at that."

"She tried to kill me today. She used dead termites to bite through a wood ceiling beam." I figured I'd tell him.

Max rubbed his hand over his face in frustrated disappointment. "I'll take care of it."

I nodded. I didn't want to argue with him especially since he had just bared his secrets to me. Elisha really would kill him if she knew what he'd just told me. Elisha thought she had an ace in the hole, and to be honest, she had. Finding out about Eva and Max was huge. I needed to tell the gang. We had been looking for a little girl with violet eyes, not an adult. Jason would no doubt scour all the footage of every attack that had happened in the last couple of weeks since Elisha was "awake." She could have been there and we would never have known it.

"Do you think Jill will be grossed out when she finds out?" Max asked.

I could see from his whole demeanor that the thought of Jill hating him was tearing Max apart. He really liked Jill. Jill! It actually made me feel happy, especially after everything Jill had been through with her parents dying and Bill rejecting her. To be honest, I had no idea how Jill would take the news. Max was less than five months old. Talk about an age difference! I knew that was unfair to Max, but Jill was a funny bird to say the least. She might be disgusted by him, or she might be okay with it. It was impossible to say.

"I honestly don't know, Max."

The look on his face showed that Max was resolved to his fate either way. He started to leave. "I better go."

"Do you want me to tell Jill or do you want to?" I asked.

Max stopped, but kept his back to me. "You tell her."

"Okay," I agreed quietly.

Max walked down the grass street until I could no longer see him.

I watched him go, not sure of how I was going to tell everyone about this. I knew Elisha was messed up, but this took the cake.

Poor Max.

I even felt a little sorry for Eva. Nope. Never mind. I'd have to keep an extra eye on Eva for Bill's sake. He always saw the best in people and falling in "love" or "like" with a coo-koo-head could cost him his life.

After a minute or two I made my way back into the house and joined a very depressed looking Jason on the couch. "Nancy still pissed at you?" I asked. I couldn't help but feel for the guy.

Jason just sighed in a dramatically exasperated way.

"She'll come around, but seriously, what were you thinking inviting Joan to the prom?" I still could not believe he'd do something that stupid.

"I wasn't thinking apparently. Joan's dad is very important…"

"Yeah, yeah, yeah," I interrupted what I assumed would be a rambling explanation of why he felt his decision was perfectly logical.

Jason wasn't offended that I cut him off. He just slumped even lower on the couch, and I didn't think that was possible. He practically looked like a turtle with its head tucked into its shell.

"I have something that will cheer you up, although it really shouldn't, but I know you too well," I announced. Telling Jason about Max, Eva and Elisha would put him in a great mood, which was kind of horrible if you thought about it. But I had grown so used to Jason perking up at all the misery in my life that sometimes it actually made me feel better to see him so excited. At least someone could enjoy the nightmare that was me.

Jason immediately sat up like an eager puppy.

See?

I told him everything Max had revealed to me.

Jason's eyes were round with interest and I swear I could see the gears spinning in his head like a couple of out-of-control Ferris wheels.

Before he could respond verbally there was a knock at the door.

Vianne yelled from the kitchen, "Could someone get that? George probably forgot his keys again."

I jumped up and hurried to the door. George usually came home with a bunch of prototypes from his work that he let Ryan mess with. George was fascinated by Ryan's brilliance. And seeing how Ryan could take an ordinary invention and turn it into something extraordinary was one of George's favorite pastimes. I'd have to tell him that Ryan wouldn't be up for his amusement tonight. Not with that headache.

I opened the door ready to help George with all his things.

Not George.

I couldn't hide my complete disbelief as I stared into the eyes of my grandfather, Vice President of Population Control, Geoffrey Turner.

I kind of just froze.

I mean, it wasn't like I hadn't seen the guy before. But it had been so long, and it was when Roberta died in his arms.

"Are you going to let us in?" Turner stared down at me with annoyance.

I noticed then that he wasn't alone.

A man about six feet tall walked into view.

Turner introduced him, "This is Dr. Johnson. He's a specialist I brought for Ryan."

I was so relieved I thought my knees would give out. I never thought Turner would bring help, let alone come himself. I guess he took my voice mail more seriously than I thought.

"Yeah, come in." Saying those words were foreign to my lips when concerning Gramps. Aside from the fact that Turner repeatedly tried to kill me when we first met, personality-wise, he was also kind of a dick.

"Where's Ryan?" Turner asked. To my surprise, he actually sounded concerned.

"Upstairs in my room. He was sleeping when I left him," I told the doctor who was now looking at me for a response.

Doctor Johnson nodded to Turner and left up the stairs.

I moved to go with him, when Gramps gently touched my arm.

"Let him do his work. I need to talk to you."

Of course he did.

Always an ulterior motive.

But maybe it had something to do with my dream of Roberta.

"You're not talking to her alone." Jason had moved his butt off the couch to stand by my side.

The thunder of footfalls came rushing down the stairs. Nancy joined me on my other side. "And not without me either." I smiled at her crazy "Nancy loyalty," which basically equated to "Mother Bear mode." Her eyes were slightly red. She had been crying.

Jason noticed it at the same time and his face fell with guilt. I could tell he just wanted to push me into Gramps and take Nancy into his arms.

That would have been awkward.

But Jason did what he always did in situations that were beyond his mental capacity. He ignored it.

"I don't have much time, so if you plan on assembling your little gang, I can't wait for you."

Turner moved his way past us into the living room.

We followed like lame sheep.

Yeah, we were real badasses.

After everyone was sitting on the couch, Gramps turned to me and pretty much pretended like no one else was in the room.

"As much as it pains me to admit it: I need your help," Turner cringed.

"Again?" Okay, not so nice, but it was kind of impossible not to be mean around him, trust me!

Gramps mumbled something unintelligible under his breath, then gave me a hard look. "I'm to be assassinated tomorrow. Is that dire enough for you?"

Assassinated?

No one had been assassinated in over a hundred years. What with Age-pro and all, no one wanted to risk getting caught or worse killed. Besides, only a handful of people knew that Turner was evil. The rest of the populous thought he was a hero. Gramps kept the population under control. Little did they know he did it by exterminating the poor and unnoticed. Most people loved him.

"I'm not behind it, if that's what you're thinking." I suddenly felt under attack. Was he coming here because he thought I was going to kill him? As much as I hated Gramps (and trust me, he killed my mother, I hated him), we had come to a sort of stalemate. He helped me, I let him, but I really didn't want to help him anymore. I'd had enough of that five months ago and it bit me in the butt. Turner had promised he wouldn't kill any of the Havenville villagers, but he murdered hundreds of them, just to rescue the twins…

I shuddered.

Turner's nostrils flared. "I know you're not behind it, that's why I need your help. I need you to stop the assassin."

"How is she supposed to do that?" Nancy interjected with her arms crossed and a scowl on her face.

Gramps didn't even acknowledge Nancy. He looked at me intensely. "With your power. If this assassin is who I think it is, she can make anyone have a heart attack by just focusing on them. The kind of energy it takes to do what she does makes a signature of sorts, like a rippling in the air. Only you will be able to see it, if you concentrate hard enough. Once you've pointed her out, my men will capture her. I assure you, you'll be perfectly safe."

Uh, huh.

Turner didn't look like he cared either way whether or not I was safe. But I could tell that this assassin meant a lot more to him than just being the intended target. He had history with her.

Her.

Obviously a girl with powers like me. But to give someone a heart attack by just looking at them? That sounded terrifying. At least the things I controlled were already dead, I couldn't kill anyone. Or if I could, I didn't want to know about it.

"I guess I can go," I reluctantly agreed.

"I'm going too."

We all turned around to see Ryan standing there with Dr. Johnson.

I jumped off the couch and ran to his waiting arms.

"I'm fine. Dr. Johnson did his thing, and I should be good. Right Doc?" Ryan gave the doctor a look that suggested he wanted him to lie.

I stopped him right there.

"Truth." I pulled away from Ryan.

"The truth is Ryan is going to need to be hooked up to the machine at headquarters." Gramps walked over to us with a terse expression.

"No way," I protested.

Dr. Johnson spoke up heatedly, "Ms. Derée, your boyfriend has over a hundred balls of energy, each with its own consciousness, all running rampant in his brain. We need to extract them and I can't do it here." He seemed angry at my attitude.

I couldn't help it. The doc meant to take Ryan back to his worst nightmare: an I.Q. Farm. Ryan had escaped that fate when he was seven-years-old. It was too horrible to think that his cure would be found there.

Ryan leaned down and kissed my forehead. "It'll be okay. I'm going in on Wednesday."

Doctor Johnson looked absolutely livid. "You should be coming with us this instant."

"I'm going with Chelsan tomorrow and there's nothing you can do or say to stop me. I can last another day." Ryan put Dr. Johnson in his place.

"I'm not so sure about that," Dr. Johnson argued back.

"What is that supposed to mean?" I exclaimed in alarm.

Gramps stepped in with his hands raised. "It means that we're leaving. You're coming tomorrow with your boy toy here, and then on Wednesday we'll take care of his little problem. Deal?"

Ryan actually nodded to Turner in thanks.

I didn't like that one bit.

"I…" I began to disagree once more.

"Deal." Ryan finished for me and gave me a look that begged me to drop it.

It took a few moments before I could finally take a deep breath and nod.

Turner's lips curled in agitation, as if staying one second longer at Nancy's house was killing him. "See you tomorrow. I'll send the details to your holo-account."

With that Gramps left with Dr. Johnson in tow.

"Dinner!" Vianne popped her head out with a smile. When she saw all of our dire expressions, she cocked her head to one side in curiosity. "What did I miss?"

Chapter 2
Tuesday April 5, 2321

Tuesday morning came like a brick smashing me in the head.

I really didn't want to go to Turner's rally thing. That was where Gramps was supposedly going to be assassinated. Some stupid rally for some stupid cause that was probably fake anyway. The location was downtown at the Staples Center, a historical landmark in Los Angeles over three hundred years old. I'd only been there once. It was huge, crowded, and I pretty much hated it. Now, the thought of trying to find one girl amongst a horde of people seemed impossible.

Ryan was already dressed and ready to go while I was just finishing up lacing my Chuck Taylors.

Vianne had already called the school, telling them (well, lying actually) that I was sick. Ryan was just skipping. He said he'd deal with his parents later. I was being extremely selfish bringing him with me, but I couldn't fathom going alone.

Ryan put his hand out for me to take and I clasped it gratefully as he led me downstairs to the kitchen.

The whole gang was there, except for Jill.

"Are you sure you don't want me to go with you guys? What if he has one of his headaches?" Bill said looking at Ryan with just as much concern as there was attitude.

"I'll be fine, thanks." Ryan didn't even make eye contact with Bill. He sat down at the table and ate the eggs and bacon Vianne placed in front of him.

We all sat down after Ryan.

That was when I came up with the brilliant idea to tell everyone about Max and Eva.

And by "brilliant," I mean idiotic.

Bill flipped out, literally flipped out. He was immediately on Eva's side and trying to convince everyone that she wasn't a complete nutball.

"Okay, okay!" Ryan held up his hands to stop the shouting match that was ping-ponging between us all. Then he looked directly at me, "You can't trust Max either, Chelsan. It's not just Eva."

Huh?

I wasn't expecting that.

After my conversation with Max, I actually felt like I could trust him to some degree. But to see the seriousness in Ryan's face…

Ryan was definitely not on Team Max.

"I get that he was basically created by Elisha, but why so adamant?" I asked him.

It was Bill that responded. "Because getting you to trust Max is exactly what Elisha wants."

Ryan and Bill made eye contact and something unsaid passed between them. They were on the same page with this one. A part of me was happy to see them being civil to each other, but the other part was kind of irked that they thought I could be played so easily.

"You don't trust my instincts?" I challenged them both.

"It's not that. It's in your nature to see the best in everyone. That's why I love you," Ryan responded. "But Chelsan, you said yourself Max's been trying to bump into your head…"

"To tell me what was going on without being overheard," I interrupted Ryan, trying to defend myself.

Nancy chimed in this time. "Now that Max thinks you trust him, see if he asks to visit that brain of yours. If he does, then he's working for

Elisha; if he doesn't, maybe we can trust him."

I didn't want to believe I could be so off about Max's intentions, but I knew they were right. How could I even think for a second that I could trust one of Elisha's "experiments"? At least Eva was straightforward in her hatred. But Max… If Max was duping me, he was more brilliant and dangerous than I could ever imagine.

"We can all agree that keeping our distance from both Max and Eva is the plan, right?" I made sure Bill looked me in the eye when I said Eva's name.

Everyone agreed.

Except Bill. "I still think Eva is the good one." He crossed his arms in defiance.

"Really?" Jason shook his head. "You're that crazy for this girl?"

"So what if I am? Even more so now. The fact that the scars on her body are stretch marks! Do you know how painful that must have been? She's been through more in five months than we have in our whole lives." Bill was definitely on the Eva train. I knew he was just sympathetic towards Eva and the horrors she had gone through, but it still sounded like he was putting her above the rest of us.

To everyones' shock George entered the conversation, "Bill, Eva is working for a monster, and possibly could be one herself, while your best friend has been tortured beyond measure at every turn. I don't ever want to hear you defend a sociopath over Chelsan, not ever. She's my daughter now, and I won't have it." George never scolded anyone. *Anyone.* Not even Nancy. And he called me his daughter. My heart sang! In that moment I could care less about Bill's loyalty to Eva. I just wanted to give George a hug.

Bill's face turned bright red. "I…" he stuttered and turned to me, upset. "Chelsan, you know I didn't mean… I just…" At a complete loss for words, Bill slumped his shoulders in defeat. "I won't hang out with Eva anymore."

Oh Bill.

Bill genuinely liked Eva and to be told she was a possible homicidal lunatic was more than he could bear.

Then another thought hit me. "The one thing I can be sure of is the fact that whether or not Max is evil, he genuinely likes Jill." I looked at

Bill with as much sincerity as I could muster. "And Eva definitely likes you. Maybe we can turn them against Elisha somehow."

Bill's face perked up at that. I knew I probably shouldn't give him hope, but seeing Bill upset always made my heart squeeze with sympathy.

I turned to George, "And thanks. I think of you and Vianne as my parents, too. I don't know what I would do without you guys."

Vianne leaned down and kissed my cheek. "We don't know what we would have done without you either."

Um, try: *you'd have a normal, safe life, free of psycho children and grandparents.*

But I didn't say anything. I just let George scuff my head like I was ten and really took in the fact that I had a new family now.

George kind of gruffed at Bill. "No harm, no foul, right kiddo?"

Bill nodded, relieved that George wasn't holding a grudge for his comments about Eva.

Ryan pulled my seat out. "We should get going," he said, stuffing the last of his bacon into his mouth.

Okay. I guess we were going. Ryan was in mission-mode.

"You guys want a ride?" Bill offered almost sheepishly. He was trying to make up for his behavior.

Ryan didn't even entertain the offer for a second. "We're going to take the Hover-Shuttle. Traffic will be a killer with this rally going on." He turned to me, "You have everything?"

"Uh, yeah," I kind of mumbled. I was a little taken aback by Ryan's need to rush. Maybe he was having another headache and was trying to distract himself.

Ryan held the door for me.

I waved to everyone with what I can only assume was a somewhat nervous expression, because Nancy hurried over and gave me a hug goodbye. "You're going to be fine. Just make sure you think of yourself first. If it's between Turner and you, don't get all martyr-like on me."

"*That*, you don't have to worry about," I replied. Although it wasn't in my nature to watch people die, even if they were the epitome of evil. But I didn't want to tell Nancy that. She'd just get paranoid that I'd sacrifice myself for Turner.

I waved to everyone else, followed Ryan through the living room, out the front door and directly to the Hover-Shuttle station.

The trip to the Staples Center was a quick one. The closer we came to Staples, the more people piled into the shuttle until we were packed so tight everyone was rubbed up against one another.

I couldn't wait to get out. The feeling of claustrophobia was overwhelming.

When we landed, I pushed my way through the throng of people until my feet were firmly on the ground. I was gasping for air outside the shuttle. And all that time Ryan's hand never left mine. He pulled me in close and held me for a few moments.

"You okay?" he whispered in my ear.

I relaxed and nodded into his chest.

There were thousands of people swarming into Staples. It was then I noticed that more than half of them were dead.

Good to know.

Turner was trying to protect himself as much as he could and using his own corpses as seat filler was a good idea. It also made my job a little easier. The fewer live people there were, the simpler it would be to spot the assassin. I was still skeptical on whether or not Gramps was right about me being able to see some wavy-energy-thingy. But I'd come to terms with the fact that Turner and even Elisha knew way more about my powers than I did.

I pulled away from Ryan and we headed toward the front entrance.

The Staples Center looked like a giant sailor's hat with its front wall being a large rectangle made of glass. Apparently, the design hadn't changed in over three hundred years. It just expanded out the back, making it capable of seating over 20,000 people. It was one of the oldest buildings in Los Angeles. The inside, of course, had been re-done and re-modeled a hundred times over, but the exterior looked the same as it did when Age-pro was invented in 2030, just with an added butt attached to its rear end.

Ryan and I placed our thumbs on the scanner at the entrance door.

The light turned green and we walked through without incident. Apparently, Gramps had taken care of everything and we were officially, legitimately, invited.

The inside of Staples was shiny and new looking. The floors were a polished marble that were almost blinding from the reflected light coming through the glass wall. And lots of state-of-the-art concession stands selling food, drinks and Geoffrey Turner T-shirts. Just what I needed, a t-shirt with Gramps's picture on it. There were photos people could buy with Turner and Roberta at State and International events. Seeing them gave me a sudden pang for Grams. Sure she was evil, but in the end there she really tried to help me. I never thought I'd be sad, but I didn't want to lose anyone in my circle, no matter how insane they were. That included Turner.

Ryan and I walked with the flow of the crowd, most of them dead and we all entered the main hallway that led to the individual entrances to each section of the arena. There was an usher stationed at every door to help people to their proper seats. We shuffled in to Section 10 and placed our thumbs on the thumb print scanner held by a wiry looking usher (yes, dead too).

"Keep your eyes and ears open. I'm counting on you," the usher said in a monotone voice.

I really hated it when Turner talked through his corpses. It was creepy, and I still didn't know how he did it. Sure, I could make corpses do anything, but that power was innate with me and he used spells. I knew full well that Turner wasn't performing spells all day, so he had to have some sort of system in place that controlled all his corpses. Every time I planned to try and figure it out, I'd get distracted, or frankly, I didn't want to think about it, so I conveniently chalked it up to "Turner secrets I'd never know." Probably not the smartest move, but I had to keep my sanity somehow.

"I'll find her, geez," I muttered with annoyance.

"Your seats are 5500 and 5501. They have the best vantage point of the entire arena. When you see her, use as many of my soldiers as you need to take her down." The usher held his hand out for us to enter the main center.

And by soldiers Turner meant his dead army.

When Ryan and I walked in the coliseum the enormity of the room almost took my breath away. It was a giant oval-shaped donut of rows upon rows of chairs with a polished wooden floor in the middle. A large obsidian stage had been placed dead center. A handful of chairs were stationed on it, behind a glass podium. No one was sitting up there yet, but I could only assume that Turner and his constituents would be arriving shortly.

The place was packed, not a single seat was empty. I surveyed the entire coliseum and more than half were Turner's dead guys. Ryan and I quickly sat in our seats and looked around. Turner had positioned us well: we were up on a balcony at the highest point of the stadium, where the whole enormous room was visible to me.

The people across from me looked like tiny specs, though, and I suddenly felt a surge of anxiety. How was I supposed to find this girl if she was the size of an ant to me?

Ryan squeezed my hand as if reading my mind. "How you holding up?"

I looked at him and tried my best to look confident. "I'm good."

Ryan reached down and kissed me gently. "Your forehead is crinkling." That was Ryan's way of telling me I couldn't fool him.

I leaned into him and he wrapped his arms around me for support.

Sigh.

What would I do without him?

The National Anthem started playing over the loud speakers. Guess we were about to start.

Ryan made faces at the obnoxious choir recording of the Anthem and I found it hard not to laugh. Apparently, Turner didn't want to have a live singer at this event and I suddenly wondered why. Did he want as few people on stage with him as possible? Maybe he was afraid the assassin would be disguised as a singer?

The recording stopped and a man I recognized stepped onstage and to the podium. His name was Grant and he was one of Turner's dead lackeys, but to the public he was Gramps's most trusted advisor. If the world only knew that the man they thought was giving Turner such great council had been dead for over a hundred years…

I was tempted to take over Grant's body and make him say something stupid, but I restrained myself. It amazed me that as serious a situation as this was my impulse was to do something irresponsible and dangerous. It was like when someone tells you not to laugh and it takes every fiber of concentration not to.

The roar of applause brought me out of my stupor as Grant introduced Turner.

A procession of five people walked toward the stage, Gramps in the lead.

"Whoa… Is that who I think it is?" Ryan's voice sounded in my ear.

I stared in disbelief.

Yes, it was.

Right behind Turner was Roberta.

Not cat-lady-Feline Roberta, but young, vibrant, twenty-year-old Roberta.

And a black swirling hole was spinning madly in the center of her chest.

What was going on?

It's me, Roberta's voice broke through the barrier of my mind like a lightening bolt. I was so shocked to see her, I'd let my defenses down and she managed to push her way in.

But how?

How was she alive and dead at the same time? I saw her old body die, but now she was in this new, dead, young body. I had too many confusing, conflicting thoughts to process.

Then I remembered my dream.

Clones.

I let my mind open only to her and asked, *How?*

I was so eloquent.

Roberta spoke inside my brain, *I'll explain after. Keep watch for Isabelle.*

Isabelle.

They obviously knew a lot more about this assassin than Turner let on.

Surprise, surprise.

I answered Ryan, "Yes, it's Roberta, but I don't know what's going on. She's in a dead cloned body of herself, but it's definitely her soul in there."

Ryan didn't respond. He didn't have to. What can anyone really say at that point? My grandparents were full of mojo and surprises and seeing a twenty-year-old-Grandma-corpse wasn't exactly a shocker at this point.

Their entourage arrived on the stage and Turner stepped up to the podium while Grams and the four other corpses sat down behind him.

The cheers slowly died down as Turner motioned for everyone to be quiet.

I scanned the audience. Back and forth, back and forth, looking for any kind of wavy-air-thing. I still didn't know what Gramps expected me to see, but I felt the urgent need to really search.

Why did I care about him again?

Ugh.

Focus.

I started to freak out.

Turner was mid-sentence when he started to stutter out his words. A faint black hole began to spin around his heart.

Oh crap.

I looked everywhere.

Nothing.

No wavy air. No nothing.

And his black hole was growing.

Gramps clutched his chest.

The crowd gasped. A growing roar of concern and chatter was quickly becoming deafening.

Roberta rushed to his side and our eyes met.

Find Isabelle! she screamed in my head.

I'm trying! I screamed back, but I wasn't even sure if she heard me.

I took a deep breath and concentrated as hard as I could.

FLASH!

I made myself see all the swirling black dust in the air. It was like a hurricane of darkness swarming around the stadium. It was amazing how dead skin cells could be so disgusting and so plentiful. Gross.

Then I saw it.

A direct line to Gramps's heart. Like a laser cutting through the air from the top balcony off to my left, the disturbance of tiny black spinning holes was a surreal sight.

"Got her," I said aloud and felt Ryan's hand squeeze mine.

I could barely see the assassin through the swirling fog of black, but it was enough.

I connected to ten of Turner's dead army and made them tackle the assassin to the ground.

Instantly the beam of…of whatever it was Isabelle-the-Assassin was beaming at Gramps stopped.

Turner's black hole immediately dispersed and he glanced up at me with a nod of thanks.

That was seriously the nicest gesture he'd ever bestowed upon me. But all the same, I found myself sighing in relief. That was close. Gramps almost died and the weirdest part was the fact that I actually cared.

I must have been going insane.

The assassin was putting up quite a fight, so I added five more men to the mix and she quickly stopped her struggle. Fifteen men to hold down one woman; she must be quite a force to be reckoned with. It made me wonder who this Isabelle was. How did she learn about her power? What made her decide to kill people for a living? I found that I had a sudden desire to meet this girl.

Turner made his excuses to the hysterical audience and hurried offstage with Roberta and his men, leaving Grant behind to answer questions and calm the crowd.

Roberta's voice sounded in my head, *Give Geoffrey control over his men, we'll take it from here. Meet us backstage. I'll send someone to show you the way.*

I didn't answer, but I disconnected from Turner's corpses when I was sure Gramps had control over them again. I led Ryan through the throng of nervous people until we met up with our usher once more. He didn't say a word as he walked to the service elevator and punched in his employee code. The elevator was clunky and old, the owner of the center not caring much about its staff, but the car managed to descend safely to the bottom floor with only a few clunks and squeaks.

When the elevator door opened, Ryan and I followed the usher through a maze of hallways. I could already see over twenty spinning black holes in one of the rooms ahead. It had to be where Turner and the assassin were. And Roberta. I still wasn't sure of what to think about Grams. What was she? I pushed aside my questions and entered the room full of corpses.

The room was huge, filled with lockers and benches and a large group shower area in the back. We were obviously in the locker room used for athletes of whatever sport was being played at the Staples Center at any given time. It had a kind of musty, sweaty smell that wasn't exactly pleasing to the senses.

Turner sat on a bench with Roberta next to him, her arm wrapped lovingly around his back.

All fifteen of his zombie army surrounded the assassin. Isabelle. She was like an island amongst a sea of swirling chasms. Isabelle wasn't struggling. In fact, she just stood there with no expression on her face.

Until I walked in.

Isabelle's eyes flickered in my direction. I could tell in that instant: she sized me up, tried to calculate my threat to her, and dismissed me, all in one look.

Okay, fine. I promised myself I wouldn't be as dismissive of Isabelle as she was of me. I knew better. This girl could squeeze my heart until it stopped, she didn't need to know what I could do. Her ignorance might just be my savior.

Turner and Roberta both stood when they saw Ryan and me.

"Chelsan, come here," Roberta called out.

I was still skeptical of Roberta's obvious black hole in her chest, but I walked over to her all the same. I couldn't stop myself. When I was buried alive, this was the appearance that Roberta had taken when she visited me in my head. I couldn't help but feel instantly comforted by this new image of her. I realized I associated *evil Roberta* with her Feline self and *good Roberta* with her young self. I couldn't seem to come to terms with the conflict within me so I didn't even struggle when Roberta pulled me in for a long hug.

I didn't exactly hug her back, but I didn't pull away either. It actually felt kind of nice. Then I remembered the image of Roberta puppeteering my mother's dead corpse, making Mom dance like a crazed lunatic, with her empty gouged eyes from where Roberta had plucked them out, and I stepped back with a shudder.

Roberta paused for a moment, upset, but then nodded that she understood.

I hated it when she did that.

I still didn't want to forgive her.

Dead, sure, I could almost remember her fondly because of her sacrifice. But alive, or at least, sort of alive? I was just as confused as ever.

I glanced over at Isabelle and I could tell she had observed the whole exchange with an impassive expression.

Turner controlled his men to part the way so that Isabelle was in clear view with no one in front of her.

Not the smartest move, but Gramps seemed to think he knew what he was doing.

"Isabelle." Turner stared at the assassin intensely.

They definitely knew each other. From the look on Isabelle's face, it wasn't a happy reunion. She probably had similar experiences to mine with dear old Gramps, and being an assassin and all, she didn't seem to be as forgiving as I was.

Isabelle took three steps forward to stand within a foot of Turner. She was a tall girl, about five eleven, almost the same height as Gramps, so they were staring at each other eye-to-eye. Isabelle was quite stunning. Dressed in black, tight-fitting cargo pants, black boots, grey A-shirt, and black form-fitting long-sleeved shirt completely unbuttoned down the front, she was a very fashionable murderer. Isabelle's face was pale with a smattering of freckles across her straight nose. Her eyes were bright blue in contrast to her medium length dark brown hair that was pulled back in a slick ponytail.

Isabelle spoke with a kind of confidence that gave her power, "Turner."

Gramps actually smiled, though there was no humor in his eyes. "Did you honestly think I didn't know you were still alive?"

Isabelle shifted slightly. It was the first time I'd seen her show any kind of fear. She was definitely scared of Turner. I couldn't blame her. He scared the bageezees out of me most times too, especially when he was trying to kill me and I was his granddaughter!

But the fear in Isabelle's face quickly turned deadly. I stepped back, even though I was five feet away from her. "We know about your army and plans for a war. You have to be stopped."

We?

And wait, war?

Months had gone by since Jason predicted there would be a holy war after our ordeal with Elisha, but hearing the word war again made my skin crawl. If what Isabelle was saying was true, maybe it was Turner that wanted the war and not Elisha, or both.

I wanted to kick Roberta, who was standing next to me. They weren't honestly thinking about starting a war were they?

Turner shook his head. "I'm not the one you should be worried about. I'm building an army of defense. You should know me better than that."

"I know you'd rather kill in secret than in the open," Isabelle's voice grew more angry and intense.

Gramps remained calm as usual. "Exactly my point."

Turner let that sink in for a moment.

He did have a point. Why would he go through all the trouble of secret exterminations if his plan was open warfare?

"You were never the bright one of the bunch, were you, Isabelle?" Turner rubbed salt in the wound. He was good at that.

And *bunch*? Were there more heart-stopping assassins on the loose? How long of a history was theirs? Did Isabelle used to work for Turner? Too many questions and there was no way either grandparent would share. I was surprised they'd let me witness this whole thing in the first place. I concentrated on the task at hand. I wanted to remember this exchange for the gang later. I briefly glanced at Ryan and noticed he was doing the same. Between the two of us we'd be able to memorize this little soiree.

Suddenly, Isabelle's eyes were on me. "Is she your new secret weapon?"

"She has more brains and talent than you ever had," Turner sneered.

Wait. What?

Did Turner just compliment me?

I was about to go in shock.

"Really?" Isabelle smiled back.

Isabelle stared at me and I could feel my heart slowing down.

Way down.

I stumbled from the force of it.

She was going to kill me.

Turner immediately controlled his dead men to punch Isabelle in the face, breaking her hold on my poor little heart.

I gasped for breath and rubbed my chest.

But Isabelle was waiting for this moment. In fact, I realized almost immediately, she'd planned it. Isabelle looked like a Kung Fu movie, swinging her arms and legs in a graceful, but deadly manner. Little did Isabelle know that her targets were dead: no amount of kicking and punching would hurt them or slow them in any way. But it was enough for her to reach her goal.

Roberta.

Isabelle held Roberta in a chokehold before Turner could control his men to stop her.

"I'm taking the girl or Roberta dies." Isabelle looked triumphant.

Um.

Yeah.

Roberta was already dead.

I almost didn't have the heart to tell Isabelle, but yeah, there was no way I was coming with her.

I spoke up. "You can't kill someone when they're already dead."

Isabelle's face showed real surprise at that. It was definitely the last thing she expected to hear.

Then a light bulb seemed to go off in Isabelle's brain. She eyed Turner with an almost grudging respect, then she laughed. "You're the one who hired me to kill you."

Gramps smiled back and I saw the glimmer of an old friendship between the two of them. "It was the only way I could be sure if the two of you were still around."

Excuse me?!

That bastard!

I was used yet again. What if I hadn't stopped her? He could have died.

Like Roberta.

Maybe his contingency plan was the same one Roberta had apparently used. Then the two of them would have been young again. I still didn't know what had actually happened with Roberta, my brain was melting from too many questions.

But Turner had said *if the two of you were still around.*

Which Isabelle attempted to deflect, "I never said *he* was still alive."

Isabelle was serious once more.

"Earlier, you said *we* know about your army.'" Turner gave her a look like he had checkmated her. "Besides, that little fire you two concocted to make me think you were killed was a little too obvious."

Isabelle still held tight to Roberta's throat. She turned to me. "I'm assuming you're the one who stopped me from killing Geoffrey."

I nodded.

"You saved a monster today. I hope you're proud of yourself." Isabelle said it in a sort of sad way, like she understood why I had saved him, but couldn't bring herself to admit it.

"Not really."

Yeah, I said that.

I could literally feel Gramps rolling his eyes.

Isabelle paused. Then I saw it. A glimmer of amusement.

"She's interesting," Isabelle said to Turner.

"She is my granddaughter." Gramps looked at Isabelle knowingly.

Realization hit Isabelle. It was public knowledge that I was Turner's granddaughter, but I didn't think Isabelle made the connection until that moment.

Isabelle tightened her chokehold on Roberta.

Roberta gasped for air.

Turner's eyes locked with Roberta.

I would have done something to save Roberta, but well… she was dead already. Turner apparently felt the same.

Isabelle placed her hand on the side of Roberta's head.

She was going to snap Roberta's neck.

"If she's already dead, then this won't hurt."

Okay, this girl was getting annoying.

I didn't care if Roberta was already a walking corpse, there was no way I was going to let her mutilate my grandmother's body like that.

So, I did something pretty violating.

I connected to Roberta's swirling black hole.

It was like nothing I'd ever experienced. The only thing close was when I was able to connect to the twins and use their power to control life. Even though Roberta was dead, she was very much alive inside. I could feel her life force flowing through me, just like when I connected to the townspeople of Havenville. And even though she was dead, I could see her swirling white light. It was confusing, I thought that white light meant life, but it was more than that…

It was her soul.

Roberta's soul was living inside a dead body.

There was no other way I could describe it.

But Isabelle was about to snap that dead body's neck, so I shoved my feelings of awe aside and acted fast.

I made Roberta grab Isabelle's hand and push it away, then I made her back kick Isabelle in the knee.

I connected to five of the dead army and had one of them pull Roberta to safety. I let go of my control of Roberta, feeling like I had debased her as a human being, then puppeteered the corpses to attack Isabelle.

She was gone.

I searched the area.

Nothing.

Isabelle had completely disappeared.

I released my hold on the men and turned to Ryan.

"Did you see where she went?" I asked him since he was *Observant Boy*.

Ryan was at a total loss. "I got so focused on Roberta's ninja moves, I didn't see her."

"That was me," I said, feeling a little ashamed at controlling Grams like that.

Ryan raised an eyebrow in curiosity, but there was no judgment on his face.

Not so true with Gramps.

"How dare you!" he roared. "Never do that to Roberta again, you hear me? Never!"

"Geoffrey, it's okay." Roberta locked her arm in Turner's. She turned to me.

"I have no control over you tapping into this corpse at any time. That's how much I trust you. I wanted you to see that for yourself." Roberta was so sincere, it made me feel even more guilty.

"What about Isabelle?" I asked.

Hello? There was still a psycho assassin on the loose.

Turner was calm once more. "She'll run back to Harry and tell him I know they're still alive."

"Who's Harry?" Ryan asked.

I knew they'd never tell us, but I felt a surge of pride that he even tried to ask.

"Oh I'm sure your little team will figure it out soon enough, the details are not something you need to know. But know this: If you think I'm 'evil,' Isabelle and Harry are ten times worse. They've been in the business of killing for three hundred years. They have no remorse and no conscience. At least when I have to let people go it's for a greater good," Turner explained.

"*Let people go*? It's not like you're laying them off from a job, you're freaking murdering human beings!" Okay. I was mad now.

"Relax," Gramps grumbled. "I'm just saying that they're worse."

I groaned, knowing I wasn't going to get anywhere with this argument. I focused my attention on Roberta. "What happened to you?" Before she could answer I waved at the dead guards around us. "And can we just send these lame butts away please."

"These lame butts saved my life, but we can go to a safer location." Turner was getting annoyed with me again. So much for his earlier affection. I guess it had just been a show for Isabelle.

Ryan and I followed the grandparents to a small office down in the bowels of the Staples Center. Gramps kept two of his dead guards with us just in case, but he let the rest of his men leave. Ryan stayed quiet the whole time and I wondered what he thought of all this. Even though he was my stoic statue today, I couldn't have imagined going through everything without him. It just made me worry that his head was killing him. Ryan was only quiet when he was trying to keep me from worrying, which of course made me worry. As if reading my mind, Ryan reached around me as we all sat down on the two facing couches. He kissed the top of my head.

All cozied up. I felt like I could face anything.

Or at least I hoped so.

Roberta and Turner sat next to each other on the couch across from us. The room was lit with ceiling pot lights. There was nothing else in it except the two couches and a couple of fold-up chairs leaning against the wall.

"What are you?" I couldn't keep it in anymore.

Roberta smiled, and it was a pleasant contrast to her previous face-stretched smile of the past. "I showed you last night."

"That *was* you. Clones," I thought aloud. "But why is this clone dead?"

"There's a reason why cloning humans never caught on. There has never been a successful case of human cloning in history," Turner interjected with an air of irritancy.

"But hello?" I motioned to Roberta proving him wrong.

Gramps looked at me as if I were an idiot child that was incapable of understanding the obvious.

Roberta placed her hand on his to quiet him and turned to me. "What Geoffrey meant to say is that cloning is very successful when it comes to the physical. We can replicate anything if we have access to its DNA. And the replication is identical. It's just that with human cloning… they end up… unbalanced… in the head."

"You can replicate a body, but not a soul," Ryan said seeing things more clearly than I did.

"Exactly," Roberta agreed. "Geoffrey and I have other means at our disposal, if you hadn't noticed."

"Voodoo." I was starting to see the bigger picture here.

Roberta nodded. "When I died, I needed a vessel to be brought back into. With the voodoo ritual, it needed to be a dead body. We've been keeping clones of ourselves in stasis for the past two hundred years. Geoffrey injected one of my replicants with poison, performed the ritual and voila… Here I am, twenty years old."

"And dead." I really didn't mean that the way it came out.

"Yes, and dead," Turner picked up on my attitude right away.

I almost apologized, but we were interrupted by one of Turner's advisors. A live one.

"Mr. Vice President, sorry to interrupt, but your hover-limo is ready for your guests," the weasely little man groveled.

"No interruption. We were done here. Have my granddaughter and her guest escorted home. If anything happens to her, I will hold you personally responsible," Turner ordered.

The man's face turned five shades of white at the possibility of being blamed for any mishap that may fall upon me.

I was taken aback yet again by Turner's strange kindness and almost... loyal words toward me. He'd never say anything like that to my face when no one was around, but it was weird hearing him threaten people on my behalf. I didn't know if it was an act for others or if it was real. I knew I shouldn't care either way, but there was still a little part of me that missed my family, and it made me cling to the shred of a string of hope that Gramps could change and maybe be a good person someday.

What was I thinking?

Seriously? He just threatened a guy.

Ugh. My brain was too jumbled at this point to think clearly, so I took the moment to stand up, bringing Ryan with me.

"Don't worry about it. We're taking the shuttle." I started to walk toward the door with Ryan holding tight to my hand.

The man in the doorway turned about five more shades of white.

"You will do no such thing, young lady!" Gramps shouted as if he was actually some sort of parent figure to me.

I whirled on him, suddenly angry.

"Don't you dare act like you care. You've had me kidnapped, tortured, and you've tried to kill me a bagillion times. Now, because former cat-lady actually grew a conscious and has some weird obsession with me, you think you can order me around and pretend to even like me?" I almost snarled at him, "Just stay away from me and my friends. And the next time you want to use me to re-connect with your old psycho buddies, leave me out of it!"

I shoved Turner's poor lackey out of the way and left the room before Turner or Roberta could respond.

Ryan kissed my cheek. "Good for you."

I was still reeling. I didn't know where all that anger came from in that exact moment, but it hadn't subsided yet. I was so angry with myself for creating a false sense of calm with my evil grandparents. And they were evil. Why did I always seem to ignore that fact and do them favors?!

No more.

They could fall off the face of the planet and I wouldn't care.

I made sure my "brain walls" were in place. I didn't want Roberta jumping in to try and reconcile with me. Screw her and her twenty-year-old-soulless-dead-clone-body!

After a few minutes of us charging through the hallway bowels of the Staples Center, Ryan started to chuckle. "We're totally lost, aren't we?"

I had been storming around so thoroughly I hadn't realized that all these hallways looked exactly alike. I started to laugh with him.

"Should we ask that guy you shoved?" Ryan kissed me playfully.

I rubbed my hand over my face in embarrassment. "Did I really just do that?"

"Yes." Ryan kissed me again. Melt. "And it's about time."

I stopped in my tracks with a horrible thought.

"You still need help! What did I just do?!" Dread started to set in. I had just burned a bridge with the only person who could help Ryan. He could die and it would be all my fault. Why couldn't I have just sucked it up until Ryan was okay? I was so selfish!

Ryan kissed me passionately, leaving my head spinning. When he pulled away he cupped my face in his hands like I loved so much. "I'll be fine. I can take care of this on my own. I think I know how. I don't need their stupid machine."

"I'm going back and apologizing." I couldn't let anything happen to Ryan. Pride be damned, I would grovel on my hands and knees if it would save Ryan's life.

Ryan held my arms with his hands and looked me straight in the eye. "I won't let you do that. You have to trust me. I'm going to be fine. I can do this on my own even if I have to build one of those brain machines myself." Then he smiled. "I'm just that smart, you know."

Ryan would sell me the moon at this point, so there was no use arguing with him. I vowed to myself that I would visit Grams in my dreams tonight and ask for their help. I probably wouldn't even have to apologize. She really was getting a little stalkery on me.

"This isn't over." I left it at that and Ryan didn't argue. He could tell by the expression on my face that I wouldn't be able to let it go, but he also knew there was no use in arguing the point further.

"Let's just try and get out of here. I think I remember the way." Ryan concentrated and used that super-memory-brain-power-thing he was so good at and led the way.

Twenty minutes later we were exiting through the back of the Staples Center. The Hover-Shuttle station was visible in the distance through the crowd of people and all the press-hovers parked everywhere. We started to head toward the station when…

Eva stepped out in front of us.

I backed up instinctively (and logically, the girl looked vicious!).

"What do you want, Eva?" I asked.

"Elisha knows Max spilled the beans, and she's ready to see you now." Eva had her arms crossed in a kind of confident defiance. She really thought she was on the winning team.

"Max telling me was all a part of her plan so don't act like it was an accident," I said, more to gauge Eva's reaction, though, than actually believing what I'd just said was true. There was still a part of me that believed Max was on the up and up. Eva's response would tell me a lot.

I wasn't disappointed.

Eva looked defensive. Defensive, not upset. If Eva had been upset it would have been because I had seen through their ruse. Defensive meant she wanted to protect Max, and more probably his reputation. It wasn't concrete proof of his innocence, but it was a start.

"Leave Max out of this," Eva scowled.

"You brought him up," Ryan chimed in.

Eva tossed her auburn hair back as if to say she was bored with the two of us. "I'll take you to her."

"No thanks." I started to walk away with Ryan.

I was not about to go to an undisclosed location to talk to a psychopath that had forced me to kill innocent people so she could gain the same power I had. It was bad enough I had to talk to her in Ms. Floster's head, but in person? There was no telling what she could do to me. Elisha knew way more about my powers than I did, and that meant she'd most likely be able to kick my butt.

Seriously, no thanks.

"Wrong answer." I heard Eva say behind us.

I saw it then.

Millions of swirling black holes coming straight at us. She was using my trick with the dust.

But this girl had only been alive for five months.

I had my powers my whole life.

Before the dust reached its intended target (our noses and inevitably our lungs), I stopped every last piece dead in its tracks.

"You really want to play this?" I turned to Eva, asking her calmly.

Ryan could see none of this, to him we were just standing in open air, but he'd been with me long enough to know something was happening.

Eva's face was scrunched in concentration as she tried to regain control over the dust.

Not going to happen.

Eva dropped her attempt and looked at me with pure fury in her eyes. "You're coming with me."

A slew of dead branches came flying at us like a sudden tornado in the middle of the Staples Center loading zone.

I acted fast and stopped all of them. They were literally hovering around us.

This Ryan could see.

And unfortunately so could the hundreds of press crews just behind us.

Eva was sweating bullets as she tried to make at least one of the dead pieces of wood smack me on the head. It would have been comical except for the fact I knew I was going to be on the evening news. Using my powers in public was not something I needed right now.

I disconnected the branches from their black swirling holes and they all dropped to the ground. Once disconnected not even I could control them anymore.

Eva's eyes widened in shock.

Apparently, she didn't know that trick.

The press reached us in seconds and started screaming out questions about hovering tree branches and what happened and was Geoffrey Turner involved.

Oy.

I wanted to crawl under a rock and then throw the rock at them.

I took full advantage of the swarm of people and jumped right in the middle with Ryan in tow, making our way to the Hover-Shuttle.

The little weasel man from Turner's entourage pushed his way through to us. "Vice President Turner insists that you take one of his hover-limos. It's right over there." He pointed to a safe haven of dead bodyguards and a waiting limo.

I guess Gramps wasn't mad at me after all. I breathed a secret sigh of relief, hoping he'd still help Ryan.

The press pushed in closer and as far as I could tell the Hover-Shuttle would be a nightmare for us too.

I sighed. "Lead the way."

Ryan gave me a half-smile of approval, and the two of us shoved, clawed and tripped our way to the safe refuge of corpses.

The hover-limo was empty, so at least we didn't have to suffer through another awkward moment with the grandparents. Roberta probably talked to Turner on my behalf. Not something I wanted to think about at the moment.

As we took to the air I could see Eva talking in front of the cameras, apparently loving the attention. She had failed in her mission, but I knew in my gut she'd be back trying to make me go to Elisha. A meeting with Elisha was inevitable. I just needed more time to prepare. Eva might not have complete control over her powers, but Elisha would. And Elisha was a lot more dangerous and far more knowledgeable about the subject. I had to be on my toes.

It was hard not to become completely overwhelmed. From Turner to Elisha to the new threat of Isabelle. Why me?

It wasn't long before the hover-limo landed at Nancy's house. I didn't even bother saying anything to the driver as Ryan and I exited. It was mid-afternoon so Nancy and Bill would be arriving soon and we could give them the scoop. I knew I was going to have to confirm to Bill that not only is Eva with Elisha, but she seemed pretty happy about it. And the fact that she tried to use her powers against me again. The evidence was in, and Eva was guilty. I was on the fence about Max. I'd have to wait and see what he did next.

Walking inside the house, I felt instantly safe. It was amazing how much an inanimate object could stir so many emotions. It was just four walls and a roof, but somehow it epitomized everything that was good in my life. Almost every good memory I'd had since the devastation of my mother being murdered was in this house.

George came running in from the kitchen. "I thought I heard the door. There's something you should see."

Uh oh.

George looked worried and if George was worried, I knew I should be too.

Vianne came in from the kitchen right behind George holding a plate full of steaming chocolate chip cookies. "You'll need a few of these."

Chocolate chip cookies? I knew I was in trouble then.

I grabbed three from the plate and bit into the chocolate gooiness.

Um. Yum.

George turned on the holo-TV and rewound this afternoon's broadcast. My stomach already started to turn when I saw Eva in rewind. What did she say? George stopped the holo to right after I disconnected the floating tree branches from their swirling black holes. It was just as I remembered it: the press swarming up to us spouting questions, then Ryan and I making our escape with weasel-guy. Since Eva was the last man standing, they quickly surrounded her.

But Eva was prepared. A little too prepared. Actually, what she said next was down right rehearsed.

Being set up part 2, party of 1. First Turner, now Eva or I should say Elisha.

Man, I was such a sucker.

Eva made herself look like she was a terrified rabbit. The crowd of press was so intense that the life-size holo versions of the reporters actually digitalized around the edges. Otherwise the whole living room would have been full of people. It was surreal watching the scene we just escaped from right in front of us.

Then Eva spoke and I cringed at every word. "You all saw it! Geoffrey Turner's granddaughter has powers! She can make things fly with her mind. She was going to kill me with those tree branches. If you hadn't shown up… I owe you my life."

The press ate it up like they were the heroes of the millennium.

Eva spoke straight to the camera, "Chelsan Derée has to be stopped before she kills us all. Vice President Turner has been keeping her powers secret, to protect her, but we have to stand up to him. If he won't turn over his granddaughter, we'll have to take her down ourselves!"

The crowd was getting riled up. I thought I was going to puke.

I never thought Elisha would do something like this. I thought that in order to protect herself, she'd have to protect my secret. But Elisha was insane-o and that unfortunately meant unpredictable as well.

George paused the holo-TV. "I'm not sure what this is going to do, but you better stay here until we sort this out."

Vianne handed me another cookie and I took it gratefully. "Jason is on his way. He says he thinks he knows how he can spin this, but he'll need Turner's help."

I let out an exasperated sigh. "I'm not sure how receptive Turner will be for doing me any favors right now. I kind of screamed at him and Roberta and told them to never speak to me again. But they still gave me a ride home after all that, so maybe he'll listen." I just wanted my favor from Gramps to be for Ryan not me. Saving Ryan was way more important than saving my reputation. Hands down. I just hoped Turner saw it that way.

George's eyes twinkled with pride. "He owes you, and he deserves any words you have to say to him."

Vianne plopped down next to me and ate a cookie herself. "You know we're behind you, no matter what happens."

I nodded and placed my head on Vianne's shoulder while I took another bite out my cookie.

"Why would Eva blatantly lie about your power?" Ryan asked, thinking it through. "I mean, it's far more terrifying that you can control the dead than you making things fly."

"Thanks," I said sarcastically.

Ryan kissed my cheek. "I love you, but your power is pretty scary. What's even scarier is that three more people have it, one of them being Elisha, the craziest psychopath on the planet."

He was right, but it only made my stomach churn more. "They don't want anyone knowing they have the same power?" I volunteered, though I was only guessing.

Ryan shook his head. "If I were Elisha I'd want everyone to know exactly what your powers are. That way she could blame you when she uses them herself. Especially, if she plans on using them for war."

There was that word again.

War.

I brainstormed, "Well, what would be the purpose of telling people that I can make things fly?"

George sat up. "She's going to blame you for something, like Ryan said, and she has to be certain everyone will blame you."

I rubbed my face in frustration. "This is all speculation. We could guess until the cows come home. With Elisha we won't know it until it's happening."

"There's got to be a way to get a step ahead of her." Ryan pulled me in and held me close.

I wished he was right, but experience told me that unless we wanted to get into the torture business we were out of luck.

"Whatever she wants to fly would have to be something dead, because as far as I know making random things fly isn't a skill set our powers have." I sighed.

We all sat there in a stupor. For smart people, we felt pretty dumb. Maybe the others would have some more input.

As if answering my thought, Jason, Bill, Nancy and Jill walked in the door. I was a little surprised to see Jill, but part of me was happy all the same. I felt like I could use a dose of her bitchy point of view right about now. Sometimes that particular skill ended up helping us "nice" people see things we wouldn't normally see.

They all plopped down around us and helped themselves to Vianne's cookies.

I was about to tell them the scoop when I realized I hadn't told Jill about Max and Eva yet. I wasn't looking forward to this conversation at all. Why couldn't Bill and Jill just have stayed a couple? It was really annoying that they both liked two possible homicidal maniacs.

Nancy could see from my face the inner dilemma I was having. "I told Jill about Max," Nancy admitted.

Ah, Nancy. This was exactly what best friends were made for.

Jill folded her arms and gave an exasperated sigh. "I knew that boy was too good to be true. Whatever."

"We're still not sure about Max yet, but Eva..." I looked at Bill, worried about his reaction. His face didn't reveal a thing.

I filled them in on everything, and tried to handle the Eva debacle as nicely as I could for Bill's sake. There was silence when I finished.

Bill was the first to speak. "You guys were right." He looked devastated, but also resolved. Bill just wasn't lucky when it came to girls. It seemed like a flaw in the universe that someone as deserving as Bill couldn't seem to get a decent girlfriend. Let alone one that didn't want to annihilate the world. Bill looked directly at me, "She trusts me. You could use that if you need to."

Wow.

That was Bill proving his loyalty to me, and I just wanted to jump over the couch and give him a big hug.

But Ryan shook his head, cautioning Bill. "After today, she'll be suspicious. You shouldn't risk yourself getting hurt or worse, kidnapped by Elisha and used as leverage."

Instead of being defensive, Bill nodded agreement with Ryan, but then said, "I'd be careful. I just want to help."

"I know you do, Bill." I wanted him to know how much I felt for him. But Ryan was right, I didn't want Bill turning into an Elisha pawn. If that happened, I knew I would do anything to get him back and I also knew that since Bill's parents were possibly the richest people on the planet, they would pay anything to get him back.

Jill harrumphed, "You guys are so dramatic. So what? Do we just hole up here until Elisha makes a move?" With both Jill's parents dead, she was pretty much living on her own. But she did love a good excuse to stay over. George and Vianne had offered her a room permanently, but Jill was too stubborn for that. She'd just turned eighteen and lived alone in her giant empty mansion. Surprisingly, Jill appeared to be handling it quite well, but she was a hard one to read. I wondered if I'd even be able to tell if Jill was hurting or not. She was flippant about Max, but I had seen in her eyes how much she liked the guy. I decided not to push, but I also decided I was going to try and have a heart-to-heart with the girl as well.

Jill and I had come to an understanding. I was pretty sure I was her only true friend.

Jason finally piped in, "You guys go to school. Act like nothing new has happened. Chelsan will stay here. I'll see what I can do to spin this." He sat thinking a moment then added, "We just need another explanation for why sticks can fly."

Yeah, not hard at all.

After that, the conversation turned to the mundane, which was a welcome relief from the chaos that was my life. Nancy seemed happy with Jason again. He must have begged and apologized profusely enough to satisfy her. She was already planning out her dress for prom. I wanted to be excited and plan everything for myself, too, but yeah…

The world was coming to an end and I was in the middle of it. Yet again.

Why couldn't I shut off for brief moments of bliss like Nancy seemed able to do? But I wasn't being fair. Nancy was probably stressing out just as much as I was, but she didn't want me to see it. She just wanted me to forget about my crazy life for a while. I loved her for that, but at the moment I couldn't get into it.

Jill noticed right away and of course couldn't keep her mouth shut. "Do you honestly think Chelsan cares about prom right now?"

Instead of looking hurt like I thought she would be, Nancy stared daggers at Jill. "It's called distraction, you moron."

Just like I thought. But now I felt bad for Jill.

Jill stood up. "Why do I even come here? Call me if you need me." She headed for the door.

"Now who's being dramatic?" Nancy accused.

Really?

I went after Jill with a quick smile and shake of my head at Nancy. Nancy shooed me toward Jill, essentially giving her permission for me to patch things up. If Nancy's temper was fire, Jill's was lava. And the two of them combined could potentially turn into an erupting volcano (like five months ago when they got into a fistfight at school).

I caught Jill on the front porch making her way toward her hover-BMW.

"Jill, would you just wait a second." I caught her arm.

She whirled on me defiantly, "What?"

"Look, I know you're upset, but I need you." I didn't exactly know what I needed Jill for, but I wanted her to feel like she was part of the team.

"Oh please! I'm just your charity case. I wouldn't even be popular again if it weren't for you. Do you know how much it sucks owing your worst enemy?" Jill fumed.

"Worst enemy? Really, Jill?" I knew she was just frustrated and let's face it, she felt left out. No matter how hard I tried to make her feel like one of the group, Jill was still an outsider. That was a fact. I couldn't erase three years of bad behavior from my brain, and neither could she.

Jill sighed heavily. "You know I'm full of crap. I'm just… I don't know. I'm tired, I guess. Look, I'm gonna go."

"Jill?" Max stepped into view. He had obviously been standing behind her car and neither one of us had seen him.

I wanted to think it was creepy, but seeing as how Max was well Max, it was kind of cute.

Jill turned to him. "Stay away from me, psycho."

Okay.

I guess Jill thought it was creepy.

"Can I explain?" Max was upset.

Meanwhile, third wheel here.

"Explain what? That you're a six-foot infant that has no soul and uses freak powers like her."

Thanks, Jill, thanks.

"I should leave you guys alone." I tried to bow out of this uncomfortable situation.

Max put his hand up to stop me. "No, Chelsan, I need to talk to you."

Jill threw her hands up as if the world had just exploded. "Of course you do! She's way more important than any of us plebes."

Max stepped forward, giving Jill a stern look. "I want to talk to you, but I have to warn Chelsan of Elisha's plan."

I thought Jill would explode, but then something strange happened. As if against her will, Jill walked toward Max. It was kind of jerky at first, like she was fighting against her own thoughts, it was so odd…

Then I knew.

I grabbed Jill as fast as I could and threw her back toward Nancy's front door.

"What the—!?" Jill snapped out of it and yelped in shock.

Max's face went from sweet to pissed in about a millisecond.

I yelled at Jill, "He's inside your brain! Get in the house and make Bill sit on you! I don't want Max influencing you!"

Jill didn't need to be told twice. She ran inside and slammed the door.

I turned to Max, "Played too hard, too fast."

Max's beautiful face grimaced in annoyance. "You're coming with me, now."

I still couldn't believe Max had been faking everything.

"Elisha will have to come to me. I'm not going to her," I answered, keeping my distance.

"I'm already here," Max snarled.

Oh man.

Okay, well it made me feel a little better about my instincts.

Elisha was using Max's body.

Duh.

I should have known that as soon as Elisha found out that Max had spilled his guts to me that she would use him to get to me.

I tried to help Max fight Elisha. "Max, if you're in there. Build a wall. You can kick Elisha out."

"Did you ever stop to think that he doesn't *want* to kick me out?" Elisha spoke through Max.

It was very surreal having a full on conversation with Max knowing that it was really Elisha nestled in his brain.

For a second, Max came through, his eyes clear and panicked and scared. "She brought others."

Then like a switch, his eyes were Elisha's again. Max's face smiled the way Elisha smiled, like she owned the world.

I ran for the front door just as five armed men raced out from cover. They weren't dead because Elisha knew I'd be able to control them otherwise. They were hired thugs and they had guns. All of which were pointed at me.

Elisha spoke through Max, "Unless you want me to have my men walk inside that house and mow down all your friends, I suggest you come back here."

I abandoned my idea of running into the house for safety. What made Nancy's house safe anyway? It wasn't a game we were playing. I didn't have a base where Elisha and her men couldn't touch me. I turned to Max and the men pointing machine guns at me.

Machine guns? Really? Overcompensating much?

I put my hands up in surrender. "I'll go with you, just don't hurt anyone."

"I can be fair. I don't need to hurt your friends, but I will if you don't come with me." Even though Max was saying it, I could almost hear the evil feminine tone of Elisha.

Before I could step toward them, Max and all five soldiers clutched their chests in pain. They dropped their guns, screaming in agony.

Black swirling holes started to form in their chests.

Isabelle.

She was here and she was killing Elisha's soldiers.

And killing Max.

"What's happening?" Elisha screamed through Max.

I ran over to Max and screamed to Isabelle wherever she was hiding, "DON'T KILL THEM!"

Then Max grabbed onto his head as if fighting off the world's worst migraine.

When Max looked up at me, he was Max again. "I don't know how long I can hold on before she takes over." He was still clutching his chest as the black hole grew larger. "Am I dying?"

Yes, yes he was.

"Isabelle! STOP!"

The assassin walked out from behind Nancy's house. "They want to kill you," she said as if I were stupid to want to her stop. She still hadn't let up. Max's eyes were bugging out.

He was going to die.

I acted fast.

I searched the area for anything dead.

Aside from dust and a few baby tree branches there was nothing… Except…

Gross.

A dead opossum.

Okay, this was about to get nasty.

I connected to its black chasm and made it run as fast as it could move its tiny little feet. It came up from behind Isabelle and I puppeteered it to chomp down on her ankle.

Isabelle's hold instantly dropped on Max and the others.

Isabelle tried to kick the opossum off, but I made it attack her to keep her distracted.

The gunmen caught their breaths and looked terrified.

I turned to them and to Max, "If you guys want to live, then I suggest you RUN!"

There were no arguments from the soldiers. They took off at a sprint, some even leaving their guns behind.

Max turned to me before he ran off himself. "Tell Jill, I'm sorry." Then he was gone, down the grass road.

I turned my attention back to Isabelle. She was attempting to use her powers on the opossum, but Isabelle was beginning to realize that her powers didn't work on dead things.

I dropped my connection.

The opossum fell to the grass as dead as a doorknob.

Isabelle whirled on me in shock and anger. "Who are you?"

"Why are you here?" Wow. I was impressed with myself. I actually sounded authoritative.

"I came to talk, but when you looked like you needed help…" She left the thought unfinished.

"Killing people isn't helping. And Max was being held ransom in his own body. You almost killed one of the good guys." I realized she had no idea what I was talking about, but I didn't care. I was tired of people like her and Elisha and my grandparents who just killed because it was an easy out. It disgusted me.

"Fair enough." Isabelle didn't even seem mad at the rabid attack from the dead opossum. She was way more interested in me and my abilities.

Just then George, Ryan, Bill and Nancy came running out. George was holding a stun gun, which I assumed was meant for the machine-gun toting thugs. I felt a huge moment of relief that they hadn't had time to charge out like the cavalry when the men with guns had actually been here. But I knew they couldn't help themselves either.

It was hard not to chuckle at the absence of Jason and Jill. I appreciated their need to self-preserve. And I definitely didn't hold it against them.

When I turned back to Isabelle to introduce her to the others, she was gone.

Typical.

"I'm all right, guys. That girl Isabelle made them leave," I informed them.

Ryan ran over to me and held me. I fell into him.

George looked over at the opossum. "Your work?" he asked with a wave over his nose.

The little critter was kind of ripe.

"I'll take care of it." I connected to the opossum's swirling hole and made him run back into the trees, dig a hole, and bury himself in it. I should start a business. No one would ever have to bury their own pet ever again.

Ugh.

"Come on inside." George motioned Ryan and I toward the house.

We all went back in.

This time I didn't feel safe.

I knew at any minute Elisha could return, or Isabelle.

We needed protection.

And there was only one person I could ask.

Turner.

My stomach turned at the thought.

Never in a trillion years did I imagine a world where I'd rely this heavily on the monster that nearly destroyed my life. I wanted nothing to do with him. But I couldn't use dead people to guard us, Elisha could just take them over and use them against us. I had to assume that she was better at using our abilities than I was. She wouldn't use Max as a shield anymore, though. She'd be coming herself next time.

I tried to imagine what Elisha looked like as an adult. Pretty stunning, I'd guess. Elisha and her purple eyes! Seriously! Purple. She was a gorgeous child, why wouldn't she be a gorgeous woman? Although… maybe she was awkward looking and that was why she used Eva and Max to do her dirty work. Yeah, right. She used them like she used everyone else. Elisha never wanted to get her hands dirty. And why should she when she could make others do it for her?

Jill came running up to me. "Is that freak still in my head? Can you get him out?"

"It was Elisha, not Max that took over your brain. He wanted me to tell you he was sorry." Seeing Max struggle to gain control over his own body made me feel for the guy. Elisha had tried similar tactics on me, though more subtle. She'd planted herself in my mind and made me make stupid decisions. Mainly decisions that involved helping her. Just a nudge here and there, but by the time Roberta taught me how to block out Elisha, I had felt like a total idiot. I vowed never to let anyone in my head again without my permission.

Jill seemed slightly placated by this information, but she still looked upset. "Well…" she paused as if not quite sure what her next sentence would be, then she surprised us all when she said, "Is Max okay?"

Jill really cared about Max.

And it was obvious that Max really cared about Jill.

I'd be happy for them both, if my life was NORMAL!

"Chelsan, Elisha won't kill him, will she?"

"I honestly don't know, Jill." And I didn't. If Elisha felt that Max was no longer useful to her, then yes, she'd kill him in a heartbeat. She had killed her father and sister without blinking an eye. I just hoped that she needed Max for her plans. Whether he went through with the plans or not was an entirely different subject.

One step at a time.

"We should help him, like you helped me," Jill said in such a vulnerable voice I nearly choked.

Even Nancy looked moved. She walked over to Jill and placed her hand on her shoulder, "We will."

The events of the last twenty minutes were apparently too much for Jill. She folded into Nancy and hugged her for dear life. We could all hear her quiet sobs.

I wasn't sure how to react. With Jill it was hard to say.

I'm nice, she's mad at me; I'm nonchalant, she's mad at me.

Either way, the girl always seemed to be mad at me.

I knew that wasn't fair.

So I tried the nice tactic, "I'll make sure we're all safe. I promise." I didn't say how I was going to do that since I knew that Jill would have a fit if she found out I planned on using Gramps. Jill still wanted to kill

Turner. Gramps was responsible for murdering Jill's parents and keeping her dad his puppet for years. Why did I want his help again?

Jill pulled away from Nancy and wiped her eyes. With each wipe, Jill's face became more and more closed off. "Good. You owe us."

Yup.

Good old Jill.

But I completely agreed. I did owe all of them. And then some.

"Let's have dinner," Vianne announced to break up any tension.

That sounded amazing. Getting lost in one of Vianne's tasty meals was the perfect idea. I could already smell the sizzling of some kind of meat, and it made my mouth water. It turned out to be burgers when we all sat down at the dining table in the kitchen. Yum.

Considering everything that had happened today, everyone seemed fairly relaxed. Nancy managed to steer the conversation back to prom and even Jill had a few suggestions, forgetting that earlier she had berated Nancy for even bringing up the dance. After everything was consumed we all helped Vianne with the dishes, then Jill, Bill and Jason said their goodnights, promised their undying devotion (well, Bill did at least) and left.

It was still early evening. George, Vianne, Nancy, Ryan and I plopped in front of the holo-TV and decided to fry our brains on some new drama series that everyone was talking about.

"I'm going to get into my jam jams," I announced, thinking how utterly comfy I wanted to be in that moment.

I hurried off the couch and headed toward my room with a slight skip to my step.

Even though Eva's statement today on the news might be calling unwanted attention to me, I was feeling a little more positive about things to come. Call me crazy. Okay, yes, I was completely insane. But denial is a great place to be sometimes, especially when it was my life.

I walked into my room and pulled down a sweater from the closet.

"We didn't get to finish our conversation."

I turned around to see Isabelle stepping out from behind the door. She closed it gently.

I couldn't decide if I should scream for help or not. I figured it wouldn't do much good since she could squeeze my heart into oblivion before I could even try.

Why hadn't I thought she'd do this?

Oh yeah, denial-land. I should really stop visiting there so often.

But honestly, she didn't look angry or upset. She didn't even look assassiny like she usually did. Isabelle just looked curious.

"Did Turner make you too?" she asked.

Make me? Turner? Yikes. What did he do to this girl?

"Um, no." Good one. Always the intelligent speaker. "I mean, what do you mean by *make*?"

Isabelle sat down on the rocking chair near the window. She looked casual, but I could tell in about two seconds she could fly out that window if need be. This girl knew her exits.

I decided to play along and sat across from her on my bed.

"You don't seem power hungry," Isabelle observed.

"Thanks?" She was trying to make connections between Turner and I.

Isabelle crossed her arms, eyeing my every move.

"How old are you?" I asked. I wanted to know exactly how long she knew Gramps.

"Three-hundred and six."

Gulp.

If I did my math correctly (which was always iffy) Isabelle would have been six when Age-pro was invented and Turner fifty.

Isabelle continued, "Turner experimented on my mother when she was pregnant with me, hence, my powers."

"Why are you telling me this?" I mean I was glad she was, but having a confession-fest didn't exactly seem like her cup of tea.

"I'm not telling you anything you couldn't find out on your own. I just need to gauge my enemy before I go into battle," Isabelle said it so intensely that I clutched my heart instinctively.

"I'm not your enemy," I sputtered out.

"You're Turner's granddaughter and he's given you some kind of power. I'd say we're enemies." Then she kind of smiled. There was no warmth in it, just calculation.

I switched into dust mode. A million swirling black holes up the nose and into the lungs was becoming a good line of defense. The only problem was that it made it hard to see clearly through the ever-shifting black fog. Better safe than sorry though. The last thing I needed was heart-stop girl to, well... stop my heart!

"Listen." I was actually beginning to get annoyed with Isabelle. "You can sit in that rocking chair and make all the threats you like, but it still doesn't change the fact that I don't know who you are or what you want from me."

Isabelle's nostrils flared and oh crap...

My heart squeezed.

Ouch.

It freakin' hurt.

Okay dust, do your thing.

I connected to the millions and millions of dead flakey skin and slammed it up her nose and into her lungs.

My heart instantly went back to beating strong and normal as Isabelle gasped for air and fell to her knees choking uncontrollably.

Is it bad that I kind of enjoyed watching her sputter and cough? She was so darn cocky and she abused her power, using it to kill people. KILL people. What did I do? Make them choke? Okay, it was still an abuse of power, but my heart was still recovering, so sue me.

I pulled out the dust from Isabelle, but kept it ready if she decided to attack me again.

It took a few moments for Isabelle to gain her bearings. Then she looked up at me with shock and... what was that? Admiration. Isabelle was seriously impressed by my powers. She put her hands up in supplication.

"Truce?" she grinned.

Why was she grinning? It was creepy and annoying. I almost slammed the dust down her throat to teach her a lesson. But of course, I didn't.

"I never planned on hurting you," I accused. I was more angry than I thought.

"I didn't think you could anyway, so we're even," Isabelle shrugged and stood up.

Even? See? Arrogant jerk!

"What do you want?" I crossed my arms in anger. "You know what?

I don't give a crap what you want! I'm so sick of you and Turner and Elisha. You're all alike. You guys think you're so different, but you're just as bad as he is, look in a freakin' mirror!" I was really raging now.

"I'm nothing like him," Isabelle said, angry herself.

"You're *exactly* like him," I countered defiantly. I was really letting my anger run wild in the last couple of days. I was tired of being the "calm one," the "sensible one," the "mature one." I wanted to be the "honest-angry-annoyed-one" in that moment.

Isabelle looked like she was going to use her powers on me, but then thought better of it. She sighed with exasperation. "If you hate Turner so much, why do you work for him?"

"It's complicated. Five months ago I would have laughed at you for even suggesting that I'd speak to the guy, but my grandparents saved the lives of my friends who are my family, and that's not something I can just walk away from. But I want to. I want to walk away from them and never look back. They killed my mother. She was the most important person in the world to me. I loved her more than myself. I'll never forgive them for that. But I need them to keep my family safe. And I'm willing to suck up and do anything to make sure that they are. *Anything*." I realized I had just rambled to someone who probably didn't give a flying rip what I said, but once I started I couldn't seem to stop myself.

"Safe from whom? Turner is the only threat to this world." Isabelle looked genuinely at a loss. I think she believed that Turner was responsible for all of Elisha's mayhem. Don't get me wrong: Turner was responsible for a lot of mayhem, but he didn't deserve the credit for psycho-girl's crimes.

I took a deep breath and decided to tell Isabelle everything that had happened to me since my mother's death. She sat there patiently and attentively. I could tell she was taking in every word I said with extreme interest. And there it was again… admiration. This crazy assassin girl actually admired me.

Isabelle sat on the rocking chair, staring at me as if trying to figure out what she was going to say next. After a moment she said, "We can protect you. You don't need Turner."

We?

"We?" I decided to just ask it.

"I can't tell you everything, but I worked with Turner for over a hundred years. He was like a father to me, but he betrayed us," Isabelle paused.

"Us?" I asked, wondering if this was the guy Turner had been referring to when he and Isabelle had their earlier confrontation.

Isabelle continued, "Me and his best friend, another General like Turner, Harry Clifton. We faked our deaths to escape. Until today we believed Turner thought we were dead. I'm still furious with myself that I gave him proof of life. He'll try and bring us back into the fold, or kill us. Turner's always been that way. Black or white."

General? I had no idea Gramps was in the military. To be honest I never bothered to find out as much about him as I should have. Jason must have known that about that part of Turner's past, but apparently he didn't think it was important enough to tell me. I made a mental note to find out as much as I could about Gramps, this Harry guy and Isabelle.

"He's gotten softer," I suddenly accused Gramps. But it was true. When he killed my mother, it was black and white for him. He thought she was responsible for his only son's death, so he killed her and tried to kill me as well. Simple for him. When I was being stubborn and just wouldn't die, instead of reevaluating and possibly trying to… I don't know… STOP… instead he was relentless. It wasn't until I was attacking Roberta with a hive of dead bees (trust me, she deserved it) that he begged for me to stop. When I did, it began a weird kind of truce. Roberta was a little reluctant to come on board the not-kill-Chelsan-train, but once she did, she completely 180-degree flipped about how she felt about me. Even though she was a psychopath I genuinely believed Roberta loved me in her own warped way. I was her last link to her son, my father, Franklin.

"Softer? Somehow I doubt that." Isabelle wasn't hearing it. She stood up and headed for the window. "I'm leaving, but think about what I offered. Harry and I can protect you. I've been alive a long time and I can see you're exactly who you say you are. I know why Turner and Roberta want to protect you, and it's not just because you're their granddaughter. There's something very special about you, Chelsan Derée, and when you've been around as long as we have… Well, let's just say it's been a long time since I've met anyone as honest as you."

Isabelle was halfway through the window when she popped her head back in the room. "Be careful of that Max character. I know you said Elisha hijacked his body, but he's been standing outside your house watching you every night. You trust too easily." Then was gone.

I wasn't sure which part of that last statement I should be more freaked out about: the fact that Max was stalking my house, or the fact that Isabelle knew about it, or the casual way she mentioned Elisha's name, like she knew about Elisha before hearing my story. It meant that Isabelle was interested and watching me way before today.

Or she'd been watching Max…

I knew I'd have to take everything Isabelle said with a grain of salt. Once I put the team (and by team I meant Jason) on the task of researching these new players, I felt that I'd have a better understanding of who Isabelle was.

The rest of the evening was uneventful aside from the initial craze when I told them I'd just had a heart to heart with a three hundred year old assassin. We all agreed not to do anything until the next morning when we could assemble the whole gang. Ryan decided to stay the night and George and Vianne had no arguments. They seemed to sense that I needed someone near me. And let's face it; if it hadn't been Ryan, Nancy and I would have been having a slumber party because I did *not* want to be alone.

My bed never felt so fluffy and inviting as it did that night. I barely remember feeling Ryan wrap his arm around me as my head hit the pillow and I fell fast asleep.

CHAPTER 3
WEDNESDAY APRIL 6, 2321

"I knew you'd let me come," Roberta's voice sounded in the darkness.

She materialized in front of me and I had to admit I was relieved. All I could think about was Ryan and making sure he could get the help he needed. I knew Turner and Roberta were okay with me when they sent the hover-limo, but I wasn't sure until this moment, when I saw Roberta's face, that all was forgiven. She looked at me with relief and affection. It didn't repulse me like it normally did.

"Ryan still needs help," I responded.

I was getting good at this whole dream-astral-thingy. Since we were on my turf, I decided to make it creative and put us on top of a mountain. We stood in a small cove surrounded by gargantuan snow-covered peaks towering over us like guardians. The sky was a deep blue and I made a couple white fluffy clouds float lazily by. The best part about the whole thing was the fact that, since this was all just inside my head, there wasn't any temperature gauge, so to enjoy being up in the mountains while really being snuggled up in bed made it all the more perfect.

"Geoffrey and Dr. Johnson are still going to be waiting for Ryan tomorrow. Your little tirade didn't stop that."

I visibly sighed in relief. Thank goodness. Just knowing Ryan was going to be okay made me want to wake up and tell him the good news, but I knew Ryan wouldn't see it that way because he'd rather not go at all. I decided I'd fish some information out of Roberta instead.

"Isabelle visited me this evening and says she wants to protect me. She doesn't like you two very much." That was an understatement, but I kind of figured Roberta knew more about Isabelle's hatred of them than I did.

"Do you know what her powers are?" Roberta asked me, eyeing me for my reaction.

"She can stop hearts?" I thought I was stating the obvious.

"That's like saying you can control corpses." Roberta shook her head.

"But I *can* control corpses." I didn't understand what she was trying to say.

"Yes, it's one component of your abilities," Roberta continued. "If Isabelle knew the extent of what she could do, this world would be in big trouble. Much more of a threat than Elisha."

Um.

Huh?

"What can she do?" I asked, not at all expecting to hear an answer.

"As much as it would fill my heart to trust you, you know I can't." See?! Though Roberta actually looked like it upset her to say that. It probably did, but it was annoying. She was such a tease. "Isabelle came to see you, which means she'll be back for an answer. She'll want to know if you want her protection or not… What are you going to tell her?"

"Um… no?"

Why was I being so wishy-washy? I didn't want to give anyone a straight answer. Maybe because I didn't have one. I didn't want anyone's protection, but now that Elisha had herself and two other people all with my exact same powers, it made me feel neutralized. Sure, I could best Eva, but maybe she had tricked me into thinking that. Actually, no, Eva's ego was too big for that. She probably would have made the dead branches fly around for the press while acting terrified and pointing her finger at me. Most likely it pissed her off that I disconnected their black holes so that they dropped to the ground.

"You don't like needing protection. You're like me," Roberta preened.

Ick. (Although it was nicer to see her preen as a twenty-year-old as opposed to a Feline. But still.)

Eew.

"Yeah, well, you better go. I guess I'll see you tomorrow when I drop off Ryan." I wanted to end this transmission. It was grossing me out. My Roberta threshold had been reached.

"Wait." Roberta reached out and touched my arm.

I felt a tingling sensation even thought I was asleep. Roberta was bringing me into her realm.

"Don't," I hissed. No really. I hissed. I shocked myself. But it upset me that she was trying to rip me out of my own world of protection and drag me into hers.

"I have to show you something, and I can't show you here," Roberta informed me.

As far as I could tell she was being sincere, but still…

"Can't you just tell me?" The tingling was lessening. Roberta was listening to me for once.

"It's important. In fact, it's the key to everything." I felt the hairs on my dream-neck prickle. "Elisha knows about them."

"Them?" I whispered. I was suddenly extremely afraid and I didn't know why.

"You're going to be upset, but believe me, we did it to protect him." Roberta was trying to convince me of her innocence, which was never a good sign.

"Who's him? Who's them?" I almost shoved her out of my head. I couldn't explain it, but I was terrified.

"Just let me show you," Roberta pleaded.

I swallowed hard and nodded.

I don't know why I agreed, but I did.

Roberta took a deep breath and clasped my hand.

The tingling sensation turned into an all out vibration until…

…We were standing in a room, just like in my dream with Roberta a couple of nights ago.

There were coffin-like boxes everywhere, but all were child size.

Clones.

When I peered inside the closest one to me, my heart nearly stopped.

A young boy about seven years of age lay sleeping inside the stasis-container.

If I could have thrown up in my dream I would have.

I recognized the boy from Roberta's memories.

It was my father.

There were hundreds of stasis-containers all holding clones of Franklin Turner.

"They all have your power," Roberta's voice was barely a whisper. "They're soulless. They feel nothing. They only take orders."

I stood in shock until Roberta said the last four words that drove a stake through my heart in terror.

"Elisha's coming for them."

***

I jumped awake and gasped for breath. It took me a few moments to stop my heart from racing when I realized something was off.

Why weren't Ryan's arms wrapped around me like they normally were when I awoke from one of my astral nightmares? He must really be tired. Normally, Ryan was such a light sleeper.

Then I heard the choking.

I turned to see Ryan.

He was lying on his back, jaw clenched, arms clenched, legs clenched and jerking violently at the same time.

"Ryan!" I yelled uselessly.

Ryan's eyes rolled back in his head and the sound of him choking was terrifying.

I didn't know what to do.

I was too scared to touch him for fear of making it worse.

So I screamed for help.

George, Vianne and Nancy were all in my room in seconds.

Nancy gasped when she saw Ryan while George and Vianne instantly went to his side.

George turned to me and said in a steadying voice, "He's having a seizure. You need to call Turner and have him send Dr. Johnson right away." Seeing the shocked state his daughter was in, he added, "Take Nancy with you. We'll take care of Ryan."

I didn't want to leave him.

He was going to die.

I was going to lose Ryan forever.

I could see the beginnings of his swirling black hole forming in his chest.

"He's dying," I sputtered.

Vianne stood up and made forced eye contact with me. "Not if you get him the help he needs."

She was right.

I needed to snap out of it and get Ryan help.

I grabbed Nancy's stiff hand and pulled her out of the room with me. Once we were in the hallway Nancy shook herself into alertness. "Where's your phone?" she asked.

Downstairs. We hurried to the phone and I dialed Turner.

Roberta answered Turner's phone, "Chelsan, I didn't mean to scare you, but you had to know."

What?

Then I realized she was referring to the room full of Dad clones in their basement.

"No, it's Ryan. He's having a seizure. He's dying," my voice cracked. I was about to fall into hysterics in less than five seconds.

"I'll send Dr. Johnson immediately," Roberta spoke with an authority that made me feel slightly better. "Ryan will be fine. I promise."

I didn't know why, but as I hung up the phone I believed her.

Nancy and I raced upstairs to see how Ryan was doing.

My heart surged in relief when I saw Ryan propped up on pillows while Vianne held a wet cloth to his forehead. I ran to the bed and crawled up next to him.

He smiled weakly and pulled me in close. "I'm sorry I scared you," his voice was hoarse from coughing.

I held him tighter. "Help is coming."

Ryan squirmed a bit. "I'll be okay."

I peered up at him. "Don't even think about arguing."

"It looked worse than it was…" Ryan began.

I cut him off, "Your black hole was starting to form. You were dying." There were tears in my eyes and it took every ounce of control I had in me not to bawl like a baby.

Ryan said nothing. For the first time, he looked scared. I felt horrible, but I didn't want him to brush the doctor off again. Ryan needed help and he was going to get it whether he liked it or not!

And before I knew it, Ryan was being led away by Dr. Johnson.

"I'll take him from here," Dr. Johnson said in an irked sort of way. He was apparently still mad about not being able to take Ryan with him yesterday. I didn't blame him. Ryan probably wouldn't have had the seizure if he had gone with the doc.

Ryan shrugged Dr. Johnson off and leaned down to kiss me.

Toes officially curled.

"I love you," he whispered in my ear.

"I love you too," I whispered back, reining in my tears.

Ryan kissed me once again for good measure, then left with Dr. Johnson out the front door and off to the main I.Q. Farm at Population Control. I imagined it was pretty deserted since all the former members of the I.Q. Farm were currently residing in Ryan's head. Still, it was a freaky place to be. I just hoped the doc would be able to fix Ryan.

We all just kind of stood in the foyer staring at the closed door. In less than an hour Ryan had almost died…

And now he was in Turner's clutches.

It made me feel nauseous. I didn't know what I'd do if Ryan died.

I couldn't think about it.

Not even for a second.

Nancy put her arm around me. "He'll be fine. Let's just try and get some sleep. Maybe we can visit him in the morning," she suggested optimistically.

I nodded. Everyone was exhausted and I didn't want to keep them up any longer.

"Can I stay in your room?" I asked Nancy. I couldn't be by myself. I just couldn't.

"Duh." Nancy nudged me affectionately.

George and Vianne gave their well-wishes and said goodnight.

I crawled into Nancy's gigantic double-king bed. After a few minutes of talking, Nancy fell asleep in mid-sentence. I stayed up for at least an hour longer, maybe even two. I couldn't stop seeing Ryan convulsing, playing the memory over and over in my mind. I thought I would go insane.

Then I remembered.

The room full of clones.

How many clones of my dad were in there? And if they all had my powers and Elisha was after them, she'd have an army of generals that could control the dead.

Elisha would be unstoppable.

I was grateful that the clones were all children. It would have been more difficult for me if his clones were older. I might have had considered keeping one, as crazy as that sounded, I knew, of course (or at least according to Roberta), that they were soulless empty shells. But they had to possess some traits that were like my dad. I never had the chance to know him, or even meet him. He died to bring me back to life. It would be nice just to talk to him.

Another truth hit me in that moment.

Roberta and Turner never experimented on the real Franklin. That was the one thing Roberta couldn't tell me because if she had she'd have to admit to the room full of Franklins. They did all their testing on the clones. That was why when I first met Turner he was always shocked at what I could do with my powers. It meant that as a result of the clones being wrong in the brain, they may not have the full extent of my dad's powers.

My brain spun a mile a minute, so I figured I should at least try and get some sleep. I closed my eyes and tried to relax.

Nope.

No good.

After a while I must have caved, because I remember dreaming about Ryan being hooked up to the I.Q. Farm machine and him screaming.

***

"Is he going to be okay?" I heard Jason's voice a few feet away.

I awoke to see Jason and Nancy talking in her doorway. She was still in her pajamas and trying to shoo Jason away.

"We don't know yet, but you're going to wake up Chelsan. We'll talk downstairs," Nancy scolded.

"Don't bother. I'm awake," I announced.

"Oh good." Jason maneuvered past Nancy and sat at the foot of the bed. "We need to talk."

"So talk," I encouraged. Jason was simply salivating to spill his guts.

"I did some digging and I found out a couple of very interesting facts about your grandfather and Harry Clifton." Jason scooted in to make himself more comfortable. "First off, Geoffrey Turner was born in 1970 in Austin, Texas. He joined the Navy when he graduated high school in 1988 and became a Navy Seal. A Seal? Can you believe that?" Jason was obviously impressed.

I had no idea what a Seal was besides a really adorable sea mammal.

Before I had to ask, Nancy chimed in, "We have no idea what a Seal is, dork boy."

Jason groaned at our ignorance. "They were the elite of the elite. Before the military became what it is today, basically a glorified exercise camp, they were every country's defense and offense. And the Seals were sent in for all the impossible missions. Trust me, you did not want to mess with a Seal."

Gramps was a badass? It was hard to picture with him being so old. I couldn't imagine him as a young, agile, gun-toting soldier.

Jason continued, "Turner served in a war in the early 1990s called the Gulf War. His team performed re-con and assassination missions in Kuwait and Iraq." Jason shook his head in admiration, "The guy was ambitious and apparently the best on his team because he made Lt. Commander in only a few years."

I didn't know rankings for the military since there wasn't really a military left to speak of nowadays. Like Jason said, army bases these days were basically places where people went to get in shape, but I knew from history class that soldiers used to be more like Isabelle. Stealthy, unafraid and driven. But I always thought of Gramps as a politician. It scared me to think of how capable he actually was of doing the killing himself and not through his lackeys.

Jason folded his arms, "Turner met Harry Clifton in the Gulf and according to everything I read: they became inseparable. So inseparable, in fact, that it was actually Clifton that introduced Roberta to Turner in 1994. Roberta and Clifton grew up together in Chillicothe, Ohio. So this trio goes back about as far as you can get. Your grandparents were both in their mid-twenties when they met. They married a week after being introduced. As disgusted as you are with your grandparents, they definitely belong with each other."

Normally a story like that would garner a few "aawwws," but Jason was talking about Turner and Roberta so I had to settle with a little throw-up in my mouth.

Jason switched topics upon seeing the nausea in my face, "Turner and Clifton were sanctioned by the U.S. government to create an elite team. A team that ended up being so good that the government propositioned them to be the President's secret right arm. They agreed and were paid extremely well. That's the team that Isabelle was part of. We can't find much on her, just what she told you already, that she was a foster kid and Turner brought her in and trained her. There were others. I'll dig some more, but nothing stood out to me as a red flag. At some point, Turner obviously wanted something more than just being a military force because according to the records, Clifton and the rest of team died in an oil fire in the Middle East. After that Turner became V.P. of Population Control. A title he created and all the world leaders signed off on."

"That must be the fire they faked to convince Turner of their deaths," I surmised.

Jason nodded in agreement. "That's all I got, but it's definitely more than we ever knew about your Gramps."

"I don't know if it'll help, but it gives us some background at least," I said.

Jason rubbed his hands together, concluding his part of the conversation. "Can we see Ryan now?"

It was nice to see Jason so concerned. Jason was obviously worried about Ryan and that made me grateful for some reason. I reached across the bed and hugged him, which surprised Jason, but he hugged me back.

"I'll call Turner and find out, in the mean time, I have something to tell you guys." I told them about the cloned Franklins.

Jason was visibly rocked. "That's bad."

"Understatement." Nancy shook her head.

"I know." I fell back into the soft pillows. "We can't let Elisha take them. She's already broken out I.Q. kids and a bagillion pregnant ladies from Baby Centers. Elisha is really good at helping people escape," I groaned. It was true. She had bombed the L.A. Baby Center and helped thousands of women escape to Havenville. And that was high security. Then she actually broke into Turner's headquarters and busted out all the I.Q. kids. Even higher security. There was nothing she couldn't do. And now that she had my abilities…

I shuddered.

I seriously considered trying to tap into Elisha's brain, but I figured that was exactly what she wanted. She'd probably have some sort of trap waiting for me. And my one ally, Roberta, who could truly stand against Elisha with super-mojo-powers, was dead! Making her vulnerable against Elisha. The fact that Elisha could control Roberta like a puppet was infuriating. It meant I couldn't rely on Roberta's help as much as I'd like. (And admitting that was difficult to swallow!)

"Now that we know we're looking for a girl of eighteen not seven, I think I spotted her on some news footage. I brought it over. You want to come see?" Jason dangled the holo-chip containing the footage in front of me like a carrot to a rabbit.

"Uh, yeah." I punched him playfully in the shoulder. "Let's go downstairs."

We all headed downstairs and were quickly joined by Bill and Jill, who had arrived together. I didn't want to pry, so I kept quiet.

Nancy and Jason had obviously filled them in on Ryan since the two of them looked at me like I was a fragile egg teetering on a ledge. I decided not to acknowledge their stares. Though their hearts were in the right place, it just made me worry more about Ryan. I didn't trust Turner. And to give Ryan over to him made me sick, even if it was for the best.

Everyone sat on the couch. George and Vianne walked in from the kitchen. I was surprised that Vianne didn't have a giant breakfast waiting for everyone as usual, but Ryan's seizure had obviously taken its toll on her psyche. She held a basket full of power bars and placed them on the coffee table for anyone that wanted one. I wasn't hungry. In fact, the thought of food made me even more sick. I just wanted to focus my attention on taking down Elisha so I wouldn't be allowed to be alone in my head anymore. It was dangerous in there and making me insane.

Jason plugged the hole-chip into the TV, and news footage reenacted itself in front of our faces as if we were there.

Jason walked directly into the life-sized holo-images and began pointing out what he wanted us to see.

The footage was on an army base, showing the boring opening ceremony of a new gym. Aside from joining the military to get in better shape, a huge part of the poorer population joined mainly for the early use of Age-pro. The government had made a deal with the military recruiters: if someone joined for five years, then that person would be eligible to take Age-pro early, fully funded by the government. Normally, the lower class wasn't eligible for Age-pro until they were thirty when National Health Care kicked in, so being able to take it by the age of twenty-three was a big deal. Thinking about how the military now was such a different organization than when Turner joined was surreal to me. It was so much more a fitness thing than a fighting thing nowadays. Sad but true. So opening a new high-tech gym that the world had never seen before, I'm sure was fascinating to health nuts, but for the lazy like me, it was a snoozefest.

Jason pointed to a young woman off to the side of the ribbon-cutting ceremony. "There she is."

And there she was.

Elisha.

She looked my age. And, like I had already guessed, Elisha was annoyingly gorgeous. Long wavy black hair, large violet eyes, perfectly sculpted face with prominent cheekbones and she even had Barbie-like curves. Hated her.

Elisha was beyond stunning. But she somehow managed to hide in the background and not bring any attention to herself.

"What is she doing at an army base gym opening?" I asked aloud. Somehow drooling over all the really buff guys didn't seem to me like it was Elisha's cup of tea.

Jason started to fast-forward through the holo-images. "Not once, but twice."

The next piece of footage was at a Naval base. It was another press conference, only about a week back, when they announced that the military was lowering the amount of service time for Age-pro recruits, cutting it down to three years instead of five. After that announcement there was a major upsurge in volunteers…

Oh crap.

"You don't think?.." I left the sentence hanging, but I could see that Jason definitely *did* think what I was thinking.

"That Elisha was somehow responsible for the age cut and that she counted on the record number of recruits? Yes." Jason paused the holo. "But how is she going to recruit them to her army?"

"Kill them?" Jill guessed.

"But Turner could control them or I could. It has to be something more," I sighed heavily.

"It can't be a coincidence that she was at two military events. She must have been sussing something out," Bill volunteered as he took a bite out of a power bar.

Suddenly the paused holo-images started to blur and made a kind of buzzing noise.

George took the remote from Jason, "Must be something wrong with the holo-player."

The buzzing sound grew louder until it was almost deafening!

"Turn it off!" Vianne yelled over the noise to George.

"I'm trying!" George shouted back, frantically trying to turn off the holo-TV.

The holo-people started to shake violently and lose their shapes altogether.

Then I saw him.

Ryan.

The holo-images shifted into his face.

His eyes were wide with terror.

The buzzing turned into Ryan's voice, robotic and loud. "Chelsan? Are you there?"

"YES!" I screamed.

Everyone including myself was standing at this point, terrified and worried at seeing Ryan's larger-than-life face staring at us in the living room.

Ryan didn't seem to hear me because he repeated, "Chelsan! Are you there?"

"I'M HERE!" I yelled as loudly as I could.

Ryan's eyes shifted in horror, looking around like a rat caught in a trap. "Get me out of here! Chelsan!"

SNAP.

All the power in the house went out.

We all stood staring at the spot where Ryan's face had just pleaded for my help.

I was frozen in shock.

Ryan.

It took all of two seconds for me to snap out of it. I picked up my phone and dialed Turner. Everyone else was silent. I could feel their eyes on me, not sure of what to say or do themselves.

George was the first to try and bring the room back to some kind of sanity.

George mumbled, "I'll go flip the breakers." Then he walked off toward the back of the house.

The phone rang and rang until Turner's voicemail picked up. "What did you do to Ryan?! I'm coming there right now!" I hung up and threw my phone across the room. I heard it smash against the wall, but I didn't care. I was so enraged I couldn't see straight. Why on earth did I think I could trust my grandparents with the most important person in my life? I was so desperate to get Ryan help, I didn't even want to consider the possibility that Gramps would betray me. Again.

"I'm driving," Bill volunteered.

Jason stepped in, "I'm coming too."

Jason was just as spooked as I was.

That look in Ryan's eyes…

"Let's go," I said, walking toward the door.

Vianne called out, "I'll call the school and tell them you're all staying home today."

I appreciated Vianne's concern for our school attendance, but it was the very last thing on my mind. I didn't want to be rude to her, though. She was just trying to be helpful in a helpless situation.

Before I knew it Bill was driving me, Jason, Jill and Nancy to Turner's headquarters. I was a Chelsan sandwich in the back seat with Jason and Jill as the bread. Somehow Nancy always managed to call out shotgun before the rest of us. Since headquarters (a.k.a. Population Control Center and Research) was open to the public, I knew we wouldn't have a problem getting in. It was getting to see Ryan that I wasn't sure about. If Turner was experimenting on him, I somehow doubted he would let me take Ryan away.

I needed to reach Roberta. Work on her a bit.

I closed my eyes and concentrated on Roberta.

I felt myself floating above my body and then I followed the strong white thread of light that I knew to be Roberta's tie to me. I could see the barriers Roberta put up against unwanted intruders like myself. It was strange. It looked like a bubble around her brain. I figured this is what it must look like when Elisha and Roberta tried to jump inside my head.

I thought about how Max would tap on my bubble and I tried to do the same on Roberta's.

A pin-sized opening formed on the surface of her protective barrier. I assumed this was an invitation to enter, so I zoomed inside. This was way more difficult to do when I was awake! When I was sleeping I'd just summon Roberta to my head and she'd appear. I suddenly knew how much work she really had to do in order to master astral projection. Seriously impressive.

Roberta's new, younger self materialized in front of me. We were in the oak forest where she'd helped me when I was buried alive by Elisha. It made me instantly calm. "We're coming to get Ryan," I told her.

Roberta actually looked surprised. I couldn't tell if she was acting or if Turner hadn't told her about what he planned for Ryan.

"He still needs Dr. Johnson's help," Roberta replied.

"Ryan was screaming for help through the holo! He's being tortured! I never should have trusted you two!" I screamed at her. I couldn't help it. I was so angry at them! But truth be told, I was more angry at myself than anything else.

Roberta placed her hands up to stop me from yelling. "Dr. Johnson is taking good care of Ryan. I promise you…"

I interrupted her in fury, "He isn't! I'm telling you, I just saw Ryan trapped in the holo! Get him out of that machine!"

Roberta nodded. "I'll go right now."

"Good. I'm on my way there already," I said, then jumped out of her head before she could tell me any more lies.

Roberta was way too good at lying. I couldn't tell the difference and that was really frustrating. It was better just to let her know we were coming and that they'd better have Ryan waiting to go.

"Are you okay? You went all slumpy," Jill's voice brought me back to reality.

"Yeah, I'm fine," I smiled at her reassuringly. Then I announced to the car, "Roberta's playing dumb, but she'll let us in," I said even though Roberta had made no such promise. I wasn't about to take "no" for an answer from my grandparents.

"We're coming up on the building," Bill announced.

The deep red maple forest that surrounded the white spectacle that was Population Control Center and Research was breathtaking. The enormousness of Turner's main base of operation still amazed me. I knew there was so much that went on in that building that I had no clue about. And probably didn't want to. A room full of Franklin clones for one. How many other people had my grandparents cloned? Themselves, obviously. My dad. I suddenly wondered with terror.

Me?

I didn't want to think about it.

We landed in the public parking lot. Instantly twenty guards surrounded our car.

Uh oh.

"I thought you said they were cool with us coming," Jill kind of gulped.

"I'll take care of it," I said with more confidence than I felt.

We stepped out of the car to find Turner himself waiting for me.

Instead of anger or irritation at my presence he actually looked…

Frazzled…?

Not a normal look for him. Not much could faze the rock that was my Gramps. He was pretty much an emotionless lump. Except for the emotions of rage and irritation. Those he had in spades.

"Ryan's not here," he announced before I could get a word out.

"Bull!" I countered. No more lies.

"I know you'd like to believe that I'm an evil mastermind, but I'm telling you the truth. When Roberta went to check on him, he was gone. Roberta's looking at the surveillance holos as we speak. Come with me." Gramps didn't even wait for my retort. He turned and walked toward the side entrance to the facility.

I glanced at the others and we all followed suit.

Ryan gone?

I wasn't sure if I could believe Turner or not, but for some reason in that moment I did.

If Turner didn't have him, who did?

No.

No.

Please No.

I said what I feared most out loud, "Turner? Do you think Elisha has Ryan?"

Gramps barely glanced back at me, but I could see from his eyes.

Yes. That was exactly who he thought had him.

Oh crap.

"What does she want with him, do you think?" I tried to keep it together.

"I don't know. Ryan has a once-in-a-lifetime mind. If Elisha found a way to harness that…" Turner left the thought unfinished.

Jason chimed in, "What about Dr. Johnson? Did he see anything?"

Turner didn't bother to look at Jason, apparently I was the only one he'd stoop to acknowledge, but he did answer, "He's dead."

Turner didn't elaborate, but the news stunned us all. Gramps didn't let anyone else have a chance to ask more questions. He moved ahead and let some of his men step in-between our party and him.

Jason walked directly beside me. "We'll get Ryan back," he said reassuringly.

I appreciated his attempt to calm my nerves, but it really didn't help much.

Nancy held on to my arm as we walked. She knew she didn't need to say anything, just having her there was enough to keep me sane. Bill, Jason and Jill trailed behind. Bill and Jason had already been inside the underbelly that was Population Control. But I could tell this was Jill's first time. Her dad had worked as Turner's second-hand-man for years so I figured she'd have been here for sure, but from the expression on Jill's face I could tell this was all new. Being here must be difficult for her. After all, most of her father's reign in Turner's court was as a pose-able corpse. Jill didn't know that, however, so she just thought she had a really horrible dad that never spoke to her. It was why she was so ornery (and that was putting it lightly!). If I'd thought my dad was ignoring me on purpose during my formative years, I'd be pretty angry and bitter as well. Not that I was making excuses for her, but over the last few months I'd learned to appreciate Jill's unique view on things, even if they leaned toward the mean.

Our journey into the belly of the beast would have been more fascinating if I wasn't totally freaking out at the moment. We walked through mazes of metal, to plaster, to marble, to glass: Headquarters was like a freak show of architecture. I stayed arm-in-arm with Nancy as we passed by every door imaginable, from intricate iron-wrought design to plain old hollow wood. I wondered why Turner had the place designed so randomly jumbly. Maybe it had something to do with how old he was. I could only imagine what it would be like to be over three hundred. I mean, for me everything was kind of the same and had been for the last two hundred years. But for people like my grandparents, and even Isabelle, they lived in a time when immortality was off the table, when there were things like paper and concrete that cars that drove on. It was an entirely different existence. So maybe this building was Turner's way of capturing all of his lifespan's history in one place. It wasn't exactly tacky, but it wasn't terribly Feng Shui either. It was just a cluster of every type of building material possible.

I decided it was becoming a weird kind of "nightmare" home, if that made sense. I'd had the most terrifying moments of my life here, but I couldn't help thinking that I had a room full of my dad here as well. I knew he was *wrong*, but it was still him to a certain degree. They were cloned from his DNA, so they were a part of me.

Stop.

I needed to focus.

Dad clones needed to be put on the back burner.

The mass that was Turner's entourage turned left, through a large oak door, and into the next room.

When we entered the room I stared in awe. It was gigantic, the size of a football stadium. The ceiling was domed and the surface was a moving depiction of the night sky. The Milky Way moving at a snail's pace (though miles faster than real life!) across the faux sky was a spectacular site. Despite the fact that by all appearances it was nighttime inside, the room itself was surprisingly bright and well lit. The floor was a swirling green marble that resembled the sea. If the room had been empty, I imagined myself pulling out a blanket and staring at the ceiling for hours on end, but it was full of holo-images all playing different footage at the moment. The images were like Nancy's house, fully life-size, so it felt like we were in a crowded room full of people doing various activities.

Even Jill made a small noise of appreciation though you'd never be able to tell from the expression on her face. She was scowling, as usual.

Jason was already watching the footage around us with a professional eye, trying to take in as much as he could, knowing the chance of us ever returning to this room was slim to none. Bill and Nancy were my guard dogs as usual. Each of them by my side, not even remotely distracted by the spectacle, just wanting to keep me safe. My besties.

Then through the packed crowd of holo-people came a solitary figure walking straight toward us.

Roberta.

Turner nodded for his men to leave and they immediately complied.

Roberta stopped next to Gramps and addressed the five of us. "You all need to see this."

Roberta swiped the air: a small holo-box materialized. She typed into the floating image and a new scene appeared in front of us.

My heart stopped.

It was Ryan.

They had just arrived, and Ryan was walking toward the entrance of the Population Control Center with the help of Dr. Johnson acting as his crutch. There were at least ten guards behind them, surveilling the area and keeping it safe.

Ha, ha.

Black figures dropped from the sides of the building, all on ropes, all silent.

Before Ryan or Dr. Johnson could react, all of their guards were shot and killed.

Ryan was too weak to fight, but he didn't stand a chance anyway. These were professionals and they meant to accomplish their goal.

Kidnap Ryan.

When Dr. Johnson tried to stop the men from taking Ryan, he was shot in the head.

They all died trying to save Ryan.

I was about to scream Elisha's name like a lunatic when Roberta zoomed in on the perpetrator taking hold of Ryan's arm.

Roberta made the face of the attacker gigantic, well over twenty feet high, mocking me, telling me I was a complete idiot.

Isabelle.

"Turn it off," I said in disgust at myself.

Roberta flipped off the holo-footage.

Turner was shaking his head, "What on earth would Harry want with Ryan? And how the hell did he know we were taking Ryan in?" He was obviously talking to Roberta. We were the forgotten four again.

Roberta responded with just as much frustration, "He must have had eyes on Chelsan's place. When your men arrived to pick Ryan up, Harry assumed he was important to us."

Harry Clifton. Isabelle's boss and Turner's ex-best friend.

"Isabelle knows that the I.Q. kids are in Ryan's head. I told her everything," I confessed. I figured full disclosure was probably my best bet on getting Ryan back.

"You what?!" Gramps whirled on me in rage.

"Geoffrey, calm down." Roberta touched his arm to soothe him.

Nancy and Bill immediately stood in front of me like pit bulls.

Turner rolled his eyes at them. "Even if I wanted to strangle that child, and believe me I do, she would have a hundred of my own men attacking me before I could lunge forward. Your little friend is entirely safe, you fools."

Nancy and Bill didn't back down. They didn't even flinch.

Jason and Jill on the other hand stood exactly two inches behind me. They seemed to be of the same opinion as Gramps. I didn't care if Bill and Nancy couldn't physically help me if I was in trouble, the fact that they'd still stand in the line of fire made my throat catch. I loved them so much in that moment I thought I'd burst. They didn't care one iota that I had just revealed all our trade secrets to the enemy. They loved my moronic self anyway.

"Isabelle made me think I could trust her enough to tell her." I tried to explain my behavior. Why had I told her everything? Because I thought if she really knew what had happened she'd leave me alone. It was selfish and it put Ryan in danger.

Turner sighed, "She's good at that."

Roberta stepped forward and I motioned for Nancy and Bill to relax. "There is a way we can find out where Ryan is located."

My body flushed with hope. "How?"

"It might be dangerous…" Roberta began.

"I'll do it," I interrupted. I didn't care what the cost, if it could help Ryan I was in.

"Chelsan." I was surprised to realize it was Jill who spoke the word of warning, "This could be a trap."

I wanted to throw something.

Yes, everything could be a trap! Everything! Everything! Everything!

I was so sick of being in a constant state of distrust I wanted to hit something. No wonder I'd spilled my guts to Isabelle, I was tired of living a life of fear and paranoia! When you've lived eighteen years with an amazing mother and a dead stepfather you control, life is pretty free of any trust issues. In the last five months my life had turned into one big freaking trap.

I just didn't give a crap anymore.

I turned to Jill and tried to smile as reassuringly as I could. "I have to do it."

Jill didn't argue. No one did.

I looked at Roberta with as much bravery as I could muster. "Lead the way."

Roberta simply nodded and walked past us out the large oak door. We all followed, with Turner behind us.

It was weird traversing the corridors once again. I couldn't keep my eyes off the back of Roberta's head and her thick black hair bouncing slightly every time she moved. It was young hair, not like the thin, weakened hair with a strand of white every so often in her old body. And her swirling black hole, spinning wildly in her chest reminding me with every twist that Roberta's soul was inhabiting a corpse. A walking, talking, breathing, corpse. She looked my age now. My age! My head couldn't seem to wrap around it.

No one said a word as we descended lower and lower into the underbelly of Population Control. I knew where we were headed: the deserted I.Q. Farm. It was where Ryan was supposed to be, hooked up to the strange brain machine that started this whole mess in the first place. If Ryan hadn't hooked into that machine, those I.Q. kids never would have been stuck in his brain when they died. On the other hand, without that machine, we would have all died at the hands of Elisha, so it was both a savior and a curse.

The machine.

That was it.

Roberta was going to hook me up to it to find Ryan.

I knew it with such certainty I didn't even feel the need to share my revelation.

Everyone would freak out soon enough.

One last flight of metal stairs and we entered what was left of the main I.Q. Farm. I'd never come in through the front door before. Normally, I was breaking in through air vents, so that in itself was surreal. But seeing the place deserted, with unused and unplugged machinery made it look like a ghost town of electronics. The sight was a relief in a sense, because it was difficult to see children strapped into machines looking all comatose and such (even though they weren't really children, just Age-pro'd adults). But still, I'd learned that the world was much safer with them in the Farm than out in society. The kids were brilliant, but they were all like Elisha.

Devoid of humanity.

It was Turner's way of using their brilliance without having to kill them off before they became serial killers. Most of the world's scientific advances were made in this I.Q. Farm through the machines hooked up to the genius psychos. A weird kind of trade-off.

Roberta moved to the middle of the room, where the largest machine rested. It was the crazy-wired mind-sucking machine that had terrified

Ryan when he was a kid. There were several hundred tubes draped from the ceiling and into a headpiece for the lucky participant that volunteered to be strapped in.

Namely, me.

"You are seriously not going to strap yourself in to that." Nancy looked at me incredulously.

I plopped down in the chair. "Nancy, I have to do this." Then I turned to Turner, "Hook me up."

Gramps and Grams began suction-cupping wires and tubes and every other nightmarish piece of machinery onto my head. I had only experienced being "in the machine" once before when Ryan brought me in through astral projection. It was kind of a rush, but I'd felt safe then because Ryan was guiding our way the entire time.

When there was one last wire to hook up, Grams turned to me and said, "When I plug this in, everything will go black and you won't hear any of us. Focus on Ryan: if he's in the system, he'll guide you to him. We're going to unplug you in five minutes no matter what, so try to get in and out as fast as you can. Agreed?"

"Yeah," I heard myself say, but my heart raced and I felt like I was having an out-of-body experience. Knowing me it might have been possible, but I needed to stay grounded if I was going to be any help to Ryan. Focus. I breathed a deep relaxing breath.

Roberta plugged me in.

Black.

Grams wasn't kidding. This was worse than astral projection because I had absolutely no power. I couldn't create an environment by just thinking it. I couldn't create anything.

A lightning flash whizzed by me and I felt like I jumped. Then I realized I was only "here" in mind, no body, so jumping wasn't exactly possible.

Another lightning flash.

Okay. This must be electricity or electronics or something computery.

I took Roberta's advice and concentrated on Ryan. I screamed his name out in my head, hoping that this magic brain-sucking machine would connect me to him.

A blinding flash engulfed me completely. All I could see was white.

It was so bright I found myself bathing in it. It felt like a weird kind of purity, since I didn't have to squint. I was surrounded by the brightness and never had to look away from its beauty, like basking in sunlight without the fear of going blind. It reminded me of the twins and using their power to connect to life. I didn't want to leave. I wanted to stay in the brightness forever.

"Chelsan?" Ryan's voice called out to me.

I tried to speak through my mind, "I'm here."

Ryan's beautiful face formed in front of me, shaped out of the light into perfection.

"What did you do?" Ryan asked. I could hear the worry dripping from his tone.

"Where are you? Do you know?" I asked. I was evading the topic of being hooked up to the machine, since Ryan would blow a gasket if he knew.

"I'm stuck. I can upload my coordinates, but they have an army here. I don't think you'll be able to get in. Isabelle took me," Ryan tried to explain.

"I'll come get you," I responded.

"This Harry guy is dangerous. He reminds me of Turner." Ryan's giant glowing face was surreal to watch.

"How do we get you out of the computer system?" I hoped he knew the answer.

"I'm not sure. As soon as they brought me here, they hooked me up to a newer version of the machine that Turner and Elisha have."

You mean the one I'm strapped into. I didn't want to alarm Ryan by admitting that that was how I was communicating with him.

"How do you know where you are?" I wanted to know.

Ryan responded, "I can see everything, and I mean everything, so their system must be plugged into satellites and surveillance holos; that's why I can send you coordinates. I can hear them talking and Isabelle seems to like you. She keeps trying to convince them that you were telling her the truth. That Harry guy hates your grandpa pretty badly though, and he doesn't trust you simply because you're Turner's granddaughter. I can tell you this: if Turner shows up here, they'll kill him."

"Is that necessarily a bad thing?" I joked.

WHOOSH!

Unplugged.

I couldn't stop blinking my vision was so wonky. Going from the brightest light imaginable to a regular old room, lighting was a difficult adjustment to say the least. After a few moments I started to make out the worried faces of Bill, Nancy, Jill and Jason.

Gramps just looked pissed. What was his problem?

Then I saw enough to read the holo-screen next to me. It had Ryan and my entire conversation typed out and floating in front of me. I guess my joke about him dying not being a bad thing didn't go over so well. Oops.

Grams started unstrapping me. She smiled gently at me and I found it strangely comforting. "We have Ryan's coordinates. We'll send a team to retrieve him."

I helped her take off the rest of the suction-cups and stood up. "I'm going. And you heard Ryan, you're not." I eyed Turner. As evil as Gramps was, I didn't want him thinking that I wanted him dead.

"Don't be ridiculous. You're not going anywhere, it's exactly what they want." Turner just looked annoyed. He was already punching the coordinates into his holo-device.

I grabbed his arm. "Send them back to Nancy's and send me with the extraction team. Trust me. I can talk to Isabelle." I was full of crap! But I needed to rescue Ryan and Gramps was the only one who could make that happen.

I could already hear the peanut gallery (and by peanut gallery I mean Bill and Nancy) arguing with me, but I cut them off. "I can't worry about the two of you. Isabelle is a killer and she knows you're my weakness." I focused back on Turner, "Just give me some dead guys and I'll be fine." Wow. That was quite a statement, but true. Even if Elisha planned a surprise ambush I was pretty sure I could best her when it came to controlling corpses. It wasn't a hundred percent, but I was willing to take the risk.

Turner and Roberta exchanged a look, then Turner slowly nodded.

It took a good hour before everyone was headed back to Nancy's and I was on my way to Ryan. The hover-vehicle was filled with a mixture of alive and dead soldiers. I felt safer with the corpses. Controlling dead people was like second nature to me, even with the compound Turner injected into his dead soldiers that was meant to keep people like me out. It used to work on me. It would make me see corpses as live people, and prevent me from using my powers on them. But I had learned how to break through it and then later Roberta taught me how to master seeing through the strange substance so that it wasn't even a nuisance anymore.

I leaned my head back against the cold steel of the hovercraft's wall. It was like a metal dungeon with benches and seat belts, two long rows on either side of the craft.

A thought kept plaguing me. Why couldn't Ryan and I catch a break? Every time things approached some semblance of normal for us, one of us was kidnapped or tortured or something. It would almost be funny if it wasn't so depressing.

And now Ryan had a bunch of I.Q. kids stuck in his brain. Did Isabelle and this Harry guy even understand what that meant?

The soldier in charge walked over to me. (And yes, he was dead, controlled by Gramps who wanted to be there even if he couldn't physically be present.) "We're almost there. Harry and Isabelle have no idea I can inhabit the dead. They won't know I'm there," Turner said almost conversationally. My how things had changed!

"You know this Harry guy and what he might do to Ryan so I appreciate you coming," I admitted. Before, when I first thought of this rescue mission, I planned on charging in alone, though determined, I felt way out of my depth. Isabelle could crunch my heart. And I wasn't sure how my "dust trick" would go over the second time. Something told me Isabelle was the kind of girl that would be prepared.

"Almost there, sir," one of the guards called out to the corpse Turner was in control of.

"Assemble the men," Gramps ordered.

Things started to bustle.

What were we really expecting? To charge in there and take Ryan? They had to be waiting for that. What did Harry and Isabelle want to happen? Did they want me to attack? I had too many unanswered questions and the closer we flew toward our destination the more questions popped into my mind. I wouldn't have to wait long, I guessed.

As the hover vehicle descended to land, I looked out a small round window and saw that we were landing in the middle of a large warehouse facility. It reminded me of the warehouses in Havenville, but much grungier and more dilapidated. Good hide-out. I would have assumed they were abandoned. Beyond the warehouses was a pine forest that went on for miles. Anyone and anything could be lurking inside the trees' shadowed protection. It made me wary. As if I wasn't wary enough!

If I could gulp any bigger I would have. Outside the center warehouse stood at least three hundred men, all with guns, none of them dead (shocker) waiting for the shuttle to land.

So much for the element of surprise. Not that this gigantor hover-craft wasn't a huge giveaway!

Yet, somehow, I knew it would go down like this.

The moment we landed I was close enough to see Isabelle's smug face at the forefront of the armed warriors. I knew rescuing Ryan was going to cost me something.

Turner's puppet turned to me, "Just tell her that I'm your personal bodyguard. She'll let me come in with you."

I nodded. Couldn't believe my "back-up" was Gramps.

The Commander-corpse ordered the men to stay and the two of us walked out of the hover together. So much for bringing an army. A part of me was relieved, though. I really didn't want anyone to get hurt, and knowing Turner, this situation might have turned into a blood bath. In his brain that would probably have been the best option because then he could control the freshly killed soldiers. Didn't Isabelle know how dangerous it was to threaten Turner with her soldiers? Isabelle hadn't believed me, I guess. Or, as Ryan had observed, Harry must have thought I lied about my powers to Isabelle. I really hoped I wouldn't have an "I told you so" moment with Isabelle later down the road.

When I was face-to-face with the assassin I nodded to the dead man next to me, "He's my bodyguard."

Isabelle didn't argue, she just acknowledged what I'd said with a slight nod. "Follow me," she instructed quietly and turned toward the open warehouse door. Her men parted for us, all statues of frightening stillness, hands grasped tightly on their guns, ready to shred us with bullets. I wished for a moment I had inhabited a dead body of my own for protection.

Walking through the warehouse's giant double doors, I felt like I was entering a metal barn, except for the fact that it was…

SHLUNK!

Steel sliding doors slid shut behind us, sealing us off from our men and theirs.

And…

Uh, oh.

I was right. Isabelle had up'd the ante.

The warehouse we were in was hermetically sealed.

No dust.

There went that back up.

I searched for anything dead.

Not much.

A couple of flies and a few harmless spiders.

Even if Harry didn't believe I could control dead things, Isabelle apparently did and prepared as such. I wondered if Harry even knew Isabelle had been so thorough.

Looking around there were a couple dozen desks with holo-computers at every table and soldiers manning each station. Probably thirty people total. The walls, ceiling and floor were all the same solid steel that kept the dust out. They must have either found this place after Isabelle met me, or had it installed like ninjas. Either way it made me even more nervous about their competence.

We rounded a desk and there was Ryan.

Lying flat on a four-foot tall bed, his head suction-cupped and wires running back into the computer system. The only movement I could see from him was his chest slowly rising and falling as if in a deep sleep.

I ran to his side.

Guns from every corner lifted and pointed at me, but I ignored them completely.

Isabelle nodded for the men to put their guns down. They responded instantly to her command and went back to their holo-stations.

I held onto Ryan's hand, but there was no response. I turned to Isabelle demanding in rage, "What did you do to him?!"

A man's voice answered. "We didn't do anything. We were told that hooking him up to the computer would help him. When we took him he was already comatose."

In front of me the man behind the voice stepped forward. He looked like he was Turner's age. Old. Deep suntanned lines around his eyes and grey hair cut short. He looked like he could have been handsome when he was young, but it was impossible to tell since he was at least fifty. I had to admit he was in incredible shape though. I could tell through his black attire that the guy was cut. I didn't even know old people could work out. You'd think they'd break or something.

I knew who he was.

Harry.

He held himself with such assurance it was intimidating, but I couldn't let him see me sweat.

"You must be Harry," I said with as much confidence as I could muster.

"And you're Chelsan Turner," Harry replied with a smile.

"Derée," I corrected him.

"Interesting." Harry looked at me as if I had done something to explain the answers to the universe.

"What's interesting?" I should have let it go, but hey… I couldn't.

"That little microscopic sneer your lip did when I called you 'Turner.' Now I know how you feel about Geoffrey. I still think you're a liar, but maybe I can use your hatred." Harry walked over to stand directly across from me, with Ryan's prone body between us.

I tried not to look at corpse-Gramps. It was quite possible I did sneer. I didn't want to be associated with my grandparents no matter what kind of truce we had come to. I guess it was to my advantage that I felt that way in this moment, but I can't imagine what Turner was thinking as he heard Harry accuse me of basically being repulsed by him. Knowing Gramps, he could give a rat's ass.

I decided to appeal to this Harry guy's heartstrings. If he had any. "Please. Ryan didn't do anything to you. I just want to take him home. He's very sick. He could die here."

"That's not what our mutual friend thinks." Harry cut me off like I was an irritating fly.

"Mutual friend?" I shuddered to ask. (And I really hoped he was talking about Isabelle and not who I thought he was talking about.)

"Elisha," Harry said as if… I don't know… Isabelle hadn't told him *anything*!!!!

"Elisha?! Are you kidding me?!" I turned to Isabelle. "Did you not hear a single word I said?!"

"Calm down," Isabelle stepped forward shaking her head. "Of course I heard you. I just don't believe you."

"Oh really? Is that why this building is hermetically sealed and there's nothing dead I could possibly use to defend myself with?" I said as sarcastically as possible.

But I could see it in her eyes. She had no clue what I was talking about. And that freaked Isabelle out a bit.

Elisha must have prepped the place. Harry and Isabelle were just gullible idiots.

Isabelle tried to defend herself, "Harry has been in contact with Elisha's people for the past two months and she's proven herself an ally."

Her people? Eva probably. Since Elisha had been in cocoon world until recently, neither Harry nor Isabelle really had the chance to see how insane-o Elisha was.

"So basically, at Nancy's house, that was just for show? You two have been working with Elisha the whole time?" I felt so stupid. And betrayed. And stupid. Wait a minute. "*Harry* was working with Elisha and not you? You had no idea."

Isabelle and Harry exchanged looks.

Isabelle hadn't faked a thing!

When Isabelle talked with me she *was* being sincere. Then, when she came back to report to Harry what I'd said, Harry told her that I had lied and that Elisha was a friend and not a foe. Of course Isabelle would trust Harry over me, she'd worked with him for centuries. And, come to think of it, she probably thought Max was just Max and not Elisha puppeteering him.

"Harry set me straight," Isabelle confirmed.

"You two are even bigger idiots than I remember," Corpse-Gramps spoke up.

Oh man.

Isabelle and Harry turned to the dead guard, slightly disarmed by his statement.

"Do we know you?" Harry asked.

"Dead thing! Remember?! I control dead things. So does Turner. Better than I do." I rolled my eyes. Talk about stubborn dummies. They hated Turner so much, they hadn't believed a word I had said to Isabelle. I had given her state secrets for crap's sake. I made a ripe smelling opossum bite her leg!

"That's Turner?" Harry didn't look like he was buying it for a second.

"No, that's a dead guy being controlled by Turner," I shot back snottily. If I had taken a second to really comprehend my situation and the danger I was in, I might not have had so much attitude, but I couldn't help it. I was a lot more angry at the fact that Isabelle hadn't believed me than I cared to admit. Sure, she was an assassin, sure she was Turner's mortal enemy, sure she had tried to kill me, but damn, I hated it when people thought I was a liar. It came from the fact that my whole life I actually was a liar. Lying about my power, lying about keeping my stepfather alive, lying about who I was. Now that everything was out in the open, I was super-paranoid about what people thought of me. Especially when it came to lying.

"Elisha said you'd tell us these lies. She warned us in advance that your true power was in making things fly." Harry looked triumphant, like he had exposed me for the traitor that he thought I was.

Aside from his idiocy, it was the second time where Elisha wanted people to believe I could make things fly. What was she up to?

"And Turner may have been clever, but he didn't have any powers. I've known that man my whole life and the last thing he is capable of is black magic. That was always Roberta's thing." Harry's face had turned angry.

"That was your own stupid ignorance," Corpse-Gramps said.

Harry went from angry to furious in a half a second. He pulled out his gun and shot the already dead soldier in the head. "Let's see how dead you really are," he said fully expecting the man to drop dead in front of us.

Nope.

Still standing.

Lamebrain.

"You were saying?" I sighed.

Harry couldn't or wouldn't believe it. He emptied his entire bullet clip into the corpse, shredding its uniform and skin.

Still standing.

But barely.

Gramps didn't have the kind of control over dead bodies the way I did. Even for me, the less skin they had the harder they were to control, but for him it was a lot harder.

The dead guy turned to me, "Little help here."

I took control over what was left of the corpse.

Gross.

He looked like a mangled zombie, but he was intact enough that I could control him comfortably.

I turned to Harry, "Look, duh, we're telling the truth. Watch." I made the dead guy jump around and do a little spin. "Elisha is lying to you. You're trusting the wrong person. I don't know why she wants everyone to believe that I can make things float or fly or whatever, but I can't. Unless it's dead, then I can. But other than that, I can't." Good speech.

"You always were a stupid fool," Turner's corpse sputtered. Considering he was still able to access this guy's vocal chords while I was controlling his body was pretty impressive.

Harry stood there.

Frozen.

Thinking, no doubt.

It was one thing to hear Isabelle talk about witnessing me controlling the dead, Harry could write it off as me tricking her. But to see it firsthand was throwing him for a loop.

Weighing what he was seeing in front of his face with what he'd been told by Elisha. He must have truly believed her because he was definitely struggling in his brain.

THWAP! THWAP! THWAP!

I saw it before I could react.

A swarm of dead flies carried three metal rods toward us: one rod whacked Isabelle unconscious and the other two knocked-out two more of Harry's guys.

"All my toys in one room. I couldn't have planned it more perfectly."

Elisha's voice echoed from the back of the warehouse.

Harry was all military.

His men had their guns out and pointed at Elisha and Eva as they approached our little group.

No Max.

I stood in front of Ryan's unconscious body to protect him.

"What's the meaning of this, Elisha?" Harry barked. He was seriously pissed.

"Um, you're stupid, like I told you." Did I really just say that? I was shocked at my own attitude, but this guy really annoyed me.

With at least thirty guns pointed at her, I'd have thought Elisha would be scared.

Nope. Too nuts.

Elisha strode over to Harry and me.

Dang.

Seeing her in person was crazier than seeing her on the holo. The girl was drop dead gorgeous. This, I thought, might have something to do with Harry's unwavering belief in Elisha. She bamboozled him with her looks. Guys! Her large violet eyes were piercing and stunning. I couldn't stop staring at her. I felt like an imbecile. Elisha looked like she could go to my high school, dressed in a tank and jeans. She even had the nerve to wear a pair of Chucks. Evil.

Why wasn't she worried about the guns?

Elisha had knocked out Isabelle because of her powers, but why the other two soldiers? Did they have powers as well?

I knew better than to ask her directly, so I kept quiet and let Harry and Elisha hash out their beef.

In the meantime, I tried to casually find a way out of this warehouse tomb!

Elisha and Eva stopped a few feet from us. Eva had a self-satisfied look on her face as she stared me down.

Elisha's grin grew wide as she glared at me as well. "Hello, Chelsan."

I was glad she was an adult now. Before, even knowing she was a hundred years old, she still looked like a kid, but as an adult…

…I was planning the ways I'd kick her butt.

"You better explain yourself, Elisha, or I'm just going to shoot you and call it a day," Harry said with such intensity it gave me goose bumps.

Elisha laughed. "You mean like this?"

Before I could react, out of the ventilation shafts a handful of dead crows soared through the air faster than I could blink.

THUNK! THUNK! THUNK! THUNK!

Each dead crow slammed into the jugulars of four of Harry's men. Blood sprayed everywhere as the men gurgled and dropped to the floor, dead, with freaking crows sticking out of their necks!

I was in shock. The crows were too fast. I didn't have time to stop them. Now there were four dead men lying at my feet. I waited to take control of the corpses, not sure if Elisha and Eva would be stronger than me and simply take control of the dead soldiers themselves.

Elisha had a better grasp on dead things than I did. I wasn't even sure I could have made the birds move that fast. My worst nightmare was coming true: Elisha knew my powers better than I did.

And she could use them to create more death and destruction.

"Fire!" Harry screamed with fury.

Every soldier in the sealed warehouse pulled their triggers.

And a bunch of harmless clicking sounds followed.

Not one gun went off.

Harry looked stunned and, actually, a little bit scared. "Charlie?" he said in horror.

Elisha smiled. "Charlie's with me now."

I saw it then.

Someone dead arriving through the same back-of-the-warehouse entrance Elisha had come through. He was about five foot ten, of Asian decent and looked like he was in his late twenties (so really he could be any age, either pre-Age-pro, or poor). He walked over to Elisha and Eva.

"Charlie, how could you?" Harry's face showed the betrayal he felt.

"He's dead, you dolt," Turner's dead puppet sniped at Harry.

Harry couldn't accept this answer, "Charlie, we've been working together for three-hundred years. I was wrong to trust Elisha. She's our enemy."

Charlie spoke, his voice low and gravelly, "You can rot in hell."

Harry physically flinched.

I felt Harry's pain. Roberta had made my mom say monstrous things to me when she controlled Mom's dead body. Elisha was being cruel for her own entertainment.

Time to see if I could beat her.

I connected to Charlie's black swirling hole.

Elisha whirled on me. "No you don't." She turned to Eva. "Eva."

WHAM!

I felt the two of them knock me off of Charlie's spinning black chasm with force.

Okay.

Two to one.

"Charlie's mine and so are you," Elisha grinned at me.

I was assuming that whatever Charlie's power was, it involved stopping guns. So, some kind of control over metal? I really didn't know. I really didn't want to know. I just didn't want Elisha to have all that power.

"What do you need with me, Elisha?" I asked. This was the third time Elisha had tried to extract me. Why on earth would she want me? She had my power already. Did she want to kill me so I couldn't stop her from using dead people? She'd have to kill Grams and Gramps too since they could do the same thing.

Besides, if she wanted me dead, she'd have killed me already.

"That's my business." Elisha made the freshly killed corpses with the birds in their necks stand up. She forced them pull out the crows and walk over to Ryan's body on the gurney.

I stepped in front of them. "You're not taking Ryan."

"Yes, I am. And…" Elisha made Charlie concentrate, I could literally feel it. What was she doing? In less than a second every soldier in the warehouse jerked their guns up to their heads and shot themselves with a collective BOOM!

Harry's entire army dropped to the ground, dead.

Harry was frozen in astonishment.

I was speechless.

I couldn't help but feel that I let that happen.

I was so enraged I could feel my brain shatter in red hot fury.

Elisha had just killed more innocent people.

"Kill Isabelle, Terence and Dean," Elisha ordered Charlie. "They're easier controlled dead like you."

No.

Elisha may have my power now, but I've had it longer.

SLAM!

I connected into Charlie's chest and snapped Elisha and Eva's hold over him like they were twigs.

I could barely hear Elisha scream orders to pin me down as I disconnected Charlie from his black swirling hole.

"NO!" Elisha screamed in rage.

Charlie slunk to the floor. He'd been dead a long time because he rotted instantly, turning into a pile of gloppy mush and bones on the floor.

Next.

I connected to every single dead soldier and made them rise and turn on Elisha and Eva.

"Guns work now," I snarled.

I made the men point their guns at Elisha.

I could feel Elisha and Eva trying to tag team it, and take over the bodies themselves.

Nope.

Stronger.

And way more pissed.

"Guess I'm still more powerful than you." I sounded more impressive than I felt. I could feel the two of them gnawing at my hold on the soldiers, but I was able to fend them off.

"Kill her!" I heard from two voices at once. I jumped slightly at the fact that both Corpse-Gramps and Harry were ordering me to kill Elisha. If it hadn't been such a serious situation, I'd have yelled jinx.

Kill Elisha.

The thought rolled around in my brain and I wanted to do it. I wanted to stop the monster that was going to destroy the world if she wasn't stopped. It would be so easy. Just make one of the corpses pull the trigger.

But I couldn't.

I couldn't kill anyone.

As close a bond as I had with the dead, killing was something I could never do willingly.

I'd killed too many times. Once when I was a kid and didn't know what I was doing, and the second time when Elisha made me use the twins. But now, here, I was fully aware of what I'd be doing.

And I couldn't do it.

Elisha saw this instantly.

And she smiled.

I turned to Harry. "Get Isabelle out of here before I lose control." Then I focused on Turner's corpse host. "Get into another body and take Ryan and everyone to safety."

Harry was angry, "I have to get Terence and Dean, too."

I had enough mojo to let Turner inhabit another body. When he was safely inside, I used the powers I had left to help him and four other dead guards carry Terence, Dean and Isabelle toward the exit. The corpse Turner controlled hurried to my side and started to unplug Ryan from the contraption.

"I wouldn't do that if I were you," Elisha said between gritted teeth, she was concentrating so hard. But she still took pleasure in holding something over my head.

Ryan started to convulse as soon as the first suction cup was removed.

"Put it back!" I screamed, and I almost lost my control over the corpses.

Turner's host put it back.

"Just leave! I'll stay with him!" I yelled.

Even though it was a dead man in front of me, Turner's eyes came through. "We'll come back for you two."

"Just go!"

Elisha and Eva were knocking on my control. I felt the dead men starting to twitch. I was going to lose my hold on them in a minute or two.

Elisha was so concentrated on breaking through my power, she merely snarled at the corpses and Harry carrying the three unconscious people out of the warehouse. I could see the spinning holes of Turner's dead army just beyond the door.

Elisha was breaking through.

I couldn't fight it much longer.

I sighed in relief as I saw the swirling black holes outside lift into the air toward safety. I hoped Turner was truly coming back for Ryan and me, but I wasn't sure he was powerful enough to challenge Elisha's ability. Only I was.

And I was waning.

How was I going to get out of this mess?

Eva smiled, "At least we have what we really came for."

Eva leapt at me and I made a soldier block her way. She looked like a crazed animal, trying to claw her way through the corpses, trying to attack me.

It distracted me for a moment.

WHACK!

Elisha's triumphant grin was the last thing I saw as I fell to the ground.

Actually, second to last.

As my head hit the floor, I saw the blank stare of Max, standing over me, holding one of the metal pipes.

Ouch.

Really?

How many times had I been knocked out in the last six months of my life?

My head pounded as I opened my eyes to see where Elisha had taken me.

An empty room.

Awesome.

No windows, one steel door, cement all around. I felt like I was in a slightly larger coffin than the one Elisha put me in before. She did this on purpose. To mess with my head.

It was totally working.

I wanted to scream.

I felt like I couldn't breathe.

Through the mouth. Through the mouth. If I just took small relaxing breaths through my mouth eventually my brain would calm down enough to make me realize that I actually could breathe. It was one of the techniques Jill taught me.

In case Elisha was spying on me somehow, I didn't want her to have the satisfaction of me freaking out.

I really hated her.

I searched for anything dead, my usual tactic in a hostile situation!

Nothing.

Of course.

I should have known.

Max.

Had he turned? Had he been lying to me the whole time? Was he under Elisha's control? I guess Max's loyalty was the least of my problems, but I just didn't want to believe he was evil like Elisha and Eva. I don't know why. I guess it was because I genuinely liked the guy. Max had such a quiet power that was both intimidating and inspiring at once. Plus, he could be a potential ally if I could break Elisha's hold on him. If that was what it was.

I wondered at the lack of anything dead.

At some point, I would have to be around dead things soon because Elisha had the same power I did.

I couldn't figure out why she hadn't killed me, though. I mean, I was happy for that, but it didn't make any sense. Why keep a person alive who could thwart your every move? Elisha always had a reason for everything that she did, and I had a horrible feeling in the pit of stomach as to why she was keeping me alive.

Elisha's lovely voice filled the room through some hidden speaker, "Good morning."

I kind of grumbled. I really didn't feel like talking to evil-wench-girl.

The steel door clunked and then opened.

Four burly guards walked in, all strapped with guns. "Please follow my boys." Elisha's voice ordered with annoying politeness.

I decided it was better than the cement tomb, so I stood up on wobbly feet and followed the guards outside.

The hallway we entered was similar to the room I just left, cement all around. I had the distinct feeling we were in some sort of underground bunker. Buried alive with style this time, I guess.

I did a quick Roberta check. I opened my mind to her, hoping she'd be there waiting to tell me they were on their way to the rescue.

Nope.

I'd have to save myself.

Again.

Where are you? Roberta's concerned voice echoed in my brain.

Relief flooded through me.

I thought back to her, *No idea. I thought you guys would track me or something.*

With what? You insisted that Geoffrey take our tracker out of you.

I could hear the *I told you so* tone in her voice. When I'd realized that the grandparents had injected a tracking device in my blood five months ago, it kind of… I don't know… freaked me out! I told Turner to take it out, but I had secretly assumed he hadn't. The fact that Gramps actually *had* taken out the tracker made me realize what a huge step that was toward trusting me. Now, of course, I felt like an idiot because they could have rescued Ryan and me by now. Ggrr.

That was assuming Ryan was anywhere near me.

The odds were for it since Elisha loved torturing me, and seeing Ryan hooked up to brain-sucking machines was the perfect way to do it.

After what seemed like hours (probably five minutes), our party arrived at a solid steel door. I needed to come up with a battle plan. Preferably one that didn't involve Ryan or me dying.

I got back to Roberta, *I'm in some kind of place with lots of cement and steel doors. Does that help at all?*

Roberta's response was quick in my brain, *Not really, but it sounds like it's underground. We'll start a search. In the mean time, keep our connection open.*

Will do, I answered.

I shivered.

What was that I just felt for Grams? Comfort? Gratefulness? Loyalty? It was sad that it actually made me shudder to think of a grandparent that way. Those feelings should be natural. Ha.

I walked through the opened steel maw of darkness into another concrete room. This one was filled with holo-computers and set up like an I.Q. Farm. Eva and Elisha stood over Ryan's unconscious body.

As I'd expected, Ryan was hooked up to the thousands of wires that plugged into the ceiling and the giant brain machine. The holo-monitors displayed his brain activity and it was off the charts. The I.Q. kids stuck in Ryan's head were going nuts in there. And from his weak vital signs, they were killing him.

There were no others in the room. Four guards behind me. Ryan, Eva, Elisha in front. And me.

Max was nowhere to be seen.

Still nothing dead.

But still… these were odds I could work with.

Elisha smiled when she saw me.

Eva didn't.

Elisha motioned me toward her. "Don't worry, Ryan will be himself soon."

I reluctantly walked over to her so that I could hold Ryan's hand.

I looked up at Elisha with as much hatred as I could muster, "What do you want with us? Why haven't you tried to kill me?"

Elisha acted as if the very thought offended her, "Chelsan, why would I kill you? I need you."

"Uh, huh. To do what? Break-in to headquarters again?" I was fishing and she knew it.

"Oh, I can do that on my own now. No. I need you to kill yourself," Elisha said it like it was the most natural thing in the world to say.

"And why on earth would I do that?" I asked, appalled at this psychopath.

"I can't tell you that, just trust me."

Um.

Was Elisha really this insane or did her recent, forced growing spurt fry her brain a bit?

"Here's an answer for you. No." Geez.

Elisha laughed. "You don't have to do it now, silly. I need you alive first." She nodded to two of the guards.

One guard stepped forward and grabbed me by the arms. The second guard opened a small metal box to reveal two filled syringes inside.

Uh, oh.

The second guard took out the first syringe and injected it into my arm.

Elisha tilted her head to the side as if observing me for the first time.

"This first injection makes you loopy so you won't have control over your power."

My vision started to blur and everything felt really sluggish. My body felt thick and heavy, every movement was a Herculean effort.

The guard injected the second needle.

Elisha's voice sounded like she was in a tunnel, "The second shot should make it impossible to communicate with anyone."

Roberta! I screamed in my head. *She injected me with something!*

Nothing.

Roberta! I used every ounce of my astral ability.

Crickets.

Elisha stepped closer to me, so pleased with herself. "That little shot works wonders, doesn't it? Did you honestly think I'd let you talk to your dear old grandmother? You're still just as dumb as I remember."

I wanted to respond. To yell. To scream. But my tongue felt like it was eight times its size and my lips were numb.

Elisha took another moment to gloat, but when my sluggish state was no longer entertaining for her, she moved towards Eva and Ryan.

Eva's eyes lit up with joy at the sight of my drugged stupor.

No matter how hard I tried I couldn't focus on anything.

"Open the wall," Elisha ordered.

Eva walked over to a holo-computer and punched in a command.

A loud clanking echoed in the room and I wanted to giggle. Why did I want to giggle? I felt so weird.

I noticed Elisha and Eva suddenly turning toward me. What were they looking at? I realized I was making strange noises as I opened and closed my mouth trying to feel my numb lips.

Eva groaned, obviously disappointed. "You said she'd be in pain."

"Patience, Eva. I never said it was the drugs that were going to make her feel bad. Let her enjoy the good for now." Elisha turned around to focus on the wall in front of me.

It was opening. I couldn't tell if it was the drugs or not, but as light started to pour into the room, yes, it was definitely opening.

Whoa.

Thousands of swirling black holes were behind the wall. I hadn't seen them before. The wall must have been made of that compound the grandparents used. I had been so freaked out I hadn't noticed.

Focus.

Focus.

Blah. Blah. Blah. My mind felt fuzzy. Unicorns.

The wall was gone.

And standing in front of us was an entire army of dead soldiers standing in perfect formation.

Elisha's army.

They were outside in some sort of canyon, or maybe it was cement. The L.A. River. I was sure of it. Darn it, stupid, slurpy drugs! I needed to talk to my grandma.

"Get Ryan ready," Elisha ordered Eva.

Ryan?

Ready for what?

How was I standing? My legs felt like Jell-O and yet I was standing perfectly straight with no guards helping me.

Eva's hands were moving a mile a minute as she swiped and swirled and punched the holo-screens in front of her. I couldn't tell if it was my muddled brain or not, but it looked like her hands were dancing.

I nearly toppled over when Ryan's whole body seized.

"Ryan!" I could hear my voice scream, but it felt like it came from someone else. Like I was standing outside my own body watching the entire scene take place.

Wait a minute.

I was standing outside my body.

My mind instantly became clear. Somehow I had jumped out of my body completely. Whatever brain-wave-stopping drug Elisha injected me with didn't work. She thought it would stop me communicating with anyone... I realized then that "talking" to Roberta was different than "visiting" Roberta. They were actually two separate things. One: I stayed completely inside my brain. And two: I was completely out of my body. I suddenly realized that calling every kind of mental communication "astral projection" was actually not accurate.

Now that I was out of my body, I didn't know what to do.

I felt so helpless.

Ryan seized again, his back arched in pain.

"NOW!" Elisha screamed.

Eva pressed a final switch.

Ryan screamed.

They were killing him.

Instinct took over.

I jumped inside his head.

It was like entering a wind tunnel full of light. Streaks of white soared past me at lightning speed.

Then, just as suddenly, it was calm.

"Chelsan?" I heard Ryan's sweet voice call out.

One second I was in darkness, the next I was in a field of the greenest grass I'd ever seen. And Ryan stood in front of me.

I ran to him and we embraced like we hadn't seen each other in years. Even though I wasn't really there, I could still feel his arms wrapping around me. Ryan kissed me and my imaginary toes tingled just like in real life.

Ryan pulled away with a smile. "They're gone. Elisha did it."

"The I.Q. kids?" I asked incredulously.

Ryan nodded. "Whatever she did to configure the machine, she took all of them out. I'm sure my body will be unconscious for a while, but I'm free. I'm actually free."

I hated Elisha's guts, but I admit I was thrilled that she'd made good on her word and helped Ryan. Of course, my body was still drugged and she wanted me to kill myself, but baby steps.

"Where did they all go?" The thought suddenly occurred to me.

"Into the ether? I dunno. I'm just happy they're gone." Ryan kissed me again and my stomach did flip flops. "How are you here? Are you sleeping?"

"Weren't you watching?" I figured he had "seen" everything that had just happened like he had the last time he was hooked up to the brain contraption.

"Elisha injected some kind of drug in me so I couldn't have free access to the machine. Why? What's happening?" Ryan had *worried-face* on.

"I'm drugged too," I informed him. "Elisha used it to stop me from talking to Roberta in my head, but it didn't stop me from leaving my body."

"Interesting." Ryan was thinking. "Do you think you can take over my body?"

Huh?

"Huh?" What was he getting at?

SWOOSH!

I was thrown out of Ryan's body with stomach-puking force. Luckily, I wasn't pushed back into my own drugged-out form.

"Clever, but you have to stay in your own body." Elisha was talking to my actual body and not my incorporeal form, so I figured I was ahead of the game. She really thought the drug would keep me locked inside my own body. Her mistake.

Ryan was out cold and I was loopy girl down below. I made a quick decision and flew out of there as fast as I could. I focused so I could see all the strings of light that connected me to everything. The brightest, as usual, was Grams. I clung to it and raced to Roberta as fast as I could while keeping an eye on the ground to see where we were.

Definitely the L.A. River. I was right about that.

Elisha had built some kind of underground facility underneath the Sepulveda Basin, which branched off from the river. I recognized the Sepulveda Dam first with its cement archways and long straight bridge spanning its way across the concrete floor. There wasn't much water, it was more for show than anything else at this point (and at any point according to Mr. Alastar). But the Sepulveda Dam was a landmark, and that helped me gain my bearings.

I was flying past it and towards Population Control in a matter of seconds. Everything was a blur of light and color until I was floating above Roberta's head. She sat in a room with Turner. Harry and Isabelle were there as well with the two other soldiers that escaped Elisha's ambush, Terence and Dean I think it was. It looked like Gramps was so angry he was about to rip off Harry's head. Isabelle stood in the corner like she was invisible, taking in the conversation. She was definitely an observer while the other two sat in cushy armchairs quietly next to Roberta.

I didn't have time to listen in so I jumped full force inside Roberta's head.

"Chelsan! You're here! I've been trying to contact you, but Elisha must have some sort of blocking device." Roberta appeared in front of me, the blackness around us melting and transforming until we stood in our usual oak forest. Apparently, this place gave comfort to Roberta as well as to me since she always created the same forest as our meeting place.

I got right down to it. "Elisha gave Ryan and me some kind of drug that stops us from communicating outside ourselves. For me it was the psychic thing and for Ryan it was preventing him from connecting to the computers. Somehow I was able to leave my body and come here, but my actual body is seriously drugged out right now."

Roberta's eyebrows furrowed with thought for a moment, then relaxed as she understood and explained, "When you talk to me directly through your mind it's called 'telepathy.' When you leave your body like this, that's 'astral projection.' They're two different things. Elisha's obviously found a way to stop telepathy, whether through minds or, as Ryan does, through computers."

It made sense, although it still made me feel like a novice. I'd just assumed they were all the same thing. It made me realize there was so much more about the whole black-magic-mojo world I didn't know.

Roberta brought me sharply out of my contemplation. "Do you know where she's keeping you and Ryan?"

I nodded. "In some kind of base under the Sepulveda Dam."

"We'll get you out of there as soon as possible. You'd better travel back to your body. Sooner or later Elisha will realize that you're not in it, despite her drugs. Probably sooner." Roberta hugged me impulsively. "We're coming, just hold on tight."

Sudden tears filled my eyes. Roberta said the words with such conviction, it made me emotional. Sometimes it was hard being the strong one. Having someone, even Roberta, hug me like that made the whole situation a bit overwhelming.

Roberta pulled back and wiped the tears from my cheeks. "You and Ryan will be fine," she smiled, "I promise."

I smiled back. Me! I actually smiled back. What was wrong with me? I couldn't help it. Roberta was giving me comfort and I needed it.

"There's something else I need to tell you," I began. Then I told her about the I.Q. kids being ripped from Ryan's brain.

Roberta's face turned white. "I'll tell Geoffrey. Now go."

I didn't like that look, it made me extremely nervous as to where exactly those I.Q. kids went. It wasn't like Elisha to do something out of the kindness of her heart. So what was in it for her? There was nothing more I could do here, though, so I nodded to Roberta and zoomed out of there, heading back to Ryan as fast as I could. So fast I made the mistake of actually entering back into my own body.

Whoa.

Drugs are bad.

Seriously.

I felt like I was going to throw up, and yet at the same time, I couldn't move. Through the whole super-sluggish haze, I saw that Elisha was busy talking to Eva, probably planning out their world domination strategy. I concentrated as hard as my muddled brain would allow and tried to partition my consciousness from the drugged out part of my brain. I tried to use the same technique I used to focus and unfocus on dust. One moment I'd see it, the other moment I didn't. If I could just separate my clear mind from my intoxicated one. Basically: shove my consciousness into another part of my brain that wasn't affected by the drug.

I felt something…

Wow.

I did it.

I was completely aware.

The only problem was.

I couldn't control my body.

Not good.

Maybe Elisha wouldn't notice?

Honestly, it seemed like Elisha was kind of ignoring me completely. I guess that, whatever she had planned next, I wasn't exactly a part of it. I was just amazed I could actually stand.

"Get in the hover and bring Chelsan," Elisha barked to the guards behind me.

Okay, maybe I *was* a part of the plan.

The guards had to carry me.

I wondered if I'd be able to reset myself once this drug was out of my system. I started to feel a surge of panic rise in my unresponsive body. Did I just paralyze myself? I was learning so many insanely crazy things I could do with my brain, it was a wonder I hadn't gone into a coma months ago!

Elisha was talking to Eva now. "They'll be here soon, so we have to leave. I can't lose Chelsan."

Lose me? They? Did Elisha know my grandparents were coming for me?

Oh! Toe wiggle. I wiggled my toe. Good first step.

"I'm trusting you, Eva. Can you do this?" Elisha was the most serious I'd ever seen her.

Do what?

Eva nodded, determined. She looked like she was about to go into battle.

The two men shoved me into the back of a rather nice hover-SUV. Eva slid-in to the seat in front of me while one of the live guards drove. Elisha and the soldiers stayed behind. That kind of scared me. Where were we going?

Fingers. I could move my fingers. I was determined to get around this whole "drug" thing. There were conveniently no dead soldiers in the car for me to test my powers on. Elisha apparently didn't completely trust the drugs either. I felt a modicum of relief that Elisha wasn't in the car with us. For some reason Eva seemed a lot less scary, probably because I'd been going to school with her for the last three months, and every time I'd gone up against her… I had won.

Of course I wasn't drugged out of my mind those times, trapped in some sort of half-in half-out of body experience. I couldn't even describe it properly. It was almost as if I was dead and controlling myself at the same time.

Eva was silent while the hover-SUV drove on. I could tell she was nervous by the way she was fidgeting. That girl couldn't sit still. She kept looking outside like she expected someone to show up at our window in mid-air.

"Where are we going?" I asked. Admittedly it sounded pretty slurred, but I hadn't figured out how to control my body properly yet. How long do drugs stay in your system anyway?!

"Shut up!" Eva barked. She didn't even turn around to look at me.

But I saw her face reflected in the window.

Eva was terrified.

That made me terrified.

What was going to happen? Maybe I should zoom outside my body and go and tell Roberta? I just couldn't. I was afraid if I did… something horrible would happen to my body. And besides, they were on their way to Ryan. Sure, they'd be upset that I wasn't there, but at least Ryan would be rescued. It was the least I could do after all the crap I'd brought into his life. Now that the I.Q. kids were out of his brain maybe he'd be back to normal. I really hoped so.

In my drug-induced prison, I didn't even want to think about the fact that Elisha had an entire army of dead soldiers. I'd deal with that later when I wasn't in a hover-SUV on my way to who-knows-where to do who-knows-what.

And I vowed to myself that, once we arrived, if I had a moment I'd jump out to Roberta and tell her where I was. The drug that stopped me from talking to her with my mind while I was in my body was really annoying. If there was any of it left in me by the time the grandparents found me maybe they could take a sample of my blood and re-create it. Then we'd have that weapon for ourselves. Elisha was one of the best head-communicators or telepathy-people out there: to stop her from using that particular power would be priceless.

Then I thought about how Ryan asked if I could control him. If that was a part of the whole astral projection business, then maybe Max really was being mind-controlled by Elisha. I really hoped so.

"Just park over there," Eva instructed the driver.

The hover-SUV landed and I tried to wobble my head towards the window to see where we were.

The Glass Mall.

Why were we at a mall? And the Glass Mall at that? This wasn't some secret or hidden location.

Eva exited the vehicle while the driver came around and pulled me out of the hover-SUV, supporting me to stand. We had landed on a large hill just outside the mall, so we had a full aerial view of the monstrous building.

Hover-packages were zooming in and out of the stained glass structure droning in the normal buzz of commerce. The Glass Mall itself was always beautiful to behold. Its five domes of intricately designed stained glass sat atop a giant canyon. A work of architectural art. It should have been a museum, not a shopping center.

"Can you make her stand on her own?" Eva asked the guard.

"Eva…" I sputtered out. What was she going to do?

Eva and the guard ignored me like I was their toy mannequin. Somehow they propped me up so I could stand without support. Better for me. It allowed me to experiment with puppeteering myself. I already had full use of my hands and feet, which they didn't know, now I just needed control over my arms and legs. No biggie. Ugh!

Eva and the guard positioned themselves next to the SUV, but within arms length of me. Then I saw something that made my heart stop.

A small device in Eva's hand. A device that would…

POP!

Yup.

Dimension displacement.

The same kind of device Turner used to disguise our vehicles when we snuck into Havenville months ago.

Somehow Elisha had stolen the technology. Now she was using it to hide her own armada. Although now that I thought about it, it was probably one of the I.Q. kids that invented it in the first place. Turner said once that pretty much all of our modern day innovations came from the I.Q. farms. Of course Elisha had access! She probably invented it herself!

The hover-SUV, Eva and the guard disappeared from sight.

Oh boy.

This was the moment I'd been dreading.

I was going to be set up for something.

That whole *She can make things float* thing Eva had been telling to the press was going to bite me in the butt and there was nothing I could do about it.

Eva and the guard had disappeared from sight, but they were still nearby.

"Watch her. I need all my concentration." I could hear Eva's voice order the guard.

Concentration?

She was going to use her powers.

And I wouldn't be able to stop her.

I tried not to lose it as I focused on all my limbs. I needed to control myself. I needed not to be drugged!

Too late.

I felt it before I saw it.

A mass of swirling black holes looming behind me, headed straight toward the Glass Mall.

What the…?

I managed to tilt my neck up to see the most terrifying sight imaginable.

A gigantic shard of metal floated above me casting a shadow over everything in the nearby vicinity. The thing was huge, well over seven football fields long, and it was jagged all around its edges. Sharp metal edges that could do some serious damage. But what was most frightening was the fact that this enormous slab of metal floated in the air because it was being held up by trillions of dead flies.

Before I could even contemplate what Eva planned to do with this razor-blade-of-terror she made it slam into one of the Glass Mall's five domes. The structure was built to withstand hurricanes, so the first attack didn't break the glass. But I could tell the building wouldn't hold up for long.

I could hear screams from the people below, and see them running from the mall as fast as their terrified legs would carry them. But there still had to be thousands of people inside. If I didn't so something quick…

They would die.

I heard the guard's voice next to me, placing an "emergency" phone call to the authorities, and knew my fate was sealed.

"Hello?! Hello?!" he cried into the phone, pretending he was scared witless. "I'm at the Glass Mall! We're being attacked! We're all going to die!" For a "frightened" person, he had a lot of details to convey, like this kicker: "I see that Chelsan Derée girl from the news on the north side hill! She's doing this! She's trying to kill us all! Stop her! Stop her!" He hung up, making his phone call sound like it was cut off in mid-sentence: all the more dramatic to whoever was on the receiving end.

But at the moment I didn't have time to care about the fact that they were framing me for this attack. People were going to die unless I could get control of the flies and move the metal to safety. Problem was:

I couldn't just drop the flies' connection to their swirling black holes because then the sharp metal shard would fall directly on the mall and on the people below.

SLAM!

Eva made the metal hit the glass wall once more. This time it cracked. One more hit and the dome would buckle and collapse.

I heard sirens from all directions.

The authorities were coming for me.

I had to do this quick.

SLAM!

SMASH!

The stained glass shattered into a million pieces.

The screams below sounded like a roar. There were thousands of seriously freaked out people down there and they were all going to die if I didn't do something about it.

SMASH!

Eva made the giant shard of metal slice down into the mall. I couldn't see what was happening, but a moment later I could see the newly swirling holes of dead bodies scattered on the ground.

NO!

Something inside of me cracked.

I felt it.

It was like the moment I had to make Roberta stop torturing my mother's dead body.

I was blind with rage, frustration and terror.

And I screamed.

I could feel my back arching as my insides boiled.

I connected to every single dead fly.

Trillions of them all mine.

"NO!!!" I heard Eva shriek in outrage.

I hurled the deadly metal slab out of the mall, making the flies soar it safely away from the Glass Mall, into the oak forest behind me.

The loud sound of trees snapping into pieces as the metal shredded through the forest was almost deafening, before it finally crashed to the ground.

I could feel Eva trying to regain control of the flies.

My momentum was gone.

The drugs were still in effect.

I was too weak to separate my mind from my drugged-out body.

Eva was winning.

With my last bit of mental strength I kept hold of the flies and did the only thing I could.

I released them from their swirling black holes. Now no one could control them.

The sound of Eva screaming gave me small pleasure as I felt my body start to fail. I was losing consciousness fast. I heard her voice harshly whisper, "Grab her! Quick! We have the holo-footage already!"

The guard's voice sounded rattled, "The authorities are too close. They'll see me."

"We can't let Turner have her! Elisha will kill me if we don't bring her back!"

I could sense more than see the hover vehicles landing all around me, lights flashing, coming to arrest me.

I saw the guard's arm materialize next to me, starting to grab.

I wasn't going back to Elisha.

I took the last reserves of my energy and forced my body to move toward the policemen running to arrest me.

"Grab her!" Eva's voice was a shriek of dread desperation.

I jumped away from the guard's outstretched arm, blackness already starting to envelope me.

The last thing I saw was a police officer grabbing my arms as I collapsed to the ground.

***

"Why isn't she waking up? The drugs were flushed out of her system hours ago. Shouldn't she be up by now? Where's the doctor?" Nancy's voice filled my heart like a beam of sunshine.

I opened my eyes: everything was completely blurred. "Nancy?" I croaked, surprised to find that my voice was hoarse.

"Oh thank goodness!" The blob that was Nancy ran to my side and grasped my hand tightly. "Are you okay?"

"I can't see anything. Where am I?" I asked. "All I see is white blobbish stuff all around me." Since some of those blobs were moving, I assumed they were people.

"You're in Turner's private hospital. It's inside the Population Center. This place is freaking huge. Did you even know they had a hospital in here?" Nancy was rambling. That meant she was nervous.

It also meant she was hiding something from me. I knew that tone.

I sat up and my head immediately spun dizzily. "Where's Ryan?"

"Lie down, he's fine." Nancy practically pushed me back into the bed. "He's right next to you. You really can't see?" I could tell Nancy was waving her hand in front of my face.

I whacked it away. "I'm not blind, everything is just blurry."

"Give her some space, child," Roberta's voice scolded Nancy.

Nancy sat back.

"Can we have some drops over here?" Roberta barked to someone in another room.

A large blob hurried over to my bed. PLOP PLOP went the drops in my eyes. It was instantly soothing and within seconds my vision came back to me. And what I saw was… impressive.

I was definitely in the richest looking hospital I'd ever seen. Not that I'd been in a lot of hospitals, but after my ordeal with the serial killer Brady, I'd stayed the night at L.A. Hospital. It was nice, but this was insanely lavish. My bed and pillows were made of the softest foam and from the ultra-smooth feel had to be covered with about a million-thread-count sheets. No wonder I hadn't woken up right away! The room was decorated with high-end holo-paintings and the pale yellow walls were framed with intricately ornate white crown molding.

I noticed my bed was placed in the middle of the room with two other identical beds on either side.

Ryan was on the bed to my right, asleep.

I started to sit up again to go to his side, but Nancy pushed me back down again. "He's fine. He's sleeping."

She had that tone again.

"You're hiding something from me," I called her out.

"I'm not," Nancy answered, looking away worriedly.

"Nancy." I grabbed her hand so she'd have to make eye contact with me.

Roberta stepped forward, her black swirling hole a constant reminder that the body she inhabited was as dead as a doornail. "Ryan hasn't woke up yet, but he will. We've done scans and there's nothing physically wrong with him."

"It's Max you should be worried about," Jill's voice came from my left.

I hadn't even noticed she was there. I turned to her.

I lost my breath.

Max was on the bed to my left, or what was left of Max. He was on life support and looked like he'd been beaten to a pulp. I felt my eyes well up at the sight of him. I couldn't stay in my bed. I ignored Nancy's protests and wobbled over to Max's side. Despite my dizziness I couldn't just lie down while Max was barely alive. Jill was on the other side of the bed, holding his hand. Her eyes were puffy and red from crying. I'd never seen Jill so wrecked before, and it wasn't until that moment that I realized there was a lot more to Max and Jill than I had ever guessed.

"Is he going…?" I couldn't finish the sentence. I didn't need to: I already saw the beginnings of a black hole forming in his chest.

Turner came up from behind me, "We're doing everything we can to save him. Unfortunately, whatever Fortski did to age him so fast is causing complications," he said it with a genuine concern that made me pause. I had only seen glimpses of Turner's humanity in the short time that I knew him. This was one of those moments.

I could hardly speak for the lump in my throat, "What did she do to him?" I choked out.

Turner kept his eyes on Max as he answered, "We found him dead in one of the rooms where you were being held, but we were able to revive him. As far as Elisha knows she killed him. We can use that to our advantage if he recovers."

Business as usual.

I gave Jill a look that I hoped told her I was going to do everything I could to help Max. She barely nodded as she focused all her attention on his still form. Max was so mutilated, it was hard to look at him. Elisha had beat him to death. To death. And remembering how she'd done almost the same thing to her ninety-eight year old twin sister, I really wasn't that shocked. Elisha enjoyed hurting people. It was what made her tick. Maybe knowing that would help me later on.

I turned to Gramps. "We have a lot to talk about."

"Agreed." He eyed me up and down, "Do you need to rest some more?"

He so didn't care if I did or not, but I could tell Roberta had made him ask.

"I'm fine. Can we go back to Nancy's to talk?" I wanted to be someplace where I felt at home, not locked up in a dungeon, even as nice a dungeon as this hospital room was.

Turner looked at me like I was crazy. "You can't go anywhere. The world thinks you're a mass murderer. I pulled every string I had to get you out of police custody."

It all came back to me in a flood of heightened memories: the giant flying piece of metal, the Glass Mall shattering, people dying, me being blamed.

My knees suddenly failed me and I nearly toppled over. Gramps awkwardly caught me with his hand. "Maybe you should rest."

Nancy gently pulled me from Turner's grasp and led me back to bed, where I sat on its edge. She sat down next to me, protectively. "Jason is handling the spin and Bill and his parents are helping. You know his mom, she's using her influence to vouch for you."

My whole body squeezed in guilt. Even after everything I'd put her son through, Bill's mom still wanted to help me. His parents were probably the nicest people on the planet, just like Bill.

Turner pulled up a chair and sat across from me.

So weird.

I could tell he felt just as uncomfortable, but I admired the fact that he was willing to suck it up and have a powwow with me.

"Our scientists are trying to figure out what was in the compounds that Elisha injected you with so we can come up with some kind of vaccine," Turner started the conversation.

Roberta walked over to us, standing behind Gramps. "The fact that you were able to leave your body speaks volumes about your ability. Elisha must have been pretty certain that you wouldn't be able to."

"I think this drug is more specific than that," I said, starting to rationalize out loud. "Elisha knew I'd jumped into Ryan's body, in fact, she yanked me out of it. The drug definitely only works on telepathy, not astral projection."

Turner followed up on my thought. "An actual telepathy-blocker," he said, nodding in agreement. "We've been developing something like that in our labs. Elisha must have perfected it."

Roberta nodded, too, agreeing, then added, "Combined with the loopy-juice she gave you, I'm amazed you had as much control as you did."

Grams was trying to compliment me, but I felt like a complete failure. My memory of what happened was: me acting like a flibberty-jibbet until I ended up passing out.

"Elisha said I was going to have to kill myself. What did she mean by that, do you think?"

I felt Nancy's hand squeeze mine when I said that. "Can't we just kill her?" she grumbled. "I mean seriously? I'll do it. I officially volunteer."

"Nothing would give me more pleasure," Gramps said in such a severe tone that it reminded me of why he used to terrify me so much. It wasn't that long ago that I was on his kill list.

"'Kay," Nancy trailed off, picking up on the lethalness of Turner's intensity.

Roberta answered my question. "The short answer is that we have no idea why Elisha wants you to kill yourself. Revenge? For her own sick pleasure? She used to convince I.Q. kids to kill themselves as sport. We lost fifteen of them to her psychotic nature."

Seriously?

Just when I thought I knew how evil Elisha was, I was hit with a whole new startling discovery.

Ryan suddenly sat up in his bed and started screaming.

We all turned at the sound. I jumped to my wobbly feet and ran over to his side.

"Ryan! Ryan!" I tried to get him to stop screaming. I whirled my head around to Gramps, "What's happening?"

Ryan's screams grew louder.

Turner and Roberta stood there, both looking just as confused as I was.

A doctor ran in. I moved aside to let him do his work.

Just as suddenly, Ryan stopped.

He was awake.

Our eyes met.

Ryan looked like he was scared. "Oh no," he said with such horror it made my fingers and toes tingle with fear.

"What is it?" I barely heard my own whisper.

"I know where the I.Q. kids went."

This had everyone in the room's attention.

Roberta shooed out the doctor as the four of us stood around Ryan's bed, waiting for what we knew would be horrible news. Even Jill stared at him from Max's bedside.

"Where?" I asked, my voice still unnaturally quiet.

"Clones. They went inside the clones of a little boy. There're at least a hundred of them."

Only my grandparents and I knew the true gravity of what Ryan was saying. Elisha had transferred the I.Q. kids into the clones of my father, Franklin Turner.

And they all had my power.

I quickly filled in Ryan, Nancy and Jill about the dad-clones. They looked terrified and sorry for me all at the same time.

The building security alarm went off on cue.

Turner and Roberta were already in strategy-mode. Gramps stared Roberta in the eye. "You are to go to the safe zone. I don't want Elisha controlling you."

"Geoffrey, I can help. No one knows this facility better than me," Roberta argued.

"Precisely my point. You don't think Elisha knows that? It is probably a part of her plan: to control you to get her and the clones out of here." Turner wasn't budging.

"Chelsan can take control of me. She's much stronger than Elisha. I'll be safe, trust me."

Um.

Not feeling exactly the strongest right now. And talk about pressure!

I decided to speak up, "If it was just Elisha, maybe, but what if all the I.Q. kids join her in trying to take over your body. I wouldn't be able to stop all of them working together."

Roberta didn't seem fazed at all by my doubts. "I'm willing to risk it."

"I'm not." Turner's position was unmoving. And I kind of agreed with him. Gramps would do anything to save Roberta if she was in danger. "I'm not going to lose you again," his voice cracked.

Even Jill looked away at that. The only humanizing trait Gramps had was his love for Roberta. I guess it ran in the family from my parents to Ryan and I. When we fall, we fall hard.

In contrast to the loud security alarm, Roberta paused for a few moments of silence. Finally, she nodded, "Fine. I'll stay in touch through Chelsan."

Turner kissed her lovingly on the forehead, then called for a couple of guards. They arrived promptly from outside the hall. "Take my wife to Section D," he ordered.

Before Grams left she turned to me one last time. "Remember, the clones aren't dead, so the transfer won't be like mine. We killed this clone so my essence could take over the body completely. The I.Q. kids are going to be sharing their existence with the Franklin clones. Maybe we can use that to our advantage." She turned to Gramps and kissed him gently on the lips. "Be careful. I love you."

Turner hugged her desperately. "I love you."

Then she was gone, out of the room and off to Section D, wherever that was.

Ryan started to get out of bed, but I pushed him down. "No. You're getting your rest."

Ryan removed my hand from his chest, firmly but not in a mean way, and I could see he was determined. "I'm obviously still connected to these kids or adult-kids or whatever," he said. "When they entered into the clones, I felt it surge through every nerve of my body. They're not in my head anymore, but I'm still bound to them somehow. If you can reach the part of the clones that's your dad and if I can reach the part of them that's from the Farm… maybe we can stop them from doing whatever it is Elisha is going to command them to do."

"He's right," Turner agreed, ordering sharply, "Let's go. We're losing time." Gramps apparently didn't care if Ryan might get hurt. I guess I couldn't blame him, though: the clones were active and trying to escape.

We had to act fast.

I nodded and helped Ryan to his feet.

I turned to Nancy and Jill. "You guys watch over Max. We'll leave a team of soldiers here with you."

Nancy looked like she was about to argue, but thought better against it. She simply nodded and sat across from Jill on the other side of Max.

"Lead the way." I put my hand out for Gramps to take us to the clones.

Turner walked out the door and, with Ryan and I trailing behind, navigated our way through the giant labyrinthine infrastructure that was Population Control. No one seemed too alarmed by the alarm. Apparently, if you didn't have direct orders from Gramps to actually do something about it, the standing order was "Business as usual."

The hallways were as eclectically designed as the whole complex. In some parts it felt like you were in an office building with generic holo-paintings and white walls and in the next you were in a modern art museum of minimalist holo-sculptures and striped wallpaper.

"We need Isabelle," Gramps said on the move, apparently deciding to let us in on what was going on inside his brain. "She's the only one who can kill that little brat."

Ryan's hand was firmly wrapped in mine as we followed Turner in silence. Gramps was probably right, but I didn't like talking about killing anyone. Even Elisha.

I shook the thought from my head. It was making me ill and I needed to have all my wits about me if we were going to stop the I.Q. kids/clones from escaping. It was almost funny in a way. The I.Q. kids had to escape from this same building five months ago and now they were back in here, having to do the same thing over again.

After a few more twists and turns through the building Turner led us into the same room I saw when I astral-projected to Roberta. Isabelle and Harry were both standing with their two other partners, Terence and Dean. They were all in a huddle, like they were already planning their own escape. I guess with the security alarm sounding off they figured it was a good time to bail.

Harry practically snarled when he saw Turner enter.

Gramps didn't even acknowledge him, though, motioning instead to Isabelle, "You. I need you."

Isabelle crossed her arms defiantly while Harry and the other two moved protectively in front of her.

"You can't have her." Harry stood in the way, forcing Turner to make eye contact with him.

"If Elisha accomplishes her goal, it will be on your head." Gramps was livid.

"What do we care if she steals something from you? We're staying out of it." Harry wasn't backing down.

Turner wasn't fazed at all. "You may hate my methods, Harry, but you at least know that population control is a necessity to survive. People have to die."

That pissed me off.

I didn't care if it was true. My mother and everyone in my trailer park died because Turner was "controlling the population." It was wrong and there had to be another way. I forgot sometimes that my grandfather killed with no remorse. He even looked proud. It made me want to throw up.

Right now, though, Elisha was worse. I didn't even want to think about what she and the I.Q. kids/Franklins were going to do if they escaped.

I needed to step in before Harry and Gramps got into a fistfight.

Apparently Isabelle had the same thought, because she beat me to it. She placed a restraining hand on Harry's shoulder. "We'll deal with Geoffrey later. Right now we need to stop Elisha. She killed Charlie. She would've killed the rest of us." Isabelle nodded to Terence and Dean. Then she focused on Gramps. "What's happening?"

Turner couldn't hide the triumphant smirk on his face and it looked like Harry was going to tackle him despite Isabelle's plea. But he obviously thought better of it and turned his full attention to Turner.

Gramps filled them in on what Elisha was trying to pull off.

"I have confirmation that she is in the building and I want Isabelle to kill her," Turner finished.

To my shock, Harry's little crew were all nodding in agreement, like an assassination order was the most normal thing in the world. Then I realized: to them, it probably was. Isabelle was a killer after all. And apparently so were Terence and Dean. It made me wonder…

"And what are your special skills?" I asked on a whim. They'd either shut me down or confirm my suspicions.

I was shocked again when Dean very openly said, "I can blend into any wall and he has true aim." I didn't exactly know what *true aim* was, but it wasn't hard to figure out. And blend into any wall??? I wanted to see!

Dean's dark brown eyes bore into me. I felt uncomfortable under his gaze. He was pretty cute as far as *soldier boys* go, what with the shaved head, being super-ripped, and a bone structure that could cut glass. Everything about him was intimidating. I couldn't imagine how Dean could blend in anywhere.

Terence was a little less intimidating, but only because his demeanor was a lot more laid back. He was just as ripped as Dean, but his shaved head was grown out slightly. From the little hair that was showing, Terence was blonde, his eyelashes practically disappearing on his face they were so light colored with eyebrows to match. Add that to his five o'clock shadow and it gave him an overall scruff that made him pretty cute too.

Terence's baby blues were focused on Turner at the moment. "I need a sniper rifle."

Gramps was already barking orders into the holo-com wall.

Everything was moving way too fast.

"Hold up!" I found myself shouting.

All eyes bore down on me.

Um.

The gentle squeeze of Ryan's supportive hand gave me the added confidence I needed.

"I know you are all in kill, kill, kill mode, but shouldn't we talk about this? Elisha should be imprisoned, not killed. You kept her locked up for how many years? A hundred? You didn't seem to have a problem keeping her in this very building back then?" I just couldn't justify murder, even if I felt like murdering her myself.

"Elisha and the I.Q. kids didn't have your powers last time and if you don't remember more than half my army is dead. So no, she will die and so will the clones." Gramps had made up his mind and I knew nothing I said would stop him.

A second security alarm went off making the blaring even more obnoxious as both sounds competed for which one could be the most annoying.

Turner looked at Harry. They were on the same page. "The clones have broken through the second security level."

Harry nodded. "How many levels?"

"Five," Turner confirmed.

"Let's do this." Isabelle took control and Gramps led the way out of the room and back into the hallway.

I let all the crazy people go first, then Ryan and I took up the rear.

We met a group of Turner's dead soldiers along the way who armed Harry and Dean with several hand guns and gave Terence a ginormous rifle with a holo-scope sight. I felt like peeing my pants seeing all those guns, but I kept my mouth shut. Apparently, Isabelle had no use for a weapon, seeing as she could stop a beating heart with her mind! Yeah.

Although we'd started out in the rear, Dean dropped back and made Ryan and I stay in front of him. I guess we were the weak ones of the group. Ryan didn't seem to mind, but I felt a bit shafted. Elisha and the I.Q. kid/clones having my powers really sucked. It made me feel rather useless.

I glanced over my shoulder to see how far back Dean was trailing, and I nearly jumped when he wasn't there.

I called out to Gramps, "Dean's gone!"

"I'm right here," Dean's voice was right next to my ear.

He suddenly materialized inches away from me.

Whoa.

"Keep moving," Dean ordered quietly.

I think my eyes were stuck in permanent "wide" mode. Fortunately, Ryan recovered first and led me forward to stay with the group. I couldn't help myself. I looked behind me, checking. Sure enough, I couldn't see Dean. Dang. I almost wished I could swap powers with him. I'd much rather be able to disappear than to…I don't know… deal with dead things all the time!

I started thinking about how many Dad clones there were. I never did find out the exact number. All I knew was that more people than

I cared to admit now had a power like mine, and they were all evil. I didn't want to think about what they'd do with that power. The question was: what was Turner going to do with the clones? Kill them? I couldn't bear to think of destroying what essentially was my father. Logically, of course, I knew the clones weren't him, but they were made from him. From his DNA, from his cells. For all intents and purposes, they were all my dad. But if Roberta thought they were *wrong* before, now with the I.Q. kids consciences planted inside them…

I shuddered.

"Up here," Gramps announced and pointed to our destination: the largest metal door I'd ever seen.

This thing was huge, and I mean HUGE. I couldn't even believe that a door this size would fit inside a building. The hallway we were just in looked distorted like it grew at its end to encompass the enormous door. It was at least a hundred feet tall and fifty feet wide. It was like someone had an enlargement machine and just hit the door itself by accident. The surface was completely smooth. There wasn't even a doorknob or latch so I assumed it was a pressurized door that would open when Turner typed in the combination. I couldn't for the life of me guess why Turner chose this particular design, but I was positive he had a reason. Psychos usually did.

"This thing crytonsteel?" Harry looked awed.

Gramps nodded. "Smallest piece I could get for level two. The walls of this level and the whole subbasement are made of the stuff."

Crytonsteel? What the…? Apparently this was impressive because even Isabelle and Terence looked amazed. I really couldn't tell if Dean gave a crap since he was invisible!

Then I noticed Ryan's awestruck face and I really felt left out. I must have looked like a kicked puppy because Ryan melted when he glanced down at me. "Don't feel bad, crytonsteel is more of a science myth than reality. Most people have never even heard of it. I just can't believe it exists."

Turner motioned for Dean to come over to him. Dean materialized and walked to Gramps's side. I really didn't think I could get used to that.

Ryan explained further, "It can't break. It can't be cut. It can't be melted. It can't be shaped. Basically, what you find is what you get."

"And it's found in perfectly shaped walls?" My sarcasm was intended to make up for me feeling stupid.

Turner spoke at that remark. "No, you silly twat, it isn't shaped like a wall. If you'll notice the door frame surrounds the metal not the other way around."

Oh.

Now that he mentioned it, it really wasn't much of a door after all. He was right, the regular door frame and plaster walls made a perfect rectangle around the metal.

I hated to state the obvious but, "How do we open it?"

Gramps didn't answer, he just groaned at my apparent stupidity.

Isabelle shot me a supportive smile, which I appreciated, but it was amazing how a man I despised could actually make me feel dumb.

Ryan explained further (in a really nice non-condescending way, not like my a-hole grandpa) "That's what makes this metal a myth. If you know the right frequency, supposedly you can walk right through it."

"Elisha already broke through the first barrier," Turner addressed the group, "She's obviously figured out how to hack the frequencies. We have to stop her here before she and the others break through. The crytonsteel surrounds the entire second level and it's our last defense. If they get past here, it'll be near impossible to stop her."

"Why didn't you just make the whole building out of this stuff?" I asked and immediately wished I hadn't.

Gramps just looked at me like I was a fly he wanted to swat. "It's a little hard to come by as you might suspect."

I restrained myself from imitating him with my *mocking face*, and decided to keep my mouth shut.

Turner ignored me and spoke to Dean, "Here's the frequency code, type it in here and you should be able to enter. Strictly re-con."

Dean nodded. He opened up the holo-com next to the doorway and punched in the code that Turner recited for him. The metal rippled outward like it was a wall of water that someone had dropped a stone into its center. A second later Dean disappeared. I couldn't tell if he was "blending" or if he had walked through the metal. Probably both.

I looked up at Ryan and he was practically salivating at seeing this crytonsteel in action. My adorably nerdy boyfriend. Sigh.

A few moments later Dean re-emerged from the wall.

"There are at least a hundred and they're all huddled in a group," he informed us. "None of them have weapons. Easy pickings. Elisha's with them, chanting something in some other language."

"That's Roberta's domain," Isabelle added.

I had to keep reminding myself that Harry, Isabelle and probably Dean and Terence had known my grandparents for three hundred years. From the way Isabelle talked, though, it seemed like she didn't have any clue that Gramps was a voodoo man himself. Maybe he'd kept that part of himself hidden from them, or maybe it was something Roberta got him into later. Either way, Turner wasn't volunteering that he was an expert. It made me realize just how long Roberta had been doing her mojo black magic. Three hundred years. It gave me a little extra confidence, since Elisha was only a hundred. Then I remembered that Roberta wasn't here and I suddenly felt the noose tightening again.

"Roberta will be monitoring the situation." Gramps eyed me knowingly. (Guess that meant me.) I nodded to Turner and let my mental wall down long enough for Roberta to connect with me.

I'm here. I heard Roberta's voice in my head. I told her everything that I knew. *I can hear and see through you, just make sure Geoffrey is safe.*

Yeah, my first priority. I didn't say that of course. I just kind of nodded internally and Roberta seemed fine with that. There was no way she didn't know how I felt about them, *him* more than her, but only because Roberta had proven an ally more often than not. She was a little delusional, though, I seriously think that she believed when all this Elisha business was over and done with that we'd all be one big happy family. I didn't want to be the bearer of bad news, but that was never going to happen.

Turner started to give orders. "We're going in and we're going in fast. Terence you'll stay against the wall and take down as many as you can. Isabelle, you'll concentrate on Elisha, she'll have some kind of protection spell barrier around her so bullets won't harm her, but you should be able to break through that."

I could tell Isabelle didn't put much credence in the words *protection spell.* Even with her own innate powers, the girl did not believe in rituals or spells. I wouldn't have either if I hadn't experienced it first hand. Hello?! How I got my powers in the first place! Though you'd think watching Turner inhabit a shredded corpse would be a serious clue about the reality of black magic, but I think she thought that was all me and my power. How do you convince someone that doesn't want to be convinced? Headache!

Turner continued, "Dean, you'll take position on the upper level balcony and shoot down from above. They won't see you so you'll have the best cover."

Then Gramps walked directly over to me and Ryan. He placed his hand on my shoulder so we were eye to eye. Intense. "Do not let Elisha into your brain. I don't want to give her any access to Roberta. You hear me?"

"I won't," I kind of stuttered out. Pressure much? Besides, the last thing I wanted in the world was Elisha in my head! Seriously!

Don't listen to him, you'll be fine. I heard Roberta try and comfort me. Oy.

Gramps turned his attention to Ryan. "Listen to me very carefully: when the I.Q. kids were stuck in your head, you were the one who kept them there. *You.* You were controlling them. Any time you had a migraine or seizure was when they were trying to escape. All Elisha did was relax your defenses enough for them to leave your head. Do you know what that means?"

Ryan looked shell-shocked, but he nodded. "I can connect to them."

"Yes. I'm not sure how, but once we're in there, do everything you can to communicate with them." Gramps was looking at Ryan like he was his son, overprotective and concerned.

With me he kind of grimaced. Strangely enough, it seemed kind of affectionate.

Turner faced the assassin squad. "We ready?"

The group of four locked and loaded their guns in response.

Guess so.

"Everyone stand in a line against the wall," Gramps ordered.

We all obeyed, Ryan and I the only ones holding hands. Ryan was beside himself with worry, but I could tell he was excited to try out this crytonsteel experience too.

Turner continued, "Once we're inside I'm locking down the exit, so

Elisha can't control any of you to aid her escape plan. Isabelle, take Elisha out fast. Harry, Dean, Terence, shoot until you're out of bullets," Gramps said cold-heartedly.

I had to admit it, I couldn't stomach what was about to happen. We were going to walk through that door and hundreds of my dad were going to be slaughtered. It was making my heart race.

Calm down, Roberta's voice tried to soothe my fears, *If you had spent the years Geoffrey and I have with these clones the decision wouldn't be as difficult. They aren't Franklin, they're evil. Worse than Elisha. No emotion. No souls. The worst of humanity because they aren't human.*

I couldn't believe her. They were made from my genes. They were a part of me.

We kept them alive in the hopes that we'd be able to fix them some day. But they aren't fixable, Chelsan. You know I would never agree to kill them if I thought there was an ounce of my Franklin inside them.

I heard her, and I knew she was right, but seeing my father... I'd never met him. I wanted desperately to know him and not just in other people's memories. I wanted my own memories of him. Maybe if we could just keep one of them alive. Maybe we could fix him and let him grow up and I'd have my dad. I knew I shouldn't be thinking about all this right before...well...battle, but I couldn't help it. I'd lost my mom and now I had a chance to get my dad back. Sort of.

"Now!" Turner commanded and we all stepped forward.

It was the weirdest sensation I'd ever experienced, like walking into a cold waterfall where the water was a thick paste. I was too scared to breathe for fear of sucking up a nose full of metal. But I soon realized that, even though the metal was fluid, it was solid as well, shifting itself to let us pass while caressing us at the same time. I found myself shivering from the feeling, exhilarated just from the pure absurdity of it all.

And just as quickly, we were in the cloning room. Over a hundred open modules in perfect rows spread out in front of us. Above us a metal-framed catwalk surrounded the entire room. All four walls were crytonsteel.

It was the noise that caught my attention first.

In the center of the room were at least a hundred children, all the same child, my dad, humming a yoga-like chant, their high-pitched voices a reminder of the age Turner forced them to stay at with Age-pro. In their center was Elisha. She was definitely speaking a different language, maybe Latin or some kind of Creole. There was serious mojo going on.

Upon seeing all the clones of my father, I nearly froze. I could feel the lump in my throat getting bigger. Dad. They were him. All of them. In front of me. Real. Not just a vision or a conversation, but real. I didn't want them dead. I just wanted them not to be psychotic. Was that too much to ask?

The seven of us stood out like sore thumbs, but Elisha and the clones didn't seem to notice. Or care. Elisha concentrated on whatever spell she was trying to perform.

Time to mess her up.

"Hey!" I yelled before I could think better of it.

Elisha didn't stop her chanting, but she looked up and made eye contact with me.

And she smiled.

Uh oh.

Elisha smiling was never a good thing.

It meant she wasn't surprised.

Then she stopped.

"It's about time you showed up. We've been waiting for you," Elisha chuckled.

I hated it when she did that.

Gunfire everywhere.

Dean had already disappeared, probably on his way up to the catwalk, while Harry and Terence aimed and fired at all the clones.

Their bullets hit harmlessly on… on air.

Elisha had created some kind of invisible force field surrounding them all.

Turner's little mini-army stopped firing.

All the Franklins turned to us at the exact same time.

So creepy.

The I.Q. kids/clones stopped humming. With faces identical to my father, Franklin, they stared at us like we were cockroaches waiting to be squashed.

Isabelle dropped to the floor, holding her chest. "Some kind of feedback loop. I almost stopped my own heart," she gasped. A few seconds later she recovered, but was still catching her breath as she stood up.

"Nice trick, huh?" Elisha was positively beaming.

I really hated that.

Elisha looked at me, her eyes were alight, "I was afraid I'd lost you. Eva has been properly punished for failing me, but it looks like your grandpa has delivered you to me with a bow on top."

Gramps had apparently had enough, "You still can't get past the crytonsteel, you little brat."

Elisha returned his gaze. "Can't I?"

Gulp.

Elisha clapped her hands.

WHOOOOOMP!

The room shook with such force that our little group fell to our knees.

Elisha and the clones remained unfazed, the bubble she'd surrounded them with protecting them from everything.

I looked behind me and saw the walls of crytonsteel rippling like crazy. The metal was giving off a sound that made me think the whole room was going to explode.

"What have you done?" Gramps actually looked scared.

Harry did the only thing he knew how to do: he started firing his gun at Elisha.

When he ran out of bullets and she was still unharmed, he turned to his team.

"Let's get out of here," he ordered.

Elisha's grin grew even bigger, if that were possible. "I wouldn't do that if I were you, Harry."

Harry stopped, not a man to ignore a psychopath.

"There's no way out, only in," Elisha said cryptically.

Huh?

Why would she trap herself and the clones inside? Wasn't their goal to…I don't know… escape!

I searched for anything dead. I know, Elisha and the clones had my same power, but searching for potential weapons was somehow a comfort for me. I'd overpowered Elisha and Eva before maybe I could overpower these reject clones and her if I concentrated hard enough.

Nothing.

When Elisha could tell that none of us had figured out what she was up to, she looked me directly in the eye. "Haven't you been wondering why you haven't heard a peep out of your dear old Grams since you walked in here?"

Double gulp.

Turner snapped. He launched himself at the invisible barrier only to be shot back with enough force to slam him into Terence. The two of them fell to the ground, almost hitting the crytonsteel wall behind them. The metal's ripples were moving faster and faster, the vibrating noise growing louder and louder. We were either going to be sucked in and swallowed alive by living metal, or trapped inside this chamber forever.

Roberta! I screamed in my head, but I knew Elisha was right. Something had happened and I'd been too distracted to notice.

From the opposite wall of where we were standing Roberta walked into the room followed by a small army of dead soldiers. As soon as they entered, the walls stopped rippling and the noise stopped.

Elisha smirked at Gramps. "As long as she's within the four mile radius, right Turner? Not even your protective metals and spells can keep your precious wife from my control."

Roberta's eyes were screaming for help, but her body was being controlled by Elisha.

"Do something!" Gramps screamed at me.

"I'm trying!" I yelled back.

I squeezed my little brain as hard as I could, but there were two hundred clones all with my power controlling Roberta and the dead army. I just couldn't break through. It was like a giant wall of cryptocrap blocking me from using my ability.

The Franklins parted, making way for Roberta to walk to Elisha's side. The dead army stood in formation at the far wall.

"They're not protected! Fire!" Harry ordered.

Harry and Terence all fired at the dead soldiers.

Really? They still didn't believe it? Even after everything they'd witnessed?

"They're dead, you morons!" Turner shouted, so enraged that I instinctively stepped in front of Ryan. If he was going to attack, I'd rather it be me than my boyfriend.

Isabelle flashed me a look that said she had my back, which both surprised and comforted me. I figured with everything that was happening, she was finally starting to trust me and everything I had told her.

When the dead soldiers just stood there with their newly Swiss-cheesed bodies, it finally clicked in Harry's brain. "I just can't believe it."

Gramps ignored Harry and focused on Elisha. "I'll give you whatever you want, just let Roberta go."

His Achilles heel. My Grams.

"Exactly the words I wanted to hear." Elisha grinned, Roberta at her side. "We want out."

Turner stood there staring at Roberta, conflicted.

"You can't!" Isabelle protested to Gramps. "Elisha will kill millions with her army. It's not worth one life. Roberta would agree."

I didn't know about that.

"No she wouldn't," Turner pretty much confirmed what I knew. My grandparents were possibly the biggest self-preservationists I had ever met. Roberta was in a dead body for goodness sake…

Wait a minute…

"You can't kill someone who is already dead," I said as if I was the smartest person in the world.

Elisha couldn't resist making me feel like a buffoon. "Of course not, but I can rip out their soul, isn't that right, Turner?"

Could she do that?

Then I remembered how Elisha had ripped out the I.Q. kids from Ryan's brain. But that was with the computer. Wasn't it?

From the expression on Turner's face, I knew what the answer was: Elisha could absolutely do *that*.

"No ritual could save her then, could it, Turner? Your precious Roberta would be dead forever." Elisha was having way too much fun.

"Get ready," Ryan whispered to me.

I looked up at him. His face was so intense I almost let go of his hand. "Ready for what?" I whispered back.

Ryan didn't answer. He was concentrating too hard, so I had to assume it had something to do with the clones. If he could distract them long enough for me to get a hold of Roberta and the dead army, maybe we could win here.

Ryan must have been doing something because I started to feel myself able to tug at their collective grip on Grams. Elisha's grin showed that she sensed nothing, but that wouldn't last the harder I tried to gain control.

Gramps wasn't about to risk losing Roberta a second time. "I'll have you escorted out of the building. I assume you have transportation?"

"Of course. They'll be waiting at the north east corner in about ten minutes." Elisha was so cocky, it made me want to punch her.

Come on Ryan, do your thing.

The clones' hold on Roberta and the dead army was definitely weakening. A little more and I was in.

CLICK.

Dean materialized directly behind Elisha and cocked his gun to her head.

Yes! Go Dean.

Elisha's face dropped.

Finally! Someone took this girl off guard!

Dean wrapped his arm around Elisha's throat and kept his gun pressed against her forehead.

"What are you waiting for? Shoot her!" Gramps barked.

Elisha looked scared for the first time. Really scared.

Before Dean could pull the trigger all of the dead army raised their guns and started firing.

Elisha was faster than I imagined as she reached down and squeezed Dean in the you-know-what. Ouch. And then she ran, escaping into the crowd of Franklins.

"Now!" Ryan shouted over the gunfire.

SLAM!

I connected to all of the dead army and made them stop shooting. More importantly, I connected to Roberta and made her push her way through the clones to Turner's side. I kept my grip on her, but allowed her to move and act on her own. She embraced Gramps and the poor sap actually looked like a teddy bear when he hugged her back. If I didn't know them I'd say it was adorable.

"I'm losing them," Ryan informed me. I began to feel my grip slipping away.

Dean shoved Franklin clones aside like rag dolls trying to get an aim on Elisha, but she was keeping her head down.

Where did she think she was going? This was one room, she was done for.

BOOM!

The walls rippled again frantically and the vibrating noise became deafening.

One more trick, little one. That was Elisha's voice! How did she get in my head?!

CRACK!

The whole room felt like it was caving in on itself. The noise was too loud. I covered my ears, but nothing could stop the pounding. I was losing consciousness.

Ryan dropped next to me.

When he went down so did my control over the army and Roberta.

I fell to my knees.

The pounding was making my bones rattle.

Gramps dropped, then Harry.

I tried to crawl to Roberta, but she went down as well.

Dean grabbed Terence and Isabelle and the three of them disappeared completely. I couldn't tell if Dean somehow used his powers to hide them from Elisha, or if he actually pulled them through the crytonsteel. Either way, they were gone.

A part of me wanted to be knocked out so I wouldn't have to be tortured by the raucous noise that threatened to deafen me permanently.

I realized then that none of the clones were affected by the sound. They all just stood there, staring…

…At me.

My arms buckled and I fell flat on my chest.

I could barely lift my head as I saw Elisha slowly walk up to me, smiling and unfazed by the chaotic noise.

"You're mine now," Elisha said.

Everything went black.

CHAPTER 5
FRIDAY APRIL 8, 2321

Ouch.

I opened my eyes to try and figure out why my whole body was in agonizing pain.

Oh.

Wrists tied together with chains.

That's why.

Oh, and I was hanging from a meat hook while my ankles were being pulled by another set of chains attached to the ground.

I felt like a giant rubber band being stretched as far as I could go except for the fact that I wasn't made of rubber. I had no idea how long I'd been hanging there. It must have been long, though, because I couldn't feel my fingers. It reminded me of when I'd sleep with my arm above my head and then wake up in the middle of the night frantic because my whole arm had fallen asleep. Only this time it was both arms and I had no way to return the circulation. Everything ached. My head hurt.

And I was captured. Again.

I surveyed my surroundings, trying to get a feel for where I was this time. It was dark, lit a kind of reddish hue that made the whole room feel even more creepy than it already was (if that were possible). The walls and floors looked wet, as if the place had just been hosed down. There were about five rows of meat hooks running parallel to each other across the entire eight-foot ceiling.

I was in the center row middle with nothing else hanging from the hooks. The walls and floors were cement, but more of a gravelly cement, lots of uneven footing and rocks. The room itself was huge, well over two hundred square feet. So much room for little old me. At least I wasn't in a coffin! Small favors.

I searched for anything dead. But I knew Elisha would have prepared this place. Like I thought: nothing. Not even dust. The sounds of air-sucking machines told me that Elisha had made sure that I didn't have that particular weapon to work with.

Next best thing…

Roberta? I called out in my brain.

Nothing.

I wondered if she was okay or if she was even alive. Before I'd passed out, Ryan, Roberta, Gramps and Harry were all spread out unconscious just like me. Elisha could have taken us all. Only Isabelle, Dean and Terence had escaped. I couldn't blame Dean for only taking his two comrades. Elisha would have had no hesitation about killing the three of them instantly so she could control them as dead people and use their powers for her own gain. I just wished Dean would have grabbed Ryan too. I'd feel a lot better if I knew Ryan was okay.

The sound of a creaking metal door filled the air, making me flinch. The door was behind me so I could only hear the footsteps walking toward me.

Oh joy.

It was Eva.

She smiled up at me as happy as I'd ever seen her. Eva really hated me.

I almost felt a pang of sympathy for the girl when I saw exactly how Elisha had punished her for my escape. Eva's body was covered in bruises and stitches. Even her beautiful face was black and blue. The fact that this girl was still loyal to Elisha blew my mind, but maybe it was loyalty out of fear. If so, I could use that.

"What happened to you?" I asked, pretending I didn't know.

Eva self-consciously touched her bruised cheek. "None of your business," she spat.

"Are you going to get me down from here?" Thought I'd ask. Ha, ha.

Eva smirked. "Yeah, right. You're going to look a lot worse than me when Elisha is done with you."

"You mean like Max?" I had to say it. I had to see if Eva knew.

She did. Eva's face crumpled. Max was a soft spot for her and she thought he was dead. Her sadness quickly turned to raging hatred, her eyes practically on fire as she tried to stare me down. "Max's death was your fault! If you hadn't hypnotized him into helping you Elisha wouldn't have had to kill him!"

"Hypnotized? Max helped me because he knew it was the right thing to do." I knew trying to reason with Eva was useless, but I had to try. Maybe if I could convince her…

"The right thing? He's dead. The only thing that gives me any kind of peace of mind is the fact that you'll be dead too before this day is over. Max will be avenged." Eva meant it.

"Elisha killed Max, not me. You're mad at the wrong girl." At that point I knew I couldn't break through to Eva. All I could do was plant a few seeds of doubt and hope that they'd grow. "Why are you here anyway?"

Eva lit up at that question. Uh oh. "To help."

Help?

Gulp.

Was Elisha really going to beat the crap out of me? To what end? For fun?

Then I remembered Elisha said I needed to kill myself. How was killing me, killing myself? Nothing was making sing sense.

That same creaking door and the new footsteps that followed made my heart jump.

Here we go.

Elisha's annoyingly beautiful face came into view as she stepped around to the front of my hanging body. Wearing a tight sweater and jeans, with her long black hair perfectly in place, made the moment as surreal as it could get. Her giant purple eyes stared up at me.

"How are those arms?" she asked, knowing full well how my arms were doing.

"Great," I responded heartily. I hated her so much. My freaking arms were on fire!

"I see, tough girl, huh?" Elisha seemed more amused than annoyed like I wanted to provoke her to be.

SLASH!

I screamed.

Elisha pulled back the small knife she'd been hiding with her hand. I could feel the blood dripping from my thigh from the shallow wound Elisha had just made. Not enough to kill me, but it seriously hurt.

"Eva." Elisha nodded to the thrilled Eva.

Eva took out a small pouch from her pocket and rubbed some kind of paste on the fresh cut.

I screamed again. The pain was even worse that the cut itself.

"The salve will keep you from bleeding out, but it's designed to extract as much pain as the body can take. Get comfy, dear, we're going to be here a while." Elisha looked both businesslike and elated at the same time.

The pain was searing. I tried to focus on something else, anything else, but when your leg feels like it is literally going to fall off, it was hard to think of anything but the pain.

SLASH!

I bit my lip, not wanting to give Elisha the satisfaction of screaming again, but tears came to my eyes against my will. She had cut my other thigh, this time at least seven inches long and deeper than before. I felt like my muscles were going to spill out onto the floor. I wanted to cry like a baby it hurt so badly. I just wanted it to stop.

Then Eva was there pasting on that damn cream. It was like she had taken a match and lit my leg on fire. I felt the sweat pouring down my face.

SLASH!

My shin.

I heard myself scream, but I had no control over it. Then the fire cream. My vision was blurring. I couldn't see straight. My brain felt more muddled than it did when I was given the drugs.

…wait a minute…

My brain clung to the only lifeline I could think of. Getting out of my body.

SLASH!

The other shin.

My voice was already hoarse from screaming. I could feel my throat getting raw and tingly as I couldn't seem to stop myself from yelling. Crying out was the only release I had.

The salve.

Then suddenly I didn't feel any pain.

I was staring down at myself like I had before when Elisha had injected me with the drugs.

I was outside of my body.

I wanted to cry from relief.

I had never felt so much pain before in my life. Emotional pain yes, even psychological pain, but this kind of physical pain was nothing like I'd ever experienced.

"She'll be grabbing you back soon," I heard a voice say beside me.

My astral self turned around to see Max floating behind me.

"Max! What are you doing here? You're not…" I didn't want to say dead, but it was the first thing that came to my brain. He kind of looked like a ghost and I'd never seen anyone floating around in astral space before. Usually I'd just see strings of light that would draw me to certain people, namely, Grams. Seeing a hovering Max made my brain jump to conclusions.

Max smiled, "Dead? No, but I'm in a coma back at Turner's. Jill's with me," he said and I couldn't help but grin. Even through all this crap, dying and coming back to life, Max still cared more about Jill. He was a keeper.

Pain. Excruciating pain! I was slammed back in my body and I screeched in response. What happened?!

"Cheating again, little one?" Elisha snarled. "What would be the purpose of me torturing you if I let you jump out of your body?"

I couldn't even think about responding to her. She had made three new cuts. One on the inner thigh and two on my ankle. I gasped for breath the pain was so intense. My eyes felt crossed. I could feel the drool falling from my mouth involuntarily.

"Grab my hand," Max's voice sounded like music against the shredded backdrop of my screaming.

My head lolled up.

I could see Max. Floating above me with his hand outstretched.

Elisha and Eva had no idea. They were so focused on slashing and salving that they couldn't see him.

My arms were dead, but I tried to pull my astral self out.

I was too weak.

"I can't," I muttered.

Elisha thought I was talking to her. "Ready to give up so soon? I thought I'd at least have a few days of this." She walked up to me so she could stare into my eyes. "Are you ready to kill yourself?"

I needed to know her plan. The throbbing of every wound on my body was unbearable. I managed to say, "Why?"

"There was one missing ingredient in the spell that transferred your father's power into you: he killed himself." Elisha actually was angry, her face kind of scrunched up. I didn't care. As long as she was talking she wasn't cutting. You'd be amazed at how much of blessing that was.

"But… you have my powers." Elisha did have my powers already, gained by performing the ritual and killing one of the babies from Havenville. After reciting the spell that my father had performed on me, Elisha had walked away possessed with my ability to control the dead.

Then I remembered the connections I had made earlier that didn't make sense at the time…

Turner never realized the full extent of my powers because he had only tested the clones. They were copies. Maybe since Elisha received her powers through me using the twins and not directly…

I knew I was growing closer to the truth, I just needed more information.

Elisha screamed in fury and slashed under my arm.

Even though it was numb I still felt the excruciating sting as the knife sliced through skin.

Eva quickly applied the paste and my body tensed in pain, and I howled from agony.

"I can't do everything that you can! I have the echo of your powers, we all do! It's like a copy of a copy, but you… you're the source and I need you to kill yourself while I perform the ritual again!" Elisha yelled in my face. She was losing it.

Even through my pain the gravity of what she'd just admitted to me sunk in. I was right. Elisha wasn't as strong as me. Her powers were weaker. Diluted. How did she even know that, when I didn't even know the scope of my powers? The more I thought about it, the more it made me wonder what I could do. Mainly, what I could do to get out of this torture chamber!

SLASH!

I felt the knife's edge cut deep into my calf.

My screams were throaty and gravelly now. I couldn't take much more of this.

Eva spread the lotion on the cut. I slumped my head. I was going numb with the pain.

I felt a hand pulling me out of my body. It was blessed release. As soon as my incorporeal form left my body behind, I felt the instant sensation of intense relief.

Max held my hands in his as we floated above the disturbing scene of Elisha destroying my body.

"I don't think I can recover from that," I said to Max as Elisha sliced the back of my heel. I was so grateful I didn't have to feel that, but terrified that she'd drag me back down into my body so I'd have to.

"You will recover and I will too, but we need Fortski's help." Max started to pull me away from the scene. "You have to hold on to me. She can't pull you back in as long as you're tied to me."

I wasn't so sure. "But I was inside Ryan's brain and she ripped me out of there."

Max looked at me and I felt instantly reassured. "It's not the same thing. Elisha doesn't know everything, even though she likes to think she does." Max pulled me further toward the wall. "I'm taking you to Fortski, just don't let go of me."

He didn't need to tell me twice. There was no way I was going to let go of Max, not if it meant I'd have to feel the pain again.

As we traveled through the cement wall I could hear screaming. I was pleased to recognize that it was Elisha, frustrated and in a rage. She had obviously tried to pull me back and couldn't. Max was right. The part that made me happiest though was the fact that she thought I'd done it myself. The more powerful Elisha thought I was, the better.

On the other end of the compound was a completely white room. Definitely a lab of some sort. Rows of pristine tables filled with glass beakers and Bunsen burners boiling crazy concoctions; it looked like a really expensive version of the chemistry lab at school. There were several scientists busy at work, entering notes in their computers while experimenting with their potions.

"Fortski is over there." Max nodded toward the famous man himself.

John Fortski. Inventor of Age-pro and pretty much the most famous man alive. He was old, like Turner, probably about fifty-something. He almost had no hair, just grey wisps on the sides of his head. Fortski had small furtive features that made him look like a mouse. He was using an eyedropper to put some kind of liquid into a beaker.

"How's Fortski going to help me?" I asked. I mean it was cool and all to meet the man, but I didn't see this guy as being the hero type.

"He's going to help us." Max turned to me. "He's developed a formula that will heal all wounds instantly no matter how severe. Elisha is going to keep it hidden from the public and only use it for herself and whoever she sees fit."

Just like Ms. Floster let slip in class. The universal wound healer. This was the invention that Fortski had been working on three hundred years ago when her dad worked at his lab. He had actually done it!

If the public ever heard about this, they'd go nuts. People lived a certain protected way because taking Age-pro meant you could live forever, but you were still susceptible to dying by other means. If Fortski had invented a new drug that could heal any wound, then it would be a lot harder to die. Like Ms. Floster had said, the only way you could actually die was if it was instant, like a shot to the brain. She specifically said that the drug couldn't bring you back from the dead. So, we just had to decapitate Elisha and we'd be all good. Uh, huh.

"There's only one prototype and Fortski carries it in a secret place at all times. He's told Elisha that it's not quite done yet, but he's lying. He wants to escape. He wants her dead like the rest of us." Max really wanted to kill Elisha, I could see it in his eyes. Or in his ghosty eyes anyway.

Knowing that Fortski had a formula that could cure Max and I of all our wounds made me want to jump inside his head, control his body…

…control his body.

Could I do that? I knew Elisha could. She had controlled Max quite thoroughly.

I turned to Max. "Max, do you think we could do what Elisha did and control a live body?"

"Elisha can't really control people. She jumps in the part of the brain that makes all of the decisions and makes you believe you're doing what *you* want to do. It's a neat parlor trick, and she made me do things I regret like hitting you with a pipe, but she can't actually control anyone. Only the twins could do that. I've tried to do the whole *influencing* thing and I can't seem to make it work. I tried to convince science guy over there to rescue you, but all I could do was make him have to pee." Max looked embarrassed and I laughed.

Max cracked a smile and started to laugh too. It felt good in the middle of all this chaos to have one good feeling. "Well, peeing is something, anyway." I smiled at him.

"I think you're powerful enough to do it. You're stronger than Elisha, even though you don't think you are." Max looked at me with a confidence I didn't feel.

I got a little embarrassed, but he was right: I didn't think I was even close to how powerful Elisha was.

"Even if I could influence Fortski, the guy is kind of a weakling," I said. I began to realize how absurd this all looked right now: two floating "ghosts" hovering above John Fortski talking about his bravery (or anything else for that matter). I felt like I was in a dream.

"He's the one who has the formula. If Elisha finds out *she'll* be the only one to have it. We can't let that happen." Max was very determined. "We have to hide it, so we can come back and retrieve it later when the rescue crew comes."

"Assuming that a rescue crew is coming," I grumbled.

"It's our only chance. If Elisha finds out about the formula we'll never see it and we'll both die." Max was certain.

I nodded and looked at Fortski. "Jump in together?" I asked. I had no idea how this was going to work.

Max nodded.

The two of us kept our hands clasped and we swooped into John Fortski's body.

Like the other times I visited people's brains, we were immediately in what I call the memory area. Apparently, the way I visualize peoples' memories was long hallways with millions of doors. Everyone sees it differently, but since I was probably more familiar with this whole process than Max, we both saw it my way. Fortski's memory doors were a lot like Roberta's, on and on forever. Age, I guess: the older you were the more memories you had. I was a little curious to peek in a few and maybe get some more info on Elisha, but first things first…

"How do we influence him?" I asked.

"I thought you would know," Max admitted.

I felt like a complete bumbling idiot. While my body was being ripped to shreds by Elisha, I was in John Fortski's head trying to figure out how to influence him like a puppet.

Maybe if I thought of his body the way I thought of controlling dead things.

It was so easy to take over the dead because I could focus on their swirling black holes and connect to them. They were like an extension of me. So, maybe, I just had to do the same thing here. Fortski didn't have a swirling black hole, since he wasn't dead, but he had a brain. A brain that told him how to move. I just needed to connect to that part of his mind. I concentrated as hard as I could, focusing on movement. I closed my eyes.

I could see something.

But it wasn't his brain.

It was his swirling bright light.

I looked up at Max in alarm.

How?

Just like with the twins, I could see Fortski's spinning white center. His life!

I realized I could only see it from the inside. I didn't have their power to see every living thing as swirling light. But inside Forstki, I was seeing his. I had no idea why. Maybe it had something to do with the fact that the twins were the reason I had my powers in the first place. I wasn't sure.

"Max…" I said in wonder.

"What is it?" His curiosity was piqued.

"Watch."

Fortski was mine.

I connected to Fortski's swirling light and a surge of power flowed through me. Intoxicating. I tried to keep my euphoric state from distracting me as I realized that I could actually see out of Fortski's eyes.

Once I took over his every move, I hadn't noticed that I had made Fortski stand perfectly still. Not conspicuous at all.

I made him put down his beaker and walk over to the bathroom.

Max's voice echoed in my head, but I couldn't see him anymore, I could only see what Fortski saw. "You're controlling him!" He was obviously shocked and pleased at once. "How?!"

"I can see his light like when I controlled the twins. It feels like it does when we connect to the dead, but stronger because he's alive," I tried to explain.

I could hear Max's sigh of awe.

"Max, do you know where he keeps the sample formula?"

"Inside his leg. He had a pouch of skin surgically added to his right inner thigh."

Gross.

But I had to give it to the guy, inventive.

"All right, eww, but once I have it, where should I hide it?"

Max apparently had thought about this. "You're going to have to leave the building. Fortski isn't allowed off campus, but he is allowed in the courtyard. We can bury it out there."

"If we can get my grandparents to rescue us, then why wouldn't we just take it off Fortski then? Why hide it when we can get it from him directly?" This whole plan was starting to sound fishy. Why couldn't we just take it from Fortski later? It's not like he was going anywhere.

"Because Elisha is going to kill him tonight," Max answered calmly.

I, on the other hand, was not so calm.

"What?! Why would she do that? This guy is a genius and probably has like a million other drug inventions in him!" I was appalled. Someone like Elisha would know better. I hated to say it, but think of all the things she could make this guy invent.

"That's exactly why she's going to kill him. She can't allow this guy to exist." Max sounded like he was spouting a prophecy. "He's too much of a commodity and Elisha knows it's only a matter of time before Turner gets Fortski back. She can't have Fortski giving Turner the drug that could potentially make him invulnerable. It's worth killing off the possibilities of Fortski's talent than to give her biggest enemy her greatest asset."

Damn that girl was horrible.

"Does Fortski know?" I asked.

"He's suspects, which is why he's keeping the sample hidden. He's going to use it on himself if she hurts him. Fortski told her he'd have a prototype ready tonight. Once she has it, that's when she plans on killing him," Max said.

"How do you know all this?" I wondered.

"After I slipped into a coma, I came here. I'm still connected to Eva and Elisha. I watched as Elisha almost beat Eva to death like she did to me. Elisha kept saying Eva needed to be punished, but as soon as Fortski had the prototype, she'd try it out on Eva. Eva is so obsessed with Elisha. She is actually proud and grateful to be the guinea pig." I could hear the bitterness in Max's voice.

"Shouldn't we be more worried about saving Fortski's life than this stupid formula?" Thought I'd throw that out there.

"Normally, I'd say yes, and if we can save Fortski, I'm with you, we should. But this formula makes Elisha nearly invincible. She can not have it." Max was adamant.

"Okay, I'll make him bury it. But I'm going to do everything in my power to save him. I'm not going to let Elisha kill one more innocent person," I said with as much conviction as humanly possible.

I re-focused on controlling Fortski. First I made sure that his memories were locked from him by closing all the doors that were opening from his newest memories. Then I made him leave the bathroom and Max guided Fortski/me outside to the courtyard.

Seeing through Fortski's eyes was strange. It felt almost blurry, but in fact everything was in perfect focus. I tried not to think about it too much, though, or it would give me a panic attack.

We reached the courtyard, which looked as if it had been there a while. Ivy and bougainvillea grew up the sides of the stone walls that were at least twenty feet high. A broken, multi-layered fountain dominated the center, moss growing all over it. It was like a scene out of fantasy book, except this place was a prison. Walking over the slick cobblestone floor made me paranoid that I would make Fortski slip and break his neck. And I noticed that there were no other doors leading out, just the one we had come in through.

"Go towards the back," Max suggested. "We'll bury it under a stone."

I made Fortski look around, making sure no one else was in the courtyard and that there were no cameras. Then I had him walk to the very back of the small space. I almost wanted to close my eyes when I had to make Fortski pull down his pants so I could grab the formula. Embarrassing.

And seriously gross. I felt around his right inner thigh until I found the piece of loose skin and peeled it back. Blek. There in his secret hiding place was a small vial full of a clear liquid. I wasn't sure how this stuff worked, but just because I wanted to make Fortski as safe as possible, I made him drink a few drops.

Max didn't argue. He knew I had to at least try and give Fortski a fighting chance. I was burying his only cure after all. I just hoped it wouldn't come to that.

I stoppered the vial and pulled back a loose cobblestone. There was thick mud underneath, so I grabbed a nearby stick and dug a small hole. Placing the vial inside, I packed the dirt on top, then had Fortski place the stone in its original place.

Done.

"Let's put him back in the lab and get over to your grandparents." Max was all business.

I made Fortski return to the lab and I left him exactly as we found him. I closed the doors on all of his memories for the last five minutes, so hopefully he wouldn't skip a beat.

Keeping my grip on Max's hand, I let go of Fortski's spinning white hole and Max and I flew out of Fortski's body.

Fortski had a moment of confusion on his face, a bit disoriented, but he shook it off and went back to his experiments.

"All right let's get out of here and get some help," I said to Max.

SWOOSH!

Before I could react I was ripped from Max's grasp and being sucked out of the room.

SLAM!

I screamed.

I was back in my body.

Elisha was glowing with pride. "Tricky, tricky. I knew I should have snagged Roberta, very clever of her pulling you out, but I'm smarter than the both of you combined and it won't happen again."

More cuts had been made since I last visited my wrecked body. I began to sob from the sheer agony of it. I'd never felt so much pain in my life. I couldn't even revel in the fact that Elisha thought it had been my grandmother who pulled me out and not Max. Max hadn't even entered her mind since she believed he was dead.

SLASH!

I bit my lip to hold back a scream and tasted blood in my mouth. Elisha had just cut my side, long and deep. Eva could barely keep up with the pain-inducing salve as blood pooled beneath me on the cement floor. I wanted out of this body. I couldn't stand another minute. Max! Help me!

I searched the room for him, but he wasn't there. Had Elisha inadvertently separated us forever? Or had she performed some kind of mojo that prevented me from leaving my body again? I tried to leave myself, even if just for a second before she'd pull me back. Just one second of bliss. I tried as hard as I could, but I was stuck in my broken body.

I began to seethe. I had never felt such rage in my entire life. I wanted to destroy Elisha. I wanted her to die. I couldn't even fathom how I ever argued for her survival. She didn't deserve it. She deserved to suffer. The more she cut me, the more I wanted to destroy her. My expression must have been screaming how I felt, because Elisha actually took a step back when our eyes met.

Then just as quickly, her face lit up in pure ecstasy.

Elisha took pleasure from hatred.

She was evil.

Pure evil.

I saw black.

Blacker than I'd ever seen before.

Elisha and Eva's bodies were covered in it, like a thick skin of tar. It took only a second to realize it was their dead skin cells that hadn't flaked off their bodies yet.

And I acted.

I connected to every last dead skin cell on Elisha's body and I made them burrow into her skin. Digging. Digging. Digging.

Elisha screamed in utter terror and pain. It was music to my ears.

Eva was in shock. She had no idea what was happening.

Deeper and deeper I made the dead cells burrow into Elisha's body. Her screaming grew louder and more intense. I loved it. I loved every second of her pain. It somehow lessened mine.

"Knock her out!" Elisha yowled at Eva.

Eva was completely freaked out. She grabbed a metal pipe and started towards me.

I burrowed Eva's dead skin cells into her living skin and watched as she dropped the pipe to grab her arms and legs in agonizing pain.

They were screaming and I wanted to laugh. I wanted to sing!

SWOOSH!

I was out of my body. Max was holding onto my hands and pulling me away.

Elisha and Eva stopped screaming.

I tried to pull away from Max. I wanted back in and I wanted them to suffer!

Max held on tight. "Chelsan, stop! This isn't you!"

"It *is* me! I'm tired of being hunted and tortured. I have to make it stop! I have to make Elisha stop!" I tried to tug away from Max, but he was too strong.

He pulled me into him. Even though we were bodiless I could feel his arms wrap around me, holding me tight. He whispered in my ear, "Chelsan, she's trying to turn you into her. Fight it. You're better than this."

And then I heard him.

Really heard him.

She's trying to turn you into her.

And, for a brief moment, Elisha had succeeded.

I had become as bad as she ever was.

I slumped into Max.

What was I doing?

What had I done?

I started to cry. Really cry. Ugly cry. Thank goodness I was a ghost.

"We have to get out of here, she'll recover soon and pull you back in," Max whispered in my ear.

I nodded into his chest. I wanted to fly as far away from this place as possible. I couldn't even look at myself I was so ashamed. I had let my anger get the best of me. I kept a tight hold on Max's hand as I pulled away from our embrace. "You lead."

Max nodded and the two of us soared outside of the building until we were hovering over it.

"Where are we?" I asked.

"About fifty miles outside of Los Angeles, near Castaic Lake," Max informed me.

If I wasn't so pre-occupied with my horrible behavior, I would have appreciated the scenery. Beautiful pines over rolling hills, all framing a deep blue lake. In other words, the middle of nowhere.

I searched the billions of strands of light that spread out before me like a network of spider webs until I found the brightest and strongest of them all. Roberta's. "Found Grams, hang on," I told Max as I led him toward Roberta at full speed.

It only took a matter of seconds. Astral projection was the best way to travel! I brought Max in with me for fear of letting go and being sucked back into my body.

Darkness surrounded us, but only for a brief second. Roberta materialized in front of us, creating our oak forest for scenery. From the expression on her face she seemed surprised to see Max, but she wasn't upset. Grams hurried over and hugged me close. When she realized I wasn't letting go of Max's hand, she pulled away. "Where are you and what's wrong?" she asked.

When I saw Roberta's concern something inside of me snapped. I didn't want to admit what I'd done to Elisha and Eva. To tell her would be to acknowledge that I had actually become... like my grandparents. Even in my incorporeal form I felt like vomiting. But she had to know, so I told Roberta everything. By the end of it, I was choking back tears.

Grams gently touched my cheek with her hand. "They deserved it. Don't feel guilty for a second."

I know she was trying to make me feel better, but it actually made me feel worse. Getting any stamp of approval by psycho-Grams wasn't exactly what I needed right now. Still, I knew she was trying to make me feel better, so I shrugged it off.

"Now where are you, Chelsan?"

"I'm in a building near Lake Castaic on the south western shore. Fortski is there, too – and Elisha plans to kill him tonight," I told her.

Roberta was genuinely taken aback by this last piece of information. "Kill Fortski? What on earth for?" she asked, trying to process Elisha's warped reasoning. But, Roberta didn't know the full story, so I told her about the prototype serum.

Roberta's eyes lit up. She might as well have been salivating. This stuff really was dangerous.

"We need to get it so we can save Max," I kept her focused.

"And you," Max added, looking at me.

He turned to Roberta, "Chelsan's body is more injured than she led you to believe. Almost every inch has been cut and salved with burning acid."

Was that what it was? Acid? Even though I was safe in Roberta's head, I could almost feel the pain, the memory was so fresh. I hadn't gone into huge detail as to how extensively Elisha had tortured me, but Max apparently wanted Roberta to know.

Grams took a second to recover from the news, then her eyes became so intensely furious I was grateful she didn't want me dead anymore. Nope. If her eyes said anything, they said she was going to kill Elisha.

Before she could fly off the handle, I told her what Elisha told me about why she was torturing me.

This made Grams very interested. "So, she doesn't have all your powers… That's good. That means that, no matter what, you'll always be more powerful than Elisha and that you have a few tricks that she doesn't. And controlling Fortski? That's something we should study further." She was very impressed.

"I don't feel more powerful than Elisha," I admitted.

"Chelsan, you made her own dead skin cells burrow into her body. Trust me, if she could do that, she would have done it by now. Elisha loves to hurt people, really hurt people."

"Maybe she hadn't thought of it yet?" I offered.

"No," Roberta was definitive. "The fact that she's using mundane items like knifes and salves means Elisha can't harness her power like you can. That's a good thing. She still has her astral skills, which allows her to pull you back into your body, but Max was pretty brilliant holding on to you like this." Roberta gave Max a slight nod of respect. "He's a human tether and she doesn't know how to break it."

If Max could blush he would have, but instead he addressed Roberta, "Am I going to live long enough to take Fortski's serum?"

Roberta didn't respond right away, which rattled me. Then she answered, "If we get there in the next few hours, yes, I think there will be enough time." Grams touched Max's arm with genuine affection. "Being outside your body is making you weaker. An hour ago we thought you were taking a turn for the worse. Now I know it's because you were saving my granddaughter." Roberta stepped forward, eye to eye with Max. "I promise you I will make sure you live. Even if your body dies I can perform a ritual to place you in another body until we can have a clone made for you. I will not let Elisha win."

Yeeks. "Let's just hope you don't have to do that," I said, wanting to focus on getting the vial so that Max's real body could be saved. All this transferring-spirits-clone-crap was a little too much on the black-magic-sci-fi-creepy side for me.

Grams got the hint. "We're putting together a rescue team. Isabelle will be leading. I can't go with them because of Elisha's power. I'll need both your help to prep Isabelle. There's one more thing I should tell you." Roberta looked pensive.

Uh, oh.

"What?" Even the oak forest couldn't calm me down. I somehow knew what she was going to say.

"It's about Ryan," Roberta continued, "Elisha took him. She left Turner and I, but she took Ryan and Harry."

I froze.

Ryan was back where I was, and I had left him. Was he being tortured like me? Was he even alive?

Max grabbed onto both my hands now, warning urgently, "Chelsan, you're slipping."

I couldn't seem to stop it. My hold on Max was growing weaker and weaker the more I thought about Ryan alone and hurt.

"Chelsan!" Max's hands fell through mine like he was solid and I was a ghost.

Oh no.

I felt myself flying out of Roberta's head like a snapped rubber band. I flew backwards in the air watching the scenery in a blur of motion until…

…SLAM!

I was back in my body.

I held in my groans as every fiber of my body screamed in pain.

Elisha was arguing with Fortski while Eva watched.

Elisha roared, "You said you'd have the prototype ready! Look at my arms!"

Her arms were smeared red from where I had burrowed her skin cells. There were patches of blood all over her face. Her legs were injured as well, I could tell from the blood seeping through her jeans. I felt almost relieved seeing her so outraged because I knew she was fine, only a few minor scrapes. And the damage to Eva wasn't nearly as bad.

Fortski's face was wide-eyed with fear. "It's almost done, Elisha. Within the hour, I promise you – but I won't have enough for both of you. Just a few drops."

Not true. He had a whole bottle. I had to respect the guy, he knew what to lie about to save his skin. Elisha would want more of the formula before she killed him.

"That's not what you promised!" Elisha screamed. "I need to test it out on Eva first to make sure it won't kill me!"

Eva didn't even flinch at that.

Then Elisha's eyes met mine and she snarled, "You're back, are you?"

"You're face is looking kind of blotchy," I smiled. What was I thinking? I just couldn't seem to stop myself.

Elisha shrieked from rage. She picked up the metal pipe Eva had tried to hit me with earlier. "Until I can figure out how to control you…"

WHACK!

Everything went black.

***

It was very surreal to wake up in total darkness. Then I realized Max was next to me. He held my hand like he was a vise. "I pulled you out when you were unconscious. We're in Isabelle's head."

"We don't have to be in the dark." Then I called out, "Isabelle!"

Isabelle popped into view, a confused expression on her face. "This is weird."

"I know, but we need to see and only you can make that happen for us." I felt like I was becoming an expert at this head-jumping thing.

"Roberta told me, I just don't know how." Isabelle shrugged.

Roberta popped in. "Good. We're all here." Then I heard her in my head only, *Do not tell Isabelle about the formula.*

I jumped from the surprise of it. Max had the same expression on his face so I knew she had communicated the same message to him. We both gave her barely perceptible nods of acknowledgement. I knew my grandparents' distrust for Harry's team and, frankly, I trusted Grams more than Isabelle at this point.

Isabelle did not seem happy at all to see three people she hardly knew standing in what was essentially her brain. "Can we just make this snappy so you can all leave."

Roberta motioned for Isabelle to come over to us. "Take our hands, Isabelle. Chelsan and Max will re-create the building she's being held in so you'll be able to access it like a memory. It'll feel like you've been there before." Roberta turned to Max and me. "Concentrate on every last detail of the building. Max you've done more exploring than Chelsan, so give Isabelle anything and everything you can remember."

The scenery around us swirled and spun until it became the outside of the building I was being held in. Just like when Roberta created the oak forest, Max and I imagined Elisha's location into being.

Isabelle was a bit taken aback by everything that was happening. Even though she had super-crazy powers, apparently she was like I used to be and the whole mojo-astral-magic-thing was beyond her scope of reality. But she was taking it like a trooper at this point. I could tell she was making mental notes on all the building's entrances and exits. Once we were inside, Max took over and led us through every nook and cranny of the entire compound.

We passed by quite a few shut doors where we assumed prisoners were being held. Namely Ryan and Harry. I could tell Isabelle was way more concerned about Harry and I couldn't blame her. They'd been working together for hundreds of years and I was sure their bond was tighter than ever. After all, she'd accepted his faith in Elisha over my word, which ultimately put us in this situation, but I wasn't going to point fingers. As long as Isabelle's team rescued Ryan I didn't care what she thought. As far as I was concerned I'd be happy if I never saw Harry and his assassin squad again.

When Isabelle was sure she knew the building and the surrounding area to her satisfaction, we all jumped out of her head.

Max and I were floaties, but Roberta stood in front of Isabelle in person. Turner had joined them while we were in Isabelle's head.

Roberta talked to the air, knowing we were there. "You two go back to the compound. If Isabelle needs help, I'll contact you and you can jump in her head."

Isabelle was adamant when she said, "That won't be necessary. I don't want anyone in my brain, thank you very much."

Roberta looked right at me, like she could see me and gave me a quick glance that suggested that I should completely ignore Isabelle. I was a little mixed on the topic. I wanted to respect Isabelle's wishes, but I didn't trust her completely either. More importantly, I didn't trust her to keep Ryan as a priority. She was *objective girl* and to her that meant save Harry, Fortski, me and then Ryan, in that order. Ryan and I were definitely last on the list of Isabelle's priorities.

"Ready to go back to the compound?" I asked Max.

Max nodded and the two of us flew out of Population Control to return to my torture chamber. It was amazing how fast travel was when you weren't in an actual body. I knew it was going to be at least a half hour before Isabelle and her team would arrive. The hover trip itself was only about ten minutes, but to break into the building? I wasn't sure. I knew Isabelle was good, but none of us knew how good Elisha's security team was, either.

Elisha and Eva were nowhere to be found. We needed to locate them for Isabelle. I knew she didn't want any head-jumping going on, but information on where the bad guys were seemed pretty important.

Still, I could understand Isabelle's reluctance. Elisha and Roberta had brainknapped me enough times to learn how to train myself to keep people out. Roberta and now Max were the only people I let in. I was sure Elisha tried every day, but so far I'd been able to build a mental wall against her. If Elisha could jump in my head she'd probably try and convince me to kill myself to complete the ritual. But the more I thought about it, the less likely that would be. Elisha needed to perform the spell herself: that meant being completely in her own body. She wouldn't want to risk it going wrong.

Max and I floated near my tortured body. It was hard to even recognize myself. I was seriously messed up. If I didn't have some of Fortski's potion soon I wasn't sure if I'd survive.

Reality set in.

I was outside my body.

Max was in a coma and outside his body.

We were practically dead already.

Max held on to me tightly, his face worried. "You're slipping again. What's happening?"

"I... I..." I was panicking. I was seriously panicking. I pointed at my body hung like a piece of meat on a hook. "That's me," was all I could spit out.

Max held onto my arms and stared me in the eye. "Yes, and the more you freak out, the more you'll be pulled back in. So calm down, I need you out here with me."

I took small comfort in his gaze. If I could have taken a breath I would have. Then the thought that I wasn't breathing sent me into another tizzy.

My hands were becoming less substantial, like before. Max grabbed me and held me close, but my body started to pull through him. I was going back to my body.

"Chelsan, we need to find Ryan." Max said the only thing that he knew would keep me grounded.

Ryan.

My ghost form solidified instantly and our grip on each other stabilized once more.

I couldn't let that happen again.

It couldn't be good to be out of my body for this long, but being sucked back into my wrecked form wasn't an option.

"Let's check those closed doors you saw," I suggested.

The door in the room we were in clanked open.

"CHELSAN!" Elisha's voice reverberated through the room and through my brain.

She was sending a psychic all-points bulletin to wherever I was. Elisha had no idea I was floating above my own body. If she wanted my attention, though, that couldn't be good.

Eva walked in after Elisha and she was holding a handcuffed…

Ryan.

Thank goodness he wasn't hurt. Yet. Oh man.

When Ryan saw my ruined form hanging from the hook, his whole face fell. He shrugged off Eva and ran to my body before she could stop him. "CHELSAN!" Ryan screamed and my heart ached to tell him I was okay. "CHELSAN!" He thought I was dead.

"She's still alive." Elisha walked up behind him.

"YOU BITCH!" Ryan turned and head-butted Elisha to the ground. Go Ryan!

Eva kicked Ryan in the groin and he went down for the count.

"You're slipping!" Max hissed.

I wanted to jump into my body and make the two of them pay.

Elisha stood up, brushing herself off and staring down at Ryan with fury. Ryan was balled up on the floor, but he was going to be okay.

I calmed myself enough to keep ahold of Max.

Elisha spoke out loud with her psychic-megaphone voice. It must have been some kind of spell. "Chelsan, if you don't return to your body, I'm going to kill your boyfriend."

Elisha nodded to Eva. Eva pulled out a knife and placed it against Ryan's throat.

Max held me tighter. "She won't. Don't fall for it."

"She won't? Are you joking? Of course she will!" I yelled at Max.

I could never live with myself if Ryan died. I wouldn't want to.

I turned to Max, "I'm sorry."

I let go.

I watched Max's expression turn to horror as I was sucked back in my body.

I groaned in agony. Even though it had only been a short time since I was last in the chamber of pain known as my body, every moment away was like harmonious peace. Now, back inside, every nerve was on fire like my cells were stinging.

I managed to croak out, "Stop Elisha. I'm here."

Eva pulled away the knife and forced Ryan to his feet. The three of them walked around to face me.

Elisha warned, "You try any more tricks and he's dead. I can still slit his throat when I'm writhing in pain, you understand?"

I nodded or at least I think I did. It was hard to tell since every ounce of my body ached uncontrollably.

"Chelsan, don't do anything she says. You can't let her use us like this!" Ryan pleaded, but he had to know I wouldn't listen to him. I'd never let Elisha hurt him if I could help it.

That's when I heard Roberta's voice in my head, *Oh dear, back in your body I see. Isabelle, Dean and Terence are there. They have Harry and Fortski and should be on their way to you now. Fortski doesn't know that the formula was buried he still thinks he has it in his leg. He hasn't mentioned the serum to Harry yet, either. Let's hope he keeps his mouth shut. I told Isabelle you were the priority, but she doesn't care.* Roberta sounded pissed.

Elisha calmly spoke to me, unaware of the goings-on elsewhere in the building. "You know what I want, Chelsan. You just have to agree to kill yourself so we can complete the ritual."

"NO!" Ryan roared. "NEVER! Chelsan, I'd die first!"

Elisha slapped him, then turned to me, "You *are* going to die, so the only thing you have to ask yourself is: Do I kill Ryan first or let him live?"

"Live. Live. I agree. I'll do it." I had no intention of doing it, but I needed to give Isabelle more time. Who knows, maybe Dean was in the room right now. Please. Please.

Chelsan! They're leaving! They have Harry and Fortski and they're leaving you there! I knew we shouldn't have trusted them! I'm sending a new team! Just hold on!

Wait, what?

No wonder Isabelle didn't want me in her head. She knew I'd see exactly what she was planning. She didn't care about me or Ryan or anyone. She and Harry still saw me as the granddaughter of their worst enemy. Isabelle probably figured Elisha and I would take care of each other.

No.

I was not about to let that lame-ass-lying-bitch leave here without helping Ryan and me escape.

My fury took over.

Nothing was going to stop me from saving Ryan.

I flew out of my body without the help of Max. I didn't know how I did it, and I didn't care. I aimed my focus on Isabelle and soared straight to her.

SLAM!

Right inside her head. I connected to Isabelle's light spinning hole so fast, she actually stumbled a bit.

Mine.

I saw through her eyes and I could hear Isabelle's thoughts shouting for control inside her mind. No way that was happening.

Dean and Terence were following behind Isabelle and they all had almost exited the building, with Harry and Fortski in the lead.

I made Isabelle speak, "We have to get Ryan and Chelsan now."

Harry whirled on her, "No, I'm not going to argue with you again, Turner will get them out and I don't want to be anywhere near him when he does. We have Fortski, let's get the hell out of here."

Well, at least it appeared she had tried to argue rescuing us before. Still wasn't enough for me to let her go, though.

"You can leave, I'm going back," I made her say.

"Me too," Dean chimed in. He didn't elaborate on his reasons, but I could tell he agreed with Isabelle... or me rather.

Fortski wasn't having it, "Now wait a minute. Elisha is going to kill me if I go back. We have to leave now!"

Fortski was right, so I made Isabelle say, "Harry, Terence, you take Fortski out of here. Dean and I can handle this." I didn't really want *them* to have Fortski, but I wanted the poor guy to live more, so I decided to let him go. Besides I knew where the formula was, they didn't, and there was enough to cure Max and me. We'd find Fortski later.

Harry took a few moments before he finally nodded. "Fine. Meet back at the rendezvous point."

Like an annoying buzz in the back of my head, I could hear Isabelle trying to talk to me, but I was ignoring her before I lost my nerve.

Dean turned to Isabelle and said, "You lead."

I made her nod and moved in front of him, heading straight for the torture room.

Along the way there was a long string of dead guards littering the hallways, a reminder to me of who I was body-jacking. This girl was a killer, maybe worse than Gramps or even Elisha. The fact was: I didn't know Isabelle. There hadn't been enough time. I just hoped she wouldn't kill me as soon as I jumped out of her body. It was a chance I had to take.

I started to worry about Ryan and leaving him like I did. Surely, Elisha knew I wasn't in my body again. But I hadn't heard any of her psychic-intercom-screaming yet, either. Maybe she was preparing the "power-transferring" ceremony.

We weren't far from the torture room: Isabelle had all the maps Max had given her right there in her head to reference. It really was more like a memory, as if I'd been to this place a million times. I couldn't see Dean, he'd faded into the wall, I guess. Must be procedure for these guys.

Arriving at the clunky door, I realized we were going to have to make some noise. Unavoidable. So I made Isabelle say to invisible Dean, "This door is loud. You go in and I'll take care of the girls."

I realized as the words came out of my mouth that there was no way Isabelle could know that there were only the girls in there, but I hoped Dean hadn't noticed.

Time to play around with Isabelle's power and see what she could do.

I made Isabelle open the door fast. It was a lot lighter than I thought and clunked violently to slam against the wall. Walking in I could see my tortured body hanging from the hook – and Ryan, handcuffed, with Eva still holding a knife to his throat.

Elisha had a gurney and table in front of her. Definitely preparing for the ritual. She looked at Isabelle with annoyance. "Shocker, the rescue team has arrived," Elisha said angrily.

I focused on Elisha's heart, thinking this would connect me to Isabelle's power.

I wasn't disappointed.

I could literally see Elisha's heart beating under her chest. It was similar to the way I saw swirling black holes. The movement had a trailing light effect, like a slug leaving a slime trail. I could see it in all our hearts, mine, Ryan's and Eva's as well.

And Dean's.

Whoa. I could see him, like an outline of him. I knew no one else could, but every time Dean moved whichever part of him moved would leave the same trail of light.

In fact, any time *anyone* moved there was a trail of light. It wasn't just the hearts. I wondered what that meant. The hearts were the only thing that continuously gave off the light because they were constantly moving. I concentrated on Elisha's heart and found Isabelle's mind grasping on to it *because* of its movement. It felt very similar to when I connected to the dead. I could puppeteer the dead because once I had control over their swirling holes the rest of their bodies were mine to move.

It was almost the same here. Because Elisha's heart was beating steadily I could grasp onto the trails of light surrounding it. I could make it stop because I controlled its movement. I controlled its movement because it was moving. This was seriously blowing my mind.

I slowed Elisha's heart rate down so low that her blood pressure dropped instantly. The girl passed out before I even made it across the room.

Eva moved the knife closer to Ryan's neck, "Don't come any closer. I'll kill him."

"No, you won't," I made Isabelle say.

Dean had snuck up behind Eva and now appeared, grabbing the arm holding the knife and making her drop it to the floor. He reached up and started to grab Eva's head to snap her neck.

No!

I connected to the movement of his arms and hands just like I did with Elisha's heart and…

…made him freeze.

Dean was stuck in mid-pose.

Eva took full advantage of this pause and wiggled herself free. She leaped to Elisha's side and crouched over her protectively.

Dean looked at me with complete shock. Apparently, Isabelle had never done anything like that before. I felt disbelief running through my mind-inside-Isabelle's system, too: she seemed to be reacting the same way as Dean. I had done something with her powers that, even after three hundred years, she'd had no idea she could do. Oops. Somehow, I knew I'd regret that. Giving more power to your enemy is never a good thing. I'd learned that first hand a few times already.

I kept holding onto the trails of light that had formed when Dean moved, keeping his arms in place. He started to walk forward towards Eva and Elisha. I connected to the trails of light his legs were making and made his legs stop as well.

Isabelle could control anything that moved.

If they weren't moving she had no power over them.

"You're not Isabelle," Dean looked at me, his eyes cold and calculating.

"I've taken over for a while," I made Isabelle say.

I quickly connected to the trails of light making Eva's heart beat and made her pass out on top of Elisha.

No killing.

I was sick of it!

I hurried over to Ryan and uncuffed him. His eyes met mine, confused.

"It's me, it's Chelsan. They were going to leave us here so I took over Isabelle's body."

Ryan hugged Isabelle/me, but refrained from kissing her. Good boy. That would have been awkward later. "Let's get you down from there," he said, looking up at my near-unconscious body.

I made Isabelle unhook my body from the ceiling. I could only imagine how much that must have hurt and I counted my lucky stars I didn't have to.

Ryan held my body like I was made of glass. He looked up at Isabelle. "We have to get you to a hospital."

"I have something better, but I can't take all of it because Max needs some too." I realized Ryan had no clue what I was talking about, but I wasn't leaving without the formula. Literally. I think my body would keel over and die first.

As Isabelle, I turned to Dean, "You're going to help me, then you're going to let Ryan and I leave. When we're far enough away I'll return Isabelle's brain to her, okay?"

Dean actually seemed more amused than angry at this point. I think he was getting a kick out of all this magic-mojo-stuff. "We're the ones who wanted to save you two in the first place, in case you didn't know."

"I had to take over Isabelle's body to come back, so I'm not impressed. Do we have a deal or not?" It must have been odd for Dean to hear Isabelle say those words, but he shrugged in agreement all the same.

"Deal."

"Ryan, you stay here and tie Elisha and Eva up. We'll be back," I said.

"Be careful." Ryan eyed Dean suspiciously. "Don't keep your eyes off that guy."

"Don't worry, I can see him when he fades into the walls," I told Ryan to calm him.

Dean didn't look too happy about that.

"What? Isabelle never told you that?" I made Isabelle ask him.

"Maybe she can't. I've never seen her do *this* either." He nodded to his frozen arms and legs. "And I've known her for three hundred years."

"Maybe she's a little slow." Wow. I was being mean, but I was really annoyed at this crack-assassin team. "Let's go."

I released Dean from being a human statue and led the way out of the room. Dean used his blend-into-walls power, but now that I could see the streams of light whenever he moved it was easy to track him. I wondered if Isabelle had ever been able to see Dean before, but I didn't really want to open the lines of communication with her for fear of her bumping me out. I didn't think she was powerful enough to do it, but when you're feeling out of control and angry... I shuddered to think of all the things I'd done in situations like that. Including what I was doing right now by taking over Isabelle's body.

As we walked through hallway after hallway, each one was littered with the dead bodies of Elisha's guards. I couldn't help but feel it was my fault they were all dead. If I didn't have my abilities Elisha would have used dead soldiers to guard this place. Because she was afraid of me being stronger than her and taking over her own men, she had hired live people. Now they were dead. Elisha wouldn't care. Either way they'd still work for her. But it made me sick to think that I was inadvertently responsible for even more deaths.

It also disgusted me that the woman I was inhabiting could murder so ruthlessly. What happened to Isabelle that she could kill so easily? I almost didn't want to know. Almost.

I opened the door to the lab and I gasped at the sight. All the scientists were dead, necks broken.

Pissed off I turned to Dean's semi-invisible figure, "You guys are sick! They were innocents!"

Dean materialized and looked a little ruffled at the fact that I had turned to where he had been standing when he was completely cloaked. He didn't like the fact that I could see him. Of course, as soon as I left Isabelle's body I wouldn't be able to any more. That scared me more than I cared to admit.

"They were collateral damage. We needed Fortski." Dean didn't even break a sweat. He really didn't give a crap. To him killing was like picking grass, something that needed to be done but wasn't a real loss.

I couldn't wait to get out of this girl's filthy body and be as far away from Harry and his team as I could. I was siding with Turner and Roberta on this one. These people were foul.

"If I was in my body I'd make these corpses torture you." No I wouldn't, but it felt good to say. And it made Dean hesitate. He was scared of my power, I could tell. Probably because Elisha had used it to control his friend Charlie after she murdered him.

I made Isabelle storm past Dean and out the door to the courtyard.

Oops.

Spread out before us was an entire army of Elisha's men, loading their guns and setting up for a major assault. They must have rallied here and planned on taking the compound back.

When they saw Isabelle/me suddenly walk in on them, they all swung their guns up and were about to shoot…

I connected to their light trails and stopped all of them instantly. At least a hundred men stood in front of me with the top half of their bodies motion-still like rocks. After a few seconds of horror they tried to charge me like I was a red flag and they were the bulls. I made their legs freeze in place.

Dean was actually amused now that it wasn't him that was trapped.

The men yelled and barked orders, but none of them could move. I just kept them standing exactly as they were. It was strange, almost like when I controlled dead people, except these guys were freaking alive — trying to fight back.

I made Isabelle move to the back of the courtyard and dig up the small bottle of serum.

"How long can you keep them that way?" Dean asked.

"As long as I'm in this body," I said and hurried to the door.

When we were both through I slammed the door shut, placing a nearby chair under the doorknob. "Ryan's going to carry my body to the escape hovers my grandparents sent. As soon as we're safely away I'll jump out of Isabelle. The men out in the courtyard will be released the moment I leave Isabelle. I don't know if Isabelle knows how to use her powers like I do. I'm sure it won't take her long to figure out, but you guys might be in trouble. Those men will be after you." As angry and disgusted as I was at Dean and Isabelle, I still didn't want them to die. They were the only two that had actually wanted to rescue Ryan and me. Maybe it wasn't their fault that they were so brainwashed by Harry. Three hundred years is a long time to take orders. Questioning those orders might not be easy for them.

"We handled Elisha's guards just fine twenty minutes ago, but thanks for the warning."

Cocky much?

"You may be able to handle the live ones, but I've seen how you guys do against the dead ones, so have fun." I was tired of helping these guys out. They were so used to being *elite* that they didn't realize when they were out of their depth. They had tried twice now to stop dead guards and guns just didn't cut it. Only Dean could disappear into the walls, Isabelle would be forced to fight her way out and she couldn't stop the already-stopped hearts. Maybe if Isabelle could remember how I controlled movement she could get the live and dead soldiers to stop long enough for them to escape.

At this point it was their problem.

I swung open the door to the torture chamber and was relieved to see Ryan sitting there safe. My body was laid carefully in his lap and he was stroking my hair. I couldn't wait to wake up in my own body and see him staring down at me. I was almost jealous of myself.

I made Isabelle hurry over to Ryan and me. Pulling out the small bottle of Fortski's wound-healing medicine, I decided I was going to be the one to pour the potion in my mouth. I couldn't trust Ryan in this situation. He'd give me the whole serum for fear of me being hurt, and I needed to save at least half the bottle for Max. He was in a lot worse shape than I was.

I wondered if Max was floating around me right now, watching everything. Probably. I lifted up the small bottle as if to toast to his floatie form. I had no idea if Max saw me, but I wanted him to know that help was on the way.

"Hold my neck back so it'll go down without me having to swallow," I instructed Ryan. After all, no one was in there, so I needed the liquid to go down my throat. Gravity always worked best.

Ryan complied and I made Isabelle unstopper the bottle and pour a few drops in my mouth.

Everyone waited.

Watching.

So far…

…Nada.

Then something started to happen.

The bubbling burns from the salve Eva had applied started to change color from angry red to a lighter and lighter pink.

We watched in shock as, in a matter of seconds, the cuts and burns quickly shrank and turned into smooth unscarred skin. (Even better skin than I had before! Jill will be so jealous.)

Ryan's face looked more relieved than I felt, and I felt pretty darn relieved. In that moment I realized that he hated to see me in pain as much as I hated to see him in pain. If I ever doubted that Ryan loved me, all of that was gone.

I also realized that Dean and Isabelle now knew about the formula and what it could do, which ultimately meant *Harry* would know. I couldn't worry about that now, though. Ryan and I had to get out of there.

Isabelle/me smiled at him, "Carry my body out front. Turner and his men should be here by now. When you're safely away have Roberta join me in Isabelle's head and we'll jump out." Then I made Isabelle/me place the bottle of serum in my real body's pocket. Didn't want to leave that behind!

"Got it." Ryan stood up and lifted my body, carrying me like a baby. He was gone in seconds and I was now stuck in a room with Invisible Guy and two unconscious lunatics.

Awkward.

Jinxing myself was always a particularly lucky trait of mine as I suddenly noticed Elisha starting to stir. I could knock her out again, but I was afraid of killing her. Yes, I know, she deserved to die, but I still didn't want to be the one to do it. Just remembering how I felt when I had made her dead cells bore into her skin…

…it made me sick. Really sick.

I never wanted to go back to that dark place again. Not if I didn't have to.

Eva began to wake up as well.

Dean had disappeared into the walls. I could see his heart beating behind Elisha. He was ready to kill if he had to. Man, these guys were worse than Brady the serial killer.

Elisha turned to me, "I know you hate me, but I just want Chelsan. We can call a truce for the moment. How long ago did they escape?"

"A few hours ago." Lies. Maybe enough to stop Elisha from sending out an attack team. I wasn't sure if Ryan was out yet.

My heart sank.

In fact, I suddenly realized that I wasn't sure if Ryan even knew *how* to get out. He'd didn't have access to Max's memories like I did. Ryan had been kidnapped the same as me, locked in a room, and brought to this chamber. The compound was all twisty-turny hallways, and he was carrying me to boot.

I had to get out of Isabelle's body now and help him.

Here went nothing.

I leapt out of Isabelle and snapped back into my body.

My eyes opened to see Ryan's baby browns. "It's me. I'm here," I said.

Ryan's whole face lit up like fireworks and he kissed me more passionately than he ever had before. My brain nearly exploded from impact. But I felt better than I ever had in my life. The serum heightened every feeling, sensation and sense. All I wanted to do was stay in Ryan's arms and be kissed like he was kissing me now…

To my disappointment he pulled away and laughed.

"I'm totally lost. Is that why you bailed early?" He kept kissing my face as he spoke, like he couldn't get enough of me.

"You can put me down now," I laughed back.

"Oh yeah." Ryan carefully placed me on my feet, his hands cupping my face like he was breathing me in. "How do you feel?"

"I feel amazing," I confided in him. "Like I just came off the factory line."

Ryan kissed me again. For a wonderful moment I completely forgot where we were and any danger we were in.

For a very *short* wonderful moment.

I pulled away this time, "We're in trouble."

"I know, it just feels like I haven't seen you in years." Ryan affectionately tucked my hair behind my ear. "Okay, let's get out of here."

I grabbed his hand and led the way. Max's memory imprints had been pressed on Isabelle's memory and now, having been inside her mind, I had access to them as well.

I knew Isabelle wouldn't be far behind if she and Elisha had called a truce. She was probably pretty pissed off at me for taking over her body. I would be. But I wasn't a killer, she was. When she got mad, she destroyed. We were so close to freedom.

"Going somewhere?" Dean appeared in front of us with a creepy grin. "Can't stop me now, can you?"

I looked around, but no Isabelle or Elisha. I searched for anything dead that could knock Dean out temporarily.

Dean misunderstood what I was searching for. "No body to jump in?"

I really wasn't thinking about that, but now that he suggested it. I whispered to Ryan, "Get ready to carry me."

Before Ryan could acknowledge me, I jumped out of my body and straight into Dean's. I snapped right into his swirling light and he was my puppet.

Ha, ha! I wanted to see his shocked snarky face, but I'd have to look in a mirror.

Ryan caught my body before it fell to the ground.

"This way," I told him and Dean/me led him forward.

Ryan didn't even question it. Our lives were so insane these days, something like this was just another drop in the bucket-of-crazy for us.

I knew Elisha and Isabelle weren't far behind and, frankly, Dean's power to disappear into walls wasn't exactly a skill that would help us at the moment. But it did give me small pleasure at making this conceited jerk have to help rescue Ryan and me. Although, Dean *did* volunteer to help us in the first place. I guess my taking over Isabelle's body made him turn against us. This schizophrenic crew was giving me a headache.

Blinking against the glaring sun, we exited the building straight into the arms of Turner and his men.

Their guns were up aiming immediately when they saw Dean.

"Ryan, get her in here." Turner motioned to the hover-SUV behind him. Ryan hurried to the car and I knew we were both safe.

"It's me, Chlesan, I'm in here," I made Dean say to Turner and it felt weird to hear a man's voice come out of my thoughts. I was starting to have serious guilt, but it seemed like the only way to stop everyone from KILLING ME!

Gramps raised his eyebrow in surprise… and… What was that?… Pride? Oh man, if doing something like this made him proud, it must really be awful.

"We'll get him locked up, then you can transfer back into your own body." Turner motioned for his men to take Dean/me into custody. I let them tie him up with some kind of flexible metal rope. Dean wasn't going anywhere.

We all piled into the hover-SUV and within seconds were in the air on our way back to safety.

In Dean's body I sat next to me and Ryan while Turner sat across from us. Gramps pulled out a small black container holding a syringe. "I'm going to knock him out so he can't disappear on us. You can go back to your body now."

I disconnected from his light and jumped back into my own body.

Dean was instantly himself, "You're going to pay for that, bitch!"

"Yeah, yeah, save your threats for someone who's actually scared by them," Turner responded, reaching over to inject Dean with whatever knock-out drug that was in his syringe.

Before any of us could react, Dean smiled at Gramps and opened the door with his cuffed hands, jumping out of the car and free-falling to the ground. I instinctively reached out to help him, but he was gone.

Turner slammed the door shut with a look of annoyance.

I looked out the window to see what I thought would be the splatted body of Dean on the ground below. But all I saw was a flash of Dean running back towards the compound before he disappeared completely.

I whirled on Gramps, "How?"

Turner sat back, frustrated. "Another skill of Dean's. I've seen him fall from an eighty story building without a scratch. You should have waited until I injected him."

"You said I could jump out!" I distinctly remembered him telling me to jump out before he injected him.

Gramps sighed heavily. "I forgot about that particular talent of Dean's. It's my fault."

Whoa. Wonders never ceased. That was as close to an apology as I was ever going to get, I suspected. Even Ryan raised an eyebrow in amusement.

Ryan took my hand and kissed it.

I smiled back at him.

We had made it.

I had survived another attempt by Elisha to torture me to get me to do what she wanted.

"There's a shoot-on-sight order placed on Elisha and all of Harry's team," Turner said as if reading my thoughts.

I didn't respond. What could I say? It was out of my hands. I just wanted to go home and snuggle in my comfy bed with Ryan's arms wrapped around me.

"Where's the serum?" Gramps asked.

"I have it. I'll give you what's left *after* I cure Max." I wanted that to be clear. Max and I had been through a lot to get this formula and Max couldn't survive without it.

"Yes, of course, but after that we need to study it. Without Fortski, though, I'm not sure my scientists can figure it out." Gramps seemed more like he was running down scenarios rather than stating facts.

"I can take a look at it if you want me to," Ryan volunteered.

Turner's face lit up at that suggestion. "Yes, that would be appreciated."

This was seriously the most cordial any of us had ever been with each other and it was just weird. I could tell Turner and I were both uncomfortable, but I preferred this Turner to the monstrous murdering one. At least this one didn't want to slit my throat.

We landed at Population Control ten minutes later and Gramps had a set of guards escort us to Max's hospital room. Apparently the world wanted my head on a pike for the shopping mall incident, and word had leaked that I was staying at Population Control. There were families of the victims there protesting that I be executed for my crimes. I wished I could convince them that it wasn't me, but I didn't see how. Sooner or later Gramps was going to have to do something publicly, because as of now the world saw him hiding me as the worst form of preferential treatment ever.

Nancy stood up and ran to me when she saw us enter Max's room. Her arms squeezed me in a bear hug that felt amazing. Just what I needed. Bill and Jason were there as well, sitting in cushy chairs a few feet from Max. After Nancy was finished hugging me they both followed suit, though far less forceful.

Jill barely looked up when she saw me. She was a wreck.

I couldn't blame her. Max's body was almost grey he was so far gone. His breath was shallow, but at least he was breathing.

I moved past everyone and sat across from Jill on the other side of Max.

Jill and I exchanged quick glances as I pulled out the small bottle containing Fortski's formula. I poured a few drops down Max's throat…

…and waited.

Jill kept looking from me to Max like she was a cat following a pendulum, but she didn't say a word.

Max started to move. His breath became stronger and deeper. And, magically before us, all his wounds healed within seconds. Max had been beaten far more than I had been, seeing as he had *died*, and watching the serum run its course through his system brought tears to my eyes. I knew how much pain Max had been in. Max's body had almost given up on him.

His eyes fluttered open, unclear for a moment. When he looked over and saw Jill he smiled with his whole face.

Tears streamed down Jill's cheeks in disbelief. She leaned in and kissed Max to his surprise and delight. I felt like I was watching a holo-movie, smiling myself. Then I felt like I was intruding. "I'll just let you guys be alone." I started to stand.

Jill pulled away from Max and came around to my side, clutching me desperately, "Thank you, thank you," she whispered in my ear. It was so sweet and sincere.

Jill turned away from me and took my previously occupied seat next to Max. Jill was an interesting person to say the least. Cruel one moment and the next she was the nicest person I'd ever met. I just never wanted to be on her bad side again. Saving Max gave me some serious leeway in that department.

As I handed Gramps the vial with the remaining formula, Max said, "Thank you, Chelsan."

I smiled down at him, "Thank Fortski, he invented the stuff."

"But you brought it to me." Max wasn't letting me out of taking credit.

"You'd do the same for me." I didn't truly knowing if that were true, but I hoped that it was.

Max seemed to sense that I needed reassurance because he said, "I would, you know, I believe you are the only one who can stop her."

Her, being Elisha, and as much faith as was radiating off of Max, I couldn't even fathom beating Elisha. She was always a step ahead of me. I couldn't out-think her and, even though Elisha seemed to think that my powers were stronger than hers, I wasn't so sure.

"Isabelle and Dean left the compound. They're not with Elisha," Max added. "They headed back to Harry and Fortski. I was following them before you pulled me back."

"They're still dead," Turner chimed in. "Just because they left Elisha's lair doesn't mean they're not trying to play both sides. I know Harry and he likes to keep his options open. I think I'm the only person in existence he's comfortable burning his bridges with."

Whatever happened between those two must have been pretty insane for someone like Harry to cut a man as powerful as my grandfather out for good. If Harry could even consider for a second to work with Elisha after everything she'd done to him, then Turner must have eaten his babies. I couldn't understand any of it.

Then it hit me: I was freaking tired.

"Can we go home now? I'm exhausted," I complained weakly.

Ryan slid over and wrapped his arms around me so I could lean into his chest. Aaahhh.

Turner's voice of reason grated at my soul, "You'll all have to stay here tonight. Nancy's place still isn't safe for you after the mall incident."

I found myself livid.

Elisha was trying to take everything away from me!

I couldn't let her get away with it anymore. Elisha would hurt or kill everyone I loved if I didn't do something about it. I needed to set things right. I needed the world to know it was Elisha and not me that killed those innocent people.

I wanted my life back.

I pulled away from Ryan to make eye contact with Gramps. "I'm on board with whatever you want to do. We need to take Elisha down before she hurts anyone else."

Turner raised an eyebrow in what I could only describe as… happiness? Go figure. "We've had rooms made up for all of you."

Roberta came rushing in at that moment and nearly cried when she saw me. "Geoffrey, you told me you'd send for me when you two arrived."

"We just got here ten minutes ago," Turner tried to defend himself, but Roberta wasn't really mad, she was relieved to see us both okay.

Before I knew it, Grams embraced me like she hadn't seen me in days. "You did the right thing. I'm so proud of you," she cooed in my ear.

I didn't really like the fact that she was proud of me, either, but at this point I was ready to drop if I didn't get some sleep.

"Roberta, let them go to their rooms. The poor girl is exhausted," Gramps said.

Seriously, bizarre.

For the first time ever they were acting exactly like grandparents should. Putting aside for a moment the threats from Elisha and Harry's team looming over our heads, it was actually quite comforting.

Nancy and Bill's eyes bugged out from the shock of the family moment, too, but they were dealing as best they could.

Jason finally piped in. I had almost forgotten he was there. "We still have a lot to talk about." Of course he wanted to keep me up, but it was probably pretty important if he did.

Ryan shook his head. "No, she's sleeping. We'll talk about everything in the morning."

Oh how I loved this boy.

Everyone grumbled agreement and we all headed to our rooms. Even Max left the hospital bed in favor of a luxury room offered by Gramps. He had a spring to his step that I could relate to. Fortski's serum made my body feel like a gagillion bucks.

We each had our own private room (of course everyone coupled off, Jason and Nancy, Max and Jill and ...Bill). Bill didn't seem to mind not having anyone though. He hugged me goodnight and gave me one of those goofy grins of his that made my heart sing.

Ryan and I entered our room and I nearly gasped at the décor. One word: rich. Everything was deep mahogany, from the four-poster bed frame to the floors to the side tables and dresser, all intricately carved and shaped into beautifully ornate pieces of art. The fluffy down comforter and pillows were a stark contrast with their white coloring, but it made the room scream elegance.

Ryan leaned down and kissed the back of my neck.

Serious chills.

But I must have been tired because not even Ryan's touch could keep my eyes open, and normally it took everything in my power not to jump him. I kind of shuffled to the perfectly-made bed and threw back the comforter. I popped off my shoes, pulled down my pants and slid into the most comfortable bed I'd ever been in. Even Ryan made a small noise of satisfaction as he crawled in beside me. As soon as my head hit that pillow everything went blissfully dark.

Chapter 6
Saturday April 9, 2321

"What are you doing here?" Isabelle's voice woke me.

Or was I awake?

Uh oh.

I opened my eyes and I was in the dark place that was Isabelle's brain.

How did I end up here?

"I didn't come here on purpose, I'll leave," I said. I didn't want a confrontation and I could only imagine how angry Isabelle was with me.

Strangely enough, she didn't look mad at all. She looked sad.

Isabelle sat down in the darkness and rubbed her hands over her face in frustration. "You don't have to leave. I'd like you to stay."

"You would?" I asked incredulously.

Isabelle looked up at me. There was actual wonderment in her eyes. "What you did…" She left that hanging.

"You were going to leave us, I know it was wrong, but I panicked. I really am sorry." I felt like I needed to give Isabelle an explanation.

Isabelle motioned for me to sit.

I cautiously sat down across from her. "You know," I said, "we don't have to sit in the dark. Just concentrate and imagine where you'd like to be and your brain will do the rest." It was weird being the teacher when only months ago I was being taught myself by Roberta.

The darkness transformed into a beautiful setting. We were now sitting on an old wooden dock made of aged pine, stretching at least twenty feet over a crystal blue lake. Our feet touched the cool water while the sun shone down on us in a perfect eighty-degree temperature. I could even feel a cool breeze wash over me as the clear waters caressed my feet.

Much better.

Usually, places like this held special significance to the person creating it, and it made me wonder what importance it held for Isabelle. I didn't know anything about the girl, only that she used to work for Gramps. In my brain I imagined that she was born an assassin and started killing her pets or something horrible like that. Thinking of her as a child didn't compute.

"I used to come down here to hide from one of my worst foster homes. He liked little girls, if you know what I mean," Isabelle confided.

"I'm sorry," I said what I thought was appropriate. I suddenly felt like I had walked in on someone's conversation. Why was she telling me this? It made me feel uncomfortable. Hearing that Isabelle had a difficult childhood, though sad, still didn't excuse her killing hundreds maybe thousands of people. My stepdad had beat the crap out of my mother and then me. I killed him by accident, in self-defense, and I never wanted to kill again. Then when Elisha made me kill all those people using the twins… I shuddered.

I wasn't like Isabelle, she had a taste for killing. She used her gift to murder people for a living.

Yet as horrible as she was a part of me couldn't leave. I wanted to know more.

Then she said, "Don't be sorry. I killed him eventually."

Okay, and on that note, "What do you want from me?" I asked.

Isabelle splashed some water with her foot. "I've never lost control before today. It was terrifying."

"I know. I'm sorry," I repeated, not quite sure that I was. I was conflicted on that particular point. There was a definite part of me that was genuinely sorry for using her so utterly, but then there was another part of me that felt justified. Isabelle had been going to desert us and I felt like I had no other choice.

"You could have jumped into Elisha and make her release you. That's what I thought you were going to do," Isabelle said flatly.

Um.

Wow.

That thought had never even occurred to me. I was always so focused on keeping Elisha out of my head I had never thought about reversing it and taking a dive into Elisha's noggin. Maybe I could control her. She was so powerful in the mojo department, I think my subconscious mind was afraid of getting stuck in there. What if that was exactly what she wanted me to do so she could trap me in there forever? No, jumping into Elisha was dangerous. More dangerous than jumping into Isabelle.

"Elisha is too powerful. It was a risk I wasn't willing to take," I acted as if I had considered the option and decided against it.

"I had no way to defend myself and you knew that. Smart." Isabelle looked impressed. She respected tactical advantages and military strategy. I was doing none of those things, but she seemed to think everyone thought in those terms.

"I'm not some soldier, I don't think like that. I lost control and jumped in your head because you were leaving us behind. I didn't even know that I'd be able to use your powers, I just needed a body to rescue us." I didn't like Isabelle thinking I was some manipulative mastermind. She already compared me to my grandparents and I didn't need her thinking she had confirmed that I was like them.

"That's how we all discovered our powers. An emotional event. Turner and Forstki experimented with the prototypes of Age-pro on our pregnant mothers. We were the result. Then your grandfather murdered our parents and sent us to the vilest foster homes he could find knowing that if we had powers they'd be triggered by an extreme emotional event. Those that survived mentally and physically ended up on the team." Isabelle confessed this as if she were talking about French fries, nonchalant, like it had been a job interview. "What about you?" she asked. "How did you find out about your powers?"

Stepdad. Beating. Killed. Yeah. I saw the pattern.

"I killed my stepdad." Then feeling totally exposed I qualified, "He was beating my mom."

"Did Turner set that up?"

"No. Maybe. Inadvertently." I thought about it for a second. "My mom only married him because supposedly he was untraceable to Turner's network."

"Bruce Lenton?" Isabelle asked with steel in her eyes.

It took a moment to recover. But from the extreme hatred in Isabelle's eyes, I was sure she knew Bruce well.

"Yes, how did you know?" I wasn't sure I wanted to hear the answer.

"Bruce was one of Turner's first experiments with injecting tracking devices into people's blood streams. It backfired and ended up making Bruce completely untrackable. Bruce fit the mold of the kind of person your grandfather picked for foster care. I lived with Bruce for a while before I knew about my abilities and before he was injected with the tracking device. I know you already know what it was like living with that man. After I discovered my powers and Harry and Turner trained me how to utilize them, I tried to find Bruce, to kill him. But I never could track him. Turner promised me he would hunt him down. Your *Gramps* made me the monster I am today." Isabelle splashed the water with her feet as in emphasis. She didn't make eye contact with me. This was not the kind of girl who shared all that often. What she was telling me was a skyscraper-sized olive branch. I just wasn't sure what to do with it.

"Well, he's dead now." I tried to comfort her. I knew how evil Bruce was, how he would beat my mother for no particular reason other than because he felt like it. As much as I knew I couldn't kill anyone it didn't change the fact that a world without Bruce was a better place.

I sighed heavily.

A world without Elisha would be better place, too.

How many people did she have to kill before I sucked it up and killed her? Even just saying the words in my head, it just wasn't in me. I realized that whereas Isabelle blamed my grandfather for who she was today, I blamed the moment I killed Bruce as the person I was today. As much as my mom and I were better off with him dead (and me controlling his body), I hated myself for killing him. I hated that I'd let my emotions take over and turn me into a murderer. Even if I was only seven at the time, *especially* since I was only seven, to feel that much hatred so young and to actually do something about it. What did that make me?

Isabelle must have made certain connections in her head because she reflected, "You used your power to make Bruce seem alive, that's how you kept Turner's anti-tracker working."

"Yeah. I didn't know I was doing it, though. My mother never told me that marrying Bruce was to protect us from Turner. She made me think that Bruce was someone she married for love. I used my power to keep him animated because I thought Mom would be devastated if he died. I never dreamed that she hated him as much I did. She only stayed with him to keep us safe," I explained.

"Why do you have a relationship with Turner and Roberta, then? After everything they've put you through, after your father's sacrifice, after your mother's death? I'd kill them if it were me." Isabelle wasn't judging, she was genuinely confused.

"Why haven't *you* killed Turner yet?" I shot back. "You said he did all those horrible things to you, too. But you haven't killed him." I figured if Isabelle could give me her reason for not killing Turner, I could maybe think of a reason for myself. I honestly didn't know why I kept going back to my grandparents. Circumstances, I guess. But I knew it was more than that. I was genuinely developing feelings for both of them. A thought that made me want to vomit and cry at the same time.

"I tried to kill him and you stopped me," Isabelle stated.

"True, but you knew he'd stop you, didn't you?" I asked what I suspected about the assassination attempt.

"Yes, we knew about you and we knew that attempting to kill Turner during his speech would be the opportunity to draw you out. We didn't, however, know what you could do. We didn't even know that kind of thing was possible." Isabelle still seemed flabbergasted at the thought of raising the dead.

It was odd to me that someone with her powers would be shocked by my ability, especially since her fellow assassination squad had equally frightening mojo.

"Your power is way more dangerous than mine, Isabelle. If Elisha knew the potential of what you could do, she'd perform the power-transferring ritual on you," I warned. I still didn't know exactly what

Isabelle's power meant. It was kind of like the twins' power had been, though not as straightforward. They could control all life. Isabelle's ability wasn't like that. It was almost as if she could control all movement, if that made any sense.

Isabelle began to lazily swirl the water with her feet. "I haven't told anyone about what happened and Dean is keeping quiet for me. We trust each other, but I'm not sure about Harry anymore, and Terence is Harry's loyal dog. Harry wants to stay out of the *Turner and Elisha feud*, but Elisha is trying to bring Harry back into the fold. I know him, he's definitely considering it. I think she's just as bad as Turner though."

"She's worse, and I never thought I'd say that, believe me." Seriously, never thought I'd say that. "Turner thinks he's doing the things he does for the greater good. I'm pretty sure he believes that whole-heartedly. Elisha wasn't born with a conscience. She's like what they used to call serial killers."

"I was around when serial killers existed," Isabelle reflected. "They would make movies and TV shows about them. Real life monsters."

"They still exist. Gramps employs them. Another form of population control for him." I was supposed to be arguing Turner's case, not reminding myself of what an insane psycho he was.

"I know. He started that program years ago. He had them all tagged so they wouldn't get too out of control." Isabelle laughed at the absurdity of it, "It was one of the reasons why Harry and our team left Turner. We had to fake our deaths."

"Now that you know what you can do, what are you going to do?" I still didn't trust the girl, no matter how much we were sharing.

"I can't do what you did. I tried. I'm not really sure if I tried all that hard though. I'm tired of this life. I'm tired of being a killing machine. I'm not all that different from a serial killer. Our motivations may be different, but I can guarantee my body count is higher." Isabelle pulled her feet out of the water and stood up on the dock. She reached her hand down to help me up and I took it warily. "I want to show you why we distrust your grandfather so much. Can I do that?" Isabelle wasn't asking permission, she was asking me how to access her memories so I could see her past.

I wasn't exactly the master of that kind of thing, but as long as I could get to the memory door section of her brain we were golden. I tried not to look too eager, but I had to admit I was extremely curious to see Isabelle's past. Maybe it would give me more insight into her – or, better yet, into my grandparents.

"Yeah, hold my hands," I instructed, and we faced each other holding hands. I concentrated as hard as I could on picturing a long winding hallway with lots of doors, hoping this would take us to that part of her mind.

But we were still at the lake.

"Is something supposed to happen?" Isabelle genuinely looked perplexed.

"I usually jump straight into the memory section. We just need to think about your memories…" As the words came out of my mouth the dock and sky and water all swirled into a tornado of color and was replaced by Isabelle's memory center.

Nice.

Isabelle surveyed the area in awe. There were millions of doors all facing each other down an infinite hallway. Each door was unique in its design: some tall, some small, some carved out of wood, and some made of metal.

"These are my memories?" Isabelle asked.

"It's how *I* see them. You should be able to sense which memory is behind which door, so it's up to you what you want to show me."

Isabelle nodded and walked forward, then her face lit up. "You're right. I know without looking what's behind each door." She tapped a few doors and started to hurry down the hallway, "This way. We have a long way to go."

I followed close behind. The older the person, the more memories they had. It looked as if Isabelle organized her memories by date. If we were going all the way back three hundred years we were in for a long walk. So much for getting a good night's sleep tonight!

After what seemed like miles Isabelle stopped in front of a half-sized door. It stood out among the other normal-sized doors so I knew that whatever was behind it had to be important. Isabelle didn't seem surprised at all at its size. She turned to me, a sad expression on her face. "You ready to see this?"

Gulp.

That sounded really scary, but I nodded.

Isabelle took a deep breath and opened the small door. We had to duck to walk in, and once we were inside neither one of us could stand. I immediately started to feel shaky. I felt like I was back inside the metal coffin I had been buried in. The room was only five feet high, and maybe ten feet wide. A single light bulb swung from the low ceiling, giving only a small amount of dim light to the room. A little girl was huddled in the corner. Isabelle. She was probably eight years old. Her clothes were torn and dirty and it didn't look like she had bathed in weeks. She was scraping the walls with her fingernails.

"I thought you should see this first," Isabelle's voice was distant. Seeing this was more emotional than she had expected.

I noticed then that underneath the dirt covering little Isabelle's skin were deep purple bruises.

"I thought I told you to keep it down!" A familiar voice screamed from outside the room.

Bruce.

I hadn't heard his voice in what felt like years, but had only been months ago. Then I realized, I hadn't heard his real voice since I was seven. Controlling Bruce my whole life, he had been the epitome of the perfect father, kind and loving. But in this memory... this memory was how I remembered him too. Inhuman.

We had to crouch to even stand in the room, and it made me feel all the more vulnerable. I knew this wasn't real, that it was just a memory, but hearing Bruce scream at young Isabelle like that brought me back to the terror of my own childhood.

I flinched involuntarily when Bruce swung the door open and grabbed young Isabelle by the collar of her dress, violently pulling her out of the room.

Seeing Bruce again made my breath stop.

Tears came to my eyes and I couldn't seem to stop them.

I remembered him hitting my mother.

I remembered him hitting me.

And now, seeing that three hundred years before I was born he was beating another little girl made me want to scream. It made me think about Turner's vicious words to me when he told me the truth about Bruce and my mother. *My only tiny bit of satisfaction was knowing that Bruce was a violent man and I hoped that he beat that murderer regularly.* That *murderer* being my mom. My brain was on conflicting overload. Turner sent kids to Bruce and men like him on purpose. On purpose!

Little Isabelle didn't make a noise as Bruce yanked her the rest of the way out of the room to have his way with her. I was afraid that Isabelle was going to make us follow him and watch, but she motioned for us to leave.

I didn't argue. I followed her out of the small room and immediately started to breathe in deep. I knew that, literally speaking, I wasn't even there, my actual lungs and body snuggly safe in bed with Ryan, but when you were inside someone else's head, it *felt* real. I needed deep breaths to calm down.

Isabelle looked visibly shaken by the memory as well. "Thank you for killing him."

I didn't know how to respond to that so I simply said, "Yeah."

Isabelle started to move back the way we came. "I'll show you how Harry and Turner were like my family."

I followed her without a word. Betrayal only happened when you trusted and cared about the person doing the betraying. It was going to be strange watching Gramps in the past. Maybe it would give me more insight into the man he had become today.

After a long trek back through the hallway of Isabelle's memories we arrived at a steel door. Isabelle opened it slowly, then we walked through.

We were in some kind of office or headquarters. Strange rectangular metal boxes with flashing lights were set on the floor. On the desks were rectangular frames playing flat images on their surface. I was pretty sure they were what we learned in history class were called "monitors," and the boxes on the floor had to be a kind of primitive computer. All very archaic and chunky.

Turner and Harry were there, staring at the screens, which played some kind of surveillance footage. From the tenseness in the room there were obviously a few missions taking place.

The door on the opposite side of the room burst open. Dean and Charlie charged in, carrying Isabelle between them. She had an arm around each of their necks and her stomach was red with blood. She didn't look like she was going to make it.

Turner and Harry nearly leapt to take Isabelle from Dean and Charlie's arms.

Turner screamed at Charlie, "Get supplies!"

Charlie ran out the door.

Dean swiped a monitor off one of the desks, sending it crashing to the floor. No one complained about it. Harry carefully laid Isabelle on the makeshift bed.

Turner took off his jacket and wadded it up to make a pillow, tucking it under Isabelle's head. He whirled on Dean, "What the hell happened?!"

Dean was a wreck himself, "She didn't have enough time to stop his heart, a guard got to us first. He was good. Really good. He fired from what had to be eight hundred feet. It was an impossible shot. He has to be like one of us."

Watching the scene from outside, Isabelle explained to me, "That was Terence, Turner hunted him down to have him killed for shooting me. But he recruited him instead."

I couldn't tell if that upset her or if she was okay with it, either way Isabelle couldn't keep her eyes off the memory.

I focused my attention back to my grandfather who was brushing the hair out of Isabelle's face. There was so much concern and worry in his eyes that it made my heart ache. I had only seen Gramps act that way toward Roberta. It was weird seeing him look at Isabelle like she was… his daughter. Especially now since he so coldly wanted her dead. How could things change so drastically?

Gramps spoke to Isabelle gently, "You're going to be fine. We're going to take care of you."

Harry was just as frantic, holding Isabelle's hand. He turned to Dean, "Did you call the doc?"

Dean nodded and watched as Isabelle's eyes fluttered in and out of consciousness. He loved her. I could see it in his eyes. Did Isabelle feel the same? Were they still an item? These memories were causing me to ask more questions, not answer the ones I already had.

The Isabelle of the past woke up briefly, "Geoffrey," she called out weakly.

Gramps held her other hand and she clasped it tightly, he said to her, "I'm here, Izzy, I'm here."

Isabelle's face relaxed slightly as if just hearing this from Turner would cure her instantly.

"We just need to see your injury," Harry said. I could tell he was a little miffed that Isabelle called out for Turner instead of him, but Harry's concern for her overrode any jealousies he was having.

Isabelle might not have caught that, but I did.

Charlie came running in with a bag of bandages and supplies, placing them next to Isabelle's body.

Dean took over. He ripped open the bottom of her shirt to reveal the damage done. There was blood everywhere with a wad of cloth that used to be someone's undershirt stemming the blood flow. He carefully pulled off the improvised bandage: a flood of blood poured out of a small hole in Isabelle's gut. Isabelle groaned in pain. Dean started to clean the wound with gauze and rubbing alcohol.

A man I could only assume was a doctor ran into the room and went directly to Isabelle's side. He wore a white coat and some kind of rubber over his hands that I assumed were gloves. It was weird watching the past: nowadays doctors operated using "alternate skin," a germ-free bio-compound that formed around their hands. I guess that before the Waste Laws doctors used to use tight fitting gloves.

"Clean those," the doctor instructed, pointing at the metal instruments Charlie had brought in the bag.

Charlie began cleaning the instruments with the alcohol. The doctor picked up a kind of prong-type medical tool and started digging into the small hole in Isabelle's stomach, trying to locate and pull out the bullet.

Isabelle screamed. Turner still held on to her hand and with the other wiped her forehead clean with a wet cloth.

Isabelle turned to Gramps with tears in her eyes. "I'm not going to make it."

Turner responded, "You're going to be fine. The doctor will fix you."

Isabelle shook her head and pulled his hand closer to her heart. "Thank you. Thank you for everything."

There were actual tears in Turner's eyes. "I don't know what you're thanking me for. Save your strength."

"You all are my family. I've never had a real family before," Isabelle's voice grew weaker the more she talked.

Turner leaned down and kissed her forehead, "Just hang in there."

Gramps really loved her.

Isabelle's eyes fluttered. She was about to lose consciousness. "I… love you…"

Before she passed out completely Gramps kissed her hand. "We love you too, Izzy."

Turner and Harry shared a look of terror.

They didn't want to lose her.

The Isabelle next to me pulled me outside into the hallway and slammed the door shut.

"I wanted you to see how he felt about me before I show you what he did." Isabelle's voice was cold. She had detached herself from Gramps so many years ago and now, seeing how much he'd loved her once…did nothing to change her hatred for him. In fact, it seemed to strengthen it.

Uh, oh.

I could only imagine what he did to her.

We walked further back to where we first started passing the wide variety of doorways along the way. Finally we came to the creepiest door I'd ever seen. It was rusted metal with thousands of sharp spikes protruding all across its surface. I wasn't even sure how Isabelle was going to open it without making her incorporeal self bleed, but she simply kicked it open with her foot.

As we entered the space it shocked my senses to find ourselves outside in bright sunlight. My eyes had adjusted to the semi-darkness of the hallway and of Isabelle's darker memories, but this flashback was on a hilltop overlooking an enormous skyline. I didn't recognize the city, but it was huge. Buildings that stretched up into the sky mixed with old stone masonry structures. The city looked like a patchwork of old and new. It was breathtaking, the expanse of the ancient city going on for miles. There was something so majestic about the place. It even had a river winding its way through the beautiful architecture of the cityscape. It wasn't until I saw the Eiffel Tower in the far distance that I realized we were standing above Paris, France.

Isabelle of the past was standing across from Harry. They were screaming at each other.

"You're full of crap, Harry!" Isabelle was enraged. "Turner wouldn't have done that to me!"

"I'm not lying." Harry's eyes were pleading, "Turner had all your parents killed, including Dean's. He's the reason you have your power. He started testing Age-pro trials on pregnant women years ago and when some of the children started showing unique abilities, he decided to build an army of them. When Fortski realized the key ingredient to stop the aging process was to literally to *stop* aging, Turner could no longer continue his experimentation because nothing can grow inside a body that can't age. Geoffrey was left with the only people who'd survived his experiments, namely *you* and the rest of our team." He held Isabelle's arms with his hands and looked at her with genuine sympathy. "Your mother was just another guinea pig when she was pregnant with you. It was his idea to kill the parents after the kids like you were born and send you all to abusive homes. He thought it would weed out the weak ones."

Isabelle shrugged off Harry's hold. "He wouldn't do that to us! He's the only dad I ever knew."

"What about me, Izzy? I consider you a daughter. I'm the one who has your best interests in mind." Harry desperately wanted Isabelle to believe him. "Turner's lost it. He's created a title for himself, 'Vice President of Population Control,' whatever that means. I don't know how, but the world leaders are acting like his puppets. He's becoming the most powerful man in the world and he'll destroy anyone who can take him down."

"What proof do you have?" Isabelle was incredulous. I could tell she thought Harry was crazy.

"This." Harry pulled out a small holo-reader (I guess technology had progressed enough at this point in their lives). He pressed Play and a holo-image of Turner and Harry popped up. They were see-thru, not solid like today's holo projections, but both men were clearly visible.

Turner was fiercely intense, confronting Harry, and even as an eight-inch holo-image he was still intimidating. "If you don't get everyone on board, Harry, I'll have you all killed."

Holo-Harry spit on Turner. "I'd like to see you try you little weasel!"

"How far the mighty have fallen. I played the game, Harry. You sat behind your console and took orders. I made sure I was the man who gave the orders," Gramps snarled.

"There's no way you can rally the U.N. to your side. They hated us a month ago. They find us useful, but they'd never let someone like you in any kind of public position of power." Harry laughed at Turner with a mocking tone.

Turner didn't flinch. "I have them all in my pocket. I can make them do and say whatever I want."

Yeeks.

I knew Gramps well enough to know that he had killed whatever world leaders they were talking about and controlled them using his black magic. The ramifications of that hit me hard. Isabelle would have no idea. She probably still hadn't connected those particular dots since this memory was more emotional for her than political. But I did. Gramps was the most powerful man in the world because he literally controlled the people who ran it.

If Elisha knew that…

Oh man.

We were dead.

Holo-Harry stopped his argument and looked sad. "Geoffrey, we've known each other almost our whole lives. I introduced you to Roberta. We built this organization together. How can you ask me to do this?"

"Isabelle is the most dangerous human alive. If you don't kill her, I will. I know you care about her, but she's never been more than a tool for me to get where I needed to go. She's dispensable and she always was, I thought you knew that," Turner said as if he were talking about a lab rat.

Harry looked broken. "I can't kill her. I won't."

"Then I will." Turner left Harry standing alone. The holo-image flickered and died.

Isabelle pulled me back into the hallway. I could see her trying to hold back emotions. Turner's words had destroyed her that day. For someone who was raised by abusive fathers, then trained as an assassin, to be betrayed by the only father figure you knew and trusted was devastating.

I understood her pain, but I was raised by a mother who loved me unconditionally. She never had that chance because Turner killed her mother too. We had a lot in common.

"I'm sorry." I didn't know what else to say. I felt horrible for her, but my mind raced a mile-a-minute. Elisha must know about Turner controlling all the world leaders. All she'd have to do was watch some old footage of them and see their swirling black holes. It made so much sense now! A policy over a hundred years ago for "security reasons" had made all important figureheads for each country stay off camera. One of Turner's main duties was to be the face of world leadership. That was why, when anything happened, he was the one everyone turned to.

I, personally, had never even seen a world leader. It was considered normal not to see anyone else but Turner. If I was right and they were all dead, then I would have known right away what Gramps was up to if I'd seen them on holo-TV.

It would have been a great way to take him down back in the day. All I'd have to do is disconnect the leaders from their holes and they'd be dead for good.

Of course, that would cause mass panic as they'd turn to skeletons in front of their constituents. Maybe keeping the world leaders "alive" was better. Ugh. I really hated this crap. Politics were not my thing AT ALL!

Isabelle was still thinking of her memory, though. "After that, before Turner could do anything, we staged a mission where we made it look like the whole team blew up. We've been running our own organization ever since. Turner never knew, though I'm sure at times he suspected. I always wondered if he'd come after me and try to kill me himself."

"Isabelle," I started cautiously, "I really am sorry my grandfather wanted you dead after how close you two were, but we've got bigger problems." I told her my theory.

Isabelle stood there, her face unreadable. Then she nodded her head. "It makes sense. The higher-ups distrusted Turner, they knew what kind of man he was, that's why they hired him. Then suddenly not only were they taking orders from him, but they were publicly campaigning for his new title. We never knew how or why."

"I know you hate Turner's guts. I do, too, most of the time. But the bigger picture here is the fact that, in all those years, Gramps has never abused the power that he's had. I mean not in the *I control the world* kind of way anyway. Elisha on the other hand…" I left that open-ended.

"She'll burn us all to the ground for sport, yeah, I get it." Isabelle took a deep breath. "Okay, we need to work together on this, you and me only, because there's no way Harry is going to work with Turner again."

I interrupted her, "There's a kill order out on your whole team." Thought she should know that.

"No surprise there," Isabelle sighed. "We probably can't meet up in person is what you're saying?"

I nodded.

"Then we'll have to meet this astral-whatcha-call-it way until we can figure it out. I'm okay with that. But you'll have to come to me. I have no idea how to do any of this stuff." Isabelle tossed her hands around to indicate how crazy she thought this astral thing was.

"Deal." I wasn't sure if we should shake hands. Isabelle didn't strike me as the kind of girl who did that kind of thing. "I know I'm related to Turner, but I'm my own person. He didn't even care that we were related when he tried to kill me."

"I know. I trust you. I don't know why, but I do. The only other person on this planet that I trust is Dean, so you're on a very short list." That was a huge responsibility! But one thing I knew: I was trustworthy. If it came down to Isabelle being on the right side and Gramps being on the wrong, I'd pick Isabelle hands down. I wasn't about to let him lead me down the garden path again. I didn't want it to be like Havenville all over again, when Turner promised he wouldn't kill anyone and then he killed almost everyone!

"Are you and Dean…?" Wow. I sounded like I was in high school. Of course I *was* in high school, but I tried not to sound like it when I could help it. I just had to know though.

"Yes. For almost three hundred years." Isabelle actually smiled at that point. So when it came to Dean she was a softie. It made me happy in ways I couldn't describe. From everything that I knew of the poor girl it seemed like her life was full of sadness and chaos. It was nice to know she had a ray of sunshine in there somewhere. Even if it was with a jerk.

I smiled back. "Just tell him not to kill me next time he sees me."
Isabelle mock-saluted me.

I took a deep breath. "Okay, I'm gonna go."

I jumped out before she could respond.

***

I slammed back in my body and the jolt made me reflexively sit up. Ryan wrapped his arms around me and started kissing my neck to calm me down. "Where were you this time?"

I turned around in his embrace and kissed him. Man it felt good to do that. Why did my life have to be full of world domination and death crap. "Isabelle's head."

"Yikes, what did she say to you?" Ryan couldn't seem to stop kissing me. From my neck to my ear to my cheek. It was giving me shivers.

"Stuff." I just wanted to ignore everything that wasn't me and Ryan.

Ryan apparently agreed: he grabbed the back of my t-shirt and drew me in for the most amazing kiss ever. I could barely think straight as I felt his lips move with mine. It always amazed me how much this boy could make my head explode. I could feel his hands touch my waist and then his grip tightened. Of course this made me want him even more.

I ran my hands across his back, feeling his muscles tighten at my touch. He let out a small gasp as I pulled him in even closer so our bodies were pressed together. I could barely breathe as every nerve in my body was on fire.

Ryan's gentle touch was maddening as he ran his hand through my hair while touching the small of my back with his other hand. I could literally kiss him forever. There was nothing like it. It was a moment of pure joy, and I could use as many of those as I could get.

When he wasn't kissing me he was telling me how much he loved me, which made me respond even more. I told him I loved him too and we made love.

***

Afterwards, Ryan and I held each other, snuggling close in pure contentment. He laid up against my back with his arm draped over my side holding my hand. I played with his hand while he gently kissed the back of my neck.

"We're going to have to have a big talk with the gang tomorrow." I didn't to ruin the mood but I knew that I'd have to wake up to reality sooner rather than later.

"I figured." He kissed the top of my head. "Let's just enjoy the moment and worry about saving the world in the morning."

"Sounds good." I kissed his hand again.

"Good night, beautiful." Ryan snuggled in closer.

"Good night," I answered back and couldn't help but feel a surge of happiness when he called me beautiful. I closed my eyes, still smiling when I fell asleep.

***

We woke up to Jason knocking on our door and letting himself in like he owned the place. "Rise and shine, lazy butts, we have a lot to discuss."

"Turn around!" I scolded Jason.

Jason groaned in annoyance, but turned around all the same. Ryan and I quickly dressed and sat up in the bed.

"All right, we're decent," I informed him.

Jason whirled around and made himself comfortable at the foot of our bed. "You guys just make yourselves at home anywhere, don't you?" He said it with a smile, but my face turned red regardless.

"Kidnap and torture will do that to a person." Ryan leaned back on his pillows to emphasize his point.

It was true, though. When you were constantly on the run, anywhere soft and fuzzy became home.

"So spill, you look like you're going to burst." I observed, noticing Jason's fidgeting behavior.

Jason tried to hide his deep worry, but I could see it as clearly as if he had screamed *We're doomed.* He focused on me like I was a patient about to hear the news that I was dying. "That fiasco at the mall...

It's been a lot harder to squelch than I thought it would be. Thanks to my superior reporting," (no modesty there!) "I've managed to convince some of the public that you may have been set up, but the majority just isn't there."

"What exactly does that mean?" I asked. Sure, I knew I was enemy number one out in the world, but I somehow just believed that Turner would take care of it. Naïve of me, I know.

"It means you're on lockdown until we can get this thing settled." Jason shrugged. "I've never seen it this bad, Chelsan. People are screaming for your execution. There's a public outcry that I'm positive is being flamed by Elisha, and I'm not sure if we can control it." Jason looked defeated.

The fact that being locked up in Elisha's dungeon may have been a safer place for me than a walk down the street seemed ridiculous, but according to Jason it was. I never thought in a trillion years that being at Population Control would be a safe haven for me. My how things had changed.

Nancy and Bill walked in at that moment and I was instantly relieved. Seeing their friendly faces made me feel like no matter what happened at least I had my amazing friends to back me up. Nancy sat next to Jason and rested her head on his shoulder, which instantly made him relax. Bill did his normal thing and kind of stood close to me, but far enough away that Ryan wouldn't think he was intruding. Boys and their territorial instincts!

Bill spoke first, "Tell us everything."

They had no idea what Ryan and I had just gone through. Ryan didn't even know it all. So I gave them the scoop. When I was done Bill and Nancy looked like they wanted to hug the horribleness out of what happened.

Then Nancy reached over and examined my arm. "That's crazy. Not a scratch on you. We need that serum with us forever."

Bill piped in, "Hopefully there are no side effects."

Nancy gave him a reproachful glare, "Bill!"

"It's too late now," I said. "It was that or die for both Max and I."

Just saying that out loud was far more dramatic than I actually felt about it, but it was the truth.

"But we're fine now," Max's voice was a welcome sound as he and Jill entered the room. It was starting to feel like a party.

Jill and Max were holding hands and I thought I would burst with the cuteness of it all. Jill looked different. Calm. Like she'd finally figured herself out and was at peace with her past and present. It truly made me happy seeing her like that.

Jill spoke, "Max told me everything that happened from his end. You're lucky to be alive."

"How did you control Fortski and Isabelle?" Max asked.

"I connected to their life force, if that makes sense. Like the way you and I can connect to dead things. It was the same when I used the twins' powers. When I'm actually inside a person I can see their swirling white light and connect to it, but when I'm in my own body I can't." I tried to reason it out myself.

"Can Elisha do that?" Jill asked what everyone was wondering in horror.

Max allayed everyone's fears, "Don't worry, that's not how Elisha controls people, or at least, not how she controlled me. She uses astral projection like Chelsan, but she can't connect to the white-light-life force like Chelsan can. Elisha nestles into the part of the brain that controls a person's decision-making process. She'd tell me what to do, trying to make me think it was my idea, when I refused, Elisha would convince me I was wrong and I felt like I had to do what she said. But she never took over my body. And she was only able to do it with me and for some reason our teacher, Ms. Floster. She tried with Eva, but it didn't work. She even tried with the guy that controlled the metal stuff, Charlie, before she killed him. Elisha was afraid by killing Charlie his powers wouldn't work. But Charlie wouldn't listen to her and tried to kill her, so she shot him. That's why she wants Isabelle, Dean and Terence dead, so she really can control them." Max was pretty certain of his analysis and it made me sigh a breath of relief.

I was terrified that I might somehow let my guard down and Elisha would take over. Thinking back to when I first met Elisha, she had tried similar "influencing" tactics on me though not as blatant as what she did with Max. Elisha gently tapped on the decision-making part of my brain and made me think things like, I don't know... breaking her out of prison and walking into her lair were a good thing! I remember thinking it was a bad idea, but then I'd talk myself into doing it anyway.

Max's information gave me some hope. At least Elisha didn't have body-control in her arsenal. I assumed the reason I could do it was due to my connection with the twins. Because I had been the only person who controlled them, that experience had given me insight to how their power actually worked.

Everyone was quiet. The enormity of what was happening had finally hit us all. I didn't know what to say. No one knew what our next move should be, or if we should make a move at all.

Nancy finally broke the silence, "So, anyone buy their dress for prom yet?"

We all laughed, even Jason.

Prom. If only my life could be that normal. It was the first time I envied someone like Joan. As shallow and horrible as she was, her biggest concern was what she was going to wear to our senior prom.

"I know it makes you all uncomfortable to bring it up, but I need to tell you: I'm going to save Eva," Max said with conviction in his voice.

I knew they were bonded, but I also knew he was blinded by his emotions. Eva was a sociopath.

"Max, she tried to kill me and she did nothing to save you." I didn't mean to sound harsh, but I really wasn't on board with a Saving Eva campaign.

"I thought you should know," he said. "I'm not leaving her behind and I'm not letting Elisha have her." Max's mind was made up and I didn't want to be the one to argue, so I let it go.

"I'm telling you right now you're not getting any help from us," Ryan responded pretty defensively. "She's dangerous *because* you care about her. She'd let Elisha kill you all over again."

Max wasn't upset by Ryan's comments, he simply replied, "I know. But she is a good person at her core, she's just been brainwashed by Elisha."

I had to say something, "That's partially true, yes, but like I've told you before, Elisha picked you two for your genetic markers. Markers that indicate that you're like Elisha. The psychopath part."

"But I'm not a psycho, you know that, so maybe Eva isn't either."

Max turned to Bill. "She loves you, you know. That wasn't fake. She'd talk about you for hours to the point where Elisha locked her in a room with no food for three days until Eva promised not to speak your name. But she still did, to me, when Elisha wasn't around. A sociopath wouldn't care. Eva would have been just using you to get close to Chelsan, but she fell for you instead."

I could see that Max's words truly hurt Bill. As much as I hated to admit it, Bill obviously still had feelings for the girl. He was just too good of a guy to bring it up, knowing how it would hurt me.

I didn't care how much Max vouched for the girl and how much Bill liked her. Eva had sided one too many times with Elisha, and she was the reason I was in hiding in the first place. "Eva killed those people at the mall, not me. Remember who you're trying to save."

My words acted like a slap in Max's face. I didn't mean them to, but they did regardless.

He kept quiet after that. I wanted to say something to him. We had been through so much together, but I knew that, anything other than "yes, I'll save Eva with you" wouldn't make him feel any better.

Finally Max said, "I won't interfere in taking down Elisha. I just want you guys to know my intentions."

Jill leaned into him, showing her support. She had kept quiet the whole argument. Jill hated Eva as much as I did, but for once she took the higher road, respecting Max's feelings over her own prejudices.

Wow. Jill had acted more mature than I had. But then again, Jill hadn't been tortured by Eva either.

Turner ran in at that moment and it took me a second to recognize him. He looked frazzled and rushed. "We found something," he announced directly to me. He ignored everyone else in the room. "Get out of bed and come to the surveillance room. John will show you the way."

John, another guard, entered the room with a small wave of the hand.

Gramps stormed out of the room like he had been a tornado that touched down briefly only to rise back up into the sky.

I raised my eyebrow in curiosity, "I guess we better follow him."

The giant group of us followed John down the hall to a large conference room with plenty of chairs surrounding a large oval table. Turner and Roberta were at the back of the room, sitting down already and waiting for us all to get situated. Not many decorations adorned the walls, just a few holo-paintings and an obnoxious yellow paint job that made the room overly bright.

When everyone was ready and staring at Gramps, he hit a button on the table. It took a moment for my eyes to adjust to the onslaught of holo-footage playing in front of us, inches from our faces. There were hundreds of different shots of what looked like an airport.

Jason was the first to take it all in, his reporter's eyes used to seeing massive amounts of footage at once, "What are we looking for here?" he asked, trying to see the connection Gramps was trying to show us.

Turner stood up and pointed to the piece of footage closest to him. "There. Getting on the holo-jet to New York."

Dad.

A Franklin clone, pretending to be a child flying alone, was being escorted on a holo-jet at L.A.X. airport.

Then I saw them all.

Every single piece of holo-footage in front of us had a Franklin clone boarding a holo-jet on hundreds of different flights. All leaving LAX. All going to cities around the world: Tokyo, Berlin, Moscow, Cairo, Rio, the list went on and on.

I didn't know what that meant, but it couldn't be good. "Why?"

Roberta spoke. "We don't know. We have analysts searching right now for any reason why Elisha would be sending the clones away. Maybe for protection? Maybe to have eyes in every major country? We just don't know yet."

"I think I might know." Jason's face had turned white.

Gramps turned his full attention on Jason. He pretty much pretended I was the only one worth talking to when my friends were around, but Jason appeared to be an exception at the moment.

"May I?" Jason asked Turner, nodding at the holo-footage.

Gramps nodded and Jason used a remote device to change what we were seeing. Now there were just as many holo-images of headlines in a bunch of different languages. I couldn't read any of them, but apparently Roberta and Turner knew how to translate enough of them to make their faces go just as white as Jason's.

"What already?!" Jill couldn't take the suspense.

I had to agree with her.

Jason explained, "The one thread all these articles have in common is the word *Missing*. Remember when the army base down in San Diego reported that their soldiers were gone?"

Oh crap.

"And they turned up in the Sepulveda Dam as dead soldiers," I concluded.

Jason motioned to the thousands of headlines. "These are all reports of the same thing happening all over the world. Smaller bases that barely make the headlines since no one cares about military any more. No one has a need to, wars ended almost three hundred years ago when Age-pro made people re-think dying senselessly. Who wants to fight a war when they can live forever?"

Nancy piped in with alarm in her voice. "So you're saying Elisha's killed all these soldiers all over the world to build an army?"

Gramps sighed heavily. "And she just sent her generals on holo-jets to go lead them."

That sunk in.

"How do we stop her?" It was Bill who spoke. He said it so bravely it made me proud of him.

"I'm not sure if we can," Turner answered, sitting down in utter shock.

Elisha had planned well and we had missed it entirely. We were so focused on her obsession with me that we overlooked the big picture.

Then I thought of something. "What about the world leaders? You control them right? Can't you make them put their armies together and stop her?"

Roberta and Turner both stared at me like I had shocked them to their core.

Oh yeah.

They didn't know I knew what they'd done.

"I figured it out through a memory Isabelle showed me," I explained.

Gramps was the first to recover. "Isabelle showed you her memories? When did this happen?" His tone was one of hurt rather than the hatred for Isabelle I had expected from him.

"Last night. She said that one minute the U.N. hated you and the next they did whatever you said. It didn't take a genius to figure it out, knowing what I know about you." It was true.

Turner cleared his throat and by doing so cleared his head. "Yes, they're all dead and I control them. They're in lock down right now because I was afraid Elisha was going to try to take one of them over and turn the world against itself. But she knows she doesn't have the reach or the resources to control all of them, so she's bet on brute force instead."

Ryan joined in the conversation. "And since her armies are already dead, the more Elisha kills, the more men join her army."

"She wants it to be a slaughter," Nancy finished Ryan's thought.

"When did the flights leave? Can we stop them from landing?" I asked, not holding my breath.

Roberta shook her head. "These were from early morning. All the flights landed before we saw this footage. We have to assume the clones are with their respective armies by now."

"So what can we do?" I was at a loss. I hated to think that we were going to lose, but it certainly felt that way.

Turner seemed just as defeated as everyone else in the room, but he brought a slight sliver of hope when he said, "We still have two things that Elisha wants: You and Fortski's formula. Maybe we can come to some sort of arrangement."

"Having Fortski would be better," Jason pointed out.

"Well, we don't have him," Turner grumbled. "Harry's got him, and considering the fact that I wasn't able to track down Harry for the past two-hundred years, our prospects are rather low for finding him."

"I told you, I was with Isabelle last night. She said I could contact her, I'll just tell her…" I started.

Gramps cut me off sharply, "You can't trust a word that girl says. Isabelle's setting you up so she can take you again. She'll betray you without blinking an eye." He was mad. Really mad.

I found it strange since technically he was the one who betrayed her, but if I was an observer just coming off the street I'd swear he was the dumpee in this situation. Maybe Isabelle's faking her own death, regardless of whether or not Turner actually wanted to kill her, was too much for him. It didn't make much sense to me, but then again my grandparents' logic was pretty unfathomable.

"She seemed pretty trustworthy. She showed me things that would compromise her position with Harry…"

Cut off again. "Isabelle's personality is exactly like her power: she insinuates herself into your heart, then she squeezes it until you die."

Okay.

Two hundred years later and this guy was seriously pissed.

I just couldn't understand why. I saw the holo-footage. He'd wanted her dead. He didn't even seem to care about it at the time. He talked about her to Harry like Isabelle was just an experiment that had gone wrong. Why all the emotion? Was it because he thought she'd made a fool of him? It seemed way more personal than that. At this point it didn't matter. I couldn't coddle Turner's hurt feelings. I went for the assertive stance.

"Well, we have to do something and Isabelle is our only option at this point. We'll just have to be on our guard in case she turns on us." I didn't leave much room for argument.

Gramps hesitated, but it was Roberta who agreed first. "Contact her. Tell her we'll make a trade. The formula for Fortski. Elisha doesn't know Fortski even made a sample so she'll want Fortski himself."

"Speaking of Fortski…" Ryan stood up. "I'd like to take a look at those last few drops of his formula if we're going to give it up, just in case Forstki can't re-create it."

Turner nodded to Ryan. "I'll have you escorted to the labs."

I still didn't think we'd be able to stop Elisha from bloodshed, but we had to do something to at least try and stall her until we could come up with something brilliant.

Yeah, right.

The meeting was apparently over and I felt far worse than I had when it started. Ryan kissed me goodbye, then a handful of guards led him down a hallway towards the lab. Jason and Nancy stayed in the conference room to brainstorm on how they were going to spin a story to get me out of trouble with the public. Max and Jill went off to their room to do who-knows-what (well, I kind of knew what, but eeww). Gramps and Grams left to plot and scheme without me. That just left Bill and me.

I sighed a big sigh of relief. Bill. My big teddy bear. (A teddy bear that was completely ripped, but a teddy bear all the same.) His goofy smile greeted me and I couldn't resist: I leaned into him for the hug I knew I needed. With his strong arms wrapped around me, it made me want to believe that we were all going to be okay.

I pulled away with a smile to match his. "Let's try and find something to eat. I'm starving."

"There's a kitchen down the hall," Bill said, leading the way. "I'd say we go to one of the cafés for the public, but you'd probably get tarred and feathered," he teased, but the fact was that was exactly what would happen.

"I'm sure Turner stocks his kitchen with lots of goodies. He doesn't seem like the kind of guy who skimps," I observed. After all, look at the architectural structure we were in. Elaborate and over the top, certainly not cheap.

Bill rubbed his hands together greedily. "Oh there are definitely some goodies. I was kind of bored last night and snuck in for a midnight snack."

I felt a pang of guilt at poor Bill being all by himself last night, but he didn't seem upset by it so I decided not to be, either. I was just glad I was able to finally have one-on-one time with one of my best friends.

We entered a ridiculously huge kitchen and found that it was completely empty. Ten long rows of stainless steel tables spread across the room with pots and pans dangling above them from the ceiling. There were probably twenty refrigerators and at least that many oven ranges. It was an onslaught of silver to my eyes.

"This fridge is the prize." Bill had a jump to his step from actual giddiness. It was really nice to see him like he used to be, a fun loving easy-going guy. Despite everything I had put him through, he still was the same old Bill.

Bill opened the said fridge and he wasn't kidding. Every sweet imaginable was stocked in this refrigerator. From elaborately decorated cupcakes, to brownies, to five inch chocolate cookies, to lemon bars: you name it, it was in there.

"Oh yeah," I gushed. I knew gorging on sugar would most likely give me a stomach ache, but in that moment it was so worth it! I grabbed the densest chocolate chunk brownie I could find and a strawberry shortcake cupcake (strawberries were at least a fruit!), while Bill cut himself a slice of blackberry pie and loaded it with freshly whipped whip cream. He grabbed a couple of forks from a nearby drawer full of silverware, but I was using my hands for this one. It was probably the best brownie I had ever eaten in my life. Maybe it was because I was starving, I had no idea, but it was like eating the richest most decadent chocolate on the planet. I was pretty sure my eyes rolled back in my head from the sheer enjoyment of it.

Bill laughed at me, but when he took a bite of his pie, I could tell he felt the same way. "See?" he said, "Jackpot."

After three quarters of the brownie was nice and settled in my tummy and I had moved on to the ridiculously tasty strawberry shortcake cupcake, Bill held out his hand for me to join him on top of the metal table next to us. We both sat with our feet dangling off the edge, eating our newfound treasures in bliss.

Bill finished his bite then asked, "How you holding up through all this?"

I wiped the excess frosting off my mouth. "I'm all right. What can I do, right?" I couldn't elaborate much more than that. Bill knew everything that had happened, if I thought about it too much I'd go insane.

"What do you think about Max saving Eva?" he asked tentatively.

Here we go.

Apparently, the look on my face made Bill feel like this wasn't a line of questioning I was up for, because he immediately took another bite of his pie and mumbled, "Forget it."

I took a few seconds to regroup. I knew that my friend was seriously hurting over this, so I swallowed my hatred for the girl. "It's just hard for me, Bill. She really hates me and when Eva hates someone, she tries to murder them."

"I'm not making excuses for her. I'm not even saying I forgive her for what she's done to you. I just... I just saw something different in her... that's all." Bill wasn't meeting my eyes. That was really difficult for him to say.

I tried to make Bill smile. "She's only five months old, she has a lot of growing up to do."

Bill made eye contact with me and we both started laughing. It felt so good just to let it out and just be normal for once. The fact that Eva actually *was* only five months old only expounded how crazy our lives were.

"Jill used to be evil too, but we gave her a chance," Bill said after we had stopped laughing.

"True," I admitted. "Look, Bill, let me think about it for a while. I'm not going to stop Max from saving her, if that's what you're thinking. I'm just not sure I'm going to participate in trying to rescue someone who doesn't really want to be rescued."

"Agreed," he paused, "And thanks."

"Sure. Now can we just pig out and pretend like we're in your house and not in the grandparents' lair."

We both laughed and Bill pulled out a perfectly decorated chocolate cake. "Hands?" He smiled.

"Definitely," I answered.

We both dug into the thick, soft cake, grabbing handfuls of chocolate-y goodness and stuffing it in our mouths.

Um, yum.

That was when Bill pelted me with a slop of chocolate frosting, right in the face.

Okay, he was asking for it.

And the food fight of the century commenced. I threw anything I could get my hands on in that fridge, and Bill did the same, until we were both dying of laughter and covered head to toe in cake and frosting goop.

"I needed that," I admitted. Even though I was sure some of the maple syrup was not going to come out of my hair any time soon, just horsing around with Bill made me feel like sudden doom wasn't lurking over my head. Even if it was just for a few minutes, it was worth it.

Bill pulled me in, wrapping his arm around me and scuffing my frosting/syrup'd head affectionately. "Me too," he agreed.

Roberta walked in and I immediately felt like I was about to be grounded for life. But to my surprise she actually smiled at the mess and our current state of grossness. "You two should probably shower. Chelsan, it's time to contact Isabelle. Geoffrey and I will be in the conference room when you're ready." She left without waiting for an answer.

Nothing like the gong of reality to break us out of our good mood. Bill gave me one last squeeze of affection and we headed off to our rooms to shower.

Five shampoo rinses later, all existence of the food fight was erased from my person. There were fresh clothes folded perfectly at the foot of my bed and I was pleasantly surprised to find that Grams had picked out items I'd actually wear. The woman was paying attention, I guess. I pulled on the tight black-T and blue jeans and saw a brand new pair of red Chucks waiting for me at the door. After I was all laced up I sat down on my bed and concentrated on leaving my body.

I felt like a pro at this point. I jumped right out and knew exactly which string to follow until I flew inside Isabelle's head.

I decided to stay in her memory hallway, figuring it would be the easiest for her to reach. Isabelle was new to this whole astral projection thing and I wanted it to be as simple as possible for her.

"Isabelle!" I called out.

As I waited, I was tempted to peak behind a couple of her memory doors. Before I had a chance, though, Isabelle popped into existence.

"Chelsan, what is it?" Isabelle had a worried expression on her face, apparently visits from me warranted concern. Not a shock there.

"Gramps wants a trade. Fortski for the formula. If you haven't already, tell Harry about the serum. We need Forstki to bargain with Elisha. We think she has some pretty nasty plans in play." I told her everything we knew about the clones and armies. Turner would kill me if he knew I'd spilled everything, but I had to trust my own instincts and not give in to Turner's paranoia. My instincts had kept me alive this long.

"Okay, I'll make it happen. I'm not sure how, but Harry will listen if I can convince Dean and Terence to side with me. Harry doesn't know that *this*," she motioned to the astral space that was her head, "is the way you and I are communicating, so I'll tell him I heard from Turner. We'll meet at Rocky Peak Park. Turner will know where." Isabelle had a flash of anger in her eyes when she said Turner's name and I had a brief second of anxiety that maybe her vengeance was stronger than her desire to help me. I guess my doubts were pretty evident in my face because she looked me straight in the eye. "I won't betray you again. We'll meet there at six."

I nodded, still feeling a bit uneasy. "We'll be there."

I jumped out of her head before Isabelle could say more.

Opening my eyes, I took a few minutes to gather myself together. I seriously hoped we could trust Isabelle. I'd really hate it if Turner was right.

I made my way to the conference room, where Turner and Roberta were sitting, strategizing over their cups of coffee. I kind of waved when I entered and Roberta stood to welcome me, motioning me to sit.

Looking at the clock, which said 5:30, I didn't bother. "We're meeting them at Rocky Peak Park at 6. Isabelle said you'd know where."

Turner stood up and his face betrayed his butt-hurt expression. Wow. Rocky Peak Park must definitely be another bump on their rocky road of a past. No pun intended. "Let's get to the hover then," he said without further comment.

We decided that only Turner and I would go. Roberta stayed behind in case Harry had decided to work with Elisha again and had brought in Eva or one of the Franklin clones to puppet Roberta into doing something we couldn't control. A couple of live guards went with us, one to drive and one to protect. For added bonus we brought along two dead guards as well. Now that I knew Elisha's powers weren't as strong as mine, I was sure I could maintain control over them.

There was a part of me that worried Elisha would be there because the formula was so important to her. If Harry was working with her, he'd have told Elisha for sure that we had it. But we'd have to cross that bridge if we came to it. In the mean time I fully planned on keeping control over the dead guards.

It took less than ten minutes to fly to our destination. I could see rock formations and a scattering of trees below. There weren't any buildings for miles, the place looked completely deserted, like an old western movie.

I observed Gramps out of the corner of my eye. He was fidgeting, which was very unlike him. Something about Isabelle made him nervous, angry and just plain hurt. Isabelle felt the same way about him. I'd like to think their whole separation was just a big misunderstanding, but I saw the same holo-footage Harry'd shown Isabelle, and Turner had definitely wanted her dead.

Our hover-SUV landed near a small cropping of trees overlooking an empty expanse of dirt and rocks. Isabelle and crew were nowhere to be seen, but I knew better than to assume they'd stood us up. It kept me more on guard.

Turner turned to me, very serious. "You take control of these guards. My network isn't powerful enough if Elisha or even Eva is here."

"Your network?" After all this time, was I finally going to find out how Turner controlled all his dead soldiers without having to constantly chant spells and perform rituals?

"Yes, my network. Can you do that?"

And, no such luck. "Yes, I can do that."

I connected to the two dead guards' black holes and the six of us exited the vehicle.

The two live guards stepped in behind us, while I made the two dead guards stand in front.

"What time is it?" I asked nervously. This whole thing was making my heart palpitate.

"Five 'til." Turner scanned the area like a soldier. Now that I knew he used to be military, a lot of his quirks made sense. Like how he was able to compartmentalize so well. Even when he was hunting me down trying to kill me, Gramps managed to separate himself from the emotion that I was his GRANDDAUGHTER. Who does that? That's right, *this* guy does. I guess I shouldn't blame the military, but there was something so mechanical about it. Roberta had been a crazed lunatic back when she wanted me dead, whereas Turner was always systematic and logical in his approach. Scary but efficient. Luckily, I was more clever than he had expected and I was able to maneuver myself out of harm's way. My mother hadn't been so lucky.

I erased those thoughts from my mind and tried to focus on the task at hand.

At what felt like eons later (probably a few minutes), Harry, Isabelle and Fortski walked out of seemingly empty space. Should have known: a dimensional displacement vehicle. They had been hiding there since we arrived, which most likely meant that Terence was aiming his gun at either Turner or myself from the comfort of being invisible inside the vehicle. Dean, meanwhile, could be standing right next to me for all I knew.

Isabelle and I made eye contact, which essentially equated to *Hey, I have your back*. At least I hoped that was what she was conveying.

Harry and Turner looked like they wanted to strangle each other, but neither made any sudden moves.

Fortski on the other hand just appeared terrified. When he saw Gramps, his eyes lit up and relief was etched all over his face. Apparently, Fortski actually liked my grandfather. I thought this guy was supposed to be a genius!

Harry addressed the both of us, "You have the formula?"

Turner pulled the small vial out from an inside pocket of his suit jacket (the guy always wore suits!) and gave it to one of the dead guards.

My turn. I made the guard walk over to Harry and hand him the serum. Harry shook the bottle with an annoyed expression. "Sampling the goods, Turner?"

Gramps grumbled, "There's plenty left for you, Harry."

Harry handed the bottle to Fortski for inspection and Fortski examined it carefully. Then he nodded. "This is it, though I have no idea how they stole it from me."

I tried not to look guilty. I did after all body-knap the guy, rip open the really gross hiding place in his leg, and steal his formula. Oh yeah, and erased all memory of it from his head. I was such an awesome person.

Fortski handed the vial back to Harry, who pocketed it in his cargo vest. So many pockets on that thing, I'd be surprised if he remembered where he put it.

"I'd like John now, please." Turner eyed Harry and Isabelle like they were going to pull out machine guns and start mowing us down.

"Of course." Harry grinned.

I didn't like that grin.

I didn't like it at all.

Fortski started to walk toward us.

BAM! BAM! BAM!

Three bullet holes to Fortski's back and he fell face down in the dirt in front of us.

We couldn't see where the shots came from, but it was obviously Terence from the cover of their dimensional displacement car.

I was in shock.

After everything, Fortski ended up dead.

I wanted to cry.

BAM! BAM!

The two dead guards were shot.

Terence was trying to take down our only defense so he could kill us.

Too bad the guards were already dead.

I made them pull out their guns as if the bullets that had ripped through them were mere scratches, which of course they were because… yeah, dead.

I couldn't believe Isabelle betrayed us. I looked at her and that was when I saw…

…She was as shocked as I was.

Small comfort considering Terence and Harry were now emptying their guns into the guards. I kept the two dead guys in a tight formation giving Turner and I some cover.

"Make them shoot!" Gramps screamed at me.

I couldn't make the guards shoot Isabelle. Crap, I couldn't even make them shoot Harry. I just wanted to get out of there. "Let's just go!" I screamed back.

"You are going to have to learn to take sides!" Turner motioned to his live guards. "You get in the car and you shoot!" Each soldier took their orders.

"Chelsan!" Isabelle yelled over the gunfire.

My two corpses were almost shredded. I was about to lose control of them.

I could barely see her behind my cover of the dead guys, but her eyes were screaming at me. She mouthed, "*Take control of me.*"

Isabelle wanted this to stop as much as I did. Even assassin girl didn't want us dead.

She gave me permission.

It was all I needed.

I leapt out of my body and shot myself directly into Isabelle's. As soon as I jumped in I took control of her swirling white hole.

I immediately saw trails of light everywhere, even the bullets had them (though almost faster than I could process). I nearly freaked out when I saw the invisible Dean about to grab Gramps from behind and most probably try and snap his neck. Behind Isabelle, Terence's heart beating and trigger finger were the only thing exuding movement.

I connected to all of it.

Even a bird flying by.

I didn't have time to differentiate.

And I made everything and everyone stop.

Completely stop.

Harry's eyes grew round with terror when he couldn't move his arms. When Harry and Terence tried to move their legs…

"I wouldn't do that," I heard Dean's voice say. He had just gone through the same tactical experience.

Once their legs started to move, I connected to the trails of light and froze them completely.

Dean reappeared and stood with his arms frozen since they had been the only parts of his body that had been moving. "I'm just going to join my team," he said flashing a kind of half smile at Isabelle, knowing full well I was controlling her.

Harry shouted at my actual body, "Get the hell out of my girl!" He, too, understood that I had control over Isabelle and wrongly assumed she was my victim.

Even frozen, Turner was more than pleased. I concentrated only on Turner and allowed him to move freely, but I kept my guard up in case he tried to kill them. And speaking of guards, there was no way I trusted Turner's guards so I kept them frozen as well.

Gramps walked over to Harry with a triumphant grin and pulled the vial of Fortski's formula out of Harry's vest pocket. "I'll be taking this."

Fortski groaned from the ground.

He was still alive!

Turner whirled in shock at the sound and hurried to Fortski's side. He carefully turned Fortski's body over and to all our amazement Fortski started to sit up on his own. He looked just as surprised as everyone else.

Turner ripped open the back of Fortski's shirt to examine his wounds.

There weren't any.

Fortski was completely healed.

Fortski's eyes were wide. "But I never took the serum."

Oh but he had. I'd made him take it. I didn't know it would still be working a day later, but I was relieved that it did.

Gramps very soothingly said to Fortski, "We'll get you back home, John, just help me bring my granddaughter to the hover."

Fortski was positively gleeful as the two of them walked over to my crouched form and carried my body to the hover-SUV, situating me inside.

I told Isabelle in her head, *I'm going to jump out of you as soon as our car is clear.*

I could feel her approval.

Harry cried out with malice. "This isn't over, Turner."

After I released the two live guards and they were situated inside the vehicle with Fortski and my floppy body, Gramps turned to Harry. "You were always a fool, Harry. I'll always be better than you."

Harry screamed. A bloody, vicious *I freakin' hate you* scream.

I had to give Turner credit, he definitely knew how to press people's buttons.

I watched, through Isabelle's eyes, as the hover-SUV flew away. I left her body and slammed back into mine.

My eyes fluttered open and Gramps was there to greet me with a smile. "You did good."

Was it weird that it actually felt kind of nice when he said that? Never mind, yes, it was weird, but I was proud of myself, too. With Isabelle's help no one was killed. Except the already-dead soldiers, who were pretty badly mangled. Gross.

Fortski kept feeling his body like he was waiting for the bullet holes to come back. "I just can't believe it," he kept repeating.

I thought I'd ease his mind and I explained to him what I had done.

Fortski wasn't upset. In fact, he looked relieved. "If you hadn't done that…" He took a deep breath and turned to Gramps. "Geoffrey, this formula, it's… it's… what we've been searching for since we met. It doesn't just cure you if you're injured. It also has the same anti-aging compound as Age-pro. The difference is that once you take it you never have to take it again, the effects are permanent. It's what Age-pro was supposed to be. Don't you get it, Geoffrey? I finally did it! I finally invented true immortality." Fortski's eyes were overly bright from emotion.

I could tell Turner was soaking it all in. He was shocked, but also something else. I couldn't pinpoint it, but I swear Gramps looked less tired. Like everything he'd been trying to do in life finally had fallen into place. Turner simply placed his hand on Fortski's shoulder with gratitude. "You did it. I can't believe after all these years…"

Fortski was on the verge of tears. "I know. I just wish Roberta could have taken it before…"

"She lives. That's all that matters now." Gramps didn't want to relive Roberta's death, not when she was still technically alive. "Anyone that takes the potion can't be killed, is that what you're telling me, John?"

"I'm proof of that," Fortski confirmed.

A thought suddenly came to me, "What about decapitation or being blown to bits?"

Fortski was positively bursting with excitement. "Your body will reform! Once the serum is taken your cells are bound forever! It's impossible to die!"

"Then we can never let Elisha get her hands on you or the formula. She could undo us all." Gramps was horrified at the thought of Elisha being truly immortal. To have an enemy that couldn't die, especially when that enemy was a sociopathic killer… It really was a scary thought.

Turner turned to me like he was seeing me for the first time. "I guess you don't have to decide if you're going to take Age-pro or not."

That was a random thing to say to me.

Then it hit me.

I drank the serum.

I started hyperventilating.

I couldn't breathe no matter how hard I tried.

Turner's arm was instantly patting me gently on the back, trying to soothe me. Trying to soothe me! Gramps! My head was going to explode.

I couldn't die.

I couldn't die.

This shouldn't be freaking me out, but it was. It really was!

"Why is she so upset? This is a miracle." I heard Fortski's confused voice ring in my ears. He sounded like he was in a tunnel. I was seriously going to pass out.

Turner's voice sounded just as distant, "Because she's a sensitive young lady."

Sensitive young lady? Who was this guy? Gramps with any kind of sympathy was just odd, but to hear him sound so worried about me, squeezed my heart in all the wrong places.

I shrugged his hand off my back and started to calm myself down. "I'm not sensitive," I said lamely. Why did I feel the need to argue with him?

Fortski had a look that had *awkward* written all over it. "You're immortal, child, enjoy it. I certainly am."

And Fortski definitely was enjoying himself. He wiped the remaining blood off his back with a handkerchief Turner handed him and kept mumbling the words, "amazing," and "miracle."

I kept my mouth shut the entire trip back, which was only about ten minutes.

Honestly, I really didn't feel like talking to Turner. I somehow blamed him for all this mess. I knew it was illogical, but he was so damned happy about me being immortal that it made me mad for some reason. I was surprised he didn't pull out the serum and lick the bottle clean for himself.

As we exited the vehicle, I could hear the screams and protests from the crowds of people wanting to kill me.

Sigh.

Too bad people! You can try all you like, but I can never die. Ever. *Ever.*

Death was scary, yes, but living forever was ten times more frightening and I couldn't begin to explain why. Just the mere thought of something going on forever, with no end… It gave me shivers. It reminded me of when I was a little girl and the first time my mother told me about outer space. I kept on imagining a big circle surrounding earth, but when Mom really drilled in the fact that the universe never ended, my little brain couldn't seem to wrap around that fact. It wasn't until I was slightly older that it hit me and I had my first panic attack.

Now that never ending concept was me. Literally.

We entered the building and Gramps told me I could go to my room to rest (gee, thanks) while he and Fortski rushed off to the lab. They were like two giddy school boys who'd bought a new toy.

I think I kind of shrugged and Turner's two guards escorted me back to my room.

To my enormous surprise, Ryan was already there, lying on the bed. When he saw me, he jumped off and leapt into my arms. Aaahh.

Ryan gave me the kiss of all kisses and suddenly thinking of doing this forever didn't seem so bad. "I missed you," he whispered between kisses.

"You have no idea," I mumbled incoherently.

I wanted to escape into the moment and not have to deal with what was coming, but no such luck.

"Did you get Forstki back?" Ryan asked innocently.

I groaned. "Yes, he's fine, he's immortal, nothing can kill him, me too, oh and Max too, how are you?"

"Say that again?" Ryan did a double take.

I fell into his chest and he wrapped his arms around me supportively. "That serum that cured Max and me, once you drink it, nothing can ever kill you. Nothing."

Ryan gently pulled away and held my face with his hands. I'd never seen him smile so big in my life. "Do you have any idea what a relief that is? I never have to worry about you dying again!" If Ryan could have jumped in the air and whooped he would have.

I never thought of it that way. My friends were constantly worried about me, and rightfully so: now they'd never have to fear that I'd die. Of course, I didn't want to bring up the fact that someone like Elisha could then torture me forever and my body would never give out. Or if she buried me alive again, I'd just rot down there and never die.

Breathe.

This immortal thing was really scaring the crap out of me.

"We just need to give you all some of this formula so we can rest easy," I confessed. It would be rather nice not having to worry if my friends were going to die or not.

"In time. I'm sure Turner has Fortski slaving over the lab right now. I figured out some of the compounds, but that man is seriously the smartest man alive. I couldn't even scratch the surface of what he put in that serum." Ryan was impressed.

"Yeah, in the whole three hours you had to examine it. You're such a dummy," I teased.

Ryan started kissing me again and my toes tingled in delight.

"Elisha's on the news. This can't be good." Jason interrupted us by entering our room. He looked scared. "Everyone is in the conference room."

We quickly followed Jason there, not wanting to miss a moment of whatever Elisha was doing on the news. Nancy, Jill, Max, Bill, Roberta, Turner and Fortski were already inside watching a giant holographic image of Elisha's stunningly beautiful face on the holo-TV.

Jason explained, "She's taken over every station worldwide. If you own a holo, you're seeing Elisha."

Elisha's demeanor was serious, there wasn't a hint of a smile on her face, not even in her eyes when she spoke, "My name is Elisha Stearne. I have taken over this little planet of ours, and frankly, it was just about the easiest thing I've ever done. Don't bother trying to fight me, my armies only grow stronger the more you fight back. And don't look to your precious Vice President Geoffrey Turner, he doesn't have the means to hurt me. He's weak and a liar, and you'll finally get to see him for what he is: a fake. I have a general in every major city around the world with armies of thousands. You *will* bow to me. You *will* respect me…"

Then she laughed hysterically, like she was in on a joke that only she knew the punch line of. "Wait a minute, I don't care what you do. I'm going to make this planet burn. Why you ask?" Elisha, being one for dramatics, paused long enough to be annoying. "Because I think it'll be fun."

Elisha blew a kiss to the camera, "Ta-Ta for now!"

There was a huge flash of light and then regular programming popped back on the holo. Turner turned it off.

"What are we going to do?" Nancy's voice shook.

I was the one who spoke. "We're going to stop her."

Chapter 7
Sunday April 10, 2321

I should be used to this by now. Seriously!

Every time I go to sleep I end up in someone else's head. It was getting ridiculous.

I was definitely in Roberta's head. She had yet to pop up to greet me, and I was surprised I'd drifted in. Usually, her guard was up.

After my rousing statement, not much had happened, so we all talked in hushed whispers of what we should do about Elisha, then we went to bed. It felt so amazingly wonderful to finally lay down that I almost didn't want to fall asleep just so I could enjoy the sensation.

I also suspected that I'd be ripped out of my body like clockwork.

I wasn't wrong.

In the last six days, I think I spent more time out of my body than in it!

"Roberta! What's up?" I wanted to go back to my body and actually have a good night's rest. Was that too much to ask for?!

Our oak forest materialized in front of me, but still no Roberta.

I felt like I was "on hold." Like she was saying, *Make yourself comfortable and I'll be right there.*

But suddenly Ryan, Isabelle and Max popped in next to me. I could only describe their faces as surprised and bewildered when they arrived.

I immediately snatched Ryan's hand and he took it gratefully.

"Where are we?" Ryan asked.

"Roberta's brain," I answered. Yeah, just a normal night of being me. Aren't you glad you picked me as your girlfriend?

Roberta finally made her appearance and smiled at all of us. "Good. I wasn't sure if I could pull you all in, but I'm glad it worked."

"What's this about?" Max asked. He didn't seem upset about being yanked out of his body for this little powwow, though, he seemed more curious than anything.

Roberta motioned for everyone to hold hands (since I was already holding Ryan's I grabbed Max's). Without question the others followed. I still had to pinch myself that I'd follow directions from Grams so willingly, but she'd definitely proved her loyalty to me lately. That I couldn't argue.

A pulsing of light traveled in a circle through our hands. It was a strange sensation, but pleasant at the same time. Every time the light rushed through my hand into Max's hand and then back the other way from Ryan's hand to my own, it warmed me from the tip of my toes to the top of my head. After a few moments it stopped.

"We're bound now," Roberta announced. "I want us to be able to communicate with one another telepathically since we won't physically be together. Max and Chelsan you know how this works, but Ryan and Isabelle aren't as familiar with telepathy. Now that we're connected, all you'll have to do is think of the person you want to talk to and they'll hear you."

Isabelle's face showed relief, while Max looked like this was nothing new. Roberta was right, Max and I didn't need the connection to talk to anyone we chose, but it would make it easier on Ryan and especially on Isabelle who was who-knows-where.

Isabelle spoke up, "We're supposed to rendezvous with Elisha tomorrow. I've injected myself with a blood tracker, the number is 88765. Follow me and you'll be able to snag her. Just so you know, I plan on killing Elisha, so if you want her as your lab rat, you better get there quick. I'm only going to give you an hour." Isabelle looked at me when she said that.

She knew I didn't like killing and she was trying in her own way to respect that. "Also, I'm pretty sure Harry's been lying to our team this whole time. He makes it sound like he wanted to stop a war and that Geoffrey was trying to start it, but I now believe Harry's wanted a war this whole time. That's why he sided with Elisha without our knowledge. He knew we'd never agree."

"I'll tell Geoffrey, and thank you." Roberta genuinely meant it, which made Isabelle squirm a little. Then Roberta continued, "I don't know what happened between you and Geoffrey, he never told me the whole story, but I hope you two can resolve your differences. He really did love you."

Isabelle's eyes lit up with fury at hearing that, but her voice remained calm as she said, "Are we done here?"

"Not quite."

Uh.

That was Elisha.

Elisha appeared in front of us with an annoyingly condescending grin. "Why wasn't I invited to this little party?"

Then her smile turned to shock when she recognized Max.

"How?" was all Elisha could spit out.

Roberta was quick: she used Elisha's momentary confusion to her advantage and with sheer force of will made Elisha lift off her feet and fly backward through the forest.

Before any of us could even strategize, though, Elisha popped right back in front of us.

Irritated and angry, she hissed, "Nice try, cat lady, but now that you're in a loaner, I'm much more powerful than you in this realm."

Elisha twisted her fingers in a quick motion and Roberta immediately grabbed her own throat, choking from the gesture.

I may have had my own issues with Grams, but there was no way I was letting Elisha strangle her in her own head. I concentrated as hard as I could, thinking only of Elisha being removed from Roberta's brain.

And it started to work.

Like a horizontal tornado, Elisha was starting to be sucked out of the space in a wind tunnel that only affected her. I could tell she was trying to use every spell or thought that she could to stay here, but I was gaining in strength.

Roberta was released from Elisha's hold and took a few seconds to gain her bearings.

Why was Elisha here in the first place? Was she trying to spy? If she was, there'd been no reason to show herself, she could have just listened and left. I couldn't believe Elisha's ego was so big that she had to gloat about it, not with all the careful planning she'd done so far. I decided I needed to ask her.

I kept Elisha at a mid-point halfway between sucking her out and keeping her in. She was just floating in space with a giant fan blowing her hair, skin and clothes back at full force.

"What are you doing here, Elisha?" I asked.

"Just bored," she lied, her face furrowed in concentration, desperately trying to gain the upper hand.

"Seriously, are you here to spy?" I tried to see if I could provoke any kind of expression or response that would help me figure her out.

Then I noticed something I'd never seen before in Elisha's eyes. Doubt.

And I knew, with a certainty I couldn't explain, that Elisha hadn't come here on purpose.

"Your connection to one of us brought you here," I said with confidence.

She didn't answer – but her eyes flashed at me briefly. Yup. Elisha had no idea how she had come to arrive here.

Max stepped forward. "It must have been me, because of our connection."

"When I bound us together, Elisha was sucked in through Max." Roberta suggested. "I can try to sever the connection."

"No," I answered before I even knew what I was saying. "We may need their connection in the future. I don't want to hurt Max."

Elisha was livid, "So sweet. Have you two bonded now?" Then she screamed at Max, "Next time I'll have to be more thorough when killing you." Elisha didn't like that she was connected to Max. It gave her a weakness she wasn't expecting.

"Good luck with that," Max said, and I almost laughed.

The punch line of Max's joke wasn't lost on Elisha.

Realization flooded through her. "You two drank the potion… that's why there's not a scratch on you." Then Elisha screamed in a rage I'd never seen before. "You're immortal!" Her eyes met mine and I flinched at her fury. "Now the ritual can never be completed!"

It must have pissed her off even more when my eyes lit up. I never even thought of that. If I couldn't kill myself, then Elisha could never take my power. Sweet.

It also told me something that wasn't confirmed until this moment: Elisha already knew that the serum didn't just heal, it created immortality, which meant she'd be after it with a vengeance.

"Time to leave now." I flicked my wrist and Elisha flew down the vortex of wind and was gone from Roberta's head.

I looked around at everyone. Ryan's hand held mine, the ever-present rock of support.

"Time for everyone to go," Roberta announced. "We have a big day ahead of us."

No one argued.

Before I knew it, both Ryan and I were gasping for breath as we returned to our bodies.

Ryan turned to me and moved my hair out of my eyes. "Check astral projection off my bucket list, and hopefully never to make any other list from here on out."

I leaned in and kissed him. "I'm not sure why Roberta brought you in, but I'm grateful."

"You have to give it to her. She knows how much we mean to each other and she wanted us to be able to stay connected. It was kind of a cool move." Ryan kissed my forehead.

"Yeah, it was. I'm not exactly sure how I feel about that," I admitted.

"Me either," Ryan admitted as well.

"What time is it?" I wondered. It was impossible to tell because there were no windows in the center rooms of the Population Control building.

Ryan reached over me and grabbed his phone, lighting up the screen. "5 a.m."

"Maybe we should…"

I didn't get to finish that sentence.

A large explosion shook the building like an earthquake.

Alarms sounded everywhere.

Population Control was under attack.

Nancy, Jason and Bill all came running in at once.

Bill yelled over the continual explosions and gunfire, "You guys okay?"

"Yeah," I answered.

Ryan and I hurriedly dressed and the five of us left the room to find Jill and Max. Ultimately, we needed to find Turner. I somehow didn't think we were lucky enough for Elisha to have brought the fight to us. I knew after we evacuated Population Control our next stop would be wherever Elisha was currently residing.

Max's voice sounded in my head, *Jill and I are fine. Turner and Roberta are with us, we're on our way to the lab. Your grandfather thinks that Elisha is coming after the formula and Fortski.*

"They're all at the lab. Let's go," I informed Ryan and the others. I didn't bother explaining how I knew this and, frankly, no one questioned it. We all just ran towards the science labs and I hoped Fortski was still there. No, he couldn't die, but Elisha could certainly hurt the poor man, *forever.* Besides, the thought of Elisha taking the immortality juice was a bigger nightmare than any of us wanted to contemplate.

We rounded the hallway just before the lab.

Gunfire!

I shoved everyone back before they could get hurt.

THWACK!

A bullet grazed my arm as I ducked the rest of the way around the corner. The pain was sharp and I grabbed it instinctively. It only lasted seconds as I could literally feel the wound instantly heal. So freakin' strange.

I could hear the screams of the shooters.

They were protesters from outside and they wanted me dead.

Elisha had planned this all out. Riling up the public against me and then attacking Population Control giving the rioters access to attack. Now that she couldn't use me anymore, Elisha wasn't going to be exactly careful in protecting me. I couldn't die, but my friends could. I needed to keep them safe.

I could see the black swirling holes of ten dead soldiers several hallways behind us, busy with their own fight. They were controlled by Turner, but I needed them more. I connected to their black holes and made them hotfoot it back to us. Since the protesters were innocents (not really – I mean, they were trying to shoot me! But they weren't evil incarnate like Elisha!), I made the dead soldiers act like a shield for us to follow.

The angry villagers (as I liked to call them), shot at the soldiers I controlled, I didn't have them fire back. I made the dead guards push, shove and punch the guns out of the crazies' hands, pretty much rendering them useless.

Although when the protesters caught glimpses of me behind my wall of men, they were like rabid dogs trying to break through to kill me.

"I didn't kill those people at the mall! Elisha Stearne did!" I screamed. I had no idea why I was trying to convince the angry mob, it wasn't likely these people could even hear me, let alone believe me. It was just that seeing their enraged faces made me want to explain myself. I could only imagine that some of these protesters were family and friends of the victims that died. Considering I was pretty much caught on tape doing the deed, I wouldn't believe me, either.

Unfortunately, the insane-o crowd was the least of my problems, because when we showed up at the lab, Fortski was there – but the newest batch of his formula was gone. And a giant hole in the wall revealed the point of entry for Elisha's men, its gaping open mouth mocking us for the idiots we were. Now we knew what the explosions had been for.

Turner was going over everything that happened with Fortski while a slew of his dead soldiers joined my dead soldiers in protecting the lab, pushing protesters away.

We had a short breather, then. I could hear the fighting and gunfire from the hallways beyond, but at least the explosions had stopped.

Apparently, the bombs Elisha's attack used were quick and decisive, placed in strategic points to make a direct tunnel through the walls of the building, leading straight to the lab. Turner's men stopped them from taking Fortski, but Elisha's crew managed to snag the three vials of the formula Fortski had made. Turner's men were chasing them down as we spoke, trying to stop them from escaping and ultimately going back to Elisha. I really wished Fortski had another bottle in hiding so all my friends in the room could take a swig. It would make my life so much less stressful. Of course, that was never my luck. If we survived through this, though, my friends were the first on the list for the serum.

Then I felt it.

"Chelsan," I heard Max's voice next to me. He felt it too.

Turner sensed something big was up because he turned to the both of us. "What is it?"

I swallowed hard. "Elisha brought an army of dead. There are thousands of them."

I could see an ocean of black swirling holes outside the building. So did Max.

Roberta walked up to us. "Can you connect to them all? The two of you?"

Yes.

I could do this.

Then we could stop Elisha from retrieving the serum.

I nodded and tried to slam into the black holes of her soldiers.

Nope.

They were controlled by someone else. Someone else either stronger— or simply, there were more of them asserting control.

Max and I shared a look of concern.

"We can't," I informed everyone.

"Let's go to the roof and see what we're up against," Turner commanded. He didn't reprimand me or even give me a disappointed glare. I could see that Gramps had such confidence in my ability that if I couldn't connect to all those soldiers there would have to be a reason why.

My gut had the sneaking suspicion that I wasn't going to like the reason I couldn't control Elisha's army, but I needed to see for myself.

Turner led us up to the roof through a series of secret hallways that were closed off to employees and, more importantly, to the warring civilians.

When we reached the top, all I saw below us was an ocean of black. Everyone else except Max just saw fighting men. Gunfire echoed off the walls of the buildings though it was much quieter from this far up.

"There, there and there." Turner pointed. "I count ten."

My eyes went to where Turner indicated.

Yup. He was right.

There were ten of them.

Ten Franklin clones, all controlling the dead army.

"Wait," Ryan announced suddenly.

He must have felt conspicuous as the entire lot of us focused on him. "I can feel them, the I.Q. kids are in the clones. I'm…" He couldn't seem to put what he was feeling into words. "I'm not sure what I'm seeing," Ryan said, distress clearly written across his face.

Roberta was the one that comforted him as she touched his arm gently, "Just describe everything, even if it doesn't make sense."

Ryan nodded, then after a few seconds said, "It's like the I.Q. kids and the clones are seeing as one, but the I.Q. kids are fighting with the clones they've been planted inside of. Some of the clones don't like what they're doing. The clones are mad that they're destroying their home?" Ryan wasn't sure he was interpreting the Franklin clones correctly, but he continued, "The I.Q. kids' consciousness's are stronger, but I feel the clones fighting them for control over their bodies."

"This could be good." Roberta seemed encouraged by this news.

I didn't know what it meant, but the more time we wasted the more black holes were forming down there.

Ryan stopped and looked at me with horror in his eyes. "One of the clones. The one that broke into the lab. He just drank some of the serum. He's going to get the other clones to drink from it as well."

"We have to stop them!" I exclaimed. Not only did Elisha want to be immortal herself, but she wanted her generals indestructible as well.

Not going to happen.

I reached for Max's hand and he took it immediately. "Tell me what to do," he said.

Connect to every single hole down there. I instructed Max in his head.

"Get ready," Turner instructed a handful of his live soldiers.

I couldn't think about what he had planned, I could only think of stopping Elisha's dead soldiers from killing anyone else.

The enormous power of the Franklins was like an invisible barrier of steel. Their strange head connection that Ryan appeared to be a part of made them stronger than when Elisha and Eva were teamed up.

"I can't break through," Max said through gritted teeth.

"Keep trying. We can do it," I urged.

I felt us connecting to Turner's dead soldiers first, since the clones hadn't had time to solidify their power over the newly dead. This seemed to inspire Max and I felt a new wave of power flow from him. I grabbed onto it and added my own strength. I could feel the Franklins' hold over the corpses start to wane.

"Almost there, Max," I said evenly, trying to maintain my concentration.

SLAM!

We were in.

"We don't have much time before they gain back control," I instructed Max. "Channel your energy through me and I'll do the rest."

Out of the corner of my eye I could see Max nod, then I felt a surge of power so intoxicating my knees almost buckled. Wow. Max had some serious mojo. It was all I needed.

Before the Franklins could take back control of their army, I disconnected all the dead bodies from their black holes.

Corpses collapsed everywhere and the decaying body stench flew up to our nostrils like it had wings. Depending on when each body had actually died determined the level of corpse-rot that lay below. Some had been dead so long they were now skeletons.

Instead of the gunfire stopping, I heard ten distinct shots blast out from right beside me.

I turned next to me to see Turner's soldiers with full-on sniper rifles shooting at...

My heart jumped in my chest.

...The Franklins.

Nine of the clones lay dead on the ground next to their rotting army.

The tenth Franklin, the one that had already taken the serum, shrugged off the bullet wound and ran to his hover-shuttle.

Turner swore and whirled on me, "Did you have to destroy all of the dead soldiers? I don't have any men to follow the clone!"

I was still in shock from Turner killing my father, or fathers. I knew they were just clones, and I knew that they were *wrong*, but they still looked and acted and were made of my dad. Seeing them lying there dead brought up emotions I wasn't expecting. And I couldn't help but feel a tiny bit relieved or grateful or…I didn't even know what… that one of them would live forever. Maybe someday there'd be some way to make him whole, to make him my dad.

The last Franklin's hover-car was in the air and out of sight before Turner could order a team of living soldiers to follow.

Before I could respond to Gramps's outrage, Roberta stepped in and talked him down. "We have Isabelle's blood tracker, she's on her way now to join Elisha. You should get going."

Turner kind of grumbled under his breath, but he didn't attack me. He was just frustrated…

Did I really just make an excuse for him?

I was seriously going nuts.

Everyone started to follow Turner to the five newly landed hover-SUVs on the roof when I made the group stop.

"Jason, you and Nancy need to stay here, spin the story. To all the civilians, it's going to look like those men out there died today. Bill and Jill, you can't come either, it's too dangerous." I couldn't let the four of them stand in the line of fire for me one more time, but Max and Ryan were needed.

"I'm not leaving Max again!" Jill was adamant.

"He can't die, Jill, you can!" I didn't mean to sound so harsh, but it was the truth and it was enough to jar Jill out of protection mode.

"Fine," Jill huffed and crossed her arms.

Jason, of course, didn't argue at all. That guy seriously hated a fight.

Nancy and Bill on the other hand were on the verge of another argument, but I put up my hand to stop them. "Please, I don't have the strength to fight you. Elisha will kill you just to torture me, and she'll do it quick. She has nothing to lose, now that she can't have the full extent of my powers. You'll both help me out best by staying put here, so just nod and say good luck."

Nancy's nostrils flared, but she didn't argue. She bear-hugged me and whispered, "Good luck."

Bill hugged me after and surprisingly said, "Look out for Ryan, he's not indestructible."

It was sweet, but it felt like a knife in my gut. Ryan wouldn't be safe and Elisha knew how much he meant to me. She could try to kill him as soon as we landed. I knew I had to protect Ryan with my life.

Then I caught something in Bill's eyes. Bill was usually so easy to read, but in that moment, I caught a glimpse of a kid with his hand in the cookie jar. I didn't know what to make of it.

"Let's go!" Turner yelled.

Impatient, much?

But he was right, we needed to stop this once and for all. Maybe taking down the head of the snake would stop the plans for world destruction. Oh boy.

I sat in one of the SUV's back seats in-between Max and Ryan, with Turner and two live guards in front of us. The driver had Isabelle's blood tracker ID number typed into his GPS. In seconds we were up and away following the little yellow dot.

It was weird sitting in the back of a car driving to your destiny. The scenery below whizzed by in a blur. My life was so peculiar. I fidgeted with the seatbelt. The most mundane of activities somehow seemed blown up out of proportion. Everything felt too real. Turner had the news blazing on the radio: reports on what happened at Population Control alternated with advertising jingles. It felt like I was dreaming.

No one spoke.

Everyone waited as we followed that little yellow dot.

The driver broke the silence after an hour of driving, "The target has stopped twenty miles ahead."

Turner didn't even acknowledge the driver. He didn't have to: we'd be landing soon and everyone was preparing in their own ways on how to approach what was to come. I was probably going to take on Elisha and whatever live or dead things she used to protect her. Max technically should do the same, but I had a feeling his mind was on rescuing Eva, if she was even there. Ryan was going to try and connect to the I.Q. kids' bodies and see if he could influence the Franklins to take over and maybe stop them from obeying Elisha's commands.

And Gramps. What was he going to do? I wasn't sure, but he'd most likely be the only one to take Harry down. Isabelle could help with that. It seemed a fight between Gramps and Harry was inevitable.

Too many people. Too many agendas. My mind almost went blank at the enormity of it.

Still, it all centered on Elisha. I mean, we were talking about a violet-eyed girl planning a terrorist attack so big and so vast that it would take out a large portion of the world's population. She'd already killed so many people. All those soldiers at all those army bases. Dead. And now poised to kill even more innocent victims.

Our hover-SUV landed near a two-story brick building in the middle of nowhere. It looked broken down and abandoned, with ivy growing up its walls and weeds that covered the entire circumference. Beyond the weeds a pine forest surrounded the structure, like the building was the eye of a storm.

And, in this case, it actually was.

We exited the vehicle. It truly did appear as if the building was deserted. Broken windows, doors shredded and worn with age and weather, the place looked like it had stepped out of a horror movie. As if to reiterate my point, a faded, cracked sign in front of the dilapidated structure said, *Willtonby Asylum*.

Of course it did.

"Trap?" Turner asked me directly.

I shrugged. "Probably, but what choice do we have?"

"Not to walk into it," Gramps stated logically.

Well, there was that.

I guess I was an act first, ask questions later kind of a gal because I just wanted to go in there and get this over with. I wasn't looking forward to doing what everyone else thought needed to be done, namely killing Elisha, but I wasn't going to stop them either. Too many people had died and my mercy was making me feel guilty about all the lives that may have been saved if Elisha had just been executed. It depressed me more than I cared to think about.

"I'll go in first with Max. She can't kill us." I didn't wait for a reply.

Max joined me as I walked through the already busted in front door.

Inside was far more frightening than the outside. This place was a dump. The walls were barely visible from all the peeling paints, like popped blisters on skin.

I wasn't sure which way to go, neither was Max, but instinct guided us forward, through the main hallway.

Isabelle's voice reached out to me, *We're upstairs. There's a sanctuary up here, it must have been an old church. I hope you two are hearing this. Okay. Bye.*

Max and I exchanged glances. We'd both heard her.

I responded back, *Is Elisha expecting us?*

Yes. Tell Turner to execute a Flamingo formation. He'll know what that means.

Will do, I said back.

I conveyed the message to Gramps and he spoke back to me instantly, *Flamingo formation? All right, that means you two are the distractions, go in and keep Elisha's eyes off the ceiling and side windows, that will be our point of entry.*

Turner didn't elaborate or give me any words of encouragement, but what did I expect?

I told him to keep Ryan safe and that I'd literally kill him if Ryan had a scratch on him. I think I felt him groan and roll his eyes if that were possible.

I relayed everything back to Max since he couldn't mind-hear Gramps and he nodded in agreement. I had to give it to Max: whether in ghost form or live in-person he was a good partner to have around. I almost felt like Max and I were super heroes walking up the stairs and toward our confrontation with Elisha. Indestructible and the power to control the dead. We were kind of bad-asses.

The wooden stairs were rickety to say the least, but they held our weight. Once we reached the second level landing I saw the double doors that led to the sanctuary Isabelle had described. Only Elisha would pick that room. She obviously felt a connection to religion because of the way she was raised, or had had that connection at least until she was seven. I just couldn't tell if she was mocking it or actually believed in it. Knowing Elisha, probably a little bit of both.

The double heavy wood doors were in good shape and arched up to a point. Might as well go in big. Max and I each took a knob and opened the doors wide.

The room inside was the complete opposite of the rest of the asylum. Pristine and modern, not even a speck of dust dirtied the floor. Stained glass windows adorned the back and sides of the room giving off a yellow/ orange tint. Elisha stood behind the minister's podium overlooking the empty room where the pews should have been.

Eva stood on her right and a Franklin clone on her left and my whole body froze when I saw the bullet hole tear in his shirt. We were too late.

As if sealing my coffin shut, Elisha wiggled the empty vial in front of me. "Now we both can't die."

I saw Eva's skin. She no longer had the stretch marks or any injuries. She had taken the formula too. But the most heartening thing that I saw in Eva was how her eyes lit up when she saw Max.

"Max!" Eva's whole demeanor changed from Elisha-side-kick-evil to beyond thrilled. "You're alive!"

Max smiled warmly at her. "Chelsan gave me the serum. She saved my life."

I noticed he was very clear when he said my name. He wanted Eva to know whose side he was on. Smart.

Eva looked more conflicted than I'd ever seen her.

Elisha stepped into the conversation, "And I gave the serum to Eva, so she's loyal to me."

I kind of wished Elisha was right, then I could write Eva off for good. But there was no denying the fact that Eva was debating where her loyalties lay. Which ultimately meant that Max was right: the girl *did* have feelings. Unlike Elisha, Eva wasn't a complete sociopath.

I suddenly noticed Isabelle, Harry and Terence standing on my right watching the whole scene like they were statues in the church. Isabelle and I made brief eye contact, but it was enough for me to see that she was going to take my cue.

Harry stood there with the smug expression of a man who thought he had already won the prize. Terence didn't wear any expression, but I could tell he was watching everything. Dean was probably behind me about to snap my neck, which wouldn't kill me but would most likely be fun for Dean. I secretly hoped that Isabelle had told Dean about her allegiance and managed to sweet talk him to our side, although somehow I didn't think that Isabelle trusted anyone enough to tell them her secrets. Not even Dean.

The bigger issue of all this being that Elisha couldn't be killed. It was funny because now that she *couldn't* die, I realized I had been lying to myself. I wanted the girl dead.

"Welcome to my home away from home." Elisha presented the room with a sweep of her arms like the host of a game show. "I spent my childhood here before dear old Geoffrey took me to the I.Q. Farm. My father," she looked directly at me, "you remember him, Roland Light?" Elisha laughed, thoroughly enjoying herself, "He put me in here. Thought I was crazy. Then, when I was taken away, he just felt guilty, and a hundred years later, it's just a lump of ruins." Elisha actually looked nostalgic. "But this was the only place I ever felt at home. I was seven when Turner took me, and I became the woman I am today."

Eva was listening with sympathy. How could that girl have any feelings other than utter terror for Elisha? She'd only been alive for five freaking months! I was surprised she and Max could even think coherently.

"What now?" I asked Elisha foolishly.

Elisha snapped her fingers and a holo-projector lowered from the ceiling projecting images in the center of the room. The news flashed on and I wanted to scream.

People being mowed down by dead soldiers in the streets only to rise up and join their ranks.

Image after image, country after country, Elisha and her generals were slaughtering people like they were playing a video game.

And, in every country, there was the stark, contrasting image of the same little boy in the middle of every battle. Franklin clones controlling the armies and killing thousands of innocents. I needed it to stop. I needed to stop Elisha.

I had to look away so I stared at Eva. The holo-footage was bothering her as much as it was bothering me. It made me wonder if she really *had* wanted to kill those people at the mall. After all, I hadn't been able to see her, maybe she'd been too terrified of Elisha to rebel. I couldn't believe I was making excuses for the girl! That was the problem when your best friend vouches for someone: you can't help but try and see the good. Sure Bill had a wounded-bird complex, but it didn't mean that his instincts weren't right.

Grr. Not the time to think about Eva.

I needed to think about stopping Elisha's army from killing more people.

At that moment, glass broke all around us as Turner and his men dropped down from the roof, feet-first shattering through the stained glass windows. They hit the floor, guns ready, quickly surrounding Harry's team and Elisha, Eva and Franklin. It all happened so fast, I didn't know how to respond.

Ryan was last to enter, walking in through the sanctuary doors and coming up protectively next to me. I felt his hand wrap around mine and felt instantly better.

"Don't be mad," I heard Nancy's familiar voice come from behind me.

I whirled around to see Nancy, Bill, Jason and Jill.

No.

"What are you doing here?! Get out before you get killed!" I found myself screaming.

Nancy spoke, "We followed you here. Chelsan, there's no way we'd let you face this alone. Even Jason agreed."

Jason didn't look like he agreed, but a part of me was glad they were there. I just needed to keep them safe. Ha, ha.

Harry stepped forward, even though he was surrounded, "Geoffrey hasn't taken the serum. Kill him."

"I'm the one with the men, Harry," Turner gloated.

Dean suddenly appeared behind Turner and…

SNAP!

Turner's neck broke like a twig.

He collapsed to the floor.

I couldn't move.

He was dead.

My grandfather was dead.

My knees started to shake.

I never expected to feel anything if he died, but seeing him fall like that…

I wanted to scream and vomit at the same time.

Elisha giggled in glee. I'd never seen her so happy. It was like killing Gramps had made her life complete.

I connected to every dead particle of dust in the room and performed the trick that never failed… I made the dust fly up Dean's nose and down into his lungs. Dean's eyes bugged out in shock, and he fell to his knees. I could hear Isabelle scream, but I didn't care. I wanted him to suffer even though I knew Dean would be okay. I pulled out the dust as soon as he lost consciousness.

Elisha was annoyed that I knocked Dean out. She or Eva could have stopped the dust like Eva had done before, but I had been quick enough that they didn't have the chance.

Harry furiously whirled on me, "That man had your mother killed and you exact revenge on his killer! What is wrong with you, girl?!"

"He was still family," I found myself saying and was surprised to hear the catch in my throat. "And Dean will be fine. He's unconscious, not dead."

Turner and Roberta were the only family I had left in the world and Gramps was gone.

Truly gone.

I heard Ryan whisper, "The clone is fighting with the I.Q. kid, he loved Turner."

A part of me knew how the clone felt. I wouldn't call it love, but working together had given me a different perspective on Turner. I actually cared about him, and now he was lost to me forever.

I found that I was furious with Harry, "You were best friends! How could you do that to him?!"

"He was a killer and a mass murderer!" Harry justified.

"You're siding with Elisha, hello!" I pointed to the holo-images of people dying by the hundreds.

Harry stopped.

It was like I'd caught him in a lie he couldn't get out of. Even Isabelle turned to him, waiting for an answer.

Harry practically screamed. "I was bored out of my mind and when Elisha promised me a war, I jumped in with two feet." He turned to Isabelle, "I knew Geoffrey was trying to stop Elisha and that's why I wanted you to kill him. We can have the old days back again. We can fight in the open like soldiers again. Not like now, in the shadows, like cowards."

So Harry wanted bloodshed all along. All that crap about trying to stop Turner from starting a war was just a way to convince his team to kill

Gramps. Then Harry and Elisha would have no resistance to their war.

I couldn't believe that Gramps had been the last hope of saving humanity. After everything he had done, Geoffrey Turner was still the man that had kept the world together.

Isabelle looked at Harry in disgust. "I'm glad Turner is dead, but I don't want a war!"

That was when we all heard it.

A groan and a SNAP!

Turner had reached up and actually snapped his neck back into place.

Gramps was alive!

Relief flooded through me.

As Turner dusted himself off and stood up, he turned to Harry. "You honestly thought I wouldn't take the serum the first moment I had the chance?"

Harry's face had gone white, but it quickly turned red in anger. "You can't stop it, Geoffrey. The war is here and I plan on fighting it."

Isabelle fumed. She was actually upset that Gramps was still alive. It was as if his very existence offended her. Out of spite, she twisted her hand and Turner fell to his knees, clutching his heart. "I may not be able to kill you, but I can hurt you!"

"Isabelle stop!" I yelled harshly.

"No!" Isabelle yelled back.

It disgusted me to see her so vengeful. If anyone should be mad at Gramps it should be me, but I was happy he was still breathing. All he did to her was betray her trust. Welcome to the club and get over it!

"You know I can make you!" I responded as coldly as I could.

Isabelle released her grip on Turner's heart and whirled on me. "Why do you keep defending him?!"

"Because despite of what you think of him personally, he actually wants to stop *that*!" I pointed to the holo-images playing in front of us.

Gramps caught his breath and slowly stood, looking at her with eyes full of anger and hurt. "What on earth did I do to deserve your wrath, Isabelle? All I ever did was protect you and take care of you."

Isabelle's jaw dropped in disbelief and fury, "Harry showed me the holo-tape. He recorded your conversation. You remember, the one where you told Harry I was an experiment and that if he didn't kill me, you would!" She was raging now. I thought a couple veins were going to burst on her forehead.

I spoke up timidly, "Yeah, I saw it too."

Turner was genuinely floored. "What holo-tape?"

And when I say floored, I mean his eyes showed zero recollection as to what Isabelle was talking about. Zero. He couldn't fake that.

Even Isabelle paused in doubt. Then she continued, "Harry recorded you."

"Oh he did, did he?" Turner looked straight at Harry.

And Harry…

…Looked guilty.

Whoa.

Drama central.

I felt like I was watching one of Vianne's soap operas.

"Didn't see that one coming," Jill said what everyone was thinking.

"I did it for your own good," Harry's voice was small.

Isabelle closed her eyes. I thought she was going to cry. It was like the weight of the world had just slammed on her shoulders without warning. "You faked the tape."

Gramps walked over to Isabelle, a genuine sadness in him. "You thought I wanted to kill you so you faked your own death."

Isabelle nodded.

Harry looked like he was going to implode. "It was only a matter of time, Izzy. Geoffrey wanted you dead, you were too powerful. I faked that tape to convince you, but that doesn't make it a lie."

Turner punched Harry in the face hard enough to split his lip. "Yes, it does."

I didn't know why, but I couldn't let Gramps get off that easy, "But you did kill her parents and send her to Bruce and people like him." Oh, if looks could kill. I suddenly felt extremely glad I was immortal at that moment.

"Is that so?" Turner seethed. He grabbed Harry's throat and started to choke him. "Tell them, Harry."

Harry clawed at Turner's hands, but couldn't break free. The man had a grip of steel. Harry spoke through choked breaths, "She never would have trusted me if she knew I had done those things."

Seriously?! That was Harry too?

My whole world spun. Was Turner the way he was now *because* of what happened between him and Isabelle? Maybe he became the hard and sometimes evil man I knew because he trusted and loved Isabelle so thoroughly that when she left him… Wait a minute. The only way for him to know she betrayed him was if…

"You knew she faked her death the whole time," I blurted out.

Gramps let go of Harry's throat and kicked him so that he fell on his rump. "Yes, I knew. Harry was never any good at covering his tracks and the fire reeked of his handiwork. I let it go because I didn't need Harry or the team anymore to get what I wanted, but I never forgot."

As emotional as this all was for them, it still didn't do anything to help our current situation. The holo-footage was still playing the horrendous killings all over the world.

Elisha seemed quite amused by the little drama unfolding before her, especially the part where Gramps had suffered for years thinking he'd been betrayed.

Eva was already starting to back away from Elisha, her eyes never left Max's.

Harry brushed himself off and stood up, facing Isabelle. "That man became *exactly* what I said he was going to become: a monster. I didn't make that up. You've seen it for yourself over the years. He may not have wanted you dead, but eventually you would have become a liability to him. He wouldn't have hesitated to take you out. He tried to kill his granddaughter for God's sake!"

"Okay, don't bring me into this." Even though I had asserted myself into the conversation earlier, didn't mean I wanted to be a part of it.

"Oh yes, please continue." Elisha was simply reeling with joy. "While you all bicker about who backstabbed who, the world is ending."

The sad part was…

…Gramps, Harry and Isabelle didn't seem to care. Their current predicament apparently was way more important.

Elisha clapped her hands to shut everyone up. "Okay, bored now." Elisha was positively thrilled though she was still surrounded. "Chelsan was right." She eyed my friends over. "I *will* kill you now." She snapped her fingers. "Surprise!"

Uh, oh.

Even Isabelle looked startled.

Whatever Elisha was about to show us was news to Isabelle, too.

Suddenly, the sound of popping filled the air. From all the way down the hallway to all around the sanctuary's walls.

And after each pop a live soldier appeared with gun raised.

We were completely surrounded by at least a hundred men, with even more pouring in from the downstairs. So yeah, Turner's soldiers were easily disarmed.

Elisha was back in control and beaming at Gramps. "I made a little tweak to your dimensional displacement device. Turns out you can make human beings displace as well. Cool, huh?"

Gramps was angry to say the least, "Very," he kind of grumbled.

Elisha pointed at Bill. "Bill first, he's Eva's biggest distraction and Chelsan's best friend. This will be fun."

Something snapped in Eva.

I saw it then.

That girl loved Bill.

"NO!" Eva cried, and shoved Elisha hard into the podium. So hard that a part of the wood stabbed Elisha in the chest. Elisha pulled herself off of the shard of wood and instantly healed. She didn't even miss a beat. "I said KILL HIM!" she screamed.

One of the soldiers pointed his gun to Bill's head and pulled the trigger.

The bullet froze in mid-air.

It wasn't me.

I turned to Isabelle.

Isabelle yelled, "I can't hold it for long!"

Nancy reached up and knocked the bullet down like it was fly. "Ouch!" she yelped from the heat, but Bill was safe for the moment.

Bill looked like he was about to pee his pants.

Elisha's face kind of crinkled in shock, then excitement. "Never mind, grab that one," Elisha pointed to Isabelle, "I want her power."

When the guards reached to grab her, Isabelle made them stop.

She was definitely getting the hang of her powers.

Then I heard her in my head, *Time to do that dust trick. I can't hold them for long.*

Oh yeah, the dust trick.

But Elisha could stop me.

I couldn't think of anything else. I had to try.

Here went nothing.

This old decrepit building was full of dead swirling dust. Time to take out an army.

I connected to trillions of swirling holes and made them fly around the building like a swarm of killer bees.

Only to be stopped right before I could make the dust fly into the guards.

"You wish." Elisha grinned.

I could feel Elisha and Franklin keeping hold of the dust, just above each guards' nose.

It felt like not being able to thread a needle. My insides wanted to burst.

"Kill them all!" Elisha ordered.

I knew Isabelle didn't have the strength to control the army.

But I did.

Through her.

Isabelle, hang on.

Do it! she screamed in my head.

I jumped inside her and connected to the trails of light and made all the guards' arms and fingers stop. When they tried to move forward I froze their legs as well.

My body was vulnerable, being in Isabelle's head, so I had to act fast.

Isabelle, I'm going to try something and I'm not sure if it's going to work. Whatever you need to do, just don't let her kill Dean.

I thought to Max, *Can you make the dust move, just a little?*

I think so. What will that do? Max, always the inquisitive one.

Elisha was more fascinated than angry at this point. She was walking around trying to see just how frozen the men actually were.

If Max could take advantage of her momentary distraction…

All the dust moved ever so slightly.

And I could see trillions of trails of light.

I almost blacked out Isabelle from the sheer power of it as I connected to every trail of light.

It was more than surreal as I realized that I could move the dust with Isabelle's power as well as mine.

But Elisha couldn't.

I could hear her scream as I made the dust fly up through the noses of the guards and down into their lungs.

Every soldier gasped, fighting for air, then dropped unconscious to the ground.

I jumped out of Isabelle's body and back into my own.

"Oh, sorry, was that your army?" I couldn't resist.

Bill stepped forward like the romantic I knew he was, "Eva, please," he pleaded. Who could resist that?

Not Eva.

She came running to him and they embraced like a sappy romance movie.

"Okay, gross, Bill," Nancy scolded, but I could tell she was happy.

Elisha, on the other hand, was beyond furious.

It took about two seconds for Turner's men to pick up their guns and aim them at her. She practically spit, "You can't kill me, fools!"

"I don't need to kill you," Turner replied coldly.

"One more surprise," Elisha cooed.

Elisha pressed some kind of button before anyone could stop her.

A green gas started to pour in from the vents.

I knew that gas.

It was the poison that killed my mother and everyone else in my trailer park.

Elisha laughed.

"RUN!" Turner screamed and they all ran out of the sanctuary as fast as they could. Isabelle grabbed Dean and carried him in her arms.

I wanted to cry when I realized that by knocking out Elisha's army, I had inadvertently killed them all. I watched in horror as black spinning hole, after black spinning hole, formed in front of my eyes. It was an eerie contrast with the green mist pouring into the sanctuary.

But I stayed.

And so did Elisha.

I couldn't die, and I certainly wasn't going to let Elisha get away.

It was an unnerving moment.

Only Elisha and I were in the cavernous room, the Franklin clone was no where to be seen. Green smoke billowed around us like evil fog.

Elisha's smile died.

I must have been a sight to behold because she actually looked scared.

And she should be.

I knew what I had to do.

I had been scared to do it for fear she was more powerful than me, but I needed to try. I needed to see if I could make the killing stop.

I leapt inside her head.

I found her swirling white light and tried to connect with it…

…but I couldn't.

Shock thundered through my being.

I couldn't connect to Elisha's light because *she* wasn't connected to it.

The implications of that were mind blowing.

The swirling white lights in people were their life force.

Their souls.

It made total sense.

Sociopaths had no feelings. Had no conscience…

…because they weren't connected to their souls.

I could see where I could connect the light to Elisha's mind.

The only way I could potentially save all the people Elisha was having her soldiers kill was to control her.

And the only way I could control Elisha was to make her whole.

This was going to be bad.

I concentrated as hard as I could.

…And connected Elisha's brain to her swirling white light.

I was suddenly gasping for breath in my own body.

What I had done was so forceful it had thrown me out of Elisha's body like a canon ball.

Then I heard the shrieking.

I didn't even recognize the sound as human until I saw Elisha on her knees, clawing at her chest like it was on fire. She was screeching so loudly I had to cover my ears.

Green smoke wrapped around Elisha like a blanket of poison, though I knew she couldn't die.

But I saw in her eyes…she wanted to.

It took me a moment to realize that Elisha was screaming a name over and over again.

Beth.

Her twin sister. She had tortured and killed her sister Beth.

Of all the horrible things Elisha had done, that was the one that obviously hit her the hardest. Twins had a bond no one could explain. A reattached conscience meant Elisha had to face the horror that she had brutally murdered the person who loved her most in the world.

Elisha had her soul back.

I'd never seen someone in so much pain.

And now she had to deal with everything that she had done over the years.

I stood there watching Elisha scream in agony. The horrific holo-images of people being slaughtered still played around us like an absurdly grotesque play.

I needed to do something.

I thought about jumping into Elisha again and controlling her, but that thought now seemed so violating. From the way she was rocking herself in a ball and yelling her voice hoarse, the girl was broken.

I walked over to her, the green smoke billowing around me as I moved.

Kneeling down next to Elisha, I placed my hand on her back.

Elisha flinched, then looked me in the eye.

So much anguish.

Tears automatically filled my eyes. I could feel the suffering radiating from her. As despicable a human being as she was in the past, I knew Elisha was different now. And I didn't know how she would ever be able to live with herself.

"Chelsan!" Elisha said my name like I was her only lifeline.

"Elisha, we have to stop what you started. Do you understand?" I had sympathy for her, but people were dying.

"Oh God, Chelsan, what have I done? What have I done?" Elisha shrieked.

I held both her arms to steady her. "Elisha, what can I do to stop the clones?"

Her purple eyes were filled with desperation and dread. "Nothing. There's nothing you can do! I didn't make a kill switch. It's all over now…" she trailed off and her eyes turned glassy.

I was losing her. She was about to go into some kind of traumatic coma.

"Elisha! Stay with me!" I shouted.

But she was gone. Her eyes closed and she slipped into unconsciousness.

"Elisha!" I shook her.

But Elisha was out cold. Her conscience was too much to take in all at once. Her brain was on overload and she just couldn't cope.

I lifted her up like a baby.

Walking through the broken-down asylum, I tried to imagine Elisha here as a little girl. If only someone like me could have fixed her then, she would have lived her entire life in Havenville with Beth. She would have been happy.

I walked out of the asylum and handed Elisha off to Turner's men, who immediately handcuffed her. I didn't know what Turner would do with her, but he needed to know what I had done.

Everyone was coughing, but otherwise okay.

Nancy and Ryan both came in for a hug at the same time.

Turner was handling Elisha's capture pretty roughly so I told everyone what had happened.

Their faces were white, especially Eva's.

"She kept screaming Beth's name." I didn't realize how traumatic seeing Elisha go through that actually was.

Nancy's hand went to her mouth from the shock.

Even Turner looked fazed, but not much. He had a way of turning his emotions off, even with a soul!

But it was Jason who changed the subject, "We have to focus. The Franklins are going to kill everyone."

Jason was right, it was far beyond Elisha now. The I.Q. kids she'd planted inside the Franklin clones were finally exacting their revenge. They were going to kill the world.

Jason had a portable holo-projector and played all the news stations outside like it was happening right in front of us. Thousands upon thousands of people were dying.

I tuned everyone out to focus on doing something *anything* to stop them.

"Chelsan," Ryan whispered.

I looked up at him and noticed at his side was the Franklin clone holding his hand.

"Why is he doing that?" I asked quietly.

Apparently after a few choice words Turner and Harry were having it out again and it became harder and harder to ignore them.

"Could someone shut them up?" I heard Jill complain.

Ryan was totally focused on me and the Franklin clone. Ryan was baffled himself at the clone holding his hand. "I don't know."

The imagery and sounds from the holo-footage was becoming unbearable. People were dying by the second. I'd never felt so helpless in my life. We were stuck in front of an abandoned insane asylum and I suddenly wished I could admit myself.

At this point even Isabelle had backed away. She looked over at me. She was in pain, but I saw something else in her eyes. Relief. All those years of thinking that the only father figure she ever had wanted her dead must have been impossible to live with.

We needed to stop all the Franklins, but they were scattered across the world. There was no way to reach them, let alone stop them.

The world was ending and I couldn't do a thing.

I wanted to vomit.

What was I missing?

Then I glanced over at the clone holding Ryan's hand.

A seed of an idea started to grow, but it was just out of reach. Something about Ryan's connection to these clones. But what? So what? Ryan could hear what they were thinking? How would that help me?

Connection.

Roberta had bound me, Ryan, Max and Isabelle together.

Max was connected to Elisha. Ryan was connected to the I.Q. kids. I was connected to Isabelle…

And Isabelle had the power to kill.

Whoa.

What my brain was piecing together, I wasn't liking.

Was I really considering killing all the Franklin clones? Could I really do that? Not just morally, but physically as well. My powers to control the dead kept me at a four-mile radius, but did Isabelle have such a range?

What was I thinking?

I couldn't kill hundreds of kids. Sure they were a hundred years old, not really kids, not really people. Were clones really people? Yes, I believed they were. For someone who was surrounded by death, the last thing I wanted to do was create it myself. I didn't think I had it in me.

I watched more and more innocents die: children, babies, mothers, fathers…

I started to cry.

I couldn't help it.

It was devastating to watch.

If I could stop it, I had to try.

I thought about Isabelle, Max and Ryan and I spoke to them, *You all have to trust me. Do you trust me?*

There was a resounding *YES* from the three of them and I wanted to cry even harder. They looked to me to fix this, and they believed I could. I wasn't sure if I deserved such faith, but I took it anyway. What I was about to do to them they may never forgive me for.

I slammed into all three of their swirling bright lights…

…And I controlled them all.

I felt the shock of the sensation from Ryan and Max, but Isabelle was used to it and completely open to what was happening. Though the two boys were surprised at their loss of control, they didn't fight it either. They really did trust me.

The first thing I did was test out Max's connection to Elisha.

I was on energy overload as I controlled three extremely powerful people.

But I could feel the strength of the bond between Max and Elisha. It was like when I was flying in astral projection, a thick bright string bound them together.

I felt a surge of adrenaline.

This was working.

It became tricky then.

I grabbed Ryan and the clone's hand to make the three of us a circle. I wanted to join directly with this clone in order to strengthen Ryan's connection with all of the I.Q. kids in the other clones.

As with Max's link to Elisha, hundreds of thick strings of light spread out from Ryan and the clone. I could feel that every string led to another Franklin, no matter where they were on the planet.

I had to take a deep breath to steady myself.

Like when I had used the twins to control life, I was essentially doing the same thing with my own power now. It was exhilarating. I could feel every nerve in my body. I was so alive I wanted to scream in utter bliss.

Ryan's voice called out to me in the light, *Chelsan, don't lose yourself.*

The jolt of his words drew me back.

But the lure of the power was so great, it took all of my willpower to pull away from the desire to tap into *everything*.

It felt like I could connect to every living thing on the planet.

The craving was so strong I could barely breathe.

Then Max's voice said, *We're here. Focus on us.*

Like an anchor, the sound of Max in my head, pulled me away from the intoxication of the power.

Then Isabelle spoke, *We trust you with our lives.*

The words reverberated in my brain.

And it was enough.

The weight of the responsibility of holding these three people that I cared about in my hands hit me like a hover-freight.

Through my light-induced stupor I could see the swirling black holes of all the dead soldiers and newly killed victims on the holos.

I had to stop them.

I tapped into Isabelle's ability and anything that moved gave off the trails of light like before. Although no one was moving anymore. Not even Gramps or Harry. They had obviously stopped fighting long enough to realize the strange slackness of body from the five of us. And I swear, Terence was made of stone, the guy didn't react to anything. He stood against an SUV, observing everything. Not the kind of guy you want to invite to a party, for sure! All I could see was the trails of light that their hearts gave off, small pulses of a reminder that they were alive and well.

Next.

I reached into Ryan's mind and simultaneously connected to every last clone around the world.

Oh crap.

The rush exhilarated me beyond measure.

Help! I cried out.

I was going to be lost.

I was losing…

…My…

…Mind.

Ryan soothed me, *We're here, don't leave us.*

Then Max, *Concentrate on us.*

Then Isabelle, *You know what you have to do.*

I did know.

And I was pretty sure only Isabelle did, too.

Ryan and Max had no idea I was about to use them to kill all the clones.

Their voices brought me back to sanity.

Although I was about to lose it after what I planned on doing.

I'd never forgive myself.

I wasn't just killing.

I was killing my father.

Before I could talk myself out of it, I connected to every single trail of light in the clones' hearts…

…And I made them stop.

Instantly black swirling holes formed in their chests.

I could hear gasps from Max and Ryan as they not only realized, but felt what I had used them to do.

I wanted to collapse in a heap on the ground, but I had one more thing to do.

Now, through my connection to the Franklin clones, even dead, I was still able to use their powers to control the corpses.

I connected to every single swirling chasm they controlled.

There were millions.

I disconnected them all from their black holes.

Including the Franklins, making it impossible for the I.Q. kids to continue to inhabit their bodies.

The devastation of what I had done was instantly visible to us all from the holo-news footage playing in front of us.

Corpses littered the ground all around the world.

Millions dead instantly with no explanation. One minute there were soldiers fighting, the next they lay dead among their victims.

I released my hold on Ryan, Max and Isabelle and I fell to my knees, sobbing.

I felt Ryan's arms wrap around me and I almost wanted to push him away. I didn't deserve sympathy. I was a mass murderer, just like my grandfather. In that moment, it didn't matter to me that it was for the greater good. It was still assassination.

I barely heard Turner barking orders. Isabelle was explaining what had just happened and Turner relayed the information to someone through his holo-communicator. It sounded like Roberta.

Elisha's body was being carted away to what I could only guess was a high security facility. Gramps couldn't kill her, but he'd probably keep her locked up for good. Sad thing was that Elisha wasn't even a threat anymore. She'd most likely welcome being shut away from the world and what she'd done.

Eva and Max were embracing.

Isabelle was gently trying to wake Dean up. He was laying peacefully on the ground next to Terence and a hover-SUV.

Harry was in handcuffs and being ushered to most probably the same prison as Elisha.

And I was still in Ryan's arms.

Ryan's beautiful, forgiving arms.

I turned to him, waiting to face his eyes. Eyes that would hold disappointment and disgust at what I did. But instead I found only sympathy and concern. It broke my heart all over again. Why didn't he hate me? I had used his connection with the clones to kill them! I'd hate me! Ryan just held me and kissed my forehead and said, "You saved us all."

What?

How could he say that?

Before I could move, I was suddenly embraced by the whole gang. A giant pile of arms wrapped around me like a lifeline to sanity. Nancy,

Bill, Jason, Jill and even Max held me until I was filled up with their unconditional support. This was my family. It made my eyes well up with tears of joy.

Jason was the first to pull away and his face suddenly appeared on every news station on every channel – reporting live from the scene. It was like watching through Larry the cockroach's eyes, about a thousand of him making an announcement.

We all listened. Jason told the world everything that had happened in the last few days leading up to the horrific slaughter everyone had just witnessed. He left out the part about me controlling the dead, the world wasn't ready to know about people with powers like me and Isabelle. Jason placed all the blame on Elisha and assured the public that Vice President Geoffrey Turner had everything under control.

It was too much.

I buried my head in Ryan's chest and cried.

Really cried.

It was over.

Truly over.

I could feel it.

Relief, sadness, happiness, guilt, washed through me.

All my muscles felt like Jell-o.

Ryan lifted me to my feet. When my legs nearly buckled, Bill and Ryan supported me to the SUV.

We all piled in and seconds later our vehicle was in the air, headed back to what I could only assume was Population Control.

I leaned into Ryan and closed my eyes.

I woke up in bed.

My bed.

At Nancy's house.

My eyes filled with tears.

I was home.

It felt so good I wanted to scream, but I knew that would have scared the crap out of everyone.

The room was empty and I wanted to see everyone stat.

As I walked through Nancy's house I could hear the clink, clink, clinking of dishes coming from the kitchen. I had another surge of happiness as I opened the door to see my family sitting around the table, eating the pot roast and potatoes Vianne had apparently made for everyone.

All of them were there: Nancy, Ryan, Bill, Jason, Vianne, George, Jill and Max. No Eva. Max and Bill probably weren't sure how I felt about her and didn't want to upset me. No Isabelle, either. Not that I expected her, but still, we had been through a lot together.

When they saw me, like a giant school of fish they all stood up and hugged me. They were laughing and joking. I couldn't help but feel the happiest I'd ever felt in my life.

We'd all made it.

Some of us would never die, and I hoped that someday soon that would be all of us.

No one needed to talk about what happened.

The wounds were too fresh.

We just needed to be normal for a while.

"So," Nancy grinned at me. "I picked out your prom dress because I knew you'd never do it."

Prom?

It suddenly sounded like the most amazing event ever. I'd pick a school dance over everything that I'd been through any day.

"I trust you," I said and sat down to enjoy the best meal I'd ever eaten.

We all talked about prom and how Joan was going to flip out because Jason told her he couldn't take her to the dance. Nancy planned on fully flaunting that in Joan's face. It was so nice just to talk about nothing and everything. As long as I had my friends I knew things would be just fine.

Later that night I tried to go to sleep, but I was too wired. I watched Ryan peacefully sleeping next to me.

I thought about Roberta and Turner and how different our feelings were now from when we first met. Our relationship was still tentative at best. I knew in my heart I'd never really forgive them for killing my mother, but we had definitely come to some sort of neutral ground. Maybe someday we could have a "normal" relationship. Somehow, I doubted it, but still… I was open to maybe…

I heard a tapping on the window.

I wasn't alarmed. I knew who it was.

I slid out of bed and opened the window.

Isabelle crawled inside.

She eyed Ryan.

I shook my head, "He's out like a light. He won't hear us."

"I just wanted to say good-bye," Isabelle said.

"Where are you going?" I asked.

"Dean and I are disappearing for a while, maybe do something different." Isabelle seemed genuinely hopeful about the notion.

"Well, I wish you guys luck. If you ever need me, you know how to contact me," I said, pointing to my head. We were bonded for life and telepathy was a part of that package.

Isabelle smiled, though there was pain behind it. "Will do. Good-bye, Chelsan."

"Good-bye." Then I did something we both didn't expect. I hugged her.

Isabelle, after a moment of surprise, hugged me back.

When she pulled away she had a slight grin on her face then she disappeared out the window.

I stared at the darkness for a few minutes before I crawled back into bed.

I snuggled in close to Ryan and for once in a really long time I fell into a deep, uninterrupted sleep.